REALITIES

VALANCOURT CLASSICS

REALITIES

A Tale.

BY ELIZA LYNN LINTON

Edited with an introduction and notes by
Deborah T. Meem

"Therefore should I
Be but the essence of deformity,—
A coward,—did my very eyelids wink
At speaking out what I have dared to think."
KEATS.

𝕶𝖆𝖓𝖘𝖆𝖘 𝕮𝖎𝖙𝖞:
VALANCOURT BOOKS

2010

Realities by Eliza Lynn Linton
Originally published London: Saunders and Otley, 1851
First Valancourt Books edition 2010

ISBN 978-1-934555-73-6

Design and typography by James D. Jenkins
Published by Valancourt Books
Kansas City, Missouri
http://www.valancourtbooks.com

CONTENTS

INTRODUCTION

In September 1850, critic George Henry Lewes wrote of Eliza Lynn Linton[1] that she would do well to "quit those remote regions of the antique world in which her thoughts hitherto have wandered too much at large"—her first novel *Azeth* was set in ancient Egypt, and her second, *Amymone*, in classical Greece—and instead "resolutely move amidst the thronging forms of modern life, and paint from *them*" (616). Linton followed Lewes' advice, and her third novel *Realities* details the life and adventures of a headstrong young woman who runs away from her wealthy family to go on the stage in London. There she is romanced by her theater manager (a villain right out of Central Casting) and her reputation is compromised; she also encounters the manager's wife and children, whom he has abandoned; and she befriends two impoverished sisters who try to earn a living by slop-work, compensating for any shortfall by prostitution. Like her heroine Clara, Eliza Lynn Linton was independent but innocent of the world and its snares, and *Realities* met with an unexpected fate which changed the course of its author's life.

* * * * *

By the time Linton died in 1898, she was known as England's foremost antifeminist. She began writing sharp anti-woman articles as early as the 1850s, but by and large her reputation as a misogynist rests upon the widely read "Girl of the Period" essays that appeared in *Saturday Review* in the late 1860s and early 1870s. In those articles she pilloried all kinds of women: those who marry for money; those who wear outlandish clothing and makeup; those who "shriek" on behalf

---

[1] At this time the author was not yet married to William Linton, and wrote under her birth name Eliza Lynn. After her marriage in 1858 she named her literary persona E. Lynn Linton, and was known by that name for the rest of her life, even after she and her husband separated in 1866. Although technically *Realities* was written by Miss Lynn, I will refer to her as "Linton" throughout my commentary, on the principle that this is the name she is known by today, the name she made famous (and infamous) during the last third of the nineteenth century.

of women's rights; those who feign youth in middle age; those who blindly follow the fashions of the day; those who are idle; and so forth. In later years she attacked the New Woman, who seemed, even more than her mother's and aunts' generation, bent on blurring gender and class boundaries—playing sports and hunting, attending university, smoking and drinking, and generally establishing a life outside the home. It is no accident that Nancy Fix Anderson titled her biography of Linton *Woman against Women in Victorian England*.

But what are we to make of observations made by many, at different points in Linton's long career, that she herself was an independent woman, the very type of woman she was so ready to castigate in her periodical essays? She moved from the country to London and lived alone in lodgings at the age of 21; she was the first female journalist in England to earn a fixed salary; she supported her husband and his children throughout their unsuccessful marriage; she was male-identified to the point that she wrote her autobiography (*The Autobiography of Christopher Kirkland*, 1885) under a male pseudonym. A detractor wrote in response to one of Linton's "Wild Women" essays, "Mrs. Lynn Linton should have spared us this wearisome iteration concerning blatant, noisy, unsexed, and wild women, few of whom are more blatant, noisy, unsexed, and wild than Mrs. Lynn Linton" (*Review of Reviews* 312). Linton's long life, which included many peculiar and unconventional episodes, and her writing, which gained her fame but also general disparagement and ridicule, were characterized by inconsistency.

Eliza Lynn was born February 10, 1822, in Keswick, in the Lake District of England. She was the last of twelve children born to Charlotte Alicia Lynn and her husband, the Rev. James Lynn. Charlotte Lynn died when the baby was five months old, leaving household management and child-raising to the eldest daughter, fifteen-year-old Charlotte Elizabeth, who also died within a year. James Lynn made virtually no effort to raise the other children, committing them to the care of servants and troubling little about their behavior or education. In her autobiography Eliza Lynn Linton recalls a distant and uncaring father, and rough treatment from her siblings. The constant "spurring and pecking" among the children caused her to grow up "as furious as a small wild beast" (*CK* I: 47, 49). She felt generally unhappy at home, "so isolated in the family, so out of harmony with them all, and by my own faults of temperament such a little Ishmaelite and outcast, that as much despair as can exist with childhood overwhelmed and possessed me" (*CK* I: 60). Many of the heroines of her subsequent fiction share with their author this sense of domestic disharmony, their "faults of temperament" depicted rather much like good qualities—Clara de Saumarez in *Realities* representing the earliest of these Eliza-like characters.

After this tempestuous growing-up, which included increasing frustration at the utter lack of formal education she received, close "alliances" with one of her sisters and a brother or two, and what her first biographer George Somes Layard calls a "bizarre" romantic relationship with a young wife who lived nearby (41), young Eliza Lynn focused all her energies on escape. Eventually she persuaded her father to allow her to live in London and do research for a novel. After months of intense work at the British Museum, she produced *Azeth, the Egyptian* (1847) and *Amymone* (1848), both set in ancient times. They received decent reviews, but the young author became convinced that future success depended upon her proving able to write of the present, not the past. Lewes' commentary had something to do with this, but two other authors strongly influenced her decision: Charlotte Brontë and Henry Mayhew. Brontë's *Jane Eyre* had appeared in 1847, and made a considerable splash despite some critical carping about the "unregenerate and undisciplined spirit" of the heroine, and the "sheer rudeness and vulgarity" of the book as a whole (Rigby 52, 51). Linton admired Brontë's novel and hoped to create one of her own that might earn "a success equal to Jane Eyre" (qtd. Anderson 56). Henry Mayhew was a journalist (founder of *Punch* magazine) whose brutally frank and often disturbing articles about the condition of the poor in London began appearing in the *Morning Chronicle* in 1849, and were published in three volumes as *London Labour and the London Poor* in 1851. During the time of Mayhew's articles, Linton was also working at the *Morning Chronicle*. She knew Mayhew's work well, and was moved by its poignant descriptions of impoverished seamstresses, vagrant children, and prostitutes. In 1851, she felt the time was exactly right for her to write something "heretical and bold" (qtd. Anderson 56).

Richard Bentley, Linton's publisher of first choice, turned down the manuscript of *Realities*. The second choice, John Chapman, consulted his wife, who objected to the book's "sensual nature" (qtd. Anderson 57); Chapman suggested bowdlerization, and Linton refused. The third choice, Smith & Elder, told Linton that "it would be best for her welfare and reputation to throw the manuscript in the fire" (Haight 133-134). Linton finally agreed to make some cuts (it is not known exactly what was eliminated, as the MS has not survived), and *Realities* was published by Saunders & Otley at the author's expense in May 1851. To the expurgated text she added an angry and self-serving preface in which she called the book her "literary Caliban" (iv) and rationalized her decision to publish despite her friends' advice to the contrary. "Few women," she wrote disingenuously, "could have withstood such a battery of condemnations" (v). In dedicating the book to her literary friend and father-figure Walter Savage Landor, she expressed the hope that the public would give it a more "candid and intelligent" (vi) reading than her friends had done.

She was destined for bitter disappointment. Within days of the publication of *Realities*, the reviews began appearing. *The Spectator* sniped meanly that when one's friends find one's literary efforts unworthy, "request of friends may generally be safely complied with in *this* direction" (499). The *Athenæum* elaborated somewhat on this point: "There is such a thing as plain-speaking presumption disguised under the garb of honest and pains-taking sincerity. In Miss Lynn's eagerness to preach, it is possible that she may have contented herself with a most imperfect ordination. In place of enlarging the world's store of wisdom, she has added another to the proofs that daring and infallibility do not always imply self-knowledge or due preparation" (626). But more damage was done when reviewers waxed more specific in their criticism. The *Leader* took the young author to task on two counts. First, and most serious, she was assumed to be writing about subjects which no woman could, or should, know about: "Singularly unfortunate we must call the choice of her subject, which, lying of necessity beyond the sphere of her own actual experience, frustrates all her efforts. How is it possible for her to know theatrical life with anything like the accuracy needed for artistic reproduction? How can a woman know enough of the slopworker's modes of existence, to give anything but a partial representation of them? Yet we are in this work mainly thrown behind the scenes of a theatre, and into the dread alleys where slopworking rises hideous amidst so many horrors" (517). The second criticism focused on the character and life of the heroine, and would turn out to be a species of critique Linton would encounter throughout her literary career, that is, how can an utterly improper young woman expect sympathy from readers? We might compare this idea to the *Saturday Review's* comments about Linton's twelfth novel *The Rebel of the Family* in 1880: "[T]he reader's attention is roused . . . by an ardent desire to find out whether what seems at moments the author's advocacy of strange views is serious or not, whether she means to sympathize with or to laugh at her heroine's convictions and inconvenient theories, and whether or not she thinks [her] example a desirable one, on the whole, to follow" (650). The *Leader*, as early as *Realities* in 1851, begins the critical thread of castigating Linton for impropriety, particularly of the kind that transgresses accepted behavior for women.

These were not, however, by any means the worst of the negative comments concerning *Realities*. The *New Monthly Magazine* leveled a far nastier critique: "the whole work is one tissue of . . . exaggeration, violence, and too often prominent writing, and . . . we do her most service when we say the least. Miss Lynn is a determined social reformer, and that our social system requires reform on many of the points which she attacks, there can be no doubt; but we shall be very much mistaken if the defective condition of our laws, and the ugly vices which she dissects with such an eager hand, are cured or mended by her novel. Amongst the many repulsive portraits which we meet within it, Emma, the abandoned wife of Vaughan, is the most hideous. From the moment of her first entrance, 'a woman, bold, ragged, and untidy,' sitting in 'a dirty room overlooking the fetid river,' to that of her last appearance, 'an old she-wolf,' 'an irreclaimable demon,' a convicted felon only saved from the scaffold by madness, she shocks and disgusts us more, perhaps, than we have ever before been shocked and disgusted by any fictitious creation" (235). The accusation that Linton deliberately created "repulsive portraits" with the intent to "shock and disgust" was the kind of comment that guaranteed that her book could simply not be widely read, especially by proper middle-and upper-class women, the core of the novel-reading public in Victorian England. *Bentley's Miscellany* wrote its final epitaph: "The perusal of the work leaves a very painful impression, and not all its eloquence can compensate for its unhealthy tone. It is a protest against the laws which bind society; a vehicle for the publication of all the immoral doctrines, the propagation of which has caused such misery in France; and a sad stain on the literary reputation of one of the most gifted authors of the day" (670).

The *Realities* disaster put an end to Linton's novelistic career for a decade and a half. Both Nancy Fix Anderson and Andrea Broomfield assume that the harsh reviews catapulted Linton into an intense "period of discouragement and depression that lasted almost two years" (Anderson 62). It did not help that she was fired suddenly from her job at the *Morning Chronicle* and found herself virtually without resources. Linton wrote in the *Christopher Kirkland* autobiography that she did not know the reason for her dismissal: "All that I do know is, I suddenly failed to please. I, who up to this time had been a kind of cherished seedling who might some day develop into the very roof-tree of the office, now could do nothing that was right. Day by day my independent articles were rejected and my routine work was undone; while I myself was rated with the peculiar force and fervency with which [editor John Douglas Cook] knew so well how to flavour his displeasure. Finally, I was abruptly dismissed, and told to go to the devil, but never to show my face in that office again" (II, 142). It is interesting that Linton is willing to write about the firing in her autobiography—even if she ascribes "fabricated" motivations to various individuals "to save her pride" (Anderson 62)—but she does not write about the *Realities* debacle. If Anderson and Broomfield are correct, and I believe they are, the negative reception of the book was so devastating as to turn Linton away from the novel between 1851 and 1865, when she published *Grasp Your Nettle*. During those years she wrote mostly journalism; as Broomfield writes, she "practiced and perfected the art of punditry" (441).

And here the fame that eluded her with *Realities* finally arrived. After decamping to Paris and earning a living free-lancing, Linton caught on with Charles Dickens' journal *Household Words* in 1854. Her first article for Dickens was titled, "Rights and Wrongs of Women," and it set the pattern for her future career. She adopted a tone that was at once opinionated, condemnatory, humorous, misogynist, and sarcastic. Dickens noted that she was "good for anything, and thoroughly reliable" (qtd. Anderson 66) and as she built up a reputation, she gradually became known for her articles about women. Deliberately abandoning the idealistic, socialistic direction of *Realities*, her later periodical journalism was conservative, even reactionary, typically protesting against the progressive movements of her day. The key moment arrived in 1868, when she wrote "The Girl of the Period" for the *Saturday Review*. So widely read and piquant was the "G.O.P." that it has been called "perhaps the most sensational middle article the *Saturday Review* ever published" (Bevington 110). Writing anonymously and from a male-identified point of view, Linton turned female speech, fashion, attitude, and (presumed) fatuousness into her ticket to notoriety. Article after article by her appeared in the *"Saturday Reviler."* The "G.O.P." was on everyone's tongue, some agreeing with the implied criticism of feminism and "advanced" women, others decrying its carping tone and (after the author's identity became known) attacking Linton as a hypocrite who lived a "liberated" life but wished to prevent other women from doing so.

From 1868 on, Linton was *the* voice of antifeminism in England. She wrote indefatigably until just before her death in 1898. By the 1890s, as the figure of the New Woman appeared, along with countless previously unimagined opportunities for women, it became clear that Linton's strident efforts to contain the advance were destined to be as useless as trying to "wall a cuckoo" (Herbert Maxwell, qtd. in Anderson 213). There was no question, as Ray Strachey wrote about "woman's advance in England," but that "the old opposition at the beginning of the nineties . . . had an out-of-date flavour even then" (262-263). Clearly, having achieved fame and financial security, Linton clung relentlessly to the formula that had worked for her in the past, even long after her particular point of view seemed irremediably old-fashioned. In her autobiography she described her 1850s self as "one of the vanguard of the advanced women" (I, 253); but, as George Layard wrote, "afterwards, as is well known, [she was] left far behind in the rush of the movement" (78).

She had hit the precise moment only once, with the "Girl of the Period" in 1868. It was more characteristic of her to be out of step with her age. Let us consider *Realities* in light of this idea. In the 1840s, as Kathleen Tillotson argued, a strain of social novels arose whose intention was to shock readers into awareness of the profound class-based inequities in England. During the so-called "Hungry Forties" novelists such as Benjamin Disraeli (*Sybil*, 1845), Charles Kingsley (*Yeast: A Problem*, 1848), and Elizabeth Gaskell (*Mary Barton*, 1848) enjoyed considerable popular success in the same decade when the Chartists were agitating for parliamentary reform. But Chartism died as a viable political movement in April 1848, after the government's rejection of their third petition and promise of violent response to mob confrontation. Not six months later, still starry-eyed with admiration for the French Republic and the Chartists, youthful and idealistic Eliza Lynn went to work for the *Morning Chronicle*. Mayhew's *London Labour* notices began appearing in 1849, and two years later a reviewer for *Bentley's Miscellany* assumed that *Realities* was strongly influenced by "the letters which have appeared from time to time in the Morning Chronicle, and which have aroused the public mind, which will not rest satisfied until the social condition of the lower classes is considerably ameliorated" (670). Yet *Realities* failed where *Sybil* and *Yeast* and *Mary Barton* had succeeded. Why?

Certainly the collapse of Chartism was part of the national change in mood. But the year 1851 is typically marked not as the year of *Realities*, or even of *London Labour and the London Poor*, but rather as the year of the Crystal Palace. The Palace, which housed an enormous Exhibition of the Works of Industry of All Nations, was crammed with astonishing novelties: shawls and tissue from India, a fire engine from Canada, a reaping machine from the United States, rugs from Turkey, watches from Switzerland, and even Sheffield steel-bladed Bowie knives for sale to Americans (who, as the Queen wrote in her diary, "never move without one" ["To the Exhibition"]). The Crystal Palace stood as a massive monument to British industrial and colonial superiority. Similarly, its resident genius, Prince Albert, embodied both Royal pride in British accomplishments at home and abroad, and the Ideal Father of the empire's First Family. The Queen and the Prince stood for benign domesticity; and the prosperous and powerful England of 1851, only three years removed from the threat of Chartism, could apparently afford to promote family values. Suddenly, as Donald Southgate writes, this was the period of "Britannia ruling the waves and London ruling the exchanges, with Britain dominating world trade, enjoying economic growth at a rate unknown before or since, and finding in social peace, political equilibrium and deepening prosperity grounds for the optimism so often wrongly thought characteristic of the whole Victorian era" (xxiv). England had entered its "Age of Equipoise" (Burn). Historians of the Victorian age see the 1850s as a "great plateau" (Briggs 1) between the social upheavals, even the possibility of out and out class war, in the 1840s, and the Woman Question, the Labour Question, the Reform Question, even the Irish Question, which came later. It is easy to swallow these platitudes wholesale, and believe—as potentially insurgent people in 1851 were supposed to—that in the triumphant Crystal Palace time, with a motherly queen on the throne, counterculture movements were in eclipse.

And this is the moment when Linton produces her *Realities*. Given the carefully orchestrated national celebration of that summer, it should come as no surprise that a running theme of the negative responses is that the book is an insult to the country. Here is the *Bentley's* reviewer again: "Fatalism, materialism, Chartism, and socialism are the doctrines inculcated in 'Realities.' When we add that the Divine Author of Christianity is here styled the first socialist, we have said enough to disgust most people" (670). The removal of Chartism as a threat to the upper classes licensed this reviewer to write contemptuously and dismissively of *Realities*. Linton's book appeared just after the heyday of the 1840s social problem novel, at the beginning of a period of "equipoise," prosperity, and self-congratulation. Its biting social critique was simply swept away in the Crystal Palace delirium.

Still, as Andrea Broomfield suggests, the very fact of *Realities'* failure was likely a hidden blessing for Linton. It compelled her, writes Broomfield, "to reevaluate her career, her limitations as a novelist, and most importantly, what her legitimate talents actually were, and how they could be better used to help her achieve fame and financial security" (448). One of these "legitimate talents" developed by Linton during the post-*Realities* recovery period was a remade prose style suited specifically to periodical journalism. Broomfield describes this new style as including "striking caricatures, short, authoritative sentences, catch phrases, shock tactics, provocative twists on old stereotypes—particularly of foreigners, society ladies, women's rights activists, and preachers—and reductive arguments" (450). The series of *Saturday Review* articles generally referred to as the "G.O.P." group represent perfect examples of this successful style. Interestingly, when Linton returned to the novel genre in the 1860s and after, she incorporated this journalistic style into her long fiction. Even her late works from the 1890s exemplify this trend—for example, her caricatures of emancipated feminist club-women in *In Haste and At Leisure* (1895), and her jingoistic warmongering exhortation to Liberal M.P. William Woodall in 1898: "Oh, let us have the war and be done with it! Lop off one at least of the arms of the Russian Octopus; strike back at that insolent stout-boy Germany; spurn, as she deserves,

France, the most contemptible nation of ancient or modern times"
(qtd. Layard 349). She even includes some of her G.O.P. categories
in the fiction itself. In *The Rebel of the Family* (1880), for instance, she
refers to "Mature Sirens," "Modern Man-Haters," the "Shrieking
Sisterhood," and "Mésalliances," always assuming that the reader will
recognize these terms. It is a testament to Linton's striking success as
a journalist after *Realities* that she was probably right.

It is also true that Linton seems to have deliberately embarked
on a pragmatic mission in search of fame and fortune, and in so
doing abandoned the progressive, idealistic principles that animated
Realities. Her friend A.W. Benn wrote that when they first met, "Mrs.
Linton . . . was a professed Communist," but her late writings showed
her to have morphed into "an ardent Imperialist" (qtd. Layard 201,
202). She also learned to attend scrupulously to the requirements of
Mrs. Grundy. No more lurid scenes of abject poverty, prostitution,
even the theatre for her! As an established author, she would never
risk introducing another dicey Clara de Saumarez. In 1885 she wrote,
"Actresses, like all other women, have to obey certain laws of social
life. If girls come up from the country, go into lodgings alone, and live
without personal guardianship or social protection of any kind, they
may be Unas and Virginias to the back-bone, but they will have to pass
through mud-heaps by the way, and their experiences will be more or
less abominable. Also they will be roughly handled by the censorious,
and loosely regarded by the vicious. The fact of being on the stage
does not emancipate a modest girl from the conditions held necessary
for her social preservation elsewhere" ("The Stage" 16). Here she not
only seems to reject *Realities*, but also her own experiences as a young
woman who came "up from the country" and lived in lodgings alone.
Indeed she publicly repented of her early daring. "I thought that the
lives of women should be as free as those of men," she wrote, "[but]
I have lived to see my mistake. Knowing in my own person all that
women have to suffer when they fling themselves into the active fray,
I would prevent with all my strength young girls from following my
mistake" (qtd. Layard 140).

What has happened to Linton here? The Anderson-Broomfield
opinion holds that the author, wounded by hostile reviewers and
intent on "success" defined in terms of fame and money, strategically
altered her style and focus after 1851. Apparently willing to relinquish
her early ideals in pursuit of this goal, Linton achieved what she

sought. The comfortable, if solitary, life she built for herself resulted, according to this view, from her own conscious choices and actions. There is certainly evidence to support this interpretation of Linton's career.

But let us approach Linton's ideological shift from another angle. In *Discipline and Punish* (1975), Michel Foucault identified an important function of modern society's power—as evidenced through its manner of disciplining miscreants—as the correction of deviant behavior. Whereas in premodern eras gruesome punishments enacted the culture's revenge upon the criminal, in the modern era the culture attempted to "reform" its misfits, through "normalizing" them to live by accepted social standards. Foucault likened modern power to Jeremy Bentham's Panopticon, an "architectural apparatus" (201) allowing a prison inspector to see an inmate at any time without being visible himself. Such a machine, argued Bentham, would cause inmates to behave as if they were constantly under surveillance, whether this was true or not. The prisoner, then, disciplines himself with a minimum of input from the "unverifiable" inspector. Foucault expands this theoretical operation of power upon inmates into a rumination on society. By convincing citizens that they inhabit "a state of conscious and permanent visibility that assures the automatic functioning of power" (201), the state creates a normalizing environment in which individuals train—and discipline—themselves.

Regarding Eliza Lynn Linton, we might ask whether the reviewers that drove her away from her early artistic and political ideals represent a kind of literary Panopticon. Those anonymous observers—able to criticize invisibly—"reformed" Linton into a mouthpiece for conservative, even reactionary, values. Thinking in Foucauldian terms, we can see Linton as having been "disciplined" by the disembodied voice of the culture, to the extent that she became its unapologetic spokeswoman. The first stage of this discipline was straightforward punishment, in the form of harsh magazine reviews of *Realities*. These reviews originated from known places, but unknown individuals; like the hidden inspector in the Panopticon, these anonymous voices passed judgment in order, to quote Foucault, to "disqualify and invalidate" (223). Linton's "crime" in *Realities* was the propagation of "immoral doctrines" (*Bentley's* review 670) associated with revolutionary movements on the Continent; Foucault points out that such crimes as the promotion of socialism were "intolerable in commercial and industrial ownership" (85). Linton was, accordingly, isolated (the next stage of discipline) and banished to France where she might be "re-educated into social life" (Foucault 112). Over the years of her exile, Linton transformed herself from a political enemy of normalizing society into a citizen who "participates in the punishment that is practiced upon [her]" (90). She returned rehabilitated, the advocate of the state and its institutions—punished, disciplined, and chastened.

Read in this way, Linton's 1851 "punishment" cannot be accidental. *Realities*—a book which openly advocates for socialism and raises the spectre of class war—simply had to be suppressed. Appearing, as Foucault writes, at a moment characterized by "the development of production, the increase of wealth, [and] a higher juridical and moral value placed on property relations" (77), a country entering an age of "equipoise" and seeking global dominion could not allow an "unruly" citizen—and a woman at that—to challenge its fundamental social and economic norms. But because this was the nineteenth century and not the sixteenth or seventeenth, the offender was not physically brutalized but instead mentally chastened. The reviewers were just as faceless as the masked executioner who operated the guillotine—acting on behalf of the culture to discipline a recalcitrant individual. Linton's "reformation" indicated the success of the disciplinary project—as it also succeeded, in different but comparable ways, in domesticating thousands of other Victorian women pushing against the straitening ties of their society.

Linton may have been successfully domesticated through the work of powerful invisible operatives of the culture—but we should not assume by this that she was unaware of how the process functioned. In her 1867 book *Sowing the Wind*, not long after returning to the novel after a decade and a half away, she created another Eliza-like character, Jane Osborn. Jane is a journalist and proud of it, and says to her friend Isola: "Ah, you may talk as you like, Isola!—babies and love and the graces and prettinesses are all very fine, I dare say, but give me the real solid pleasure of work—a man's work—work that influences the world—work that is power! To sit behind the scenes and pull the strings—to know that what one says as 'we' in the *Comet* is taken among thinking men as a new gospel, when if one had said it as 'I, Jane Osborn,' it would have been sneered at as women's babble—to feel that strange thrill of secret mental power—no, I would not give up that for all the happiness of your so-called womanly women!"

(III, 27-28). Note that in this passage Jane refers twice to the idea of power, making it clear that this power originates from "behind the scenes" and its author can be identified only as "we." This is the kind of anonymous power that "influences the world," even creates "a new gospel." This is Foucauldian power, which is both "secret" and "mental," precisely because it is normative. Linton here reveals that she knew perfectly well how she had been disciplined, and more, she acknowledges the "strange thrill" of taking on the inspector role herself. The author of *Realities* has been replaced by the representative of public morality.

Twenty-first century readers will likely prefer *Realities* to Linton's later fiction and journalism. Most people who are acquainted with Eliza Lynn Linton at all think of her as an unreconstructed "woman against women." This early work provides an introduction to an unfamiliar side of Linton. During the past decade or so, one novel (*The Rebel of the Family*) and a number of essays by Linton have appeared in print. Most of these, however, come from the G.O.P. years and after. Readers are thus trained to regard Linton as "a sort of literary swashbuckler" ever "at war with the Advancing Woman" (Layard 224, 289). The Linton who wrote *Realities* was an ardent advocate for social justice on the basis of both class and sex. Her book described events and ideas considered entirely *outré* for a woman author, and these were the basis for much of the harshness of the contemporary reviews. With *Realities* Linton ventured onto untrodden ground, and was informed in no uncertain terms that she did not belong there. Yet today we recognize a kindred spirit in that young woman; she deserves to have her early ideals read again.

DEBORAH T. MEEM
Cincinnati, Ohio
February 22, 2009

ABOUT THE EDITOR

DEBORAH T. MEEM is Professor and Interim Head of Women's Studies at the University of Cincinnati. Her academic specialties are Victorian literature, queer studies, and the nineteenth-century woman's novel. She earned a Ph.D. in English from Stony Brook University in 1985. Her work has appeared in *Journal of the History of Sexuality*, *Feminist*

Teacher, Studies in Popular Culture, and elsewhere. Her edition of Eliza Lynn Linton's 1880 novel *The Rebel of the Family* was published in 2002 by Broadview Press, and her co-authored (with Michelle Gibson and Jonathan Alexander) *Finding Out: An Introduction to LGBT Studies* appeared in 2009 from Sage Press.

Works Cited

Anderson, Nancy Fix. *Woman against Women in Victorian England: A Life of Eliza Lynn Linton.* Bloomington and Indianapolis: Indiana University Press, 1987.

Bevington, Merle. *The Saturday Review, 1855-1868.* New York: Columbia University Press, 1941.

Briggs, Asa. *Victorian People.* New York: Harper & Row, 1963.

Broomfield, Andrea L. "Blending Journalism with Fiction: Eliza Lynn Linton and Her Rise to Fame as a Popular Novelist." In Linton, *The Rebel of the Family.* Edited by Deborah T. Meem. Peterborough Ont.: Broadview Press, 2002: 441-455.

Burn, W[illiam] L[aurence]. *The Age of Equipoise.* New York: Norton, 1965.

Foucault, Michel. *Discipline and Punish: The Birth of the Prison.* Translated by Alan Sheridan. New York: Vintage, 1995.

Haight, Gordon. *George Eliot and John Chapman, with Chapman's Diaries.* New Haven: Yale University Press, 1940.

Layard, George Somes. *Mrs. Lynn Linton: Her Life, Letters, and Opinions.* London: Methuen, 1901.

Lewes, George Henry. "Literature." *The Leader* 1:26 (21 September 1850), 616.

Linton, Eliza Lynn. *The Autobiography of Christopher Kirkland.* 3 Vols. London: Bentley, 1885.

___. "Mature Sirens." *Saturday Review* (9 January 1869), 46-47.

___. "Mésalliances." *Saturday Review* (26 September 1868), 419-420.

___. "Modern Man-Haters." *Saturday Review* (29 January 1871), 528-529.

___. *Realities: A Tale.* 3 Vols. London: Saunders & Otley, 1851.

___. "Rights and Wrongs of Women." *Household Words* (1 April 1854), 257-260.

____. "The Shrieking Sisterhood." *Saturday Review* (12 March 1870), 341-342.

____. *Sowing the Wind.* 3 Vols. London: Tinsley, 1867.

____. "The Stage as a Profession for Women." *National Review* 5 (March 1885), 8-19.

"The Novels of the Day." *New Monthly Magazine* (June 1851), 231-235.

Rev. of *Realities. The Athenæum* (14 June 1851), 626-627.

Rev. of *Realities. Bentley's Miscellany* 29 (1851), 669-670.

Rev. of *Realities. The Leader* (31 May 1851), 517-518.

Rev. of *Realities. The Spectator* (24 May 1851), 499.

Rev. of *The Rebel of the Family. The Saturday Review* 50: 1308 (20 November 1880), 650-651.

Rigby, Elizabeth, Lady Eastlake. Review of *Jane Eyre.* In *Women's Writing of the Victorian Period 1837-1901: An Anthology.* Edited by Harriet Devine Jump. New York: St. Martin's, 1999. 51-56.

Southgate, Donald. *"The Most English Minister...": The Policies and Politics of Palmerston.* New York: St. Martin's, 1966.

[Stead, William Thomas.] "Some Illustrated Magazines: The *Pall Mall Magazine.*" *The Review of Reviews* (September 1893): 312.

Strachey, Ray. *Struggle: The Stirring Story of Woman's Advance in England.* New York: Duffield, 1930.

Tillotson, Kathleen M. *Novels of the Eighteen-Forties.* Oxford: Clarendon Press, 1954.

"To the Exhibition" (excerpts from Queen Victoria's diary). *Crystal Palace.* 14 February 2009. Available at http://www.mcgill.ca/mchg/pastproject/cristal/.

NOTE ON THE TEXT

The Valancourt Books edition of *Realities* is based on the first edition, published in London by Saunders & Otley in 1851.

Linton's sentences tend to be extremely long, stitched together with what would today be called highly idiosyncratic punctuation. I have retained her punctuation and spelling throughout, making a silent correction only when there is a clear error in the original.

The editor would like to thank Jenny Grubbs, the Women's, Gender, and Sexuality Studies second-year MA student who assisted in the preparation of the text.

REALITIES

A Tale.

BY E. LYNN,

AUTHOR OF

"AZETH, THE EGYPTIAN," AND "AMYMONE."

"Therefore should I
Be but the essence of deformity,—
A coward,—did my very eyelids wink
At speaking out what I have dared to think."
KEATS.

IN THREE VOLUMES.

VOL. I.

LONDON
SAUNDERS AND OTLEY, CONDUIT STREET.
1851.

TO WALTER SAVAGE LANDOR.

My dear Mr. Landor—

The unvarying kindness with which you have treated me from the first hour of our happy meeting, has never been more manifest than in your acceptance of the dedication of a book which has received so rough a baptism as this. It would be endless to enumerate half the critical dangers undergone by the production which I now lay at your feet with every feeling of reverence and affection. Nor is it to drag strictly private matters before the public that I allude to them; for, by a series of misfortunes, all the censure which else might have been confined to me alone, became current in the different circles in which I move. For three months my book has been a species of literary Caliban to my friends—a monstrous thing of wickedness and deformity—advocating all that was abhorrent to reason and good morals. Many sought to terrify me with dark pictures of evil consequences to my reputation—many to deter me from publishing by censure of the story as a work of art. Timid respectability converted the most cherished thoughts, and the boldest endeavours after good which I have yet attempted, into questionable forms of dulness or of vice; while hard names flew like hail-stones round me when I adhered to my unwelcome social doctrines, and still determined to publish them against all advice to the contrary. In truth the very diversity of opinion helped to give me strength; for no two of my self-constituted judges pronounced the same sentence. One objected to my style, but approved of my sentiments; another thought the style might pass current, but the opinions were little better than libel or high treason; a valued friend suddenly withdrew his aid when most needed, because the "construction of the book was not ingenious;" and an able critic condemned sentiments, style, and characters, but thought the "story slightly interesting." Few women could have withstood such a battery of condemnation; yet though of no illustrious nor aristocratic race, my father holds good blood of courage and independence in his veins, and I should blush to turn traitor to the characteristic of moral bravery, which has been to our family a greater blessing than ancient lineage or ample rent-roll. Firm in my conviction that the undaunted utterance of truth—as it is to each—ought to be the first duty of every author—conscious of the sincerity of my wish to do good, how far soever I may wander from my aim by ignorance—conscious, too, that I have not written one word which I do not believe with all my heart and soul, and to uphold which I would willingly suffer any amount of pain and social dis-esteem—I stood up against the storm, and neither bent nor broke before the critical simoom that threatened to lay waste the brightest hopes of years. By the kind aid of a relative, whose noble exertions in my behalf I can never fitly repay, my unhappy book is at last presented to the world: I would fain hope, to receive a more candid and intelligent sentence than those privately passed on it.

If you ask me, dear sir, what are the opinions which have called forth such a concert of reprehension, I answer simply— the recommendation of a law which works well for morality both in America and in Prussia—the truth that religion comprehends sectarianism and is not comprehended by it—and the advocacy of the SOCIAL DOCTRINES TAUGHT BY CHRIST.

Such as my book is then, my dear Mr. Landor, with all its faults magnified by conservative antagonism against innovation, and with busy tongues proclaiming in it vices which I, the author, know not of—I offer it respectfully to you; sure, that though unworthy as a composition of your name and high place, it will receive your indulgence from the sincerity of belief and the earnestness of affection with which it has been written, and now is dedicated. Accept it as a tribute of esteem and of gratitude from one whom you have publicly honoured by your praises and privately blessed with your friendship; and let it stand between us as a loud and public word of affection from your

Obliged friend and faithful servant,

ELIZA LYNN.

London, March, 1851.

REALITIES.

———

CHAPTER I.

THEY had ridden far and the evening was coming on, when young Clare de Saumarez turned her horse's head homeward. It was a pleasant sight to see her gallop so merrily through the lanes and woods, her light hand scarcely holding the rein, and her pliant form bending to each motion of her horse, "like as if," said the country people, "she'd a been born on his very back." And pleasant was it to see her naughty skill, as she checked and fretted and otherwise maltreated the high spirit of her bright bay blood, and made him kick and prance as if some unblessed elf—cherub-mate of Gilpin Horner[1]—and no sweet thing of buoyant girlhood had mounted him. She made a pretty picture as she scoured along the road in her round low hat, with the drooping feather blowing all across her eyes and curling in among the chestnut ringlets down her face—with her baby cheek flushed and fair, and her large blue eyes bright and clear. Like a burst of sunlight she passed before your sight; like a joyous note of merry music. Care had not cankered one leaf in her blooming garden; sorrow had not dimmed one gem in her brilliant crown. Essentially a thing of impulse and all wild warm sensations was this young maiden child, pouring such a prodigality of feeling into the smallest circumstances of her existence as would have served many for a lifetime of emotion.

Clare de Saumarez—it was a high-sounding patronymic enough, suggestive of lengthy genealogies and courtly breeding—was of the great De Saumarez family of Shorne. She was the only child; heiress to the vast estates, and keeper of the name and honour, which had flourished so long in pride and purity. She was the centre of all the knights and 'squires and gallant gentlemen who, for so many generations, had maintained unbroken the legitimate transmission of the De Saumarez virtues. We shall soon see whether she is fitted to keep up the family name and add lustre to the family shield in the prescribed fashion of the De Saumarez race.

She was now at a very interesting age, having celebrated her thirteenth birthday about six months ago by presenting her mother with a copy of verses, vilely done and shamefully spelt, and entitled "A Thank-offering for Life." But her mother criticized the metre and counted the feet, and made poor little Clare cry by her ridicule and her Zoëlian[2] objections uttered in such a cold and stony manner of literary superiority. Yet there was so much energy, life, and beauty about Clare de Saumarez that, in spite of her ready aptitude for tears, you could not picture for her an unhappy future. Melancholy mania in a bird of paradise, or the death by jaundice of a Brazilian butterfly, were as little within the range of probable contingencies as was cold dead misery possible to her. She seemed to set at defiance the ordinary accidents of humanity, and to hold love and happiness in perpetual leash, guiding them before her wheresoever she turned. There was such a lavishness of life about her! It was a mere gambler's chance whether all that unformed energy would shape itself out into the virtue of the angels or the vice of demons. Any way there would be an entireness of choice; there would be no halting midway at respectable compromise between law and instinct—no pale hypocrisy of wise speech and stealthy indulgence—no coward sinning afraid of the consequences of sin, and unwilling to accept the punishment with the pleasure. There would be none of all this half-heartedness. An enthusiastic upholder or a brave denier—setting her foot firmly on the traditions of society or following fervently in their shadow—she would be all, not half a life. And this might be read, as in an open book, in the broad brow—the deep eye so frank and fearless—the full lip and strong jaw—the glossy hair, bright and warm—where intellect, will, affection, and passion, showed themselves through these tender features of youth, as queenly lilies in the bud. For though all is only indication at present, it is indication in such a positive form that the perfect development may easily be prognosticated.

A terrible creature to manage was this same Clare de Saumarez! Various methods of nursery discipline, based on nicely calculated nursery theories, had been tried; but without success. The mystic shibboleth[3] had not yet been pronounced, and Clara was still, as she had ever been, beyond all control and superior to every influence. No one exactly knew what was to be done with her. She openly rebelled against cold authority; the severity of moral condemnation had no reformatory power whatsoever; threats fired her rebellious blood, and extorted defiance; neglect made her careless—punishments obstinate; and Mrs. de Saumarez at last pronounced her incorrigible, and hinted at a "strict system of correction," and the diligent "whipping out of the offending Adam." At thirteen years of age to be given over incontinently to the spirit of evil, and to be discarded from the affection of one's mother as too criminal to dwell in her wide heart, is not a recommendation of character. But happily for our Clare she had some slight excuse for her naughtiness, intense as it was. No one had experimented on her education in the only spirit which gives success, namely, the spirit of Love. No one had tried to win her to goodness— no one to charm her into gentleness. All her characteristics were overlooked or directly opposed. And what but imperfection could be the result of such a false system? Until this spirit of Love has been employed, and until it has failed, she may be considered conditionally condemned only; she has not yet fallen bodily into the boiling caldron of sin irredeemable.

Mrs. de Saumarez excused her educational failure by complaining of the violence and obstinacy of this scourge to strict propriety. And she was partly justified in her complaints. Baffled in her more serious endeavours she tried a lighter method. She stripped philosophy of her serge and clothed her in motley instead. All Clare's amusements must be made educational and intellectual, "developing her mind," said Mrs. de Saumarez; "while pleasing her fancy." She hoped this would prove an immense success. She bought a perfect magazine of maps, conversation cards, little books of poetry on science and natural history, German puzzle boxes of utilitarian object, &c. But Clare tore up the pictures to make paper frills for her dogs and kittens, and could not be induced to learn the puzzles or the poetry by any possible amount of temptation. While the lady mother sat waiting for her to repeat some sweet little bit of versified geology, or a page of Roman history in a dialogue between papa and Laura, Clare was "messing about the rabbits," or coaxing the pigeons to eat out of her hand, or teaching her big dogs to beg—which they did with a very bad grace, and an unmistakeable protest against such canine frivolity.

The person liked the best in the world by Clara was old Hugh Clayton, the hereditary groom of the Hall. By this confession I allow the grave charge of vulgarity against my little friend. It is too true.

Nine times out of ten when missing from the drawing-room, she would be found in the stable among the horses' heels, or buried in a world of dogs' heads and ears, or by the favourite rabbit-hutch, experimentalizing on cuniculine food and having more than one fight with nature on the battle field of cuniculine digestion. Her ragged hair, so brown and curly, was always covered with straw and oats; her dirty pinafore was always smeared with green traces of cabbage leaves in a state of vegetable dissolution, or blackened with the cobwebs and dust of the hayloft, the granary, and harness-room; but her fresh cheek was so rosy, her young face so bright and beautiful! Often when she believed herself most secure from the tall windows of the Hall, which seemed to have human eyes in every pane incessantly watching her movements, she would be caught by the prim ladies' maid or severe housekeeper as she was following the gardener while he dug up the spaces between the currant trees and gooseberry bushes, teasing him for his spade and fork, and making illegal descents on the same if laid down unwarily. She never could be kept in the house or away from the yard and stables; though Mrs. de Saumarez did her best both by intellectual incitement and intellectual punishment; and Mr. de Saumarez spoke to her as gravely as if she had been convicted of shoplifting, or any other immoral fact.

Of all in this plebeian section of the household, as I said before, she liked old Hugh the best. In times of real difficulty he was almost the only person to whom she would attend—certainly the first to whom she flew for advice or protection. As this predilection was a capital crime in the eyes of one so essentially a gentlewoman as Mrs. de Saumarez, Clare's conferences with old Hugh were generally carried on by stealth, though their fruits were borne on her riotous vocabulary which at all times and in all places was interlarded with the phrases of a jockey, and the knowledge of a Harry Hieover.[4] Diana Vernon[5] herself was not better acquainted with the stable and the kennel than was this young lady of gentle birth, who ought to have learnt the harp when she studied farriery[6], and mastered the sciences when she pondered over the evidences of Blood.

Here then was the key to the discordances between Clare and her mother. The one loved the rudest, the wildest exhibition of Life; sensation and love were the great things necessary for her affection: the other bowed before the still wonders of Art, and carried the Artistic Feeling into the smallest details of domestic life. Moreover,

Mrs. de Saumarez was a Woman. By this I mean she was a person who took her stand on her womanhood, and treated it as a moral qualification. She cared not to ask herself whether her opinions and feelings were intrinsically right or no; she simply asserted that they were "womanly", according to the conventional ideal of that characteristic; full, as her admirers said, of the "nice feeling" and "right-mindedness" which Mrs. Ellis[7] has made so popular. She did not much value the affections and instincts of womanhood; she did not think these were characteristics to be specially preserved. Her affections lay exclusively in her morality—and her morality was the product of her intellect; and thus there was not much room for the luxuriance of natural forces. It is easy to be understood how such a mental condition as this must have been opposed to Clare's passion and impulsiveness, and how much mutual affliction must have sprung from such mutual dissent between mother and child.

The great peculiarity of Clare's domestic existence was this; she was incessantly scolded. It was a wonder certainly that they had the heart to be so stern when she crept close to them, looking into their faces with those deep blue eyes of hers that demanded pardon by their very audacity of innocence. But they were bored by her innocence and made angry by her audacity. She was never out of mischief; and people grow tired of this in time, even with the most beautiful child in the world. Go where she might, and do what she would, she was always about something disastrous to her domestic peace. She was always doing wrong, apparently for the fun of asking pardons never granted. She offended while words of good resolution were warm on her lips and tears of contrition big in her eyes. She promised to become a very El Dorado of steady matter-of-fact virtues, and the next moment she had jeopardized the whole household by some wild prank, or had done some clumsy and outrageously benevolent action which became a stereotyped laugh against her. She was the plague of the whole neighbourhood; more scolded, spoiled, and petted, than ever before fell to the lot of one individual to undergo.

How could this luxuriant life be the product of such parentage as that which Mr. and Mrs. de Saumarez supplied—a laboratory and a moral essay—a pedant in science and a pedant in morals? By what law of nature had they brought forth a being so unlike themselves? It was a strange physiological fact; not easy of solution as matters stood. Yet she was their child sure enough; for when she was born the whole village had been thrown into an uproar in the search for a healthy young mother to be the poor babe's nurse. Mrs. de Saumarez was unable to perform this office herself. Ethics and metaphysics had dried up more than the natural instincts of her heart, and left her like a stranded sea-weed without one germinating point remaining. When the decision of nature was fairly understood, and Mr. de Saumarez had absolutely received the fact that his wife was but half a mother, he complacently smiled his reliance on science, and speedily brought up to the nursery a chemical compound based on the best analytical principles. Unluckily it disagreed with the child. The saccharine matters, the phosphate of lime, the chalk, albumen, and other pedantries of the laboratory which he employed, were found ineffectual to preserve that delicate life; though the father swore they were better than mother's milk, being subject to no disturbing causes. The baby pined; the doctors ordered a healthy nurse; and Mrs. de Saumarez shuddered when she thought that a peasant's milk must nourish the blood of her high-born child.

No one was to be found. All the young married mothers seemed to have suddenly buried themselves alive, and an Herodian massacre might have passed over the baby world of the village. No one could be found; excepting a young daughter of old Hugh's, who—oh, shame!—had brought into the world a beautiful baby unsanctioned by the marriage ceremony.

Vile Martha! where were the judgments of Heaven that thou didst not die in thine hour of trial?—that thy stricken form did not crouch beside thy child's unblessed corpse, and acknowledge thy sin in the visible wrath of the Infinite? Alas for the slack arm of justice! The child lived and throve and laughed up in its mother's face, untouched by plague or leprosy or scaring wound of shame. And in that young unwedded bosom love and woman's pride poured through the deep channel of maternal affection in a rich stream of fertilizing happiness. And when she ought to have pined for shame, and shut out the light of heaven from her blighted brow, she sat beneath the clear sun, as bright and brave and joyous a heart as ever beat within its rays.

Proud too she felt, for her child's father was a grand nobleman— handsome and generous—wild perhaps—but then how great a gentleman!—and she, the humble village girl, believed herself honoured when she traced and retraced his likeness in the rosy face of her little one. For if like to him, how great and beautiful she would be!

And so poor Martha, though reviled and cast out, was very happy, and looked upon herself as much blessed in her maternity as a diademed queen when she hears the voice of her first-born, and knows that she has brought forth the lawful heir to the throne of half a world.

Martha was very sinful doubtless—very presumptuous, impenitent, and bold in her guilt. But authors only relate facts; their readers apply principles.

Though the last of his family, Martha had been discarded by Hugh when her illegal maternity become patent to the village. Indeed Mrs. de Saumarez had insisted on this sacrifice to moral justice, under pain of instant dismissal. The hereditary servitor balanced his place against his paternal affections, and gave the preference to the former. Martha was turned out of doors, and the faithful groom was rewarded with an increase of wages.

However, no one could be now found for the pining heiress of the Hall but this same blooming, sinful, happy Martha. With great repugnance, and after much internal strife, Mrs. de Saumarez at last consented to an arrangement so fraught with iniquity. But it was too much for her. She could not bear to see her child—the offspring of such chaste morality—nourished by one so criminal. It agonized the soul which no affection and no fear had ever stirred so deeply; it harrowed the heart to which propriety was the great all of creation. Was it not better, she used to ask herself, to let her child die in the unstained purity of her inheritance, than to keep her in life by the pollution of that life—the corruption of the very springs of being— the interfusion of all the passions and guilty propensities of her nurse? It was a knotty point; a very godsend to Mrs. de Saumarez; affording her mental food of a tough if not nutritious nature, that sustained her for many days without the aid of metaphysics.

It ended in a compromise. Martha's services were retained, but Martha's presence was discarded. The rosy-cheeked sinfulness was once more sent away—her foster little one with her; and then Mrs. de Saumarez sat down comfortably, and drew up a strict code of educational discipline to counteract the moral effects of this pernicious lacteal influence. We have seen how it worked.

At the proper time Clare was returned home. Her mother, truth to say, was pleasantly startled at the improvement wrought in the pale puny changeling she had sent out. It could hardly be recognised. It had expanded into a fair, fat, rosy thing, with great blue eyes, and great red cheeks, and dimpled hands, and rounded legs—just the kind of thing that mothers delight to exhibit nude for the better display of the fat and the fairness of the baby creature. Tumbling about the room like a larger ball—a soft round fluffy thing all pink and white—with wilful propensities of noise and mischief even then—laughing, if it saw but a bird fly across the lawn, as if it had been suddenly seized with a merry madness—even when unnoticed and silent, rolling its heavy little head like an idiotic toy set in perpetual motion—ever muttering pleasant thoughts with its red wet open lips that kissed all they came near, and left large stains on painted doll and dog—crowing with insane delight when it fell, for the twentieth time that hour, in the marvellous sitting posture of a clumsy baby—holding up its short white frock with both its dimpled hands as it came shyly to the call—pointing to its new shoes or its broad ribbons with a bird-like note of unconscionable pride, as it strove to hug its little feet when scrambling over your lap— asserting its own wayward will and raising its shrill voice in passion or in pleasure on the smallest occasion—the most self-important, self-willed thing in the world was this same infant heiress; of more bustle, noise, assertion, and trouble than all the rest of the household combined.

But Mr. de Saumarez said it was noisy, and Mrs. de Saumarez said it was vulgar; and both felt that nature had conferred the order of paternity on them in a decoration of questionable shape.

Martha Clayton alone declared it was the most beautiful baby ever seen: and more than one neighbour spoke low, and whispered of foul play, when they compared the pale little one on her knee—for which she seemed to have no special affection now—with this boisterous off-shoot of such trim propriety. Physiology might have demonstrated necessities long before it could have reconciled these anomalies with any known rules.

Poor Clare thus grew up under a daily ban which time only increased, as the characteristics repugnant to her educators developed themselves. For if she was noisy as an infant, what must she have been as a strong, high-spirited, growing girl? If wilful at four, must she not have been utterly unmanageable at fourteen? God speed those who attempted to control her! Nothing more wild, untamed, and impulsive, had ever existed; and Mrs. de Saumarez really deserved pity for her disappointment in this only trial of her theories and perpetuation of her nature. For one who valued art above all things, to know herself the mother of so fierce a disciple of nature—it was really an infliction! But she read a certain Treatise on Compensation[8] whenever she felt particularly unhappy; and she found it very consolatory and convincing.

Gaily and bravely Clare galloped forward on this summer's evening from which my story takes its date, until she came to the brow of a steep hill. The road had been repaired in such fashion as, by a fiction of the surveyors, passes for scientific macadamization.[9] Consequently it was very dangerous, and the acknowledged "bad bit" of the neighbourhood. Of course Miss Clare prepared to gallop down this hill twice as recklessly as on the level ground. Hugh knew her wilful ways, and riding hastily to her laid his hand on her bridle rein, and told her, in rather authoritative accents, to walk Fleetfoot gently down the steep. It might be that the heiress was not disposed to be commanded by the groom; it might be that her fate had been marked out beforehand, and that she was acting under the decree of a special destiny; be that as it will, she heeded nothing of Hugh's remonstrance, but taking off her hat with a saucy smile, waved it round her head; and rising in the saddle, dashed down the hill at a murderous pace.

A sudden turn in the road hid her from the servant, who came down cautiously, walking his sleek mare with all that care for a valuable life which grooms display, and emigrant shipowners ignore. As he turned the angle, he saw Fleetfoot quietly grazing by the hedgerow; while something that he thought to be Clare, in an undistinguishable heap of blood and rags, was lying on the ground close to his head.

Inexpressibly shocked, the old man flung himself from his horse, expecting to find her dead or maimed for life. At that instant his young lady's voice called imperiously for "water," and insinuated that he was an old fool for standing gaping there when he might be so much better employed. When Hugh returned from the wayside brook, with his hat running over in all directions, he found a child, pale and bleeding, resting against Clare's lap.

She was a slight sickly little girl of about Clara's own age, but much less in size; with features sharp and delicate—a mouth of no vulgar but of no pleasing expression, vain and querulous in its thin lines—pale blue eyes, which had a hardness in their fixed look scarce so admirable as strange in one so young. Her hair was beautifully kept; it was long and glossy though thin, and of that peculiar straw colour which bad judges call flaxen, and anxious mothers assert to be golden. This hair is seen only with a certain complexion and a certain character. I never knew an enthusiast with hair of that particular inanimate tint of which I am speaking; and I never knew it combined with passion, even where the temperament was nervous.

Clara, flushed and frightened, did not hear old Hugh's surprised exclamation as he returned: that girl was his grandchild, little Alice Clayton. If Clara had heard those words then spoken, another page of life than the one she now turned would have spelled out her fate—another cast than the one she now threw would have assigned her a different lot. It was, unknown to herself, the turning-point of her destiny, for all her after-life was referable to this small moment—this minute event of chance.

Hugh had just so much experience of human ailments as to know that a swoon is not death. He reassured Clara by saying roughly; "Oh she'll do well enough!—she'll soon be as brisk as a terrier pup in a rat-hole; and it's of no good Miss carrying on like that; even if she be dead! Crying can't bring her to life again," and then he turned away muttering, "the varmint deserved it. What call had she here!"

Clare dried her tears and looked at him wondering; and, as a circumstance worthy of note, it must be told that she believed what he said without question or contradiction. Hugh took the little girl on his knee and bathed her face afresh. She opened her eyes and began to cry piteously.

"Oh, I have hurt you very much!" sobbed Clara, bursting into tears again, and kissing that pale face, mud-begrimed as it was.

"Never mind that!—but you've torn my frock and dirtied my hair," exclaimed the child, pushing her aside. Hardly intelligible from tears and terror, her first words were lamentations for her disordered person.

Instinctively Clara shrank from a nature so opposite to her own; but old Hugh laughed and grumbled to himself, "Ah! she was always a lady!"

A sudden glow of pity and benevolence soon swept away this instinct of repugnance; and once more Clare's generous heart beat with the impetuous kindliness of her nature. She sprang on her horse, and in a loud voice commanded Hugh to take up the child and ride quick to the Hall. She then struck Fleetfoot sharply, and never drew rein till she came to the old lodge gates.

She kept so far ahead that she heard nothing of the instructions the groom gave the frightened girl. To conceal her mother's name—to be in the Hall Alice Forster, a beggar and an orphan—to deny all previous knowledge of the place, and to make the best of what had befallen her—were the hurried rules the old man laid down. He knew that he was doing wrong to teach her these lies; but then—it might turn out a good thing for Martha's child if properly managed, and he would put sixpence in the poor-box and go to church twice on Sundays for a month to come. Such compositions were unanswerable; and the Angel of Truth was silenced.

Alice promised implicit obedience, and old Hugh's lecture on conduct and propriety ended just as they came up to Clare waiting for them at the lodge gates, and wondering why they could not ride as quick as she—what a lazy old man he was!

CHAPTER II.

WHEN they rode up little Alice was crying bitterly, but more from a vague terror than from pain. Clara thought that the old man's rough arms hurt the child, and ordered him, in tones too peremptory to be disobeyed, to place her on Fleetfoot's back. How was it to be done on a lady's side-saddle? Never mind. By dint of management the feat was accomplished, and the young heiress of the De Saumarez family was locked in the arms of the wandering beggar girl.

Through the open gates—with a beaming smile for all answer to the gatekeeper's wondering look—up the long elm avenue—up the broad gravel walk—across the lawn, though fresh mown to-day and forbidden always—and clattering past the tall windows of the dinner room, did Clara de Saumarez take her way. Her hair streaming in the summer breeze, and her young face turbulent with ungovernable excitement, she flashed upon the grave party assembled in the Hall as a passing meteor or a wandering whirlwind. Panting and eager she made the old place ring with her voice, calling the hurrying servants to her assistance. Astonishment and condemnation might be read on their faces as they saw her so strangely accompanied; and one footman, who had gone through a longer London education than the rest, flatly refused to touch the "dirty beggar's brat." He had been told to lift her down.

Clara bade the child be still. There was a strange accent in her voice when she spoke. She sprang from Fleetfoot's frothed back, and, with her own strong little arms, took down Alice safely and placed her in the porter's hall chair; much to the dismay of that respectable functionary.

The servants stood clustered together, dumb with surprise, and visibly reprehending their young lady's "wicked familiarity."

Great in her own strong sense of Right above Law, Clara confronted them in open defiance of the conventionality of which they were now the type. She knew by the instinct of her heart and the teaching of her conscience that she was doing right, and she could brave any amount of censure when she believed herself acting conscientiously. And standing thus our young friend was in truth a heroine; for it requires more moral courage to despise the social martyrdom of disesteem than to endure all the racks and tortures of the Inquisition. God's blessing on the brave heart that dares uphold its way of right in spite of opposition, censure, or rebuke! God's blessing on the strong faith that can override the barriers of conventional form and conventional morality, and trust in something higher! The time has come for the truthful manifestation of great principles, and with it the endurance of much social persecution—God strengthen all who hold the Better Faith unacknowledged yet by society!

Clara's heart beat fast in spite of her courage, as now, holding the little girl's hand in hers, she hurried through the long galleries to the drawing rooms where the ladies had assembled after dinner. The blood mounted into her face and blinded her eyes; but with a loud exclamation of "Oh, mamma!" she burst into the room as tumultuously as a young Newfoundland dog.

It was the best drawing-room, hung with amber satin and silver. The walls were covered with gilded mouldings and with pictures of costly kind; with mirrors and brackets of tasteful design—the last supporting expensive gauds; the carpets were of velvet, covered with flowers of bright colours and in exquisite taste; the whole atmosphere was redolent of luxury and state. And dispersed through these gorgeous rooms were groups of high-born ladies—some with aristocratic titles—all of the upper classes; dressed in the latest fashions, and sparkling with jewels; scattered about in picturesque attitudes of ease and elegance and high-bred indolence, speaking in low soft voices like flower leaves in the wind, far too refined to use a natural tone wherewith to express a natural emotion.

Amongst them all—so calm and polished, so richly decked and softly speaking—rushed Clara like a whirlwind; flushed and hurried; her voice echoing through the stillness like a storm through a summer's night; her hair disordered, her habit torn and covered with mud, her gloves soiled, her whip broken, her whole air one of untutored ardent life. And in her hand she held the ragged beggar child—pale, squalid, covered with blood and filth, yet standing on those costly carpets and in that supreme assembly, by the side of the future heiress of it all. It was a striking scene, suggestive in the highest degree to those who had brains wherewith to think, which unfortunately was not a popular characteristic among the present spectators.

"My child—Clara!" cried Mrs. de Saumarez, her thin cheeks flushed, and her hard blue eyes darkened by the flash of anger darting from them. As if recollecting herself, she then smiled—in grim and ghastly fashion enough—saying softly, "What new act of outrageous kindness is this, Clara?—what new proof of injudicious benevolence? I do not scold you, my child, but I would that you had more wisdom, and more self-control. Youth is beautiful, but how foolish!" she added aside to a lady near.

Nothing abashed, nor even checked in her boisterous energy by those courtly manners and slow, smooth, smiling words, Clara stood and told her story. How she had ridden over the poor child and hurt her grievously—whereat Alice began to cry—and how she had brought her home to have all this evil repaired. Clara's voice was louder than ever, her face of a deeper crimson, and she seemed less and less conscious of the manners appropriate to the presence in which she stood.

"And what am I to do with her, unthinking child?" said Mrs. de Saumarez, in the same voice, without intonation or emphasis; "am I to make her your adopted sister—perhaps your superior? What historic revolution would you create, my impulsive Clara, to repair the damage done to a mendicant?"

Clara felt the sarcasm; she continued to blush till neck and brow and cheeks were all of one deep burning crimson.

"Can you not give her food and shelter?" she said passionately but pleadingly. "I have plenty of clothes, mamma!" she added, looking into her mother's face with her own look of audacity and affection— "there is my old black silk, and my striped blue muslin that is too short for me, and my pink——"

"Are you going to enumerate your wardrobe, Clara?" asked Mrs. de Saumarez, icily polite, and bending courteously as to an equal.

Clara's lip quivered. She grasped the child's hand more firmly, and said in a tone of intensest feeling more expressive than any words of all she felt—"Mamma—from you!"

Mrs. de Saumarez had a part to play in the society of which she assumed to be the leader and the model. She had been ever heard to speak æsthetically of charity, and she had a strong idea of womanly tenderness. She had several groups of maternal love, guardian spirits, Niobes, charity, &c., in her house, indicative of her feelings; and these, together with a model infant school and a picture of the Madonna, had given her the character of extreme benevolence.

The ladies by this time had clustered round the young speaker, and every word that passed between this ill-matched pair became public to the room. Clara's temper was rising against the sarcasm and the cool survey taken through so many eye-glasses levelled at her; against the ridicule and the injustice. Mrs. de Saumarez was afraid of pushing matters too far; yet how could she yield? She could not turn the Hall into a nursery for all the little beggar girls Clara might choose to ride over. It was a dreadful precedent: what a pity all these people were here to see and mark it!

"You *must* take her, mamma," then said Clara firmly. "It is only right—only your duty! God says we are to be kind to the poor; and He says there is no distinction of persons."

"Do you lecture your mother!" said more than one voice. "Is this your duty, Miss de Saumarez?"

Clara's tears fell fast. The storm was rising. She drew her breath hard, and with an hysteric sob flung herself into her mother's arms, crying; "Mamma, you must—dear, good, noble mamma, you will take her for my sake!"

Mrs. de Saumarez put her away coldly, and smoothed her dress after the contact.

"I hate scenes and affectation," she said in an under voice.

Clare hung her head and sobbed stormfully; then, wiping her eyes with her soiled gloves, she covered her wet cheeks with dirt.

The beggar child went slowly and timidly to the lady of the house, from whose face she had never once withdrawn her eyes since she had entered the room. She walked carefully; for she was lame and her bruises pained her. She held forth her small hands, and in a gentle voice, very calm and sweet in its tones, begged earnestly to be taken as a servant—to be amongst the lowest of the dependants—but to be sometimes allowed to cross that dear lady's path, and to bless her every day of her life. She spoke earnestly and fluently, but without passion. She raised her blue eyes to the face of the cold woman above. She knelt down and clung to her dress. Her fair hair broke over the deep purple of that gorgeous velvet, and the long, straight, silky tresses fell on the lady's feet.

The guests were enraptured at the beauty of that living picture. They spoke of Raffaele and of Canova,[10] and said this group excelled the maternal embodiments of both. Mrs. de Saumarez was pleased; her vanity was touched and her moral position raised. It was an æsthetic moment, and she made the most of it. In defiance of the rags and dirt, she raised the kneeling child with her white-gloved hand; and her touch lingered kindly—more kindly than a moment before it had fallen on the person of her own child. Bidding her be God-blessed, she gave her permission to remain in the household until something better could be done for her.

The guests did more than applaud: some of the more sensitive fairly wept with admiration.

Chilled, sore, wounded, she knew not why, Clare came forward to thank her mother for this kindness. She spoke cheerily and heartily, and would have taken her hand to kiss it, but Mrs. de Saumarez drew it away, saying coldly; "Your gloves are dirty, my dear!"

Clare shrank as if she had been struck; but with a sunny smile, determined to believe the best and to see only goodness and charity in this chill repulse, she cried, "Oh! I forgot, mamma dear!" and shook her head, and laughed loudly. She then dragged little Alice from the room to invest her in a certain black silk frock and scarlet sash which she particularly admired for herself. However, the housekeeper interfered, and put the child to bed, after sundry bathings and rubbings and internal administrations, mixed up with "wonderings at the strange fancies of grand folk."

Mrs. de Saumarez, in tears of despair at the untameable vulgarity of their child, related this scene to her husband. Mr. de Saumarez dived into his study. Till past midnight he was employed in drawing up tables of chemical proportions by which he hoped to combine such food as should lessen Clare's sanguineous superfluities, and make her paler, gentler, and of more artistic development.

"Man, Mrs. de Saumarez," he said, when he retreated for the prosecution of this design, "is a mere chemical laboratory. Fill the retorts with certain fluids, mix, reduce, combine, and you have an inevitable result. If there be any truth in science, your daughter shall be thus modified by the simple application of agents which must effect certain results. Acting on the blood and other physical conditions, these agents will change the quality and the quantity of the nervous fluid; this, in its turn, will modify the action of the brain, and thus the moral character will, by physiological necessity, be thoroughly transformed. Good night; be tranquil. *I* will discipline this wild off-shoot of rude nature."

And he believed himself capable of doing so.

The De Saumarez were what the world calls "desirable acquaintances." They were an old family—having come over with the Conqueror according to genealogical traditions; not directly noble, but allied on both sides to members of the nobility, and thus claiming a sort of relationship with Debrett.[11] Their society lay exclusively among the higher classes—the well-born and the wealthy: for, being themselves extremely rich, all that they did was in good style, and therefore suited to those who require "correct taste" and "perfect appointments" in payment for their presence. The Hall was famous for its internal arrangements: so much so, that every house of any pretension in the neighbourhood had some copy—or imitation if not the copy—of furniture, ornament, picture, statue, &c.: much to the lady's annoyance at times. For like most women she was very sensitive on the matter of exclusive possession.

It was emphatically the mark of respectability—the sanction of a local court—to be received at the Hall. Nothing was so much desired by newcomers as an invitation from Mrs. de Saumarez; sure that if once admitted into the penetralia of this temple of respectability, they might take a certain stand hereafter among the visitable inhabitants of the place. Mrs. de Saumarez gave æsthetic entertainments—not many of them certainly—but the more truth-telling part of the society said they were quite enough. Low voices, subdued manners, rich appointments, vapid amusements which no one on this side the adytum[12] of fashionable intellect can find in the least degree amusing, were the order of the day there. But a genuine burst of feeling, a hearty laugh, an enthusiastic word, or a passionate pulse, was never known. If any one had been so lost to all sense of propriety as to have indulged in the same, he would have been looked on as a polar bear, or a rampaging wolf. Any way he would have been a monstrosity among these polished cubes of social humanity, with whom virtue and coldness were the Siamese of civilization.[13] It would have been impossible to have walked fast, to have talked loudly, to have felt excited, to have been even hot or cold or hungry or thirsty in those rooms of Mrs. de Saumarez. The carpet was so thick that even Clara's noisy feet were dulled; and there was that excessive stillness throughout the whole house which subdues like mesmerism. He would have been a brave man who could have allowed his own voice to be the only sound in that atmosphere of silent luxury. The careful arrangement of the very furniture would have rebuked him. Everything was so calm and quiet—so much in repose—that no one could be aught else for very sympathy.

Mrs. de Saumarez was a religious woman: indeed I may say a very religious woman: taking Christianity at all times under her especial patronage, and assuming it a personal affront if "unsatisfactory doctrines" were held in her presence. She was a kind of nursing mother to the Bible, and was ever on the watch against insult and aggression. It never seemed to occur to her that any one but herself had a right to an independent opinion concerning matters of religious faith. Unitarianism, deism, philosophical abstractions, and Kantian logic, were much beyond her code of allowance. Within the range of Christianity she tolerated most sects. Without, she stretched a fearful cordon of condemning spirits. She scorned to be confined by sectarian views; but there *were* limits. And though she prided herself on the comprehensiveness, or what, being a German scholar, she used to call the "many-sidedness" of her intellect—yet even she "must draw the line somewhere." So she drew it on the cover of the Bible, and wrote the Universe inside.

And priding herself thus on her many-sidedness, she essayed various schools of reasonings. Metaphysical explanations and Swedenborgian supernaturalism alike were impartially examined, and the truth of both extracted. "She rejected nothing," she said, "and believed in everything." She had learnt the outlines of many sciences, and understood the main part of the "Vestiges of Creation."[14] She delighted in collecting minerals, shells, and plants, and in a correspondence of tastes with Sedgwick and Faraday.[15] For she was essentially a clever woman. Phrenology and Mesmerism she had also dabbled in—pitting the last against the first, as counteracting its materialistic tendencies. Physiology she condemned as an "undesirable study for ladies," though she knew a few of the leading facts of anatomy, and could distinguish between a bilious and a sanguine temperament, and between the nerves of motion and those of sensation. She prided herself on her own individual power of gaining good from what was generally evil—this flattering her exclusive propensities; and therefore she boldly ventured into depths over the surface of which she would not permit others even to skim. She had, in short, a capacious brain—large in its intellectual division, smaller in its moral region, and in its animal portion cut sheer off to the neck; thus she was simply an intelligent being, but not a loving nor an impulsive one. She was self-conscious too to a painful extent. She could tell you, in the midst of her most eloquent discourse and most fervid feelings, what organs were then excited, and why. This induced the same sickliness as is induced in plants and seeds when children pluck them up to see them grow. The worst of many bad effects was the intolerance which it generated. Consciousness was followed by subjection of emotion: and virtue and subjection of emotion meant the same thing with Mrs. de Saumarez. She had attained the last, she believed that the first came with it; and that her mental state was eminently satisfactory because she had stiffened her muscles and mutilated her impulses. And believing this, she knew neither pity nor tolerance for those who suffered or who sinned by reason of their passions. Why could not all subdue themselves as she had done? Ah, Madam! you have never known the temptations which assail the passionate temperament! You have never felt the fierce blood rush through your veins till it maddens your brain beyond control! Cold and unimpressionable by nature, your work of subjugation is easy—beginning and ending in the false taste of an artistic and well-bred manner.

In consequence of this mental composure, Mrs. de Saumarez was harsh and severe in all her relations. For instance: she was wonderfully particular in the character of her servants, and nothing could possibly induce her knowingly to take one whose fair fame was not immaculate. Merry and allowance she knew not. The inflexible Rule of Right was that by which she governed herself and measured all the world. Moreover, she was too refined to tolerate the vulgarities of vulgar people. They disgusted her even more than the immoralities of the great. And yet she condemned these too in terms of strict abhorrence. We must do her this justice: she did not weigh virtue against rent-rolls and coronets—she did stand up for equality in morality, at any rate! So far indeed did she carry her dread of vulgarity, that she at last prevailed on Mr. de Saumarez to refuse his park for the annual village-games which, for generations past, it had been the family custom to encourage. She disapproved of these village-games. Horse-racing led to drinking and other unpleasant practices; running in sacks, climbing greasy poles, bobbing for apples, &c., &c., were evidences of an unintellectual and unformed state of mind, which she would do her utmost to reform. Cricket was not so reprehensible in itself—but then the bowling-green was always more or less the door-way of the public-house; and were not tracts, and lectures on popular astronomy, popular science, and popular history, better employments for a summer's evening than the idleness of sport? Schools, Mechanics' Institutes, and large educational measures generally, Mrs. de Saumarez thought should supersede all other occupations, save those which were purely industrial. The consequence of her prohibition against the healthy and instinctive desire for physical amusements, was to be found in the increase of drunkenness in Shorne—the public-house being now the only place of recreation—in Saturday-night fights, with their accompaniments of swearing and profanity—in the erection of a dissenting chapel and the consequent division of the village into two parties, to the enduring destruction of friendship and kindness—in short, in much demoralization throughout the place; as was natural, seeing that the only pleasures left to the people were vice and religious dissent.

In all things well suited to Mrs. de Saumarez was her husband, Bellenden de Saumarez, Esq. He too was cold and intellectual; proud of his wife's moral position in society, and undesirous of any fonder sentiment. His laboratory was his home; and in German metaphysics and chemical experiments he believed to work out the end of his existence. Intellectually he was opposed in some degree to his wife. He was a thoroughbred sceptic while she was an artistic believer; not less conventional than she, but not so bitter in his judgments nor so courteous in his manner; bearing himself manifestly above all who had not reached his standard of knowledge, and taking the acquisition of facts as the last development of human power.[16] He had the air of a literary, she that of a moral, pedant. The strangest thing of all was, that Clara, with her great heart and bounding blood—her passion and her impulse—should be the offspring of such a union!

The little so styled beggar girl, Alice Forster, was not kept in the outhouses and about the servants' offices as Mrs. de Saumarez at first intended. There was so much delicacy of appearance, so much tact and quickness about her, that she was at once promoted into a kind of body attendant on Clara. From this the transition to playmate was easy. Clara's generous spirit found no sin in this democratic familiarity. She insisted on an equal division of all her good things—finery and all; and exulted daily in the sacrifice of possession and inclination at the shrine of pure benevolence. Which meant simply this: when she had been more than ordinarily wayward, she would go to Alice (whom she had very likely mortally insulted and tyrannized over to a frightful extent) and do penance in her own way. Which penance, for the most part, consisted in a magnanimous permission to the child to do what she liked without let or hindrance, or in the generous gift of a smart frock or bonnet, from her own wardrobe—too grand a thousand times for the wearer.

But the frock and the bonnet did not make Alice forget, nor did they change her growing enmity to Clara into anything more grateful and more affectionate. For it must be confessed that my Clare, like all of her age and temperament, was neither more nor less than a magnificent tyrant; and Alice had the sense to understand this peculiarity of her republican mistress, and the tact to yield to it, else the collisions between them would have been endless. As it was, but a very hollow peace shook beneath the heavy blows which Clara's passionate character gave to it. But, oh! the deep well of hatred gathering silently in the heart of that gentle dependant! How little did Clara dream of the track of bitterness her footsteps were leaving in the heart of one she fondly thought to love her, and vainly tried to love!

Mrs. de Saumarez began to see a great deal of Alice, for Clara was now required to be more with her mother, that she might be chastened into a propriety suitable to her age and rank. The contrast between the two girls was very striking: wherever the lady turned, the sharp delicate face of Alice was before her, watching her humbly but not inquisitively; and when Clara, flushed and tumbled, was deep in some enchanting story book which she would rather have died than lay down unfinished, or was lost in meditation, composing an

Homeric Epic or historic drama, the little orphan girl was studying
her every expression, and anticipating her every wish. Whatever she
wanted Alice brought, long before Clara—who was busy liberating
a fly from a spider's net, or warming a fainting bee in her hand, or
crying,

> "Lady bird! lady bird! fly away home!
> Your house is on fire; and your children will burn"

—in perfect belief that the lady bird would so fly away home—had
made half a dozen dragging steps across the room. When Clara fumed
and fretted at the rain which kept her a prisoner in her mother's stately
rooms and chilly presence, Alice, meek and patient, seemed to be
happier there than in all the amusements of childhood, so long as she
could creep near Mrs. de Saumarez and look into her face unbidden.
And when they had leave to retire, and Clara had bounded away with
a noisy cry and eager step, little Alice would go sorrowfully, looking
back in regret at the liberty which was her desolation. Many times
did Mrs. de Saumarez wish that Clara had been fashioned in the same
mould as this poor beggar girl; and many times she compared their
two natures with sorrow to her own motherhood.

By degrees Alice gained permission to attend on Clara during her
lessons. Before this Clare had rigidly set apart certain hours of the
day in which to teach her dependant all she herself knew. There had
not been much practical good in this scheme of education, for the
hours of instruction generally ended by the little maiden spouting
some most wretched poetry of her own, or reading the wildest
passages on love and liberty from Byron, Moore, and Scott, which
she had procured by stealth, to the utter neglect of Pollok, Cowper,
Cary's Dante, or Goldsmith—her prescribed colts of Pegasus. Else,
if in a prosaic and political mood, she would break out into a grand
and flowery speech against kingly governments in general, but against
Russian and Austrian despotisms in particular. She even went so far in
republicanism as to defend the French Revolution; and to have a secret
approbation of Mirabeau and Danton. Robespierre was too chill and
pale. Couthon was paralyzed—though the way in which he became
paralyzed somewhat redeemed him. Lafayette was pedantic and too
much of a gentleman—too much the pseudo-Bayard; Bailly was too
respectable; but the Leonine heroes she much admired. Madame

Roland was the grandest woman (except Corday and Joan of Arc and the maid of Saragossa) that the world ever saw, and she envied her fate and grew warm on her virtues. Camille Desmoulins she adored: he was a beautiful apostle of liberty to whom she gave her first love— shared perhaps by the living hero of Moore's Lalla Rookh, the girl's dear idol Hafed. All this she had learnt from Mignet's "History of the French Revolution," which she tried hard to understand in its scientific politics, and which she believed in far more than in the Bible. She worshipped this book, and went to sleep with it under her pillow; and dreamt one night of Mignet, who was the embodiment of Hafed and the likeness of Camille.[17] She would have been an easy conquest now to a handsome young republican!

Alice would listen to these furious outbursts for the most part in silence; a pale smile, sarcastic and condemnatory, her only answer. Clara's loud voice disturbed her nerves; and her vehement expressions and ultra opinions were painful to her calm and even nature. Sometimes she would interpose a chill remonstrance, which, as it had neither instruction nor heart in it, only made matters worse; for Clara would rather have had a stand-up fight for their respective opinions, than simple repression only of her own. There was some life in the one; the other was essentially a negation, a death. After all she erred only by youth's passionate adherence to the virtues which it knows, ignorant of others that may be contradictory. She erred by such wild love of justice and freedom as made her forget the claims of those who opposed her. Youthful and ignorant as she was, all that could be expected of her was fidelity to what she did know, though misdirected for the present in specialties.

"Kings," cried Clara one day, rising from her seat where she had been composing an essay on equality and universal suffrage;—"kings, Alice, have been the bane and the curse of all nations. Read history— what good ever came from a crowned head? What noble action or generous concession? Alice, the purple robe of monarchy is the pall of a nation's welfare!" That was a fine expression, Clara thought— Byronic and grand—but Alice let it pass unnoticed. "They are all grasping despots," she continued, blushing at her oratorical failure, "grinding the poor to the dust to supply themselves with luxuries, and caring no more for blood and life than if these wore different coloured threads in their weaving machines. All—all are the same! There is not a whole part in the crowned body! There is not a good man among them! To be a king or a noble is to be vicious without redemption, and so I can prove it!"

Now all this was in her essay—a kind of preface or peroration to the body of the thing. Alice raised her eyes with a wearied look; then, slightly shrugging her shoulders, began a piece of work for Mrs. de Saumarez with a kind of tranquil desperation, as if taking courage from the fact that time was not eternity, and Clare could not talk for ever; which reflection had more than once helped Alice to a marvellous amount of endurance.

"Look at their laws!" continued Clara, using much action, and speaking very loudly. "Look at their dungeons—the same in all countries! The tortures of the Inquisition; the infamous Bastille that our brave people threw down"—(Clare always identified herself with the French Revolutionists) "the fortress of Spielberg where that glorious Silvio Pellico[18] was confined—the Star Chamber—Siberia— oh! all that man could devise of most wicked, most infamous, does the world owe to the noble class! And this is the giant idol I am to worship!—this is the race to which I am expected to pay the homage of obedience, because I am unfortunately born one of them! No, Alice! when I am a woman, I will find out all the poor and sick, and those that other people despise, and these shall be my companions! I will not choose my friends among the vain, proud, heartless things that come here, so rich and noble—nor will I reject affection that is not offered in a golden cup. There are plenty of people to court the rich—I will defend the poor."

"No one doubts your kindness," said Alice quietly. "But you were talking about kings and princes. Now what you will be when you are a woman has nothing to do with dungeons, and nobles, and oppressed republicans. You wander so from your subject!"

"Yes, but it has to do with it!" cried Clare still more vehemently. "I am one of the superior class, and what I feel, others ought to feel also. You, Alice, have all your sympathies for the poor by birth, but mine come from reason."

"Thank you for reminding me that I am a beggar's daughter," said Alice, turning pale, for this was a point on which she was very sensitive. "It will not be your fault, Miss de Saumarez, if I ever forget the distance that is between us. But though I *am* one of the plebeian class, and you of the aristocratic, yet I don't think as you do, and I would blush to hold such dreadful opinions. I think them positively impious! We ought to submit to authority. We didn't make the world; and if there are these grades and distinctions, we ought to uphold them. It is told us so in the Bible, and I don't suppose you would deny *this* authority!"

Alice spoke harshly. She had seldom used this tone of severity, and Clare opened her great blue eyes in wonder. Now Clare, though religious in her own way, was so only in her own way. All biblical quotations, if against her theories, were abominations: and especially those which upheld constituted authority she flung to the ground at once, and would have nothing whatever to say to them.

"How can you talk such nonsense, Alice!" she exclaimed; "as if it was ever intended that we should submit to any tyrant because we had made him a king. Why, who makes kings and nobles but the people?"

"Oh! Miss de Saumarez, for shame!—are not all the powers that be ordained of God?" cried Alice hastily.

"No, they are not, Alice! They only exist by the people's sufferance, and it is of no use to deny it! If we did not like them, of course we should not have them! We would soon get rid of them if they were unpopular!"

"I know that Cromwell cut off good King Charles's head, and that Robespierre guillotined Louis—mild, patient Louis—and the beautiful queen," said Alice spitefully; "but I don't think they did right, though the nation upheld them. You may approve of murder if you like; I do not."

Now Clare prided herself on her humanity. This last speech made her furious; it was such an unjust sarcasm, and struck so deep! She walked about the room in great wrath, using many angry words and much vehement gesticulation. Never had she been more excited, never more beautiful. Her hair flung back from her flushed face, her eager manner, her bright eyes, the tremulous motion of her lips, the earnest words, formed a beautiful contrast to that slight figure bending so tranquilly over her work, unmoved and graceful.

"It is a disgrace to human nature," cried Clare, fetching her breath in gasps—for she was strongly agitated. "What!—you to uphold that bad class so much! You, who are one of the people, to have no sympathy, no love for them. You, who have seen the miseries they suffer, to care only for the luxuries above them!—Alice, I am ashamed of you! I, who have never known want, would give up all I have to save one poor being! And then you call such men as Voltaire and Rousseau, and all those great fathers of liberty, wicked, because they took the cause of the poor to heart, and loved them more than they loved the great! Oh!" she continued, clasping her hands and speaking more and more ardently, "if I had now the choice to suffer in fame and life as those men suffered, and do what they did for mankind, I would accept all their disgrace rather than the throne of worlds! Oh, Alice! how can you be so blinded by a little golden shine! How can you—a child of the people—be so indifferent to your class, and make yourself false idols of what is so hateful—so abhorred! I wish there was not a poor nor an oppressed person in the whole world, and that all the rich and proud were made slaves to the meanest of the poor! I do, Alice—I do!—and I would go to the stake for what I say!"

And, excited beyond her measure of control, Clare burst into a passionate flood of tears; in which tempestuous drownings her thunders of oratory generally ended.

Alice looked at her for a moment, in a quiet sarcastic way, and then pursued her work with a small still smile. Oh! no words that she might say could tell the contempt which she felt for that fiery enthusiast, nor have rightly expressed her calm sense of superiority over that untamed passionateness. Clara was to her like some furious animal, whose ragings she endured because opposition would have been destruction, yet with whom she had neither sympathy nor affection. All the warmth and life of that young heart went into this bitter drop of enmity. Even her love for Mrs. de Saumarez fell short of the intensity of her dislike for Clara. A dislike arising from purely physical causes, and therefore not to be treated as an independent moral crime. In after-life it was easy to be understood.

Mrs. de Saumarez heard the wordy tumult, and hastened up stairs. She found Clara all passion, haste, and fervour—in tears, and sobbing violently; and Alice quiet and lady-like, undemonstrative and subdued, just what all ought to be who have a true sense of propriety.

Without pausing to ask who was in the wrong, or why this wordy war had arisen at all, Mrs. de Saumarez, with the instinct of moral sympathy, went to the beggar's child and kissed her, while Clare's large tearful eyes met only a heavy frown.

Alice glanced triumphantly at the disgraced little democrat, and Clare wondered where she had been to blame, and what she had said that was wrong. Mrs. de Saumarez vouchsafed no explanation. She was determined to crush this rebellious spirit. Holding the hand of

Alice in her own, she said coldly to her daughter, "For today, Clara, you are confined to your own room."

"But, mamma!" interrupted Clara, her tears arrested by astonishment.

"And if you answer me in such a disrespectful manner as this," said Mrs. de Saumarez still more coldly, "you shall remain to-morrow also in confinement. I am determined to break this passionate temper of yours, and you will find opposition useless."

She took the little beggar girl with her gently, and both together left the room; she locking the door after her, and giving the maid express orders, within Clare's hearing, "not in allow Miss de Saumarez to leave her room until she returned."

In a few moments the carriage drove down the avenue. Alice, for the first time, seated by the grand lady's side in Clare's peculiar place.

Clare sat down and took herself severely to task. She chid and rated her naughty heart, with all its boiling blood and passionate impulses; but she did so falteringly; for how could she help it?—and why was it thought such a sin? She could not exactly understand the nature of her crime to-day. She had said only what she felt, and what she knew to be right. Yet mamma said she had been naughty; so she must accept the sentence on trust. She only wished that she could understand it better, then she would improve sooner; but when they told her that she was wrong and did not tell her how or why—it was impossible that she could do better by herself!

Many a tear Clara shed that solitary hour, and many a vow she made to herself not to allow her temper, as she had been taught to call her impulsiveness, to get the better of her. She must be calm!— it *was* very unlady-like to make such a fuss always, and to cry and sob merely for opinions! Mamma was right, and Alice was right, and she had been very naughty, and would ask pardon when they came home. And then, satisfied with her self-condemnation, she began to recompose her essay on equality.

This occupied her for a long time; but the sun poured into the windows and dazzled her. As she went to draw down the blinds, she heard the birds singing among the ivy and clematis twining round the casement. The blue sky was wide, and the air was fresh; and there was a sense of imprisonment for her alone of all that free creation. She stood for some time by the opened window, the fresh breeze fanning her heated cheeks and cooling her burning eyes. Her heart was sick at the silence and constraint of that narrow room. She longed to be away, unfettered as the boundless elements—away into fresh free life, where she might feel without sin and speak without rebuke. And for the first time came up in visible shape, in known truth and definiteness, the desire for sympathy, the consciousness of mental solitude.

Her blood, which had grown calmer, again rushed wildly through heart and brain. Vague desires, shadowy wishes, floated before her; she longed to be far hence, she knew not where, with something to love her, she knew not what. The mental dependance of childhood was swept away in the torrent of newly-awakened feelings; she was a woman, solitary and unloved.

The thought of self-destruction flashed across her, for she could see no way out of her misery. But the songs of the birds, the beauty of the scene, the bright sunlight and scented flowers—LIFE, in all its strong magic of sympathy, repelled that cold vision, and she turned from it, shuddering at its hideousness. But she would escape, she knew not where nor how. She did not measure distance nor compute impossibilities; she only felt that she must leave this hateful house. A thick cord, which she had bought for some boy-like purpose, lay in the corner of the room. She fastened one end round her waist, the other she tied to the iron stanchion of the window; well and strongly made were both knots; and then, utterly reckless of the certainty of being seen, she swung herself off, and putting in practice one of her masculine accomplishments alighted safely on the ground—into old Hugh's arms.

A scene of tears, entreaties, struggles, remonstrances, ensued; but the groom held her fast, and would not yield even to her prayers. Clare flung herself at his feet, weeping passionately; and just as she shrieked rather than said, "Let me go, Hugh! let me go! Let me starve, beg, die, only let me leave this horrible place!"—the carriage drove up, with Mrs. de Saumarez as a witness.

Solitary confinement for a week in her own room, which this time was well secured, was the practical result of Clara's attempt to run away from home. But deeper effects than the mere ennui or pallor of confinement were left; and thoughts, passions, wishes, were awakened in that young heart which nothing now could still. It was her lesson-time of life, and she had to learn in sorrow, as must we all, the truth of what she felt and the value of self-reliance; she had to learn how best to gain her independence; how, by self-help and self-nurture only, can strength and power come to the soul of man; how the lonely mind in youth must bravely bear its loneliness, and come out in maturity all the grander, all the stronger, for that solitude.

CHAPTER III.

SUCH scenes as this soon became of daily occurrence. As Clare grew older, and her opinions gained strength and her feelings intensity, she gained also a boldness of utterance which drew on her the redoubled censure of the household. The violence of her republicanism increasing in exact ratio with her reverence for truth and her recklessness of integrity, she believed that her whole code of morality consisted in steadfast adherence to what it pleased her to call her "political principles." In all places, and at all times, Clara de Saumarez was sure to make herself unfavourably conspicuous by her furious advocacy of some monstrous doctrine of equality and liberty, where most tabooed. She would rhapsodize on the French Revolution before a party of county magistrates, and inveigh against the iniquitous oppression of the Protestant Church in Ireland, in the very teeth of grave divines. She canonized O'Connell[19] at the table of a Tory member, and burst into tears over the wrongs of the Poles before a Russian intimate of Nicholas. In short, she did so many extravagant things, that she began to be regarded as insane by some of the kinder sort, and as innately depraved by those of stricter morals. For opinions are crimes in England; and if you oppose your clique in politics or religion, or even in simple social views, your head is in a moral halter, and you dangle a convicted felon against the holiest laws of ages.

About this time too, (she was just sixteen) she conceived the most violent admiration for John Mitchell.[20] She had read of him in the papers, and, in spite of the ridicule and misrepresentation of the Times, and others of the Tory press which her father patronized, she believed him to be the brightest star that had risen over the Green Island since the quenching of Fitzgerald's[21] glory and the setting of O'Connell's sun. And perhaps she was right. She had a long, long day-dream about John Mitchell, in which a camp—a brave band of rebel warriors—a disguise, of course in the cavalier dress of Charles's time—the enlisting of a beautiful young soldier chosen soon to be the leader's bodyguard, to watch him while he was asleep, and to keep the door of his tent always—a skirmish—the rescue of the leader by this beautiful young soldier—a wound—a discovery—and then something very vague and wildering—she knew not what—formed the elements of the programme. This day-dream was her chief mental existence for a long time. It was the development of the Hafed and Camille idolatry—her first devotion to a present cause and living man. How she longed to see her beautiful Irish hero—(for of course he *was* beautiful!)—how she used to dream of him—of his dark blue eyes and long hair, and wonder why she was so miserable when she woke! It gradually became a very vivid part of her life; and as she wandered alone about the fields and gardens, she used to think over all possible and impossible plans of realizing this dream—of running away from home (her staple thought,)—of getting to Ireland without harm or ill, passed on for love of the cause and universal charity to all men— and of flinging herself at John Mitchell's feet, and beseeching him to make her his cookmaid, secretary, or generalissimo, she did not care which—only to make her something by which she could advance the good work, and drive out the Saxon at the point of the bayonet. For years after, her heart would throb at the sound of the Irish accent, even from a beggar: and many a tear of passionate excitement has astonished Protestant and Tory sons of the Green Isle when they sneered at Ireland, and she electrified them with her abuse of England: all to be distinctly traced to these days of romance and dream.

As Clara thus deteriorated—at least what Mr. and Mrs. de Saumarez called deterioration—becoming more concentrated in her mental turbulence, so to speak, and more vehement and impassioned every way, Alice improved so rapidly that the very servants learned to call her the "most ladyly" and the "best mistress of the two;" for servants are excellent judges of conventional breeding. Her natural quickness enabled her to make use of every opportunity of improvement; and in point of artistic accomplishments she was already far beyond Clara. She drew with more neatness and precision, though not with so much boldness; and she played much more correctly than the young heiress, who used to improvise half her lessons. But she did not know so many languages, nor so much of history, nor could she understand Kant and Fichte,[22] which Clare asserted were mere A B C to her, not to speak of the first book of Euclid,[23] which the bright little pedant would boastfully go through at any given moment of the day, and which she had "learnt all by herself," she used to say. Neither did she ride so well, nor read so well, nor make such vigorous verses, nor write such original letters; but she *crocheted* better, and worked worsted-work better, and was a marvel in silk purses and steel beads; all of which were unknown problems to Clare.

Alice was a striking girl in her way. Her manners were retiring, but graceful and self-possessed; very refined and very gentle; her face and figure were delicate and well formed, and her hands were positively beautiful. She was extremely like Mrs. de Saumarez; so much so, that strangers continually made the mistake of remarking on the resemblance between the mother and daughter; much to the open grief of the lady when obliged reluctantly to introduce the fine, glowing, brilliant, but most noisy Clare, as her child, instead. Even the Treatise on Compensation failed then!

One fine spring morning, when just enough of winter lingered in the air to make it fresh and pure, Clare and Alice went out to walk. They had for their body-guard old Hugh Clayton, and for their moral overseer a meek young governess, who, it was a superstition with Mrs. de Saumarez to believe, would "keep Miss Clara in order." Poor weak wavering Miss Turner!—she had as little control over the girl as a weather-vane over the wind! All things to all men, she was Clare's echo when with her, and the accurate reflection of the mother when with her. And Clare, not possessing any experience of life, and therefore deficient in the comprehensive sympathies which experience alone gives, and, being ferociously virtuous—a perfect savage of truth— showered down as full a measure of contempt on the poor girl as her heart could bestow, and loved nothing better than to convict her of palpable dishonesty, and to make her small in her own eyes.

As they rambled along, Alice walking gently by Miss Turner's side, and Clare always far in the van or in the rear, flushed with her own thoughts or declaiming aloud with eloquent fervour, they met a tall, stylish, theatrical-looking woman, who inquired mincingly "the nearest way to the Hall."

The two ladies in front turned to old Hugh to explain; but Clara ran up, and not only answered all her questions while very much out of breath, but gratuitously informed her who they were—how she was the only child of the great De Saumarez family—how Miss Alice was her friend and companion—how Miss Turner was the governess, and old Hugh the faithful servant of the household.

The stranger flung back her head affectedly, clasped her hands, and exclaimed in a manner to which no words can do justice, and nothing but Astley's or the Surrey[24] represent; "No agate vilely cut is this fair scion of a noble house!—what grace, what majesty, what nobleness, in all her parts! Fair lady, I kiss the hem of your garment, and am in all things your most humble servant."

Clara's colour mounted at this address. Miss Turner seemed to dread some mysterious fascination or improper influence, and motioned her away; a sign of which Miss Clare took no sort of notice whatsoever. Alice bit her lip, yet looked provokingly tranquil, as the beaming burning face of her young patroness turned triumphantly towards her, asking for her applause of this flattering commencement.

The lady then went on to say that she was Miss Kemble—a distant connexion of the Kembles[25] of immortal memory; and here she paused and blushed in gentle shame, unwilling to paint more plainly the fashion of that connexion. However, her audience was far too innocent to understand her, or to eke out her delicate allusion into intelligibility. "She had come," she said, "to this sweet nest of doves, to give her celebrated modified representation of Shakespeare. She was well known in London; she had appeared before the queen, and had received a royal bouquet at her benefit; her 'fortune had kept an upward course, and she was graced with wreaths of victory.'" Altogether, by her own account, she was a most respectable sort of person, not at all according to the conventional idea of an actress—a very Lucretia to the Tarquins[26] of the green-room.

She was a tall person, with finely formed but haggard features. Her voice was now harsh and strained, but must have once been full and sonorous; her dress was of stylish cut, but poor in its materials and tawdry in its arrangements, and her manners those of a queen on a fifth-rate stage. Yet Clara, caught by the witchery of her profession— for she had always longed after the stage, in her innocent conviction that every actor must be a second Pericles, and every actress a very Sappho—believed it all genuine, and that she, Miss Kemble, was immeasurably superior to Mrs. Siddons or Miss O'Neil[27] of traditionary fame. So far went the alchemy of youth.

Without a moment's hesitation she promised the De Saumarez patronage in a torrent of assurances. She then drew forth her purse with its whole fortune of six shillings, and thrust it into the hand of the actress with an enthusiasm of generosity that overpowered herself much more than the recipient.

Alice touched her arm. "Will your mamma approve of this?" she said in a low voice.

"Of course! What a foolish question, Alice! Is it not right to encourage talent?—and is not this a glorious opportunity of paying our homage to the Immortal Poet of England and to the Dignity of the Dramatic Art? Of course mamma will be pleased—why should she not?"

Alice drew back with a small smile lurking at the corners of her delicate mouth, and Miss Kemble, taking the hand of the young heiress, kissed it, or rather the air about two inches from it, saying—

"Oh that I were a glove upon that hand!—or that I might be my lady's tricksy spirit—her minister of grace—to stand between foul harm and her, so that the very winds of heaven should not visit her check too roughly! What recompence can I make thee, beauteous girl? May thy generosity, like 'camomile, which the more it is trodden on, the faster it grows,' increase with the using! Shall I prove ungrateful to thee?—'shall the blessed sun of heaven prove a micher,²⁸ and eat blackberries?' two questions not to be asked! I thank thee, lady, and these gentlest companions of thy youth; and I trust that when ye honour me with your presence, ye will find Miss Kemble no mean interpreter of the golden words of our brave old Will!"

Her feelings overpowered her; she made a profound reverence—stage-fashion—which Clare practised afterwards for full three-quarters of an hour before the large cheval glass—and swept from their view; once turning round to raise her hands high above her head, involving a mute blessing—and then, clasping some invisible being to her breast, she rushed forward with long strides, until the trees of the hedge-row effectually concealed her.

When fairly out of sight she examined the contents of her reticule, and enumerated her possessions, beginning with, "six shillings from that little fool——"

Clare loudly pronounced her perfect—"with a face like a Greek tragic mask."

"And the same square-cut open mouth?" interrupted Alice quietly.

"Manners fit for a Juno," continued Clare, highly incensed, but too proud to show it; "a figure like Catherine de Medicis."

"It was in our reading-book to-day, that Catherine first introduced the fashion of riding on horseback sideways, because she had such a beautiful figure," again interrupted Alice with the same quiet manner and still face. "Clare's learning is not very profound!" she added with a slight laugh.

Miss de Saumarez finished her speech to Miss Turner; and when she had run through the names of Cassandra, Cleopatra, Mademoiselle Mars, and Mrs. Siddons, she had got to the end of her subject, and so had leisure to walk home tragically indignant and very ill-used—stalking apart in most heroic silence.

When they reached the Hall, the two girls—or rather Clare first—rushed into the presence of Mrs. de Saumarez; Alice following in her usual manner—graceful, noiseless, and composed. Clare began a fast and furious account of "a most beautiful woman—so lady-like—so beautifully dressed—so grand—who was a celebrated actress in London, and a sister of John Kemble's—and had come direct from the Queen to give plays in Shorne—and to whom she was going, having paid for front seats."

Mrs. de Saumarez made no reply, but calling Alice, asked her pointedly: "What does all this mean, my dear?—is it of a strolling actress that Miss de Saumarez is speaking in these extraordinary terms?"

"Mamma!" exclaimed Clara, "how strange of you to ask Alice, while I am here, what kind of person this is!"

Still Mrs. de Saumarez took no notice of her. Keeping her eyes fixed on Alice, she repeated her question, as if she had not heard Clara's voice.

"It is, ma'am," replied Alice; "she *is* a strolling actress, and not a very nice person, I should think. But I am no judge, only I did not think her nice."

"In what way, my dear?" said the lady kindly.

"She was affected and bold and ill dressed."

"Oh, Alice!" remonstrated Clara in great wrath.

"Were you spoken to, Clara?" said the mother severely.

The impatient little lip quivered, and the thin nostril dilated. "At sixteen to be ordered like a child—it is too much!" she exclaimed.

"Do you, Alice, think that she was genuine?" continued Mrs. de Saumarez; "and would you have thought her worthy of such violent patronage and ardent admiration?"

"No, ma'am; I am sure she was not a lady. If you saw her you would see at once that it would be very unfit for your daughter to be among her audience."

"For shame, Alice!" cried Clara, unable to contain herself. "You know that you are only trying to gain mamma's favour by saying all this! I am ashamed of your cruelty and meanness, trying to do an innocent person harm, just to please another. Mamma, she was good, for she was poor! Her cheeks were hollow, and she looked ill. She was deserving of kindness from her talent and position; and as for Alice," she continued, her eyes flashing with indignation, "you might hope for love from a stone before one kind or tender thought came from her! *She* is never too much carried away by her feelings to forget to censure! *She* will never be blinded by pity nor silenced by affection!"

"Is this your mode of manifesting charity and generosity?" said Mrs. de Saumarez very sternly. "To forget the affection and respect due to the members of your own household, that you may defend an unknown and most probably disreputable person, does not, I confess, seem to me the most satisfactory kind of benevolence! I am shocked!—this is worse than even I believed of you."

"Oh, do not scold Miss de Saumarez, ma'am!" said Alice patiently. "I am accustomed to these attacks on me when she is out of humour with anything else. It saves you, dear ma'am, many an undutiful word, and so I am pleased to bear them. Besides," she added with a sharp glance, "it is her prerogative; for she is my patroness."

Mrs. de Saumarez drew the girl to her bosom, and kissed her forehead; and an expression of the truest maternal love made her harsh features almost beautiful.

There was a dead silence for a few moments, during which Clara struggled hard for the show, at least, of calmness. At last she spoke.

"Alice!" she said, "do not think that I have not seen, almost from the first, the arts by which you have gained my mother's love from me, and placed me always in a bad light before her. I have seen and known it all throughout, and I have suffered it to go on in silence, thinking that if you were so base, and mamma so credulous as to believe you when you spoke against me, it was far beneath my dignity to counteract your evil doings. But it has come to a crisis now; on a foolish cause; but anything will serve. I *will* go to Miss Kemble's representations, for I have promised to go—and it is only from what you say that mamma would forbid it. I am too old now to be kept under by a girl I brought into the house myself, and who but for me would have been now begging her bread. I am sixteen years old, and a menial shall not be my mistress even with my mother's sanction and under my father's roof."

The first taunt that had ever issued from Clara's lips!

Alice turned sharply round, but she did not answer; only underneath her shawl and dress might have been seen every nerve and muscle quivering. The bolt shot, Clara prepared to quit the room.

"Stay, Miss de Saumarez!" said her mother, rising from her seat; "before you quit this chamber, down on your knees to ask the pardon of this 'menial' for the wicked words you have just repeated."

"I will not, mamma!" Clara returned firmly. "I have done nothing wrong—said nothing untrue—nothing that you and Alice do not know to be true. She has been my enemy from the first," she added vehemently, her long pent-up feelings at last finding utterance; "and though I have tried to make her love me, and tried to treat her as my own sister, and have done all I could for her in every way, she has always hated me, and always made me appear selfish and bad to you. Have I not seen it!" she repeated bitterly, "and suffered from it, and found all my misery in it!"

"There is but one way to end this painful scene," said Alice, coming up to Mrs. de Saumarez and speaking gently and tearfully; "let me leave this house—this dear house—where I have been so kindly treated by *you*," with emphasis, "dearest and best Madam. I have been happy here—far beyond anything I have deserved—but"—and she raised her eyes with a Madonna look—"it will only teach me that earth is not the place for happiness, and that imperfection must entail suffering."

"You must not speak foolishly, my child," said Mrs. de Saumarez gently; "you are my protégée and kind complying companion, and I will not part with you, Alice, for any storm of such imperfect and wrongful nature. You belong to me, and you shall not be separated from me."

Alice knelt down and kissed her hand, and Mrs. de Saumarez bent over her smiling. It was the old group as formed three years ago.

At a little distance stood Clara; and the scene of that child's first introduction to the Hall, when forced by her on the lady's care, rushed to her mind. Large tears came into her eyes, for she could not but confess to herself that she was misunderstood and unhappy; and she pitied herself so heartily! There was not a creature in the world to whom she could turn for sympathy or advice. She, though the heiress, was the Pariah in the house, and lived alone in a forbidden atmosphere into which no loving heart dared to venture. Never had she felt so truly solitary; never had the wide world seemed so entirely one vast blank—holding neither happiness nor affection for her. Eagerly creating opportunities of mortifying her, her mother and her dependant taught her that she was of less consideration than a hired servant would have been; that, nominally the superior, she was in reality the lowest of the household; not only solitary in mind, but banished from their affections and neglected in every social detail of their lives. Poor Clara! she hung her head, and sitting down on a low stool, burst into such a passion of tears and sobs as seemed to rend her very being.

In the midst of this wild storm the butler ushered in pompously "Miss Kemble."

"Who told you to admit this person?" said Mrs. de Saumarez sternly, though the poor faded actress was not many feet from her.

The man was awed and silent; but the visitor, making a sweeping courtesy, besought the lady's "gentle judgment on her."

Clara could have rushed into her arms and fairly kissed those hollow cheeks. She did go up to her frankly, and hold out her hand as if to an old friend.

Nothing abashed, and holding the young girl's hand between her finger and thumb, as you may see nightly represented on the stage—symbolical of various kinds of emotions—Miss Kemble came forward, handing in a very folio of testimonials, three tickets, and two or three programmes; and speaking in a peculiarly stage-bred manner, half deferential, half familiar, she informed Mrs. de Saumarez of her literary and histrionic intentions, and how she had now come to secure the patronage which this "sweet cushat dove"—meaning the sobbing, stormful, tearful Miss Clare—had promised her.

Mrs. de Saumarez answered coldly and curtly; smoothly, without accent or deflection in her voice, she declined the honour of this patronage; and with perfect good breeding expressed her determination not to allow any member of her household to attend these modified readings of Miss Kemble's.

Miss Kemble made no reply, but, standing from Clara at the distance of their two arms jointly extended, she made a sweeping flourish with her disengaged hand; indicating by this act that the young lady being the cause of her application was also the guarantee of its success. The girl's face was crimson; she felt the necessity of being very calm and womanly, and therefore she spoke gently, but with an accent of such determination that Mrs. de Saumarez herself was surprised at the boldness of her opposition.

"I might have been rash, mamma," she said, "but I promised Miss Kemble that some of us would go to her readings this evening. I even secured places. If you have no *real* objection, Miss Turner and I will attend, for I have a great wish to see something of this kind, and there can be no impropriety in my doing so."

"You may be sure, my dear Madam," then inserted Miss Kemble, clasping her hands at a considerable distance from her, while she drew back her body and put her head a little on one side; "you may be sure that the morals of the young with whom it may be your gracious will to entrust me, shall suffer nothing at my hands. I have carefully excluded all such passages as could give gross sense to the understanding, and taken due diligence to extract those which shall elevate the mind and refine the sentiments. Alas! for the imperfection of even the best of men—the weeds in the fairest garden of intellect! I travel, my dear Madam, with a moral purpose—to remedy this imperfection, and to remove these weeds: and I trust I am not defeated in my aim. The Bible first and old Will Shakspeare next; I hope I am not profane—I hope not; but my reverence for the Avon Bard increases with my reverence for religion; and this, dear Madam," and she sighed, "I have found my great comfort and support through a chequered career." Miss Kemble had been in church on christening or matrimonial occasions sometimes; but never on any other. As for religion, she knew just as much of it theoretically as she did of geometry. She stumbled on a virtuous action as she did on a perfect hexagon; but not from scientific rules in either case. "Old Will was nature's poet, and Nature and the Bible are, you know dear Madam, the lock and key to the door of truth," she added with an oratorical flourish.

Mrs. de Saumarez knew too much of life and the highest models to be deceived by this coarse daub. She saw at once that Miss Kemble was a very inferior actress; probably the prima donna of some second-rate theatre, or one of the supernumeraries at the Royal Theatre; and so in truth "playing before the Queen." It was not a matter of charitable consideration with her whether this poor faded piece of finery was starving or not, or whether she was struggling to keep herself "correct" by a few "white lies." She was not "genuine" in her profession; and this stern stickler for truth refused to patronize where it was not the patronage of art, but merely the simple gift of charity.

Mrs. de Saumarez was indeed a stern stickler for truth.

Miss Kemble was bowed out—coldly enough—and her three tickets refused; likewise the six shillings which her pride made her offer to return. And by her manner of refusing Mrs. de Saumarez inflicted a still greater insult than before. The poor actress thought of her unpaid lodging, her scanty fare, her empty rooms, her unsympathizing audience, and so smothered the rising indignation and the apt quotation, and, as many others have done before her, repressed her pride for the sake of her pocket. Clara, in open defiance of her mother, accompanied her to the door—accompanied her to the gate—and down the lane for more than a mile. Talking of the excitement and the glories of a theatrical career—of the intellectual pleasures of conception and delineation, which pleasures Miss Kemble knew by hearsay only, having never understood more in her profession than the coarsest technical business and the most parrot-like imitation of conventional models—of the vivid delight that rushes through heart and brain when pit, boxes, and gallery applaud—when you feel that you have stirred the hearts of all those hundreds, and made them beat and throb as *you* chose and willed—of all the intoxication of that gas-light life which lures on its victims as the candle attracts the moth. With greedy ears and heated blood Clara listened to these gorgeous pictures, and when they parted she wrung Miss Kemble's hand almost convulsively, saying in an agitated voice, "Should I make a good actress?" and looking into her face as if her whole life depended on the answer.

"I would guarantee you an European reputation in a year," Miss Kemble cried fervently, and without her usual affectation.

Clara turned away, and walked thoughtfully home; such burning wishes and passionate sorrow awakened in her heart as must surely soon bear fruit in action of no mean importance.

CHAPTER IV.

THE dinner bell rang. Clara prepared to descend, when she was stopped by the lady's maid bearing a small tray which contained her solitary meal. Henceforth she must consider herself an outcast from the family, until she condescends to apologize for her late ill conduct. In Clara's present state of mind this was an injudicious request. The cord had been already strained nearly to breaking; it needed but the slightest additional pressure to make it snap like burnt flax. All the love of that affectionate nature; all the strong influences of early habit and of childish memories, when a divinity which nothing could break through hedged round those awful dispensers of fate, the father and the mother; all the clinging instincts which bind the heart to Home, were tottering before the onward rush of wild desires for freedom, which the consciousness of an unloved and desolate solitude had aroused.

A few kind words might have saved Clara from herself to-night. This severity sealed her fate.

At the proper hour she rang her bell. The maid answered it. She told her to prepare to accompany her to the village, about a mile distant, and to bid Hugh be in readiness to guard them home at ten o'clock, when Miss Kemble promised that her reading should be brought to a close.

The maid looked important and left the room. In a few moments she returned with her shawl and bonnet.

Clara was soon ready; the door was opened, and she walked slowly down stairs; slowly through the gardens and down the long avenue; all in sight of the dwelling rooms. It was a bright evening, still light and clear at the closing hour of the day. Without remonstrance or hindrance the girl went forward, wondering as much as rejoicing at this strange lull in the usual battle of domestic opposition.

The reading passed off respectably enough. Miss Kemble "did" Lady Macbeth extremely well; she essayed Beatrice,—but it was a pert and vulgar Beatrice even to Clare's ignorance of stage perfection; she read the balcony scene in Juliet's brief career, and made the whole a very farce. And then she turned back to the Grand, and did not disgrace herself in Constance. The audience applauded as village audiences generally applaud—when there was a rough joke, or broad delineation made with such coarse splashes that no one could fail to recognise the meaning; but all the finer shades were lost on them; and, as Miss Kemble said, "the country louts did not relish her delicacies."

It might have been very petty and very small, but Clara did feel a certain degree of pride when she, alone of all the audience, was invited into that mysterious little retiring room where the actress was retransformed into the woman. This may seem more than puerile to those of the London world who stroll behind the scenes of the opera, and hear the prima donna swear sweet Italian oaths, and see the *première danseuse* drink porter while she chalks her shoes. But Clara was only sixteen, and she had never seen an actress before, and had scarcely ever been beyond the precincts of her native village. And to her it was a *privilege*, as is every new experience that you make, if exclusive to the rest of the world then surrounding you. And this little incident, coupled with Miss Kemble's kind manner, completed the fascination which sorrow first created more completely than even prepossession.

"And when do you leave Shorne, Miss Kemble, dear?" asked Clara, when she rose to bid the actress good night.

Her face grew pale when she asked this question, and her hand, which rested on the table, trembled beyond her power of control.

"By the eight o'clock morning mail, my dear young lady. I shall reach London somewhere between six and seven in the evening. Can I do anything for you?"

Clara was silent. Her agitation visibly increased.

"You are not well, my dear young lady?" said the actress, alarmed at her manner and appearance.

"Yes I am," returned Clara; after a short pause she added, "but I am very miserable;" and then she betook herself to her old resource of violent tears.

Sincerely concerned, Miss Kemble made the young heiress re-seat herself. Bidding her open her heart unreservedly—she would not betray any kind or amount of confidence, and she might be able to comfort her—she placed herself by the girl's side and did her best to soothe her. And the old robe of tarnished affection fell from her, and left the pure core of Woman's Tenderness undefiled.

The girl was overcome. With mingled tears and grateful words she poured forth her flood of sorrowful confidence, till even the actress felt her eyelids moist at the picture of that young heart in its lonely greatness—its strong sense of power and oppression—its yearning thirst for love and its solitude unbroken—battling down its griefs for so many long months with a heroic grandeur, most beautiful, most rare—and oh, how misunderstood!

When she had finished her mental story of such suffering, Clara, clasping her hands on her breast, cried in the most passionate manner—"Oh that I were free! Miss Kemble, I would give my whole existence to know but three years of freedom and of action! This life will make me mad if I lead it much longer! I must, I will be free, and so change it! I must go out into active life, and learn from others what I am; if I am the unworthy thing I have been taught to feel myself at home, or if I may not be something less criminal than my mother and Alice believe me!"

"The time must come for this in the due course of events," said Miss Kemble; "in five years you will be of age, and then——"

"Five years!" Clara exclaimed with horror—"oh! that is an eternity!"

The actress smiled. "Ah, I forgot the difference between us! With me, five years are less than five months used to be before I had learnt what the future *must* bring. I grant you—five years are an eternity to you—and you must have a change before that time. Have you a wish?"

"Yes: one always strong—and since I saw you, stronger than ever."

"And that, I need not ask——"

"Is the stage."

The actress was not surprised. She had seen this part of Clara's nature at once; and she felt sure that any false light of excitement which might flare up in her face, would be accepted before the gray dull twilight of inaction in which she now lived. And yet she started as from a sudden chasm before her feet, when this bright young heiress gave shape to her own thought. In vain she urged on her the pains and sorrows of an actress's life; in vain she expatiated—how feelingly!—on the misery of poverty, the helplessness of a solitary womanhood, the social ban which still lay on the actress class; in vain—and all in vain! Clara's young heart was too strong to warp, her young fancy too warm to chill; she shook her head at all that Miss Kemble urged, and reiterated her desire and her intention, as soon as convenient, of carrying out this desire.

"Take care!—take care! For God's sake my dear young lady, be prudent and careful!" said the actress with real feeling. "So young, so beautiful, so innocent, so unpolluted—my God, what crime and misery would befal you!"

Her voice had such an accent of genuine womanly feeling in it, that Clara's heart cleaved to her in almost child-like impulse. She took her hand and pressed it to her lips. "Miss Kemble, dear," she said, "I am as you see me; you know who I am, and why I would leave home;

will you promise me that if ever I do leave home to go on the stage, you will take care of me and be kind to me?"

Miss Kemble hesitated. There was an appearance of foul dishonour in thus tempting away, or offering facility to her wild fancy, a girl born in such a high station as that which Clara held. And yet, again, who could be more unfortunately situated?—who more miserable, with a misery ever increasing before her? It was the hesitation only of a moment; the next, she had taken Clara to her heart, and kissing her cheek, said; "Yes, sweet girl, I would take care of you!—I would be your mother and your guardian, and defend you against every sorrow and every danger with my own happiness and my own fame."

I don't know that she would have done quite all this; but she was really sincere at the moment, and would have borne a great deal from pure interest in her young friend's character. There was perhaps another reason for her fervour; the certainty of her own advantage from Clara's introduction. Few feelings are entirely pure and unmixed; none where the heart has been long deadened by a clashing conflict with poverty and oppression.

Clara murmured her blessings and her thanks; and now, something calmer, remembered her of home which she had utterly forgotten during all this long conversation. She rose to go, and as she bade her new friend once more "good night," the clock struck twelve.

"I am late!" she said with a scared look. Then a smile broke over her face as she added, "I do not care now: I have a home and a friend for the dark days that will come."

She raised her face to her companion, and Miss Kemble never forgot that look. In after days, that burning cheek wet with tears and glowing with excitement; that flashing eye, so full of life and love, every ray from the dilated pupil bearing a world of poetry, hope, and warm emotion to her soul; the parted lips of eloquent promise; the strength and enthusiasm in her attitude of upraised hand, bent form, and head erect; the very atmosphere around her eloquent of life— in the long dull days of her cheerless end, that transient scene often came before her like the glowing memory of a brilliant sunrise. And a sunrise in truth was it: the first flash of the young spirit as it leapt up from its sea of slumberous darkness, and broke over the world in energy and action.

In silence, and deeply agitated, Clara flew home. The maid looked gloomily portentous—Hugh much distressed. The household had retired (ten o'clock was the orthodox hour) and only the old porter, who grumbled much to himself and at last told Clara gruffly that her papa wanted her in the study, waited her return. Clara went immediately, fully expecting to be scolded, yet feeling too womanly to rebel to-night. She went prepared to submit to any amount of chiding he chose to inflict. Perhaps a consciousness that she had done very wrong in staying out so late helped her good resolutions of patience and forbearance.

She entered—her father was alone. "So, Miss de Saumarez," he began, "is this the conduct you deem fit for a gentlewoman?—is this the respect you owe your parents, the respect you owe your station, the respect you owe yourself? Not content with the most flagrant act of disobedience of which you—habitually disobedient as you are—have ever been guilty (yet which act might have been overlooked and pardoned on a becoming repentance)—you add to it such a disgraceful freedom of conduct as, I tell you once for all, I will not suffer in my house. The clock points now to a quarter past twelve—no, I am wrong—twenty minutes past: you have only just returned home. Ten o'clock is the latest hour of ingress generally allowed to my household; you have exceeded that time by two hours and twenty minutes. What have you to say for yourself? What excuse to offer, for bringing a scandal and a disgrace on your family through the whole county?"

"I am very sorry, papa," began Clara, "but I forgot the time: I was talking."

"Talking were you?—and to whom, pray? What associates worthy of a De Saumarez did the heiress of the De Saumarez find in the audience of a profligate actress?—or did she find that actress herself fit companion for her youthful age and high position? I am anxious to know the taste of one who, though our only child, I both blush and rejoice to say has derived no part of her nature from her mother or myself."

"It was with Miss Kemble that I was speaking," said Clara, in her secret heart much frightened, yet maintaining a calmness of manner which unfortunately irritated her father still more against her.

"And you found her so fascinating as to beguile your senses for two hours and twenty minutes?" Mr. de Saumarez returned, with increased severity of look and voice.

"I did, papa," said Clara modestly, but firmly.

"This is not to be borne!" cried Mr. de Saumarez. "If all the kindness lavished on you from your birth—if all the care and attention, daily, hourly, momentarily paid to you by your mother and myself—if no thought of self-respect, no impulse of modest pride, no principle of honour, can restrain or correct you, I will try what a harsher punishment will do. Vile girl that you are, would you be a curse to your family, and the first and only blot on its shield! Sooner than that, I will inflict its dishonour, in the hope that this light mark may obviate one deeper and more indelible!"

He seized his daughter by the arm, and with a small dog-whip that lay near struck her twice or thrice across her neck and shoulders.

"Now to bed and say your prayers, and to-morrow beg my pardon—and your mother's—for your wickedness of to-day."

He thrust her from the room, and locked the door as she turned her tearful face of horror on him.

I will pass over this night of Clara's terrible agony, mingled as it was with fierce flashes of joy coming in between her fits of madness and despair. For now there could be no ingratitude, no coldness, no sin, in escaping from a home where personal brutality had been added to moral harshness and the coldness of indifference. All night long she busied herself in arranging her wardrobe and in choosing such things as were indispensable for her flight; adding so many favourite relics that her work had to be done over again hundreds of times, until she learnt, at last, that in leaving home she would have to leave all that had made that home dear and loved. Clara was no waverer. When she thoroughly comprehended her inability to carry away in a parcel a whole roomful of personalities, she stoutly resigned them, and confined herself, as I said before, to the necessaries of her wardrobe. But there was more heroism in this stedfast resignation than appears on the mere face of it. To such a childhood as Clare's, and with such a nature, it is easy to understand how dear her own little world had been—how her own garden, her own books, her playthings, and private treasures of all kinds, had been more entirely her companions than they are to others. And in leaving these, she left the only brothers and sisters and gentle friends she had ever known—she left all that had made up her outward life.

The morning broke—the house began to stir. The question was now, how she might escape without being seen. If boldly through the hall, and then directly down the avenue, she must surely be discovered. Besides, her father was sometimes taken with a fit of afflictive restlessness, and he might be wandering abroad too. That would be awkward. But all must be ventured. It was now half-past seven o'clock. There was not much time to spare. The mail passed through Shorne at eight o'clock, and waited for no one. The house was thoroughly awake. Mrs. de Saumarez rang her bell, and Clara heard her father's measured tread pass down to his laboratory. She also heard Alice, who slept immediately over her, draw up her blind. She too was stirring. It was no time for fear. Taking her bundle in her hand, she stole down stairs and gained the hall-door unperceived. The servants were at breakfast. She remembered now that this was their breakfast-time. Instead of going through the avenue, which was the direct way to the village, she cut across the fruit garden into a large meadow belonging to the estate, where she was concealed from the hall windows by a thick hedge-row. She had to cross the avenue once, far down, and close to the gate. This was her only point of peril. And yet, at that distance it would have been difficult to recognise her. The moment came. Turning her eyes up to her old home, she saw her father pacing on the terrace immediately before the house. His face was toward her, but he was looking on the ground; and so she flitted by unperceived.

Bewildered and terrified at what she had done, yet breathing more freely than she had ever breathed before, Clara rushed up to the small inn where the coach changed horses, just as Miss Kemble prepared to enter that primitive vehicle.

The ostlers and loungers standing about gaped in wonder, for the young heiress was well known and much loved in the village; and the comely landlady even ventured to remonstrate with her on her evident intention. Clara attempted to pacify her fears—with ill success; for that open brow, little accustomed to falsehood or concealment, betrayed the faltering lip in its flimsy endeavour to utter the unnatural lie. However, as no one had the power, no one made the attempt, to stop her, and Clara seated herself by Miss Kemble's side but a moment before the coach started forward.

Her flight from the Hall was not discovered for a long time. Her absence at prayers was not remarked; for, as she had been placed in solitary confinement by the authorities themselves, she could not be present. It so happened also that the maid waited for the ringing of the parlour bell to receive her young mistress' breakfast from the family table, and Mrs. de Saumarez imagined that the housekeeper would send up what was proper; and, as breakfast was a very lengthy meal at the Hall, the little fugitive got a fair start before her absence was known. Though when that absence was known, suspicion was not long undetermined where to point for the companion, at least, of her flight.

Advice now came up from the village; the whole neighbourhood was astir, swarming like bees about the Hall. The servants made a holiday, and left off their work to stand in chattering groups, sure that no domestic order could be observed on such a frightful day. But they were mistaken; for Mrs. de Saumarez, paler and colder than ever, ordered them to their business in accents that said without words, "What is the matter? do you think I suffer either grief or surprise?"

Mr. de Saumarez was more demonstrative in his own way. He talked a great deal of his father's shield and defective analyses; and jumbled up ethics, chemistry, and heraldry, in a very odd manner. He talked too of a special train; but then he did not know the direction which his daughter would take when she arrived at the railway station—whether to London or farther inland—and he did not like to be subject to an undignified defeat. Mrs. de Saumarez also negatived the "special," and expressed her belief that sorrow and reflection would restore Clara to her right mind; in which she gravely asserted she had long ceased to be. Alice thought that perhaps the mother's anger might glance on her as the true cause of this disaster and disgrace; but Mrs. de Saumarez, reading her fears, called her to her, and told her she must not think herself to blame.

"It is a severe dispensation for the time," she said, her hand on the old Treatise on Compensation; "but I doubt not that ultimately it will work good. I am no optimist, Alice, nor am I a visionary, yet I feel that beneath this mask of misfortune lies some unknown benefit to my family."

Gradually she inoculated her husband with this belief: and offended pride coming in to stifle what feeble affection might have escaped the pressure of "incompatibility of temper," Clara's flight grew to be regarded as a sin rather than as a sorrow. And so the calm life of the inmates of the Hall went on its usual even way; more stagnant now than ever, since the only bit of healthy nature had withdrawn.

Soon Clara was almost forgotten. Every one said that Mrs. de Saumarez looked in better health and spirits than she had done for years past; and she did in truth feel an immense relief, as if a boisterous wind had been lulled or a turbulent crowd dispersed. The only things that missed poor Clare were the beggars and the dogs, Fleetfoot, the bees, and old Hugh. The dogs whined for several days, and Fleetfoot used to turn his head wistfully whenever the stable door opened; the bees too were restless, and twice they stung Alice and the lady: but excepting for this mute regret of those dumb domestics, and the neglected state of the weed-grown patch of ground that had been her garden, every trace of the young heiress was in time obliterated. Her own room, cleared of all its deserted treasures, was newly papered and painted, and the arrangement of the furniture totally altered; and one day, after old Hugh had said a few words very low and mysteriously to the lady, Alice was instituted mistress of the apartment, as if this was a kind of acknowledgment of her importance. And Mrs. de Saumarez was seen to watch her young friend more narrowly than ever, and to treat her with increasing respect and affection.

Thus time wore on; and while Clara was studying under a theatrical elocutionist, preparatory to appearing on the boards under the name of Miss Clayton—for she had taken Hugh's name from a lingering love of the old place—the father mourned over his abortive analyses, and the mother prayed that the hope to which old Hugh's mysterious words had given birth might be found a reality.

But Martha had long since left the neighbourhood, and even Hugh did not know her address nor where she had gone. No one else could substantiate the lady's vision of delight, and make her belief, that this mask of misfortune covered her ultimate advantage, a true and positive fact. Therefore she must wait in patience the turning of the next page in the great book of the future.

CHAPTER V.

THE manager of the theatre to whom Miss Kemble introduced Clara, was a naturally kind-hearted, but capricious and violent man. He had led a life of self-indulgence mingled with much mental exertion, and had gone through the further hardening process of signal success in his official career. He had thus grown to consider himself so superior to the rest of mankind that, had he not been physically humane, he would have been always intolerably tyrannical. As it was, where his affections were not concerned, he was overbearing, cruel, and unfeeling, in the same proportion as he was kind and gentle when actuated by fancy or desire. He was a dangerous enemy and an uncertain friend; for he was so easily offended, and he required such unlimited obedience from all with whom he had any kind of connexion, that few people could attain to that degree of self-denial which his tyranny demanded. Yet, as a friend or lover, no tenderness was too excessive, no generosity too great for him to show. This sounds a paradoxical character; but a physiologist could explain it, and prove its credibility.

Mr. Vasty Vaughan—the great V. V. as he was sometimes called—was no longer young. He was rather more than forty years of age: just dreaming of baldness and contemplating a few gray hairs. But he was youthful in feeling, and of an elastic temperament: and these two characteristics soften down the asperities of bare heads and silver locks. Agreeable, gentlemanlike, a systematic roué, and a thorough-going atheist sceptical of all virtue and all goodness—he was a dangerous person to become the arbiter of a young girl's fate. He was handsome too; one of those manly, frank, benevolent, and pleasure-loving people, who win women sooner than any other class of men. He had a certain protecting, almost fatherly, manner inexpressibly delightful to the young; and he boasted often that he never knew a woman who was proof against this manner. As for Clara—though the precepts of her early education formed a slight counterpoise to her natural imprudence—yet she soon regarded him with the confidence of a daughter; feeling that anything was "correct" if she could say, "Oh! but Mr. Vaughan was there!"—"I am going with Mr. Vaughan—" "that handsome man you met me with late last night?—why! that was Mr. Vaughan!" Let a man once establish this feeling and, *ceteris paribus*,[29] he may walk over the course at his leisure. It was Vasty Vaughan's particular method, and he had never known it fail.

Miss Kemble rejoiced in the evident partiality of the great V. V., their omnipotent manager, for her young friend. The strictest of the theatrical world have but lax notions after all; and Miss Kemble, though a green-room Lucretia, did not hesitate to trust this inexperienced child with a man whose list of *bonnes fortunes*[30] included almost all his female friends of every station and condition. Yet had he not been in power, and the dispenser of reputation and position to his actress world, Miss Kemble, who was a good woman at heart, would have guarded her protégée from his presence with the care of a mother. But the curse of subordination had fallen on her, as on us all in more or less degree; and from her chief—though from none other—she would have borne profligacy, tyranny, and insult, and deemed it only in the way of her profession; part of the daily bread which the gas-light and its false world gave her. The theatrical population is not alone in this subservience to its leaders; it is the brand stamped on most of those who are dependant on others.

As for Clara herself, she was far too innocent to suspect evil in any one—least of all in Mr. Vaughan who was so gentle and protecting in his manner to her. It was sad but beautiful to see this poor child's confidence in all sorts of people. In the green-room, for instance, she might be seen accepting the attentions of the vilest of the supernumeraries as she would have accepted the attentions of a hero; and she would speak to the most notorious of the ballet dancers in the same hearty manner as that in which she spoke to Miss Kemble herself. And when told what characters these people had, and that she must not be on terms of social charity with them, she would pass, when she next met them, with a brow bent and crimsoned as if she had been the guilty one. Poor little Clare!—she stood in that green-room world like a damask rosebud in the midst of flaunting weeds and rankest refuse. It made one sad to see her in such unsuited atmosphere; credulous of all, and fondly taking paint and tinsel for nature and rich jewellery. As yet she could not use her unaccustomed freedom with judgment, but, like a blind man suddenly gifted with sight, had to learn the difference between reality and appearance in bitter shape of hard experience. She knew nothing of the world—suspected nothing of the evil nature of man; and Miss Kemble shrank from the task of instructing her in that evil.

"It will come soon enough," she used to say to herself, when Clare had made some of her egregious blunders, and failed to see what lay manifestly before her; "and if she does burn her fingers, I will take care that she does not really damage herself. I don't like to tell her all that villany which she does not know now. She must learn it by experience. She is so young yet, that she has some good years of innocence before her eyes need be opened."

Whether wise or not, one could not but respect this determination of the actress, marking, as it did, the lingering footsteps of a delicacy which somehow or other most women retain in the very heart of crime and degradation. It may be half forgotten; it may be buried under a heap of positive and present sin; but it seldom dies out utterly; never while one impulse of maternal instinct remains.

Clara's theatrical studies must now begin. She was placed under the care of a famous elocutionist; and Vasty Vaughan himself superintended her studies. Percival Glynn was the name of this new master: a name henceforth inextricably woven into the web of her existence, chequering the whole of her future.

He, as all the rest, was delighted with her. The power of character and grasp of intellect which she displayed enchanted him in his world of conventional imitation and limited comprehension. It was like a burst of sunlight in a darkened room. And bright and glorious were the pictures of success that he drew before her dazzled eyes. Hour on hour Clara would listen to his scenes of future triumph, her whole soul burning beneath the impress of those glowing words. Then she would study with redoubled diligence, and pass long days in a state of ecstatic blessedness, while taxing the coldest of her mental powers in learning technicalities and professional business of the most uninviting character. Yet though undergoing the worst drudgery of her education, she was so entirely absorbed by her impassioned fancy as to believe that drudgery pure poetic pleasure. So true is it that the mind creates its own world, and that the meanest condition can be transformed into the most exalted by hope and fancy. Like magicians, who call up the living light of gold and gems and fairy flowers from the worthless landscape of weeds and stones, are these gifts of hope and fancy. This is the bright side of the picture. When sorrows come, the same mind which floats in a sea of gleaming brightness and drinks in deathless glory if but a bird sings in the hedge, gives a gloom and desolation to the passing summer cloud which wraps the whole world in one huge pall of death. The simply sanguine man laughs always. His heart is large and his digestion good. But those who feel deeply add such passion and intense sensation to the circumstances around them, as heighten their joys to madness and deepen their sorrows to despair. These are the people who exhaust life while still in early youth. These are the people who revel in burning pleasures where colder natures find only weariness, or who die of broken hearts where others of weaker brains live on unmoved; these are the people of whom success makes gods, or who perish in their fierce passion of disappointment. And of such as these was Clare de Saumarez. A many-stringed harp that gave out sounds to every passing wind,

whether scented-shrub or carrion laden—a flower that blossomed
forth or faded if but a rushlight[31] shone or was withdrawn—a being
emphatically in the power of every hand that chose to strike a rough
chord out of tune, or to pluck the blossom budding to the sun. Call
it what you will—lack of dignity, of pride, of self-control; brand it
with what harsh names cold dulness ever gives to unknown feelings;
yet sure it is the faculty which threw on Sappho all her beauty, on
Shelley all his power. Make poets unimpressionable, and poetry is
a withered weed tangled through the slack strings of a broken lyre.
And all who feel with much intensity are poets with more or less of
rhythmic power. For her selfish calmness—go bathe yon maiden child
in chill apathy; for godlikeness, pleasure, power, for poetry of life, for
majesty of thought—wrap her in a quivering robe of strong emotion,
and thrill every nerve with tenfold faculty of sensation. Give her the
poisoned ashes of hell if ye also give her the golden fruits of heaven,
and with one hand pour the curse of sorrow's bitter gall freely into
her cup, if, with the other, ye shed the fleeting drops of joy divine in
its intensity. Such is the only existence worthy of the name of Human
Life.

   This Percival Glynn, under whose tuition Clara was placed, was
a man of no ordinary character. Justice—or, as the philosopher calls
it, universal toleration, as the religionist, latitudinarianism, was his
grand characteristic. The equal right of every opinion to utterance
and of every principle to recognition—the equal right of every instinct
to preservation and of every individual to unrestrained action—the
civil laws of the country the only circumscription of his sphere—these
were the great truths he taught under the simple name of "Justice."

   "Justice," he used to say, "is virtually unknown. We recognise her
under the form of prison discipline only, and in the black cap of legal
retribution alone do we clothe her features. Toleration—which name
I for my own part repudiate, as assuming a right of intolerance or
individual repression, but which the world understands in the sense
in which I use justice—is our only word representing true social
and moral freedom. And yet by what right have we the power of
intolerance—of constraining our fellow-men in aught beyond the
disallowance of acts inimical to the rest of the community? We have
certainly no right to forbid the utterance of any opinion, or to stifle
the birth of any passion, because subversive of the present state of
society. Rather ought we to change this present state, and reconstruct

our social relations on a basis broad enough for the whole of human nature; not so narrow as to exclude the majority of its instincts. Which is the case now. What I claim for myself I claim for every man—namely, freedom in its widest sense, bounded only by the chain of common laws stretched round the country. Within this I recognise no narrower circle of social laws, social usages, or social prejudices, which stultify the instincts of humanity; for I hold the wildest savage life to be grander and truer than the stunted growth and abortive products of social formalism, which checks natural impulse and nullifies the independence of individual free will."

This was the man chosen to be young Clare's instructor.

Percival's enemies used to say that he had no moral standard at all, and that vice was of equal value with virtue in his eyes: in fact, that he ignored the existence of virtue altogether in his "equal right of every instinct to preservation." The accusation looked like truth, and yet was truth distorted out of form. True it was that in all cases, even of the most flagrant crime, he ever reflected on the concurrent causes which might have met together to produce that particular action. And where specific causes were not manifest—such as madness, drunkenness, or others so self-evident that the most stupid must acknowledge their influence—he thought of other unseen but no less powerful physical agents, such as temperament, organization, an evil education, the pressure of disease, &c., to which physical agents all crimes are more or less distinctly referable. And then he would show the irrepressible force of physiological conditions, and modify such hasty words of censure as condemned on moral and spiritual grounds without consideration of material influences.

For these opinions, with their wide philosophy and deep truth, Percival was called a Materialist; which men take to mean much the same thing as a socialist, a freethinker, a thief, a cheat, or a murderer: namely, the concentration of every species of moral villany under heaven. Though what is materialism and what spiritualism, and how we make out one part of the Creator's work to be bad and another good, he, as well as many others, left to those who lay down the laws of GOD with mathematical precision, and detail the counsels of the Eternal with as intimate knowledge as they would speak of their neighbour's business.

Percival was a man of naturally strong feelings and violent prejudices, and long and severe discipline alone had schooled him to his present state of toleration and recognition. In manner he was undemonstrative, almost to coldness; yet he did not leave the impression of indifference on his hearers. Few were so dull as not to feel the living warmth of his affectionate nature flowing beneath the chilly surface of still appearance. Calm as his manners were, there was a look of thought and love in his mild grey eyes that touched the heart far sooner than ardent demonstrations, or excessive expressions. His penetration into character, and his sympathy with all kinds of instincts, made him a valued friend to the most opposite natures; though strangers often wondered what there was in that silent, reserved, unlovely man, to call forth such affection as he always gained when well known.

Moreover, he was politically a socialist, religiously a non-sectarian—a freethinker in the positive sense of the term—and practically the unshrinking protector of such poor sinners as a moral society has discarded and a Christian people anathematized.

Born in a higher sphere than the one in which he now moved—educated with the leading men of the day—he was, from the two causes mentioned—namely, immoral associates and unconventional opinions, a castaway from among them. Still he was good enough for the lax theatrical world, and there he was regarded as an easygoing man who never found fault with anybody. But from what deep-lying principle of true religion no one ever gave a thought. The depraved little ballet-dancer would go to him when she wanted more money than that which her multifarious professions gave her; and he would bestow it on her with an earnest exhortation, and sweet serious words falling like balm on the sear and the scar of sin. He was told of her ingratitude perhaps—of her drunkenness, her immorality, her worthlessness—and he answered gently; "Poor thing! she was once pure, and might have been kept so, but for neglect, or harshness, or other evil causes which she could not herself control. Yet bad as she is, she has a human heart, and is one of GOD's children. And while the Father of us all does not desert her neither will I; if she may breathe His air and retain His life, she may claim the kindness of man."

Brave, good, noble Percival!—were men more like thee, my friend, sin and sorrow would disappear from the world like snow before the sun. Harshness, stripes, imprisonment, and death, have been tried in vain as the world's tutors. But none save One, whose words are not yet understood in half their force nor his actions in half their meaning, used Love as his weapon of extermination.

Percival Glynn was said to be no Christian. He certainly did not believe in many dogmas; he took no part in the Gorham case nor in the Papal Aggression[32] when they came; he thought that salvation lay in quite another direction than through church-doors or church-services; and he enlisted in no war of words within or without, not helping a jot in the Christian labour of flinging up eternal hell-fire on those who cannot believe certain mysterious dogmas, inexplicable, incomprehensible, and often contradictory. But though of no positive sect, none followed more faithfully or more unweariedly, that example of charity which modern Christianity has drowned in an icy sea of formulas and doctrines—an icy sea that turns to burning lava if a breath but flutters the rags of their idols—an icy sea whereby men are said to sail down to hell if they cannot find its barren waters pure and good. Ah, no! this is not the Religion that Christ believed; this is not the Christianity that He bequeathed!

To care for the poor first of all things—to aid them, not by that magnificent aid of the high gentleman who stands like an archangel above man, and daintily patronizes a shivering multitude—but to care for them as one with them—to love the very vilest sinners through every crime and degradation, and to save them as a brother would save his mother's sons—to help them because of the equality of nature—to sympathize with and to comfort them—to improve them by the holy influence of charity—this was Percival's endeavour, and this was the life of Him who preached on the Jewish Mount, and forgave the Jewish sinner, nineteen centuries ago. Yet how are those lessons forgotten! The lips which said so often, "Thy sins be forgiven thee"—which pardoned all, and bade the condemning Pharisee cast the first stone if he too were without sin, though the guilty one was so frail and he so strict and moral; the eyes which wept for the unrepentant—which looked kindly on the Samaritan, the adulteress, the thief—those lips and eyes gave forth their teaching all in vain: a church, a dogma, a mystery of jangling sound and hidden words, a subtile creed, a narrow code, condemnation, and abhorrence—these are modern Christianity, but Christ's example is set aside.

Too surely was Percival condemned for this plain speaking. But he spoke the TRUTH; and for the sake of truth he could well bear any disapprobation, any slander, any scorn; sure that in time the deeds of Christ must and will rank in importance of imitation and of reverential understanding before the dogmatism of a creed, or the self-constituted authority of a church.

By degrees a change crept over Clara. Her brilliant fancy paled, and her enthusiasm seemed to have died. She was restless and unsatisfied, petulant at times and irritable, and quite unconscious that she was so. She lost her appetite, her colour went; she became thin, with a slightly care-worn look in her baby face; her eyes were sorrowful, her buoyancy gone, her riotous laugh subdued; her reckless love of liberty stilled; she spoke mournfully of the future and forgot to hope for success; the stage itself had foregone half its witchery, and Percival Glynn's Visions of Success became intrusive impertinences and hateful mockeries. Miss Kemble often found her sitting alone in some neglected corner, with big tears in her large eyes that hung there like dew-drops on a bed of violets, and with that pretty pouting look, half childish half womanly, which would have made an anchorite kiss her into smiles again.

"Why, how now, sweetheart?"—she said one day as she returned from rehearsal with Mr. Vaughan, (who by-the-by was seldom absent now,) and they found their young favourite in some such melancholy mood as this—"What bee has lately stung thy cherry lip to make it so like a naughty child's? What angel's wing has swept over thine eyelid, love, and filled the orb with tears of blinding? I must not have thee, Clare, throw such foul discredit on my maternal management as to weep like a child forbid—and all for nought! Come, cheer up, sweetheart; care must not swoop over thee yet!"

It must be remembered that it was only on the rarest occasions that Miss Kemble forgot to be theatrical. It had become such a second nature with her that she was totally unconscious of it, and it required deep emotion indeed to make her break through this mildewed crust of false tone and false appearance. Her present speech was an ingenious piece of rhetorical patchwork, composed of fragments from various plays and characters strung together like broken pottery; for her poetic flights were always far beyond her powers of original composition.

Clara started up and blushed deeply.

"No, I am not unhappy," she said, and the most radiant expression beamed over all her face, to give confirmation to her words.

"Well, I can't say that this face is very dolorous," Vasty Vaughan said, laughing as he took the girl's hand and turned her crimsoned countenance to the light. "But you certainly did look very unhappy when we came in," he added, patting her cheek; "so come, be a good child, and confess to me. You know, Clara, I am your father confessor in ordinary, and it is your religious duty to confide in me. Isn't it, little witch?"

He sat down and drew her, still standing, to his side. His arm was round her waist, and her hands were clasped in his.

This sounds very lover-like; but then Vasty Vaughan was famous for his paternal manner to young women of every rank.

Blushing and not looking into his face, but fixing her eyes perseveringly on his cravat, on his forehead, his hands, or his shirt-studs—anywhere but on his eyes—the now happy Clara parried his questions with playful sauciness, or boldly told manifest untruths, denying that she ever knew what unhappiness meant, and that since she had been in London, no "lark at heaven's gate"[33] had been more blithe than she.

"I should be very ungrateful if I were not so," she then said more gravely.

"Ungrateful? Why ungrateful, my child?"

"I have had so much kindness lavished on me," returned Clara. "Dear Miss Kemble, how good, how kind she has been; and you—what other man would have taken me by the hand so frankly as you, dear Mr. Vaughan? Indeed I should be very wicked to be desponding or unhappy when you have done so much for me."

"But I am kind to you only because I love you," Vasty said, pressing her hand tenderly; "and is not this selfishness?"

"It is from your goodness, which would make your benefits to me less evident, that you say this," said Clara, turning her eyes suddenly on him with one of her own looks of intensest gratitude and enthusiastic affection. "You cannot but think that I receive all your kindness as so much gratuitous benevolence; for what have I that could reward you in any way?"

Vasty smiled. He was silent for a few moments, and then said in a lower voice; "Your affection, Clara, would reward me for any sacrifice, and pay back any benefit with trebled interest. If you will always feel for me as you do now, you will reward me more than I have ever been rewarded. Will you, Clara?"

"Why should I not?" she said warmly. "You will be always good, and I must surely love goodness!"

The tender lingering accent of that trembling voice went to Vasty's inmost heart. He looked at her with eyes so full of love that they became almost sorrowful from the very excess of emotion. But Clara had drooped her head on her bosom, and did not see that tell-tale look; else it would have interpreted even to her the untold mysteries of the heart within.

"Come! come! this is folly!" he then said suddenly, "where is your part, my little queen? Glynn tells me that you have been idle lately, and I want to hear you, that I may scold you if you have not learnt as much as you ought."

"Oh! I can't say it to you!" laughed Clare, blushing as she spoke.

"And why not?"

"I don't know—I can't—" with the bashfulness of a child.

"But you repeat to Mr. Glynn daily—and he is younger and more formidable than I!" Mr. Vasty Vaughan looked at his comely features in the mirror as he said this, with no small satisfaction.

"Oh! Mr. Glynn!" Clara exclaimed with the most profound indifference in her voice; "but I don't care for him!"

Vasty smiled. "So much the more reason—if you do care for me— to have confidence in me," he said.

Clare shook her head; but when pressed to explain this apparent contradiction, she could do nothing of the kind; she could only reiterate the fact, and beg with clasped hands and loving eyes to be let off the dreadful task of repeating her part to the omnipotent manager.

It ended in her having her own way, on condition of giving Vasty a kiss. Oh, the torrent of blushes that overwhelmed her when Vaughan held her tightly with one hand—in the other was the copy—and gave her the alternative! How she struggled to be free!—how she assumed to be angry, with lips that woke up all the dimples in her cheeks, and eyes that clung to the ground, too heavy to lift up their world of love into the face of the tormentor!—how she refused stoutly, and then would bend forward as if about to offer the ransom, when, if Vasty bent his head too, she would start back as if something horrible had risen up between!—how she then essayed her task, but faltered over the first line and could not remember a word following! It was an eloquent comedy that this young innocence played, all unconscious as she was what she was revealing; and Vasty felt that he could have watched her for ever in this expressive declaration of her love.

At last he grew peremptory, and Clara was awed; and when he told her, more as an executioner than as a friend, that he would leave her if she did not give him that kiss, she offered her lips cold and trembling and despoiled of all their blushing beauty.

But Vasty turning suddenly grave patted her cheek instead, and saying, "You are a little fool!" left the room hastily. And so the first kiss was not given yet, though the manager was more than forty and she not quite seventeen.

CHAPTER VI.

"*SHE* is in love, Mr. Percival," Miss Kemble whispered in the tone of a stage aside; and then she drew herself up and nodded, frowning portentously.

"Since when, my good Lucretia!" asked the tutor, with a slight nervousness of manner he could not wholly suppress. But Miss Kemble was so much taken up with her own importance in giving out such an interesting secret that she did not notice it.

"I have observed it long and long, not rightly understanding—even I—the meaning of what I saw. So far removed do we become, sweet Mr. Glynn, from a right interpretation of youth's fresh feelings! I might have known the fact by sundry signs—much time bygone—but I was ignorant, and the heart's hieroglyphics were unread."

"And with whom is our beautiful young friend thus in love?" Percival returned, not raising his eyes from the book, the leaves of which he was cutting open as it lay on the table before him.

"The front of Jove—I cannot add and his Hyperion curls, because he has none," Miss Kemble answered waggishly, "hath bewitched her youthful senses. The great V. V. lives in the breast—nay, in the heart's inmost shrine—of gentle Clara Clayton."

A slight shudder passed through, rather than over, Percival. He was silent for a few moments, and then, turning the page of his book, asked in his quiet voice: "And how do you know this, fair Lucretia? Has the gentle Clara made you her confidante, or have you not perhaps drawn great conclusions from small premises? May there not be some mistake, think you?"

"Mistake, Mr. Percival!" exclaimed Lucretia, interrupting him hastily. "Mistake did you say to me? No!" she added, oratorically. "No!—I, standing in the place of mother to that noble child, with eyes sharp-visioned by the power of love, do here make affirmation strong that she hath placed her in the blind god's cruel power. Nay, more: oath upon oath I heap—pile Pelion upon Ossa, in asseveration that not only doth she love, but also that she loves our Vasty Vaughan. And who indeed so fitted for her choice! The fairest floweret of the garden may well turn upward to the sun."

"And you are glad at this fancy?"

"I tremble for her peace, for Vasty has numbered many summers where but few have lightened o'er her head. Fain would I chide, but when harsh words——"

"Good heavens, woman! You forget that you are speaking to *me*, not to a playhouse audience," Percival exclaimed almost irritated, for he was in a state of painful nervousness. "Tell me in so many words, and without all this farrago of nonsense, do you encourage her foolish passion for this man?"

"I do not," said Lucretia, a little startled at this unceremonious clipping of her poetic wings, but obeying the grave elocutionist in a manner that was very creditable to her powers of versatility. "Vaughan is too old, too heartless, too dissipated for her. She would soon awake from this fancy to her utter and life-long misery. I would often speak to her and warn her, but she avoids the subject. I want to show her the folly she would commit if she were to marry him even. And la bless ye! I don't suppose he dreams of making her his wife. He has had the pick of more established actresses than her, and look, he has not chosen one; though I believe he has never been out of love with some one or other! Even as little unknown Clara Clayton, she would be far too good for him; and when she is well known and thoroughly celebrated—oh, it would be madness to think of such a thing!"

Not that Lucretia believed all this. She merely took the cue which she thought would please Percival, and waited then for him to follow her lead.

"This wants careful management," said Percival, with a firm and distinct accent, pronouncing each word clearly as if he wished to impress every letter on her mind. "Do not frighten her, nor make her feel that she is committing a folly—not to speak of an indiscretion—in her love for Vaughan. Regard it as a sad but inevitable disease, and treat her with the tenderness due to an invalid—but one from whom it is necessary to keep the knowledge of her sickness——"

"Then you agree with me that it would be a bad match?" said Miss Kemble anxiously.

"He will never marry her," answered Percival, slowly.

"Surely yes! What makes you say this, Mr. Percival?"

"Simply because I *know* it," he replied emphatically. "Vaughan means only her ruin. I have heard him boast of her already; and that, too, in a party of half-drunken men who congratulated him on his new mistress, and speculated on her length of reign. This is a secret between us two," he added; "for *her* sake, as well as for your own. But now you know why I have spoken so gravely and thought so seriously of Clara's fatal love for Vasty Vaughan."

Miss Kemble was struck dumb. Though she had affected to condemn the notion of Clare's marrying Vasty, yet in her secret heart she speculated on its possibility as a lucky hit for the young *débutante*. She knew that eventually she would have large possessions, but in the meantime this prospective affluence did not fill her purse, nor make her coming *début* a success. And then Vasty was so much older, and had led such an irregular life, that there were not many years left in him, and Clara would in all probability be a desirable widow while still in her early youth. Vasty was fifty if he was a day, and she was only near her seventeenth birthday. And so the affair wore a better aspect to the calculating Lucretia. She was therefore inexpressibly shocked to hear of Vaughan's treachery, for she had seen his evident attachment to the young girl quite as plainly as her enthusiastic love for him. And she shuddered to think of how that love might end, when villany and warmth—heartlessness and innocence—met in such unequal union. She might have lax notions generally, but she had too true a woman's heart to calmly contemplate that poor child's ruin, or to wish to see her the prey of a profligate man in reward for her devotion to her first and earliest lover. Lucretia's face betrayed her, and Percival sat watching her.

"Guard her," he then repeated in the same distinct voice, and with an inexpressible tenderness and majesty of manner; "watch over her with care, but oh, with trembling delicacy and love! Do not tell her of Vaughan's boast—hint nothing of his probable proposals—oppose no barrier to their meetings—but without parade or effort be always with her in his presence. But what folly in me to advise a woman on matters of tact and heart! You will do all that a careful woman ought to do, who has voluntarily taken on herself the responsible guardianship of so much youth, passion, and inexperience. Poor Clara!" he added very gently, "poor child!—thy feet have strayed into a track which ere long will blister them, and the anguish of thy pain will strike into thy heart!"

Percival's eyes were again cast over the pages of his book, and an unobservant bystander would have said that he had ceased to think on the subject of their conversation altogether.

Miss Kemble forgot to be an actress. Pressing his hands she thanked him with fervour, truly grateful for his counsel, and feeling a strange influence of tenderness and virtue which her artificial life and degraded companions had well nigh stamped out of her soul. But this was Percival's privilege. Few people left him without a certain consciousness of improvement—a certain purifying influence—such as the young and tender-hearted feel when they have listened to a touching sermon. What sermons do for religious youth, Percival's nobleness of character and sentiment did for his audience.

Miss Kemble returned home hoping to find Clara there; but her mind misgave her, for she had heard some whispered arrangements, yesterday, for "Windsor" and "to-morrow." She looked up to the small windows of the "first pair front"[34] where she and Clara lived, and almost trembled when she saw that the blinds were lowered. This was the usual sign of non-occupation, for Clare loved the light so much that she had more than once almost blinded poor Miss Kemble's strained organs—to say nothing of faded carpets and pallid curtains— with the floods of sunshine she would let in. Floods of sunshine?—a hyperbolical expression for the dim rays that struggle through a London atmosphere!

She entered. Clara was not there. The servant said she had gone out with Mr. Vaughan, and they had left word that they would not be back till late. Perhaps not at all that night, as they were gone to Windsor, and Mr. Vaughan thought he might have business which would keep him there.

"Did Miss Clayton say this?"

"No, ma'am, Mr. Vaughan did."

"Did she hear him say it?"

"No, ma'am, he turned back after they had got off the step, and told me in a whisper like."

"Were they alone?"

"Yes, ma'am. I heard Mr. Vaughan ask Miss Clayton if they should take Miss Clarke with them," (a very undesirable person,) "and she said 'no, that she would rather go alone if he would allow her.'"

"Very well, that will do. Bring up my dinner and open a fresh bottle of porter."

It may have been seen that Lucretia—kind-hearted soul as she was—was not the most sensitive nor the most reflective of mortals. She soon reasoned herself into calmness. "There was no earthly cause whatever to go on fidgetting herself like that. Besides, it was done now, and she could not bring them back again at any price; and then Vasty had so often taken girls out whole days alone, and no harm had come to them—at least no one knew that any had—why should she fret and worry about this in particular? It was all along of that old maid Percival, who was always thinking everything that no one else ever did. After all it was much better that they *had* gone alone. Miss Clarke was a thorough little jade, and would have been sure to have made mischief somehow, and she would have been sure to have told and perhaps exaggerated the whole affair; and if Clara had been seen in her company by any one, it would not have been so well. Things were better as they were, and who would know anything about it?"

And with such reasonings as these Miss Kemble dispatched her chop and "relished it" with porter. And porter always *was* a great soother of the nerves and helper to digestion. I don't know how the theatrical world would get on without it. Miss Kemble then slumbered off into a lazy doze; that state of existence which is rather a pleasant consciousness of luxurious happiness than the actual presence of delightful dreams. In this guise the fair Lucretia sat; her feet on a high stool, her body reclining in an old soft easy-chair, her head flung back, and a faded yellow silk handkerchief thrown over her face to protect it from the flies. Her cap was off, her black hair untidy, her dress disordered; and thus she lay and slumbered—the ideal of careless sensual ease.

Dressing-time came at last, and our actress must betake herself to the theatre. She was to play in a "running piece"[35] that night the character of a grand queenly majestic mother; one of those women of whom, by a poetical fiction, it is said they are "better at forty than at twenty." In this character she had made a "hit" worthy of her earlier career; one that consoled her for many theatrical mistakes and the acceptance of many inferior parts. To-day all went smoothly. Her gown fitted her to a hair's breadth, and by frequent repetition the dresser knew how to dispose her whole attire to the best advantage. She could repeat her part in her sleep, and she loved herself in it—a great feature with elderly actresses; and she was just beginning to feel more than a mother's interest in the pale smoky Lover who was assumed to be her son. All these things co-operated with the soothing effects of that black bottle, and made Miss Kemble forget Clara and her perilous position.

The piece was played, the applause bestowed. Beyond a very natural though emphatic adjuration at the General who tore her mock point flounce with the rowel of his spurs, nothing went amiss; if we except one obstinate quarter of a house with trellis-work and trees, which would stand obtrusively in the midst of a Louis quatorze drawing-room. The stage manager swore a little, and a royal body-guard lent a helping hand, and so the house was slid off amidst the laughter of the pit and the jokes of the gallery. These *contretemps* well over, and the last scene just commencing, Lucretia stood in the wings by the side of the heroine—the stage *fiancée* of the pale-faced Lover—Prince Antonio to the audience; to his landlady, Mr. Buggins. She was a clever little thing, this *fiancée*; with small brown eyes, a *nez retroussé*,[36] a thin pert body, but with plenty of good humour and talent in her. Lucretia hated her. They were deadly rivals in heart, for the Prince was so royally general in his attentions that neither knew which he preferred, the *style sévère* or the *style riant*. Lucretia thought of course that he must admire her more than that foolish little plain uninteresting Miss Gray:

"A person, my dear," she said to a masked Duchess in tin strawberry leaves and cotton velvet train, "of no sort of mind or character whatever—though I admit she has talent. But talent—mere mechanical talent, my dear—though it pleases for the moment, cannot stand. It is like the blue light as against gas. It gives a sudden glare—a temporary flare-up—and a prettiness perhaps—yes, a prettiness decidedly; but when you come to steady seeing, why then the gas, my dear—and when you come to steady acting—acting that is to last—a cut and come again sort of thing—then you want character and person." Lucretia drew herself up, and smoothed her gown over the comely bust for which she was still in debt to her milliner. "Mere talent with small eyes and no person—with smartness and no strength of character—dies into a chambermaid of genteel comedy, or into a fairy of the pantomime. Depend upon it, my dear, it is so; whatever some people may think in the heyday of their trumpery success." All of which, said for the benefit of Miss Gray, the little *fiancée*, was received by her with provoking good temper and irritating equanimity.

Mr. Buggins was sitting on the supports of a canvas column which formed one of a series—the peristyle of a Grecian temple called in the playbills, "The Church of San Geronimo," and situated in the heart of Spain, in the midst of Swiss, Neapolitan, Elizabethan, and Castilian wardrobes. He was engaged in an amicable chat with the villain of the play; he who in a short time would stab him to the heart, and consign Miss Gray to madness or a convent: but he overheard these remarks of the Siddonian Lucretia.

"What a deuced shame!" he said to the villain, who was adjusting his property rapier and smoothing his Mephistophelian beard. "No one can be more good-natured than little Gray, and for that old hag Kemble to run her down like this—upon my word it is too bad! I'd rather have little Gray to play with any day than her, with her heavy mouthing way! She's just like an elephant floundering through her part; calling herself Siddonian indeed!"

"But her birth, good Prince—her birth! The true current runs in her veins though it does spring from a side branch of the stream! Hath she not the Kemble blood unmistakeable?"

"Good lord, no! She's the daughter of a cheesemonger in Ratcliffe Highway. I know her family well, and owe her old father a good score yet. I thought every one knew the truth of the Kemble dodge! She only calls herself somebody Kemble's daughter because she has a hook-nose and is five feet ten without her shoes. I believe it was put into her head somewhere in the beginning of last century by her only lover. So they say here. There's the bell!—Come, old cheeseparing," he said to poor Lucretia, "and make the flats believe that you are Siddons revived—a new edition revised and corrected, with additions ad lib.!"

And then they went on and played at heroes and queens in all the stately lordliness of virtue and refinement; and when they came off they drank porter and made unseemly jokes, and acted to the life their enduring *rôle* of degradation and vulgarity.

CHAPTER VII.

"WHAT made you blush so much, Clare, when the waiter came in?" asked Vasty Vaughan.

They were at Windsor, at the —— hotel, waiting for dinner.

"I don't know," answered Clara, her voice trembling very much and her eyes cast on the ground. "I have never been to an inn before, and it seems so strange—I don't know what they must think of me."

Vaughan smiled.

"Do you imagine they think of you at all?" he said caressingly. "Are you such a vain poppet as to believe that every one must be as much bewitched with these sunny locks," taking them in his hand and pressing them to his lips, "and these crimson cheeks, as I am? Must you have a world full of Vasty Vaughans, darling?"

As he said the last word—so low and soft—the blood flew over Clara's cheek and neck; her head drooped, she visibly trembled, and her breathing was checked and slow.

Vasty took her hand; it was cold as stone, and lay in his grasp motionless but not inexpressive.

"The sun is very powerful to-day, and yet your little hand is like ice. What makes you so cold, Clara? Is your hand emblematic of your heart?"

"I don't know," she repeated, scarcely audibly, "I don't think though that my heart is cold."

"Come here—let me see." He drew her towards him, and held her close; his own heart beating strong and loud. Clara hid her face on his bosom, and felt as if her life were dissolving into a rapture of spirituality. At this moment the door opened with a noisy jar, and the waiter dashed in as if a lion were at his heels; as hotel waiters do dash in and out of rooms—especially when they are not looked for.

Vaughan muttered something more emphatic than euphonious, and began to talk in the most unmoved voice possible; while Clara, too inexperienced to conceal her real feelings, looked much as though she had been taken in the act of burglary or the commission of a murder. She could not command herself, but trembled so evidently and changed colour so rapidly—flushing to the deepest crimson one moment, and paling to a marble whiteness the next—that even the lion-hunted waiter noticed her, and formed his own conclusions on the subject; which pointed to the fact that either her father had been scolding her, or her bridegroom had been complimenting her—he didn't know which.

The dinner passed off in a strange halting fashion enough. Vaughan had ordered all sorts of delicacies for his little favourite; but for once he had misunderstood the lesson of years. Had Clare been older or calmer, I doubt not that all these adjuncts to pleasure would have had their due effect on her. As it was, they were simply distasteful. She wanted no fish, no fowl, no fruits; the champagne made her ill; the pastry nearly choked her. The dinner seemed interminable, as she sat with her blue eyes bent ever on the ground, and her young cheeks burning through her curls; and when Vaughan praised the oyster patties, or pressed on her strawberry ices, she wondered how he could expect her to lose his eyes and voice for such horrible substitutes. She looked to the window wistfully, longing for the fresh air, and for his dear presence beneath those spreading trees. She wanted to be out in the thick glade—on the soft smooth moss. She wanted to have grass and leaves and flowers about her, and the bright sun overhead; and then she would be happy in her home, and with her ——. Her lips gave no name to that beloved image, but her heart supplied the word and whispered a heaven of changeless bliss in the echo.

At last the waiter tore away with his last load of cloth and tray-stand, and once more Vaughan and Clara were alone and safe from interruption.

"Do you like to sit there?" asked Vaughan; "or will you be more sociable and come near me?—here;—" and he drew the couch across the windows—"we may sit here and look out if you like. Would you like it?"

"No," said Clara timidly, rising and walking with a peculiarly soft step to where he stood. "I do not care to look into a street. If it had been a wood or a garden, yes; but not a dirty town."

"You shall have your own way," said Vaughan kindly, removing the couch as he spoke. "Remember this, Clara," he added, taking her hand and making her sit by him, "you are always mistress with me. I will never ask you to do anything you don't like to do, and I will never control your wishes in any way. So long as you give me the privilege of—of—liking you—so long as you give me only the least fragment of your affection—you will find in me a ready acquiescence in all your desires. Never be afraid to rely on me. Make me your confidant in all things, and I will not abuse your trust. I am much older than you are, and of course I know more of the world than you do, and you may be perfectly safe when you have told me anything and I have given my permission and my sanction. I have your happiness at heart, and all I ask for is—reliance and affection. Do you hear me?" He turned her face to him with his hand, and kissed her forehead gently.

"I always will," said Clare in a low voice, as if she had been repeating a lesson.

"That is right!"—patting her waist round which he kept his arm, but so lightly that Clare soon forgot it altogether. "You will never have a truer friend than I am, Clara; never one who will guard you more carefully or respect you more tenderly."

She leant nearer to him, and touched his shoulder with her hair.

"Another thing I want to say to you," continued Vaughan. "You need never be careful of what you do with me. I should not like you to come down to Windsor alone with any other man—now don't start and look so frightened!—there is no earthly harm in it, my dear child—it is simply a thing not usually done by young ladies—but there is no real harm in it; and with me, you know, you are as safe as with Lucretia. You may always trust me, Clara. If I ask you to do anything—do it without hesitation. Be sure of any action if I approve of it. At all times you may throw away your own responsibility and take my knowledge of the world and my affection for you as your best guides. Will you do this too, as well as—love me?"

The head sank lower; the girlish form bent nearer. The beating fingers on his own pressed themselves involuntarily yet unmistakeably; the parted lips, trembling and slightly swollen, seemed eloquent of words.

"Will you, Clare?" he whispered.

She turned her face towards him and answered, "Yes." And in that little word seemed to her to be comprised the confession of a life. She cared not to analyze, to sift, to understand; she cared only to feel. And now, not one pulse but brought such tumult to her heart—such delicious madness to her brain—such vague, impalpable, but heaven-born ecstasy—as made her feel her gift of life a gift that brought divinity as well. Now, and for the first time, young Clare de Saumarez knew her full power of emotion, and felt tenfold repaid for all her past suffering by the counterbalance of this present hour of bliss.

Vaughan flung his arms round her almost wildly. He strained her to his breast; he looked into her face with a painful mixture of sorrow and of passion. His lips were warm against her own—when suddenly he released his hold, and starting up from the sofa, cried: "By Heaven, I will protect her!"

With a heavy sigh Clare roused herself as if from a dream, and tried in vain to collect her thoughts. But she looked anxious and bewildered, and could not understand herself or him.

"Go up stairs, darling child, and put on your bonnet," said Vaughan in an agitated voice, "we will go into the fresh air."

Clare made no answer, but left the room sadly. For the first time she had hoped consciously that Vasty would have said he loved her; and the disappointment was excessive. She was afraid he found her very stupid and childish—perhaps altogether unlovely—and she was nearly heartbroken at the idea.

At last she came down stairs after a long absence, very pale and dispirited; and then they went out into the park, and wandered about under the trees and on the grass; both quite silent. Not that the blank of silence was between them; it was, in point of fact, the most eloquent communication they could hold.

"You are tired," at last said Vaughan; and he led her to a low seat beneath the trees. It was placed far back, not in sight of the broad walk.

Clara was rather tired. She sat down; but the bench had no back, and she lounged in an uncomfortable way against the tree.

"I will support you," said Vaughan, and he placed his arm round her. "Lean against me—that will be as good as a back to you."

She laughed a little and blushed more, but did as he told her and leant against his arm.

"Are you comfortable?" whispered Vasty after a short time, bending down and looking into her eyes.

A sudden start, a sudden crimson glow, a swift shy pressure, and the gentle voice still lower, told Vasty more than words what his young companion felt. They told him to her hurt—to her misery—to her ruin; they told him to the strong enkindling of his half-smothered passion—to the utter wreck of all his principle and good; they told him to the after strengthening of her character, and to the grandeur of her mind in all the destruction of her position; they told him to the fulfilling of her painful mission, the teaching of her long sad lesson. It

was a mystery that Evil should have had such power to tempt her—
but let us pray that in the end it may be well!

"Clara—Clara!" said Vasty, his own voice low and broken—"do
you love me?—do you love me, darling, as I love you—with half the
fondness, half the truth that I, a *blasé* man, have poured out in a very
childish prodigality? Clara, could you be happy with me?—could you
be content with me?—could you live only in my love, and care nothing
for the flattery of the world? Tell me, darling—tell me, my own sweet
child—can this young guileless heart give me back one tithe of what
I have lavished on it? Oh, Clara! if you will love me—nay, if you do,
for so I hope and so I believe—my only study will be to make you
happy. Not a thought but shall point to that—not an energy but shall
be directed there; your peace and success—your happiness now and
for ever—shall be my first and sole care. Only tell me that you love
me—tell me that you will live for me and in my love as I in yours—tell
me that you will not place my forty years between your young heart
and me—and that you will be true to me as I to you—tell me this,
Clara, and then earth has nothing left to tempt me—heaven nothing
left to give me!"

She listened with held breath and parted lips; she murmured
something that fell like seraph music on the air; she saw nothing but
a golden gush of sunlight—heard nothing but soft harmonies, not on
the earth but in the heaven where her soul was rapt; she knew nothing
of actual life; clasped to her lover's heart, his arms pressing her to
his bosom as to her dearest home, his rich voice whispering love and
promising eternal happiness and joy—her future his alone—all else
but this went from her. Clinging to him she sobbed one small sweet
word, and then she only knew that he fondly pressed her lips, and
called her "his own beloved Clare."

Her flushed cheek covered by one burning hand—the other clasped
in Vaughan's nervous hold—throbbed still beneath the impress of his
touch. All life, all heaven, all power of sensation were concentrated
in that moment—the first wherein her innocent lip had gathered up
a lover's kiss—the first wherein her ear had heard a lover's magic
words. The ardour of her fresh sixteen years—the wholeness of her
most unsuspecting adoration—the halo which her imagination threw
around her lover, chief as he was in the society wherein she moved—
the bright summer sun in its golden hour of setting—the scene and
place where the whole voice of nature was love and love alone—the

glad knowledge of sorrow ended and happiness begun—the quivering delight of joy such as even she might name intense—all these swept away reflection, prudence, fear, and shame; and looking into the burning face bending over her with a gaze that startled even Vaughan, practised as he was in all the varied expressions of love, she raised his hand to her lips and stole her arms about his neck.

Silent they both sat some few moments longer. The sun shone its last rays over her happy head, pure and fond as young Haidee's,[37] and saw her the fancied possessor of the keys of Paradise. With the guilelessness of a child, but with the fervour of a woman, she poured forth the rich treasures of her boundless love—a love that almost sanctified the object by its own power and purity. And Vaughan's heart, not all corrupted though sorely warped and sadly stained, beat with large pangs of pain when he beheld the truth and purity and virginal devotion of this loving, innocent, deceived heart.

It was not often that remorse had checked him in his downward path. It was not often that he had regarded women as other than the mere playthings of an hour—heedless of the wrecked hopes, the shattered affection, the blighted life of his poor victims, when, wearied with the love he had sought so eagerly, he flung them coarsely off and left them to the desolation he had made. It was not often that Vaughan was stayed in his career of vice; but to-day this child made him pause and tremble.

"It is not too late yet," he muttered to himself, rising suddenly. He raised her tenderly, and strained her to him with a convulsive pressure. Clare's whole soul vibrated with divinest pleasure at that mute caress; for she thought how he must love her to be so much moved! Poor Clare!—that passionate embrace had something of a love thou knowest not of, but more of pity and regret in its touch! But the life of woman ever passes thus: in one wide web of deception and fond fancy, which, when she understands and breaks, she dies.

They reached home by an early evening train, and Vaughan conducted Clara safely to her lodgings; enjoining silence on her, and secrecy, until he should give her leave to speak.

But even this did not startle her nor awaken the faintest suspicion. "He has his own reasons," she said, "and they must be good."

And so she laid her young head on her pillow in an ecstacy of feeling that raised earth into heaven. With thoughts that made her brain reel and swim—with words repeated softly till every nerve re-echoed them—with hopes that blazoned the dull night with pictures of unfading bliss and charmed every sense to heaven-born madness; such was the night to her. To him we will not ask what were the emotions that companioned with those fiery hours; what struggles were between the two principles of his nature; what evil promptings were battled down by virtuous resolves; again rising to be again cast down; what a Hell made contrast with her Eve-like Eden.

CHAPTER VIII.

A WOMAN, bold, ragged, and untidy, sat in a dirty room overlooking the fetid river. Just before her window the Thames, heavy with refuse and clogged with filth, heaved up and down beneath the swell of the many holiday steamers that cut through its dull waters; but the woman looked out listlessly on that gay world sweeping by, too much a thing apart to feel even the interest of a common humanity. What had she to do with the sunshine of society? In her stifling chamber, where the only furniture was rags and rotten timber—where disease lay crouched in heaps of filth that neglect and hopelessness had left to accumulate as they might—where the atmosphere within scarcely surpassed the atmosphere without for noxious noisomeness of smell and substance, and the skinny fingers of poverty lay in the burning palm of vice, inextricably interlaced—where a broad line of separation marked her out from the rest of the world and showed her to be discarded and abandoned—where she had only want and shame here, death and annihilation hereafter—why, from such a point of degradation and of suffering, should she regard the holiday dwellers in the sunshine as of her own race and class? Nothing but a common form bound them to a common interest. All else in their several portions was unlike.

This woman must once have been very beautiful, and even now she might have been called handsome, but for the coarse depravity of her face which forbade such a desecration of terms. Her ragged hair, matted and uncombed, was long and of jetty blackness; her eyes, hollow from vice and want together, were open, large, and once had been divinely lustrous; the transparent nostril of her well-formed nose was of that quick dilating kind which adds so much expression, but not always of the most pleasant sort, to features already of themselves full of character; her lips were thin but handsome; and her figure, even through the reckless toilet of a public woman of the lowest class, was finely turned and artistically moulded. But oh, that face!—the hardened lines of profligacy that stood on the broad bold brow—the fierce stare that gleamed from eyes whose beauty of shape and colour and lengthy lash gave a sadder power to their maddened look—the sneer that sat on lips where sin had left black stains more eloquent of her ruin than all the rest—the desecrated temple of a once fair womanhood that she stood, when not so far back in the calendar of time the very nobles of the land had courted her, and modest maids had envied smiles an outcast's pence could buy to-day.

Sad sin to her doubtless, that she thus flared in the light of Heaven the pitchy torch of her soul's degradation. But was she wholly and alone to blame? Had circumstances and social laws nothing to do with the downward stream which had landed her here? Was society guiltless and she the sole guilty one? Surely she had sorrows as well as crimes in her long catalogue of suffering!—surely she had been also sinned against, though so fearfully the sinner!

Something of feminine instinct yet remained with her. Her gentle voice and manner to the squalid children round her made good her claim to some remnant of womanhood, which the unsexing power of vice almost denied. One baby at her breast, a second little one prattling at her knee, and a third, many years older, and of strangely beautiful form and intellectual character of face, sitting pensively at the window, and trying to understand why all that outer world was so happy and this within so wretched—stood as last frail links between her and purity.

It was sad yet beautiful to see this woman's love for her offspring. The only things she ever spared in her wild fits of drunken madness— the only beings that she loved on earth—the stars to which her heart pointed true through every scene of burning guilt and howling misery—were these three hapless little ones—the nameless offspring of a shameless life.

That woman was Mrs. Vasty Vaughan: the children—Heaven alone could say of whom!

When very young the beautiful Emma Hardy was married to Vasty Vaughan, the only son of her father's oldest friend. It was a marriage approved of by the world in the most undoubted manner; one after the stereotyped pattern of proper matches. Both were well born, both well educated, both beautiful: and Vasty at twenty-five was a fitting age for his dark-eyed bride of eighteen. But Vasty at twenty-five, with his smooth brow and smiling lip, was old in soul, withered and decrepit beneath the weight of vicious experience which he had already heaped on himself; as old, if not older than the man who sat beneath the Windsor oak and heard the innocent words of young Clara's love.

Vasty was eminently an unworthy man. A libertine without principle, a philosopher without faith, he had gone through life with the most fatal doctrine which man can hold; namely, that virtue and religion are both mere state engines of policy without any living echo in the soul of man. He regarded them as an archæologist would regard the gods of Greece, as a jurist would speak of the maxims of kingcraft: things useful but false—wise for their generation but bygone and worn-out; at all times beneath the acceptance of a philosopher who looked at *truth*, and beneath the respect of a man who cared for the enjoyments of life. His cold scoffing spirit checked not for youth, for reverence, for innocence; his coarse jest cared little for the delicacy it wounded, his libertine habits for the virtue they destroyed: Self was the great centre of his life, and all which ministered to his own sensual gratifications the absolute necessities of creation. For beyond this self, and beyond these gratifications of sense, he acknowledged nothing.

Vasty's conversion to spiritual truth had been often attempted. But he never rose from a religious controversy without becoming harder in heart and more contemptuous of the opinions of others. Original thinkers are not easily converted, because of the narrowness of mind with which most men meet them. If it can be clearly shown that you have thought up to, and beyond, the mental state in which your opponent exists—something may be done; but where you begin by assuming the influence of an universal Spirit of Evil as the cause of all dissent with received opinions, you lose every chance of success. The mind revolts at a dictum so false, and clings to the wider truth with increased tenacity. This was one cause of Vasty's adherence to his desolate, his terrible, life of brute denial; he had not, when plastic and capable of conversion, met with one who had ever shown him a truth which comprehended his. The laws of nature, and its instincts, were not placed by those clerkly combatants within the details of the Universal Plan: they were assumed to lie without—to be something in opposition to the dealings of the Eternal—interpolations made by Satan in the great book of humanity writ by GOD. And for this false creed, one soul from the multitude parted company with love, with hope, with virtue, and with GOD.

Emma, when she married, was vain, wilful, and passionate—emphatically of an evil temper—giving but little happiness to those with whom she lived—a dangerous wife, young and lovely though she was. But she was pure-hearted and ignorant of the world; and by proper treatment might have been made a valuable woman. With affection and strong moral principle influencing her, all her worse faults would soon have been repressed and virtues raised in their stead.

Neither of these did her husband supply to her. Sated with her beauty in less time than a pretty bird would have wearied a child, and alienated by her untoward humours, Vasty soon neglected her. Infidelities too glaring to be overlooked made the girl's proud heart throb with the indignation of a neglected wife, cast aside for the vulgar toy of the moment. Hatred gradually took the place of the pleased vanity she had mistaken for love; and all attempts at reconciliation and affection yielded to the enmity of mutual reproaches and mutual dislike.

Time after time her accusations were met by sneers at her feminine jealousy; by forced caresses, more insulting still, to appease her wifely wrath; by profligate reasonings; by licentious jests; and last of all by coarse retort. When that base word of suspicion first fell on Emma's ear, the child sleeping now on her bosom was not more free from such shape of harm than she.

And as the tempest woke up from one small cloud no bigger than a man's hand, so that word of Vasty's roused up in Emma's soul a fierce and fiery devil that nothing now would lay.

From that moment she forbore every word of reproach. She met her husband when he came home, feverish with wine or prostrate from excess, with calmness truly, but with a bitterness of disdain far worse than any accusation. But Vasty cared nothing for this queenly mode of anger. Provided he might escape a scene, it mattered little to him what formed the elements of that escape.

He was still proud of her as of a thing belonging to himself. Her beauty was the talk of the season and her virtue the wonder of the clubs. Both of these characteristics flattered Vaughan's self-love—as the thorough breeding of his horse or the acknowledged superiority of his cook would have flattered it. The woman was his property, and her excellencies were his advantages.

However, if they could they would willingly have been divorced on more efficient terms than those which Doctors' Commons[38] supplies. Their marriage had long been a mere mockery; and a most unholy one. For by the very constitution of their union other vices were necessarily added to the many already seething in Vasty's soul. Hypocrisy and falsehood—a broken vow and love degraded—came in side by side with the violation of a false law and the rejection of a social superstition. But they were bound by ties that it has pleased men to name too holy to break, save for one cause, and that the lowest of all which ought to dissolve these ties. And what evil soever may follow on this holy indissolubility, this ignoring of all the characteristics and necessities of human nature—what evil soever may follow on the false and fatal compromise of separation—it is deemed immoral to prevent this evil by a previous release. Our age is too spiritual to contemplate the possibility of conjugal disunion after the sacred vows of the marriage ceremony: it is too pure to accept the fact of human inconstancy. A legal contract—for such is marriage—must not be legally dissolved save for one low moral crime; the instincts of human nature must not be suffered to exist save under the name of crime. No personal cruelty, no brutalizing vice, releases the unhappy bearer of ill-fitting matrimonial fetters: but society makes a compromise with law, and permits a separation which of itself *necessitates* the very fact that society condemns. Is this wise? is it true? is it just? Would it not be better to act honestly in the face of the world, and to allow divorce where legal separation is suffered now? A frank and perfect disunion would be better than this half-hearted compromise; honesty under any conditions would be better than these unflinching falsehoods.

Vasty at last discovered that his wife had followed his example and imbibed his principles too accurately for even his free tastes. She took a lover, and the world pitied the husband. Angry as he was, he could not be so unjust as to chide her for the want of a virtue he had always ridiculed and never practised. He, so handsome and agreeable, was perhaps a little stung by this open preference to another not nearly equal to him in manner or in person; and wounded vanity for a moment piqued him into something that was not love, and yet was more than fancy. He upbraided her very gently; on social not on moral grounds; spoke to her of the "folly of this public *exposé*;" paid her vast attention in public; was her devoted husband in private; and for a month everything went on well. Alas! a pretty little milliner, and Emma's unlucky temper, separated them again.

And now began the career which ended as we have seen. Mrs. Vaughan's *affaire* was undisguised, for the law was on her side now. Once forgiven and taken back under the specialities of their reconciliation—Vasty's character itself so tainted and her proofs thereof so indubitable—not Messalina's self could be divorced by English law. When Vasty threatened her with the dreaded House of Lords, she brought recriminating accusations too strong to be despised. Her blood was fairly up; she *would* not be released under their present conditions—she would not be disgraced as a divorced wife, when her husband, who had first corrupted her, was so rich and high. No, before his very face she would live his own life, and in the arms of another dream of the love he had denied her. Vasty was forced to submit; our wise laws were against them both; offering no relief to him, and no way of repentance to her.

At last the climax came. She left her home with her lover, and was henceforth the vile degraded outcast; he, the injured husband about whom fair ladies grew romantically sympathetic. On the death of her mother, Emma would receive a small pittance sufficient to keep her above absolute want. This was all on which she had to depend for the future; but reckless and improvident ever, she sold her reversionary interest to buy fine trappings for her baby; and soon wanted food. The gallant gentleman for whom she left her husband's house deserted her; the little money that she had was spent; her mother had discarded her; Vasty cared not if she died for very hunger. She had not a friend on earth, and often she thought not one in Heaven. Lower and lower she sank; heaping vice on vice and misery on misery, till now, at thirty-four—just ten years since her separation—she was the wretched thing that we have seen; the haunter of low theatres—the frequenter of low gin-shops—the strolling walker of the midnight streets—one of the moral fungi that have spread out so thick and loathsome from the rottenness of society.

Under other conditions Emma Vaughan might have been saved. If, as in America or Prussia, when she discovered that her marriage had been emphatically a mistake, she might have gone back to her mother's house with the unsullied name and undisturbed prospects of a young widow, the seal of shame which now burnt into her brow would never have been set there. A kinder fate might have mated her with a more suitable companion; and so by affection, noble teaching, and the bitterness of experience, she might have learnt better things of life and have become a worthy and an estimable woman. A timely divorce, I say, might have made her this; with the indissolubility of the marriage tie she became what she was; and once more human nature showed the nullity of laws which pain but do not control it.

But this is called an immoral doctrine; and so men go on adhering to theories which eradicate the substance.

In the same room with Emma Vaughan sat a girl and her young sister. They were two orphans, the children of respectable but painfully poor people, who, from poverty, had been unable to give them more than the coarsest rudiments of education. They were slop-workers;[39] unfit for any other occupation, and getting but little remuneration from this. Both together they did not earn three shillings clear in the week, deducting all outgoings for working implements, candlelight, &c.; and for this they must labour sixteen hours out of the twenty-four. Cold, sleepy, hungry, weary—they must still work on in desolate toil—no hope before them, no pleasure behind, no part of happiness in all this great wide beautiful world given equally to all God's children. Three shillings for the week's nurture of two human beings! Bare life could not be supported out of this! The eldest, a girl of about nineteen, a gentle blue-eyed thing, used to make up the deficiency in the terrible hours of night. But how, her sister, apathetic through work and want, though so young, neither asked nor cared. The meat was bought, the bread was got; and money that supported the necessities of nature must be at all times welcome and well got. But heaven alone knew how truly it was a deed of heroic sacrifice, when that girl stole out to buy her sister bread and keep her virtue unsullied by the sale of her own worn shrinking self. By heavens, this is no fancy portrait! It is to be seen nightly in our wide Christian city with its thousand churches and its countless Bibles; and the world turns in loathing from the girl whose self-immolation places her by the side of stately heroines, and whose painful shame of life lies heavily on false principles of social government and falser codes of moral rule.

"How many hours have you worked to-day, Sarah?" asked Emma suddenly, turning to the elder sister after a long pause, during which that heavy brow had hung with deepening clouds. Bad thoughts were at work within those clouds to-day.

"Ten already," she answered with a sigh. "We have six more before we finish the work."

"And you will not earn sixpence each?" returned Emma with a kind of tiger's growl and a bitter sneer.

The girls looked up, and even the pale thin cheeks of the phlegmatic Jane flushed with a momentary crimson.

"Ah, it is too bad!" she said, with a stupid look, "but the masters are cruel, and the law does nothing for us!"

"And for sixpence a day—for less than four shillings a week, you slave your lives and souls out! By heavens! girls, I had rather cut my master's throat and be hanged for it, than live like this. Live!—it isn't life!" she added with a short hoarse laugh, "it's death and hell in the living skeleton of starvation!"

The elder girl glanced up uneasily. The maternal love with which she guarded her dull half-witted sister took much the place of education; and the sensitiveness of affection made her conscious of evil which no awakened intellect pointed out.

"But patience will help us on a great bit," she said hastily, laying her wasted hand lovingly on her sister's cheek; "and we shall have in the next world all we want here. At least they say so in the churches, out of the Big Book. Besides, there's worse off than us," she added cheerfully. "The poor old lady below who has lived these three days on a penny loaf—the widow and her children who went out begging in the streets for four days and got only twopence halfpenny a day—and hundreds more than even we know of, Jane—who can't work as well as us—they're all worse to do than we Jane, and please God, we'll do better some day!"

"That word's always in your mouth, girl!" said Emma fiercely. "And what good does it do you?—does God ever help you?—does he give you food and clothing, or leave you here to work at the starvation wages of the sweaters? I can understand the rich believing in a God," she added with a bitter laugh, "for they have it all their own way, and it's pleasant to believe that one is specially cared for; but the poor— they are cowards as well as slaves for taking things so easily, and canting about a heaven they don't see, and I believe never get to!"

Jane laid down her work and seemed to think. A heavy leaden brain was hers, but unchangeable in its dull ideas when once they had entered there: one of those brains which follow an evil guide with the dogged perversity of a brute, and by this very doggedness are formidable engines of ill.

"Work now, Janie dear, and maybe you'll think clearer after," said Sarah anxiously, for she dreaded the effect of Emma's fierce atheism and licence on her sister: "don't you see Emma there is mad to-day?" she added in a whisper. "What a little fool you must be to believe what she says!—you have all your wits, and she—poor thing—drink has crazed hers!" which was not far wrong, adding other vices and evil counsel too.

Emma was in one of her most diabolical tempers to-day. She was fevered with excess, and half mad with drink; and with the craving for more. She scarcely knew what she wanted. Drink, drink—this was all she could fly to; but this was not enough for her present humour. She felt that she would like to see blood on her own very hand—that she would like to murder some rich man—no, some saintly Christian— and wet her lips in his heart's drops. Her eyes were flashing wildly: her hands were strained, and their grasp convulsive. Thoughts crowded on her—thick, thick, and maddening—till the baby at her breast looked up and moaned at the checked and fevered flow. Not even this soothed her.

"You make me sick, girls, with your beastly trade and beastly patience!" she cried, standing before them like a crazed maniac. "If you were decent companions I would stay in more than I do, and talk to you instead of to the men at the corners there; but you are disgusting—Sarah with her cant, and you, Jane, with your ass-like temper—your broad back scored with blows, and you contented still, eating your thistles as if they were golden oats! Curse you both!—you make me worse than I should be. If I had but women—human beings and not brutes—as my mates, I would be better!"

Pacing through the room she continued a torrent of frightful oaths and vituperations, till even Jane was moved. Then out she rushed for drink, and still more drink; and not many hours elapsed before the girls heard her voice, strained and cracked, in loud blasphemous curses—a mad, wild, drunken woman, scoffed at, jeered and insulted by the lowest rabble of the lowest quarter.

"That comes of drink, Jane," said Sarah, as Emma Vaughan hurried through the streets in such disgraced disorder. "Jane, we have a hard life of it my girl: we have to work and never stop a bit for any pleasure—we have to do as others bid and not as we would like—we have to toil for wages that can't let us live; but Jane, if we keep sober and honest, and thou be a good girl and don't go after men, and wait and wait, it'll all come right in the end Jane, and we'll find ourselves happy at last!"

"But Emma said right, Sally, when she said that no God helped us," returned Jane, slowly. "Why can't he?—why won't he?—we are honest girls, and we've done nothing wrong—we get our own living and never wronged nobody. Why are we left so poor if God could help it? Why does he let us be so hungry?" and she looked up in a hopeless helpless way.

"Hush, lass! you mustn't talk so! They say in the churches, I've heard, that it's all a riddle like here, but that the poor will be better off yonder; and the poorer they've been here the richer they'll be yonder."

"But this is here and the yonder don't come, and maybe never will," the girl persisted doggedly. "Give me a drink, Sally."

The broken pitcher was handed to her. It was nothing but Thames water polluted with every filth and refuse of this mighty city, that they had to drink.

"The water's worse than ever to-day," said the poor girl with childish peevishness. "It's like a churchyard! I'm very dry and yet I can't drink it. They say the men what lay it on have fine houses and carriages. They shouldn't give the poor this stuff then. Will they be poor and drink ditch water in the yonder world, Sal?"

"I hope not, Janie," the girl answered, with a sweet sad seriousness that gave her pallid face a look almost sublime.

And then a deep silence fell between them, broken only by the ceaseless ply of their busy needles.

When the work was done there was no supper. There was not a halfpenny in the house; not a stick nor a rag that could be pawned. All had gone long ago for food. Jane began to cry. She had stitched hard all day—she had been long hungry—and now she must go hungry and thirsty to bed. These were the wages of her hard day's toil!

Sarah bent over her affectionately as she lay sobbing among the rags that formed her bed, and then kissing her she said; "Don't ye cry Janie dear—don't ye then. You'll have some supper and then you'll sleep lighter: don't ye cry—it will come directly."

She put on her bonnet, went out without another word, and after some time brought her sister a pot of ale and a piece of hot meat on bread. But she herself was sick and pale and could not eat any. She gave her share to the children, who cried to her for it, and then lay down in her bed. And while Jane ate her meal greedily, the poor girl who had just bought it—at what a price!—wept silently and bitterly, once or twice moaning faintly as if in pain, and trembling like one suffering from ague.

CHAPTER IX.

Up early the next morning, so soon as the broad sun fell on the world, rousing one part of the great family of man to painful toil and creeping over the soft slumbers of others born only to pleasure and to indolence—up early, to a long day of work and want, the two girls began their dreary task. Needle and thread—oh, how hideous those words had become to them! It was like stitching at an endless shroud, this incessant ply of those hated needles! But work! work! work!—till the wasted hands fall powerless from the wrist, and the very bone lies bare beneath the point and the knot—in sickness and in health—in hunger, in cold, in weariness, in very death—work! work! work! for these wretched children of a wealthy nation. And when all is done, what gain? When the throbbing head lies down at night on the rags and the straw, what is earned? Perhaps not sixpence; perhaps not enough to buy food if the lodging is to be paid for, or to pay for the lodging if food is to be bought. Thames water to drink; if fortunate beyond her fellows, a small portion of tainted offal to eat: no more than this to keep body and soul together does the female slop-worker earn by sixteen hours' toil. And then men wonder that modest women should be so rare among the poor, or that poverty should ask from vice that which labour will not grant.

Oh, the wisdom that applies quack salves of political economy to dress the wounds of a corrupted core—that drones forth theories of ultimate prevention while the famished labourer groans for hunger, and woman's virtue is sold perforce for bread—drones forth theories and gives no present practical aid! Oh, the true religion that preaches from its thousand pulpits once a week sublime dogmas of ineffable mystery, yet stays not the plague eating through the very temple itself, still less steps out into the foul hovel to clear that of its vice and filth! Oh, the free philanthropy that spends its blood in slaying unruly men who rise up to gather back the little space of their forefathers' graves, and its treasure in teaching these men a religion of love and peace and justice; while it leaves countless acres unreclaimed where food could be grown to feed all the hungry, and recks nothing of the degraded heathen of the metropolis! Might it not be as well, think ye, magnates of the realm political, if ye would put your shoulders fairly to the wheel and work honestly for the people and their welfare? Might it not be as well if ye would look at facts existing, and legislate for them and for human nature as it is, and not by such theories as might be brought to bear if human nature could be changed? How long must useful measures meet with the sneer and the scoff of lazy conformity; and practical evils be enforced for the sake of the science of political economy? Startling truths come up every now and then with the deep howl of a rising storm, and the world below ye quivers to the centre as they sound. Hear them in time, and be wise in the deed! Clear away such national sins as oppressive taxes on the industry, and oppressive hindrances to the self-help, of the poor. Build houses where they may live in the decency ye give to your beasts in the stall; drain the foul courts where they lie huddled together like swarms of greater vermin, and break through the thick walls which keep in their pestilent atmosphere and shut out the light and the air; give schools to their children, and suffer the great family of the poor to rise up into the broad light of civilization: cast water before them that they may wash and be clean, and give them other to drink than the great river-sewer of the city; treat them as Men, ye legislators, and lay aside your pedantries and your theories; and then perhaps, with such practical reforms as these, and such just regulations in the labour market that life cannot be sold for less than life's worth, ye may do without Model Prisons and Union Houses, and govern a wise and happy people, instead of as now, watching jealously over the impulses of a discontented populace.

And up from their bed of rags to work through the long hours of a summer's day, these two young slopworkers addressed themselves to their business. The sunlight fell on their pallid cheeks and wasted frames, their thin hair and scant attire, in sad mockery of its own brightness showing forth such misery.

The house in which they lived was one of thousands on thousands like to it in the back streets of London—unholy places where "respectable" men never enter, where the very police are strange, and where one wild interchange of want and vice and misery makes up

the chain of life. It was a narrow stifling court; a *cul-de-sac*; the closed
end abutting on to the river. The houses were old and crazy, set so
close that you might literally join hands across the street. In the midst
of the broken pavement ran an open sewer, oozing slowly into the
river. From this sewer—the general property of the court—many a
child eked out its flickering life by the fragments of putrid meat and
decayed vegetables found therein. Bad food for a child of man that
which was too bad for a noble's dog! A stand-cock at the upper end
gave a scanty supply of water at intervals; and there the people rushed
like wild beasts to a well—fighting, swearing, screaming—to catch a
few drops into their buckets. The water itself had passed through the
churchyard near, and was often green and foul. Originally Thames
water, it seemed to have accumulated a very prodigality of filth and
unwholesome substances in its way. Yet this was all they had to drink
in the court; and of this only an intermittent supply. The houses were
undrained and unrepaired. The ricketty stairs—broken and dark,
swarming with vermin and covered with filth, against which the black
wall rose dripping with moisture thick and slimy—led into rooms
where scenes of crime and bestiality and wretchedness, common
as the flowers in the fields, make England's prosperity but a volcano
beneath the vines, and her trumpet-tongued cant of religion and
morality but asses' brayings to hide the lion's roar.

Many of the houses were trampers' or casual lodging-houses.
What these were I may not say. I dare not, in a book like this, write
plainly of the scenes of daily and hourly occurrence in these rooms:
neither can I fitly reveal their misery. Strong men with thews of giants
lying down on the black bed of straw, and sobbing loud for hunger;
women whose breasts gave nothing to their babes, and whose weaker
bodies seemed sinking into death from famine; children, wasted and
wan, crying piteously in their dreams, and waking up from such sleep
as childhood ought never to know to ask for bread they could not get.
Such things as these, with vice and blasphemy and bestial brutalism,
were the revelations of the lodging-houses of this court; and I dare
not draw a more vivid likeness. Every available space was filled with
reeking humanity, crushed up together without regard to sex, or age,
or loathsome disease. Beds lying thick on the floor were tenanted
by many of both sexes and all conditions; in one the wail of hunger
came mingled with the riot of maniac drunkenness, and tender youth
sucked in the poisoned breath of vicious age. Oh God be merciful

to them!—they are a frightful set! And they are not all to blame! Revolting as these rooms were—who had forced those inmates there? Whose oppressive laws and taxes kept them there that state puppets might be paid with more than national fortunes and courtly luxuries bought with the price of human blood? Who built those houses, and left that court undrained, and laid on sewer water, and forbade the light of heaven by taxation, and left that swarming horde without food or instruction? Not the poor themselves. They only suffer for those things which other men have done.

The young slopworkers had a room slightly more decent than these of which I have been speaking. It was very small and low and dark; the floor was worn, the walls moist and begrimed, and the vermin ran thick over the floor and walls and ceiling. The window was small, and its broken panes were filled with rags and paper: it looked on to the river which threw up a deep bank of mud and filth close beneath; but there was a trifle more freshness from the water in the winter time— though now the hot sun bred miasmas and innumerable life when beating down on the rich mud below. But though so stifling—so thick with smells that you fairly tasted the air—it was a better room than most: for the two slop-workers and Emma Vaughan inhabited it alone without male inmates.

Of furniture there was not much. A broken round table propped up with a clod of earth stolen from a neighbouring churchyard, two cranky chairs, and two heaps of rags for beds, were the only items in the place. No more for comfort or for show. A broken pitcher, one rusty knife, and a delf⁴⁰ plate completed the list of the possessions; all the rest had long since gone for food. What more was wanted was borrowed. The washing day—what a mockery in the name!—when it came round, saw some poor wretch depriving herself of her solitary possession to lend it to others still more poor: and so on with all the aid that could be given among such a poverty-stricken race: for the poor are proverbially kind to each other. If they were not—GOD help them visibly, for no one else would! This was the room where the slopworkers toiled, and Emma Vaughan suffered the punishment of society. This was the room where life fought with gold and sank disabled at the touch. This was the room of which thousands parallel to it are to be found in the bye-streets of London, and in which a moral plague is seething, to break out over the high and the grand who know not now as equals those who in the future they must know as enemies.

The other portion of the house was filled with slopworking tailors, with large bodies of sempstresses, ballast-heavers, and river-men; all working hard when they could—and when they could get nothing to do, going out to beg. If this too failed, then they must hunger and thirst, and suffer cold and pain and weary suffering as patiently as they might—nothing could be done for them if they did not commit a petty larceny or a felony, and so come into the only circumstances in which the paternal care of the government is shown. In some houses there were above a hundred people divided among the rooms. What a mass of misery and crime! It makes the heart sick to think of it—and then to go westward, and pass through Belgrave Square![41] Surely such a division as this is not GOD's parting of the earth! Surely it is not in the laws of Him whose laws are justice, love, and mercy, that two sisters should live thus, the one in such profuse luxury, the other in such profuse misery. No, no! Man holds a better creed than this in his heart, if he will but take courage and read it aloud, so that all the world may hear.

"Emma not home all night?" Jane said as she glanced round at the children where they lay. "And who's to dress these poor brats if she don't come to do it? I'm sure I can't. The sweaters don't leave us time enough to be nurses to other people's children!"

"I'll get it done, lass," said Sarah kindly. "Mind thou thy work, and I'll do the rest!—and that's as much as she can do, poor thing, with her cold and cough, and that nasty pain in her side," she added in an under tone.

"People only impose on ye, Sally," the girl said after a long pause. "They don't thank ye for all your trouble a bit more than they do me for leaving them to themselves. Nobody cares for us; why should we for them?"

Jane's questions were sometimes very puzzling to her sister. She had but the blessed instincts of her sex to fall back on; yet these, if left to themselves, will generally bring the mind right. It is a mistake to think that intellect can do all things. Instinct and character do more.

"We ought to do good to all people, Janie dear," she said.

"Why ought we when no one does good to us? Our masters don't think of us at all, and they know well enough what we go through to get the work done at such prices! The sweaters get every penny from us they can, though they know we can't live with what they leave. What with fines for no faults, and lower wages for more work, Sal, they'll grind us down into the grave at last, and then grudge us a shell to bury us in!"

The girl spoke petulantly.

"Why Janie," said her sister looking up. "where didst thee get all that from?"

"I've been thinking, Sal," she said, sullenly.

"Thinking, hast thee?—and of what?" and her sister tried to smile, but the effort stopped half way, and tears came into her eyes instead.

"Emma talks true, Sal."

"No dear she don't; she ain't a slop-worker, and can't know what it is."

"No," exclaimed the girl with a brutish frown, "but I do, and I won't work any more at it! If I take to the streets I won't! I've got nothing to eat and only this beastly water to drink, and I can't and won't!" She flung down the shirt and folded her hands.

"Well dear, rest a bit," said Sarah gently, "I'll make it up at night for thee. Thou'rt sleepy dear, I dare say. Go to bed a bit, and think better than what Emma tells ye. Go to bed dear, and I'll call ye soon, if ye sleep too long like." And she went on with her sewing, stitching up seam and hem with as calm a face and as clear a smile now, as if an addition to her labour of sixteen hours were a mere bagatelle of pleasure.

Jane's heavy face betrayed a gleam of feeling. She looked at her sister with a kind of inquiring scowl that was very expressive: and then she took back her work and went on with it quietly, muttering to herself in an idiot kind of way—"I wonder which is right, Emma or Sally."

It was about nine o'clock when a man's feet were heard coming up the stairs that led to this unwholesome garret. They were unlike the footsteps of the inhabitants of the house. Light and elastic, they were easily distinguishable from the dull dead step of hopelessness in the weary tread of the overtasked labourer; for there is a physiognomy in the foot-tread as well as in the eye; and a skilful observer could never confound the different expressions.

These footsteps attracted the whole teeming population to the doors, in wonder how a man of the privileged classes could venture into such a quarter. He did not pass in silence. Loud clamours for bread rose up around him like wild winds from the depths of deserted caves. Hoarse murmurs, low sobs, piercing shrieks, and sometimes threats, broke the stillness of the morning air; till the whole house became a very Babel of misery.

Rags and remnants fluttered round him. Mere first sketches of humanity, forgotten to be filled up, crowded on him; unclad, begrimed, emaciated, destroyed with vice, destroyed with want—there stood a hideous section of the great empire, from which the supine legislature may well fear! Of all these human souls how many had the state tried to save socially?—how many the church spiritually? No one gave them work when they asked for it, or took care that their wages were apportioned fitly when they got it; no one guarded them from ignorance in their youth or held them back from vice in their maturity. The pauperism that then was punished was forced on them by circumstances, the crime that then was deepened was made by laws. Alas! the influential classes have had a work to do, and have not done it; and so are traitors to their trust before GOD and the high court of heaven.

Women with haggard faces, and children grown old in the very cradle; men with gaunt starved looks whose giant bones rattled loose in the slack sinews and softened muscles—girls, youths, children—the grey head and the baby's soft locks—all clustered round the stranger—all with one cry; "Bread—give us bread!"

"Can you not work, man?" he said to one, who would have been a hale powerful man had he but sufficient food to keep up the mere animal consumption. "What! you to beg? It is not right!"

"Work, master!" said the man sorrowfully. "Look here, if we work or not—sixteen hours a day in such rooms as these, with fever below us and fever above, and starvation everywhere; sixteen hours of even this can't give us enough to live on!"

"Is it work, sir, you want us to do?" asked another, a lean hungry-looking fellow, with long yellow teeth and thin hands like a skeleton. "Ah! if the law would only give us work for wages that would buy us enough to eat, you'd see whether it was idleness we suffered from! There's not work to be had, master, for us all; and for those who do get it, there's not wages enough for them to live on. I lie about the streets all the day, and half the night; but I bring my children back no bread, and I'm hungry myself. It's bad to be so hungry always," he added, in a half soliloquy.

"Plase sir, remember the faderless childer!" howled an Irish woman, with a colony of little ones huddled round her. "It's a beggar

I am, and I won't desave your honour no how; for no stroke of work, nor a bite, nor a sup for the earning can I get, your honour. And my poor faderless childer, your honour; I can't let the craturs starve, with the goold on the carridges, and the iligant shops that there be! But we's hungry, your honour, and we'll bless your name, sir, for ever— may the blessing of the Almighty be yours, sir, if you help the poor widdy and her childer this morning!"

The stranger took some money from his pockets and gave it to the applicants. Oil never raised a flame higher than this act raised the clamours of the people. A perfect yell of supplication burst from them; and when large and still larger gifts had quieted them, they retreated back to their dens, gloating over the silver that was to buy them food as wild animals growling pleasantly over their prey. When the way was something clearer the stranger turned round to a woman who had accompanied him, and said to her in a gentle voice, "Which is your room, Emma?"

She pointed sullenly and silently to the door; and Percival Glynn entered.

The girls looked up, alarmed at the sight of a stranger. Their first thought was of some new misfortune; for they had become so accustomed to misery that they could not contemplate the possibility of good luck. Jane left her chair and crouched behind her sister.

"You needn't be frightened, fool," said Emma, hoarsely. "He'll do you no harm. I don't think you need fear any increase of your misery," she added bitterly. "It's pretty near as bad as can be!"

She drew her hand over her blood-shot eyes, and through her tangled hair which lay in long rough masses about her neck and shoulders, and then staggered to her children's bed. Her gait was unsteady, partly from fatigue and partly from intoxication, for she had been wandering about all night without sleep or rest, and at intervals drinking fiercely. She laid the baby down out of her arms—poor pale sickly thing, it looked even now half dead—and flung herself on the rags. In a few minutes she was asleep.

Percival turned to look at her—at this wreck—this shattered column—this fair flowering bush uprooted and trodden down, to be abhorred of all the good, scorned of all the virtuous. And the question forced itself on him; is this a picture of what men call innate depravity, or is it not rather a consequence of discrepancy between social laws and the human nature they would govern? When he met Emma this morning, in her madness and her misery, and while leading her to what poor home she had and to what comfort he could create, she told him that she was the wife of a "gentleman." In her half intoxication she spoke freely, throwing off the surly pride with which she generally concealed her former life. She related to him the main circumstances of her early married years. Though she avoided his name, she gave such a graphic sketch of her husband's nature, and of her own career, that Percival felt she had told him the truth. She told him that this man held a high position in society: that his vice, the same as hers, only increased the interest of that society in him: that where she was covered with shame and disgrace something like a glory clothed him. Remembering this, he asked himself if society metes out justice when it gives such a different rule of measurement for woman's virtue and for man's—making that a seal of perpetual exclusion in her, which in him but adds a certain kind of piquancy?—and if the fact of this poor creature here—with all her guilt and degradation and passionate wrong-doing, left to her own misery by the virtuous abhorrence of a virtuous people—was consistent with the respect paid to the man whose life was the counterpart of her own, yet whose manhood alone was allowance of his acts?

All these things crowded on Percival as he watched that haggard face in its pale unconsciousness of sleep, and thought of what she might have been were laws more consistent with human nature, or were the condition of the sexes more equal in the social rule of England. And thinking thus—though the present life of Emma was so bad—though what he saw on that face, with its blood-flecks here and there—its lines of coarse debauchery—its want of all care and modesty—was nothing but evil—he could not but pity her as much, ay and more, than he condemned.

"You live with poor Emma?" he then said, taking a chair and sitting down near the two girls; and it was strange to see the effect of this simple action on the younger one.

"Yes, sir," answered Sarah, "always."

"Then you can tell me whether she suffers want or not. I could not get it from her this morning."

"At times she is near starving,"—the girl replied. "I have seen her half famished, lying for days on the bed yonder, till she is so weak she can scarce stir. And we are too poor to afford much—else maybe she'd be better off."

"But why does she lie there and starve, and do nothing to help herself?"

"I don't know, sir; she sometimes has fits of lowness. She raves about what she was, and her mother and her friends; and she says she would go to some Magdalen[42] if she could get in, or to the House[43] and learn to work; but she can't leave her children—which she'd have to do at both places."

"Does she ever work with you?"

"Slop-work?—sometimes she does, sir—but she soon tires of it."

"And no one helps her?"

"No, sir. Maybe a poor neighbour gives her a bit now and then. But she's very proud for herself. She likes to see her children fed, but she don't care to eat other people's bread she says. She'd rather break windows and go to prison."

"Has she ever been in prison?"

"No, sir, not yet," answered the girl; "nor none of us three."

"And she cannot get into an asylum that is not a prison? I mean a Magdalen, or some such place?"

"Not that I know on, sir. I believe you want a ticket or a letter or something; any how they're not open;—and then they cut the hair and keep you very close, and make you feel that you are very wicked, I believe. But I don't know any as has been in them," she added simply. "There are very few—and women don't like them unless they are hard put to it, and can't do nothing else."

"No one to find her out—no one to give her a crust of bread to save her from a fate worse than starvation—no one to endeavour by kindness, and by showing her that degraded as she is, humanity has charity and GOD mercy large enough for her, to raise her up from this pool of misery—no one to save her—it is according to social law and modern Christianity doubtless, but Christ taught differently," said Percival to himself. Then after a pause: "And you yourself, he said; "what kind of living do you get?"

"Not a very good one, sir," said the girl, a faint blush gradually rising over her cheek and forehead.

"You are slop-workers?"

"More's the pity, yes," said Jane.

"Now how much can you earn a day," he asked; "working fair hours, say from eight to eight?"

The girls smiled to each other. "Nothing at all, sir," they said, as if answering such deplorable ignorance.

"How so?"

"We must do a partic'lar lot of work by a settled time; else the sweaters—they are the people who give us work they get off the master—would fine us and get others. We work sixteen hours, winter and summer. And it's a long day's work anyhow."

"And you earn what?"

"Not sixpence a day each. But out of that we pay for needles and thread and trimmings of all kinds, likeways coal and candles. It does not leave much for lodging, food, and clothes," said Sarah patiently.

"Why you cannot live on that!" exclaimed Percival. "You surely must have something else to live on! You both look hungry enough, thin and wasted—but you would die on such wages without some addition. Don't you get more?" he asked anxiously.

There was a dead silence.

"*She* sometimes brings me in a supper," said Jane stolidly, pointing with her needle to her sister.

Percival looked at the sister. Large tears were trickling down her faded face, falling on her thin hands as they worked and worked so endlessly. He looked at her attentively. She had so good, so innocent a look, he could not believe that she stole to make up the deficiency. If ever there was truth in physiognomy there was truth in this girl's honesty and sobriety, ay, and modesty too.

"Is it painful to you to ask?" he said gently.

"Yes, before her," whispered Sarah, with quivering lips.

Percival comprehended it all. It struck him like a blow; and if the girls had looked at him more narrowly they would have seen tears in his eyes, brave man as he was. But this simple speech, accompanied with that patient, grieved, not all ashamed but still not hardened look, completely unmanned him. What a state of things in a wealthy and a civilized land!—what a desecration of the first principles of morality in a society teeming with mystic spiritualisms and theories of progress!

"Buy no more such suppers," said Percival hastily, taking more money and laying it before them.

"Use this with care, and if you are good I will not let you want."

Sarah took up the silver; it was ten shillings. Tears came into her eyes as she looked at her sister.

"Now thou shalt have enough to eat, Janie dear!" she exclaimed, kissing her face over and over. "I cannot thank you, sir," she then said, turning to Percival and speaking with much emotion. "But you will be thanked best by the good you have done—the harm you have hindered. Oh, sir! it is not only us that live like this—but hundreds and hundreds of poor girls starve on the same such wage as we get for just as much work. And hundreds—ay, almost all—scarce one not so—make up at the week end as I have done, what they can't earn by work no how." She spoke now below her breath.

"Sally," said Jane, interrupting her and pointing greedily to the money, "Sally—mayn't I have a pot of ale? The water's so bad, and I get so dry."

She asked like a child.

"Thou may, Janie," said the sister fondly. "Run thee and get it, and maybe a bit of bread for Emma's children."

"No! no!" answered Percival, "I have given Emma money for that. You are a good girl, Sarah," he said warmly, "and you will find your account in your own virtue. But, remember, you must take care of yourself! Get tea, girl," he said to Jane, "and bread, milk, and sugar, and a bit of meat, and let me know that you have had one good meal this week!"

Jane rushed down stairs, looking back with an idiot laugh, as she exclaimed; "And a pot of ale too, Sally!"

"I did not like to speak before her, sir," Sarah said timidly, "but you deserve to hear the truth."

"I understand it all, my poor girl," Percival answered, "and I feel how deeply you deserve to be pitied."

"Oh, sir! if some one would but take us up!—if the great people what makes laws would only hinder the masters from giving us such low wages!—it would keep the prisons, and the streets, and the House clear of a vast many, sir, who are driven there by want now."

"But, Sarah, the great people who make the laws say that they must not interfere with your liberty; that if you choose to give your time for so little money, you must be allowed to do so; and that laws must not hinder an English man or woman from doing what they please with their own labour."

"Oh sir, isn't this an excuse like?" she said anxiously; "we don't do what we like with ourselves. The masters are too many for us, and there are so many workers out of employ, that they under-sell each other, and work for lower wages every one than another, and that's why things have got to such a pass. Everything's lower than it used to be, and is falling still. I don't know where they'll leave off."

"I am not one of the Great People, Sarah, else I might raise my voice against this state of things. I do not think it right to let people starve because they are afraid of saying a few words too much in Parliament. I think that Government ought to look after you; but, as this isn't so, you ought to look after yourselves."

"How sir?"

"By union amongst yourselves," answered Percival. Then, after a short pause, he added, "the whole of the working world—men as well as women—ought to unite to protect themselves, since no one else does it. By all this under-selling, and not standing by each other as you ought if there was a right feeling among you, you give the masters and sweaters power to do what they like with you. Do you understand me?"

"A little, sir."

"And you think what I say right?"

"Indeed I don't know sir; but most of the working people do. They are all talking now of what they call the rights of labour and the equality of man, and they say they are socialists, I think, and go to John Street[44] for their rights: but I don't know well what they mean when they talk so. I only hope nothing bad's in it all."

"Nothing, bad, Sarah, if men understand the true meaning of socialism, but everything that is most evil if they use it as a cloak for violence and selfishness, and mischief. The men who live in model lodging-houses have one of the advantages of socialism; the men who talk of setting up in trade for themselves, in large bodies—as the working tailors and shoemakers, and others that you may have heard of—would be socialists in practice. People are foolish in thinking that a few political opinions about charters and universal suffrages, make socialism: it is practice; the practice of helping one another by every way in one's power, and by caring more for what we believe to be right than for what people say is wise. And in nothing more than in combining labour, and dividing equally, according to the value of the help, the profits of that labour, is the true meaning of socialism to be found. Let the working-classes be true to themselves, form a world within themselves, supporting and assisting each other by combination, and they will soon make better times for their labour. Remember what I have said, for you may have to act on it."

He spoke very seriously; and as he ended Jane entered with the provisions. Receiving thanks, deep, tearful, heartfelt, from the elder girl—the shy and awkward acknowledgments of the younger—Percival turned away to leave the room; when the eldest child of Emma, who had long lain listening to all that was said, started up, and speaking very rapidly, exclaimed; "But sir tell me why we are so unhappy!"

She was a graceful and very intellectual-looking child, apparently about nine years of age.

"That is Emma's; her eldest," said Sarah.

"I cannot tell you why, little one," answered Percival kindly; "unless I knew all your lives, I could not tell you this part of them."

The girl shrank back. "I want to know this, and I can't," she said sadly. "It seems so queer, when there is so much happiness among other people, that we have none of it!"

Poor child!—she had asked the question which has puzzled all the thinking world for countless generations past. It is of no use for that young head to try at its solution.

He left them; the heavy breathing of the sleeping woman mingling with the short moans of the poor baby and the unconscious prattle of the second little one; while the elder gathered herself silent and overlooked amongst the rags, and laid down to think, as she ever did, why she had been born to such a state of hopeless and enduring misery when others were so blessed. And as he turned from this scene of misery, of filth, of wretchedness and vice—past doors that shut in isolated worlds worse even than this—past rooms that held crowds clustered thick on the floor, in one undistinguishable heap—as story after story poured out the same living hive of squalid vice and showed how many were their ripe recruits for the ranks of the Criminal Population—the elocutionist thought of the Nazarene Teacher, and of all his gentle lowliness and practical good among the leper and the sinner. And then he remembered the purple episcopacy and jewelled morality of our Christian laud, and watched a bishop's stately carriage, and a senator's proud bearing, as they passed through the better streets of this tainted quarter on business of their own—neither of mercy nor of good. And thinking thus, he wondered which fulfilled the example of that Teacher best—the white-gloved respectability of to-day which will not touch nor recognise the vicious as brethren in aught, but which has left them to be what they are now or the scorned and scoffed-at socialist—the man whom political economists sneer at as visionary and unpractical, and whom the churchman pronounces infidel and heretic—the man who, on the faith of humanity and by the power that spoke in Christ, preaches mutual cooperation with all men whether they be poor or whether they be fallen: love and fundamental equality building up the temple of fraternal aid under every condition. If the social doctrines of Christianity be true, then Percival was right; for SOCIALISM, in its purest form, is the only result that can be extracted from those doctrines.

CHAPTER X.

"DOES our star expectant grow in lustre?" Vasty asked Percival, as he entered, unceremoniously enough, while Clara took her daily lesson at the elocutionist's house.

This was the first time that he had seen her since the Windsor scene—now three days ago; and strange as it may seem, practised lover though he was, and accustomed to all kinds and degrees of excitement, yet he felt thankful that he was not to meet this young fond child alone, in their first interview after that eventful day.

The girl suddenly trembled so much, turned so pale, but yet with such a happy smile brightening over her face, that Percival saw at once some explanation had taken place. How sick at heart this made him!

She did not raise her eyes to Vaughan at first, but gave him her hand with nervous haste, attempting to cover her embarrassment by that well-known assumption of indifference which betrays the truth sooner than any amount of undisguised confusion.

Vaughan retained her hand in his, pressing it tenderly when Percival was not looking, and making Clare thus understand that his love had suffered no abatement by these three days' silence. Looking down and blushing at her own boldness, Clare returned that pressure; and Vaughan then relaxed his hold for a moment—only for a moment: the next she was drawn nearer to him, and he, in his celebrated paternal manner, had taken her round the waist, calling her his "little pet—his dear child!"

"I tell Miss Clayton that she has only to will it, and the highest honours of the profession are within her reach," Percival answered kindly. "If she will but open her mouth when she speaks, and forget to blush when she is praised, she will not have a point at fault."

"How she will blush, Glynn, as she is led on after her *début*; with bouquets and wreaths showering at her feet when she curtseys to the plaudits of a house crammed from pit to ceiling, acknowledging by rosy smiles the waving of handkerchiefs, the clapping of hands, the hearty hurrahs, the homage of the whole audience! And then she will have raised up such a world of enemies behind the scenes, who would willingly poison her before she leaves the theatre, and against whom I shall have to stand her Theseus of the drama! Won't she grow two inches taller—our bounding beautiful *débutante!*"

"So I have been telling her to-day," Percival replied, "and yet I could not make her believe me."

"But she believes *me*, Glynn," said Vasty boastfully. "Look at her little grateful glance and brilliant blush. There are faith, hope, and charity, for you, all in one!"

A shade of sorrow crossed the features of the elocutionist; but he concealed his face behind a vase of flowers, and Clara was too happy, Vasty too vain, to heed him.

"If I do succeed," returned Clare in a trembling voice, rich and low, "it will give me as much pleasure for your sake as for my own. I should like to succeed, to please you, and to show you that your kindness has not been thrown away on me."

Clare did not remember that she was *in love* with Vaughan, and that she ought to be very stiff and cold, according to time-honoured traditions on such occasions. She only felt that she *loved* him; and, acting on that feeling, she took his hand and kissed it without any disguise. Vasty glanced round to Percival, but he was looking in another direction with perfect unconsciousness and philosophical abstraction. His face was pale—that was all.

"Little fool!" whispered Vaughan with tenderness. "Take care!"

Covered with blushes, Clara would have made a precipitate retreat, but the man of the world held her fast, and again addressed Percival.

"When do you think she may come out, Glynn? Remember her royal disregard of rules, and how she flies at the highest game before she even tries her wings. A London audience at first starting!—what an eaglet it is! Why, my child, the very best actresses we have ever had have all gone through the education of the provinces. Yet you—you rare country gem!—must needs shine before metropolitan footlights without any previous polishing! Now are you not a bold forger of

histrionic bills of exchange? Ah, you are a bad child!—utterly spoilt!—
and I am to blame in no mean degree!"

"Ask Mr. Glynn if I am spoilt," said Clara prettily. "Now am I not
very modest and obedient, Mr. Glynn?"

"I have never seen any fault in you, Miss Clara," answered Percival
with a darker eye rather than a brighter cheek—"though I have been
three months looking for one: and very anxious to find the imperfect
as well as the perfect in you."

Both the men spoke with softness and affection; but Percival with
tenderness, Vaughan rather with the fervour of passion. At sixteen the
fervour of a handsome man will always be more welcome than the
tenderness of one neither attractive nor handsome. It is a condition
of mind natural to youth.

"But you have not answered my question, Glynn," said Vaughan
haughtily, for he was quick enough to see somewhat into the feelings
of the elocutionist, and like all men of his character he was fiercely
jealous and passionately suspicious while his love lasted. When it was
dead—a weed lying down-trodden among carrion would have moved
him as little as his late idol flaunting by the side of another.

"I think she will be fully capable of appearing in three months'
time," answered Percival quietly. "Let me see—that will be six months'
hard and daily study."

"A ridiculously short time!" cried Vasty rudely. "It is absurd to think
of it! She'll never do by then! It is worse than absurd, and extremely
wrong to Miss Clayton to buoy her up with such fallacious hopes!
Clever as she may be, she is not quite a prodigy! She cannot find a
royal road to fame any more than others!"

Clara was struck to the heart by the changed tone of this speech.
Since she had lived in London—for these three, long, happy months—
she had never heard the sound of an unkind voice; and now this
sudden severity, recalling her to the old life of censure, filled her with
a strange dread. It was like the cold air of a vault coming up in a
summer's day over the happy face of a laughing reveller.

Vaughan felt her creep closer to him, and lay her hand gently on
his shoulder. It was the action of a child, with just so much of the
woman's love in it as to give it warmth and expression.

"Well sir, I will give her a whole year if you please," answered
Glynn, taking up a business tone. "I have hurried her principally
because I believed you wished her to appear as soon as possible."

"Folly!—as soon as possible!—why—do I want to make the girl fail? Am I such an impatient child that I cannot wait? That could not be your feeling, sir!"

Vaughan spoke very harshly. His temper, always irritable, was doubly so to-day.

"What other reason could I have had!" cried Percival deprecatingly. "But we can give her, as I said before, a year if you like!"

"Pshaw!—would you have her wrinkled before she comes out!" exclaimed Vasty petulantly.

Clare looked up into his face. "Oh fie!" she said, endeavouring to smile; "so cross for nothing!"

The manager looked down gently. He stooped his tall head condescendingly and bestowed a paternal kiss on her forehead; pushing off the hair and looking at her as one looks at a child or a picture.

"No, not cross," he said caressingly; "not cross to you, little witch—only anxious. Though not more anxious than your friend and admirer Percival Glynn!" he added with a sneer and a heavy frown.

"Poor Mr. Percival!" laughed Clare, holding out her hand to him; for she felt that she had somehow—she could not tell exactly why—caused him to fall under Vasty's censure; and she thought that of course every one must feel as unhappy as she herself under this misfortune.

Vaughan quietly took the extended hand and folded it tightly in his own.

"You must have no other protector but me," he said; "I must not have you a flirt, my *débutante*—casting the sweetness of your affection to every gale that blows. You must abide by your election," he added meaningly in a low voice, and with an undefined accent of menace in it.

Clare shrank timidly from the elocutionist; and Percival, taking his accustomed place, bade her coldly continue her reading.

Vaughan also seated himself, and "commanded a rehearsal;" leaning back in his chair and half shutting his eyes, scanning her with ardour and interest.

The girl obeyed; but she spoke so badly, made such mistakes, declaimed so coldly, forgot the best points or murdered them so foully, that Vaughan lost all patience with her.

"Shocking! horrible!" he cried every now and then: "say that speech over again."

She repeated, blundering over the words, and making all sorts of queer sounds which were intended to express passion or tenderness or anything in the range of human emotions to which they were most unlike. And the more she tried to speak plainly, the more she blundered.

"Upon my soul, Clara, this is frightful!" cried Vaughan. "God bless the girl! has she pebbles in her mouth!"

Clare looked up from under her eyebrows with a half-terrified half-beseeching look; trembling; her hands and feet stone cold; and undergoing all the pains of excessive nervousness.

"Now come here," he said pompously, and taking her hand with the air of a man who forgives a delinquent, and assumes the responsibility of her improvement on himself. "Now give me that whole scene again from the beginning. Be calm; and do for mercy's sake child, open your mouth! You have a very pretty voice, but you quite murder it by this inarticulate way of speaking! Begin here,— 'Oh! could I ever live'——"

"Clara did begin again, and tried very hard to do well; but she was now thoroughly frightened and could not command herself.

"At this rate," cried Vaughan in a loud passionate voice; "in about three years' time Miss Clayton may come out as a silent lady at a court ball. And even then she'll fall over the throne!"

"Vasty!" said Clare in a piteous way, but in a very low voice.

"I am afraid, Mr. Glynn, you have been employing your hours any way but profitably or honestly!" he continued in the same tone; "I must have this changed, or Miss Clayton must find another tutor— one who will spend his time in something more practical and positive than you appear to have done. One or the other it shall be."

Before Percival could reply, the manager had taken up his hat and flung out of the house, leaving Clara utterly miserable, as if wrecked for life.

When he arrived at home he scolded his housekeeper so violently for no fault whatsoever, and swore so hard, and knocked the chairs and tables about with such an utter recklessness as to fractures, that the woman ran down stairs, and said to her fellow-servants; "Take care how you go into the drawing-room—the devil is out;" which was not an uncommon figure of speech, as applied by his domestics to Vasty in a rage.

"Vaughan is not well to-day," said Percival quietly, when the front

door had been slammed with great violence, and Vasty's tall figure
had stalked down the street in a manner most tragic and overawing.
"I dare say he has had something to annoy him this morning at
the theatre. You have no idea what a life the manager of a theatre
leads! You cannot imagine the thousand petty annoyances that beset
him; the rivalries, the jealousies, the discontented selfishness, the
disappointed vanity, the impossible requests and rampant interests, all
fighting furiously for themselves, that he has to steer through. Fancy
for instance a tall gaunt woman, with a voice like a Chinese gong and
a face like a gorgon shield, insisting on a part written for a Mab-like
thing of gossamer and gauze. Imagine her powerful tones echoing
through his little office, with the one incessant cry of—'Mr. Vaughan,
you promised me full scope for my powers. I insist therefore on the
part of Titania, or Juliet, Olivia, Beatrice, or Desdemona, as the case
may be.' Then comes a muffin-faced youth who talks hexameters
by the hour. He cannot recognise the possibility of any Romeo but
himself at the theatre; yet if Juliet had ever seen him—still more,
had ever heard his voice—Tybalt would not have been slain, nor
would the fair flowers of Capulet and Montague have withered in
their prime. The wit of the company objects to a rival, but won't play
the part assigned him; the belle of the company trusts all to her eyes
and nothing to her intellect; the villain of the company complains
of the damage done to his social reputation by his characters, and
sentimentalizes over his deep voice and straight eyebrows. These are
the scenes in which Vaughan lives; and you cannot wonder that they
make him irritable. You must not mind his temper occasionally. I have
seen him much more savage than he was to-day. You know he does
not mean half he says when he is in these humours."

Percival went on talking in this strain for a much longer time,
never once looking at Clare, as she sat industriously destroying the
tassel of her parasol, and evidently wishing to give her time to recover
herself before she spoke.

"He is right," she said at length, after a long pause; "I have been idle
lately, and I am very silly and tiresome to him. I cannot repeat before
him as I do when with you. I do not know why, but something seems
to take away my memory and my breath; I cannot help it, foolish as
it is."

"But that is a very pardonable nervousness," Percival returned with
a false attempt at serenity; "remember he is your manager—the arbiter

of your theatrical destiny—the man whom you must please above and beyond all. I do not wonder that you are nervous. But you must try to overcome this, my dear young lady, and try to look at him as the manager only." He spoke now with emphasis, and Clare's breathless attention hung as if for life on every word he said. "Forget all but this; and at all times strive to think of Vaughan as nothing but the judge of your capabilities and the assigner of your professional position."

She looked down and was silent. She felt the meaning of her friend's words, and could not appear brave or cold against them.

"You have entered on a profession," continued Percival, "in which you must submit to no middle course. It must be success of the most decided character, or annihilation and despair. You are young to have thus thrown yourself into active life; but having done so, you must not shrink back nor fail. Above all—and now I speak with redoubled earnestness—do not allow your feelings to interrupt your career. The passion of ambition is not generally the passion of youth. Before this comes love: and it is only when age or disappointment has left the soul stranded on the barren shores of coldness that ambition springs up to fill the slack sail once more with energy and hope. You have chosen ambition first."

"But is it impossible to unite them?" Clara asked in a low voice.

"For a woman?—yes. Clara, attend to me. Love is only for the passive life; the active has no part in it. Least of all an active life in woman. She, usually so still, so contemplative, so secluded from the realities of society, has full leisure left her for love. She seeks no other passion, knows no other life. Obedience, constancy, devotion, entireness of affection, make up her whole existence, and are to her what ambition is to man. But let a woman step out of this secluded life—let her essay the activity of a profession and the excitement of ambition—and she has forfeited her place in the world of love."

"Oh no!" cried Clara involuntarily.

"Do you know what is the love of most men, Clara? Do you know to what extent they require devotion and self-abnegation to be carried?—what narrow sphere of thought and action they allot to woman? Do you know how she must control her mind, her very thought—divine gift as it is—to suit their prejudices and please their fancies? And, knowing this, can you believe that a woman with strength and power of character would do well to love, when that love will cripple her strength and destroy her power?"

"But it is more natural——" began Clara.

"Oh! I grant you its naturalness, and I grant you its necessity. But Clara, what I want to impress on you is, the importance of a correct judgment as to the man you love. I tell you, most men require both mental and practical slavery in their wives; and if I know your character at all, this life of suppression would never yield you happiness. Dazzled for a moment by some bright fancy, you would wake to the fading of your rainbow—to the knowledge that you had worshipped a dim grey cloud instead of the glorious sun of heaven!"

"I do not think that you quite understand me," she said, looking full into his eyes.

"No?—and where do I fail?"

"In this. With all my love of independence and noisy riotousness— at least what used to be noisy riotousness, but lately I have been so much quieter that I scarcely know myself; for I am never now in the boisterous spirits I used to have sometimes at home!—yet with all this I cannot live without affection. If they had been kind to me at home, I never should have left for any temptation of fame or action or even love. It was because no one loved me, and thus I was in a manner thrown on myself, that I longed for an active life. And now, if I had not met with such friends as you and Miss Kemble and Mr. Vaughan, I should not have the heart to study a word. Oh, no! I cannot live without being loved!"

"I did not say that you could. I know too well that you cannot."

"Then what do you mean by saying that no woman in an active profession ought to love? I am sure she would never succeed in anything if she had no heart!"

"What I told you: simply that most men are essentially narrow-minded and tyrannical towards women. Even liberal men are so; and the most so of all are men of the world."

Clara coloured deeply.

"And what would you do, Clara, if you found yourself married to a man who refused you all kind of mental and personal independence? How would you like it?"

"I should not like it," she said, "but I would try to bear it properly. I hope never to be made cold or selfish, and a woman must be both who cannot submit in little things to a person that she loves."

"Ah! you think so now, but I know you better than you know yourself."

"I'm sure you don't if you think me so very turbulent," she cried eagerly. "I should hate any man to be afraid of me, and I like to be kept in order a little—only a little though: not too much."

"So you think yet, because you are a child. When you are six-and-thirty you will give me a very different account of your likes and dislikes. You will then have found that what I said was truth; what you believed, fancy. I tell you again, you are not fitted to give the kind of love which most men require from women, and you are more essentially independent than you believe. I have given you now my old man's opinion, and it is very good of you to receive it so patiently."

"But what makes you so like an old man, Mr. Glynn?" asked Clara. "You are quite young still. Miss Kemble says you are only about forty."

"In ten years' time Miss Kemble will have spoken truly," answered Percival smiling. "I am not quite so old as she says."

"Thirty only?—and you speak like an old man and look so grave and experienced?"

"Because I have felt. And feeling ever leads to a knowledge of the hearts of others. That is all. Those who feel strongly, must, if they have any power of intellect, necessarily understand human nature better than men without hearts or brains. Must not they?"

"Oh, yes, of course! And shall I be unhappy then? You said so."

"If you allow your fancy to run riot you will be very unhappy," replied Percival; "if you control yourself by reason you may do better. But I doubt if you will ever be serene and calm and all that kind of thing which passes under the name of happiness. You, too, feel more than most people; and you must pay a proportionate price in suffering."

Clara looked down. "It has begun already," she said, her pretty lip quivering.

"Then end it," urged Percival, taking her hand. "Put out the fire before it spreads too far; quench the flame before it rises too high. You possess your own soul now; tottering, but still standing, the image of your power yet rests on its pedestal. Do not shatter it at the feet of one who——" He hesitated. Clara, much distressed, wrung his hand.

"Shall I warn her openly against Vaughan?" thought Percival. "Shall I tell her how cruel and base and wicked he is?"

Something whispered to him that his wish to serve her was not unmixed with other feelings; that disappointed love held no little space in his word of reprehension for Vasty. Percival's conscience was too delicate to suffer even the semblance of dishonour. "She must be guarded unknown to herself," he said. "By noble teaching and high principle she must be taught to shrink from such shallow pretensions and empty jargon as Vaughan supplies to her. She will soon find out his nothingness; and in the meantime the lesson will not be lost."

Clara rose to leave. "No more to-day," she said, turning from him as one in pain and weary sickness. "Vaughan's displeasure and your mournful words have quite unnerved me. Do not think that I am affected—but indeed I feel almost ill, I am so unhappy!"

"Yet you forgive me?"

"Oh, yes," she said affectionately; "but you have made me very—very miserable!"

"No, no, Clara! think of your fame—of your glorious future; think of your power over thousands—your voice stirring the hearts of multitudes to their depths—your words raising up noble feelings and generous impulses from the throne to the mechanics' workshop. My child! shall a passing cloud blot out this sunshine?—shall a foolish fancy destroy all this bright-burning reality? Cast such folly from you, Clara!—rise up against it as a brave man against a tyrant; cast it down and tread it under foot—it dwarfs and fetters you!"

"I cannot," said Clara, weeping. "Oh, Mr. Glynn, do not despise me; but I do indeed love him!"

She turned away disconsolately, burdened with such a weight of speechless sorrow as she had not known since the memorable day on which she first awoke to the knowledge that she was alone in the household that made her world.

"Poor child! poor child!" murmured Percival, as he watched her fading figure. "At sixteen—her first love—with all that dazzles her untaught imagination—with hope and passion and fondest fancy in her soul unchecked—poor child!—and she so innocent and warm! She has a hard life before her; one wherein she must learn in sorrow what is the bitter baptism of tears, the fiery passover of anguish unsupported!"

Percival was right; Clara's time of trial had begun; the initial of the long programme of misery that was to follow had been now stamped on the young soul all too plastic to receive it, and nothing could efface it in time or in eternity.

All that day Clara passed in sorrow of that vague kind which is more painful to endure than the presence of any one sharp affliction;

a sorrow that compels the sufferer to self-rebukes for folly and for weakness—self-rebukes which leave no strength and inspire no wisdom. Twenty times she asked herself why she was so wretched?— Vaughan could not be *really* angry with her. She had studied as much as she well could, and if she had been idle—love for him had made her so. He could not visit this on her so severely! She would remember what Percival said of his annoyances at the theatre, and believe that he had been discomposed there to-day. But she had known him now for three months—had seen him almost daily—and yet had never seen this irritation, though his manager's office had been as onerous as now. No, no, there was something wrong that she knew nothing of. She had done some harm, and Vaughan was angry with her, and had taken this way of punishing her: perhaps—and here her blood all crept as if in listening fear about her heart—perhaps she had not the power she believed she had; perhaps she never would make a good actress—and Vaughan was disgusted with her and wished to be rid of her. And then by degrees this thought grew larger and larger, and at last swallowed up all the rest, gaining such consistency and strength that her reason had no power against it.

That weary evening! The whole of those dull and lagging hours— with the ghastly sunlight stalking through the street in long lines of funereal whiteness—Clare sat by the window, her eyes fixed immoveably on the opening which Vaughan had so often crossed on his glad way to her. No one came. The hours droned on in a frightful succession of painful minutes, till each small division of time became a register of agony that pressed her down as one stricken with disease. The horrible thought that he wanted to be freed from her forced itself on her more and more. Shall she not then be generous, and give him the opportunity he is perhaps too noble to create? Shall she not write to him, and offer him back the glittering hopes he has held out to her?—offer him back the blessed love he has bestowed on her?—offer him back all the golden treasures which have made her life of late such a priceless regalia of hopes and glorious thoughts? And then once more go out into the world a beggar and an outcast. It would be more honourable: at any rate, he would like her better for making him feel how loose and fragile was the tie that bound them : and how one little fleeting breath of his could break it for ever.

Time was becoming eternity—linking out in lengthening chains of agony. The girl's misery was insupportable.

"Oh if he would but come!—if I could but see him!—if I might but promise him to be more diligent, more careful, more painstaking!—if I might but ask him to forgive me—if I might but hear his voice, and read his smile, and feel that I am near him once again—and know that he will not give me up—then I should be happy! But this—oh, it is worse than death!—worse than any torture!"

Such was the girl who had to buffet through a stormy life, alone and unprotected. When the accidental coolness of her lover could work such havoc in her happiness as this, what might be expected in the hour of real misery?

Suddenly it struck her;—"I will go to him; I will see him, and receive his forgiveness, and renew again the broken chain. Why should I not? He knows me—he knows that I am true, and that I mean only truth and confidence. I will go!—Why should I not?"

This thought was like an electric light flashing through her. A wild star outrunning its set course she started from the house, alone in the dark streets; the lamplight falling on her eager face, and showing her disordered step and bewildered mien to more than one of the theatrical *troupe*; alone through the thick crowds, and past and among the hurrying conveyances that rattled on the way she must cross; alone in the dense heart of London, and at night, this misguided child hurried on her way.

At last, by the miraculous power of instinct rather than by knowledge of her course, she reached Vasty's home. Her hand on the bell she hesitated, and asked herself; "What will he think of me? How strange—how bold—how un-maidenly he will think me! Shall I go in?—shall I not disgust him if I do? But then to see him once again, to be with him even in anger is better than to be alone—shivering on the outside of his world! I *will* go, and let the worst be mine; at least I shall see him again."

She rang the bell; the servant answered "Yes" to her question of whether Mr. Vaughan was at home or not; and she was ushered into his presence, pale, trembling, more than half dead from terror and excitement, speechless and powerless.

"Clara!—my God, what brings you here!" cried Vaughan, himself terrified at her state.

He held out his arms and hurried to her.

"Oh, forgive me! forgive me!" sobbed Clare, "only be the same to me or I shall die!" And she flung herself into his arms with a wild cry that rang through Vasty's very heart.

"Poor child!—what misery I have caused thee, what misery yet to come!" he whispered to himself as he stooped down and pressed her livid lips.

CHAPTER XI.

VAUGHAN comforted his young dove till she hid her pretty head on his shoulder, smiling through the long tresses that lay on her wet cheek like the glossy wing of a brooding bird. He chid her very gently; each word of reproach but further evidence of his love; and cautioned her against such an act of imprudence in the future for the sake of appearances only, not for any intrinsic harm in the act itself.

"You need not mind what you do to *me*," he then said. "I am not like most men who would take advantage of your innocence: but you must be careful, even with me, of servants and such people. They talk and do a great deal of harm with the narrow-minded and censorious."

"I know it was very wrong—but then I was so unhappy! I never did anything of the kind before—so you must forgive me this once," she said in the most winning coaxing way.

"Forgive me—what?" Vaughan returned playfully.

She blushed and was silent.

"Say 'dear Vasty'," he said, bending down and kissing her cheek.

Still silent: only blushing so deeply that she was fain to hide her face again—fain too, to make her concealment more secure, to throw her disengaged arm across his breast, and so rest her hand on his other shoulder. And in this attitude Clare lost herself in such a maze of delicious delirium that she could not speak.

"Say it," whispered Vaughan; "call me 'dear Vasty' once in your life at least."

He held her hand on its resting-place, his other round her waist.

"Dear Vasty," said that soft sweet voice, whispering up from the curls and the blushes, the smiles and the delirious love, like a gentle breeze stirring among flower leaves. And then she clung to him shyly, abashed at the sound of those unusual words.

So, Clare, happy—oh, beyond all words!—leaning childlike in her confidence on his arm, went home a different creature to the being who rushed so distractedly to ask pardon for no offence; as passionately happy as she had been passionately miserable—the golden glory of her sunshine equaling the pitchy blackness of her night. But she gave Vaughan a sleepless night; one wherein he clenched his hand and set his teeth often as some painful thought crossed his mind, like a trailing snake that could not be driven forth.

Vaughan had never, from their first acquaintance, liked Percival Glynn; but his antipathy to him was now becoming more and more evident. He was excessively jealous of him, for he suspected that he felt more for Clara than the mere master's interest in his pupil; and he dreaded the influence which he might obtain over her mind. He knew that Percival was more intellectual than himself, though he affected to sneer at him as unpractical and visionary; he laughed too at the strange and foolishly philanthropic notions, which he both despised and condemned; but yet he feared that this intellectual, Utopian, loving heart might one day destroy the influence which his own knowledge of the world, his superior position, attractive accomplishments, and gentlemanlike manners, had established over Clara's young fancy. Vaughan knew perfectly well that Clara's love for him was not of that eternal kind which is based on a holier sympathy than mere personal affinity, strong as this is; he knew that she must wake from her early dream, as youth wakes from all its crude imaginings and immature life; and then she would see him with other eyes than those in which poetry and inexperience had built up the prism of adoration. Vaughan was no fool. Few men deceived themselves less than he.

He had need to be jealous of Percival. Slowly and surely he was gaining a peculiar influence over Clara. It was not love; it was not even affection: she never cared to see him; she never thought of him when absent; his image was a dark blot in her heart, excepting when the light of presence fell on it. But she was beginning to respect him. What he told her she remembered without remembering himself; when he reasoned with her she yielded; she began to think as he thought; to regard him as a being infinitely superior to the rest of the world, and one whose opinion was, even before examination, more worthy than that of any other; in a word, she was falling under his mental influence in no ordinary degree. But all this without the slightest love for him. The nearest approach to it was a certain painful feeling when Vaughan ridiculed him, or when he grew sullen with her for her kindness to him.

It was evident that things would not remain for ever in their present position. No woman can be long happy in a love which does not claim her mental allegiance as well as her personal sympathies; and Vaughan knew his own power over Clare to be incompatible with the perfection of Glynn's influence. Percival knew this too; and his sole endeavour was to attach Clare indissolubly to himself by making her feel his intellectual superiority. Hitherto he had treated her as a pretty child, or, when more reserved, as a ladylike woman; now he treated her as an intelligent but imperfect mind, to which he would supply a better teaching. He knew that ardent truth-seeking character of hers well enough to be sure of the ultimate success of this plan, how much soever it might be temporarily checked by passion or poetic fancy for another.

In this design of Percival's there was no craft—no selfishness. Secure as a younger sister under the care of her brother would Clare ever be with him. He would teach her nothing but what he himself believed—holy and pure, though it might be unconventional, doctrines. He would correct that imperfection of passionate partisanship which so often leads youth into such injustice, and prove to her earnest errant mind a wider truth than the narrowness of a one-sided advocacy; he would show her wherein she might oppose the world; wherein she must obey; and draw forth the splendid faculties which needed only cultivation to make her one of earth's grandest heroines. It was indeed from no selfish, no crafty, motive that Percival endeavoured to gain this exclusive influence. For of her love he never dreamt; save sometimes, when drawing ideal pictures of heavenly happiness, he would check himself as he discovered that Clara, trusting and loving, formed the principal figure in that vague picture from the celestial cloud-land.

"Would you like to have any practical work among the poor, Clara?" he asked one day. "Remember though, it is not all rose-water and gilt-leaf but stern reality as people say; painful sights of misery without the faintest tinge of poetry in them; every sense outraged; every feeling of refinement wounded. Would you like to help even under such conditions as these?"

"Above all things!" exclaimed Clara fervently. "I have often longed for some opportunity to do real good. As yet I have been only a theorist," she added smiling.

"A true-hearted but a short-sighted one," Percival said gently.

"How so?"

"Do you not hold sundry wild and most youthful opinions touching kings and nobles?" he said. "Do you not ascribe all the misery in the whole world to forms of government? The aristocracy and the gentry I believe are your sole causes of crime and tyranny; is it not so?"

Clara blushed very much.

"Yes," she answered slowly. "I think they have always been wicked; the rich I mean. As a class they are very bad; of course there are exceptions."

"But, Clara, did it never strike you that men have powers superior to laws—if they choose to exert them?"

"What do you mean?"

"That tyranny is not so omnipotent as it appears, if a nation is but true to itself."

"Oh! Mr. Glynn!"

"Yes—I am right. All national institutions are expressive of a certain state of public feeling and public intelligence. If a nation is strong enough for liberty it gains it by the natural progress of the national character; though an arbitrary rule may keep it in its nonage longer than is just. Still in the end it gains it. And thus in many countries, the most arbitrary rule is the most popular one—the simple expositor of the national spirit."

"That does not take away the blame of oppression," she said warmly.

"In individual cases of excessive tyranny, no: but tell me—cannot you imagine circumstances in which the arbitrary form, which you think a crime of itself, may be the only one suited to the country where it is exercised? Nations are like individuals; and like them they have their period of childishness wherein they require a strong governing force irresponsible and unlimited. This shocks you?"

"Rather," she said timidly.

"But remember," he continued, "no governing institution can exist long without the consent of the people. And none without being somewhat suited to their condition of intellect and strength. When they need him, the Hampden or the Tell[45] is sure to rise. A man who attempts to force an arbitrary and foreign government on a free state, by means of a stronger extraneous power, is a criminal for whom death is too good. I am not speaking of this class of tyranny. But the hereditary autocrat of a slavish nation is not to blame for his autocracy. He is simply the offspring of a certain social condition, and the fault of his form of rule does not lie with him individually."

"Then you approve of arbitrary governments?" said Clare, opening her great blue eyes in wonder.

"Have I not been explaining how and why? In some countries certainly. The people would understand nothing else; they have not educated themselves yet to the desire of liberty, nor would they have the power to use it if bestowed on them. The autocracy of one man, in all likelihood better educated than the rest, is surely preferable to the anarchy of a mob of ignorant serfs. Democrat as you are, you must acknowledge this. Nicholas, as Czar of all the Russias—and I owe him no love!—is a better form of government in himself than a republic formed by slaves without either the instinctive love of freedom or the power of using it—or even by nobles, many of whom are little better than their slaves."

"Certainly—but then—"

"But then, supposing all Russians to be well educated, patriotic, and full of noble feelings, a republic would be better for them. I grant you. With such ifs as these we should soon arrange the universe to our satisfaction; but taking facts as they are, I think I have spoken the truth."

"But Poland, Mr. Glynn—and Hungary?"

"I give to you. These fall under my permit of abuse—a foreign rule imposed and upheld by brute force. But even here, Clara, the treachery of their leaders destroyed the cause. Had Poland and Hungary been true to themselves, Kosciusko's spirit would not have died when his body fell, nor would Kossuth[46] be now a prisoner in the hands of the Turks. These are not national disgraces certainly; they were the crimes of individuals who betrayed their respective countries; but they have nothing to do with the internal administration of Russia or Austria."

"Only this!" cried Clara with sparkling eyes.

"If Russia and Austria had been free countries, they would never have attacked Poland and Hungary, nor have despoiled them of their liberties."

"Would they not?" said Percival drily. "Have the English never despoiled a nation of its rights? Have the French never invaded a free country? Have the Americans never annexed an unwilling territory? No! no! don't let us look for justice to others from the freest internal form we have ever seen yet on earth! Men are very much alike in their passions, under every form of government whatsoever."

"I see you think me a child, and that is true too," cried Clara laughing. "But if I were to talk very long to you, Mr. Glynn, I should perhaps lose some of what *you* call my one-sidedness, and I, my ignorance. You are the only person who has ever spoken to me as a rational being, and shown me that I am wrong by the greater truth of your own views, not by simply ridiculing what I say without giving me anything better."

"I do not say that you are wholly wrong. Your present state of mind is as natural to your age as those bright eyes and rosy cheeks; I only say that it is imperfect; and I would hasten its development as I would feed you with food to strengthen and assure your bodily health. Like all the young, you look only at effects without studying the true causes; and what you do not like for your own part, you condemn *in toto*. It is this one-sided advocacy that I would have you lose—this spirit of uncompromising condemnation that I would have you overcome. You must learn to see good in everything."

"What, in tyranny?" she exclaimed, interrupting him.

"No, not in cruelty. For that is what you mean by tyranny. But even in the forms of arbitrary rule under such social conditions as they suit with. Believe me, they are not always the causes of social demoralization. You think they are?"

"Yes," she said, more as if asking a question than asserting a fact.

"Surely not!—if you were to speak of the condition of the English poor, would you drag in poor little Victoria, the House of Lords, and the whole bench of bishops, as the only possible causes, near or remote, direct or contingent, of all the wretchedness they suffer?"

"Not as the only causes—but as very powerful ones. I think it very wicked that they should have so much luxury and money while the poor suffer such frightful want. It is not religious, it is not fair, it is not philosophical. Oh, yes! down with them all!" she cried passionately.

"Well done, my little Chartist! After all, youthful as you may be in your views, you are right staunch and honest in their utterance!"

"Now you are laughing at me!" she cried, blushing dreadfully and half hiding her face.

"No, on my honour, I am not! On the contrary, I admire your frankness and warmth! When I speak to you playfully, it is not because I fail in respect to your intellect, but because that young bright beauty seems to ask for something more genial than cold honour!"

She looked up with a delighted smile; and then something came over Percival's face and he was silent.

"I must end my political lesson," he then said in a lower voice, and with a saddened air as of a man leaving the sunshine for his work again. "Institutions change with the people and by the people. It is but a blunder that gives forms in the hope of awakening the spirit therewith. Men are not so plastic as to be moulded at the will of every government master potter, and institutions imposed by mathematical line and rule, and not developing themselves gradually from a new order of things, will never fit well with the country on which they are so imposed. Do you understand me? I want you to see clearly that forms have not, under any conditions, the whole value of national effects; that laws affecting the well-being of sections of a community in time are modified; and thus by incessantly clearing away rubbish from the base—by continually adapting partial reforms to partial necessities—the whole work is done at last; as far as a work can be done which is perpetually changing its character. Do you not understand me?"

"Oh yes!" answered Clara eagerly, "I see so plainly what you mean!"

"I am glad of that, as I believe that when you go home and think over it, you will find what I have said to be a step in advance of your present instinctive hatred of power. Or rather, it is giving you a wider field and more special objects; concentrating your interest while enlarging your view."

"But the poor?" said Clara. "What can I do for them? Though not in their own station, I could not tell you how strong the ties are which seem to connect me with them! Our families on both sides are of high rank," she added, looking ashamed at what might seem a boast; "but for all that, something—I cannot tell what—seems to make me cling to the people much more than to the gentry. To me you know the term—'of the people,'—'a man of the people,'—'a woman of the people,'—is the grandest title that could be bestowed. I like their heartiness and simplicity so much better than the polished coldness of the aristocracy! I often wish that I had been born—just what I am— yet one of the people myself."

She spoke with much animation; with all her old passionate warmth, her old self-forgetfulness, and intense feeling. She looked so beautiful, so strong and true!

"Then feeling this," said Percival. "you must next learn to overlook the minute marks of separation which, to smaller minds, are so gigantic, and to feel that your common humanity makes you of itself one with all classes. The distinctions of rank in a civilized country are so exceedingly minute, and are founded on such trifling differences, that they are unworthy the consideration of a thinking person. I would have you feel yourself as much the equal of the queen as the equal only of the beggar. But this enters on another and a wider question; one for which you are hardly yet prepared. Tell me, Clare, would you visit a poor person of known bad character—a woman, say, or man—drunkard, thief, or murderer?"

She shrank back. "No," she said hesitatingly. "No, I should not like it at all. The poor that I like are the good poor, not the wicked. It is very wrong to have anything to do with wicked people; mamma used to tell me so, and read passages from the Epistles about it."

"Did she never read passages from the Gospels which show a different line of action in the founder of her own very religion?" asked Percival gravely.

"Yes," she answered with great hesitation. "But then Christ was GOD, you know, and we must not presume to follow his example in all things. What he might do we ought not to attempt. We have the Epistles for our guides."

Percival was silent.

"Did your mamma teach you this?" he asked after a few moments.

"Oh yes! She was very strict in her acquaintances. She would not have had even a servant with a bad character. I believe that one reason why she and papa never liked me was, that I was brought up as a baby by a very very wicked woman. They always said I had imbibed her coarseness and wickedness."

"Was your nurse married?"

"No," said Clara, looking shocked.

Still Percival seemed to hesitate. He evidently wished to say something about which he was not quite sure. He looked into the face of that young bright girl, and appeared to balance her youth and inexperience with her strength of character and breadth of intellect, and to hesitate whether or not to try the last with doctrines unwelcome to the first.

"And do you also think your nurse so wicked?" he said after a very long pause.

"Not so much as I ought," she answered shaking her head. "I am conscious instead of an intense longing to see her and to kiss her; and I cannot connect any proper feeling of abhorrence with the picture old Hugh used to draw of her. She was very beautiful, I believe; and so good-tempered he used to say! I saw her once; when I was a very little girl; but still I can just remember her. She had large blue eyes I remember, and brown hair, and was tall and stout. They used to call me like her; and mamma was so angry when they did! But I ought to hate her, only I can't; and I have always believed this to be a sin in me. Some distinction must be made between right and wrong," she added gravely.

Percival had been watching Clara intently during this speech. Her eyes brightened when she spoke of her nurse—poor sinful Martha!—as they had never brightened before; with such a lustre of love in them! And he could not help smiling when she bewailed this beautiful natural instinct as a crime.

"And you have never seen her since?"

"No, mamma and papa were so much annoyed with her that they sent her away, I don't know where; and then she left that place, and no one knows now where she is; not even Hugh."

"Hugh was her father?"

"Yes."

"And did he desert her too?"

"Oh yes!" she answered seriously, "Hugh was a very good old man."

"Was that a proof of his goodness, Clara?"

"Yes, surely yes! He sacrificed his own daughter to his principles. Oh, he was very good!"

"Well, don't be shocked, but I think you are much better for loving your poor nurse, even in spite of your education and all that which you choose to call principle, than he was for deserting his daughter, however guilty she might have been."

"Do you?" cried Clara, turning on him a face beaming with a thousand happy feelings. "Oh no! but I am not," she then added sadly.

"Well, my child, I will not press this subject on you to-day. Remember my political lesson—that is enough for you now; the moral one I will give afterwards."

"You are displeased with me?" she said affectionately.

"Not in the least! Displeased? Dear child, I honour and respect you more to-day than I did yesterday! That is not like displeasure, is it?"

"But your poor people that you want me to see—where are they?" she said, reverting to her long-cherished desire to do some positive and practical good—which was also a desire for experience and for influence.

"No, not to-day," answered Percival. "You must work for yourself before you think of others. You shall do something when you are older."

"But why not now?"

"Because you are not equal to it."

"But I am; I am stronger now than I ever shall be again. I am equal to any fatigue," she persisted.

"It is not fatigue that I spoke of."

"What then?"

"Mental sympathy."

"Oh! tell me what you mean," she pleaded earnestly.

"Well—I will then. The woman I wanted you to see is very poor, and of very bad character—as far as the world judges."

"Oh!" said Clara, drawing back.

"Now you are alarmed?"

"No," she answered. "But Mr. Vaughan—"

"What of him?"

"He has always told me to keep away from all low people, especially those of any bad character at all."

Percival did not speak at first. "Very well, dear child, do what you think right and obey him; at least yet," he then said.

"I should be so sorry to offend him!" she said, her voice and manner full of the most intense affection.

"And you shall not, at least through me," Percival answered kindly. "And so, for this reason also, I will not let you see my poor woman. When you are older, if you let me still be your master, you will perhaps think rather differently to what you do now. You will then look back on to-day's conversation as you now look back on yourself, when, a happy child, you scoured the country with Fleetfoot and old Hugh."

"I feel changing," replied Clara, ingenuously. "I scarcely recognise my old self now."

"You have had so much to alter you of late! The very fact of rising at once from a checked and misunderstood childhood into an admired and loved womanhood, has had a strong transforming power. You left Shorne a child—you stand before me to-day—so few months after—a woman, free and ambitious—loved, and aiming at popular distinction. What a change for you! No wonder that you feel its action on your character. There is also another cause." Here he paused.

"What is that?" she asked.

"Love," he answered quietly. "And this, first and most of all, changes the nature of childhood into the nature of maturity."

"I feel it does," answered Clara in a low voice, leaving him.

And then she met Vasty; and in meeting him all remembrance of what Percival had been saying to her disappeared from her mind, and she was again nothing but the loving, happy, child-woman whose whole existence seemed to hang on his affection.

Vasty, fonder than ever, was in an embarrassing position. He did not know what to do with Clara. When he first tried to win her, he never contemplated the possibility of being moved by her fondness and innocence to the extent to which they affected him. He saw that she was enthusiastic and warm, and her beauty pleased his fancy; for the rest he had no thought, neither for himself nor for her. It was perplexing; for he neither liked to live in this present unsatisfactory way, nor to reveal his real intentions to her. Indeed, he was not at all sure of her reception of them. So little so, that he carefully guarded her from himself, uncertain what to do or how to act; and feeling that one step too far, one word too bold, might lose her for ever. Independently of this more selfish reason, he shrank from harming her. Few men are so utterly bad as to be insensible to real virtue and real purity.

Thus went on the double antagonism both with Vasty and with Clara. With him, passion and principle at an endless war; with her, fancy and truth, as embodied in himself and Percival. He exerting all personal influence over her, Percival all intellectual; he possessing her heart, Percival her mind; he filling up the natural, Percival the spiritual, portion. But how long such an imperfect state of division would continue, time only could show.

CHAPTER XII.

EIGHT months had now elapsed since Clara's flight from home. No attempt had been made to discover either her place of residence or her mode of life; certainly none to induce her to return to Shorne.

It was well known that when she left she could not have had more money than was just sufficient to pay her expenses to London, and therefore must have been under pecuniary obligations to some one. So inexperienced as she was, it was impossible that she could support herself by her own exertions even now; therefore, in all probability, she still existed under the same pecuniary obligations. But the model moral woman, who could not bear an unlicensed mother on the estate, let her wilful child go wandering where she would; though where that unprotected and unaided wandering might lead she never cared to reflect. She gave the child's imprudent act no harsher name than a "mistaken view of life." She spoke of her character as one made up of "undesirable impulse" and "imperfect passionateness;" and never used a bitter word or hasty epithet of condemnation. Had she been speaking of one dead she could not have shown more solemn charity than she did for the memory of Clare. For Clare was, to all intents and purposes, practically dead to Mrs. de Saumarez; and thus all that had annoyed the lady in her lifetime might well be suppressed now. It never could occur again.

The world loudly praised the sweet forgiving disposition of Mrs. de Saumarez. Her ladylike forbearance was a proverb in Shorne; and the criminal life and hideous vice of Clare, the moral bugbears held up to scare away the young ladies of the place from the forbidden grounds of independence and individualism.

Mr. de Saumarez, not knowing the anchor of hope on which his wife rested, and not possessing her self-control, suffered more than she from the public shame and disgrace which he believed Clare had entailed on them. He once shed tears about it, when he spoke of his ancestors, his family pictures, and his family tomb; and he expressed a decided belief that the old marble effigies in the De Saumarez mausoleum must feel the stain on their respected name very acutely. This was his tender point, and could not bear the smallest abrasion.

Well; eight months had come and gone, and Clare was still uninquired of. I cannot say that she regretted this neglect. There was no sympathy between her and the people at home, and consequently there was no love: for natural affection is only a name. If, when the child has out-grown the mere instinct which unites the female parent and the offspring—if moral sympathy does not then supply its place, natural affection, so called, will have but little uniting power; for after all, the love which exists between relatives does not proceed from any mysterious spiritual connexion, but simply from early education, long habit, social union, and physiological affinity: the last the strongest of all.

During these eight months Clara believed that she was spending prospectively the future millions of her professional career. She believed that Miss Kemble supplied her with food, clothing, and lodging, on credit of her bank of intellect. But in reality Vasty Vaughan, unknown to her, paid Miss Kemble a large sum weekly for her fit and proper maintenance. He had done this from the first week of his acquaintance with her, though she herself was utterly ignorant of the arrangement. Not that she would have objected to it, perhaps, had she known it. It was so natural to be supported without trouble or responsibility, and to find everything done to her hand, that she did not see her own position in the light in which another person would have seen it. She did not know the meaning which the world would attach to the fact if known. Secure of her own purity of intention, she never dreamt that she could be misunderstood, or that actions in themselves innocent would be condemned for their equivocal appearance. Partly ignorant by youth, partly careless by temperament, of the opinion of the world, every step that she made plunged her farther into the social quagmires of independence and nonconformity; and her present teachers were not the best guides to a sounder social ground. Percival taught her the wildest lessons of self-reliance in principle and of freedom in act; Vaughan taught her, so far as he durst, the valuelessness of all moral restraint, while urging on her the strictest observance of social rules. Between her admiration for Percival's deep insight and wide views, and her unconscious shrinking from the moral littleness of Vaughan's strict observance mated with his want of principle and thought, she was in a fair way to cast down every barrier and break through every law that society had set up. Though she may be pitied for what it must bring on her, yet she cannot but be admired for her courage, her truth, and her bravery, in this instinct of independence.

But now the time was drawing near when she was to take the initiative of her future fortune, and try her fate on the boards of a London theatre. Full of hope and energy, she panted for the day; feeling that she *could not fail*. Another bright star of happiness waited on that day. The mysterious seal of silence would surely then be removed, and Vasty would publicly acknowledge his engagement with her; for she imagined that, being lovers, they were of course duly engaged and would be married some time—she did not care when. It was not of marriage as an event pleasant in itself that she thought, still less desired; she merely wished to be free from all secrecy and deception, and to live her life of love in the honesty and openness which were her sole congenial elements. And thus for affection, for ambition, and for generous compensation to Lucretia, she looked forward to her *début* as to the magic spoke in the wheel of fortune, which would make it henceforth revolve only to her advantage.

All time must end. Clare's furious democratic essays used to end, after a fashion. Her life of thraldom had ended; this interval of suspense must also end. The day did really at last arrive. It had certainly taken a longer journey than any other day since the creation of time; but that did not much signify now. Here it was; and blessings on its sunny eyes!

The morning never passed her rosy fingers over a happier brow than that which greeted her from yon garret window, with its upturned look of passionate delight; nor did the hours ever flutter by a lighter heart than that which beat loud music of hope and love and confidence in the coming evening stealing on so gently. Her bridal day would have been tame monotony, compared to the intense ecstacy of this professional baptism. The flushed abandonment of a Bacchante revel would have been chill languor, compared to the divine passion of life which filled her whole nature, and seemed to float her in a golden sea dyed rainbow bright. Earth was no longer earth—no longer this cold clod of clay, this dull mass of inert matter. It was a glowing spot of heaven on which she trod, and where she reigned, as a queen on her regal throne. All nature seemed to have conspired to do her honour; all humanity seemed to have desired to form her triumph. Wherever she looked, she saw bright faces speaking eloquent love; she saw the glowing sunshine that for her had taken back a summer's warmth into its autumnal house; she saw gay flowers lying in rich profusion round her chamber, and met great gifts and fond affection wherever she might turn. No wonder that she felt as if earth and heaven both wished to do her honour on this fateful day! Young and unworn, each new emotion was a glimpse of Paradise to the fresh heart which preferred any kind of feeling to the negation of calmness—to the death of indifference. How much then must she have felt, when such mighty emotions concentrated themselves together in so small a space of time!—when love, ambition, the flushed pleasure of young vanity, and the proud consciousness of superiority, all revelled in that burning soul, unchecked by doubt or chill staid knowledge of the nothingness of life!

I have no words to express Clare's sensations to-day. My leaden hand's dull trace blurs the page which only sunlight should inscribe and rainbow tints emblazon. The delirium of poetic rapture that filled her brow and throbbed through her heart like lightning quivering through a summer's evening sky, can be as little examined as the delicate pleasure of the nautilus, or the palpitating happiness of the floating butterfly. When I say that it was godlike—that it was rapture which might have made heaven itself more bright—I have said all that language has to express the intensity of her blessedness.

Good Miss Kemble, who thought of the footlights as just so many glowworms in a gold mine, and who cared for her profession only in ratio with her income-tax, was perfectly amazed to see the intense feeling which Clara exhibited. It was not the mere excitement of nervousness—not that small fluttering of the heart, which people who know not how to feel think so great and warm; but it was a kind of divine madness or intoxication which utterly transformed her. Her very stature was increased as she trod so swiftly, yet so stately; and an expression of dignity, that was neither pride nor selfishness, gave her a majesty beyond the grave grandeur of age. Her eyes were like great blue gems swimming in light, as they flashed out their worlds of boundless joy; and one word alone seemed written in every feature and spoken in every movement—"Success—I will succeed!"

All those who saw her throughout the day predicted this success. The lustrous light which shone on her brow was bright enough for even the dullest to perceive. A few of the women perhaps hinted vaguely at pride and discomfiture, and many sneered at her excitability and enthusiastic temperament. Miss Gray loudly accused her of humbug and affectation; and Mr. Buggins spoke familiarly of her as "little Clayton," and endeavoured to make his good understanding with her apparent.

Clare let them all say what they would. She was too happy to be moved by any meaner feeling than the ecstatic raptures revelling through her.

The quick hand of time brought round the hour at last. Evening came. With it the most experienced dresser, the maid, the milliner, a host of other officials, and Vasty—all attending on her at the theatre. The manager indeed had scarcely ever left her side. He had been walking in and out of the house all the day on a succession of important errands. Now it was to hear a certain scene over again; she had not given sufficient emphasis to a "that," or a "which," or some other equally important word. Now it was to re-arrange a certain attitude; the elbow must be a thought more bent, not to interfere with the tire[47] of the chair; or the hand must be a couple of inches higher, not to cover the curve of the neck. Again, her flower-wreath had a shade too much of red in it; a dash of yellow must come here, and a bit of blue there, and a mass of green yonder, to throw out the whites and the pinks. Disguise it he could not. The great V. V. was painfully nervous.

And then Clare would stand before him like a child, and say her part so obediently—for she had overcome her nervousness to him now—and feel more than repaid for all her former troubles when he smiled and kissed her kindly.

It was six o'clock. She was deep in the mysteries of the toilet. Dresser, milliner, Lucretia, and many others, were all crowded into her shabby dressing-room, where real gems and false, gorgeous robes and paltry trimmings, fresh flowers redolent of heaven, and dirty bits of crumpled muslin libelling their beauty, lay scattered wildly about. And through the din of many voices talking all at once, were heard Vasty's deep tones calling impatiently every five minutes—"Clara, have you not done yet!"

He might have been an unburied ghost waiting to take vengeance on his murderer, for the unwearied diligence with which he paced those creaking boards.

This ended too. With a rapid rush of lights and rustling robes and fragrant scents and clinking chains and small soft twittering feet, young Clare descended to Vaughan's private room, where he, Percival, and a large assemblage of friends, waited her. As she entered they cheered her lustily, and drank to her success in brimming bumpers.

"Success to the fair Ianthe!—success to the beautiful Greek!" they cried.

Vaughan dashed his glass gallantly on the floor when the toast was drunk, saying—"No meaner service shall profane what has been consecrated to you!" But Percival kissed the lip of his, before answering to the toast, and murmured something that was a blessing rather than a compliment. Both actions expressed the same feeling in the two men; and Vasty was not slow to understand what would have been evident even to a less acute observer. He treasured up this action as a nucleus of future accusation, and so was content to smother his present indignation for the sake of that richer future.

But now that the time had actually arrived, Clare lost something of her enthusiasm. She was pale in spite of yon hated rouge, and she trembled painfully, even though Vaughan held her hand in his and spoke to her with lover-like familiarity before them all. She was failing too in confidence. She began to feel herself very ungraceful and very ugly. She forgot her part; once, when she tried to remember it, her brain was a perfect chaos of words—like an exercise on a slate, half rubbed out; and she cried in terror; "Oh! how does my speech begin!" For she could not remember a single syllable. Not all the whispered caresses of Vaughan—not all the hearty assurances of Lucretia, nor the brilliant prophecies of dramatic critics mingled with the higher thoughts and proud advice of Percival, could bring back her fading fire. The tears came bubbling up into her eyes, and she turned to her master, exclaiming piteously; "Mr. Glynn—can I fail?"

"If you try very hard you may perhaps manage it," returned Percival laughing. "But it will take a great deal of energy and determination."

"Fail! the thought is blasphemous!" said Vaughan pushing rudely past Percival. "Pshaw! yours will be *the* success of the season! It will be a great *coup* for me, bringing you out!" he added in a true manager's voice.

"Drink a glass of wine," said Glynn, pouring out a glass of champagne. "This will quiet your fears and re-string your nerves better than a whole dictionary of words."

With a trembling hand, Clare took the glass, and drank to Vaughan with her eyes and moving lips.

The call-boy's voice was heard; and she must go. They accompanied her to the side-scenes, where she stood, half supported by Vaughan, quivering like an aspen-leaf—with only flashes of memory passing across her brain like dawning sunshine over a book. She could not command herself; her nerve and courage had entirely gone.

"Good God, this is dreadful!" cried Vasty in an agony. "Clara, for Heaven's sake compose yourself! This is frightful! On my soul you will send me mad if you don't calm yourself! Here! water!—Percival, Gray, Kemble!—Quick, quick! Some of you devils there, bring her water!"

Little Miss Gray laughed outright and said; "Lord love you, it's only a show off! She's a good actress anyhow."

But Mr. Buggins tightened his Albanian scarf, and answered; "Poor little dear, she told me how it would be!"

The water was brought; or what should have been water; but it was another glass of champagne. My little Clare, who never touched wine, drank it hurriedly—nearly half a tumbler full of it.

In a few moments the blood shot like a purple thread through her veins; she raised herself from Vaughan's arms, looked up with eyes wild and bright again with hope, stood firm and free, and cried out bravely; "No! no! I *will* not fail!"

The prompter waved her on and Clare appeared. A dizzy maze of lights and upturned faces; a sea of countless eyes before her, open and unwinking like the eyes of a haunting spectre; a seething cloud of mist broken through by splashes of red and white and black, like Turner's maddest picture; a loud noise that might have been the expression of any hostile feeling as well as that of pleasure, greeted and bewildered her. And then she curtsied to a house applauding her first appearance.

Vaughan and his friends ran up the private stairs to the manager's box; and far above all that Babel of loud tumult she heard his dear voice crying cheerily; "Brava! brava!"

She looked up with a glance of fervent love that thrilled to the very soul of the enraptured manager; and then, the uproar subsiding, she began her part.

Her voice was rich and low, clear and sweet, with much of that peculiar carrying power so essential on the stage: its sweetness therefore was not destroyed by over-straining. Her beautiful young face, to which the picturesque style of the modern Greek costume gave additional beauty; her graceful figure with its undulating lines and easy movements; her thorough-bred manner so rare on the stage—all predisposed the audience in her favour. And had her intellectual conception of the part been worse than nothing, and her acting of no power and no worth, they would have forgiven all for sake of her beauty and her grace.

But when, added to these gifts of person, were an energy of passion that betokened no common character in one who could so strongly feel and vividly portray—a fine discrimination of the smallest shades, delicate lines delicately touched, faint shadows gently marked—when intellect and feeling went hand in hand with so much youth and loveliness, where might not their enthusiasm go?

The character assigned to Clare in this play of "Ianthe" suited her exactly. It was that of a young Greek wife whose life was made up of but two passions—love of her husband and love of liberty. And these two passions, in their warring and alternate victory—in their depth and strong conviction—brought tears to the eyes of the young actress while she spoke, as well as to the eyes of the rapt audience while they listened. Coarsely drawn as was the character in the original, yet Clare's own poetry and warmth shed such refinement over it, that the author scarcely recognised his work under the graceful moulding of her hands. The cold soliloquy became a monody of fervid poetry; the meagre dialogue a treasure-house of passion and of love; what was coarse and poor in the original was transformed into rare delicacy and rich eloquence by the mind which represented it. What was small became grand; what was inadequate became perfect. The character grew under Clara's transforming power into a poetic delineation, equalling Shakspeare's fairest ideal.

Now beseeching her husband to fly with her far from Greece and its hapless cause—now veiling her face and bidding him forget her foolish fears, they were but woman's weakest part, and out into the brave ranks of the gallant patriots—again that wild despairing shriek, calling him back as he attempted to part from her—and then, after yon brief struggle of eloquent silence, her last firm act of heroism, forcing on him the arms he had flung down, and bidding him go forth to liberty and his GOD, and leave her to the heaven which arched over them both; in all these alternations, so perfectly expressed by her acting, she carried the audience along with her; and when the scene closed, and the curtain fell on their parting, the whole house echoed with enthusiastic applaudings of the young actress.

"It is not finished yet," she exclaimed when they congratulated her behind the scenes; when Vaughan called her his "brightest jewel," his "dearest treasure," and spoke of his own good fortune in obtaining her; when the women looked askance and found out gigantic faults which must inevitably destroy her sooner or later, and the lower actors affected to believe her considerably overrated; when Percival, the good quiet Percival, came to her with his gentle eyes and beautiful smile, and told her how proud he felt that she had done so well; when all the bright blood danced and played within, like a fountain of light springing from her bounding heart, she looked up merrily and laughing cried; "No! do not praise me yet—wait till I do succeed!"

On again; the misty haze this time cleared partly away, and the sea of staring eyes more star-like and more kind; on again, her beauty and her passion winning her green wreath of fame from the hearts of the gracious public; on again, not a shade yet fallen on the glory round her, and the gleaming atmosphere of hope about her more radiant than ever; the young *débutante* again came forth.

This time it was a monody of love. If Clara had been beautiful in the combat of her feelings, in this absorption into one she surpassed herself. Her hands clasped on her bosom and her large blue eyes cast upward, her place on that stage before the glaring footlights and eager crowd forgotten, and she alone with her own heart and impassioned love—she poured forth her speech with such intensity of emotion, that men forgot it was an actress they had come to see.

And in truth she was then no actress! For to Vaughan, to that bright idol of her hopes, that dear god of her worship—to that high spirit which had become enshrined in such body for this present time—to that uttered thought of her love and poetry, all the meaning of the play was addressed. And when she knelt and invoked heaven's blessing on him, and prayed for him to the exclusion of herself and her own well-being, she forgot all round her now, and remembered only the man who had first said "I love you," and first obtained her frank young heart in return.

It was no wonder that the audience applauded such excellent acting which came so near to nature.

The third and last act was the most stirring of all; less purely poetic perhaps, even under Clare's handling, but admirably adapted to call forth the powers of an energetic actress. One scene where the Turkish soldiers offered her husband immunity and pardon, if she would but guarantee his neutrality, was admirably portrayed. Her affection struggling up in unexpressed mode of look and gesture through her patriotism, made a picture especially touching to an English audience. Every line of steadfast refusal was applauded to the echo; every retort flung back in the teeth of tyranny drew thunders from the house. And Clare, identified entirely with her part, stood before the Turkish soldiers with flashing eyes and floating hair, lost to the consciousness that this was acting only. She heard not an echo of the loud applause round her; she saw not a face of friend or stranger there. The daubed scenes were strong realities; and she moved and lived, for the moment a true Grecian heroine worthy of Marathon and Thermopylæ.

The man attempted a familiarity. Clare drew forth her dagger to stab him to the heart. It was well for the actor playing with her that the dagger was a "property" weapon only. As it was, the blow was harder and given with more hearty earnestness than he liked. So entirely rapt away from her profession was she; that when he fell, instead of standing, according to her instructions, in the stage attitude of defiance—terrified at what looked so like to death inflicted by her hand, she uttered a cry and rushed to raise the body.

The actors, thrown out, laughed and whispered with each other; and Vaughan swore loudly from his place. The audience, who knew nothing of the matter, cried "Turn him out," and "Throw him over;" and made poor Vasty writhe with rage, the fiercer because so impotent. However it did not make much difference. Clara could not recall herself from her mistake, and as she had the rest of the scene to herself she did no damage by false cues. It ended by her lifting up the head of the wounded man instead of spurning him with her foot—which, as it was a more feminine action and the spontaneous expression of nature, was more admired than the orthodox conventionality of a stage revenge.

Clare underwent a shower of reproaches, sneers, congratulations, and encouragements, at this unlooked-for interlude. Lucretia was really angry, and Percival was loud in his admiration; Vaughan swore between his teeth and said something about the "mischief of want of self-control." For though he admired his young friend's impulsive character and ardent temperament, he did not wish either of these characteristics to interfere with her professional success or his own comforts. But Clare was so much excited that she scarcely comprehended what they all meant when they praised and blamed her thus.

The last scene arrives. Here she meets her husband for the first time since the war. A man, pale, haggard, and wounded, approaches her with tottering steps. In the distance, parties of Turkish victors are scouring the country, and carrying off troops of doomed wretches whose crime has been their virtue. Ianthe herself, an outcast and a wanderer, escaping almost by miracle from the hands of her captors, is out on the stony plains, searching for her husband, if happily he be yet among the living. Pale and trembling the wounded man draws near and nearer; and as he arrives at the blasted tree where she rests in her pilgrimage of despair, she recognises the wasted features of her beloved, and rushes wildly to his arms.

Under what delusion she laboured I cannot say; but the man who played the Greek heard her distinctly utter the name of "Vasty" as she fell sobbing on his shoulder.

The end was at hand. The Turkish soldiers spied them out, and straightway a band came hurrying down to link them to the crowd of prisoners they had already made. But no force could separate this pair. With the tenacity of desperation they clung to each other, and neither blows nor curses could disunite them. From the veiling mass of disordered hair Clare's pale face looked out her love, in all its strong reliance on itself and contempt of foreign power. Her sobs were rising high—though by right of book she had no business to sob at all. She clung convulsively to her young husband—to this painted, padded, beery Greek—and when the Turcoman's blunt spear passed on one side, by the way of piercing them both, she gave a sudden cry of pain and fell senseless on the stage.

The audience did not perceive the temporary reality of this sham death. She simply appeared to fall, as she had acted, more entirely true to nature than any one who had ever appeared before. A hurry and a confusion behind the scenes, a loud cry for help, and many voices talking all at once, gave those near the stage an idea of something unusual. But the call for "Ianthe " grew loud and louder, and Clare, after a long interval, was at last led on to receive, half dead, the approbation of the gracious public.

Bouquets, and a simple wreath prepared and thrown by Percival, were showered on the stage. Pit and gallery rose; even enthusiastic boxes forgot to be polite and became expressive; while stalls stood loungingly, and cried "brava" in small mincing voices. Men cheered and waved their hats and clapped their hands; while the poor pale little girl causing all this uproar, stood shrinking by the side of the actor who held her hand, bearing scarcely a trace of resemblance with the glorious being whose energy had filled the house and roused the hearts of all present.

There she stood and curtsied; more frightened than pleased, in her dizzy state of half unconsciousness, at the fierce applause cast like red-hot balls in the air. But the audience cared nothing for her fear. They liked to look at her, and see her modesty, and watch the timid glance of her full blue eye, and see the heaving of her young bosom. They liked to study the evidences of such warm free nature as she displayed; and they kept her there to be stared at as long as they chose. Vasty too again appeared in his private box, and applauded her with voice and hand; till wearied by her acting and her swoon, and overcome by all the emotions which had possessed her for so many hours, her nerves gave way. While with her trembling hand endeavouring to express her gratitude for this great and genial reception, the poor child's heart and brain again failed her as she turned to the actor, whispering; "Take me off!—take me off!" in the first agonies of an hysterical fit.

And thus she was led off on the day of her triumph—her own emotions the only cloud on that triumph. So sure was Clare, throughout her life, to bring distress and pain on herself from the uncurbed violence of her passions and the susceptibility of her feelings.

She woke next morning to read her "undoubted success," set forth glowingly in long columns of the leading papers. Vasty had procured them all for her, with strict injunctions laid on Lucretia to give them to her, and to place all her bouquets within sight, the instant that she stirred. The wreath he had destroyed with an oath, and ground its leaves to powder.

She woke from her long calm sleep to an hour of more than Paradise realized—her sweet lips murmuring, as if they had caught the echo of an endless song—"I have succeeded! I have succeeded!" And all her thoughts then turned in one rich stream of joy and love to Vasty, her great, her glorious Vasty!

Vaughan kissed her hands and forehead tenderly when she descended. He had not the faintest word of censure for anything—not even for her mistaken impulse after the murder of the Turkish soldier. Indeed, so far from that, he had already sent his orders to the stage-manager to erase the standing instructions of that scene, and insert Clare's version in their stead. He had only congratulations for her and for himself; sweet whispered words of honied love; and many a fond soft phrase, reminding her that she belonged to him, and him only.

He then drew out a lawyer's paper wherein she, Clara Clayton, set forth that she promised and agreed to remain in Vasty Vaughan's theatrical company for the next five certain years—at a fixed but not sufficiently remunerative salary of so much a week. It was a simple act to sign it; soon done and soon witnessed; and Clare never thought to ask—she would have esteemed it a crime to have dreamt of such a thing—whether this deed of agreement contained any clauses of corresponding advantage to herself.

"Of course you play all the principal parts in genteel comedy," said Vasty, when she took the pen carelessly to sign it. "You are not afraid to trust my word in this, or in a steady increase of salary? I would have mentioned these in the agreement, but——"

"Afraid!" interrupted Clara, looking into his eyes, and seeming as if she were kneeling before a god rather than speaking with her lover. "Can I be afraid of trusting to the very soul of my life? You could not deceive me any more than my own heart could deceive me! Oh Vasty! I should expect the very sun to fail before your noble soul suffered the least thought of wrong to rest on it! Vasty, dear Vasty! how glorious you are to me!—the true embodiment of all my ideas of goodness!"

Vasty kissed her and smiled graciously; called her a little fool and bade her playfully beware of him—she would find after a time that all was not gold that glittered. But he shook also with a sudden spasm, and bit his lips till the blood started. While Clara, resting her head on his shoulder and kissing his hand with tenderness, went on pouring out a whole world of innocent fondness; little dreaming that every word was a very dagger in his heart.

CHAPTER XIII.

I would do Vasty all justice where he deserves it. He had no evil intention of defrauding Clare—no mean desire of paltry saving—by fixing her salary at so low a rate. His only idea was, simply to keep her dependent on himself, so that all her pleasures and extra indulgences should spring direct from him, as pure gifts of love for which she must be grateful and affectionate. Not that he had any settled plans for the future. Merely vague pictures of a constant succession of surprises and unexpected delights—merely fond looks and gentle kisses and dear soft words for thanks—floated before him as the consequences of his power.

As for Clare herself, she looked to Vasty for everything. Had he been her own father or her lawful husband she could not have accepted his benevolences with a clearer conscience, or have been more happy in her entire dependence on him. Carriage-hire, riding-horses, milliners' bills, flowers, books, pictures, statues—all came out of Vasty's inexhaustible purse: and to be thus obliged to him for all she possessed was the happiest feeling that she knew.

"You want a new bonnet, darling."

"Thank you, Vasty dear."

"Do you like this figure, Clare? Shall I give it you? It is only four pounds."

"Oh yes, please!—it is so beautiful!"

"Shall we ride to-day, Clare?"

"Thank you; I should like it so much!"

"Do you want a new dinner dress, my child?"

"I think I do, if you please, Vasty dear."

These were the conversations that took place between them every day; and these were the things that placed her in Vaughan's power beyond the hope of extrication. Without friend or adviser, she scarcely knew, and certainly did not heed, the strange appearance of this mode of life. She was Vasty's own Clare—why might he not do what he liked, and give her anything he chose? There was no harm in it; and when Clare could say this to herself honestly, she never cared for what the world might add plausibly.

"Now that she is in my power so entirely I can make her more obedient," thought Vasty, after the people had begun to talk and joke about them both; "and the first act shall be her total renunciation of that fellow Glynn. He is about her far too much. I will soon put a stop to his career!"

And this was the way he took.

"Clara, you require no more teaching," he said to her one day, after he had interrupted her usual lesson with Percival and carried her off very roughly. "Glynn does you no good in the world. I'll pay the fellow, and then you'll have done with him. I'm sure my Clare would rather receive her lessons from me than from that pedant!" he added fondly.

"As far as I am concerned, indeed I would darling," she exclaimed. "But then dear Vasty, I don't like to offend poor Mr. Glynn! He has been so kind to me and has taken such pains with me! It would not be right to desert him now!"

Vaughan's lip quivered. "Oh! very well!" he said angrily; "of course if you prefer Glynn's company to mine, and Glynn's favour to mine, you are quite right to keep on with the fellow. I only tell you that I will have nothing whatever to do with you so long as you are under him!"

"But, Vasty dear," urged Clare, not knowing that it is an insult to manhood for womanhood to argue with it, or attempt to disabuse it of a mistaken impression, "you introduced me to him so warmly, why do you dislike him now? Is he a bad man—or why?"

"I suppose it is not necessary for me to give you reasons for all my actions," said the manager haughtily. "I am not accustomed, Clara, to be asked 'why' from any one in the world: nor will I suffer it even from you. You must not presume on my affection too much," he added with emphasis, and frowning sternly.

"I do not wish to vex you, dear dear Vasty," she said affectionately, "but all this is a puzzle to me! I do not know what I have said to annoy you! Indeed, indeed, I would rather do anything than make you angry with me! Why you know that—do you not?" and she looked up so prettily, that even the irritable Vaughan could not gaze back savagely into those great deep eyes, like purple lazules glancing before him.

"I have asked but very little, Clara, from you," he answered, still retaining the magisterial air of one aggrieved, "and if you love me as you say you do, it would be no sacrifice to grant *any* request. Certainly not such a rational and proper one as this! I merely say—leave Percival Glynn and I will pay him off for all your past lessons—for you know quite as much of stage technicalities as *he* can teach you, and what more instruction you require I myself will give you. In this there is surely no such great sacrifice!—I did not expect that you would oppose me on such a trifle!"

"I don't oppose you, Vasty, from any bad feeling," persisted Clara, sorely divided between her love and her sense of right. "I only beg you to remember how kind Percival has been to me, and how much I owe to his careful training. I have no fault to find with him, Vaughan dear, and it would break my heart to act unkindly and ungratefully to him."

"Upon my soul this is too much for any man to bear!" exclaimed Vaughan exceedingly irate. "You may say a great deal Clara, but when you come to an open confession of such passionate attachment to a beggarly teacher—a superior kind of usher—and that to my very face—it is too shameless—too impudent!"

"Vasty!" exclaimed poor Clare, looking up alarmed, as if he had been a madman; which indeed at this moment he was not very unlike.

"Make your choice, madam, here and now," he continued in a hoarse voice. "Choose between your beloved Percival and me. Of course *I* have never been kind to you—*I* do not love you—nor would *my* estimation of your ingratitude break your heart. Of Percival's affection you are, and must be, much more sure than of mine; but if you are so fond of him you had better keep to him. What business have you with me!" he added, flinging off her hand: "What shameful coquetry this is—you cannot want us both! Nor do I want anything with you, if half of your heart belongs to another! I care nothing for your divided affections, and hold myself rather too high"—and he drew himself up proudly—"to be at any time the rival in love of Mr. Percival Glynn! I should not have looked for such an insulting comparison from you, Clara, of all women!"

"But indeed you are mistaking me painfully," pleaded poor little Clare, terrified and inexpressibly shocked at the coarse tone and coarse thoughts of her lover; "I do not love Mr. Glynn in any way—you *know* that—and you know that I care only for you—that he is nothing to me!"

"Then you tell me I have spoken a falsehood?" said Vasty turning full upon her, for at this moment nothing that she could have said would have been able to soften him.

"Vaughan! for Heaven's sake, what does all this mean?" cried Clara in despair. "What have I said?—what have I done? I am bewildered!—it is all like some horrible dream!"

"You can soon end it, madam," he said coldly, with a spiteful accent on the 'madam;' "you have but to say that you will give up Mr. Glynn as your teacher, and now—after your unwitting revelations—as your friend also—and you have regained your former place in my heart. If you do not do so, you may bid farewell to me in every shape but as your manager. I will not be even your *friend*. I will not be even the *acquaintance* of a woman who could deceive her best friend and affianced lover, for such a beggarly fellow as this 'Percival Glynn.' You are too shameless, Clara—too ungrateful!"

Clare was silent. Much inclined to purchase peace at any sacrifice, and really feeling no special affection for Percival, but held back by an undefined sensation of wrong—a vague consciousness of dishonour and cowardice—she was uncertain how to act.

"Your silence then is your answer, Miss Clayton?" said Vaughan after a moment's pause. "I understand you—you refuse me. It is well! Better that our connexion should end thus, than drag out a lingering life of disease and coldness. I might perhaps have expected a different mode of action from you—but I have never yet placed my heart on what I believed a rock that it has not broken itself against the edges of a wrecking reef." (Vaughan had once been to sea.) "I will not annoy you further. Here is your house:—good morning. I will send my treasurer with your first month's salary to-morrow. I wish you good morning, Miss Clayton."

"Oh! this is something dreadful! I cannot believe it all! Vasty!—dear Vasty—you are jesting with me!—oh do not leave me like this!—Vasty!—Vasty!"

Her voice had risen to almost a scream. Vaughan was at some distance; walking majestically down the street.

"I think you had better compose yourself," he said, turning back very coldly, "else people will perhaps wonder at the scene. What do you want with me? How can my disapprobation move you to any feeling at all? You have Mr. Glynn to comfort you if you feel dull. For you are too young to be such an accomplished hypocrite as to have deceived me entirely. You loved me once I believe!"

"And now, and now," sobbed Clara, dragging him into the small passage of the house; "More than ever now, Vaughan!"

"Then grant my request—and prove your love," he returned with a fierce kind of growl, pressing her arm till she almost shrieked from pain.

"Indeed I will!" she cried clinging to him, and forcibly placing his arm round her waist. "Only love me again—look at me as you did—kiss me once, and I will do anything you bid me!"

Vaughan kissed her, not once nor twice but a thousand times; calling her every tenderest word which his copious vocabulary could supply to him, and pressing her to his heart with all that fervour and passion and gentleness of affection which he knew so well how to use and mingle.

Clare tried to feel happy, but something whispered to her that she had committed a sin: for to her, cowardice and, still unconvinced, the yielding of her own sense of right to the unjust dictum of another, were the worst sins she could commit.

"Now were you not very wrong to make so much fuss about such a trifle?" said Vaughan with an air of superiority. "How much better if you had spared yourself and me all this pain, and had yielded at once like a good girl!"

Clare was silent.

"Was it not so, little witch?" he continued, playing with her hair. "Were you not very wicked to deny me so small a favour? Why Clare, when you are married you will have to give up more than a beggarly master I can assure you."

This was an artful hint. He knew how it would work.

Clare's heart throbbed at this allusion, which of course she took to mean himself. It was the very first time that the word "marriage" had ever passed his lips. How often had she listened for it and longed to hear it!

"Ah! it will be different then," she said blushing, and with a choking sigh of happiness.

"Why? or how? Am I not as much your lover, and your master too, my pretty independence, as I shall ever be? Are you such a little fool as to believe the ceremony makes the marriage?"

"Of course!" she said looking up.

"Of course not!" he answered laughing. "And so you'll find some of these days! However, I will not let you off your scolding. You must take this, our first, and I hope our only, misunderstanding my Clara, as a warning and a lesson. Remember that your part is to obey me, whether you have sworn the word or not. I am the active and the responsible agent in our union now and hereafter; and whatever I tell you to do"—here he was exceedingly emphatic—"though it may war against your own ideas, and even against your firmest principles—you must still obey me. We shall never agree under any other system than this. I am, as you know, strongly in favour of a fixed and rational autocracy, while you, my young democrat, are a perfect savage in your untaught notions of liberty. However you may think as you like, provided you act as I like. Now do you hear me, little rebel? You must subdue that naughty spirit of yours, if you intend to live happily with me; and again I give you the advice to obey me implicitly in all things—mind in all things—even when most repugnant to your contracted notions. If you wish me to love you long, or to be happy in your love, this must be your unvarying rule of action."

Clara was silent. This doctrine did not much suit her; and, blinded as she was by her affection, she had still a glimpse of reason and common sense remaining.

Vaughan perfectly understood her silence. He did not remark on it, but left her presently, with a meaning look and an emphatic—"Remember, Clare! obedience in the strictest sense of the word!" to meditate on the lesson he had just given her, and to apply it as she best might.

Poor little Clara was fairly puzzled how to act. She would willingly have done right, but she did not know what would be right. She felt excessively uneasy at forsaking Percival, so good and noble and true as he was; and yet how could she oppose her lover—the man who was to be her future husband? She had always heard that obedience was the first duty of a woman, and she hoped that she did well in paying it to Vaughan. Then again, the sense of independent judgment, and the virtue of honest action, somewhat counteracted this educated idea of womanly duty, and she felt that to Percival also, though neither husband nor lover, and only a simple friend, she owed something. What should she do? Obey Vaughan and disregard the promptings of her own heart, or cling to barren virtue and lose her dearest treasure? She was completely at a loss; and, an unusual thing for her, accepted a compromise.

She took pen and paper, and wrote the following hurried note to Glynn; which, as his house was very far off, she put in the post.

"Dear Mr. Glynn. If I am cool and estranged to you do not blame me. I may not say much; I may not give you the slightest hint of the cause—only remember that it is not my fault—not my unfettered action. For all your kindness accept my best thanks—my grateful earnest thanks. Had I been free I would have repaid you better than with coldness and neglect! Again I pray you not to impute this change to any feeling in me unfriendly to you; I am not free—indeed, indeed not! Pray pardon me; and still think kindly of one who will always remember you with true friendship and heartfelt gratitude.—CLARA CLAYTON."

When the note was sent Clara felt a little relieved, though by it she had failed both parties, as is always the case with those who make compromises.

Glynn read that note again and again before he would believe the evidence of his senses. That his bright sunlight should be withdrawn, so suddenly, so strangely! Oh, no, he could not believe it! He had suffered his love for Clare to grow silently and surely so deep in his heart—striking its roots into the very centre—that to pluck it out would be death! He would not credit this lying paper! He would go to her at once, and insist on a personal rejection of his unobtrusive friendship! No false pen should lead him thus, like a marsh-light to his ruin!

Never had the calm elocutionist been so wretched! Great drops stood on his forehead; his lips moved convulsively; the sinews of the clasped hands pressed against his brow were strained and cracked, as if resisting some heavy weight. His whole being was stirred to its very depths; and the bitter waters of anguish broke over his soul, as the waves broke over the hurrying Egyptian, and overwhelmed him.

After some time spent in the bewildering death of a sudden sorrow, Percival hurried off to the house of good, friendly, foolish Miss Kemble.

She was not at home; but he entered.

Clare sat alone in the drawing-room. Lucretia had gone up-stairs to dress, for it was time to go to the theatre, and she had not a moment to lose. Clara was free to-night. Indeed she could not have acted had she been promised.

"Not a moment, an' ye would save my life!" Lucretia cried hurrying through the room. "A horse, a horse, my kingdom for a horse! There's Vasty in a fret, and Miss Gray whispering serpent-tongued in his ear! I must be off ere the cock crow again; and so good den, and comfort ye one another!"

With which *pot-pourri* of words, Lucretia shuffled out of the room; and Clara had no one to help her in her most embarrassing position.

"You wrote to me, Clara, to-night?" said Percival after a moment's pause, and with a very sorrowful voice.

"Yes, I did," returned Clara, not daring to raise her eyes.

"And am I to believe that you really and truly intend to abandon me to the enmity—the causeless enmity of Vaughan?"

"Oh, Mr. Glynn! do not distress me so much! I cannot help myself—I must do as I am told!" said Clara in extreme distress.

"No, no, Miss Clayton! you need not be forced to commit an injustice and a cruelty," returned Percival bitterly.

"But I did not tell you that Vaughan said I was to give you up!" she said, endeavouring to shield her lover with the true instinct of a woman.

"I did not need it. I knew it without your telling me in so many set words," he answered. "You cannot deny it, Clara—it is by Vaughan's command that you must desert me. Tell me the truth—is it not so? What! are you afraid to trust *me?*"

She hesitated, blushed, wept; and at last said suddenly; " I *can* trust you; and you will not betray me. Yes, you are right. Vasty makes me do this."

"I knew it," said Percival with a groan, flinging himself on the sofa and burying his face in the cushions.

There was now a deep pause. Percival did not know whether to counsel her to obedience and peace, or to advise her to rebellion, discord, and stern right. Up to the present time he had not felt much uneasiness at the connexion between Vaughan and Clara. He had regarded it as a childish fancy on her part, which she would soon outgrow; and for him, he did not believe him such a villain as to take advantage of her innocence. Had he seen any progress to alarm him, he would have trusted to his own influence and Clare's early education to keep her free from all that was undesirable and hurtful. But if he was to be entirely separated from her—what might not then take place? Unknown to her, he had long been Clare's surest defence!

"You think me base and cowardly to give way to Vasty in this matter?" said Clare timidly, holding out her hand to him with a caressing air.

"No, not such harsh words, my dear child—but still, apart from any personal feeling of disappointment or sorrow, I do not think it right to forsake a friend for any consideration whatsoever. Friendship has its duties as well as love, as well as relationship, as well as marriage. And for none of these should you sacrifice the truth—for no one feeling should you abandon another."

"But what am I to do, Mr. Glynn? Vasty said I was to give you up both as a friend now——"

"Why as a friend?" he interrupted suddenly, fixing his eyes on hers. She was embarrassed.

"Why?" he asked again very gently.

"You make me tell you everything," Clare answered, "as if I were under a spell. He is jealous of you."

A crimson flush crossed the pale face looking into hers. The feeling of giddy rapture that shot through him at that simple word almost repaid him for this last hour of suffering.

"It is very wrong in him to be so jealous of every one, I know," continued Clara innocently. "But what am I to do if he is so?—I cannot change him now, and opposition only confirms him!"

"Then abandon me to my fate!" exclaimed Percival. "I would not cause your young heart one moment's sorrow, nor cloud your transitory happiness with a very gossamer shred hung between the sun and you! Abandon me, my child—though I shall never forsake you—and never cease to watch over you, unseen and unacknowledged; for if you were not safe and happy, Clara, I should die!"

Clara trembled at the voice in which these words were said. She was too much a novice in such matters to distinguish LOVE as the moving power of Percival's present feelings, but something that was not knowledge—it might have been intuition—filled her with alarm and sorrow—and yet with pleasure too.

"I shall never forget your kindness to me, dear Mr. Glynn," she said with much emotion. "If you are not angry with me for acting thus, and will forgive Vasty, perhaps some day you will visit us, when he cannot have any cause to be jealous or afraid." She looked into his face pleadingly.

Percival started. "Do you mean when you are married?" he said with energy.

She blushed very much. "Yes," she answered hesitating.

The elocutionist was frightfully agitated.

"Does Vaughan talk of marrying you?" he asked, covering his face with his hand.

"No," answered Clare modestly and timidly. "He only mentioned the word to-day for the first time."

"Clara!"—began Percival, and then he stopped.

"What is the matter with you, Mr. Glynn? Why do you look so wildly?—what has happened to you all lately!" she exclaimed in a kind of childish despair. "I do not seem to recognise any of you again! It is like another world to me!"

"Never mind now!" answered Glynn, calming his agitation by a strong effort of his will, "you will not do any good by asking, certainly none by knowing! I will leave you now Clara—now—though not for ever; and oh! let me remind you once again of my firm and faithful friendship for you—let me implore you to trust in me—trust in me always, as you have trusted me to-day! I do not change, and I do not lie. I will be always to you what I am now—always as truly and devotedly your friend. I look for no reward, Clara—I ask for no friendship from you in return—I wish no promises, no vows—all I wish for is your trust and your confidence, so that when I can be of use to you, I shall be summoned—summoned too, before all the world beside! Near you, and ever anxious for you—guarding you unseen from all dangers that may beset you, and that I can preserve you from—loving you as I do now, with a brother's pride and protecting care—think of me, Clara—of your old master—with affection, and never fail in your trust in me, as I shall never fail in answering to that trust!"

He took her hand and kissed it fervently. Clara was weeping very bitterly. She respected him more now than she had ever done; and, strange to say, for the first time she thought him handsome. Whether his emotion set off his plain features, or hers made an atmosphere beautifying and ennobling, I cannot say; but as the lamplight fell on his face she was perfectly startled at the beauty she had so long overlooked.

She felt him her brother; of herself she would have clung to him as such for ever; and now, as a recompence for all his attachment and patient care and respectful love, she flung him off at the base desire of a false suspicion! She was beginning to feel such a dreadful culprit; uneasy and restless, and not knowing now what to do, any more than she did four hours ago.

"Good bye my dear dear child!" then said Percival fondly. "Remember all that I have said, and act on it. Treat me with what public coldness you will—I shall care nothing for that so long as I possess your secret reliance and secret affection!"

He still retained her hand, looking into her crimson face.

"Good bye Mr. Glynn," said Clara through her tears; and then, without thinking of the effect such an action might produce, she threw her arms round his neck and kissed him.

"God bless you!—God protect you!" he cried fervently, returning her embrace with the purity of an elder brother, not shocking her by his warmth nor reproving her by his coldness. "Oh, Clara! be thou careful, my dear child, of many many dangers which beset thee!— God keep thy young heart, and guide thy steps aright!"

Again straining her to his bosom he rushed from the room, leaving Clare startled as at something strange, and in a sadly excited state of mingled pleasure and sorrow. Pleasure that she had such a friend, and sorrow that she must treat him so unworthily: and terrible excitement from her boldness in giving that unasked-for kiss!

And as Percival stumbled headlong down stairs, he met Vasty ascending. Not a pleasant meeting for either of them.

They passed each other in silence, and then Vaughan went up to Clare.

To find her in this strange bewildered tearful state; crouched in the corner of the sofa—like a crimson rose-bud crumpled in the hand; and he so fearfully jealous and coarsely suspicious!

"This shall soon be put an end to," he said to himself, as he saw her in vain attempting to conceal her embarrassment; "I will have no such poachers skulking over my manor for the future! This shilly-shally work shall end in some way, for I am not to be baulked by a silly girl or a pedantic fool. They shall find my will no trifling matter to deal with."

To Clara's great relief he made no remark on her evident excitement—for she knew that he must see it all; besides she had heard them meet on the stairs. But had she known Vasty better, she would have felt more terror at this unusual show of patience than at any amount of outspoken passion.

And yet she had done no wrong! Had she been an infant at the breast, that kiss could not have been more purely given; but when Vaughan fixed his piercing eyes on her, she blushed all over, trembling like a leaf, and feeling as if he had seen every action and heard every word of that meeting. More especially feeling that he had seen with his own bodily eyes that naughty kiss, which she was so sorry—no she was not, she was very glad!—that she had given. In fact, my young friend was lost in a mazy world of many feelings, which she could not well disentangle nor distinguish.

"You quit this house next week," Vaughan said authoritatively, when he rose to leave her; "I will have no more such pretences as 'Miss Kemble' for that impertinent fellow's intrusive calls. I will get you lodgings near me, Clara, and until some better arrangement can be made you shall occupy them. Make no opposition—I say it, and it shall be done."

And Clara remembering the duty of obedience assented, and felt grateful to be kept in favour at all after her late escapade.

CHAPTER XIV.

LUCRETIA's sorrow at this new arrangement was extreme. In the first place she was really fond of Clare, and loath to part with her sweet company; and in the second, Vaughan's handsome weekly allowance eked out her own scanty income very comfortably, and the loss of it would be heavy to her. So what with the exciting causes of affection and poverty poor Miss Kemble's heart was in deep mourning to-day.

"Can it not be avoided, Mr. Vaughan?" she said. "Can I not still hold my maternal place of guardian over this poor child, and yet keep clear of all offence with Mr. Glynn and your lordly self? I will deny my house to yonder Percival—I will stand sphynx-like between this child and your disliked intruders—I will be your subservient handmaid in all things, Mr. Vaughan—in all that is fitting for you to ask and me to grant—I will obey your behests to the letter, if I may but keep my place in this dear infant's world of friends!"

"It's of no use making any objection," returned Vaughan surlily. "You have forfeited your claim to a trustworthy guardianship, by allowing this fellow to come about Clara as he has done—making love to her at every turn!"

"I assure you, gentle lord——"

"D—— you, hold your tongue!" cried Vaughan, with a sudden shout that shook Miss Kemble's nerves like a powder-barrel exploding. "Can I not do what I like with my own? Miss Clayton belongs to me, not to you!"

No one knew what Clara thought when she heard herself so savagely appropriated. Perhaps she liked it. But yet she must have felt rather horror-struck at this broad view of her thraldom—she whose very life was liberty.

"Are you not mine, Clara?" he asked, still in the same savage tone—turning to her.

"If you will keep me yours," she answered timidly, creeping into his arms.

"There! I told you so!" he said with a coarse laugh. And then he kissed Clara harshly—more like a slave-driver than a suitor.

His lips were traitor to his deeds to-day. Master Vasty had been drinking; not enough to betray him into any indubitable acts of intoxication, but just sufficient to make him insolent and reckless. Clara shrank from him, hastily wiping her lips. He let her go, looking at her with a heavy scowl as he saw this innocent act of maiden disgust.

"Give yourself airs as long as you can!" he muttered between his set teeth. "In a year's time you won't think the smell of brandy on your lover's lips an offence against the laws of morality!"

Clare felt that something was wrong. It was not for her to make it worse by temper of any kind. She therefore went back to Vaughan, in her creeping coaxing way; and dragging him on to the sofa with gentle force, sat by him, playing with his hands and talking in her own childish enthusiastic manner, till Vasty himself, ill-tempered as he was to-day, began to smile.

"Now you are good again," she said, patting his face.

"When was I ever anything else to you, Clara?" he answered, turning suddenly on her, with a kind of muffled ferocity.

"Never, but when you are cross and jealous, and not like my own old Vasty," she answered, quaking at her boldness, but looking up too; much as she used to look into her mother's face when she was peculiarly audacious.

"Percival Glynn would have suited you better!" exclaimed Vaughan savagely. "You are like all women, Clara—you cannot understand real love when you have it! You would be better pleased with a talking doll than a man. It's a cursed sex! as greedy as it is indiscriminating!"

"Percival Glynn before you!—No, no, Vasty!" cried Clare blushing at his coarse manner, and looking down abashed.

"I hate that crimson face—crimson at the very mention of another man's name!" he said rudely, pushing her off and turning his back.

Poor Clara! she seemed to be in a large net, which the more she strove to unloose the faster it tightened round her. The more she tried to make all smooth and peaceful, the deeper she stirred up the elements of discord.

"Now don't be such a naughty old man," she said, her timid voice contrasting strangely with her confident words. "You shall not be cross with your poor little Clare, and you shall not forget all your smiles and pretty graces for these black Jupiter-tonans[48] manners. I will not allow it, so don't do it any more!'

And then she made him turn his face to her, and kissed his forehead and buried her eyes in his hair.

He could not resist this. They were too early days yet for all fascination to be lost. So after a time this shoal was safely steered by, as others before it had been; and Vaughan once more made Clare's happiness and wafted her love over a halcyon sea.

But they were rough shocks to her. Coming so often they must in the end have some signal effect. And Clara felt a wretched undefined sense of insecurity, such as she had never felt before, creeping like a blight over her happiness. She cried that night till she was quite ill, and yet she could not find out where she had offended, nor how she could have changed so much as to have changed Vaughan in such a frightful manner. She might have cried and thought to the Last Day, poor child!—and she would have found no satisfactory answer until she had gained more experience of real life.

It was very lonely in her lodgings. True, Lucretia came daily to see her, and Vaughan was scarcely ever absent, excepting on necessary business. Still her sense of abandonment was not much alleviated by these visits. It was in the solitary breakfast—the empty room with no familiar face to greet her in the morning—it was in the solitary evening when, after any pleasure or excitement whatsoever, the deep black hour of loneliness *must* come; it was when she crept up stairs like a deserted child, without a good night spoken by the fire, or a motherly kiss given in her bed—it was in all these things, little as they were, that she felt the change. But she never complained; and the only evidence of what she felt was her increased affectionateness to the good-hearted, tawdry actress when she came to "chat a bit" with her, and a certain tender clinging to Vasty when the time of parting came.

Vaughan was very attentive to her. It was now winter, so that their country excursions of last summer were impossible; and as she must be careful of cold for the sake of her voice, she was often obliged to remain in the house whole days together. This fretted her sadly, and made her pale and melancholy; for it was like caging a sky-lark to keep her in-doors in London. Vaughan would then come and sit with her— bring her what flowers or fruit the season afforded—buy her books and pictures and pretty playthings for grown-up children, till her rooms were a perfect wilderness of nick-nacks. All this helped a little, but very little. She missed something, she knew not what. Over and above air and exercise she missed some dear adjunct to her pleasures. She never dreamt that she missed Percival!

Among other things Vaughan took her much into society. He was a great favourite in certain circles—of the free-thinking fashionable kind—and he was careful that his pretty *protégée* should stand well in point of character; speaking of her always as a child—professing the most fatherly interest in her, and nothing more—and telling her romantic story and unexceptionable birth wherever he went.

By these means Clara obtained a position seldom given to one of her profession and independent life; and much amusement it afforded her. What extraordinary people she was introduced to! Mysterious refugees of princely birth and unexplained misfortunes—leaders of unheard-of sects, each one of which was to regenerate the world and remodel universal empires—heroes of whose feats she was as innocent as a baby, never hearing of their battles, nor of their very existence, before they were introduced to her by their titular decorations of "the hero of Metty Nutty," "the General of Cowasjee Jeebbjhoy," "the commander at the pass of Mont-d'or," "the great warrior of San Desperado," &c. &c.; to all of whom she did her best to look as if she had known of them from her cradle upward, and had been familiar with their fame ever since she could remember. The shameless little hypocrite!—they thought her blushes and embarrassment tributes to their greatness, and her very acknowledgment of guilt was but another proof of her admiration. Then, there were men of science, all of them "the greatest men of the day," and all of them famous for some sublime discoveries to which an ungrateful government was criminally indifferent:—"Mr. Jones, the great geologist, who discovered the traces of mummulites in the carboniferous stratum;" "Mr. Green, the theorizer on electric currents—connecting their position with the tides and their force with the winds;" such and such a mesmerizer who always tried to appear absorbed, and made it a point to look half maniacal, as if aiming at the realization of the popular notion of Mephistopheles; with sundry others of like misty fame; all drawing-room lions—those worthless, lying, sham beasts, whose own roar fills their ears to the exclusion of all other song and speech in heaven and earth.

And to many more of the same class was our Clare duly presented. Pretty little poets who did look so poetical with their straight hair and unclean complexions; nice young novelists, "dear creatures, so clever and agreeable," who played charades and wrote in albums— and were suspected of contributing to Punch—and who, on the strength of their fame, appeared with uncommon heads of hair, moustaches, and audacious necks; authoresses too of all styles—the severely intellectual and personally negligent chiefly—those who go about in faded garments of ill cut and garnitures of extraordinary uses, with odd chevelures and undesirable jewellery, and who are very metaphysical and "talk ably," and are down on you like a sledge-hammer, if you cross their path—and others of the poetic and artistic style, who get themselves up like pictures, and have a sublime contempt for fashion and general modes of habilitation—preferring the ideas of Watteau, or Lely, or Lawrence,[49] to the notions of a court milliner—pretty to look at but terribly affected in the design; singers who murder bravuras, and attempt the national songs of every people in their own language, with a moral hardihood one can scarce admire too much, provided it be not imitated; respectably born and respectably conducted actors and actresses of fashionable fame, who sit in attitudes and talk in hexameters; these, mixed up with a proper proportion of handsome guardsmen, belles of the season, rich old bachelors selfish oily and caressed, rising barristers, "able writers in the Times" and elsewhere—who if you were to believe them, are behind the tapestry of every cabinet council in Europe, and are the real levers of public opinion at home—"people you ought to know"—"people who give nice parties"—"people who know nice people"—"people *bien placés*"[50]—Heaven help her! amongst such a mass of folly and of falseness was our young Clare taken in the hope of making her like unto it.

In the which hope I did not join; for I would rather have seen her offend against every known rule in her large Newfoundland fashion, than have had her trimmed and cut and pared to the quick, to be shaped into any one such form of distortion as we see in London drawing-rooms. No no; art and civilization are grand words doubtless, and all must honour them who honour the Power of Man; but one frank impulse of nature is before them all, if one is required to love or even reverence a character.

Clara looked at all this in utter astonishment; at the boldness with which men practised, and affected to believe, such self-evident lies as were current. She panted for nature and truth in this artificial state, as she panted for fresh air in a sickly forcing-house; but Vaughan was angry when she spoke thus to him, and called her an ignorant country child, and bade her be silent on what she did not understand. So she was. But she only felt and thought the more, which was not exactly the result he wished to produce.

Being a lioness of no common order, Clare soon attracted a large circle round her, as amber attracts straws and dust and other worthless things. But the deeper she was encircled, the more intense grew her dislike to the component parts, till the very name of an "At Home" made her miserable.

They began to talk too about her connexion with Vaughan, notwithstanding his forty years and her extreme youth; but as yet the manager's paternal ways and words, with the public knowledge of her high birth and future heirship, kept her free from much scandal. However it was beginning, though she knew very little of it; and only sometimes wondered why Vaughan did not say openly that he was engaged. It would be much better if he did!

Some event in the future unnamed, Vasty did often allude to; but of an honest open rational marriage, not a breath. Did he dread her youth, and the instability of an impulsive nature? Did he mistrust her love? This fear made her very unhappy, and she fretted sorely. Had she known the real cause of this silence she would have done more than fret.

She had another cause of sorrow. Vasty was one of those men, unhappily too many, who lay aside their gentlemanlike habits at home. It was not that he was unkind; he simply ceased to be refined. In society he was remarkable for the polish and ease of his manners. At home, or when with intimates, he laid all this aside. He would do rude things, say coarse words, act roughly, without a trace of resemblance to the refined and polished gentleman of the drawing-rooms left in his savage indelicacy.

This shocked Clara much. Often at the fondest moment she has drawn herself away from him, chilled to the heart by some rough words or rougher action; and often she has felt her face grow crimson with shame at some coarseness until now undreamt-of.

How ardently she wished for the blindness of the past! How she turned back to the happy hours when she first loved, and saw her lover, like some glorious god above her, descending to earth to make that earth a better heaven! How she would sit and think over the graceful ways that were so fascinating to her—the gentle words, so delicate and tender, that carried away soul and heart as gems launched on a golden river; how she wondered whether he was changed or she grown cold; and how she wept at the altered feelings which she both saw in him and felt within herself!

Vaughan understood it all. One thing only he did not understand:— how near he went to lose her by thus continually shocking her sense of propriety. She would rather have known his real intentions, and he still remain the high-bred gentleman in the confidence and retirement of home, than thus believe him honest in his wish to marry her, and transformed to such horrible coarseness. Yet he did not dream that her love was undermining because her fastidious education, as he called it, shrank from those rude attacks. He merely thought to fling down what he felt to be a strong outpost of defence; he never thought to lose the whole.

If men did but know how much a woman's love rests on her delicacy, perhaps they would be more careful how they wounded that delicacy. At any rate they would then understand the reason of much apparent inconsistency to which they have now no clue. For to their constant ignorance of this strong characteristic—almost instinctive in woman—more unhappiness in marriage and more estrangement in friendship is owing, than to any other cause in the world: not even excepting natural inconstancy of temper.

Under the altered circumstances of Vaughan's conduct, Clara was becoming excessively unhappy. A terrible feeling possessed her: *she felt degraded.* The bright halo round everything was fading away to ebon blackness. She had not a confidante, not a friend, in the world. She could not speak to Lucretia of what she felt. It would have been a foreign language to this porter-drinking lady. And she knew no one else with any degree of intimacy. Percival indeed she might have spoken with; but Percival was denied her, and there was none to take his place. No; she had brought all this on herself and she must bear it alone and without relief.

It was a painful lesson the poor child had to learn; but she had more moral power than she knew of herself, and it was in such trials as these that the strength of her nature was perfected.

Vaughan had established a strict authority and surveillance over Clare. She could do little without his sanction, and less without his knowledge. The restraint of home was wildest liberty compared to this government of love. But because it was the government of love, she submitted with a better grace than one could have believed possible. One thing Vaughan never allowed. She must not under any pretence whatsoever walk out alone. Though his general overseership was excessively tyrannical, in this the manager was right, for Clare scarcely knew even the principal streets. She has been heard to assert the Strand to be Regent-street; and when she was first in Holborn she could not understand how Oxford-street had gone so far off. It would not have been fit then, in any way, for this pretty piece of ignorance to wander about alone, even in our well-conducted metropolis, where no woman need be annoyed unless she seek it by dress or manner. But once she ventured forth when Vasty was engaged at home.

She thought there could be no harm in going! She felt suffocating for air and liberty; and the old wilful spirit of independence rose up against the chains that love itself would bind her with. She must go out into the fresh air; and Vasty might scold when the deed was done. Come what may, she must have her own way now. Naughty wilful Clare! She ran out of the house with the old home feeling of escape from thraldom; and with the same luxuriant joy, while pacing the wards of this mighty prison, as when revelling in the flowers and the sunshine, the hearty gallop of dear old Fleetfoot, the cry of her dogs, the song of the birds, and, dearest of all, the consciousness that she was breaking the domestic law and out of sight of domestic eyes.

She walked on a long way, till at last she lost herself. She knew the localities pretty well for some distance, but two unlucky streets, both having draper's shops at the corner (for these were landmarks to her), puzzled her when she came back; and as she walked by direction, not by signature, she was thrown out. Of course she took the wrong turning; and went bravely forward for a long way.

The street gradually became more dirty and more neglected. Squalid children played about; dark courts, like large conduits, broke through the line of dull brick; ragged women, slipshod and bareheaded, mingled with smart ladies whose lace and velvet and gaudy dress contrasted painfully with the evident wretchedness about; working men lounged round the doors, with pipes or straws in their mouths— half-naked some of them were, though it was now mid-winter; all the signs were rife, which to an experienced Londoner would have plainly enough betokened the peculiar character of the quarter, but which to Clare seemed only "very odd;" "she could not make it out," and "she did not like it." But further than this she was not much moved.

Dirtier, narrower, darker streets; a more wretched population, growing thicker and thicker round her; more attention paid to her as she passed; once or twice rude words addressed which she could not fail to hear; not the slightest knowledge of where she was;—at last all this made her uneasy. She was now sure that she was far wrong, and in a very undesirable locality. Had she seen a cab—though she had never done such a thing before—she would have called it, and driven home. But nothing passed. She was really uneasy, tired, and thoroughly bewildered: when, as she was standing at the end of one street, in despair at seeing the way before her worse than what she had just passed through, a woman came up to her.

Clare's face was toward a narrow passage, through which she saw many people and carriages passing the other side. She made a few steps forward, when the woman, who had been watching her, came to her and laid her hand on her arm.

"Do not go there, my child," she said authoritatively, pointing to the passage.

Her voice was good even through its hoarse tones, and its accent was pure. Her face was fine even through its dirt and neglect, and her manner essentially that of a mother—kind, but with an air of womanly command.

Clara looked up gratefully into that haggard face, and thanked her very warmly. She asked her further way, and the woman with evident interest set her right.

"I am much obliged to you," then said Clare, drawing out her purse.

"No! no!" exclaimed the woman hastily; "no! do not pay me for such a simple act of kindness as this! Thank God, I am not so bad yet!" she added in an under tone. "No, give it to those who want it more than I do! It was not for what I could get that I kept you from that passage!"

She turned away hastily and was soon lost in the crowd.

Clara threw herself into a cab—a Hansom's patent too!—which happened to drive up at this moment, and poor Emma Vaughan strolled off as usual to the gin-palace.

"Where are you going to-night, Emma?" asked one she met there—a woman of her own sad class and infinitely more degraded.

"Where?—oh! to the —— theatre to be sure, to see the new mistress there! I hear she's young and good, and I want to see what other piece of God's work that devil of a manager will blast and destroy! There's a grand story about her—of her birth and education—and I want to see her before she is thoroughly ruined. There's where I'm going—and a pretty good errand too!—to see a live dissolving view of morality!"

And Emma went to the theatre that night—to recognise the girl she had directed on her way in the morning—to see the same innocent face and fervid expression which had so interested her then—and to groan in agony at the picture which she made to herself of Clare's miserable future—when she should be like to her.

"But I'll break his nets yet!" she said fiercely. "He thinks me a fiend—and so I am—but not such a fiend as to wish the young and good to breathe the same air with him, and to see them sacrificed to his brutal passions! If I can I will protect this child! It will go hard with me if I am thwarted, the first time I've wished to do good so long! No! no! a strong will is never baffled—and I *will* protect that poor young innocent! Bad as I am to-day she shall never become, if Vaughan dies at my feet and I swing for it!"

And by her face it was evident that she had made no idle threat

REALITIES

A Tale.

BY E. LYNN,

AUTHOR OF

"AZETH, THE EGYPTIAN," AND "AMYMONE."

———

"Therefore should I
Be but the essence of deformity,—
A coward,—did my very eyelids wink
At speaking out what I have dared to think."
KEATS.

IN THREE VOLUMES.

VOL. II.

LONDON
SAUNDERS AND OTLEY, CONDUIT STREET.
1851.

REALITIES.

CHAPTER I.

DEEPER and deeper hope struck its roots into the heart of Mrs. de Saumarez. The more she observed Alice, the more certain she felt that Nature herself endorsed her suspicions as true; the oftener she remembered Clara, the firmer was her conviction that she was not her child. The mere resemblance of feature—not to speak of the mental sympathy between herself and the young dependant—was startling; while in Clara not a line seemed to be the mother's copy—not a thought the mother's echo. In Alice was the same open eye of pale cold blue; the same thin lips, delicate and querulous; the same slight build, which would have been so wonderfully graceful had there been more *abandon* in its movements, and more fulness in its outlines; the same long lithe hand and narrow foot; the same small throat; the same light straw-coloured hair: essentially casts from the same mould were Mrs. de Saumarez and her young friend—her daughter, as she called her in her secret heart, though she dared not yet pronounce that word openly.

Had not Providence too interfered in a most signal manner? How, but by special design and special intervention, could have taken place that strange accident which brought Alice to the Hall? What a long train of concurrent causes must have been pre-arranged before that simple circumstance could have occurred! There was no chance in this, but the finger of a special Providence openly marking her importance in the designs of the Infinite. Mrs. de Saumarez felt that it would be impiety to doubt it; and as it gave her comfort to believe herself under such private and peculiar guardianship, it would have been cruel to have convinced her of the contrary. So long as the private convictions of our fellow-men do not interfere with the liberty or happiness of the community at large, it is no business of ours to gainsay them.

All Clara's wild ways came back before the mind of the gentle lady; all her passionate impulses, her bold thoughts, her extreme views. But she could, granting her hope to be true, account for everything now, as well as for her own indomitable dislike—for such she acknowledged her inmost feeling had ever been—for that so-called heiress. It was no marvel to her, under her present condition of belief, that she had thus disliked a nature so discordant with her own, nor that Mr. de Saumarez and his laboratory had been able to exert so little modifying power over that wayward character of stranger blood. If they had no connexion with or knowledge of the fundamental parts, how could they sympathize with or influence the whole?

An illegitimate child sprung from the strong source of the people, mingled with the refined blood of the aristocracy, could easily, from physiological rules, be such an impulsive, ardent, energetic, and untamed being as Clara. Indeed it would have been difficult to have arrived at any other result from such a union.

To her mother she owed her strength and health of frame; to her father, her grand intellectual powers, improved and solidified by that maternal gift of physical soundness; to both, her strong passions, her intense affections; to both, also, her lawlessness and unquenchable desire for liberty. To her mother was due her warm sympathy with the people; to her father, her appreciation of beauty, her refinement, and her delicacy. To her, the outspoken frankness of the peasant; to him, the sensibility of the gentlewoman; to both, her personal beauty and mental hardihood. And to other circumstances of her birth, her governing characteristic of passionate love.

Mrs. de Saumarez saw it all. For once her physiology stood her in good stead, and aided her natural instincts.

It may be remembered that old Hugh whispered mysteriously to his lady on the day of Clara's flight. What he told her then was simply the fact of the connexion of Alice with his daughter Martha. He said he had only just discovered it, which, as we know, was a falsehood; and he said that he had his own private suspicions "that his wicked child had palmed a lie off on his lady, and changed the children when she sent Miss Clara home;" which he had very good reason to believe were more than mere suspicions.

"She thought, belike, it would be a grand thing for her misbegot," he added, "to be brought up at the great Hall, and as heiress to all the fields and woods about. I know nothing for certain, my lady, but I have my own thoughts on't all; more 'special since I see Miss Alice there grow up so like your ladyship, that she might have been spit out of your ladyship's own mouth."

Which expression, though more pictorial than elegant, was very illustrative of the facts of the case.

No one would commend Martha, if this should be so; but yet many might find excuses for her in the servile respect to rank and wealth in which our poor are educated. From their earliest years they are taught the one long droning lesson of humility to those above them: not because they are more virtuous or more wise than themselves, but because they are "grand folk"—that is, rich and well-born. Do they give their children good scholarship? It is not to make them learned for learning's sake, nor to enable them to be more useful to themselves and the world at large: it is to make them "one with the quality," and "as good as they be." Martha thought she acted a motherly and unselfish part by her child when she thus changed her fate, and withdrew her from the warmth and fostering cave of her own heart to place her in the cold grandeur of the Hall; and most women of her class would have thought the same—taught as they are that wealth and station are the chrisms which anoint to divinity, and that "the quality" are essentially, *ex officio*, superior.

Martha had long since disappeared from Shorne and its neighbourhood. As soon as the little one was returned home, she had been "warned off" the estate, and no one cared to inquire her destination. Hugh indeed had once taken Clara, when a little girl of about six years of age, to her cottage by stealth; and after that— not so very long ago—he had told her that her "old nurse was living in a good place as housekeeper to a gentleman." This was shortly after Alice came to the Hall. Since then nothing had been heard of Martha, and her father himself could give no tidings, though Mrs. de Saumarez would have bestowed no mean reward for the discovery of this despised and sinful peasant-woman.

However, one day Hugh came up into the drawing-room, unbidden and unrepulsed. He knocked at the door, and was told to enter; the lady trembling much when she saw him.

"If you please, my lady, may I speak to your ladyship?" he said, touching his grey hair and shifting his position uneasily.

"Leave the room, if you please, my dear child," Mrs. de Saumarez said, turning to Alice who sat quietly working by her side: for she was a very Penelope in fancy-work of all kinds, was our young Miss Alice.

The girl rose and with a slight courtesy obeyed. As she passed the old man, the likeness between her and the lady never struck him so forcibly. She was Mrs. de Saumarez in little—looked at through the small end of a telescope.

"She is your ladyship's very marras!" he cried, meaning to say that she was her ladyship's very match or copy.

"What have you to tell me, Hugh?" asked Mrs. de Saumarez, with less acerbity of manner than general, and with painful interest.

"I have heard from my sinful child, my lady," he answered, looking round carefully, though the door was shut at his back and no one but the lady of the mansion stood before him. Yet it was such a secret—it behoved him to be careful!

"What!—what!" exclaimed Mrs. de Saumarez eagerly, her lips and face ashen white, and her hands clasped nervously within each other.

"Here it is, madam," he said gravely, producing a letter of miraculous shape and ingenious tortuosity of foldings; something dirtier than when it left the stationer's shelves; and with an extravagant waste of coarse red wax, sealed with the Britannia side of a sixpence by way of signet ring.

Mrs. de Saumarez took it hastily from his hand, and read the following:

"Honoured Father This comes hoping you are quite well as it leaves me at present and hearing that Miss Clara has fairly left the old place and Miss Alice in her room and I very sorry for what I did but meant to tell before I died when my Miss Clara had been a great lady and master was safe in his grave. and I change them at nurse and thought I do right to give my child who was fathered by a great gentleman the chance to be a lady and not wishing to harm Miss Alice too. but when mistress send for Miss Clara back again I thought her baby would die and I not save her and then my baby might have the Hall and perhaps if I had known that little Alice would have lived I might have thought better of what I did but it be all done now and my Miss Clara gone to London for good and all and Miss Alice is in her room and every one has got their own and I no more to blame. and if my lady will look at my Miss Clara and look at her Miss Alice she may see that I speak now the truth and that she has her own and my poor child be sent on the world alone without no mother or no father and no one to care for her when she be ill or mend her clothes nor nothing and as I go to South Australia next week with the good gentleman as I lives with and things have fallen out different to what I thought I write the truth that no more may be give to me and all may get to rights. and give my duty to my lady and tell her that I did my best for her Miss Alice and made her a steady girl and always kept her clean and brushed her hair mornings by evenings and made her mend her stockings which she can do equal to any girl that ever went to learn a schooling which I could not give her and so no more from your dutiful daughter to command MARTHA CLAYTON. PS.

"Honoured father if you should see my dear child Miss Clara tell her that she has a mother and that I love her and she need not fret for her father he was a real gentleman and had brown hair and we shall meet in heaven but no more on earth for my life is not so long now I am leaving England and all. M. C."

From which original composition, after much trouble in deciphering the audacious calligraphy and phonetic orthography—which trouble we would not inflict on our poor readers, Mrs. de Saumarez gathered the indisputable fact that Clara was not her child, and that Alice—the good, the gentle, quiet, lady-like Alice—was indeed heaven's blessing and nature's copy to her. Her own dear daughter—her fitting heiress!

Mr. de Saumarez was called up from the depths of his laboratory, and Alice was also sent for. The letter was read to both as they stood in such strange emotion—strange at least to them, quiet as they all were by nature.

The scene which followed had not much demonstrativeness in it: Mr. de Saumarez put on his spectacles, and scrutinized Alice as if she had been an agglomeration of crystals or a specimen of fluor spar.[51] He even took down one of the broad smooth shining bands of hair and gravely compared it with his wife's. He looked from one to the other, minutely inspecting each different feature, and then, satisfied of his paternity by the physical resemblance of the child, took her hand and kissed her forehead.

Alice bent her head gracefully for that kiss, and curtseying said gently, "Thank you, sir."

And this was the way in which the first paternal embrace was given and received.

"I acknowledge you our child," then said Mr. de Saumarez

pompously, "Nature has stamped her seal too legibly to be misunderstood, even by those who cannot read her code of laws. We want no lexicon *here*," he added, turning to his wife, "to help our reading. No wonder we could not comprehend the dialect of that misguided girl we thought our child, when not one point of affinity, not two words of cognate languages, so to speak, connected us. I leave the publication of this strange romance to you, madam, in such shape as you shall think best. For myself, I will be content to adduce it as an example of material influences in my treatise on the Laws of Moral Sympathy. This ought to convince you!" he continued triumphantly, "This ought to be, to your mind, an unanswerable proof of the power of matter as opposed to education and so-called spiritual influences, ignoring as they do the plain rules of chemical affinities and the negative action of human magnetism!"

He would have retreated back to his study now, but Mrs. de Saumarez stopped him.

"Stay!" she said gravely. "This is an important event for our house, and it must be met with solemnity. Seat yourself in this chair, Mr. de Saumarez, while I explain the facts to our household."

She rang the bell, and summoned the whole body of domestic retainers, even down to the stable-boys, who brought a strong atmosphere of the manger into the room. They ranged themselves round the wall like soldiers at a review. She then took Alice in her hand, saying in a slow calm voice:—

"I have called you in here, to-day, to say before you all, that from henceforth you are to consider this young lady as your future mistress, and to pay her the respect due to my—to our—daughter. This is Miss de Saumarez. The person you were so long accustomed to regard as such is the illegitimate child of Hugh's youngest daughter, Martha. The children were changed at nurse. I trust that I shall never find you wanting to my daughter in the same dutiful obedience as that which you owe to me and to your master; and that you will remember Miss de Saumarez is your present mistress and your future lady. Now you may go."

The servants filed out in order, making a deep reverence to Alice as she stood by her mother's side, which she returned with more haughtiness than, as a dependant, they believed her capable of. Her cheek was slightly flushed, her eyes darker and oh, so little loving!— and more than one of the under-servants whispered outside the door; "We've made a bad exchange, anyhow."

But the superior ones praised her very loudly.

"*You* must stay, Hugh Clayton," said the lady, as Hugh prepared to shuffle out with the rest.

Her voice was very harsh, her countenance severe. Hugh for the first time began to quake. Should he be rewarded or condemned?—should he find his prosperity or his adversity in his zeal? He hoped the first; the lady's face betokened the last.

Mrs. de Saumarez went to her writing-desk and took out a roll of money; also a small marbled book, with "Servants' Wages" written legibly on the cover.

"I think there is owing to you now, Hugh Clayton, the sum of fourteen pounds ten shillings, being the balance of your wages due since your last payment," she said, turning over the leaves.

"Yes, your ladyship," Hugh answered, horror-struck at her manner.

"Here is the sum then," said Mrs. de Saumarez. "Be kind enough to sign the book. I have no further occasion for your services."

"Oh, madam," began the old man, "am I, your faithful servant so long, to be turned out in my old age like a dog? What have I done, madam, to displease you so?"

"It is painful to me, Hugh, to act thus," said the lady coldly, "but it would be more painful to see about my house the father of the woman who has brought such sorrow, and almost shame, on that house. I am sorry to part with you, Hugh Clayton, but it is my religious duty; and it is useless to attempt to alter my determination. Take your wages and sign the book."

Crying bitterly, in spite of his manhood, the old groom obeyed her; and thus for his zeal was rewarded with dismissal: a reward he had not calculated on, else perhaps he would have left the two girls in their misfitting positions, without troubling himself to adjust them better.

So much of gratitude, kindliness, and justice, had our Christian, moral, chaste Lady of the Hall.

Alice came hastily to her mother; she took her hand and kissed it, saying; "I thank you, ma'am, from my heart, for your dismissal of this wicked family. I should never have felt your daughter while evidence of my robbery still lingered round the Hall. Nor would I, as your daughter, have commanded any respect from the servants while there remained among them one who had dared to call me his grandchild!"

At the mention of that hated word, Alice drew herself up proudly. She had never spoken with so much feeling.

The old man remembered Clara, the greathearted generous Clara, who would have suffered any misery herself rather than have allowed the slightest shade of annoyance to another. And he contrasted these two girls, with such a feeling of pride in his own descendant as dried up his tears speedily.

"My daughter, Miss Alice, was kinder to you than you are to me to-day," he said hastily. "If she did you wrong, not meaning it, she was a true mother to you afterwards."

"Madam—mother! send this man from my sight—from the room—from the place," cried Alice passionately. "Must I be for ever reminded that my early life was passed in a beggar's hovel—that the stain of a shameful birth rested for years on me, though innocent?"

"You are right, Alice," Mr. de Saumarez here interposed, "and I am glad that you have such a strong family feeling in you. In this I recognise my child; while in that mischievous deception we nourished so long to turn, viper-like, against us, I never could arouse one sentiment of honour worthy of the De Saumarez; Hugh, you bad old man, you must acknowledge the justice of the sentence against you. Ask yourself whether it would be possible for Miss de Saumarez to bear the sight of you, remembering that in her early days you took her on your knee and fed her with lollypops? By-the-bye, the superfluity of coarse saccharine matters has rendered her very pale: this must be remedied."

"But sir, I did not change the children," urged the old man: "I would have done anything in the world for your Honour and your Honour's family; and I have done my best to get the truth out of my unhappy Martha, as I was more careful like for all of your Honour's family, than for my poor girl's own child. Your Honour, sir, knows how I loved the dear young lady that's gone, and how she loved me; and it's like I would have done all for her by nature. But I have done all for you, sir, and it's hard to be made to bear other people's blame." He looked down, as if going to shed more tears.

"Hugh," said Mrs. de Saumarez, sternly, "we have proved our kindness to you by suffering you to stand and expostulate so long on an act natural, moral, and impossible to be avoided. It is not at any time your place to thus expostulate, and I must put an end to it at once. Without another word, leave the room; and leave the house at your earliest convenience this evening. You have our full permission to join your graceless granddaughter in her too probably profligate

career. I wish you good morning, Hugh, and advise you to leave
Shorne as soon as you can."

Awed and compelled to obey, the old man left the room to burst
into an agony of grief and rage and grief again, at this unlooked-
for barbarity. An old hereditary servitor, as he had been—the last of
his generation—serving the Hall so long and faithfully, that he had
become as much a part of the estate as the very buildings standing
on it—he could not at first realize the fact of his dismissal. It seemed
to him impossible that he should live anywhere but in his old room
above the coachhouse; that he should be forbidden the fields and yard
and stables of the Hall; that his horses should fall into the hands of
another master, one who would not understand them nor be kind
to them; that the dogs should fawn on a strange keeper, and the
dominion of the yard pass into another dynasty; he could not believe
the whole affair; surely it was a dream! Why, you might as well root
up that old cedar, the ornament of the park, as root out him! Poor
old Hugh! old as he was, he understood no more than a child the
natures he had just been dealing with—still less that self-sufficiency
of coldness which clings to no habit however ancient, and regards no
affection however long existing. He had loved the family: he thought
they must also love him.

But the hours drew on, and he must learn the truth of that fabulous
fact. He must in earnest leave. It was tearing his very heartstrings,
but it must be done; and the moon rose over no being more desolate
and heart-broken than old Hugh, the discarded groom of the De
Saumarez.

All night long he wandered about his old beloved haunts. How was
it that they looked the same? How was it that the dumb animals did
not moan and pine and lament his disgrace? It seemed so cruel that
all should go on without him as tranquilly as for so many years under
his even order of strict propriety. He thought something at least might
have regretted him.

Poor old man! the crash of falling thrones would not have been so
loud a tumult in his ears as this domestic revolution at the Hall, which
sent him wandering through the world. It will be some days yet before
he quite understands and believes in his present position; and more
years than he has to number before he could be reconciled to it.

In the morning, Hugh was found still wandering about the old
place—bent, pallid, stricken: a very pauper in look compared to the

hale and proud old man of yesterday—the respectable servant of the great family!

CHAPTER II.

THE disgrace of the De Saumarez had been public—the abolition of that disgrace must be also public. Their friends had compassionated them not many months ago "for the stain which had fallen on the shield of their house," as Mr. de Saumarez used to say; they should now congratulate them on the washing away of that stain. If Clara had held them up to scorn, Alice should redeem them back to reverence; and if they had been jeered at for incapacity in their education of the one, they should be honoured for the unsullied nature they had imparted to the other.

The De Saumarez therefore gave a ball to commemorate their child's restoration. It was a second edition of the old Montague-House romance, bound too in fairer shape. A delicate little romance, full of pretty pictures and gilded edges; full of smooth verses and moral thoughts; but without one bold touch of life-likeness, one grand sentiment, one large feeling, one true thought of poetry; a pretty little romance, well got up and suited to the capacity of correct young ladies.

And now prosperity waved its golden wings over Alice also—if in different shape to those which fanned Clara's fervid brow, yet in one more congenial to her nature, and giving her as much happiness in its advent. She too had climbed the dark hill which had lain between her and her promised land, and she too had descended into the plains of that promised land and found its waters sweet and pleasant.

A stately baptism was this commemorative ball—an initiation of no mean value; leading her by paths of dazzling splendour and intoxicating adulation to the inner place of social grandeur, by the door of which she had so long stood and worshipped.

Would the day never arrive? Would the great sun never break out into noon-splendour? Oh, these weary hours! Would the twilight never pass?

How different was this longing for her day of triumph to that which had possessed Clare's ardent being. What a wide chasm separated the poetic rapture, the fond love, the pride of a self-obtained success, from the cold ambition which demanded social superiority alone, and cared for nothing that was not barren glittering "position." It was painful to see the chilly haughtiness of this young girl's pride—so moral and so cold as she was—at a time when passion would have been beauty, and warmth but poetry of feeling. The base desire of superior station had so warped her heart and mind that not one pulse of natural emotion was left its room of action. It may be that such ambition is good for the constitution of society at large, but it is manifestly degrading to the individual.

The day came in its due order of succession, and Alice touched the summit of her hopes. Guests courtly, stately, richly-attired, grandly named, thronged to the Hall to do her honour whom but so short time since they would have ridden by in disdain, splashing up mud and dirt—as who should care what befell a wandering beggar-girl?

One blaze of lights and gorgeous dresses, of gleaming jewels like sunlight rays over dark clouds of velvet and rich brocaded silks—one tangled mass of flowers and evergreens twining round the walls and lamps and pillars of the lofty halls—one moving crowd of grace and beauty and high-born names—all gathered there to pay their homage to the new-found heiress.

Alice remembered the scene when the true misbegotten peasant's child had led her in, to the contemptuous pity of her own mother—to the gracious condescension of those who owed her the recognition of equality. And this memory made her slight figure prouder, her slow step more firm, as she moved through the throngs crowding to congratulate her.

A picture of Clara—a full-length oil-painting, representing her as a child of about twelve years of age, with dogs and horse and birds and rabbits round her—had hung in the drawing-room. All the other pictures were encased, so to speak, in flowers and evergreens; but the place of this was covered with a black cloth, and not a blossom nor a leaf bloomed near it.

This fancy had been granted to the prayer of Alice, else Mr. and Mrs. de Saumarez would have removed it and substituted another in its stead.

A small cabinet of shells and pretty specimens belonging to Clara had also stood in the drawing-room. It was now gone, and in its place stood a *prie-Dieu* chair covered with the same black cloth as that hanging on the wall.

The guests noticed these arrangements, and spoke in great praise of the "nice feeling" which dictated their mute expression of Clara's erasure from the family records.

It may as well be said now, that Alice had employed herself for some days in destroying every vestige of Clare's former presence in the house. All her books were burnt, all her "treasures" broken and destroyed; her garden was dug up and sodded over; her favourite dogs were sold; Fleetfoot was first degraded to the plough, then given for a mere song; her rabbits were killed and the hutch broken: all in which she had taken pleasure was laid in ruins, and another order of things raised in its stead. Her little moss-arbour, which she and Hugh had built together, was taken down and a yew-tree planted on the site. Her wardrobe was distributed to the lowest people that could be found; her old child's toys burnt by Alice herself. New paper and new furniture had long transformed her room; and, as far as possible, every trace of her former existence was obliterated. Her name was forbidden to be uttered before Miss de Saumarez on any occasion whatsoever; and a word of commendation, regret, or remembrance from the servants would have cost them their situations.

These were the first small fruits of the deep feelings of hatred which Alice had so long nourished in her secret heart. Let Clara but try the impression she has left—it will blister her hand to touch its burning lines!

Now we will return to the ball.

Every available space thrown open to the guests was filled with flowers and lights. The drawing-rooms were like fairy palaces—a bewildering mass of gold and gems and flowers and brilliant colours, flooded in warmth and lustre. The large chandeliers were fairly lost in garden-festoons; the mirrors and pictures showed only glimpses of their gilded frames between the wreaths of green and large autumnal blossoms twining round. Tables made in compartments so as to represent small gardens—tall vases with their single glory of some rare hot-house plant standing among Sèvres china, or-molu,[52] precious things from the East, old French relics of fanciful beauty and fashionable value; wherever the eye turned was one broad mass of colour and of light, which the large mirrors reflected to an indefinite extent of gorgeousness.

In the midst of all, moved the cause of all, Alice—graceful, self-possessed, and blessed beyond words.

In a cloud of gauzy white without admixture of any colour—white roses looping up the skirt—white roses drooping in her hair—a band of pearls round her small fair throat, and broad bracelets of the same upon her arms—the type of purity and chaste propriety was this little fête-day queen, giving occasion for no small measure of commendation from the assembled guests.

As for Mrs. de Saumarez, in her gems and her genoa,[53] she looked the very matron of morality—the proud possessor of such correctness in her true child as recompensed her for all that she had suffered in the wilful wildness of the false. It was a happy day for both; and for the withered inmate of the laboratory—the old pedantic father—one of the best emblazonments on his family shield. The incorporation into that shield of a whole peerage of quarterings[54] would not have pleased him more than this reception of an heiress of whose nature he approved, and whose strong physical likeness left him no room to doubt his theory of material influences.

"There," he said triumphantly, pointing to his daughter as she stood by her mother's side, "there is the best refutation of your unbelief in my theory that I can make! There is no spiritual influence *here*. Matter—matter, my dear sir, has done it all!"

And perhaps the old pedant was right.

"How blind we have been!" cried one lady. She had been present at the memorable group four years ago.

"Well;—it is absurd to predict *after* an event," said another. "No one believes in presentiments told only when they are accomplished: yet in spite of the general ridicule attached to such a course, I declare now I always thought there was something strange about that vulgar girl! She was so unlike this dear little creature!"

This speaker was a lady priding herself on her penetration and her truth.

"Oh! I think it was so evident that something was wrong," another in the same group exclaimed, making a bold dash at the subject. "That wretched girl was manifestly a peasant! Her whole character, actions, and manners, were all essentially plebeian. I have often said to myself—there is no true blood here. Ah, how great are the ways of Providence!'

"The De Saumarez affair has borne strange testimony to the materialistic doctrines of Mr. de Saumarez," a younger lady said in a tone of reverie. She was something of a rival to the lady of the

Hall, reading deep books, and talking beyond her own depth and the comprehension of her hearers: one of those strange-coloured rag-bags of unordered intellect which you sometimes find in country places, very pedantic, very vain, and very intolerant.

A look ran round this little knot of feminine orators. They began to disperse, frightened by the probable torrent of learned eloquence preparing to descend on their devoted heads.

"And this child," cried the first lady, meeting Mrs. de Saumarez as she moved with quiet voice and noiseless step among her guests—"this gentle little girl!—how well do I remember the sweet maternal smile that welcomed her to your heart—though still unknown her claim on that heart—through all the distance of such wide social separation! How strong must maternal instinct have been in you!—how powerfully its influence affected you!"

"It was a special providence, undoubtedly," chimed in the lady who had seen Clara's peasant birth so clearly in her younger years, and who liked amazingly to lay down the law. "In fact, it would be impious to doubt the evident design in it all. First, you were deceived by a woman whose unworthiness you had reproved; then, the cause of her deception brought back your own child; and so she was frustrated by the very pains she had taken to succeed. Is not this a most evident truth?" she asked with a look of unanswerable triumph, as when you have propounded a logical axiom and demonstrated it.

"Have you heard from that fierce, bad girl?" said the first speaker. "Where is she?—and what is she doing now?"

Many who heard the question pressed nearer to hear the answer.

Mrs. de Saumarez drew herself away in a manner to which no written words of description could do justice: it was such a polished, cold, lady-like, and impenetrable manner of reproof!

"No," she replied, "I know nothing of her, and I desire to know nothing. Her place and her conduct are alike utterly concealed from me, nor do I wish to raise the veil between us. Her very name is painful—any communication, however remote, would be more painful."

This was said with a countenance of such severity that none dared mention the subject again.

"I hear she is on the stage," whispered one, as if she had been approaching an improper subject—nearly as bad as religious infidelity or a runaway wife.

"Oh, but I heard worse than that!" said another bolder spirit, with a melancholy shake of the head, and a malicious dancing of the eye. "She is leading a most disreputable life, I believe; very, very bad—far worse than I could tell you!"

"How dreadful!" exclaimed the whole audience. "What a shameless, abandoned girl! But she was always bad."

"*I* can tell you something of her," a lady exclaimed with the most joyous face imaginable, revelling in the excess of scandal she was about to detail. "A young friend of mine—you know him—Edward Mantell?—has seen her in London, and knows all about her."

"Pray tell us, Mrs. Graham!—pray tell us!" cried many voices at once, several ladies pressing round her.

The lady—she was a portly woman of a mysterious age—looked up with a meaning smile. She smoothed her dress; flirted her scarf and folded it out over her knees; looked inquiringly at her bracelet, and studied the locket as if she had never seen it before; then folding her hands within each other said with a desperate calmness—half shutting her eyes while taking such a frightful leap into this sea of immorality—"She is living under the protection of the manager of a theatre, and he is a married man!"

A thrill of horror ran round that moral circle; and had Clare heard the strong expressions of disgust and shameful reproach which were then heaped on her devoted head, she would have stiffened with dread at her own portrait.

And who had taken this false character to Shorne? Who had set afloat this heavy freight of calumny, to spread the pestilence of falsehood and slander wherever it might touch? Who had dared to blacken the innocent love that an angel might have felt, yet not lost his high place among the pure of heaven? Who had thus distorted her guileless actions, and thrown the foulness of his own mind over her unspotted heart?

The name of this informer betokened nothing. It was a common name enough. Edward Mantell bore no patronymic evidence of wilful slander; nor in his thoughtful face and gentle manners could you read the evidence of a calumniator. Why then had he so distorted truth, and set forth such fearful lies in their stead?

We shall meet him soon where this report will be recalled to his memory: but I doubt if it will be welcome to his conscience.

He is speaking now with Alice; talking to her in his gentle voice and melancholy half-abstracted manner; yet looking every now and then into her face with so much inquiring interest, that even her cold blood warmed beneath his eyes.

He asks her of her early life; and, though the subject is forbidden, she cannot repress *his* questions. He asks her of her first introduction here and of all the minute circumstances attending it, as if he asked for a pretty story. He spoke of Clara; but the girl started back at the word with such visible horror, that for kindness' sake he said no more. And then he turned the conversation on religion, and spoke feelingly and beautifully of the spiritual good which she ought to derive from her past trials.

He was young to speak thus to a girl of seventeen; but he dared, from sincerity of conviction, what no superiority of station, birth, or fortune, would have given him the right to do. Alice listened patiently, and with a certain kind of pleasure, to his calm exhortation; and though her still face betokened nothing, yet her heart felt a strange influence of softness towards this, the first, man who had stood in her path and spoken prophet-like to her soul.

Her silence, and the gentle manner of her well-bred permission, pleased him. He was much with her the whole of the evening; speaking in the same quiet tone of exhortation; asking her in his tranquil voice, and with unimpassioned interest, of thoughts and feelings she had scarcely acknowledged to herself, and making her answer him truthfully by the inquisitorial, though kindly, superiority he assumed over her.

Edward Mantell was handsome, young, and rich; a theological student preparing for the church; sincere in his views, but extreme and stern; ever at war with himself, and ever exorcising the evil nature he attempted to overcome, by dogmas inconsistent with that nature. He was one of the class who take the world and all it contains and hand it boldly to the devil. From the child in the cradle to the corpse in the tomb, to him it was all the possession of the king of hell; and but a few of the chosen stood out from that seething sinfulness in fitness for the kingdom of heaven.

Something of this tinged his conversation with Alice to-night; though he only alluded to his melancholy faith, not approaching it openly. Indeed he felt the inconsistency there would be in enunciating this creed at the present moment; and though he also felt strongly the duty of instant and unceasing testimony, he made peace with his conscience by reflecting that insinuation would have more effect than broad dogmatism in such a scene as this, and that he would do greater service to the cause by biding his time, and speaking only when he should be heard.

This then is the man who has brought down news of Clara's transgression; this is the man who said, with his calm face troubled and his dark eyes cast down as one grieving while he condemned, "She is the profligate mistress of a profligate husband."

Yet had he known her?—had he ever spoken as unreservedly as to Alice to-night, with that misguided child? No: he had merely repeated to others the character given by others; he did not know Clara Clayton even by sight.

The ball ended, and Alice was now baptized into the world of the social elect. Henceforth her life was one long way of smoothest lawn and flowery borders. Sorrow could not touch her now, for she had no affections by which it might strike her, no passions by which it might wound. She had place, birth, riches, and these were the sole gems she coveted for her crown of happiness.

Yes, in spite of the spiritual doctrines of Edward Mantell. And though her cheek would gain a deeper tinge on its pallid fairness, and her blue eyes glance a brighter look through their still gaze, when he came and spoke to her eloquently of religious things—yet in spite of this her heart clung to the barren land of her social grandeur, and thought no flower in any other worthy of the plucking.

In a short time Edward Mantell left Shorne to return to London where his family lived; yet leaving, as he fondly believed, good seed in the heart of his young friend.

CHAPTER III.

DARKER grew poor Clara's day; less and less desirable her intercourse with Vaughan. His fits of tenderness and grace became more rare than ever—his insolence of tyranny and coarseness more apparent. She still tried her best to make all pass smoothly. She endeavoured to soothe him when he was irritable—as indeed when was he not now? And though she generally failed, because of her ignorance of the cause of this irritation, yet the attempt was useful to herself, teaching her the value of self-subjection—to which virtue she was not naturally prone.

To borrow a phrase from our neighbours, she was in a false position: essentially false. She lived in an atmosphere of deception in all concerning her present condition and future prospects; and her love only increased the want of fitness between her character and her circumstances. She wished to yield such obedience as he demanded, but the incessant struggle going on in her heart—love warring with original propensities, and the remnant of early education standing forth against the strength of passions and desires—made it but a poor distorted business; affording no happiness to herself and no satisfaction to him. When she is older she will change this present unnatural state of half-heartedness. She will either yield entirely—her sense of right, her sense of delicacy, her free-will, her very individuality—or she will resist the weakness of her affections, and walk forward relying on herself alone. She will find that in wholeness of action and in completeness of purpose lies the sole power of happiness: she will find that in a false attempt to piece together incongruous materials lies the main cause of misery. She will learn that she must shape circumstances to her own mental requirements, not compress her character into the mould of circumstances: and so stand superior to the force of outward accidents. But as yet she is too young in the school of conscious self-reliance, and too much under the influence of her first passion, to act on principle and not by impulse and feeling. Wait a few months and years yet: we shall not find her halting then as she halts to-day.

No harm had arisen from the last violation of Vaughan's commands. Though annoyed and rather alarmed towards the close of her walk, Clare looked back on it now with immense pleasure. The excitement was agreeable; and most of all, the consciousness of freedom, though for such a short time, was delicious beyond words. She did not confess it to herself yet—but Vaughan's watchful care bored her terribly.

She was going to a large assembly to-night (it was her off-night at the theatre), at the house of one of her new friends, and she was in want of some feminine trifle—ribbon, lace, or flowers. She might have sent her maid on the errand; for Vasty allowed her that functionary always; but she was busy, or Clara chose to fancy that she was so, to give herself a prospective excuse for her disobedience; therefore our little maiden put on her bonnet, and walked out by herself.

She had not gone far when she met a woman, who was wandering about as if waiting for some one. She remembered the face as hers who had so kindly directed her once before.

Clara could not avoid a smiling glance of recognition, and the woman hurried up to her.

"Tell me," she said hastily, "are you married to Vasty Vaughan? I have been waiting about for you many, many days. I would have written to you, but I knew you would not have received my letters. He is too clever for that! They tell me you are soon to be his wife. Is it so? Speak the truth, and openly!"

Startled at this address, Clara drew back proudly. "No," she answered, anxious to get away; "I am not married to him."

"But does he promise marriage, as I hear?" Emma persisted, placing herself in the path as the girl attempted to pass her.

"What right have you to ask?" returned Clara haughtily. "You are a stranger to me—what interest have you in my affairs?"

"More than you dream of, poor child!" said Emma sadly. "Do not use this tone to me," she added in a gentle voice; "I do not deserve it, and I have your welfare at heart."

"This is some trick to frighten me," Clara said, shrinking from the woman who came so near that her breath passed over her lips. "It is useless; I am braver than you believe me."

"It is not a question of bravery, my poor child," said Emma, "though one of courage and fortitude. Listen to me. You must not marry Vasty Vaughan."

Her voice was calm and clear, her manner one of inexpressible authority. Her frightful trade was almost lost in that womanly tone and air.

"I cannot suffer this!" exclaimed Clara, turning away. "It is too evident why you have spoken to me."

"It is not evident to you, Clara Clayton—ha! you start!—I did not then know your name? My poor child, I know your every footstep as you pass along the pathway of life! Others watch you; so do I—so do I—the WIFE of Vasty Vaughan!"

Clara started, then stood suddenly still; for she had been walking rapidly forward to escape her companion. Her eyes dilated, her lips asunder, her cheek blanched to a marble paleness, she stood and gazed silently into that woman's face.

"It is true!" exclaimed the woman vehemently,—"it is true! I am Vasty Vaughan's wife. The vile thing I am—the scorned of all the world—the outcast from heaven—the crushed worm not wholly stingless—it is all true—I yet am Vasty Vaughan's wife! Now marry him if you dare!—now love him if you can!"

Her hatred and her madness swept boiling back over the desolate track from which tenderness had driven them one little moment. She seized the girl's hand; she dragged her along the street—the one half mad, the other nearly dying; she bore her like a tigress with its prey to the door of her house, there to meet Vaughan standing till that door should open and admit him to his love.

"Here is your victim, devil!" she cried, flinging Clara from her. "Here is the deluded wretch you would marry and so exalt into a virtuous wife! Here is the last pure flower you have transplanted into your garden to make into a weed, then throw it out to feed carrion with as you have thrown out *me!* Here is your poor Clara Clayton, and here am I your wife; bringing her back to you that she may burst her bonds before my eyes, and learn to loathe you as I do—in one swift lesson of terrible truth! Here is your deluded mistress—and here is your discarded wife!"

Her accent was fearful because it was so true. Clara felt it burn into her soul like fire.

For a moment Vaughan stood irresolute—only for the shortest moment. A policeman passing, he gave Emma in charge for "riotous behaviour."

Shrieking, screaming, swearing oaths that curdled one's blood, and imprecating vengeance on Vaughan in tones of such frightful intensity of feeling that they affected even him, sceptic and atheist, Emma Vaughan was borne off; and then Vasty had time to look to Clara.

Without a word he led her in. She tottered forward like one weak from sickness, stumbling at every step. He took her in his arms, and carried her up to the drawing-room. He laid her on the couch, removed her bonnet, brought a glass of water, and smoothed back her disordered hair—all without a word. Clara was weeping bitterly; in passionate hysteric sobs.

There was a long unbroken silence. Vaughan sat by the couch, at a little distance from it—not embarrassed, not violent—wearing a cold authoritative manner—the air of an offended superior.

When relieved and a little wearied by her passion, Clara held out her hand.

Vaughan took it, still silent. He held it loosely and coldly. His manner went to her heart, and startled her into suppression.

"It is not true, Vasty, is it?" she said sobbing; and at the sound of her own voice she wept afresh.

He dropped her hand.

"Is it Clara Clayton that asks me if I am a liar—a villain—a very monster?" he asked in a calm, quiet, but deeply-wounded voice.

"Oh, Vasty, dear Vasty! do not hate me!" she cried. "I was bewildered with that woman! I do not believe her—I do not doubt you! Do not be angry with me, Vasty! I do not believe her!—indeed, indeed, I don't!"

She turned her face to the pillow in a heartbroken kind of way, as if giving herself up to helpless suffering.

"Then why those tears, Clara?" he said, still in the same manner— at so immeasurable a distance from her! "Why that question? In spite of your contrary assurance your whole conduct proves that you *do* believe this wandering, drunken woman—believe her after months of intimate friendship with me—after months of my unwearied love! I have not deserved this from you! Clara, I have had many trials in life, but none have wounded me so sorely as this unfounded doubt from you—you on whom I have hung my whole, whole heart."

Self-accusing, penitent, sadly grieved, Clara rose from the couch, and went timidly to her lover.

"Oh! will you not forgive me? But I was startled and frightened!" she exclaimed, placing her hand on his shoulder, and though still weeping kissing his forehead with her poor little wet feverish lips.

He took her hand from off his shoulder, and very quietly drew himself away.

"It is not forgiveness," he said, "but forgetfulness that you ought to ask for. I am not angry with you; not even for disobeying my express injunctions never to walk alone in London. I am not going to say one harsh or unkind word to you—but, Clara, we part for ever. You have suffered suspicion of my honour to pass over your soul, and that suspicion has sealed our separation. I have loved you; I have trusted you; I have believed you superior to the rest of your sex; and if I have kept you in ignorance of the real motive of my actions it has been from kindness to yourself, not from any dishonourable cause of concealment in me. But all is over now. You have distrusted me; and although I may forgive you, and do, yet I can never confide in you again nor rely on your faith in me. If such a woman as the one you met to-day can make you a slave to her drunken follies, what security have I for the future? Ask yourself if I am not taking the wisest course for both?"

"Vasty! Vasty! do not break my heart!" cried Clara falling on her knees before him, and holding out her hands in supplication.

He let her kneel there in a long sad silence, himself trembling, or appearing to do so, while he veiled his face with one hand.

Again and again her passionate pleadings for pardon broke through that silence. Still kneeling—her hair, loose and disordered, falling in broken masses about her face—at intervals stormful sobs and burning tears interrupting those beseeching prayers—her whole being delivered up to wild emotion—she knelt and prayed for pardon, and again and again for pardon.

Vasty's triumph was complete. He had convicted her openly of wrong. He was now the ill-used and the victim: to him belonged the place of forgiveness—to her, that of penitence. He would not lightly lose this glorious opportunity of forging his chains more firmly than ever.

"Your position degrades you," he said, with that manner of forced indifference which men sometimes assume when they wish to impress on a woman the belief that their anger is from principle, but much opposed to their own inclinations.

He raised her. She had pleaded so long and so vainly—with such truth and earnestness—and really not feeling that she had sinned in proportion to her punishment—that she in her turn grew weary, and let him place her again on the sofa; still unpardoned.

"I shall call for you at ten o'clock," he then said, "and you will be ready."

"I cannot go!" exclaimed Clara; "it is impossible!—I cannot!"

"This is absurd," returned Vasty sternly. "I will not allow this temper to me! Besides, it is useless. You have lost the power now to bring me back by all this theatrical appearance. You must and shall go this evening. Say no more about it: my mind is made up."

"My heart is breaking!" murmured poor Clara. "Mother! mother!"

The intense despair in that voice—in those words! A childish superstition still hung about that blessed name of mother. She invoked it as the name of a god, not remembering that it was a false and broken idol.

Even Vasty was moved at this desolate young thing—alone in the world—at the mercy of his falseness and his cruelty—at the mercy of her own impetuous nature—this broken, passionate, weary child—so wretched, so misunderstood, yet so desirous to do right!

He sat down by her; he took her head and laid it on his bosom.

She turned her face inward like a child, and clung to him convulsively, kissing his hands and breast.

He let her lie there for a long time—till she slept; and even then he held her gently, at times forgetting that she was in his arms, so deeply was he buried in thought.

At last she awoke, and looked up with a smile like gentle sunshine over her face. He kissed her forehead, bade her be a good child, and compose herself; and then, still preserving an indescribable manner of superiority and wounded affection that yet was too manly to complain, he left her till he should call for her in the evening, to take her to Mrs. Dunn Lorton's.

At the appointed time she was ready. All visible traces of her tears had disappeared. Her cheeks were bright with one burning spot in them, and her lips were feverish and red: so far her grief had improved her beauty.

She was dressed very prettily to-night. Her gown was white; the trimmings were bouquets of camellias; she wore camellias in her hair; and altogether there was an atmosphere of warmth, simplicity, and youthfulness about her which, independently of her beauty, attracted much admiring notice.

In a few moments she was surrounded by men; some paying open compliments; some only looking their admiration; some making her feel an unpleasant influence of disrespect, others treating her with marked courtesy and honour. She spoke and laughed and blushed even more than usual, for, as with many persons, the reaction of Clara's feelings was always equal to the foregone pressure. The more miserable she had been, the more feverish and intense was her after-excitement.

Among this knot encircling her—but listening, not conversing—stood Edward Mantell. This was the first time he had met the young actress; and though Mrs. Dunn Lorton did certainly gather strange people about her, and did not demand a very strict roll-call of morals in her associates, still he did not expect to meet Miss Clayton in her society. He thought she had been far too notorious for the most "liberal" drawing-room!

He listened to her voice. It had a sweet natural sound. There was nothing of the mincingness of guilt that wishes to appear innocent, nothing of the boldness of defiance that cares not for detection, in it. It was a flexible, modest voice; and its tones struck on his heart strangely.

He asked for an introduction. It was granted. And he met her gentle eyes, as they fell on him with an inquiring expression, with a curious feeling of sorrow.

She looked too innocent for her reputation; fearless but not bold; with a guilelessness of freedom in her manners that might and did mislead many, but which any man of penetration could understand. There was an indescribable influence in her ingenuousness and warmth which attracted more than any amount of coquetry could have done. Edward Mantell felt that influence, and yielded to it.

He did not mention Shorne. A natural instinct of delicacy kept him silent. Had he known that she was yet ignorant of the changes which had taken place there, he would have thought it a matter of painful, but most necessary duty, to have told her how fallen and destroyed was the temple of her young life. He would have told her of the social stain on her birth—of the desolate solitude in which she stood: he would have arrested her in her career of worldly glory by the terrible words of disgrace that he could have poured forth— in her career of vice by the awful words of divine denunciation on sinners. And then he would have turned to the creed, which to him had such melancholy consolation in it, and have bidden her remember the sinfulness of all humanity—the foul presence of Satan in all the concerns of life—the terrible hell that awaited the prosperous and the careless. And ending this, he would have exhorted her to look upward if she wished to escape the everlasting torments of the damned. Such would have been his language to her, had he known her ignorance. As it was, he spoke generally, on matters suited to the place; but, when he best might, mingling such theological hints, such spiritual if not sectarian exhortations, as made Clare attend to him with great interest.

He asked her address, and demanded permission to call on her. Clara forgot Vaughan's jealousy, and granted it to him with such a bright smile, and such apparent facility of approach, that Edward Mantell, like most men, at first felt almost disgusted at the very permission he had craved.

And so they parted; he sorely distressed that this young creature should be so deeply fallen as he had been given to understand, and she wondering why he took such accurate heed of all she said and did, and what he had ever heard of her to make him so mysterious at times, so interested always, in his manners.

"I will speak to her openly," he said to himself. "She is too young and impressionable not to be easily influenced. I will master her mind, and train it up to good. Her frightful profession shall be abandoned—the snares of youth and beauty and talent broken loose. I will show her the danger of her affections, the trials and temptations which she is sent to endure and to conquer. I will show her the worthlessness of all human nature, the sinfulness of our hearts unregenerate. I will lay out before her the world groaning in wickedness and sin, and lead her forth from that herd of the condemned where she stands now, to the bright band of the Elect. I will save her soul, and in her very affliction she shall be blessed."

CHAPTER IV.

A DIRTY crowd of the lowest class standing in thick groups about the doorway—policemen moving amongst them, respectable and important—here and there an inspector or a serjeant with a look of command worthy of a general officer, to whom those of the rank paid evident respect—fragments of straw littering the steps the passage and the street—plaintiffs and defendants with blackened eyes and bruised faces—the usual accompaniments of a police-court received Emma Vaughan when brought before the magistrate for riotous behaviour.

When fairly in the hands of the police she had changed her tone. Out of Vasty's sight she became calmer, and as sullen as she was generally. Her offence was inscribed on the police-sheet; and, as it was after the hour of the sitting magistrate, she was taken to the station-house, and locked up for the night.

On the cold stone floor, without light, fire, a bed, or protective clothing, she had leisure to reflect and to repent if she would—to reflect and harden her heart still further, as was more likely. She heard her baby cry for her. With that keen instinct of the mother, she *felt* the hunger of her little one—she heard its plaintive sobs—she knew it uncared for in its thousand baby wants—she knew them all hungry and unfed.

She flung herself on the stone floor, with her face ground against the flags; prostrate as one dead.

Not a limb stirring, not a groan, not a sigh—only every nerve stretched and every muscle quivering—it was thus she passed that dreadful night. The sense of imprisonment was madness to her; the sense of failure still more keen. But only for this once had she failed! Another time she would make wiser plans, and effectually thwart that wicked man's most wicked purpose. Most madly and absurdly she had attempted her design. She ought to have taken credible witnesses; to have brought proofs which Vasty could not deny nor Clara disbelieve. Was it likely that Clara would credit her as it was—an unknown woman and of such a class—unsupported in her denunciations, against the assurances of Vaughan, her lover? It would be wrong in her to be so soon turned! She could not hope such plastic malleability of nature! No; though she had spoken truth, Clara Clayton ought not to credit her! Passionate and prejudiced as Emma was—more like a wild animal than a human being—when she did reflect, which was not often, she was not unjust.

And then the cry of the baby broke through her breast—the wailing of her children filled that silent cell with anguish. She pressed her burning hands over her eyes, and twined them like restless snakes among her streaming hair.

When taken before the magistrate in the morning, no one appeared to press the charge. She was kept there for a short time—for the public to stare at, and whisper among themselves—for the reporters to eye and smile as they compared their notes which detailed the case—for the magistrate and clerk to speak to her in brutal tones of virtuous abhorrence, and be prepared to commit her under the slightest evidence—for her acquaintances among that degraded crowd to say, one to the other, that she had got it at last, but that she would be game to the end—for her to remember the day when she had stood in a different court to this, as much observed as now; but how widely changed; and to bury her face once in her hands, as the remembrance of her presentation flashed like a picture lit up by lightning before her: for all this she stood at the bar and waited for her accuser.

Vasty never meant to appear as plaintiff or prosecutor. He did not wish his name dragged into the newspapers in such degrading connexion. Not many people knew that he was married at all: none of his own theatrical *troupe*; not even Percival; and it would upset his plans entirely to have it made public. He therefore contented himself by getting rid of that unhappy creature for the moment. For the future he must provide for her in a different mode than by her committal to a temporary gaol.

Emma was kept in the court for a short time, and then pardoned, seeing that no one accused her.

She turned away quiet in manner enough, but with such a fiery demon in her eye that instinctively the crowd—even of men—gave way.

She answered no one of the many who addressed her. She turned aside for nothing; crossing the streets in a sullen recklessness, indifferent to the cabs and omnibuses and carriages that rattled by her. Those of her acquaintances who spoke to her as she met them drew back when her fierce face glared on them, and her clenched hand suddenly upraised itself with an irrepressible movement and a smothered oath. On she went, like a tigress stalking through the streets—a thing of death and fury retreating to its den of little ones to feed them tenderly, while its jaws yet reeked with blood.

The wretched quarter was gained; the black alley with its crowded population, its filth, its misery, its vice, was entered; the lodging-house with its countless inhabitants swarming like reptiles was reached; and Emma, in the same fierce haste, mounted the stairs till she came to her neglected, filthy, disordered room.

The children lay knotted in a heap asleep on the bed. Percival had removed the two slop-working sisters some time since to better lodgings; Emma would not stir; and their place had been taken by women of such natures as GOD has not sent among the brutes.

Her heart beating in large full gasps, and that strange consciousness still in her breast, the woman hurried to the bed. She shook the children roughly, from agitation not unkindness. The two elder woke; but the baby was dead.

In trying to still its cries—in trying to keep it warm throughout that long cold night—the eldest child had overlaid it; and the little one was a corpse beneath the care that would have protected it.

Without a tear, without a groan, without a sigh, Emma took the dead child and laid it on her breast. Stark and stiff hung the cold limbs. No smile answered back her cares—no gentle pressure of those little hands—no staring wonder of those closed eyes. Dead—dead it lay— and she was its true murderer.

She threw herself on the bed, and covered up the little one warmer in her bosom.

"Mother! mother!" said the eldest, "we are hungry!—we have had nothing to eat since you left us yesterday morning. We have not had even a drink of water, for the water ran dry. Mother!—we are so hungry!"

"I have no food for you," said Emma in a voice so changed that the children both started away with terror, as if it had been a stranger speaking.

The little one began to cry.

"Go out and beg!" she said hoarsely. "I have nothing to give you, and I must take care of the baby. Go out and beg—or die."

The elder girl crept closer to her, trembling.

"Mother," she said plucking her dress. "Mother—is that you? Where have you gone to? Where are you?"

Emma slowly raised herself. She passed her hand over her forehead, but could not recall her wandering thoughts. Still this strange cold burden rested on her heart; and she did not understand yet why it was so cold.

The well-known face quieted the children's fears. The younger rushed eagerly to her lap. She hid her little face in her clothes and laughed, saying in childish fashion; "Mammy back again! mammy back again!"

Slowly and surely the terrible truth came clearly before her. There she sat, the mother of these little ones. The baby dead—stone dead— on her breast; the two before her starving for food; unfed since the coarse meal of yesterday morning; she the author of their existence, of their misery, of their death. This was what she had come to at last—practically the destroyer of her children.

Still that dead baby at times bewildered her. She could not look at its placid face and small shrunken body. She could only press it closer and closer, and try to warm it—it was so cold. She knew it was dead: yes, she knew that well; but might not maternal love restore it?

Closer and closer she pressed it, while the other children clung round her and asked for bread. A dark hand came down within that room. It came on gradually; chilling to the heart all living things it touched, blotting out all where it passed. It came on and on; now shutting out the sun-light, then the window, then the scanty furniture—the walls—the floor. The whole room soon shrank to the little space where she sat—her children round her. The hand, the black grim hand, came on. Narrower and narrower grew the circle of her vision—colder lay the dead child; the voices of the two living ones grew so faint she could not hear them; their touch so shadowy she could not feel them: the dead thing only lay like a grave-stone on her heart. One vigorous effort she made to repel this ghastly presence. She tried to rise and thrust it back with her outstretched arm; but the hand was too powerful;—it came nearer and nearer, and seized her own heart. With a sudden short loud howl of misery unspeakable, she fell backward on the bed, and for a time lay as utterly lost to life as that pallid thing cradled in her arms.

The terrified screams of the two children brought such assistance as wretchedness lends to wretchedness. In rough fashion enough women tended this miserable sister. They laid her gently down and placed the lifeless little one beside her, as if it had been a thing new-born. The hunger of the others they could not appease; for all, gathering so thickly in that room, were hungry too. Want, want, in the hollow eyes and fleshless cheeks of all: want and overtasking work in the gaunt famine-wasted frames and tense nerves of all. They could not still those piercing cries of hunger. They might offer the fetid waters of a city's sewer-river, but food for man, such as GOD willed him to have, not one amongst that numerous throng could give.

Oh! do not think because this book goes out in the form and under the name of fiction, that *this* is fiction! Crowds—crowds— in our great luxurious city live out their lives in such a condition as this—in one unceasing state of famine not quite intense enough to kill; hovering ever on the borders of death, but too miserable to be released. This frightful truth is real, though no visible judgment on our land from Heaven attests to its reality. What exaggeration soever imagination may give to lesser woes, this one is true—that English men and women, in the heart of our wealthy Christian city, cannot live by their labour—cannot support life on the wages of life—but die a lingering death of years, wasting to the grave under work and starvation together.

In the midst of all this tumult, the same step that had ventured once before into this wretched place came up the creaking stairs; the same kindly voice and gentle manner which had spread about such peace and happiness as rooted misery *can* feel—was heard; and Percival Glynn entered the room, like some beautiful angel of mercy among the wandering crowds of hell.

He restored her; he stilled the children's famished cries; into many a miserable room that day he sent warmth and cheerfulness and plenty. He asked not if they whom he succoured were the virtuous or the criminal. He knew that they were the needy, and he gave to their necessities. To the Judge of all the earth he left the sole right of retribution and of judgment; to himself belonged but the duty of charity and of help.

When Emma was recovered, and had somewhat exhausted her first grief for her child, she told him of her anxiety for Clara. She told him also—glaring in his eyes the while—that she was Vasty Vaughan's true, lawful, wedded wife.

And it was strange and frightful to hear the savage exultation with which this wretched woman again and again proclaimed that she was the wife—the real wife—of Vasty Vaughan. Degraded outcast as she was, she bore his name—she wore his indestructible ring of marriage; though unseen she walked by his side through life, like a stalking spectre; she stood in his path, invisible but all-powerful to prevent; she was the evil genius he could not subdue, the Atè he could not escape. Yes; this poor flaunting woman was the equal of that caressed and courted gentleman for whom fashion opened her saloons, and beauty dressed herself in smiles. Through all—through all—moved yon grim shadow, yon nameless wife; falling like a noiseless pestilence across a gleaming way of light. She had cursed the law of marriage for fifteen long years; to-day she blessed it over the corpse of that unburied child.

Percival was not left to doubt her; she produced too many documentary proofs of her marriage—proofs that she had hoarded so long, with such a greedy hate! It was true enough. He could not and he did not doubt her; for such things as she showed him, such letters, settlements, and deeds, were unanswerable, and so they must prove to Clara. When Percival left her, he had sworn not to suffer Clara to remain longer in ignorance of the truth. At any transient cost of disappointment or sorrow she must know in what peril she is walking. If she choose then to continue on her way, her destruction will be her own work and she must abide by her own decision.

It was still early in the day. He knew that Clara would be at the theatre at this hour, rehearsing. A new play was to come out in a few days, of which she was the heroine. It was a pretty part in the original, but Clara had made it something more than pretty. She had endowed it with such fervour and truth of feeling that the author himself—

vain as authors are—confessed the superiority of her reading to his original idea.

It was a matter of consideration how Percival should meet or communicate with Clara. He knew that writing was of no avail, for Vaughan inspected all her letters and intercepted those of which he did not approve; he had also provided too wise a maid for his young favourite to be afraid of any untoward communications that he might not see.

Percival gathered so much from Emma. Writing then was worse than useless; it was betrayal where secrecy was absolutely necessary. If he went to her house, he should not be admitted. If he went to the theatre, he should not be allowed to speak with her. Vaughan had forbidden him the rehearsals and the green-room; and even if this were not the case, how could he speak to her at all in *his* presence? If he took Lucretia into his confidence, she was sure to do more harm than good by her affectation and her blundering love of management— by her want of tact and delicate handling. He was at an utter loss. Vaughan was a good general and not easily outflanked.

He was perplexed. But as he had plenty of time, owing to the peculiar divisions of the theatrical day, he sat down and began to reflect on his best step.

His eye fell on the morning paper. Without thinking much of what he did he took it up; when a paragraph headed "Romantic History," attracted his attention. Some names in that paragraph stood out in such large prominence that the whole paper seemed merged into those few lines. With much agitation he read the following announcement in true provincial newspaper style.

"Romantic History.—Since the days of the Montague-house romance, no such occurrence equal to the following, for interest or for strangeness, has taken place. Some seventeen years ago an heiress was born to the wealthy family of the De S——z, in the village of Sh—ne. It was found necessary to procure a nurse for the child, and one Martha Clayton, a relative of an old retainer of the Hall, was taken into that responsible office. In a few months a wonderful change was worked in the infant heiress, and when she returned home few would have recognised her. At that early age features are not very individual, therefore the change in the child was attributed to improved health, the transforming powers of an absence long for such a tender age, the vigorous infusion of peasant strength, and many other like reasons which would occur to most minds. As the child grew up, it displayed a most extraordinary want of likeness with its illustrious progenitors. We have heard it was remarked by more than one visitor at the Hall, how unfit in habits, temper, and pursuits, the reputed heiress threatened to prove with her position. Her tastes were essentially plebeian; and her temper of such violence as to render her parents miserable and all control over her impossible. We will not enter into the details of the chance which brought a young girl, Alice F——, to the Hall, nor dilate on the beauty, elegance, propriety, and modesty, which she displayed under the most disadvantageous conditions. She was received with maternal affection by Mrs. de S——z, though no suspicion of the truth had been breathed; and we hear that a beautiful instance of the power of natural instinct might be adduced from the intercourse of this unrecognised mother and child. After some time, the young lady who had filled the place of Miss de S——z so long, ran away from home in company with a dissolute, strolling actress. Every endeavour to reclaim her was in vain. She resisted all entreaty to return; ridiculed all care and all affection; cast off, still believing them real, all the bonds of home; and clung to her disorderly associates and disreputable life, with a tenacity unaccountable were it not hereditary. For we neglected to mention that this nurse to the De S——z, this temporary mother to the infant heiress, had been seduced by some wild young nobleman, and made the mother of an illegitimate daughter. It is due to the lady of the Hall to state that she was not aware of her transgression when she hired this woman to be her child's nurse. She believed, as she had been informed, that Martha Clayton was an honest married woman. The *dénouement* is now at hand. By some accident the truth was discovered, and the gentle Alice F——, whose place had long been in the inmost heart of Mrs. de S——z, was proved the rightful heiress to the estate, and the legitimate child of the noble parents: while Clara Clayton, the reputed heiress, was proved at the same time the child of the peasant woman. She—Clara Clayton—is, we understand, still in London, acting in some low theatre—her reputation gone—her conduct more reprehensible than we would willingly portray—the public mistress of one, if not of many—the fitting daughter of her abandoned mother.

"A ball was given at the Hall last week, to commemorate the joyful event of this discovery, to which all the *élite* of the neighbourhood were invited. The De S——z filled their house with noble names; so that, since the memory of man, so many coronets were never before collected together in Sh——ne. Long may the sun of his illustrious house shine with undiminished lustre! Long may the beautiful and accomplished heiress of a proud line continue in her own person all the glorious characteristics, which have placed the De S——z, for generations past, among our best and brightest names!"

The paper fell from Percival's hands, and all the blood eddied round his heart in large heavy waves, rushing like sea-side billows.

Was it joy or sorrow that made his heart beat so thick and fast? Was it in joy or sorrow that he saw Clara helpless and friendless before him, and he her only true support? He would have rejoiced over her prosperity, even if it brought him annihilation in the records of her life: but he could not stifle a pardonable feeling of intense delight—now that sorrow *had* come on her—at the vision which presented itself before him, wherein he stood forth as her nearest and unwavering protector against a slanderous world that did not know her.

Was this selfishness in Percival? I think not. Of the many faults in the catalogue of human infirmities he deserves the reputation of this least of all.

He hurried to the theatre. It was just the hour when rehearsal usually ended; though this is an uncertain and unequal exercise too. However, his calculations were right to-day; the actors and actresses were leaving the theatre as he arrived at the stage entrance. He lingered for a short time, writing some words in pencil on a scrap of paper in the meanwhile; and when they had all gone, the door opened again, and Clara, led by Vaughan, came out.

He saw by her face that she had seen or heard of that newspaper paragraph.

She was pale as a marble statue—her very lips white; but she walked with such an air of strength and superiority, that he knew at once how she had received that intelligence. Crushing as it was, it had not struck down her great heart, which yet the cold eye of her lover could agonize to madness. No: stunned at first, and deeply moved now, but erect and strong ever, she passed before him; not a tear, not a sigh, not a drooping lid, to say she grieved. And yet she had lost all: aye, and more than she knew of; for with her birth and her prospective wealth she had also lost her maiden fame. But Vaughan had kept the paper from her, only telling her the contents of the fateful paragraph, and as yet she was spared this second blow.

As she passed Percival—not seeing him, else she would not have moved on with that stately step and firm bearing—he crushed the paper, on which he had just been writing, into her hand. She started, turned, and saw him, and then concealed her hand beneath her shawl.

Vaughan turned too: and Percival, raising his hat, went on his way. He caught just a passing glimpse of Vasty's face, and saw in it such a frightful flash of triumph as made him tremble at the power in which that poor child stood.

She, leaning in such confidence on his arm, forgot to see that flush. She only noticed that he was the gentle tender Vaughan of her early acquaintance—that he seemed to love her better than ever—to be more respectful now when respect was charity than he had ever been before—to guard her from every kind of annoyance however small— that he had been attentive and kind before the assembled actors and actresses, all of whom by their looks and words and whispered secrecies had heard the news; she only knew that she loved him to-day with a warmth and truth that made her almost indifferent to this discovery if she could but stay near him.

All this Percival read like an open book. To-morrow—and how will that brave young heart bear up against its heavy burden *then?*

CHAPTER V.

THE paper which Percival pressed into Clara's hand contained the following words:—

"I *must* see you to-morrow morning early. At eight o'clock I shall be in —— Street [where she lived]. If I may not be admitted into your house, you must meet me in the street. Do not be startled at this request. You know that I always have reasons for what I do. You need not fear me.—P. G."

Now Clare was one of those unfortunate people who think their own consciousness of innocence sufficient warranty for any imprudence. She knew that, according to conventional laws, it was a heinous crime in a young unprotected woman to make an assignation with any man. She knew that, whether in the open street or in her own room, it was the same thing—a gross violation of social usages which would bring no small disgrace on her if bruited abroad. But she supported herself by her old fatal words;—"It is different with him!"

These words had been Vaughan's best friends; and to what had they brought her?

However, Clare was not easily taught practical wisdom. Mrs. de Saumarez used to complain bitterly of her obstinacy. This unteachable characteristic would be much the same thing under any milder and more metaphysical term. And whether it is called the necessity for a strong nature to work out its own experience, or as Mrs. de Saumarez stigmatized it, stubbornness and perversity, it will come to much the same result—namely, that it was very difficult to manage Clara Clayton, and that it did not much signify who attempted it—she generally had her own way in the end.

She locked herself in her own room, and read again and again that crumpled scrap of paper. She read it with such intense pleasure! Had Percival been her lover a brighter gleam of happiness could not have lit up all her features than that which now welcomed her old friend.

She had so often longed to see him again! Since forcibly separated from his society she had learnt to prize it better. She wanted to hear him talk to her; to be enlightened by him on so many difficult mental questions which puzzled her, and for which she could get no satisfactory answers either from her own ignorance and distraction or from the false views of the people about her; she wanted to hear him put her right—so firmly, yet so gently—when she broke forth into any of her thousand mistakes; she wanted him to show her how narrow were her own views while she railed against the prejudices of others, and how far on one side she left the truth while deprecating falsehood; she wanted to be made "good again" by him; for she felt now—though she had not been conscious of it at the time—that her mental being had grown and expanded under his teaching, "like a sea-flower unfolded beneath the ocean,"[56] and that he had had a more ennobling influence over her than any one else in the world.

With Vaughan she felt dwarfed and degraded. She could not understand how a man who assumed to be liberal should be so afraid of the opinion of the world—that awful Idol which smites with the leprosy of conformity every noble thought that else would oppose its tyranny. In religion and morality Vaughan took an independent course, because he was proud and sensual, and could neither stoop to authority nor control his appetites. But in general, the dictum of society was upheld as greater than the sacredness of any fundamental moral right which might war against that dictum; and when she spoke of truth and justice he answered her with "social laws," and "the opinion of the world."

What therefore she missed in Vaughan, Percival supplied to her in his earnestness and the recognition of moral principles as superior to social customs.

This is translating into plain language the unspoken consciousness which was the only expression her mind had yet attained: for while people love they do not criticise.

In spite then of Vaughan's hatred and express injunctions, Clara determined to meet Percival to-morrow, and to hear what he had to say that was so important.

She believed that he wished to tell her of her changed birth and loss of home. If so, she would please him so much by the bravery of her indifference! She would show him how well she carried out in practice the republican principles he too had laughed at as crude and immature. She would prove her sincerity by the openness with which she would acknowledge her peasant birth, and the courage with which she would proclaim herself divorced from the aristocratic class. Yes; she would make Percival respect as she had made Vaughan admire her great endurance. Self-deceiver!—she knew not that it was love—the concentration of her hopes and passions and whole existence on another object—that gave her more than half this practical republicanism! What young heart repines at any outward circumstances, so long as love remains its own, and the dear face smiles upon it? Ah! if we strip our motives thus of all the flowers of fancy and self-deception wreathed around them, what strange undreamt-of cores would be revealed!

In this determination to meet and surprise Glynn with her greatness Clara went to bed; and after a strange feeling of solitude, and yet of increased grandeur from that very solitude—of loss, and yet of gain from that loss—of independence so great as to be even without the recognition of the law—she fell asleep: to dream of Percival and Vaughan under various shapes of natural enmity.

The morning came. With it the startling remembrance of her early meeting. It was eight o'clock when she awoke, so there was no hope of joining Percival out of doors now. She supposed he would leave in disgust at her indifference; but as he *might* come to the house, it was as well to prepare for it. She rang the bell, and told the maid that if a gentleman should call he was to be admitted: she would be down immediately.

And true enough, after waiting for her rather more than half-an-hour, Percival knocked at the door and was shown up stairs.

In a few moments Clara came.

Their meeting was expressive and affectionate. In spite of a little embarrassment on both sides, there was an open-hearted frankness about it that proved their reliance on each other more than anything else would have done. Both hands extended, Clara hurried to him, calling him, before she well knew it; "Dear, dear Percival!"

Deeply touched, Percival took her little hand and pressed it to his lips. Clara remembered the last time when that brotherly action had led to her exceeding and most reprehensible boldness. She blushed, laughed, and drew her hand away,—only to place it again within his, with a sudden, trusting, fond manner which made him love her so much better for its innocent confidence!

"Things have changed since I saw you last, Mr. Glynn," she said. And then she coloured at the platitude of her speech.

"But you are the same, Clara!" he answered.

"How strange to hear your voice calling me by my name once again!" she exclaimed, blushing deeper than ever; as if she had said that it was pleasant.

"And you are not cast down by your sudden reverse of fortune?" he asked, after a pause.

"No, not the least!" and she looked up with a bright brave look. "On the contrary, I feel more womanly, more strong and independent than I ever did. It is true I have not a tie in the world—not a relation that can help me. I have only my own brains between me and the workhouse," she added laughingly; "but I do not feel either so desolate or so poor as I could have expected, had I foreseen the truth. In prospect it would have terrified me; as it is, it does not seem to have changed me in the least!"

"You are happy then? Yet you do not look quite the blooming, joyous, riotous girl I first instructed in the art of speaking. Are you really happy? Tell me this in your own spirit of truth and reliance."

"Yes—no—oh yes, I am!" she answered, hesitating and looking down. "Vaughan is substantially very kind to me yet;—very," she added with emphasis.

"And you love him as much as when I knew you?"

"Yes, I do, I believe. We are not quite suited to each other in some things. He does not always understand me, and I offend him sometimes seriously, without having the slightest idea how. To this hour I do not know the cause why he has been angry many times. If I knew, I should be able to avoid it in the future; but I am perpetually doing something that he disapproves of; and yet he will not tell me what it is."

"And your—marriage?" asked Glynn, with difficulty.

She looked down, shook her head and sighed. She turned rather pale. "I know nothing," she said in a melancholy voice; "I sometimes think it will never take place at all."

"And that grieves you?"

"Yes; I should like to belong to him."

"Why, Clara?"

"I should feel so safe then! Now—though I scarcely confess it to myself—I feel so utterly alone in the world! I belong to no one; and except Vaughan, not a creature seems to care for me or to think of me at all!"

"There is Lucretia," began Percival.

"Oh! she is Vasty's echo! If he is angry, Lucretia is grave. And I cannot blame her. Her whole existence depends on Vasty; for she could not make such liberal terms with any other manager—at least, he says not; and of course she would rather please him than me! No; Lucretia is my good friend in her heart always: but practically only while Vaughan continues so."

"And have you then forgotten your promise to remember *me* always as one who would never forsake you?—as one who would be, through life and death, your friend independent of all the world? You promised to regard me as such—have you forgotten it?"

"No! no!" she said, rising from her seat and going to him. "No, dear Mr. Glynn, I have not forgotten it; but when we see people so seldom it is difficult to believe that we are remembered by them."

"I understand you. At your age this distrust is allowable. When you are older you will know on whom you may rely. Tell me more of Vaughan. Does his nature—his mind—satisfy you as much as ever? Do you still believe him the perfect being you did when I last saw you, and still feel as much a child in his hands to be moulded into what shape, mentally, he may choose to impose on you? Is all this unchanged in your young heart?—Is this chaos of first love still there?"

She was silent.

"Nay, do not fear to speak to me. Have you discarded me from my old office with you?—and do you never intend to trust your father confessor again?"

"No," she said softly, tears coming up into her eyes, "not that; but I don't know what to say. I am not always happy."

She stopped. She feared the appearance, however false, of speaking against her lover.

"He is kind to you?" said Percival.

"Oh, yes!"

"But you do not suit each other, you said?"

"Not always. His manners are sometimes very strange."

Again she hesitated.

"How?—in what particular are they strange?"

"He is rough, and says things that he ought not to say; at least, I do not like them; rude things; and not always proper."

She looked down and then looked up again. The first in bashfulness; the second in a kind of inquiring affirmation.

Percival's face grew crimson. "And what do you do? Try to make him see his impropriety?—or how do you manage him?"

"Not at all," she said innocently; "I dare not find fault with him. He is very violent even to me now."

"And yet you wish to belong to him, Clara; and by such frightful laws that you could not break them again—that you could not regain your freedom? Are you mad?"

He spoke in a tone of severity.

"If I were his wife," she answered with simplicity, "I could make him happier and therefore gentler. I should have more influence over him than I have now."

"And the mental being of this violent imperfect man would satisfy you as his wife?"

"What can I do? I cannot change him! If I could, I would make him more serious in his views of life and less afraid of the world's opinion in little things. But I cannot have everything; with all his faults he is good and generous, kind and noble. How many faults I have! I ought to be the last to blame him!"

"And if you found, Clara, that he was vile, base, wicked, cruel? What then? Nay, do not turn so pale at a simple suggestion!"

It was more than a simple suggestion. She felt there was meaning in it.

She quivered in every limb. "I should hear it," she said in a low voice, "and then die."

Percival was silent.

Clara knew that something was at hand. She gazed into his face with its dark cloud of sorrowful mystery resting on it; and there she read, as in the opened scroll of the grieving prophet, words of lamentation, and mourning, and woe.

"What do you mean, Mr. Glynn?" she asked, shrinking nearer to him. "It seems as if a death had come! Are you going to speak of Vasty?"

Her voice was calm, but he distinctly heard her heart beat.

Still he was silent, betraying in his face and manner excessive emotion. At last he spoke.

"You must nerve yourself," he said slowly. "It is of Vasty that I would speak!"

"Tell me, Mr. Glynn, out openly what all this means!" she cried, her voice falling to the low distinctness of pain. "I am becoming used now to such terrible things—such sudden sweeping away of all my hopes and fancied security—that I can bear sorrow better than I did at first. Habit is reconciling me," she added with a sad smile that went to Percival's very soul. It was so unnatural for her, that bright young thing, to look subdued and patient!

"And I *have* sorrow for you, Clara," he said in a tone of exquisite compassion. "Whatever misery you have suffered hitherto, I fear you will think it all mere child's play compared to what you have to suffer now!"

"Let me sit near you, Mr. Glynn," she interrupted him. "See! I am not weak, nor passionate, nor tearful. I feel a stony strength in my heart to-day, as if I could bear any amount of pain!"

"Clara, listen to me. No, do not shade your face. Give me your hand, and do not tremble so frightfully. You have a trial before you of no common order. Listen calmly, and bear it bravely. Do you remember a woman speaking to you in the street—not so long ago: it was but three days since? Do you remember it, Clara?"

A low moan broke over her quivering lips: her only answer.

"Can you believe that woman spoke the truth?" asked Percival, holding her hands tightly. "Can you believe that every word she said was true?"

The girl rose slowly from her seat. She put back her hair, and looked down into his face with dilated eyes terrified yet inquiring. Her lips were glazed, apart, and all the lines drawn sharp in agony and terror. Her look was one of dreaming madness slowly awakening to recollection; but with no positive knowledge as yet. She peered into his face; she held back her hair as if listening; her cold breath passed over his burning eye-balls as she said in a low whisper, "Was it true?—is it all true?—really true?"

"Clara! do not look like that!" exclaimed Percival, much shocked. "Clara! my child!—my sister! do not look at me so strangely! Do you not know me, Clara—your own firm friend—your old master, Clara?"

She took no heed of what he said. He might have been a stranger speaking to her, or the winter wind rushing past. She did not seem to read a feature, though her eyes were fixed so steadily. Her lips only went on their murmuring sound; "True—true—it is true!"

This was the first time that sorrow had had this kind of effect on Clara's brain. Hitherto it had stimulated her feelings; to-day it seemed to paralyze them. The saddest proof that could be given of how much had gone before.

"Sit down by me," urged Percival; and he would have placed her in the chair near him, but she repulsed him mournfully, shaking her head and saying; "No, no; I do not want rest! I must walk—I must go on. It is a long way I have to go—very long—it is time to go now—it will be dark soon!"

She paced up and down the room, her hands pressed on her forehead. Up and down that narrow room in her sad hopeless way—stunned as by a blow—without a tear or loud exclaim—with cold fingers busy at her heart, and chilling it as they touched.

A step came hurriedly up the stairs. It was Vasty, to whom Clara's maid had flown as soon as Percival arrived, to inform him that a strange gentleman sat closeted with her mistress.

The door was flung open violently, and he entered.

"Scoundrel!" he exclaimed on seeing Percival; "what right have you here? Have I not expressly forbidden you to enter this house or to speak to this lady? What insolence is this that you should dare to disobey me?"

At the sound of his voice Clara flung herself into Glynn's arms, concealing her face on his shoulder. "Oh do not let him see me!" she cried convulsively. "Keep me! keep me!—if I see him he will take me away! Keep me, keep me, Percival!"

"Clara!—my God, what madness is this?" cried Vasty seizing her hand rudely, and endeavouring to force her face upward. "What devil's pantomime are you both playing off before me? For shame, for shame, you wanton girl—in this attitude before my face! What business have you here at all, thief and villain?" he added, turning fiercely to Glynn while he attempted to tear the girl from him.

Percival held her close, and warded off Vasty's plucking hands.

"I have the right of her friend to protect her against you, her enemy and her ruin!" he said calmly. "I have come to tell her that you are married to another woman; that I know that woman and have spoken with her; that I possess the evidence of your marriage; and that she, this poor deluded child, must abandon you before you ruin and abandon her."

Vasty started. Was the game so far gone?

"Married! married! and I must leave him!" murmured poor Clara, looking up into Percival's face with such desolate misery that even Vasty pitied her. "I must not love him now—I ought never to have loved him. I have been sinning so much!—and I must leave him!"

"Clara! listen to me! By Heavens, but you shall!" exclaimed Vasty.

He dragged her from Percival as if she had been a child: always powerful, passion braced his muscles to redoubled strength.

"Listen to me!" he said fiercely; "and leave off these fool's tricks."

She turned from him, holding out her hands supplicatingly to Glynn, crying, "No! no! let me go! Mr. Glynn, take me away! take me from him! Let me go, Vasty; I am not your wife!"

Vaughan only laughed coarsely. He pressed her to him like a giant—hardly, harshly—and kissed her lips and forehead with wild impassioned kisses.

Percival's heart was all on fire; yet he stood still and silent. What could he do? Clara must be her own deliverer.

At the touch of those dear lips the love of the girl woke up. Thoughts flew in giddy eddies from heart to brain, whirling in frenzied memories of hopes so long believed in—now struck dead. All her love, her passion, her despair, broke loose like demons wrestling for her soul. Turn where she would the blackness and the pangs of hell alone met her. She uttered a cry, such a one as Vaughan did not soon forget—a cry of anguish from the very heart—and then she threw her arms round him and clung to him in agony, as she paid back those fierce caresses with others yet more feverish and maddened.

Vaughan looked at Percival triumphantly. He pointed to the girl in such terrible agony within his arms, and said with a sneer that made his face a very fiend's, "Break *this* influence if you can! Under any circumstances Clara will not leave me! My bonds are woven far too strong for your sickly morality to loose! Passion and youth are not to be daunted by the morbid preachings of a dreaming sentimentalist."

He held her now as her master, her possessor—carelessly, loosely— as if satisfied of his power and not caring to exert it openly.

"Do you willingly remain there, Clara?" said Percival in a cold voice. "Do you willingly belong to him—married as he is?"

She shrieked at the word, put her hands before her face, and fell on the sofa sobbing in frightful passion.

She started from Vaughan's hand when he would have soothed her, as though it had been of fire. Percival also she pushed aside feebly; but as if she wanted liberty, and could not bear the smallest pressure.

This lasted for some time. All was silence, excepting those convulsive sobs rending her very life.

At last she grew calmer.

"Tell me," she said turning to Percival, "in so many words, is it all true? Is he really married—and to that dreadful woman?" She shuddered violently.

"It is true," said Percival firmly.

Vaughan paced the room.

"It is false!" he vociferated, halting in his rapid walk and confronting Glynn.

The girl looked up with a bright quick glance. Was the victim to be reprieved?

"I have proofs," returned Percival quietly but with emphasis. "It is of no use to deny them," he added; "one glance would convince the most incredulous."

"And you do not deny this?" Clara said, lifting her face toward Vasty but not looking at him—her eyes on the ground.

He was silent.

"No, Clara," he then said suddenly; "I do not deny it. But hear my reasons—hear me as you have heard him. You cannot refuse me common justice."

"No! no!" she interrupted him; "I do not want excuses or reasons. Only the fact, only the fact. You are married to another: that is all I care to know; that is true—the rest is nothing."

Her manner was hurried and restless.

"Yes, Clara, it *is* true."

Vasty's eyes glared darkly. His voice was determined, his manner brutal.

"That is enough," she then said; "I wish you both good bye. I shall not see you again. I am going home."

She moved towards the door, speaking as if her mind wandered.

Vasty placed himself in her way.

"Home!" he exclaimed with a sneer; "and where is that, Clara? An outcast from home—without a friend or protector in the world— where would you fly, if from my arms?—who will receive you runaway from me?"

The shaft struck true. For the first time she tasted the full bitterness of the cup of her desolation. The sneer roused her pride: it checked the choking tears.

"I will make myself a home." she said, standing in a firmer attitude than she had yet assumed. "I will work, and so live."

Again she would have passed him—this time more collected.

"I will not suffer this folly!" cried Vasty with sudden passion, forcing her back with his arm. "You are mine, Clara, and mine you shall remain! What good will it do you to leave me now when the whole world believes you fallen—when the very newspapers print you my unlicensed wife, and no one would believe that I had been fool enough not to have made you so? Your character is ruined for ever, and your only chance of happiness or common respectability is to stay with me—as long as you can," he added coarsely.

Percival, who had not spoken for a long time, keeping his eyes fixed on the girl, seeming to trust rather than to foresee, looked frightfully uneasy. He feared the effect of this more than of any other blow.

Clara's face flushed crimson. For a moment she seemed to droop under the picture, so horrible, so false; then the blood retreated back to her heart; she raised her head proudly, and said with distinctness and calmness—

"Is this true also, Percival? Do the people believe me bad as he says?—and is my reputation ruined?"

"If they speak against you, Clara, so much the more reason for you to prove your innocence," he answered. "Come with me. I will protect you from all slander, from all misery! Come! leave this house; you have been in it too long already. I will care for your future reputation and establish it."

He took her hand. She clasped it in both her own. Brave Clara! Virtue then has triumphed over passion—the high has beaten down the low! Had it not been so, thy soul would have died to purity for ever; hadst thou chosen Vaughan thou wouldst have lost thy heaven of future good!

Vaughan laughed loudly.

"This is the prettiest farce I have seen off or on the stage!" he cried with an oath. "On my soul, Glynn—and you, you cursed piece of folly—you both deserve credit for the masterly boldness of your conduct! Your plot is glorious! So, Glynn, you must come, and before my very eyes make proposals to my mistress—in my very presence—in the very rooms I have hired? You must talk of respectability and virtue while asking her to give herself to you as a better protector to her than I should be? And she must act a puling abhorrence of me, only to transfer herself more quickly to your arms? By my soul, it is an exquisite piece of rare diversion! Go on!—go on!—it will give me a hint for a new comedy. Clara Clayton shall be the heroine—this modest, tender, clinging dove!—this greedy kite!" he added savagely— "that feeds on every meat down to such carrion as that! I might have expected as much from the bastard of a dissolute peasant!"

Clara uttered a low cry and covered her face.

"Stand up," said Percival in a tone of command; "stand up, Clara, and fling back those slanderous words! Tell him that he lies—that his own false heart convicts him—that from the villany of his own nature he judges you!"

"I cannot bear this!" cried poor Clara, her womanly pride, her courage, her dignity, all giving way. "Let me go from you both for ever!"

"Will you?" sneered Vaughan, clutching her shoulder. "Do you forget your bond, my modest maid? I am sorry to step in between you and your pleasures, but your theatrical life at least belongs to me! For the five coming years you are my servant, my hired jester, my paid mime—a thing that paints and dresses and mouths to the gaping multitude as I would have her—my hired servant," he repeated, "and you cannot escape. Do what you will, you cannot escape! I have the mastery over you, and this moral man of words, who seduces by religion and lies by ethics, cannot prevent it! So far I am your superior!"

It was too true. Clara was in his power, turn which way she would.

By his brutality she gained strength.

"Percival, I will go with you," she said with strange and sudden calmness; "the world may talk if it likes—I am innocent and I am indifferent."

Vaughan came up to the elocutionist. He struck him in the face, saying in tones of intensest rage, suffocating blinding rage, "you shall answer to me for this, and you shall die for it!"

He turned to Clara and laid his hand heavily on her shoulder. She bore the marks for weeks after. He forced her face to him; and then he stooped down, and in low hissing tones cursed her with an oath that made her very heart turn to stone.

He was a strong man. Before Glynn could interpose he lifted her from the ground, flung her heavily on the floor, and with the same fierce curse rushed from the house.

For hours that man was mad—pacing his rooms like a caged lion—his veins all starting like knotted whipcord through his skin, and every nerve stretched to its extreme tensity.

He was baffled; he was repulsed. He loved her, and she was gone. Oh! how he loathed his own folly that he had not made her so entirely his own that she could not have deserted him for any such discovery! Why had he not lowered her to his level, and made his deepest villany but equality with herself? This was his reward for his sincere affection!—this her gratitude for being spared!

He tore his hair, and blasphemed till the air grew loud with frightful oaths. He loved her, and she was gone. He loved her, and he had struck, spurned, reviled her—her for whom every pulse was beating—every thought devoted. Fool! fool! how had he let the game slip by so easily!

Yes; mad as a man of his passionate ungoverned nature must be, when his desire is checked and he has been the framer of his own disappointment, was Vasty Vaughan! To see Percival lifeless at his feet, and to hold Clara in his arms, were the sole wishes that the universe possessed for him. And for these he would have sacrificed his own existence.

He strode from the house. Clara at least he will see again. But when he came to the well-known door, all was in confusion; the girl had gone, and no one knew where.

Gone!—gone!—and he loved her with such frightful burning intensity!

There was no need to imagine any other hell than that in Vasty's breast to-day; for nothing more hideous could be pictured, add what torments you would!

CHAPTER VI.

THE next morning it was arranged that Percival and Vasty should stand as targets to each other in a spot convenient for the honourable murder of a civilized society.

Does it seem strange that Percival, who claimed to be so far in advance of the prejudices of his time, should be a duellist—a thing essentially of the past? In an age which sees Peace Congresses held in the midst of distracted states where war is a religious duty and peace would be most shameful treachery; in an age which would square passions by theories, resist oppression by submission, and control universal nature by hypothesis, Percival will seem worse than an "imperfect being," by this duel of jealousy and brutality. However, it was true. Of course he approved of universal peace as a distant and beautiful picture, but he had no desire to submit to present tyranny because of that picture. He thought it as foolish for a man to travel through the gold digging districts of California without arms, and try spiritual mesmerism on the marauding Indians and cut-throat Spaniards, as to reject the tribunal of honour belonging to his time and console himself with "the conscience of the aggressor being his worst scourge." While men are brutes they must be kept in order by brute means. A sermon preached to a hungry tiger would not leave you much chance for your life; neither will moral maxims, as resistance to the Vasty Vaughans of the day, leave you much chance of quiet or of social honour. No: Percival was a duelist under certain circumstances; and the present was one of them. I do not think that any man who has what the Scotch call "red bluid" in him, will say that he was wrong. This red blood may be the "animal part" of us; but it has nevertheless made us what we are; and many of us would be sorry to see ourselves theorized into pale meek slaves, submitting like sheep in a slaughter-yard, because "opposition and war are exploded."

The space was measured; the men placed; the word was given, and sharp went the click of the pistols. Percival's ball went wide, Vaughan's struck home. The wounded man fell on the grass, the blood streaming from a gaping hole in his side.

Fortunately no vital part was touched; so it was to be hoped that after a time, and with careful attendance, he would recover.

This was Glynn's first practical experience of dueling. It certainly was not a just decision of fate; but then fate never was just since the world began, and never will be in the mind of any man till she dispenses prizes only and burns all her blanks.

He was taken home; and then he had a fever which lasted for several weeks, and when it was subdued left him so reduced that he could not raise his head from the pillow. He had a nurse who neglected him and stole half his property; he had a doctor who forgot to write him down in his list three times out of six; and he had a servant who gave tea-drinkings in his parlour when she ought to have been at the chemist's for his medicine. In short, poor Percival was a bachelor; a bachelor, sick and solitary, in lodgings; and what can there be more forlorn, more neglected, more miserable, on this round earth! An Indian dying among the brakes and bushes alone in the great solitude of the forest where his enemies have struck him down; a wounded man who sees the condor and the vulture swoop over him in preparation for their living meal; a wretched laggard in a retreating army; a strayer from his caravan in the desert with half a dozen Bedouins looking inquisitively at him; all these are very miserable positions for a man to be placed in; but a sick bachelor in London chambers is even worse off than they, for he has the solitude and the bird of prey, the skirmishers and the robber, all in one; and he is just as helpless as any of the more romantic heroes.

God help the poor wretches! They learn the value of womankind sometimes.

Well, we must leave Percival groaning in his sick bed, in the hope that this will be his last duel. He has had enough of its summary phlebotomy to be satisfied for the future. The "red bluid" is not always at boiling heat. A long sickness from an ugly wound cools it wonderfully. Poor Percival! with his pale cheeks and light brown mutton broth! Let us hope that he will escape the double action of hemorrhage and hired London nursing: if he does, he is a stronger man than most.

By this duel, with its subsequent illness—of both which facts Clara was ignorant—she was left wholly unnoticed, and as it seemed to her uncared for by Percival. Since her removal from Vaughan's lodgings she had not seen nor heard of him, though he had promised to be with her again the next morning. Days passed, and still no Percival. The poor child began to feel her solitary position very painful. If she went down to the theatre, no kind voice greeted her—no respectful attentions reminded her to herself that she was a gentlewoman—no loving cares raised her above the miseries of her profession. Vasty she did not see at all: Lucretia avoided her with a hurried "good morning" and a secret pressure of her fevered hand. The rest of the actors and actresses either forced on her a horrible familiarity, or treated her with studied disdain, accordingly as they had felt for her in the days of her prosperity. Those even who pitied her—such a desolate thing as she looked—and who would have willingly paid her more than common respect because of the sudden change in her circumstances, were restrained by the floating consciousness there was throughout the theatre of Vasty's desertion; and they were too much in his power to dare a kindness to one on whom he had set his seal of displeasure. No one took any care of her. She came alone—passed alone through the scene-shifters, carpenters, and Jewish-looking dirty smoky men who are always to be found lounging about a theatre, and they by their familiar looks and half-insolent manners made her feel that she had no protector; she sat by herself when not annoyed by the attempted familiarities of the lower actors; went away unaccompanied and on foot in the driving rain and gusty wind, like a lost bird in a pathless wood; she who had been a queen among them in the delicate cares showered on her! She came and went as one who brought an infected atmosphere—deserted by all that theatrical world.

But yet it was a relief not to see Vasty.

The theatrical orders concerning attendance, rehearsal, &c., which she received now, came from the stage-manager in true business form. Hitherto Vasty had told her everything himself. His little notes in their fanciful envelopes, scattering a cloud of perfume as she opened them—those cherished little notes, with their pretty devices of shields, painted flowers, initials, coloured and cut borders, which she had studied and kissed so often, as if they had been sentient things—were at an end; and instead of them came only managerial commands, which seemed contemptuous insults after their tender words. "Miss Clayton is to attend at the theatre at ten o'clock to-morrow morning," was a bad continuation to "Will my own Clara be ready at twelve to-morrow? I have put off the rehearsal to that hour for her lazy little self," &c.

How miserable she was! The whole company noticed her altered looks—her distracted air—her listlessness and hopeless weariness. When she spoke, she spoke as if in a dream; and many times the sharp voice of the prompter angrily recalled her to herself as she went wandering away in unfathomable depths of sorrow when she ought to have been standing in some ecstatic attitude, or uttering some wild cry of bliss. A more heart-broken thing than Clara Clayton for the last few days at the theatre could not well be seen!

Her Ianthe had made a hit and had a run. Night after night it was produced. At first it had been played three times only in the week; now it was given every night—lately as an afterpiece.

How Clara loathed that character! It had been always a poor sketch which her enthusiasm and passionate poetry had filled up with rainbow lights; of itself, without this inner life, it was of no poetic value. But now, when the lamp by which she had lighted her young soul had gone out in dust and ashes, the character came before her in its true daubed lines—harsh and unlovely.

She lost all pleasure in it, and played it—I must confess the truth— very badly. The papers began to notice it as a falling off; but they spoke as yet mildly and compassionately, alluding to "recent disclosures," and "evident depression," as the cause of her failure, night after night, in producing the enthusiasm of her earlier career. Her health too gave way; and she had violent nervous attacks, like tic douloureux,[57] through her head and face: still she bore up as bravely as she could, and did her best on the stage; though in poor fashion enough.

Clara's intellect depended much on her affections. When she was happy she was a giantess; when miserable, a dwarf. Under the stimulating power of love she could undergo any amount of mental labour—she would attempt and perform the hardest task that could be set her. If kind words, praises, confident reliance, and perhaps a dear half hour of caressing affection, were to be her rewards, oh! the whole earth lay as a small pebble which she could carry in the palm of her hand! She was made what those whom she loved believed her. When

Vaughan and Percival told her that she could succeed to the utmost limit of her ambition, she felt they spoke truly; when they chid her for incapacity, that incapacity swallowed up all her former powers. Under the light of Vasty's love she could have walked fearlessly through any intellectual wilderness; deprived of it, she was a weakling that tottered in uncertain circles and advanced not. This too will clear itself in the future. She will grow out of this weakness of love when her character has gained more simple self-reliance; and then affection will be merely an auxiliary, not as now the foundation of her powers.

Thus things continued in their wretched desolation for a fortnight or so, without the smallest interim of sunshine. Her lodgings were mean; her domestic arrangements of the lowest order. She had dismissed her maid, as too expensive a luxury to be kept on her unassisted income; and the lodging-house keeper cheated her in every possible manner, as well as made her thoroughly uncomfortable by dirt and neglect.

Meat, vegetables, tea, sugar, bread, and butter, were all at famine prices; and the amount which this solitary girl, who sometimes had no dinner at all, consumed in comestibles of all kinds, was appalling. Her weekly bills were frightful; less than three pounds never covering the outlay on chops, potatoes, candles, and other things. Besides Mrs. Trimmer, the landlady, put such strange things into her dishes! Do mutton chops generally use up several shillings' worth of spices, flour, currants, and raisins? Yet she never had anything but mutton chops. How then came the extra condiments in the bill? She thought it all right but very dreadful. Her small income would hardly bear such heavy calls on it for one portion only of her yearly existence. She had stage dresses to buy, lodgings, cab-hire, and a multitude of minor contingent expenses, all to be paid for out of the paltry salary at which Vaughan had engaged her. How it was to be done without debt, in the proportion of her daily consumption, she could not imagine. Unless some kind gnome come to her assistance, I fear the poor child's chance of landing at the Queen's Bench[58] is as ninety-nine to a hundred.

She was sitting one day in her rooms after rehearsal—the rehearsal of her new part in which she tried to take so much interest and could not feel any—when a knock came to the door, and Edward Mantell was announced.

He fairly started when he saw her. Was this weary, pale, broken thing, the joyous beaming girl he had met not so long ago, whose bright eyes and brilliant blush had haunted him like a sunny landscape?

"How paint destroys the complexion!" was his first thought, explanatory of the change.

Ah! it was not paint, nor late hours, nor want of exercise, nor any of the platitudes with which people try to explain away the altered looks when the loving heart is wounded! It was sorrow in a deep concentrated shape that had thus eaten like a cancer through the freshness of her beauty, and bowed the pride of her youth so low.

She met him timidly; her cheek paling and flushing alternately. She did not know how or when he had heard of her strange history, or if at all; and when she blushed as he thought so guiltily, it was because she wondered if he had ever believed the frightful report that assigned her in vicious fashion to Vaughan.

"I am glad to see you again," said Edward Mantell. "I have had trouble in finding you, for your present address is not the same as that which you gave to me."

"No," answered Clara, "I have changed my lodgings—for some time now."

"Do you live here alone?" he asked abruptly.

"Yes," she said looking into his eyes, "quite alone."

She felt the blood gather into her face as she spoke.

"That is wrong for appearances and unwise for realities," Edward cried after a pause.

"What can I do, Mr. Mantell? I am now truly alone in the world! I have no one to live with me—I have no one that I can live with. There could not be any one more solitary in her whole life than I am; and living by myself is only one phase of my loneliness."

"Have you no female friends?"

"Not one. Miss Kemble is the only woman that I know intimately throughout the world."

"Who is Miss Kemble?"

"An actress at my theatre," she answered simply.

Edward Mantell was silent.

"Have you many male friends?" he then asked.

"None."

This was said in a tone of such melancholy that it went to the young man's heart like a reproach. The prosperous in sin are never so unhappy as that accent betokened Clare to be. And yet he had told them at Shorne that she was publicly a profligate and abandoned woman!

"Miss Clayton, will you make me your friend?" he said suddenly. "You must forget that I am still young, and look on me for my profession's sake as an old man—your adviser and your pastor. Let me speak freely with you; let me speak as to my own sister. I am deeply interested in you, not only in your temporal but in your eternal welfare which I fear—I fear much—is in awful jeopardy! Will you let me be frank to you, and will you in turn speak openly to me?"

Oh, how Clara welcomed those friendly words! Her heart opened to them as a flower to the sunshine. She leant forward, half held out her hand, a smile of something almost like happiness spread over her face, and she answered, in a voice choked with emotion.

"Oh! Mr. Mantell, if you knew how I prized the least exhibition of interest now!—if you knew how utterly lonely I felt—how set aside by all the world—how miserable—how lost—you would understand what a few words of kindness are to me! Indeed, indeed, I prize them!"

That eloquent face could not be misunderstood—that moved voice could not utter falsehoods. Edward Mantell saw the impress of truth too clearly to be deceived. His interest in her was not misplaced.

"And I may question you?" he asked, "and you will not feel offended, however strange and unconventional my questions may be?"

"No," she said with an accent that was in itself a caress. "No; you may say what you please to me. Ah! I value friendship too much now to be easily displeased! There is nothing like experience, and I—I have had bitter experience by loss of its value."

"What mean you—by loss?"

She looked down.

"I have no friends now," she said.

"Not the manager?"

"No." She blushed painfully, and tears rushed into her eyes and dropped slowly down her cheeks.

"Why have you lost him?"

"It is too long—too sad a story!" she exclaimed, covering her face.

"Tell me," said Edward Mantell in a tone of command, taking her hand forcibly from before her face. "If I am to be your friend, this confidence must first be made. You loved this man?"

She wept, and murmured something that by manner more than sound passed for "yes."

"And why did you cease to love him?—if indeed you have ceased this guilty passion!"

The girl started. Edward Mantell's voice was stern though kind; and when she looked at him in horror at the naked truth he had pronounced so ruthlessly, she saw his countenance looking down on her with such a mingled love and severity that she felt awed, humbled, and attracted, at the same moment. It was the face of an apostle denouncing the sin, but offering pardon and salvation to the repentant sinner.

"Why?" she said faintly; "because he deceived me."

"In what way did he deceive you?" again that earnest voice asked, shrinking not from the pain it was inflicting; as one who must conclude a duty.

"He was married," answered Clara. She did not shed tears when she said this. Her whole heart was chilling; growing preternaturally calm beneath this new influence.

He sat down again, for he had risen in his earnest endeavour to make her confess to him. He seemed deeply moved.

"Did you not know this from the first?" he then asked.

"No; else I should not have——"

"Loved him, do you mean?" he said, supplying the sudden pause.

"Yes," she answered sorrowfully.

"You left him when you knew it?"

"Yes."

"And have not seen him since?"

"No."

"And if he came to you—would you receive him again?"

"No."

Her colour was mounting higher and higher.

"You would not love him again?"

"No," she said much shocked and distressed.

"Did you ever expect to marry him?" asked the young man after a pause.

"I believed myself engaged, from the fact of his saying he loved me," she answered.

Edward Mantell took her hand. He wished to ask her one more question; but that innocent brow, with its sorrow and its love, made him hesitate before he offered her so gross an insult or woke up such unavailing remorse. For one or the other effect that question must have. Anxiously, earnestly he gazed into her face; then dropping her hand he said, not knowing that he thus thought aloud—

"I *will* trust her. She must be innocent!"

For a moment Clara remained silent; then asked in a low voice very calmly; "Have you heard anything of me, Mr. Mantell?—I mean anything against me about Mr. Vaughan?"

"I have," said Edward.

"You believe it?"

She held her breath for his answer.

"I did."

"But now?" she said impetuously.

"I do not, Clara Clayton. I believe you pure as a sleeping babe."

His voice was solemn; his manner impressive.

"Thank God!" she exclaimed passionately. "Thank God I am not yet so far lost in the minds of all the good!"

"Bless you for that word!" cried Edward. "Of the good? Oh! then you feel the sinfulness, the degradation, of your present life and present associates? Oh! come out from among them! Come out from that fearful pit of darkness where you lie—the chained servant of the devil—up to the blessed heights of faith and love beneath the accepting smiles of God! You are young, you are beautiful; God has given you great talents, and a heart which might be made a full vessel of holiness overflowing with the blessed measure of grace bestowed. But never while you are in the position that you hold now—never while you breathe the air poisoned by the pestilent breath of vice, and pass through the world linked with the crowd of Satan's emissaries! Think of your eternal soul! Think, that if you died to-night, you would have for your everlasting portion the worm that dieth not and the fire that is never quenched; that you have betrayed the Saviour who gave himself for you, and gone over publicly to the army of his enemies; that you have perjured yourself in your baptismal vow; that you have ceased to belong to God, and have become the sole property of the devil! Oh, if I could draw in palpable shape the state of your soul, how you would shrink in horror at the frightful picture! In the claws of the demon—a charnel-house of dead men's bones, of rottenness and corruption—yourself working deeds of iniquity unspeakable—while you see a phantasm of glorious shape scattering flowers in your way and luring you on to the dignity of fame! Luring you on to the edge of the precipice from whence you will be cast down—torn, mangled, dead—the prey of the devil and all his angels!"

His voice rose to a loud melancholy wail. As he stood in the darkening winter twilight, his hand stretched forth, his eyes burning through the gloom with the fire of his fanatic faith, Clara felt as though the spirit of divine wrath had taken visible shape and come forth to claim her.

Her heart beating, her knees knocking together with terror, her weakened nerves subdued, she listened to his denunciations as though he had been something more than man—the accredited arbiter of her eternal condition.

"You are silent!" he then said. "Are you touched? Do you feel as if the lamp of love and grace could be trimmed for you also, as if you could cling to the cross, and forsaking all else give yourself up to the service of the Saviour? If so, rejoice with me my sister, for God is speaking in your spirit; and provided you give heed to what he says, and quench not the holy breath, you may yet be numbered among the elect! Oh! remember how short a time this life is!—how soon the very highest of us all must fall! And then remember that in this short time we work out our salvation or consign ourselves to damnation irretrievable! No after time of repentance is allowed us. As the tree falls so it must lie. Blessed are all those whose tree falls sound in heart and full of fruit! There is but one way in which to cure the wounds which sin has made in the whole life of the earth; from the cross alone flow the waters of healing. They who believe in their efficacy will be saved; they who believe not will be damned. There is no alternative here! A plain distinct truth is enunciated which admits of no cavilling. Faith, and faith alone, will change our corrupt tree of death into a goodly fruit-tree bearing much fruit; faith, and faith alone, will give to us also the waters of healing and bind up the open sores of sin. This is no trifling matter I have presented to you; no common subject. It is one you must think of—one that you must pray for strength to be able to continue; and so work out your salvation with fear and trembling and by the power of faith. Will you read some books on this subject if I give them to you?"

"Yes," she answered timidly.

"And you will promise me to read them carefully?"

"Yes, indeed I will!"

"That is well! And oh! if you could but be brought to see the fearful danger of your present state!—how near you are to the edge of the pit—how great is your eternal peril—how sinful your life!—if you could but be brought to see the enormity of your ways as clearly as I see it, how thankful should I be to the great goodness of Providence that threw me in your path—an humble instrument of such exceeding good!"

He took her hand.

"Dear sister, you will endeavour after this faith which you have not now?"

"Yes," said Clara, interrupting him, very eagerly and innocently; "Yes, but I have faith! I do believe in the Bible and all it says. I am very bad, but not so bad as to be an atheist!"

"Ah, my child!" said Edward Mantell sorrowfully; "that speech, more than anything you have said, shows the unconverted state of your mind. You think a bare profession of belief is faith? Oh no! faith is the living principle by which a man feels his election sure—faith is the power by which a man leaves this world and all it contains for the cross and its sharp afflictions, yet feels that exchange to be a gain— faith is the consciousness that cannot err of a oneness with God— that while in life we are sanctified by the Spirit and the Blood—and from vessels of wrath, by nature doomed to damnation, are made vessels of divine grace, by faith exalted up to heaven. Naturally we all—all without exception—from the naked new-born child first wakened to the day, to the gray bearded sage whose life has been a series of practical moralities—all groan in the bondage of sin; and nothing but faith can loose that bondage. Deeds are nothing, Clara. Humanity is steeped in wickedness. The first breath that we draw is one of pollution; and the best act that we perform, if done without faith, is redoubled iniquity. It is of no use to point to intentions in our maturity, or to ignorance in our childhood. These are the excuses of the unregenerate man. The regenerate—he who is wise by the wisdom of the Spirit—knows that both are alike the offspring of sin; that the whole life of the earth is one of iniquity; and that all we do or say or think under any guise whatsoever is deformed and distorted by the same evil influence. Death, death and damnation are over all in the world; behold the cross—at the foot of this alone can you escape these fearful lords of earth!"

Clara shuddered. Would this mournful wail never cease? Was its frightful doctrine true? Was it really true that this whole beautiful earth, with its glories and its pleasures, belonged only to the antagonistic power, and that God was thus divorced from his own work?

She did not think these words in so accurate order; but a dreamy consciousness that this condemnatory doctrine was not the sole truth of creation, kept her from the abject spiritual terror which else would have fallen on her.

"You do not understand me fully yet," then said the young preacher in a mournful voice, "but you will soon know better what I say. I have hopes of you. You have only to give earnest heed to the divine intention that I see struggling in your soul against all the arts and wiles of Satan, and I shall count you yet among the bright band of sisters in heaven! I will send you the books I spoke of, and you will read them very carefully—those passages that I have marked the most carefully—and when I see you again I will question you about them, and explain what you may not understand."

"Thank you," said Clara, speaking very sweetly, but with a novel feeling at this youthful patronage. It would have been a feeling of pride in one less affectionate and less lonesome.

The clock struck six.

"It is time for me to go," she said rising; "My piece comes on the first to-night. I have some distance to go now; and I am rather late."

He groaned. "Oh, when will this fiery pit be left!" he exclaimed in a tone of deepest sorrow.

"But am I so wicked because I am an actress?" asked Clara anxiously.

"You are lost both here and hereafter!" he answered in a denunciatory prophet-like voice. "While you suffer yourself to tread those accursed boards you are delivered over to damnation, without help or reprieve! The devil has you! You worship in his temple—you seduce others to his shrine—you cast dishonour on the God who redeemed you—and you sacrifice to the tempter who destroys you. There is no hope for you while you are an actress!"

Clara was startled. Was he right? Did he speak truths indubitable, for all that they were so abhorrent to flesh and blood, and came in such unfriendly shape and rugged language?

"And who companion with you there?" he added vehemently. "Atheists, socialists, profligates of both sexes, freethinkers and free-livers—the choicest flowers of the garden of hell! Oh! my sister, escape from their pollutions! Fly them as you would fly the tortures, the rack, and the chain; for as sure as the sting of death lies in the glittering snake, so surely does everlasting destruction lie in your present profession and in your present companions. But I will come again, and show you more plainly the frightful sin in which you are living. Till then, may God keep you, poor victim! I weep for you, Clara. I weep as for a dove in the talons of the hawk—for a hind in the claws of the lion. But you must not be left to perish. God has sent you a messenger to herald you to his courts; and in rejecting my words remember that you reject the chartered agent of heaven."

He turned from her and left her with a kind of apostolic mournfulness and yet superiority, that had a peculiar fascination for the poor child he had been seeking to convert.

Clara had not been stimulated by this long conversation to any great exertions to-night. She was wearied physically by her long lecture; and doubly chilled now in professional enthusiasm.

She played coldly—without heart or animation; and the stage-manager spoke to her very sharply more than once, and told her that she "disgraced the theatre."

Neither did the audience applaud as they were wont; and more like an automaton than a living passionate woman she crept home, bewildered, humbled, and saddened, beyond anything she had felt before.

How different was the dejection of yon pale wet cheek resting on its hard pillow, to the burning happiness of the youthful face which lifted up its glorious love like a heaven-flung banner beneath the Windsor oak! Ah! time has wrought with a greedy haste in thee, Clara! He has crumbled thy fairy palaces of hope in quicker space than with most, and dug thy young joys all too early a grave in the chill court of sorrows. Sleep, sleep, wearied heart!—thy home will not be always so far off.

CHAPTER VII.

BOOKS, frequent visits, ceaseless exhortations to repent and turn from the evil of her ways, fierce denunciations on the careless liver as well as on the open sinners, added to intense brotherly interest, and natural affections breaking through and softening down the asperities of his faith, had their due effect on Clara. Deserted by all the world— this faithful preacher her only friend—no counteracting influence weakened the growing power of Edward Mantell over her mind.

Percival, on whom she had relied so entirely, was still mysteriously and scarce kindly absent; Vaughan was a pathway-light extinguished;

Lucretia drew away timidly from the disgraced favourite, fearful
that disgrace like disease would communicate itself by contact;
the theatrical people disgusted her with their depraved and vulgar
manners; her home had shut her out; the fashionable world discarded
her; none save this brave Christian man spoke kindly to her desolate
heart! And she welcomed him as the only ray of truth and light still
left her, giving herself up to his influence with all her will, if not with
visible success.

It was a mournful faith that of Edward Mantell's; intolerant, stern,
condemnatory; the presence of evil ever blotting out the evidence of
good, and that narrow chink of protestantism, over which the spider
has spread her net, and the thick dust woven a veil, the only light in the
universal temple of religion by which to worship the Lord and Giver
of all. The terrors of damnation haunted him like a ghastly spectre;
the sinfulness of man accompanied him like a blighting pestilence;
everywhere he found the one same sad presence blurring out all traces
of beauty.

All was evil; all that we felt, did, thought, or saw—all showed the
slimy trail of the serpent, and by special revelation alone was the natural
life rendered sane and whole. Pleasure was damnation unmasked; the
prizes of earth—fame, riches, power—were so many golden balls that
lured men on to the deep chasm of hell. The very affections were
snares, snares too of wilier sort than these more palpable lures. The
mother's rapturous love over her first-born partook of idolatry, and
she was lost irredeemably unless she could feel not only resignation
but joy if its little soul were rapt away by death—for was it not God's
will?—the sister's fond faith in that other half of her life, without whom
she would not contemplate an existence as possible, was dangerous,
stealing the heart from higher things; the blessedness of a happy
marriage, that complement of all natural desires, was a favourite device
of Satan to bind souls to his service and the earth; and nought was
holy save the stern faith which cuts man off from every joy and every
love of humanity, and gives him only the cold tomb for his gateway
unto happiness. The sciences were well nigh blasphemous; the love
of nature was an idolatrous transfer from the rights of revelation; the
belief of internal holiness, of progression by eternal law, of man's own
power of good—were all so many clauses in the creed of devils; and he
alone could be saved who buried all of nature in the grave of sin, and
planted the cross above that grave as the sole resource for mankind.

It was a teaching ill-suited to a girl whose whole being was made up of passions, affections, and sensations: whose divinest pleasures sprang from material sources, and whose intensest sorrows had birth only in her wounded loves. A purely spiritual grief she had never yet experienced. She was too young for that. Her feelings and instincts must first be fully expanded and used before the later world of spiritualism can be opened to her.

What then was the effect of these doctrines on her? As yet but the imperfect *endeavour* to believe—the attempt to constrain her mind into a shape unsuited to it;—but no hearty reception of a faith to which by nature she was inclined—no fitting mental result of her physical formation.

Edward Mantell had one strong argument for the truth of his religious ideas—the unworthiness of most of Clare's associates. Vasty's character he painted in frightful colours; refusing him the smallest redeeming trait. Where, among the elect, could be found such treachery, such cruelty, such heartlessness?—where, among men animated by the vital faith of Christianity, such open defiance of the first principles of morality? The want of that faith, Edward Mantell said, was the sole cause of Vaughan's evil deeds. He gave no force to natural temperament—no power to accidental circumstances. The presence of a mental idea, he insisted, would have controlled the strongest combination that organization and temptation could have formed together.

And Lucretia—would a Christian matron have shrunk in servile fear from the side of an unprotected girl? Would she not rather have thrown over her the broad blessing of her maternal guardianship, purified by the creed of the Redemption, and have protected her the more carefully because others despised? See, too, how the gay world— those painted pages of the Devil's court, as he used to call them—had turned against her! Not because she had lost her reputation. While she possessed social advantages *this* was overlooked. But simply because she had lost the *prestige* of birth and fortune, and such romance in her history as the morality of society could endorse. The church— the little band of the faithful—would have rallied all the closer round her. They would have guarded her in such sacred ranks of love that disgrace and sorrow could not have found her there, to hunt her from among them. Oh! that she would come out from that rank world of corruption wherein she now dwelt, and shelter in the Ark where alone salvation rested!

And Percival—when she mentioned his name with lingering accents, and with sorrowful endeavours to trust in him, and to be convinced that some good cause must have kept him from her—what was this Percival—this freethinker—this accursed socialist—this ambassador of Satan let loose on the earth for men's eternal woe? A wordy windbag—a very thistledown of faithfulness! What friendship he had professed!—what a wealth of words he had wasted!—and now, when this friendship would have been so useful, so dear, had he not left her in the solitude he had helped to make, nor paid her even the civilities of ordinary society?

Could she not read in this opened scroll that he spread out before her, the folly of resting her love on such brittle reeds as would break and pierce her hand while she leant on them?—the sin of casting in her lot with such smoking flax,[59] ready for the eternal fires?

Clara listened, trembled, and believed, while his words rushed on like a boiling torrent sweeping down the foundations of the earth; but when he was gone, and the voice was silent, and her own heart spoke up in whispered denial, she shrank from this dreary faith as from a form of death with which life could not companion; and remembering her early girlhood when nature gave her such enjoyment, instinct more than reason convinced her, against all the fervent eloquence of her friend, that Nature was good, and that man was not born in sin—the heir of condemnation for eternity. For this steadfastness she may thank her large heart and the very power of passion and sensation against which that preacher flung his heaviest curse. Without this consolidating power, and with her energy and imagination, I know not into what frightful quagmire of spiritual fanaticism and mental depression she would have ultimately sunk.

But notwithstanding their different minds, the girl used to look for his coming anxiously; and the brightest hour of the day to him was that wherein he strove to convert to his gloomy views this young thing of vivid life, formed by nature to be canopied by sunlight only. Clara believed sincerely that her pleasure at his presence arose from a holier state of mind; he, that his feverish anticipations of this daily visit, from his zeal in the labour of the vineyard. They deceived themselves in no small degree: a little plain-spoken philosophy would have put them both right.

Edward Mantell had taken up this case heartily. Something about Clara, both in her character and her position, touched him deeply. Her affectionate gentleness won upon his admiration; in no otherwise—of this he was sure—than as fitting ground for the reception of the good seed. Her beauty charmed his eye; but then chiefly for the thought how fair a present he should be the means of bringing to the temple. Her powers of mind enchained his attention and commanded his respect; but not for themselves. No: while, as now, dedicated to the service of sin, they were only so many more causes of sorrow for her state. But when they should be devoted to the glad service of heavenly righteousness, they would then, and then only, do their appointed work and be of real value; then, and then only, should he love them without fear. Now, he viewed them with a prospective appreciation alone; rejoicing in them as engines rather than as possessions of good.

It was a glorious beginning to his sacred mission. To call out this lost lamb from the flock of goats among which she herded, feeding on the food of death, was no mean initiative to his future profession of saving souls!

He believed in all this. Self-deceived, but sincere, he was as firm in his faith—narrow, gloomy, intolerant, as it was—as Percival was in his. He believed himself GOD's echo on earth; working out the Divine Law in his fierce anathemas against all men not holding the same express articles of creed with himself—even against different sections of the same temple. But the law of love he ignored in all its wide conditions, reserving it only for that small band of the elect who held his principle, that faith alone gives salvation to men.

Percival, on the other hand, believed in the law of universal progress; in the internal energy of man's mind; in the power of humanity, under development, of effecting all things; in the fixity, eternity, and universality of the laws by which physical and moral results are worked; and in the consequent negation of special creation and special providence.

This, joined to the untiring practice of charity, was his belief; but Edward Mantell named it heresy—atheism—the belief that led to hell—the belief accursed by Heaven.

Clara's room presented a strange medley at the present time. Religious books, all of an inflammatory and highly spiritual character, were scattered about among dirty copies of "parts;" stage adjuncts; here and there a book on farming, gardening, botany, or farriery; here and there a print of a prize terrier, or the winner of the Derby; pots of rouge, in various stages of consumption; a mass of spangles, paste pearls, and other habilitatory[60] falsehoods, which would have sent a genuine artist hopelessly mad. In the midst a bunch of winter flowers reared their pale heads; or a handful of laurel, of holly thick with red berries, of ivy, laurustinus,[61] or anything green and shining that she could procure, cast a mock freshness round; while a dish of grapes, more for show than pleasure, or a yellow and very sour-looking orange, threw in a bit of colour and a dash of sunlight. It was a strange mixture altogether.

But the inflamed spiritual books were read carefully—perhaps while the very rouge was applying; and more than one page was blotted with the grieving tears of a self-convicted sinner, while the trembling hands had been fastening on the last ornament of her theatrical pomp.

Did she ever think of Vaughan now? Sometimes with abhorrence, or what she tried to stiffen into such; but it was a limp hatred anyhow, and fell sadly out of shape; sometimes so sadly as to take the form of a pining and a nameless grief; not so bold as to be a living wish, and yet not so craven as to be put to death by the chill breath of absence.

He might have been dead for all she heard or saw of him. She never heard his name, even from the actors: she never saw him at the theatre, at rehearsals, or in the evening. If he was there, he kept out of her sight entirely. Her performances went on in the new order. The "Greek Wife" was made an afterpiece, and played every night; and the stage manager sent his commands without the shadow of courteousness in their framing. The people about the theatre grew more and more insolent in manner. Many of the very second-rate men—men who wear decayed garments, and smell of smoke and beer—had made open love to her; and when she repulsed them, had muttered something about goods at second-hand not fetching first prices. Some of the gentlemen too, who had the entrée,[62] had spoken to her in a way more undisguised than desirable. A lonely, pretty, youthful woman—she was fair game to our honourable countrymen; and no stratagem would have been unlawful which could have secured so shy a bird.

Where was Vaughan? Day by day she asked herself this question. Day by day she wondered, as she wandered to the hateful theatre, whether she should see him there or not. And though the thought of meeting him had much of terror in it, it had also something of longing. She felt as if she could rest better satisfied if she might but see him once again. Not in love. No; she was fully secure now in her abhorrence of his sin—in her proud disdain of his unworthiness—in her firm reliance on her faith. No; she longed to see him, but not because she loved him; rather that she might plainly and distinctly renounce him for ever.

It was a dangerous experiment, yet still she wished to try it. So strange, so wayward, so inexplicable is a woman's heart to all those who possess not its key.

Where was Vaughan? She would sit by the small window of her shabby parlour, and gaze through the blind for hours. She was not looking for him; she was not even thinking of him; but how strangely like him, in walk and height and general appearance, was every man at any distance! She could not understand how like to Vasty Vaughan the whole adult male population had become. Though, indeed, when they came nearer she saw how much she had been mistaken; and then she laughed at her imagination, which had made her heart beat so with fear. I never heard that Clara was short-sighted, but undoubtedly her power of vision was not of the most accurate description.

Edward Mantell's last awakening book on her knee; tears of contrition—at least, she thought they were so—in her eyes; desolation busy in her heart, gnawing side by side with disappointment; thus by that small window she would sit and gaze on the wintry sky and streaming streets, the most melancholy and unsatisfied thing in London.

Percival away—Vaughan worse than dead—and the wild anathemas of a faith wholly antagonistic with nature thundering in her ears—she had not much likeness with the saucy girl we saw, four years ago, dash down the hill so recklessly. The young sapling in its first robe of green, and the blasted tree shivered by lightning, are not less alike than the Clare de Saumarez then with the Clara Clayton now.

CHAPTER VIII.

A MONTH had passed. To-night the new play was to appear. Clara was the heroine and the whole weight of the drama rested on her part.

How she dreamed over again the burning hours of her first

appearance on that dazzling stage! How she recalled the faintest
circumstances with such minute remembrance that each instant of
yon time stood out in isolated form, with glorious halos round it! How
she brought back every feeling in such distinctness of memory that
her head swam with dizzy rapture at but the second and the fainter
arc in her heaven of sensation! How she wept at the grey twilight of
the present which had followed so soon on the brilliant sunrise of the
past! The day of her triumph how short—the sunset of her happiness
how rapid!

Her head lay on the opened book. Her feverish forehead was
pressed against its leaves. She had forgotten all the actual life
surrounding her for the maddening pleasures of that remembered
past: she heard no step through her darkening chamber; she heard no
voice calling her by name; nor counted the thick gasps of the heart
beating loud and near. She knew nothing till a hand touched her
shoulder; when, starting up with nervous dread, her eyes fell on Vasty
Vaughan standing mournfully before her.

Her first impulse was to rush into his arms—forgetting all the
strong barriers of pride and virtue that kept her back. Nay, she had
sobbed forth his name in accents too full of passion to be mistaken;
she had taken one eager step towards him; her burning hand had
fallen on his arm outstretched to receive her; when the truth came
blinding back on her loving eyes, and smote them down to earth again
in agony and shame.

"Married! married!" she murmured, turning away and hiding her
face within her hands.

How changed they both were! Vaughan's hair was perceptibly
whiter, and on his face was carved many a deep hard line which had not
been there when she last looked upon it. He seemed to have lived years
since they had met; as if a blight of perpetual sorrow had passed over
his inmost soul. And she—pale, trembling, depressed beyond the power
of language to portray—her glorious beauty saddened—her brave
young spirit broken—her love, her poetry, her enthusiasm quenched—
the very ghost of her former self she appeared to him, as she turned
away from the mocking waters which had once baptized her into such
blessedness, and broke their spell by the harsh talisman of truth.

"Clara! hear me!" said Vaughan slowly. His very voice was altered.

"No! no!" she exclaimed, shaking her head mournfully. "No; it is
best not!—nothing is to be done!—No! leave me!"

Her excessive agitation calmed him.

"I have a right to demand a fair hearing, Clara," he said with an accent of reproach. "It has been denied me hitherto—harshly and unjustly. You have rejected me on one-sided evidence alone—you have never suffered me to plead my cause against my enemies. Is this fair?—is it kind or just?"

"What can you say?" she exclaimed, strongly agitated. "The fact is the same, and you do not deny *that!*"

"But may I not perhaps modify it?" he asked mournfully, bending on her eyes strangely troubled.

"What, your marriage?—Ah! no explanations can modify that stern truth! No reasons can change the fact! Of what good are they then?"

She spoke in the wailing voice of one lamenting the dead. Her thin hands plucked nervously at the leaves of the sickly chrysanthemum she held; her white lips muttered words, meaningless and low; her head drooped forward on her breast, as she stood in her painful wreck of passion and of hope.

"Clara," then said Vaughan, coming nearer to her, and speaking very calmly. "I need not tell you how much I loved you. A better acquaintance with men in general—especially with those who have led such a reckless life as mine has been—will show you how true and deep must have been my affection for you—how more than the mere fancy it might seem—that I should have so saved you from myself when most in my power. I loved you, Clara, as I never loved before. Instead of the mere plaything, which too often the mindless toys I have gathered round me have been, I loved you truly, devotedly, unchangeably, and with oh! how much more of purity than I believed myself capable of feeling! Clara, you called up what wasted remains of virtue were left within my heart, as waters dug in the desert by the feet of angels; you made me better, bringing back the freshness of days long past, when love was indeed salvation from the scorching fire of the world. My very being hung on you—my best feelings twined round your affection for me—my whole soul was in your keeping. Clara! an unhappy fate has long marked me out for sorrow, and for such disgrace as can fall on me collaterally from the evil deeds of another. With you I forgot that sorrow, and felt the disgrace wiped off. Oh! this is vain pedantry!" he then cried, suddenly changing his manner, which until now had been collected and calm, to one of most passionate excitement. "Clara, I love you now more madly, more entirely, than before! I cannot live without you! Life is worse than death to me! For four long weeks—weeks that have been years, Clara, I have struggled against this love. I knew its madness—feared its vanity. I have battled with the passion which wrought me misery unspeakable and poured fever through my veins like fire. I have resolved to be calm—to forget you—to forget one whose love for me was so cold, so scant, as to yield at the first breath of accusation—under the first small knowledge of frailty! Frailty rather than sinfulness!" he added passionately. "But no, it cannot be!—it cannot be that you have repulsed me for ever from the gates of heaven!—Clara! Clara! this is madness—it is death! Kill me at once rather than desert me, now when you have crept in among the roots of my being. Clara, dear, best beloved Clara, kill me with your own hand—or love me as you once loved!"

He came still nearer to her, and in his fervid way threw his arms about her.

Almost shrieking with sudden pain, she tore herself away, and crouched into a corner of the sofa.

Vaughan's brow grew dark.

"Not one embrace—such as you would give a father—a brother?" he said moodily.

"No! no!" she cried, raising her hand as if to repel him—"not one to you!"

He flung himself at her feet.

"Clara, look at me!—look at me once again!—By the love I gave you, when you first dawned on my sight—by the love I feel for you now, eating into my heart like a famished wolf that nothing stays—by the love you felt for me, dearest, dearest Clare, I beseech you for one look only—one such look as you gave me Clare, when you first told me that you loved me! Oh! remember that hour, that moment! Call again to you the golden sunshine that hallowed our affection—the hidden nightingale that hymned those words of union! Can you forget all the past, with its rich stores of hope and memory—its boundless treasures of love—for one small flaw, one little flaw, which from love alone I could not bear to show you?"

Clara did not speak. Between her consciousness of wrong and her love, she was undergoing a frightful struggle. All the sign of life she gave was a convulsive quivering of her limbs, and now and then a low faint moan, as one who suffers torture.

Such evidence as this emboldened Vaughan to more than hope. A light smile played round his lips and gleamed in his eyes; and he said to himself, "I have conquered! She is mine now! I thought she could not resist me if I bided my time!"

Is there such a thing as spiritual transmission of thought?—or what then sank cold and chill on Clare's heart and stilled its turbid passion?

"Oh, Clara! cease this unnatural separation!" he continued, still kneeling, "cease these unnatural fancies! Come to him whose life you alone make perfect, and without whom you yourself, Clara, are solitary and lone. Come to me!—to this heart that will never betray nor desert you! Do you not think that nature gives more sanctifying power to love than men can give? Do you not think that a marriage, such as ours, would be more pure and holy than those which depend on the mere ceremony for their rite of purification? My love! what argument can I use to chase away doubts that obscure your better reason!—what can I say—or how can I show the gross ignorance and prejudice with which you are rejecting happiness and choosing misery in its stead! Come, come!" he added, taking her hand, "this trial has lasted long enough with us both—it is time to end it; and end it in such blessedness as we shall appreciate better for this long apprenticeship of desolation. What misery is about you here! It breaks my heart to see the wretchedness in which you have lived; the wretchedness in every form which has come on you since you broke from my care. Come, dearest love—dear Clare—dear *wife!* Your home has been too long empty! you must return to it, and never leave it again!"

What, during this speech, had so strangely calmed our Clara? Why did she no longer tremble—no longer lose her power of self-control in the tumult of excited hopes and fears? Whether Vasty's voice had a tone that spoke of victory secure—or whether, by some spiritual magnetism, this conviction of his roused her pride—may not be said. It might be that fear of the results, if she yielded thus helplessly, woke up shame and virtue to do battle with her weak compliance: it might be that she was in truth no longer mastered by the passion which seemed to hold her its slave, and that this excessive agitation had more of memory than of present love in it: of this no one could speak. All that could be seen was her gentle face gradually calming as a lake when the wind falls off, and her soft eyes looking clear from beneath their brows, as stars through a rent cloud. How Vasty cursed that steady manner!—how chill it blew on his fervid passion!—how dark it showed in the light of his fierce love!

She rose from the sofa; and, as he had besought her, looked him fairly in the eyes. Though very pale, and still retaining much modesty, almost timidity, of expression, there was a sad collected air about her that destroyed his hopes at once. She gazed down on his face, with all its love burning like a torch-light out from a spirit in which he had no part; that his influence had passed from her soul for ever.

He was right. It had gone. Substantively her love had long since died—died when she knew him unworthy. Born of instinct and of fancy, it had struck in no deeper ground, fed on no higher food. True, its birth was of mighty parents—controllers of a universe; but something stronger even than they had been lately crowned within her, and the giants were in turn overthrown.

"No, Vasty," she said, looking firmly into his burning eyes; "I may not do such a sin as this. I did love you. But it has gone. You deceived me; and I was roughly but entirely awakened from the most delicious dream I can ever know. It is over now, and we are both free—but no longer lovers; friends for life I hope, Vasty—but nothing more."

"You reject me then!" he cried angrily, springing to his feet.

"Reject you? I have not the power to reject a married man," she answered in some surprise.

"Pshaw! What maudlin folly is this, Clare?" he cried, something of his old coarseness returning. "Can you not love except by licence! What old woman's stuff have you been hearing lately?"

"I cannot love except by the licence of virtue, Vasty."

"Virtue!—a word for the nursery—an exploded fable of the olden times! Virtue! Can priests and churches make it; or did not nature and instinct first?"

His manner was no temptation to Clare to recognise the truth which might lie within this creed. True or false, she felt that he had adopted it only because of its convenience; not because of its reality.

"It may be so, Vasty; but I have been brought up differently; and I cannot love a man when the very name itself seems a shameful crime. Oh! let this end!" she added earnestly. "We are separated now, Vasty, and for ever! It has been a pang—to you as well as to myself; at least I believe so. To me it is like an ever-present death—a thing that I can scarcely yet live with. But it must be borne—even to the heavy aching of the heart, the weary faintness of the brain! Do not condemn me as cold or inconstant. I am neither. My heart is weaker than my belief, and struggles against the decision I am forced to make."

Vaughan was silent; looking gloomily on the floor.

She laid her hand on his arm.

"We are friends, Vasty?" she said pleadingly.

He let it lie there, taking a savage pleasure in the consciousness that he could yet wound her—that he could yet refuse.

"Is this your answer?" he then said, turning full upon her, and speaking with clenched teeth and a frightful concentration of manner.

"It is," she answered.

"And for one indiscretion—one small fault—you can forget the long days of love and mutual confidence that we passed? You can pay back such heavy retribution for a trifling wrong, but pass by the claims of untired affection and unchilled devotion?"

"I must not commit a crime, even for gratitude!" said poor Clare, her heart dying within her.

"And is it a crime to love, Clara?"

"A married man? Yes, yes!—one most grievous!—one disallowed by religion, by society, by morality! Oh, the very thought is frightful!" she cried hiding her face. But through the delicate fingers might be seen the deep crimson blush that shame brought over her brow, staining it like an evening sky.

"Can nothing soften this fanatic creed of yours? Am I then distinctly answered?"

"You are," she said softly.

"And this is to be our last interview?"

"No, not our last!" she interrupted him earnestly.

"The last time," he continued, not heeding her remark, "that we, such firm fast lovers for so many months, speak that dear word between us?—the last time that we tread the glorious world where we made our home and found our joy? Henceforth we must track the grey shadow of a past blessedness, and warm ourselves at the reflection of a distant fire only!"

"Yes, Vaughan. It would be better for us both that all thought of love should be buried between us. It would only distress you to ask and me to refuse again," Clara said simply.

This touched the manager's pride.

"Me to ask again!" he repeated with a scornful laugh. "That will never happen, Clara, while the earth holds Vasty Vaughan on its surface! I only want to understand distinctly, and without the possibility of a mistake—do you absolutely and unequivocally reject me as your lover from this moment for the whole of the future? This is my last sole question."

He looked anxious and disturbed.

"I do—I must," said Clara firmly.

"Then all is over!" he said turning from her and speaking through his teeth. "All is over—so strangely, so unforseen! What lies these angel faces tell! What might of love and depth of passion—what earnestness of thought and womanly abandonment to her affections—I believed to read in her face! The cloudless sky was not less prophetic of a storm than those deep eyes of such shameless coquetry and stony cruelty! Well, nature joins the devil in deceiving man! Then it is all over," he continued, addressing her; "and we part for ever. But you have not done wisely for yourself, Clara Clayton, in thus heroically sacrificing your love to that sickly shade you call virtue! You say we are to be friends? No! no! Vasty Vaughan receives no beggar's dole, when denied the lawful possession he deserves! Perhaps, when you have learned what is the rage of a rejected lover, you will repent a folly that no repentance can repair. It will be too late then—too late then!"

Shocked to part from him thus, Clara held out her hand.

He looked first on the hand and then into her face. He half raised his own hand. Had he used it, he would have struck her; but, with a short laugh and a contemptuous epithet, he turned on his heel and left her.

Clara sat down to reflect on the past scene.

She had now tested her religious sincerity. How she thanked Edward Mantell for thus interposing the adamant of his faith between her and this fiery enemy of her soul! She could scarcely draw out a clear image from the chaos of her feelings; but over all the confusion reigning there she felt conscious of one—a deep and sacred thankfulness to her young Christian friend.

Yet much of that gratitude which she gave to Edward Mantell was due to the natural progress of her character, already advanced beyond the purely instinctive form of girlhood in which she had hitherto lived. For thoughts, and modes of reflection, and moral and mental views, are, in our first years, the result of such instincts as we have in greatest force; though people who pride themselves on their spirituality—not knowing what they mean—would be shocked to believe this. Clara's rejection of Vaughan was due also somewhat to offended womanly pride—somewhat to outraged womanly delicacy, and to the faint footsteps of undeveloped antagonism to a tyranny unsuited to her nature. All these were the real causes why she passed through that fiery ordeal so well; and her religious ideas helped to establish only, they did not compose, the whole works of defence.

It has been said that the new play was to appear this evening. Clare had tried hard to like her character—harder still to imbue it with some of the fire of her own nature, and to make it both delicate and forcible. And though chilled and cramped by the unceasing anathemas of Edward Mantell against her studies, her profession, her success, and all connected with her stage career, for the last few days she had succeeded in her embodiment better than she had dared to hope. She trusted now to the excitement of the moment for her further inspiration; and she went down to the theatre calmer and stronger, notwithstanding the late scene, than she had been for a long time.

I cannot explain why this positive renunciation of Vasty should have made her thus calmer; yet I can understand its possibility.

Vaughan was at the theatre to-night; for the first time since his duel with Percival. That duel by-the-bye had been kept so secret that no one had ever heard of it.

Clara met him with a courage that startled even herself. Though her heart beat fast, it neither blinded her eyes nor checked her breath, as in general. Whatever she felt she showed little in her face and less in her manners; and many of the by-standers said scornfully, "What a thorough humbug that little Clayton is!"

The manager took no notice of her salute as she passed him; but when she had gone a few steps, he called her by her name roughly—

"Miss Clayton, you are wanted here!"

She came back and bowed slightly. She was very pale now, and looked timid and distressed.

Little Miss Gray, with an arch smile on her lips—Lucretia, studiously avoiding that pale face, though herself so fidgetty and disturbed—the stage manager—and one or two more, redolent of tobacco and antiquated garments—were standing near.

"You will not play Violet to-night," said Vasty in a loud voice.

Violet was the name of her part in the new play.

She bowed. "Very well," she said quietly.

Had he not been so rough and rude in his manner, she would have felt more. As it was she was piqued, and so gained a factitious strength. She would have retreated.

"Stay!" he cried; "I have not done with you yet. Miss Gray plays Violet, and you are not wanted at the theatre at all!"

For a moment she knew that she staggered as if she had been struck, and that her hand wandered up to her eyes to clear off the thick mist which had suddenly come over them. But she recollected herself, and stood perfectly still and apparently composed.

The actors and actresses all preserved a dead silence. Nothing, but the careful steps of many hurrying forward to witness the late favourite's public disgrace, was heard through the noise of the carpenters and scene-shifters.

She felt that a fracas was expected, and she determined to be the high-bred gentlewoman, self-possessed, calm, and passionless. And this was the most difficult character of all for Clara to sustain.

"Do you know the part perfectly?" she asked, turning to the little *nez retroussé* and speaking very calmly.

"That is not your business, Miss Clayton!" cried Vaughan. "I beg that you will confine yourself to your own studies, which, from all I hear, are more than you can perform creditably. I shall be obliged also if you will not interfere with my arrangements. In three nights' time you play Susan in the present play. Now you may go. But stay," he added, as if a new idea had struck him; "on second thoughts you must not go to-night. You may be wanted for some business of the house. Go down to the green-room, and wait for your orders."

Susan, it must be remarked, was not even a character. She was a servant who came in during one scene, said two sentences, and then passed off to the shades below, to emerge no more from their inky depths. It was a part properly given to the very lowest of the supernumeraries.

Clara felt great and proud and independent in her disgrace, to an extent which dried up all tears of love, and choked back all sighs of sorrow. It was a mental tonic to her; bracing her heart and mind, if with bitter yet with most wholesome medicine. She looked calmly at Vaughan, and said with a steady voice and unshaken equanimity:

"I shall be ready when I am called upon."

She made Vasty bite his lip with vexation, when she passed him so haughtily, though she was so pale and thin and shrunken, and forced him to feel that his revenge had not blasted the young head whereon it had lighted—it had not shivered the brave heart over which it had passed. Vaughan believed that he understood Clare's character. He understood it as little as he knew the language of angels! He had known her only as a loving, passionate, dependent child; he has to learn her as yet as an honourable, proud, self-sustained woman. He had known her only when prostrate by her affections; he will scarce recognise her when he meets her face to face—great in her native dignity. A harsh word—a cold look—a frown—the angry silence of a moment from her lover, went nigh to break her heart: from her enemy and her social master she could bear unbroken the fiercest storm of degradation and contempt. This was what Vaughan did not understand; and this was what so staggers him now.

Clare went down and sat in the green-room very quietly. She took up a book that she had brought with her, and read to her own satisfaction and the uncontrollable annoyance of the manager. Nor did she wince, even when she heard the actor deputed to that duty go forward on the stage, and tell the disappointed public that "sudden and alarming indisposition prevented Miss Clayton's appearing that night in the character of Violet, but that Miss Gray had kindly undertaken the part at the shortest notice." (She had been studying it for a long time past at Vasty's suggestion.)

She bore it all like a heroine. And though she was avoided by the whole troupe—Lucretia herself at their head—as that wretched thing a disgraced favourite, she sat like a sea-bird on the waves, borne always up and never submerged; in the midst of spray and foam and furious billows, not a feather wetted to the sight.

Under her affections she was a weak frail bud which the hand could crush to powder—under her pride she was a crystal sphere which no force could break, no mist could dim. But few people comprehended these two points of her nature. To one this was most apparent—to another that: to scarce any were both manifest in their whole strength and comprehensiveness. And therefore were so many mistakes made in popular judgment on her nature.

CHAPTER IX.

PERCIVAL GLYNN was not a fashionable man. Indeed few people were less imbued with the animus of caste than he. Consequently he did not care to make himself very wretched and practically disreputable for the sake of keeping up conventional appearances. Amongst other things, he did not care to establish himself in the heart of dingy and uncomfortable streets—often too of questionable vicinity—because they made up a fashionable quarter. Indeed, having but a very small income, and finding more pleasure in generosity than in personal luxuries, he was obliged to be as economical in his domiciliary position as in his other domiciliary arrangements. He did not consider it indispensable to respectability to spend a large sum on a mere name at the corner of the street.

This preamble is apologetic as well as explanatory—a kind of outrider to the crowning sin of all his social misdemeanours—namely, that he lived in Islington. It is a startling truth; and but a bad letter of recommendation for the poor, reserved, unlovely, and heterodox Percival Glynn.

However, in Islington Percival did really live. In one of those long long terraces, where every house is a lodging-house, and where they are so exactly alike—such true architectural twins—that the numbers only distinguish one from the other. Perhaps though the colour of the curtains or the style of the blinds may be dissimilar. In these terraces every house has its little light iron balcony; every balcony its pots of flowers—geraniums chiefly, musk plants, and mignonette. Some may attempt a sweetbrier or a dwarf rose; but these soon die, or become such floral caricatures—such very monomaniacs of nature—that they lose every characteristic of their tribe. In such houses as these there is an area, so dark and deep and narrow, that we shudder at the idea of what the kitchen underneath must be. We know without positive demonstration that armies of black beetles, red ants, and other voracious parasites keep their sabbaths there. We hear imaginary footsteps scrunching imaginary legions; and we think of the cooking—and keep awful silence.

These houses, and others like unto them, are horribly deceptive. Enter one, in your search for temporary lodgings, and probably you are charmed beyond words with the white curtains, the spotless sheets, the fair toilet-covers. You rejoice in the anticipation of rustic cleanliness. You riot in the prospective pleasure of lavender-scented linen, with perhaps a dried rose-leaf found in the heart of a fold. You think how cleverly you have combined the town advantages of cab and omnibus close at your door, with the rural delights—unheard-of in the city—of fresh air, clean linen sweet-smelling and newly washed, of a valetudinarian garden and a soot-laden vine. Rashly—most rashly—you engage these seductive lodgings for a week certain; "and for a contingent permanency," you add in a soft voice to the landlady. Nay, if you are extremely impulsive, you take them by the month— or, if rather insane, by the quarter—without trial. You send up your worldly goods, arrange your possessions, deem yourself lucky beyond words—so cheap as the ground floor is, too! only fifteen shillings a week!—and you go to bed earlier than your usual hour, eager for the unwonted bouquet from pillow and sheet.

You go to your bed, but a population rises from theirs. If you are tolerably hardy, and can survive the onslaught and harassing skirmishes of the first week—and if you are also moderately agile in your movements and dexterous in manipulation—you may live over the term of engagement. But if you do, you will know what cheap lodgings in the suburbs mean; and provided you have an isolated fibre of charity left in you, you will pity those poor hapless wretches whose misfortune keeps them in the "desirable localities," and "genteel residences," which stretch like a mighty belt round the whole of London.

In one of these terraces, then, Percival lived. Being a quiet and sweet-tempered person, not at all irritable and a great deal too patient for prudence in his domestic arrangements, he was one of those delightful lodgers from whom landladies make their fortunes; living on their produce as rats in a farmer's granary, in a happy confusion of the possessive pronouns.

He had survived the heavy troops and the light artillery; in fact he had almost exterminated the enemy. He had even survived his landlady's cooking, and preserved a remnant of his property from her depredatory excursions. The chemist had not quite destroyed him with mistaken drugs; the nurse, though frightfully after the pattern of Betsey Prig,[63] had left him just an offshoot of life—a sucker of existence, so to speak; and the servant had been obliged to give up her tea-drinkings in his parlour, because he himself was removed therein. She vacated with a bad grace, evidently thinking herself much ill-used, and disapproving loudly of Percival's usurpation. All these rocks and shoals had been safely steered through, when one day a knock at the parlour door ushered in Lucretia Kemble.

It has been said before that nothing was known at the theatre of

Vasty's duel. It had been one of those quiet private affairs of which neither policeman nor relative takes cognizance; and as the surgeon pronounced Percival in no immediate danger from the wound—fever supervening the future hostile chance—Vasty had not given himself much concern about the matter.

Lucretia came to-day partly to see Percival himself and partly to hear and talk of Clara. She felt ashamed at heart of her own want of moral courage in standing so apart from the poor child in her day of trial; but, as she said to some of her intimate friends, "What can I do? I—mean and lowly—how dare I obstruct the wrathful way of Vasty Vaughan? The thunderbolt launched against her would strike my poor head and level it with the dust, if I stood in its path by her side. I am retained only by the week; how could I hope for that week to be lengthened out into months, if I thwarted the great V. V.'s passage of destruction?"

Lucretia was not singular in this postponement of abstract right to the doctrine of expediency. Nor can she be blamed—the poor actress with her lean lank purse! It is hard to find those who will support truth against personal disadvantage; for the martyr spirit is given to only a few of the sons of men.

"Angels and ministers!" cried Lucretia, when she saw the invalid as he lay on the hard, shiny, black sofa, which was his only couch of removal from the sick bed. "And what foul fiend of disease has come to rack thy bones, sweet Mr. Percival, since last I saw thy comely form?"

"I have had a fever," said Percival smiling faintly.

"A fever, man? You seem as if you've had a plague of fevers! Not one could have done all this damage! Why, where are your cheeks?—and your hands—they are only shapeless bits of bone! And mercy me! the crows might dig themselves out of sight in your eyes! You are a very skeleton, sweet Mr. Glynn, or my name is not Lucretia."

"Why, yes; I might give tolerable lectures on the human structure, aided by illustrations in anatomy from the living subject," he answered.

"But he's not to talk ma'am, if you please," said a short thickset woman, suddenly emerging from behind two folding doors that led from this "parlour front" into the "parlour back," which was the bedroom.

Percival would have laughed outright, had he been strong enough, at Lucretia's majestic astonishment confronted with this woman's hardy vulgarity. As it was, a very pale faint smile came over his wan face; but he put it down in his mind as a subject-matter for mirth when he grew stronger.

"That is my nurse!" he said to Lucretia in a tone of quiet enjoyment.

"Gracious powers! and you have lived her out, and will live her down! Well, the vitality of the human frame—ah it is wonderful!" she returned musingly.

"And here's your dinner," said the nurse, dashing clumsily into the room, and setting down on the table, in a heavy dragoon fashion, a large tray with a small and particularly dirty cloth partly covering it.

"What are you suffered to imbibe and to masticate?" asked the actress, curiously peering into the tray.

A small blue dish of the willow pattern, which looked as if it had been set to cool in the draught of the chimney, like smoke-dried hams, contained a piece of meat which butchers call a mutton-chop off the prime end, and doctors recommend as nourishing to invalids. It was an irregularly shaped viand, surrounded by a thick yellow fluid meant for gravy. It must have been broiled in primitive fashion on the coals, for a number of small black cinders adhering to it made it look as if cooked in bread-crumbs, though the result was not quite so pleasant and rather more indigestible. A long strip of fat made an unctuous but uninviting coda to the more solid nucleus, and gave a certain flavour of tallow candles which no sophistry of Harvey's sauce could disguise. On a round plate, also of the willow pattern, were three potatoes. One of them was diseased, the second could not have been boiled five minutes, and the third had only a coating of mealy substance, which you scraped off from the hard core as whitewash from a wall.

A tumbler of questionable transparency; an old pint decanter ground down into a carafe—the discoloured wine-rim still round the inside—filled with unfiltered and uncleanly water; and a very stale piece of bread, which some inhuman monster had cut with an "oniony knife," completed the prandial arrangements of Percival Glynn.

"Can't you eat something more than this, Mr. Glynn?" the actress asked, a slight glimmer of common sense showing her the misery of her friend's situation; for in general her womanly faculties were not very acute.

"Oh! it does not signify," answered Percival with a melancholy equanimity. "They cook here atrociously, and I cannot eat half they do for me; but I shall soon get well, and then they must do better!"

He tried to rise against such black bolsters, disembowelled pillows, and uncomfortable adjuncts of large cold camlet cloaks, dirty woollen shawls redolent with the peculiar odour of dirty woollen, and unmanageable coats whose arms and tails would not fold up properly, as had been pressed into the service of the sofa; but Miss Kemble was obliged to help him like a child, before he could be propped up to the necessary angle.

All the time she kept saying, "Dear! dear!—oh dear dear!" in the most piteously surprised tone possible; something like a person who does not exactly know whether he is awake or asleep. She was sadly grieved to find him in this state; "all alone too, and no one to chat with him or help his weakness on," as she said when she went home. And it was the more melancholy because he bore it so patiently. Had he been irritable and nervous, as men generally are when they are sick, she might not have pitied him so much perhaps. But "he bore it so like a blessed angel," she said, "that she felt shame to herself for all her sins ever committed."

The interdict on speech being still laid on Percival's lips, the actress allowed him to eat his miserable dinner in peace; watching him the while as if it was a matter of jugglery that he was performing. She helped him too to salt three several and undoubted times; and accompanied each saline donation with the words, "Salt is the life of the earth,"[64] which she had a confused idea came somewhere from the Bible or else from old Will Shakspeare.

It was ludicrous, as well as strange, to see her struggling to masquerade her feelings in her old affected ways, like a man endeavouring to thrust himself into a coat that is too small for him. But ever and anon a disobedient member of charity and feminine softness broke through the strait garment into which she fain would confine her nature, like arms and muscles rebelling against sleeves that are too short or bands that are too tight.

After a short sleep—the postprandial necessity to our poor invalid—he woke up much refreshed and apparently stronger. Lucretia's visit might have really done him good. He had been so long confined to his massive nurse and slipshod servant, the guerilla visits of his enemy the doctor alone intervening, that the sight of that old Roman face, with its rouge and its dye, was positively refreshing. Besides, did she not bring with her a very atmosphere of Clara? Did not every word, albeit so stilted and false to nature, recall some happy moment when Clara's merry voice had made the whole place alive with music? Did not every movement, artificial as it was, bring back some precious hour, isolated from all the other hours of the day in a golden band, alone and royally superior, when Clare's lovely face lit up with feeling that *his* words had awakened, or eloquent of thoughts that *he* had helped to create, made earth something more like to paradise than reality?—a large fair garden, full of running brooks of pleasant sound—full of gentle airs and scented grass—wherein she moved the divinest thing of all—the better Eve! And therefore he loved to know this matronly Lucretia near him, that he might wander at his will in the backward paths of memory.

They both longed to speak of one subject, and neither dared approach it. Lucretia, though not dreaming that Percival cherished any feeling for Clare fonder than friendship, was unwilling to bring evil tidings to a sick bed; and Percival dreaded his own weakness too much either to ask or to hear of her. And yet how many burning hours had borne this one only thought with them! And now, when he might drink at the fountain, he stood by the brink and thirsted.

At last Lucretia took the initiative. She was dying to talk of her young friend, and there could be no harm in asking, you know!

"Have you been visited by your old pupil?" she inquired, trying to look indifferent, but succeeding very badly.

A hectic flush crossed Percival's face.

"No," he said, succeeding just as ill in the same attempt.

"Does she know you have been ill? My life on it, Mr. Percival, that rare cushat dove[65] would have cooed her notes of healing by your couch ere now, an' had she known! Throw physic to the dogs then, Mr. Percival! Our Clara were worth half-a-hundred prescriptions! What say you?"

"She does not know that I have been ill," returned Percival almost in a whisper. "At least I have not told her."

"You would like to see her?"

He clasped his thin hands nervously.

"Would I like to see the Pole star when benighted on a pathless common?" he cried.

"You're not to talk please," said the nurse suddenly appearing.

"Good nurse, I prithee fear not my discretion!" retorted Lucretia majestically. "My life has not been wholly without knowledge of a sick chamber; and perhaps superiority in the gentle art of leechcraft may be assigned to me without much detraction to thy character, though thou do rise highest to the beam! Mr. Percival, you shall see her! I myself will tell this wood-bird where she may sing to the pleasant reception and soothing influence of her song. In a day or two you shall see our Clara Clayton."

"In a day or two!" cried poor Percival. "I could not wait so long, Lucretia, for salvation!"

The actress looked at him inquisitively.

"Fever! fever!" she muttered, laying her forefinger on the side of her nose, like one who studied deeply.

It was fever; but not of the kind she thought.

"You will bring her to-morrow?" urged Percival, like a boy pleading for a holiday.

"Humph! As for bringing her, good sir, she may e'en find feet and walk on them her own way. My hours are taken up to-morrow in the service of the Eternal Art; and if she comes at all, she must just come alone."

"Alone, Lucretia? My good soul, she can't do that! What will the world say!"

"Can't!—and why not? Who's to say her nay? Marry, my young lady is my young master also! She is as free as any outlaw of romance. Not a tie binds her—not the veriest silken thread fastens her to the pillar of obedience. If she likes to come, not even Vasty will prevent her now. There!—that's hint enough for one day," she said to herself, watching Percival keenly.

He understood more than she dreamt of. She wondered afterwards why he looked so boundlessly happy—boundlessly for a sick man at least—and what there was in Clare's freedom that could possibly affect him? Why he was not in love with the girl surely?

"Then I'll tell her to come?" she asked, rising to depart.

"No," answered Glynn; "tell her that I am ill—nothing infectious— and if she asks to come and see me, do you bring her like a good old soul as you are."

"Nous verrons!"[66] said Lucretia, striding from the room like Lady Macbeth when she rushes in after the murder, and sweeping past the red-headed girl cleaning the door-steps—at four o'clock in the day.

Exhausted with his long conversation—long to him in his child-like state of weakness—and exhausted still more by the excitement of his feelings—Percival very quietly fainted as soon as Lucretia disappeared.

As no one came to his assistance, he remained there for some time in a state of half-unconsciousness, trying hard to remember who he was, and where, and wondering whether he was alive or not, and whether this was not death. At last he gradually emerged from his infantine state of ignorance; and then the nurse came and rated him soundly for his visitor, his chattering, his bad dinner, and his ill-usage of herself generally.

Lucretia was puzzled for a long time how she could best communicate to Clare the fact of Glynn's indisposition. If the child had had the black fever in her house the old actress could not have been more afraid to venture within its doors. What should she do if Vasty were to hear of it, or to see her there? Her weekly agreement would not hold out then over many Sundays! As it was she felt it hang over her head in a rampant state of perpetual *in terrorem*. Conscience and cowardice were at open war; but the last gained the victory, and beat the other off with fragments of old saws, prudential axioms, proverbial staves, and others of the serviceable forces in the army of selfishness. No; she must not for her own sake go to the house; but she might write to the disgraced favourite. So, true enough, after she reached home, she sat down and wrote the following note.

"My well-beloved child—for I would have you judge by conscience, Clara Clayton, and not by sight—the first will hardly lead you wrong, the last most rarely leads you right. I have been to our mutual friend and most dear neighbour, Percival Glynn. Him I found on a sick bed— nay, to speak more accurately, on a sick couch. He hath suffered from a fever, and blood hath been let in such quantities that his cheeks fall inward with a cavernous tendency less beautiful than melancholy. I asked of your health from him, thinking that he might have had later news of you than I, poor feeble sinner, am able now to claim— but he assured me of your ignorance of his present condition, and that he prayed your presence to chase away his gloominess. N.B. His nurse is an old devil; and if I had time I would find him a better. Now Clara Clayton, I do not counsel thee, so youthful as thou art, to betake thee to the sick man's chamber. Nor can I advise myself to go with thee, seeing that various professional duties keep me chained to the rock of —— theatre. Thou must use thine own discretion anent thy visit. I have delivered my message correctly—done my spiriting truthfully, if not gently—and thou must decide for thyself. I would say in conclusion, that thou need'st not fear the crawling influence of infection—his fever hath been on the brain—the mind—not in the disordered juices of his body. Farewell, and credit me sweet maid still, though I may seem a very bankrupt in the market-place of love. I would have thee but remember these few words—'I am poor, and I am not independent.' Thine in heart and truth, LUCRETIA KEMBLE."

Clara was not long undecided after she read this letter. In the first place it created in her a feeling of the most intense thankfulness, selfish as it seemed. Percival's desertion of her had wounded her deeply, and had been the strongest point from whence Edward Mantell launched his invectives against the whole of her infidel and socialist companions. For Percival's life was so pure and so benevolent, that it did not present many openly vulnerable points, even to a fanatic of Edward Mantell's school.

It was very late when Clara received the note; after she came from the theatre; where she was in constant attendance now, without ever being called on to act. Thus she lost the chance of seeing Percival to-night, for even she, with all her impetuosity, felt that it would be hardly decorous, not to speak of useful, to pay a sick man a visit at half-past twelve o'clock at night. Had she received the note at eight even, the old nurse would have had another "nervous attack," from the "dressed-up madams that came and half killed that blessed man."

Up early the next morning was Clara Clayton. A feeling as of spring-time—as of the return of childhood—possessed her. Not that she loved Percival Glynn in any special sense, but she had found him true when she believed him false—and was not this spring-tide *renaissance*? And she was to hear old friendly accents that so long ago, and with such a gulf of circumstances between, had spoken kindly to her soul—and was not this the return of happy girlhood?

She was very sorry he was ill. Of course she was: but she could not help feeling happy too. And though Edward Mantell insisted so strongly on the danger of the affections and their satanic tendencies, she could not think with him. For her part she was always so much better, holier, more grateful and obedient, when her heart overflowed with love! And she was not casuist enough yet, to prove to her own satisfaction that her very consciousness of truth was evidence of falsehood; and that when she felt better in moral health and holier in spiritual impulses, she was therefore in greater spiritual danger and filled with worse moral disease.

She was up early; yes, and down into the middle aisle of Covent

Garden Market. For all the crowd of half-familiar men and unpleasant women—she walked bravely down; looking for fruit and flowers of the best wherewith to delight her dear old elocutionist. True, her purse did not hold much; but she made a rapid calculation as to what she could reduce in her weekly expenditure to cover the frightful extravagance that she was about to commit. And though she generally found that her economy profited her nothing, and that a couple of hard-boiled eggs somehow mounted up to the same price as a rational dinner of meat and vegetables, yet she still allowed herself to be deluded with the hope that she could save.

She might be an easy victim to theatrical managers, to milliners, and landladies, but the flower-sellers found her no such accommodating customer. The best she would have; and when they offered her withered things doctored up in all manner of unholy ways, with their unhappy heads gibbetted on wire—very simulacra of nature's children—she detected the cheat and pointed out the flaws, and insisted so earnestly on a better supply, that whether for the sake of her botanical knowledge, of her beauty, or her strenuous demands, I know not—she got her flowers in tolerable preservation, and her fruit was magnificent.

Cabs and their luxuries were unknown now to Clara. She held her purchases delicately in her little hand, took good heart even for the dreary winter morning, and not reflecting that it was hardly probable that an invalid would be astir at ten o'clock, she walked up to Islington without missing her way *very* often. Though in general she was a perambulating query to all shopkeepers and policemen, being naturally extremely obtuse in her organ of locality.

When the nurse—that dreadful bit of strong humanity—said that the "blessed gentleman was in bed and could not be seen," Clara began to cry.

Sickness has sharp ears. Percival heard the dear voice; he knew the very footfall as it sprang up to the door! Lying in his back chamber he could distinguish now her very breathing—he was sure he could! With a feeble hand, nervous and feverish, he rang his bell; and Clara did really, with ears of flesh and blood, hear him say in weak trembling accents—

"Ask the lady to sit down till I can see her."

Now, all you who are very moral and conventional, turn over this page unread: it is a shocking fact that is about to be related, and one that our daughters must not hear, else they will perchance be "going and doing likewise."

When Clara was fully convinced that those were the words actually spoken by Percival himself, she sprang past the nurse who was coming to meet her—rushed through the narrow hall in her old style of rapid feet and rustling garments—and, without a thought as to the strangeness or impropriety of her conduct, was in the sick man's room and by his side—her hands in his and her gentle lips on his forehead—crying; "Percival, dear Percival—my darling friend!" before she well knew what she had done.

And not even when Percival's thin arm, all exposed and bare, touched her soft throat as he pressed her to him, did she reflect that she was doing very wrong, and that the world would have blamed her for this act of charity as for a crime against good morals.

Blame her, ye who will! Cast stones of censure, ye who measure virtue by social rules and deem that to be vice which is not custom. In the truth, as it is before heaven, she was as free to visit yon sick man—nor relative nor husband though he was—as a sister is free to watch over her wounded brother, a child to nestle to the arms of her sick father. Ay, and as pure in the deed was she as an angel who comes down to console the stricken and the weary.

But these were the things which had rubbed off the tender bloom from her maiden name. These were the acts, substantially right but conventionally wrong, which had banded her with the world of the lost and degraded. People could not believe that she was positively pure, when they knew for certain that she had openly done things which no woman of character and station is ever known to commit. Appearances are so entirely morals in society, that scarce a dozen in a million can divest themselves of this superstition, and believe of the core what they see not in the husk. Clare's very innocence was her condemnation; her very purity of thought and passionate impulse to good sank her still lower in public opinion. Yet had she suspected more of evil she would have used more of caution: had she lost in heart she would have gained in lip. Those who are most careful in outward conduct are oftentimes least pure in mind. Those whose thoughts are always dwelling on wickedness—even to condemn it— are less to be admired for their censures than pitied for their aptitude. Prudence and strictness are virtues in their way—but who would not prefer the confidence of innocence to the measured propriety of guilty knowledge? Who would not love the frankness of purity rather than the distorted severity of guilty thoughts? The keen scent after vice does not belong to the really pure; for those who discover evil where no evil was intended themselves create the sin they condemn, and owe to their own foulness what they ascribe to another. "To the pure all things are pure;" an emphatic truth sometimes lost sight of in our criticisms on others.

From this point of view then, Clare's loss of character was a testimony to her moral worth. Had she really deserved her reputation, she would have been careful not to earn it by public imprudence; for innocence alone is bold, in women who have any virtue at all.

CHAPTER X.

CLARA was not the only person in Percival Glynn's circle of friends who had suffered both in mind and position by his illness. More than one hungry lip and aching heart lamented the sudden disappearance, which had been the withdrawal of food and the quenching of fire in the wretched home. More than one miserable mother watched from her murky room, or wandered down the reeking alley, to look for the good gentleman who had been so kind and hitherto so punctual in his bounty. But Percival never came; and the widow hungered and the children wept unsolaced. For the scant charity of an overseer but ill replaced his full-hearted bounty; and the cold protection of the House, though it kept its wretched inmates from starvation, was neither so ennobling nor so sweet as his large generous gifts, which flowed with all the sanctifying plenteousness of a sacred stream of life. This was bad political economy, but it was true Christianity, in our Percival; yet it somehow happens that all which is most consonant with the laws of Christ, is ever most opposed to the laws of this Christian community of ours.

In one small room, above all, was Percival's absence most severely felt. The young slop-workers, Jane and Sarah Walcot, no longer lived in the low neighbourhood to which poverty had pressed them inch by inch—first from off localities of respectability, and then of health, and then of common decency. They were now in a better quarter, and Percival had promised to look kindly after them, and to pay their rent; for he had been the means of their removal. He was not able to do much more than this for any of his *protégés*. What he gave was given freely—with that wholeness of charity, that great unselfish generosity, which has some mesmeric quality in it independent of its practical effects; and what he gave was saved—every farthing of it—from his private expenditure of pleasures and luxuries. Still, all that he bestowed, and twice as much as he possessed for his whole income, was not much contrasted with the poverty whereon it fell. It only served to lighten, not remove.

Indeed, he had that true wisdom of political economy which endeavours to elevate and not to pauperize the poor. He gave his charity as aid not as substitution; something to help out the frightful wages of our competitive systems, and not to abolish the necessity of work altogether. He would not nullify by pauperization the exercise of such virtues as self-denial, forethought, endurance, industry, courage—virtues which are the very marrow of an empire. He did not whine over the hardship of work as work: on the contrary, he held it high in dignity, and looked on it as the best moral regenerator of humanity. The spirit of aristocratic idleness, which views labour as degradation, was to him essentially a false and uncivilized spirit—belonging to a time that worships forms and not realities, a false and therefore a degraded time. But if he did not whine over the necessity of work, yet the labour which toils so hard for wages that cannot support life—taking out the strength of a man for less than a brute's subsistence—he did his best to prevent, in all the individual cases which came under his knowledge. And in doing this he sinned against the recommendations of poor-law guardians, the theories of political economists, the favourite essays of public speakers who stand out for Spartan severity and ridicule all maudlin philanthropy, the best views of commercial prosperity, and the best systems of commercial management; but as he did what was substantially right, he let the rest pass by.

Day by day, with trust growing gradually fainter till at last it died out like a blackened ember, had the two girls awaited Glynn's return. But when their hopes slowly changed to grim corpses of despair, and nothing was left them but the deadly sickness of disappointment, his desertion came on them rather as a remembered lesson than as a new experience: for how could they—lepers of poverty—meet with enduring kindness from one of the favoured classes, one of the aristocratic and the wealthy?

It was no marvel that they mistrusted him. Reliance is born either of general ignorance or of special knowledge—as in a child, or in a proved friend tried by years and fate. The unfortunate, and those who have found men hard taskmasters and false brothers, do not easily trust even to a succession of kind acts. And though Sarah tried hard and long to believe that all was right, at last she too failed; and shed some bitter tears at being again deceived by the false appearance of false kindness. She had once received work under the guise of gratuitous benevolence; but her benefactor turned out to be a Jew sweater, and from that hour she and her sister had gone downward in the path of life. They never recovered the crushing effects of fines and inadequate wages and returned work, that had overwhelmed them from the very first week of their commencing slop-work.

Jane had long since decided in her own mind that the strange gentleman was a rate collector, or a police inspector, or a turncock,[67] or disguised landlord, or Hebraized outfitter, or some one of those mysterious persons who seem to the poor born only to distress and harass them individually and collectively. Mysterious people, who are to them what the hawk is to the sparrow—as fierce, as unrelenting, and as destructive.

"Nay," said Sarah, "he ain't quite so bad. Belike he's something worse than we thought him at first, Janie, for he was like a lord to us at first; but it seems to be a trick too. He maybe had some reason of his own why he wanted us out of the alley and put us here. He wants to get us into debt belike, and then he'll have us in his power entire. Ah dear, it must be so!" she said to herself, "else why are we left so lone when we most want help? We were less badly off in the alley with Emma—though the air was very bad and Janie's cough came on there—leastways it's as bad now! But it *is* strange that the gentleman has led us into such expense and then left us altogether!"

And then she thought of the horror which Percival had made her promise to renounce, and shuddered as she remembered that her sister must have bread by the old means, if more lawful ones failed.

Percival had made this renunciation arbitrary; and she had promised—oh, how gladly!—to give up a condition of life that had ground her to the dust. Like a voice from the loved thing you thought a corpse—like a reprieve to a condemned criminal—like all that humanity can feel of most blessed in its transition from misery to security, was that arbitrary condition of Percival's to her! How many tears of thankfulness yon girl had wept, when she knew that the hideous sale of more than flesh and blood might be laid aside—even though the alternative were alms and practical pauperization! How happy she felt that now she might meet the eye of man without a blush, and stand near her sisters without reproach! Life?—he had given her more than mere life! He had brought her back to the possibility of peace—to the power of virtue. And are not these better than the mere breath of the lungs—the mere pulsations of the heart?

The whole class of unfortunate women are not so keenly alive to their disgrace as was Sarah Walcot, neither are they all the heroines of virtue and angels of purity which Gallic romance would make them; nay, many of them would not abandon their trade, even for the alternative of an honest and a virtuous livelihood. The most part would, and gladly; but still not all. But though they are not *ex officio* heroines, a large section of them—the slop-workers—are FORCED loathing on to the streets for the food, clothing, and lodging, which their long hours of work cannot give them. This is a fact positively known to those who care to examine into such foul pools as bad social management has allowed to stagnate underneath our stately temples of prosperity. It is a fact written of by poet, by statician, and lately by the brave old journal that has so nobly redeemed its fallen honour; and knowing this, is it not worth our while to aid, each in his own sphere, in one of the greatest works of the day—namely, the juster apportionment of wages, and the consequent annihilation of many sections of crime? Those who ignore the influence of physical facts on the moral condition of man—who assign all evil to the depravity of the human heart, and believe that a spiritual and dogmatic creed can alone destroy this evil—need but study the difference between those classes of labour which afford a cleanly and respectable existence and those which are not adequately remunerative, to judge whether crime, as a social characteristic, is born of some mysterious spirit of evil, or of ignorance, want, and social dis-esteem.

"This is the sixth week, Sal!" said Jane, "and no one here. Depend on it he is a government man or a water man. He was never no friend!"

Sarah was silent. She could not defend Glynn, and she did not like to strengthen her sister's doubts.

"Is there anything more to pawn, Sal?" asked Jane after a short pause.

"No, Janie," said her sister mournfully, looking round the bare room.

All had gone! The last stick of furniture, the last rag of clothes that could be parted with—gone for food and rent; and still they were hungry, and still in debt.

This last fact disturbed poor Sarah more than anything else. She had always kept herself honest; through the most frightful times she had eventually paid what she owed. But now—how could she ever get enough to clear off such long arrears? She owed her landlord fifteen shillings—where was it to come from? Yet until she paid off this she could not take a cheaper room, which she would do directly if she could leave their present house.

She had been growing paler and sadder day by day—falling back from the happy health of their improved condition under Percival's management into the desolate squalor of former times. As for Jane, she had been long gradually declining—very gradually but surely; and her thin hands, almost transparent as they were, and hollow eyes, foretold an end not very far off. Her strength had much decreased. She could not work hard; nor indeed every day. The pain in her side, and the troublesome cough, kept her weak. But in the spring, when it was warmer, why then she would get better again! She felt confident of it; and Sarah tried to believe so too.

And now what was to be done? Jane's increasing weakness had wrought them much ill; for she could not take back her work by the stipulated time, and the masters fined her, or returned the article on her hands and made her pay a usurious price for it. Sarah helped her as much as she could; but there was not much human energy left after sixteen hours close work.

It was a dark wet night. Jane laid down to rest a little. She had been very ill all the day, and her cough and pain had troubled her much. She was now thirsty rather than hungry, and had a craving for porter—more instinctive than sensual. But they could not afford porter. Luxuries cannot come in where the first necessaries are shut out.

The wind howled through the streets, bringing great dashes of rain against the window, that startled the sick girl and made her nervous and irritable. The fire burned low in the small grate—a mere handful of sullen cinders—and the name of the candle flared in the draught with momentary gusts of brightness. You heard out of doors a few feet pattering through the rain, hurrying to what home fortune might have given them; and sometimes a child crying for the wind and wet and deathly cold—and sometimes a woman shrieking at the brutality which nothing checked to-night—broke through the monotony of the driving rain and howling blast.

The sick girl groaned.

"What be it, Janie?" said Sarah looking round, the flaring light falling on her pallid face with every feature traced sharp by famine and wasted by labour; and still as she looked her long thin hand plied that hated needle mechanically.

"Sal!" said Jane moaning.

"Well dear, and what is it now? Wait a little, dear, till I finish this waistcoat, and then I'll come to you."

There was a little silence. At last Sarah's ear distinguished something else. She flung down her work, and kneeling by the low trestle bed, put down the covering rags and looked into her sister's face.

That sick, sad, sullen face!—bathed in tears, feverish and hectic bright—a face of want and pain and brutish lack of intellect together! She was sobbing painfully; her cough almost choking her.

"What is it, Janie dear? What is it that's to do with thee?" she cried; "what can I do for thee that thou cries so like that? Tell me, Janie dear. Thou knows I would do all for thee I could! Tell me like a good lass what's with thee to-night!"

"Sally," said the girl, raising her pale eyes to the gentle face bending so lovingly over her; "thou said once thou'dst get what I wanted—why doesn't thee now? Is it because I'm sick and can't work that thou'st angry with me?"

Had a dagger pricked that girl's heart she could not have felt more sudden anguish.

She sank down—her head on her sister's bosom—and trembled from limb to limb. But she did not cry nor say a word.

The girl made a movement of pain.

"Thou hurts me!" she said sulkily, pushing away her head and chafing her chest.

And no wonder, poor thing!—with her lungs so full of sores and disease, and her thin chest giving so little protection to them.

"What dost thou want, Janie dear?" asked Sarah kindly, struggling to subdue her dread, and rubbing the thin and shrunken flesh.

"Oh! I'm so thirsty always! and I want anything I can drink. Gin, if thou like, Sal; but I'd like ale!"

"Very well, darling! thou shalt have it soon," she cried, rising from her knees and going to the table where she worked.

She finished her job, nervously, hurriedly; her cheeks were pale; her lips parched and quivering; her limbs trembled. It was a rough night, but she would do it—she would go out and beg, and if that failed, why then——.

The promise soothed the poor girl; she had never known Sally fail her, and she trusted to her word as implicitly as to an oath.

The work was done, and flung on the bed to help as coverlet to the sick girl; and Sarah, putting on her bonnet and wrapping a shawl round her as well as she could, went out into the street.

What a night it was! The rain came down in streams from the hanging eaves, and poured along the streets in small rivulets—rushing through the gratings of the sewers with the noise of a minor waterfall. The people gathered into their houses—such as had houses to go to; but here and there whole families were gathered under a broad archway or house-porch, trying to escape the frightful weather. Families of destitute Irish, weavers out of employ, agricultural labourers from Sussex and elsewhere, who could not get even their six shillings a-week as farm-servants—all of them flocking up to London as to an El Dorado, in utter ignorance of its ways, its resources, its necessities—all of them swelling the turbid tide of pauperism already flowing through its black heart. Women too of every age might be met with, wandering about like wood-birds out at sea. In the markets you would come upon them crouched under the lee of the vegetable carts, or sleeping in the corners of the aisles, or perhaps burrowing among the wet musty straw left in large hampers and baskets. Some of them might be singing to get a few pence for a bed; others weeping in forlorn misery; and others again, reeling from the gin-shop, were happy for the brief moment—in the terrible happiness of a drunkard's paradise.

True, there are places for the utterly destitute. There are unions, houses of refuge, and such-like. There is the prison also for the lucky felon, who will exchange his freedom for food and warmth and clothing. But strangers do not know of these places; and any one who will go out in a winter's night into the by-streets, courts, and large markets, will find ample verification of the fact, that numbers of our fellow-creatures lie in nameless misery about our feet, without a hand stretched out to aid them, without a penny spent to help them. Yes, though we, the sleepers in those luxurious beds and princely houses, are both christian and wealthy Englishmen.

Sarah passed by such shivering crowds as these. They were as bad off as she, and it was losing time to stop there among them. Some spoke to her as she passed; many asked charity of her; some of the men addressed rude ribaldry perhaps, in frightful mockery of their wretchedness. But she hurried by them, until she gained the larger streets where there was more chance of help from the passengers always thronging them.

But who could be out such a night as this? The very poorest only would venture abroad, and they could not help her. With a sad heart she glanced down the wide deserted streets, where the gaslights shone coldly, and the shop-fronts—such as were open—were blurred with rain, and dim. What chance had she of getting money to-night in any way? The shopkeepers would most likely give her in charge if she begged of them, and she saw no one else about. She could not go home without her sister's drink. Though no doctor, she knew that it was food and medicine to her now, and she felt a double necessity—both from love and from humanity—to do all she could for her welfare.

No one met her. The few policemen that she saw looked savage and surly. Some eyed her as if she had been the embodiment, in her one solitary person, of all the thievery and vagabondism of London. Others told her to go home—what was she doing out here?—and one, younger to his trade and softer hearted, said "God bless thee, girl, it's a rough time for thee!"

She wandered on in the rain and wind and bitter cold of the night air, through streets that might have been plague-smitten, they were so tenantless. At last a small knot of cabs and carriages, and a few people lounging about an open door, attracted her among them.

The door let out a flood of light. A public-house was near, and a blazing fire helped the brilliancy of its gas burners. Men were grouped about, covered up in heavy coats that could turn any amount of rain—fairly waterproof by their stoutness; many, almost all, were smoking, and some were drinking. There was such an air of cheerfulness and warmth about it all!

She stood there, wet to the skin. Her thin gown clung round her, dripping with the rain. From her tattered bonnet the wet ran off in driblets, and her shawl, soaked through, lay heavy and cold on her shoulders. She stopped and begged. Some answered her with a curse, others with a false affectation of good-tempered "regret that they had not a rap with them." No one gave her anything; though in such a wet cold night, and with the flaring comfort of the ginshop before her.

Presently a rush was made at the door, and several people hurried out. Many of them threw themselves into private carriages; some hired cabs; a few prepared to walk even through the rain; while low women, hardier than the rest, gathered in knots of two and three, talking and laughing amongst themselves.

It was at the door of Clara's theatre that poor Sarah had arrived, and the people were the audience leaving at the conclusion of the performance.

No one gave her anything. The policeman warned her off. Sick, broken-hearted, she was moving away, when a woman caught her hand and turned her face to the lamplight.

Sarah started as the tall figure of Emma Vaughan darkened on her. She was well dressed; her cloak and bonnet and gown were flashy and new. Her face, though wilder and more desperate in its expression, harder too and fiercer, had not that famine-wasted look it used to wear. She was evidently prosperous—prosperous, that is, for her and her frightful trade; and if sunken deeper still in vice, raised somewhat higher in fortune.

"What, girl!—why what brings you here?" she cried. "What are you at?—the old thing, or begging?"

"I am begging, Emma," said Sarah, with a wearied accent in her voice. "Jane is sick, and we have nothing in the house to pawn or to buy with."

"Why where's the gentleman that wanted to take me along with you?" asked the woman with a hoarse laugh. "Has he too turned out false like the rest—false like the devil, who is father to them all?"

"I don't know about that," she answered; "but I've not seed him for six weeks now. And the rent's run on, and we've had little work—leastways little profit—for Jane's illness made her slack, and then the masters fined us. And it has been a hard time, Emma. But if I can get Janie comfort to-night, she'll maybe do stronger to-morrow."

"And you've come begging such a night as this, fool, have you?" said Emma coarsely. "Much good it'll do you!—much wool you'll get such a time as this! Here!—I've got credit here—come in and have a glass of gin."

She took her hand again in hers.

"No, no!" said Sarah shrinking back; "give it me for Janie if you like, but not for me. Besides, Emma, have you got up so in the world? You are dressed smart, I see—hast been in luck?" She looked up with a face so guileless and free from every trace of envy, that it struck even the degraded heart she spoke with.

"You're a fool, Sal!" she said, turning away and clearing her eyes from the blinding rain—"a very fool!—if Heaven ever let one out down here!"

A policeman came up. "Move on! move on!" he said harshly, but not touching them.

Emma turned round with an oath and a curse; and then they sauntered on, out of the sheltered place where they had been standing, into the open street. They went on—round the corner, for a little distance—then round again, into a street parallel with the one where they had stood. Another door with a feebler light, another public-house, and another knot of cabs and cabmen, told them it was the stage entrance to the theatre.

"That's my husband!" cried Emma close in his ear, as Vasty Vaughan, who had been detained at the theatre to-night, sprang past them into his Brougham.

He turned and saw her, and made a menacing motion with his hand. She answered with a savage laugh and a coarse oath, and then he passed away.

"Let me go and speak to *him!*" said Sarah. She pointed to a tall figure pacing the other side of the street uneasily, evidently watching the stage entrance.

She broke away from her companion, and crossing the street besought him for alms.

"Go away! go away!" exclaimed the man impatiently. "I have nothing for you, girl! Will that hell never disgorge its prey!" he added, his eyes fixed ever on the stage door, and his hands plucking fiercely at his breast.

"Oh, sir! my sister is ill, and we have had no food to-day!" cried Sarah, following him.

"I have nothing for you!" he returned angrily. "If you persist in annoying me, I will give you in charge. How dare you, brazen woman, speak thus to me? I tell you, I want nothing with you! For shame! for shame!—go home! Oh! will she never come!" he continued, speaking to himself and clasping his hands. "Will the mouth of that fiery pit never open to the release of its spotless victim! This is agonizing! Can I have missed her, and some of those servants of the Serpent taken her home through this frightful night? I cannot have missed her!—I have watched so long!"

He crossed over now, coming close to the door.

Only a few stragglers were left—carpenters and workmen, and some of the lowest actors. At last a young girl ran down the steps, with that peculiarly elastic tread of youth, and bravely prepared for the storm and the darkness and the solitude of the street.

Edward Mantell was standing not far from the threshold; on the other side Emma Vaughan, with Sarah leaning against her and weeping bitterly, seemed waiting for something.

Clare came forth. She looked out on the pitchy sky and streaming streets with a shudder; then, turning to unfold her umbrella, she saw Emma Vaughan and Sarah close by her side.

She knew the woman instantly, and started when her eyes fell on that handsome hardened face. A quiver as of pain ran through her, but she stopped, saying quietly—

"Have I not seen you before?"

"You have," returned Emma boldly but not insolently. "And now I wish to see you once again, to ask you if you are not thankful—thankful, lady—to have escaped the nets which Vasty Vaughan, my husband"—with emphasis—"laid for your young soul?"

The girl trembled, and turned pale.

"You are really his wife?" she asked in a low tone, more involuntarily than intentionally.

"Really!" laughed Emma loudly; "true as the stars, unalterably as the way of the sun! Such as I am, I am really the wife of that man! And such as I am you might have been, my child, when his fit of passion had wearied itself out!"

"Where do you live?" said Clara, with a strange mixture of feeling. "I should like to come and see you."

The woman turned away for a moment. Sarah felt the heart which beat against her own clinging arm leap with a mighty bound; then throb in large thick gasps, quick and great.

"No, no!" she then said, "you must not come to such as me, lady!

You must not enter the very street where I live! Do you remember
my once warning you against a court? My child! you would run into
worse dangers even than those I perhaps kept you from that day, if
you came to see me. Robbery and murder are not unheard-of in the
homes of such as I am!"

"It is wet, now," said Clara, "and I cannot talk to you here; but if I
can do anything for you—if I can be of any use to you—I will try my
utmost. I am very sorry you are so poor!—will you let me give you
this?"

She drew out her purse with its slender all of three shillings, and
offered them to Emma.

Big tears rose up into that woman's deep black eyes. They veiled
them like a curtain—they came down on her cheeks in large drops—
from her very heart. She put the girl's hand aside, then caught it and
pressed it to her lips, feverish, blackened, sin-stained as they were.

"God bless you!" she cried fervently, "Mr. Glynn tells me how true
and good you are!"

Clara started. At that moment she felt as if the whole of London
had been watching her, discussing her, arranging for her. She shrank
as from the sudden discovery of Jesuitism or a secret police.

"You know Mr. Glynn, then?" she said after a nervous pause.

"Yes! He has been a kind friend to me!" answered Emma; "and to
this poor girl, too. But he's out of town now, I think; I have not seen
him about at all, and this girl and her sister have nearly starved for
want of him. He has done a great deal for them."

Sarah turned her face to the young actress.

"Indeed, my lady, it's true! My sister's ill, and I came out to beg
to-night, to get her a morsel of food. It is hard to hunger so long, my
lady, working as we do early and late;—and then sickness and the rent
falls in, and we can't get help except we go to the union. It's true, my
lady, and Emma knows it!"

"This is all I have about me to-night," said Clara hurriedly, for
she heard the laughter of some of the people about the theatre close
behind her. "But if you will meet me to-morrow here, at two o'clock,
I will do something more for you."

She turned away into the rain and the howling wind, the darkness
and the loneliness; for they had been standing in shelter under a rude
kind of porch by the stage door. The next day it was the current joke

of the theatre "that little Clayton had been imposed on by two flash women."

All this time Edward Mantell had suffered agony of mind almost past endurance, watching the young actress, as she stood thus, talking in her gentle dignity and mercy with these two wretched women, and thirsting to rush forward and pluck her from their hated atmosphere. And yet a stronger power than his own will held him back.

Edward Mantell had unwittingly worked Clara much ill. Soon after he had become acquainted with her, he had adopted the habit of waiting for her at the stage door and taking her safely home after rehearsal and representation. This had been noticed in the theatre, and Clara had been jeered at by some of the more vulgar actors—and that too in no very unequivocal terms—for the punctuality of her new lover. Their jokes came to Vaughan's ears; and consequently, Clare received a double portion of his tyranny and contempt, expressed in the most public fashion that ingenious cruelty could invent, and coupled with hints and open accusations of a disgraceful nature. When she knew what effect the kindness of her new friend was producing, she requested him, with many blushes and much embarrassment, not to come for her again; though when he pressed her for a reason, she could only shake her head and look down on the ground and whisper faintly; "They speak about it at the theatre."

Her least word was now command to Edward. He obeyed her faintest suggestion with an eagerness, a fidelity, which she alas! never understood in half its meaning, but which only added to the fire already burning into his own soul with uncontrollable passion. And yet how he loved to obey her! How he treasured up each word of praise, each word of blame, each indication of a wish; and flew to gratify her every desire as a bird that seeks far for precious seeds for its young mate. He never dreamed of violating her commands; and if she had ordered him to his own destruction he would have blessed the lips that sealed his ruin. To-night, though it was anguish unspeakable to see her standing there in the light of that unholy ginshop—the crowd of vulgar men laughing and scoffing at her through the open doors—talking with women whose frightful lives he knew, though she might be ignorant of them—yet he never thought of freeing himself from this anguish by disobedience, and by coming in between as a guardian and a guide. He stood within the shadow, suffering silently and fiercely; trying to pray, but the words turning to fire on his lips.

The cold night wind came hot on his brow—the gust-driven rain brought no refreshment to him. The burning misery that consumed him changed the very elements, and transformed to scorching lava all that chilled to the heart those who were less tortured. Turn where he might, he saw that loved, that glorious, being weaved in with such foul threads—such hell-spun threads of sin—that he trembled for her fate in the present—and oh! for her salvation in the future how much more did he than tremble!

For her place here—for her very purity even, if that place were rent from her—for her soul hereafter under any circumstances, he feared. And all that he saw of her life, her acts, and her surroundings, added to his terror: all seemed conspiring to drag her downward and still downward. And then, when lost for ever in the world's estimation—when sullied, trampled on and torn, how could she rest on the bosom of a sacred minister of truth—how could she be associated with one whose whole life ought to be an unhesitating lesson of purity and holiness? It was impossible! She might never be his wife if she lost her fair fame—as he felt sure she must eventually lose it, should her life continue in its present path!

And yet he believed her innocent and good—then why not fit to be his wife?—why, though the ignorant despise her, might not truth make her fit to be his bride? His?—that scorned actress—that peasant's foundling—that woman born in double sin, in more than the natural iniquity of humanity—that painted toy living in scenes of vice, such as the Prophet of Israel preached against in words of thunder out of heaven—this thing the wife of a Christian minister? What! *he* league himself with sinners by the ties of holy love and Christian wedlock, then go forth to denounce others less guilty than the one he had so honoured? No! it must never be!—he must not love her other than as a pastor seeking to win her to the fold—as a physician seeking to save her leprosied soul. He must not love her as his wife, nor have her to be his wife—this consorter with the foul women of the streets! Misery! misery! would this spell never be broken!

At last that long long conversation, which, though it had scarce occupied minutes, seemed to him to have lasted hours, came to an end; and this beloved thing broke out, like the moon of heaven from behind murky clouds, and walked forth in her own purity and beauty unblemished. Joy, ye angels in heaven! her soul hath escaped the net of the snarer yet this once again! Joy, ye spirits of the just! she is not yet lost for ever!

At a distance, following her humbly with jealous care and ardent love, Edward Mantell saw that Clare arrived safely at the door of her own house. As she stood on the step, holding up her coarse umbrella against the rain that drove into her wearied face, and trying to shelter herself from the wind that wrapped her garments round and round, and left her feet and ankles bare to the pouring rain, she looked more than once at the dark figure standing in the distance, and seeming to watch her so intently. She wondered who it was; and turned her head again as she passed into the house; and her heart beat fast as she whispered to herself—"Can it be Vaughan watching over me? Can he still love me so tenderly?"

Long hours after the door had closed on her—long hours after the feeble glimmer of her candle had been extinguished in her small window—Edward Mantell wandered through the street; stopping every now and then before her house—listening if she called for help—called on his name the first of all to save her—shuddering to think that she was in some mysterious danger from which no power but his could save her.

This fear was almost a monomania with Edward Mantell. He would start up at night from his sleep, under some horrible impression of her suffering or death; or rush madly home when out on his very duty, thinking that she might want him for some sudden distress. He was ever tormented with one enduring spectre of her danger when parted from his side.

Little did Clare know what self-constituted watcher paced so often through the night before her door! Little did she dream of the consuming fire which she had lit up in the heart of one of whom she thought but as a religious enthusiast, and cared for but as her holy, patient friend! His first love was she; the only woman who had ever stirred one pulse, or stolen away his thoughts from heaven; a thing that he adored so frantically yet so grievingly—dreading to acknowledge to himself how much he loved her, and masking it under all sorts of religious disguises that yet could *not* keep out the truth. He feared to look steadily into the depths of his tortured heart. He knew that he should see there, supreme over all, the form of one for whom at the most he ought to cherish but a melancholy regard. He knew that he loved yon graceful, lost, and sinful woman, and he shrank at the

task of steadfastly regarding that love. Poor Edward Mantell! he was
terrified at the novelty of his feelings. He thought that it had been
given to Satan to tempt and to destroy him; and he prayed against
the strange tumult of his soul as he would have prayed against the
impulse to commit a crime. He wept heavy tears of contrition and
despair; and finally sank down, still protesting, beneath the power of
a love he had been taught to name a sin—a backslider yielding to the
snare, and struggling still while falling to sleep in his silken bonds. It
was a sin—a fearful sin, that he was committing!

And then the wrath of the Eternal, and the glaring flames of hell,
came up before him in visible shape; and he would rush madly home
to spend long hours of tearful agony—endeavouring to conquer
what was unconquerable—to beat down the force of nature with the
shadowy mace of an idea—and to pray against a heinous crime when
obeying the principles of nature's first law to man.

CHAPTER XI.

It was a bright but chilly morning when Clare went down to rehearsal.
Though, indeed, the poor child had not much to rehearse now on
the boards where not so long since she had been supreme controller
of all their best resources. For when Vaughan loved her—or as she
phrased it—"was kind to her"—there was not a privilege, not an
honour, that she might not have had for the asking. Now she was
nothing but a confidante to little Miss Gray the heroine—neglected
by all who had once paid her court as the highway to Vaughan's good
graces—insulted by many, treated contemptuously by Vasty, denied
the possibility of appearing well with the public, even if she had the
power; disgraced and discarded under every shape of professional
ignominy.

Clare as a dramatic confidante! All that passion and love and high
nobleness of thought pressed down into the animated automaton
which comes on trailing after the heroine, and which clasps its
hands and utters "ohs" and "ahs" in parenthetical consideration of
pneumonic failure—a thing that is dressed in rechauffé[68] trains of
questionable satin, with a plume of dirty feathers lagging to the neck
of a Roman matron, or a Louis Quatorze head-dress surmounting the
Joseph of the crusades—a thing that has less individuality than even

the Greek choruses, without distinctive character or dramatic vitality.

This, then, was the lowest point to which the once popular Clara Clayton had as yet sunk. There were others deeper still in the vaults of professional disgrace, and Vasty might thrust her down at his pleasure. For the bond which held her his paid servant gave him all authority and left her only dependence. She fully expected to be made a pantomime fairy—a huge insect or monster toad—perhaps a witch, or flitting elf with a lantern on its head—with her name in large capitals; as was once done to an eminent tragedian not long ago. But she felt that she could support any blow with courage now; she had drawn deep of the inspiration of endurance, and the more Vaughan attempted to crush her pride, the firmer and the stronger it became. This was a part of her character which few people understood.

After rehearsal—when she was rebuked and sworn at by the stage-manager more than once—she escaped from the theatre with the joy of a prisoner set free. All her artistic love had died. Perhaps it might be re-awakened in a new house, and under more favourable circumstances; but in her present situation, had the best character in the roll-call been awarded her, she could not have played it; so chilled to her heart was she by all the injustice and brutality she had undergone.

She noticed to-day that she was watched and looked at maliciously; that men and women laughed to each other as she passed them; that impudent words were spoken so that she must hear them; and that she was more than ever the licensed object of all that contempt and insolence which coarse minds love to shower on the disgraced. When Vasty came, she saw that one of the higher actors spoke to him seriously, and that both then glanced at her as they talked; and she heard the actor say earnestly and passionately—"I assure you, sir, it is true—she was seen with them; a regular boon companion at the ginshop!" Vaughan's face grew harsh, as if a midnight shadow had swept over the daylight; but he only nodded, as when one says "Very well—very well—I'll see about it!"

And then, rehearsal ended, she turned away and ran out of the theatre, choking with sobs that she would not allow to be transformed to tears.

Waiting near was Sarah Walcot. She was alone, and Clara did not see a dark face watching her silently through the chink of the gin-palace door; nor did she hear a stifled blessing that turned into a moan of pain, as that dark face buried itself in two quivering hands, and memories of a forgotten purity, and the pangs of an unavailing remorse, swept over the soul that no man sought to save.

"Oh, you are there!" cried Clara. "Have you been waiting long for me?"

"No, my lady, not so very long," answered Sarah cheerily. "There was a fire there, and they let me stand a bit back." She pointed to the ginshop.

"And how is your sister to-day?"

"Very bad, my lady—very bad indeed."

"What is the matter with her?"

"I don't know exact, my lady. She has a cough, and her side pains is bad, and she burns terrible, and sometimes baths at night, and gets weaker like, day by day. We've had a hard time for the last three years, and it's took more hold on her. She was younger nor me you see, and couldn't bear up so well."

"Have you no doctor?"

The girl shook her head. "No, my lady, such as we can't afford doctors," she said mournfully.

"But there are hospitals—workhouses"—urged Clare.

"Yes, but she isn't hurt you see, and it isn't no fever she's got. She has a consumptive, I believe they call it, and there's a consumptive hospital at Brompton; but you want a letter for that, and I don't know any one as has a letter. But if she gets on so bad as she is now, I must get her in somewhere. If work was better she'd mend fast enough."

"But the union?" said Clara; "why not go there?"

The girl blushed. "I don't like it, my lady," she answered with a courtesy. "We keep out of the house as long as we can. I don't want to see her there. Father never let us be in it. If work was slack we tramped; but we never went into no house yet."

"Then what will you do?"

She shook her head. "I don't know," she said. "Perhaps times will mend, and then we'll have more work and more pay. Both's been going down for a long bit; but things can't go down always, my lady. If they does, we'll all have to starve together."

"Was not Mr. Glynn very kind to you?" asked Clara, turning rather red; for she was aristocrat enough, proud wench! to feel half ashamed of mentioning Percival's name to a poor common begging-girl like this. Her democracy had always been a curious compound

of principle and feeling mixed up with aristocratic instincts that came
in as the scent of a hidden flower. They were instincts in the true
meaning of the word; mysterious in their origin, and irrepressible in
their expression.

"I didn't know his name, my lady, before last night when Emma
told it me. Are you ill, lady?" she added suddenly. "You are so pale!—
you look so sick!"

"No," answered Clara with drooping head and downcast eyes.
Then she raised herself bravely and added; "It was just a passing
faintness—nothing more. And Mr. Glynn has done a great deal for
you?"

"Yes, lady; he paid our rent a long bit; but he's left us lately."

"He has been ill," said Clara.

The girl's face brightened. She turned such a happy smile on the
young actress—in such evident joy at finding that her first impulse
of trust had not been misplaced, and that she had not found in the
"good gentleman who had been so kind to them" another instance
of the cruelty and indifference of the quality—that Clare felt quite a
sisterly feeling towards her. For had she not distrusted Percival just in
the same manner?—and had she not felt, when she found him true,
just the same delight?

"I am sorry the poor gentleman's been sick," said Sarah demurely.

"But," smiled Clare, "you are glad that he has not deserted you?
You would rather that he had been kept away by sickness than by
forgetfulness?"

"May be," said Sarah, dropping a courtesy.

They had been walking on slowly all this time towards Clare's
lodgings, which were not very far from the stage entrance to the
theatre.

When they reached the door of her house, Clare turned to the girl,
saying; "Come in with me, and I will give you some old linen that I
have. Perhaps it will be useful to your sick sister."

Now came the time of danger! If Clara Clayton be like the old Clare
de Saumarez of not so many years ago, Sarah Walcot will come in for
a rich reversionary interest in her wardrobe! With no one to check her
generous impulses by small whisperings of prudence—with no sort
of scruple in her trust, now that she knew the character of her new
protégée had been endorsed by Percival—her mirror of moral good—
she is in imminent danger of finding herself to-morrow morning the

possessor of sundry frocks and petticoats less a decent outfit given away to-day. It will be no miracle if she searches through her theatrical trunks, and forces on the poor pale slop-worker bodices of velvet and crumpled ball dresses of gauze, wreaths of faded roses and tiaras of coloured crystal; she would have done it three years ago—and people don't learn much wisdom generally in thirty-six months' time.

The landlady opened the door herself. Ensconced on Clara's sofa drawn up by Clara's fire, she could see all that passed in the street. She looked dreadfully indignant when she admitted the young slop-worker. If she had known more of her lodger's private history, she would have known that Clare had a kind of predilection for vulgar poverty, and that this was not the first time she had "lost her self-respect in her undesirable associates,"—as Mrs. de Saumarez used to say.

"Bring up some luncheon," said Miss Clayton to the woman, "and two plates and knives. And do you come in here," she added, turning to Sarah. "There is a nice fire in the room, and you must be very cold."

Wondering what she could be at that she was so kind to her, Sarah followed bashfully; treading on the threadbare carpet as if it had been a cloth of gold laid down over the narrow floor, and feeling sadly ashamed of her poverty of appearance in a lady's room. Mean as the whole appointments were for the home of a gentlewoman—faded, coarse, and torn as were the carpet and the curtains—worm-eaten the chairs—ink-stained the checked table-cover—to Sarah Walcot it was all a very fairy palace. There was a common blown-glass blue vase on the chimney-piece, flanked by two painted china pots such as are used for hair pomade or tooth powder; but they were Golcondan gems in Sarah's eyes; and not the finest picture by Raffaele could possibly have surpassed the loveliness of a rough chalk drawing of the lady in a queer dress, hanging over that narrow slip of mirror which turned everything into a sea green, but which made the poor girl quite bashful—it was so queer like to see so much of herself!

This drawing was a portrait of the "popular actress Miss Clayton, in her original character of Ianthe." It had been done by Vasty Vaughan in the happy days of her ignorance and love—before she had eaten of the tree of knowledge and been expelled from her Eden of security.

"Sit down and warm yourself," said Clara kindly, drawing a chair close to the fender; so close that it was impossible for anything but a mathematical line to find space of lodgment between it and the seat.

But it was such a cold day—a chair could not be too near the fire, you know!

"Oh my lady, you are so kind!" cried the poor girl, almost in tears of gratitude; " I never seed any one so good as you and that good gentleman!"

"Don't say so much about it," returned Clara; "it is only right to do all we can for each other. To give you help is only to do my duty towards GOD. We ought not to be thanked for that, you know! Christ did more for us."

"Ah my lady, not many quality think like that for us poor people! Not many would have done for one of us that was starving what you have done to-day! It is a truth my lady, and a hard one any how."

"They would if they were christians," said Clara very gravely. "Those who believe the Bible—and those alone—do their duty to their fellow-sinners. All the rest use only mocking words."

Sarah was silent. She simply looked up with a kind of wondering inquisitiveness, as if she had heard a strange language, or had come upon a scientific book full of hard names, of which she knew the letters only, not the sense.

At this moment the woman of the house brought in the tray.

She was an ingenious person this landlady, and thrifty, apparently, in her gastronomic arrangements. Yet if thrifty—to judge by the sum total of Clara's weekly bills—of extraordinary ill-luck in her shopkeepers, or else of fanciful notions of arithmetic, of which she must have had a purely private conception. Two dishes were on the coarse tin painted tray, which had a deep ledge or barrier all round it to prevent errant crockery from coming to the ground unwarily. One dish was what is called a pie dish. It was of yellow ware, burnt black and brown in some places—in others left quite pale, as if it had been blistered with the heat, and the blisters had never healed. This dish held the fragments of a beef-steak pie, which had once been both younger and more consolidated. A mass of oleaginous stuff, half jelly, half water, was mixed with suspicious-looking cubes that might have been the sodden parts of the crust—they looked like unmitigated fat—and with fragments of honest meat in a fibrous and unconventional condition, more curious than tempting. Then she had added the rejected tails of Clara's monotonous mutton-chops in an infinite number—bits of brown hard ham and bacon, which one shuddered to contemplate—a few cold small potatoes, such as

are commonly called "pig potatoes,"—and an audacious limp leaf
of bluish green, which once had belonged to a cauliflower in a state
of verdant surplusage. The other dish held all the tops and bottoms
and outside crusts of a generation of loaves. Hard shiny bits with a
sickly suspension of butter glazed sparingly along—knobs that had a
refreshing odour of onions about them—imperfect rounds of toast—
venerable antiques dating back many baking dynasties—dirty slices
with part of the crumb picked out by fingers innocent of water—
with a general presence of mice over all these portions of the staff
of life, as if that dish had been a musine union, where rats got sleek
on pauperization, and mouselings learnt gastronomy without danger.
To these dissections of loaves she had generously added a few scraps
of butter, of every possible hue that butter is made to assume by
chemical combinations known only to the traders in vaccine produce;
and all these things together made up what housekeepers call "broken
meat," and which is generally thought to be superior fare for the poor.

This womanly landlady was cross to-day. Being cross she was
savagely honest; determined that the parlour should not have any
right to complain that she was robbed of her fragments—as, being a
lone woman, she might perhaps have thought she was, if she had not
seen the very contrary before her own blessed eyes.

She placed the tray on the table with an air; and then left the room
in a curious cloud of chocolate-coloured gown, that always went out
behind in a very odd way.

Clara was in a state of great wrath when she inspected this olla
podrida.[69] She rang the bell; three distinct times before it was answered.
At last Mrs. Trimmer came; her small sharp face was very red, and her
eyes were particularly bright.

"Have you nothing better than this?" asked Clara quietly, pointing
to the "broken meat."

"Oh my lady, it'll do beautiful!" chimed in Sarah; "indeed ma'am
it's grand," curtseying to the landlady.

"No miss, there ain't nothing more," said Mrs. Trimmer in a crisp
decided manner.

"There *must* be more," urged Clara; "I sent down a large piece of
neck of mutton yesterday. Bring up that if you please."

"Neck of mutton miss?—neck of mutton? Let me see," said Mrs.
Trimmer, putting on an algebraic look, "I think Miss you eat it all,
didn't you?"

But Clara said "No," in a very positive manner, her haughty little face betokening no slight anger at the whole affair; and then Mrs. Trimmer gave way, though she had prepared herself to take her stand on the matter, and to prove that "Miss must have eat all the mutton unbeknown, or that vicked hussy Ann, had give it to the policeman."

However, she succeeded at last in discovering the relict somewhere in the twilight of her kitchen; and so the matter ended; and in another moment Clara was busy haggling off half a dozen bones for Sarah, who looked so pleased and yet so wistfully hungry all the time, and who did not seem to know that her young hostess's education in carving had not been given in an anatomical school—to judge by the perversity with which she would try to cut through bones and not through joints.

Leaving her to make as good a dinner as famine sometimes snatches from abundance, Clara then went into her own room, to look for sundry shawls and gowns that might be useful to the girl, and were not absolutely necessary to herself.

While thus employed, Mrs. Trimmer, who looked more than ever like her name, dashed open the door; and there entered simultaneously Percival, pale and weak, leaning on a stick and tottering like an old man, and Edward Mantell, stern, erect, beautiful, resolved, as a prophet of Israel in the days of his holy youth.

Sarah Walcot started when she saw them, and turned paler than ever beneath the young clergyman's severe eye of rebuke. Percival was looking for Clara, and did not see the slop-worker at all.

Clara almost shrieked for joy as she rushed from her bed-room, leaving the door wide open—an action that horrified Edward Mantell—to welcome Percival with enthusiastic pleasure. Her hand on his arm, she looked up into Edward's face gazing gloomily on her brightened countenance, with a whole world of girlish pride and fondness on her brow, crying; "Look, Mr. Mantell—this is Percival Glynn!"

Had Edward been a Catholic he would have crossed himself, and so put the sign between himself and that human fiend. Being a Protestant he simply shuddered, and drew back as from a scorching furnace fire; for so it seemed, to judge by the sudden flush that made the subsequent paleness so much more marble-like.

Percival too half started.

"And this is Clara's new friend?" he said holding out his hand frankly.

Edward took it, or rather laid his own, cold and dead, into the extended palm. He bowed, but did not speak. Clara saw that something was wrong, and her woman's instinct warned her that perhaps more annoyance than she dreamt of would be struck out, as sparks from a collision, from this unapt meeting of two such diverse natures.

"And you too!" cried Percival, now recognising Sarah Walcot; "why how many old faces have you gathered round you, Clara, since I had influence over your social life?"

Edward Mantell started. Oh! what a warp of evil was woven in with the woof of that dear life! He began to fear that Clara was marked out by Providence for reprobation—given over to the power of Satan without redemption!

"I have no other faces I think, Percival," she answered, drawing a chair near to the fire—her easy chair, such as it was—something inexpressibly like a singed dogskin.

At other times Edward would have flown to prevent her gentle hand from any labour, however slight, before him. Now he allowed her to move that lumbering chair without an attempt to help her.

"I cannot offer to assist you, Clara," said Glynn with a smile, "nor can I apologize for my weakness. It is nature's verdict for an offence against her laws, and so it must be borne patiently."

They laughed—both of them; and he sat down with a pleasant allowance of the invalid's necessities.

"And you, Mr. Mantell—won't you come to the fire? It is our best friend on such a day as this!" said Clara, trying to make all her guests happy and comfortable, and feeling that she did not succeed the least in the world. "Go on with your dinner, Sarah," she then added, addressing the slop-worker; "these gentlemen will not object."

"Oh no!" cried Percival kindly. "Nor will you Mr. Mantell—will you?"

"Miss Clayton is the mistress of her own room," he returned stiffly.

Poor Clare knew the accent of displeasure too well not to recognise it in that cold constrained voice, which seemed as if it would not relax its tense strings for any breath of southern softness whatsoever.

"Oh! you look so solitary out there!" she exclaimed smiling, but uneasily. "Do come into the magic circle!"

Her sweet voice! Though on the brink of destruction, luring him over the steep edge as a mountain spirit beckoning the doomed shepherd, he would follow where it led, and welcome even death if it came in any shape of her likeness! He did as she bade him, and sat down near her—Percival on the other side.

Sarah Walcot was perhaps the most uncomfortable of the whole party. She could not be prevailed on to remain; so after Clara had forced on her some antiquated raiment, princely to the poor girl's ragged wardrobe, and made her take with her all the "broken meat" which Mrs. Trimmer had brought up, she went away; Percival promising to see her as soon as he was able, and slily slipping a few shillings into her hand.

"And I will go with you!" said Clara, with a bright smile; "we will take care of you and your sister."

"We!" muttered Edward; "we—with an infidel and a socialist! Horror, horror, multiplied!"

Edward Mantell was to be pitied. How strained and false soever his views might be, he was earnest and truthful in them, even to the last result of martyrdom. He believed that all which he saw about Clara was sin in the very worst form, and therefore he was right in his renunciation and abhorrence. He knew no middle way of rejection for himself yet allowance for others. Denying the liberty of choice, the man who swerved aside from the strict creed which he believed to be alone truth, was emphatically anathema maranatha.[70] And in this he thought to do God service, and to fulfil the law of heaven; forgetting those divine attributes which man has named love—mercy—long-suffering—in his zeal for abstract right and justice; by which last he understood the truth and holiness of Vengeance.

He had a painful duty before him now, but one from which he must not shrink. To Percival's very face—confronting boldly this man of sin—he would denounce the criminal associates and unbefitting works of that unsuspecting girl, and call on her to cast from her the seductions by which she was surrounded, and to follow him to the temple of salvation.

When Sarah Walcot left the room, Edward Mantell drew his chair nearer to the fire, and turning to Clara said gravely—

"Do you know the character of the woman who has just left you?"

Clara looked at Percival as if to help her out of her difficulty.

"No, I don't know much about her," she said; "nothing in fact beyond her poverty."

"And that is sufficient for you?" he asked, his very tone a condemnation.

"Yes," returned Clara decidedly; "if people are poor they must be assisted by those who are richer."

"You are right, Clara," said Percival.

"Pardon me, you are wrong, Miss Clayton," said Edward coldly. "If people are *virtuous* and poor, they ought to be assisted by such legal means as the government has created; if they are vicious and poor they ought to be left to their poverty. To aid them is simply to encourage vice at the expense of virtue—to care for the wicked to the neglect of the good."

"But don't you think, Mr. Mantell, that men are made vicious by circumstances—especially by the neglect and the oppression of the higher classes?" said Clara with a flash of her old unreasoning republicanism. For though she spoke the truth now, she did not know the whole value of it.

"I am sorry to hear such a sentiment from you, Miss Clayton," he answered severely. "I did not expect you to utter an opinion which, to say the least of it, trenches on materialism."

"Yet it would be hard to disprove it," said Percival. "When you have a criminal population exclusively among one class, in a nation composed of the same race and under the same natural conditions, it is self-evident that accidental circumstances must create this class— that crime is owing solely in the mass to social or physical causes; in England to both combined."

"You forget the evil heart of man naturally," said Edward; "you forget the influence of Satan on the earth, and the want of vital religion. The power of the Prince of Darkness may be strengthened by social circumstances, but it never can be created by them."

"I do not forget the want of religion, but I place this amongst the results of an education which the poor do not possess. Had they education, they would have more spiritual religion; for this is essentially the handmaid of intellectual development, following on its steps as certainly as practical improvement follows on a more intimate acquaintance with scientific rules."

"I cannot allow this, sir. Religion is not the product of man's own mind. A truth handed down to us by divinely inspired men—a book writ by GOD himself—is a thing apart from and beyond human development. To understand Christianity, faith and pure heart only are required; chemistry and geology are not the keys to the door of life. And out of Christianity there is no religion; all the rest is a delusion and a snare—cunning devices of the great enemy of souls."

"And yet I think that even you will acknowledge that in the Dark Ages as they are called, many of the specialities of Romanism crept into the practice of Christianity simply from ignorance; and are supported to this day by ignorance. If the people were enlightened, even to the understanding of a few of the simplest natural laws, you know perfectly well that the religious miracles of the Romanists would fall to the ground as applications only of these natural laws—and as impostures in assuming to be supernatural or superior to them."

"That is no argument," Edward answered harshly. "In Rome is the power of the devil supreme. His seat is on the Seven Hills, and the wrong and crime and misery which flow round those bases are to be traced not to local causes, but to his dark rule in the hearts of men."

"Then how is it, Mr. Mantell, that, taking any nation or section of a nation, we find local peculiarities the sole causes of distinction between different classes? How is it that among the ignorant, badly fed, hardly paid, idle, and those who dwell in filth, uncleanliness, and indecency, you have, as a certainty, the result of moral depravity? If these were not creative causes, how is it that from these sources, almost wholly, you draw the criminal population of the country, while you find in the opposite social conditions the very reverse in morals? In these cases crime is not a simply spiritual effect."

"There are worse crimes than legal offences," said Edward, evading the question. "The poor are not the most guilty of the land. The world, the flesh, and the devil, have wider nets for the rich than any of those which are spread for the poor."

"But it is of the social criminal that I am speaking—it is of the ignorant and the depraved, not of the luxurious and the intellectual."

"One great cause of the present depravity of morals," cried Edward sternly, "is the pestilent presence of your so-called liberal opinions. Your chartists and your socialists—your penny publications and penny theatres—these are the wells of much of the vice which inundates the age. At the day of judgment, the hard-hearted infidel who never felt his blood warm with gratitude for all that GOD has done for him through Christ, will stand in a worse place than even the burglar or the murderer."

"But as the infidel and the socialist do not violate the laws of their country, nor the moral code of civilized nations, they must be laid on one side. The present discussion touches those only who fall strictly under the denomination of the criminal or dangerous classes—those who suffer here. And with these we have quite sufficient data to show that the want of domiciliary advantages of the humblest and most practical character, the want of education, of better wages, and of a truer position in the social world, are the exciting causes to crime. Practical reforms, based on purely physical grounds, would lessen both moral and legal offences, leaving but a very small residue for madness and imbecility—in other words, for disease and mal-organization."

"Do you make man a god? Is this the impious result of an impious creed?"

"If you mean the unlimited application of infinite powers, then I do make him a god! I make him capable of attaining to the same perfection as that which exists in nature, by the study and use of her laws. I make him capable of attaining a place in the visible creation as much beyond what he now possesses as his present condition is superior to that of the brutes. I find nothing in his history contrary to nature—nothing beside the universal plan; and therefore I assume his power to be in exact ratio with his knowledge, and his moral development in true relation with his knowledge of GOD through creation. As far as we have yet gone, we have seen this to be true."

"And what make you of evil?" asked Edward, as one who kept his calmness by a great effort of the will.

"I deny it as an independent existence," replied Percival quietly. "At the worst it is but a condition which displeases *us*, and which we therefore agree in condemning. We never think of its necessity, and consequently of its importance and ultimate general good, in the scheme of creation."

"To me your ideas are so chaotic—so entirely those of an unregenerate heart—that I cannot answer them. You ignore the Bible; and this is my only landmark. All beyond is but a sea of death and darkness, into which I care not to venture. On the Bible I take my stand; and the universe of nature and of man—of matter and of spirit—I measure by this rule alone. If I find certain principles consistent with its teaching, then do I know that they are true, and approved of by GOD: if opposed to this, then are they the work of the devil. I know no other standard—I wish no other guide. And there I find that for one man's disobedience all men are born in sin and unto death, and there I find also the means of cleansing from that sin and the way of everlasting life, given to us by GOD, manifest in the flesh."

"Then why has it not made the world better?" asked Clara innocently. "If the Bible is all that men want to make them good, why is there so much vice in the world yet, eighteen hundred years after it was first printed?"

A look of pain, gradually hardening into condemnation, crossed the young preacher's beautiful face.

"Why?" he said; "how often must I tell you why?—because of the natural perversity of man—because of the influence of Satan."

"Oh no!" cried Clara, drawing nearer to Percival.

"And those who do not receive this truth," continued Edward, his voice more than ever mournful, his bearing more than ever stern, "are given over to a reprobate heart, and the sin of pride of intellect; which last has ruined countless souls since the fall of Lucifer! It will be my endeavour to preserve at least one young lamb for the flock! It is my duty to assure you, from words that cannot lie, that you are in more than mere danger—that you are prejudged and already condemned, if you suffer yourself to be led away by the false doctrines blatant now around you. Born of man's pride and want of faith, they are essentially doctrines of the enemy of man. The simple way of trust in the offer of salvation held out by GOD, and of acceptance of the means which He has prepared, is your only way to heaven. All others lead to the pit of eternal death. At your own peril you refuse this way. Remember—once made, your determination cannot be recalled! In the grave is no repentance, neither amelioration, nor life. GOD hath spoken these truths by the mouths of his holy men of old; is it for man to reject the counsel of the Infinite?"

Clara was pained. She looked at Edward affectionately, and said, "I do not dream of arguing with you, Mr. Mantell! I leave that to Percival. You will be my mental champion, will you not, to save me from certain defeat by this onslaughting giant?"

"Cannot you defend yourself?" answered Percival, looking down on her fondly. "You have truth on your side, and this ought to conquer any giant in the whole world of argument."

"What do you call truth, Mr. Glynn?" asked Edward Mantell suddenly.

"Perhaps I can define it best by negatives," he answered. "At any rate this seems to me to be the truth—that man is in no wise distinct, physically or morally, from the laws governing the rest of the universe, and therefore his being is to be referred to these and their action only;

that he has no special part allotted to him, and therefore cannot go beyond nor against the whole; that he has as much power as exists throughout nature, if he will but apply the laws; that evil is essentially imperfection or preponderance; and that the material world, and human nature—its product—could not exist as they are under different component parts, but are to be improved by adjustment and balance. Therefore from this I deduce the belief that all is good, and that it is but ignorance and egotism which imagine evil as an abstract existence, making our finite senses our only gauge to the plan of universes and of spheres."

"Do you deny the soul?—its punishments and its rewards? For to this your rejection of evil as an original condition must at last come."

"No; I do not deny the soul—but I cannot believe in an infinity of torture for a finite fault. More especially since our so-called faults are almost always the result of organization or disease."

"And I do!—furnaces heated seven times seven!—seven times seven! The people of the Lord must be purged with fire, the chaff winnowed from the corn with a strong blast! It has gone forth in wailing and gnashing of teeth—in blasphemy and despair—but it *has* gone forth!—and woe to them found naked in the day of trial!"

"And I," cried Percival fervently, "believe in a deep mysterious good reigning supreme over all the appearance of ill. I believe in an end of greater worth than the condemnation of a world for the childish fault of one man—I believe in the inter-dependence of universal creation, and that we do not stand apart and alone, but are links in the whole—a chain we cannot see!"

Edward buried his face in his hands, and remained thus for some time praying silently; while Clara put her hand into Percival's, and looked up into his face with a mute admiration that went like a sweet song to his very heart.

"But to come back to my original question," said Edward, suddenly. "Do you know the character of that young girl who was here, Miss Clayton?"

"No," said Clara.

"Then I do. I was passing through —— street last night, when I saw this young woman in company with another female, whose character and class were very evident. They begged of me—they begged of you——"

"They!" interrupted Clara, with quivering lips. "Did Emma Vau—did the other woman beg?"

"No," he corrected himself. "No, she did not. This younger one only. I made a mistake."

"Go on," said Clare. "That is all—go on."

"I saw *you* speak to them, for I was near the stage door when you came out. I then, after you left, went to the women and took down their addresses. From no idle curiosity I visited both places this morning; and I find that they are women of the very worst, the lowest class—that they are both to the last degree disreputable and abandoned."

"Is this true, Percival?" cried Clare. "Is it true, and did you know it before?"

"Calm yourself, my dear child! There is no need of any agitation or distress. Yes; I know the whole lives and histories of these poor women——"

"And knowing them you could suffer this young innocent thing to become interested in them—to breathe the same air with them—to contaminate her fresh purity by the foul contact of their sins? Oh! this is monstrous! this is devilish!"

The young clergyman was much agitated.

"Yes," said Percival quietly; "I wished as far as my influence extended, to make Miss Clayton judge for herself, and from higher ground than that on which the rash verdicts of the world are based. I wished her to throw off some of that pharisaical horror of the criminal which had clung to her—though so foreign to her own nature—from the false education of her early life. I wished her to find by experience that crime is not always so guilty as it seems, and that one fault does not vitiate the whole character: in a word, I wished her to feel the beauty of the Gospel of Mercy, and to have done with the fierce code of retribution and vengeance. For this reason I allowed her to become interested in this young slop-worker before I told her the truth; and for this I wished her to prove that Emma, though one of the worst of her class—is not wholly degraded, but that a germ of goodness yet remains in her seared heart, from whence mercy and gentleness might educe a green and healthy plant yet. These were the great truths I wished to teach her, or rather to leave her to find out for herself."

"Truths do you call them!" exclaimed Edward bitterly—"fiendish fallacies—mocking lies—snares and pitfalls for the soul, covered with false flowers and withered grass! Tell us, Miss Clayton—do you now, on the first pure impulse of your heart, feel that Mr. Glynn has been a true or a safe friend in this act of his?"

Clara laid her hand on Percival's shoulder.

"I must always trust him, even if I do not understand his motives," she said very fondly.

"That is not an answer to my question," he returned, with a quick spasm across his face.

"Then honestly, at the very first I felt shocked and wounded that he should have done such a thing. But when he explained why he did so, I felt with him—and that he was quite right, and that I had been often very very much to blame for uncharity and coldness towards those who did wrong! I am afraid, Mr. Mantell, we sometimes worship ourselves when we believe to worship any particular virtues!"

Clara said this with the air of one who had made a profound discovery undreamt of since Adam. Percival smiled.

"That was a wise aphorism, my child," he said gently. "Where did you hear it?"

"Nowhere but *here!*" she answered, laying her hand on her heart. "On looking back I can see so well that often when I believed to love goodness simply for its own sake, I was admiring myself in the reflection of many fancied virtues, none of which I had perhaps."

"And because you have convicted yourself of mental dishonesty on some occasions, are you to rush into the opposite extreme, and for humility's sake companion with the vilest refuse of the populace, that you may not have temptation to such vanity? I confess this seems to me an unphilosophical and illogical (to apply your own terms) and eminently an unpractical method of self-subjection! Do you approve of these extreme views, Mr. Glynn?"

"In this instance. For every excess into which inexperience may lead this impetuous heart, it will learn a far greater truth, more valuable and more grand, than a little personal inconvenience can blemish. I never expect Miss Clayton to take a moderate view or a middle course—at least not for many years yet. It becomes then only a question which is the best thing to give her—which extreme will lead her the least wrong?"

"Oh, that is cruel!" laughed Clara.

"But true."

"Now, is it true, Mr. Mantell? Have you found me such a mental savage?" She appealed to him playfully.

"I have found you, Clara Clayton, an artless, pure, unspotted soul—unspotted save from the birth-stains of inherited sin; I have seen you in the hands of men who have laboured night and day to destroy that purity, to take advantage of that artlessness, to corrupt that soul. Under various guises I have seen this. But you have escaped as yet; escaped with some life of virtue left in you. I have been cast in your path by a merciful Providence, unwilling that you should be wholly lost—unwilling that you should suffer without redemption from the evil doing of others. If you do not listen to me, the sin is your own; if you do listen to me, you will escape from this frightful condition where you are placed, and gain the door of faith and salvation. I have no more to say, but that I repudiate for ever all intercourse with this gentleman, your self-constituted guardian; that I call you again in the name of Him who loved you and gave himself for you, to escape while there is yet time, and flee to the city of refuge. If you will go unto Christ he will receive and heal you; if you keep back from him he will deny you in the last day, and cast you out among the devil and all his angels, where shall be weeping and gnashing of teeth. This I am commissioned to tell you. If you turn a deaf ear to my solicitations, your blood be on your own head; for you have refused the heavenly salvation that was offered you, and preferred the blind reason of humanity instead. I do not condemn you personally," he then said, turning to Glynn, "but I protest against you as an unfit associate for this young girl. I protest against your opinions, your actions, your godless life. I care not for your philanthropy of temperament: what profits it if you save a world, if it be not done from the right motives, and to the glory of GOD? Not a very hecatomb[71] of charities piled up will secure you from the wrath of the Eternal, whose will you have despised and whose Son you have rejected. I do not condemn you personally, but as a faithful minister of the word I cannot associate with you. We are strangers in faith and strangers in lot, and we must be strangers in life. GOD decide between us! To you, Miss Clayton, I shall have much to say at some future time. Until then I commend you to the mercy and the grace of the Holy Spirit."

He raised his hands, invoking on her a blessing that at least was pure and holy in its intention; and then he left them, more broken-hearted than he had ever felt before.

"Clara," said Percival suddenly, "do you love that man?" pointing to Edward rushing down the street.

"Love him? No!" she exclaimed, looking much surprised. "Why do you ask?"

"Simply because he loves you."

"Oh, Percival, no! He cannot love me! He is so strict, and believes that my profession is so sinful. He cannot possibly love me!"

"Would it please you if he did?"

She shuddered strongly. "No!—indeed, no!" she cried. Then creeping closer to her friend, she sobbed rather than said; "I shall never love any one again!"

To soothe her, Percival laid her cheek against his shoulder; and she stayed there, sorrowing at the desolation of her heart and the death of love in her young life, while clinging to him—her dear—her patient friend.

"Then be prepared, my child," he continued, after a short silence, "to receive a confession of love from him, and that at no distant date. His affection for you is quite evident to me, and would be to you also, had you had more experience in such matters. You must make up your mind, Clara, whether you will accept him for your lawful spouse or not."

He looked down into her face. Suddenly her cheek flamed like the eastern sky, and her blue eyes took a darker tinge: yet why I know not. Percival's face was calm—full of its usual sweetness and gentleness and affection. She had been so long accustomed to this brotherly manner of his, that surely the fact of resting on his arm need not so derange her maiden modesty! Yet for some reason, whatever it might be, she blushed thus bashfully, and then looking up, exclaimed—

"It would kill me! Indeed it would!"

By a great effort—a very great effort—Percival refrained from kissing her forehead. He felt this innocent speech deeply. It seemed to give him new life, and to burnish up his sickly face as gold in the crucible. He did, unwittingly, place his arm half round her crouching shoulders, and then hurriedly withdrew it—his fingers tingling, and his heart beating, as if he had committed robbery.

There was a long silence; during which Clare was comparing the two men who had lately essayed her conversion from such different points, and asking herself which she thought the truest doctrine: the one which was so stern, so high, so lofty in its very severity, so condemnatory, so narrow—or the other, which left the destinies of man something chaotic, and blurred out the traditional lines between vice and virtue; which uprooted old rules of life, and replaced them with such wide and indefinite allowance as to make any one path equal with the other, and any one end of life as true as another. But the liberality and the freedom and the love of Percival attracted her more than the stern asceticism of Edward Mantell; and she was more than ever inclined to take what shape her old master chose to impose on her, if he left her time to adapt herself and did not force her simply to imitate.

Percival knew her too well to make this mistake of constraint or premature assumption. He detailed, as she could bear them, portions of his belief; assimilating his lessons with her mental age, and giving her only what she could adopt naturally, leaving it to herself to work out the full truth of what he might propound. And he never found that she swerved from the line. Surely, by self-examination, reflection, and reason, she came round to the opinion he wished her to receive; and so much progress in the development of her character was gained, so much waste land reclaimed. He hoped greater things though than those already attained.

He now rose to go. He stood irresolute, though his leave-taking had been made, and she had promised to see him to-morrow.

"Clara," he then said, "I have something to suggest—to advise, if you like."

"What is it?" she asked, looking into his face.

"I am half afraid of you though."

"Why? Am I not always very obedient?"

She laughed as she spoke, and blushed a little; remembering in what she had not been quite so obedient not so long ago.

"But this is a painful subject," he returned gravely; "and I am afraid that you will not like me to mention it."

She thought he alluded to Vaughan, and felt much distressed.

"Oh, yes," she said affectionately; "*you* may say anything! What is it?"

"Your grandfather."

She stalled, changed colour, looked proud, abashed, fond, repelling—everything in turns, and nothing definite.

"Well?" she said coldly, after a pause.

"You loved him always, as a child? I think you have said so to me?"

"I liked him as a groom," she answered haughtily.

"More than that, Clara! You loved him as a brave and good old man—as one of the worthiest of the people—as one who loved you well! Come!—put off this haughty air!—it does not suit that frank republicanism of yours! Remember dear, whatever you may feel, he is your real, true, undoubted grandfather. Now come!—look that fact steadily in the face, and give me your answer."

She was silent; then going up to Percival, said caressingly—

"You are right, Percival, and I was base and mean; but it is passed now. Just one little spark of the De Saumarez pride!" she added laughing. "You know I can scarcely believe that I am not still the heiress!"

"That's my noble Clare! I knew she would come to her senses on a moment's reflection! And now, when the De Saumarez pride is banished, what will Clara Clayton do for her old grandfather?"

She looked into his face puzzled.

"I don't know," she said.

"Don't you? Will you not write to him—a letter from your heart—and ask him to share your fortunes? Peasant as he is, will it not be well for you to have his presence and his sanction? Birth does not give nor take away the respectability of such an age as old Hugh's. If I had not been ill, I would have told you this long ago."

"I will!" she answered bravely. "I will write to-night! I have never had any communication with the Hall since I left; but I will positively write to-night to Hugh, and do as you tell me; for I like to please you, Percival!"

He pressed her hand and left her; and she watched his feeble steps for so long a time as she could see him—as she used to watch Vasty's noble figure.

But with what a different feeling!

CHAPTER XII.

THE letter was something of a trial to Clare, for it was the first practical test of her republicanism. Hitherto this had been condescension only; its very social equalization morally exalting her; now it was strictly fraternal—no longer a merit but an obligation. And Clare liked obligatory virtues as little as most people.

Boast as Clara might of her democratic principles—"radical to her very heart" as she used to say—she had no mean dash of the aristocrat's pride in her. This she partly inherited from her Lotharian[72] father—partly had been taught by circumstances. She was too refined, too fond of beauty, had been too long accustomed to believe herself one of the privileged classes—not to feel a certain consciousness of distinction, which, to do her justice, she tried hard to suppress. The fact of her peasant birth had never been brought clearly home to her. It had not yet exerted any individual influence over her life. She had left the Hall before it had been revealed to her, and was in just the same position since its publication. No sudden nor apparent difference kept her constantly reminded of the change. If anything, she felt relieved that all blood connexion with the De Saumarez was at an end, and that she might henceforth build up the temple of her fortunes unopposed by prejudice and undelayed by duty. Though the last, as families render it, had never been very patent in Clare's turbulent life of independence.

This feeling of relief had been while she rested under the shadow of love. When that was gone, she knew then what her real position was, and how painful in its loneliness; how that she belonged to no one person in the world—how that she was nameless, friendless, uncared for—with no portion in the allotments of affection—no share in the established order of society. She stood on one side of it all; an excrescence, not a member.

It was a painful feeling; shattering her innocent pride with a rude hand all too heavy for the light thing it had to destroy.

When she found that she was not so wholly alone as she supposed—that though she could not claim kindred with noble names or lengthy genealogies, she still had ties of birth as sacred as those which society endorses—for the instant that small spirit of pride woke up in her soul, urging her to reject the love that was offered in such coarse cup of vulgar peasanthood. What!—she, a gentlewoman by education and position, to be linked for life with low minds sodden with vulgarity—to be hourly agonized by unrefined deeds—untutored words, which her former training had taught her to abhor? It was horrible! Was then her wish, once spoken to Percival, that she had been "born one of the people," nothing but empty verbiage? It seems so, indeed, by this instinctive shrinking from those of the people to whom blood had bound her. This was for the first few moments; before she had well considered what she was called on to do, and by what high principle of good. The next half-hour saw her sitting by the table, writing to her grandfather a tender noble letter.

The village of Shorne contained almost all the characteristics of a miniature town. It had two or three inns, as many public-houses and beer-shops as a Scotch village, and an immense number of those rural nondescript shops where everything is sold, including nails, cheese, bacon, fruit, grocery, and feminine finery. It contained also a pair of antiquated stocks, still kept for the terror of vagrants and evil-doers, but not much used now; to the open grief of the old Tories of the place. At a little distance from the main street was a pound for stray cattle; in the marketplace was a large market-cross; close beside it a lock-up house, with bars in the door, by which prisoners could see and communicate with their friends outside—like caged animals for show—to the manifest frustration of the ends of justice; and near this again was the workhouse.

The authorities of Shorne were not destitute of humanity. The parish was of course included in a union, since the operation of the new poor-law;[73] but they still kept their own old workhouse for the reception of the aged poor—those whose hearts had become so rooted to the place as to make a removal from the village the worst feature in their bitter lot of pauperism.

The house would not have held many people at any time. It was a low rambling old place, only one story high, with small square casements that let out a little of the interior darkness, rather than let in much of the external light. It was damp and mouldy, more picturesque than inhabitable—a greater prize for an artist's sketch-book than for an English farmer's last home. The low roof, badly thatched and pervious—the wood work mouldering away from dry rot, and the plaster peeling off the walls, both inside and out—the thick ivy forming a pretty-looking nest for earwigs and spiders—all made it very admirable for the lovers of scenic effects, but very uncomfortable for a human habitation. The floor was of clay. In some parts the clay had delved into deep hollows, in which was a supply of standing water that gave unexpected pediluvia[74] to the inmates, and offered burglarious temptations to entomologists. It would have been difficult to find a more populous hydrogenous world anywhere than that which the workhouse floor at Shorne supplied. But this was the fashion of the country; and the old folk did not mind it much. At least they did not grumble. And as men in power make the loudness of a complaint their only gauge to the impropriety of a law or custom, the workhouse floor was thought good enough—else the paupers would have complained. A curious way of management! Something like teaching a dog to bite before you give him his daily food— an employment more ingenious than profitable, but of frightful universality now in Europe generally.

It was exactly a year and nine months ago to-day, since Clare de Saumarez, as she was then, had run away from home, and launched herself alone on the stormy sea of a professional career. It was the circumstance of the twenty-first lunar anniversary that made yon knot of men, standing by the quaint market-cross, remember it at this particular moment, and begin to discuss the characters of the past and present heiresses. For it had been a stirring time for the neighbourhood at large; and people in country places do not soon forget such a mighty epoch in the annals of their great family—such broad flat landing-places, where they may stand and take breath for a long time before they go on to the next large event in their small lives.

This was just the kind of thing of which age would make an historic miracle. Had it occurred in the olden times, we should have had legends for every hill and grove and greenwood lane in the county. Here would have been the Lady's Leap, where the true heiress, fleeing from the persecutions of the usurper, would have bounded over the black chasm—the sleuth hound at her heels, and belted men with cross-bows and arquebuses[75] pointed to her destruction. Here we should have seen the identical spot where she was ridden over, the wild fierce falsehood spurring on her with her gallant steed and jessied[76] falcon; there we should have wept over the frightful stains on the wainscot of yon small dungeon-room, which still remained in attestation of the cruel ill-usage of the gentle maid: and in the gallery, traditional pictures would have given us the dark malignant Moorish features of our bright young Clare in a blaze of oriental gems, and stiff with velvet luxury; and there, a heavenly angel clad in white, her fair hair reaching to her heel, and her blue eyes cast upward to her home above, would have idealized the cold, graceful, loveless Alice of to-day.

It is odd how necessary it is for the symmetry of a traditional heroine that she should be fair. Virtue and flaxen hair have always had a strange union in the minds of the poetic world; and a brunette angel seems as incompatible with seraphic physiognomy, as a dove with a hawk's bill, or a lily with a nettle's sting. Yet one cannot exactly make out why colour and morality should be paired, nor what good philosophic basis can be given for the belief.

However, time had not dimmed the fresh colours of reality to such changed hues as these. Clara was still the free brave young girl, who had a smile and a word for every one, and who knew all about every man's dog and every woman's child: and Alice was still the haughty, and to rustic eyes, inexpressibly lovely lady, who trod the earth as though she honoured it by her touch, and who made her dependants feel how strong was the barrier of birth that had lately raised itself between them; though they could not help sometimes remembering the time when they were all on an equality.

But common people do somehow love a little haughtiness in the great family of their place. And what they deny to simple wealth without lineage, they will always give to poverty and blood. In this they are unlike the people of the towns, who court gold allied with any amount of vice or vulgarity that may chance to be connected with it.

And so a knot of idle men—such men as are always lounging about a village, especially when the coach is expected—were sitting on the market-stone this bright February day, talking of Clara and Alice, and how they liked them both, and what they thought of them.

"Well, Miss Clara for my money!" said one, a rough honest-looking fellow. "There was allus good in her, though folk do say she has fallen out of the right way terribly."

This was said as if she had committed murder and was waiting to be gibbeted.[7]

"Poor lass! she was very young like, and had no one to give her no word," said another, an old man with white hair, who had dandled Clara slily without the knowledge of Mrs. de Saumarez many a day. "Dear! sure! I remember her when she was nobbut a brat running round Martha's floor, and making every one wait on her like slaves like. She grew up a fine lass. She would have done better I've heerd tell, if they had been kinder like at the Hall. They wouldn't have found no Miss Alice then, for the poor young lady would never have set off with that play-actor woman."

"But if she's bad now, Tom, she was bad then," chimed in a stern-looking man of about fifty. He had been a soldier, and had seen some service under the 'Dook;'[78] his ideas consequently were more ship-shape and disciplined than those of the clodpoles he had to deal with. And his influence was in proportion with his superiority. He spoke now with authority, and most of his audience seemed prepared to listen with humility.

"Yet she looked good enough," said Tom, the old man.

"So many a one does that ain't no better for all their good looks. She couldn't have gone wrong all at once you know. You can't make a blood into a mongrel."

"But is it sure true?" asked the first speaker.

"Ay!" they all cried; "they say so at the Hall."

"What, man? What do they say, for I've not heerd plain yet," asked old Tom.

"Nay, what I can't say grand words," answered the ex-soldier; "but I fancy it's as bad as may be. And it's a shame and a sin of those as has been drilled better to fall back in the ranks, and turn out bad after all. What's the use of drilling if it ain't to make a good soldier?"

"You're right, Ben," cried the first speaker.

The old man shook his head. "I'd be loath to believe any ill of her," he said; "she was a brave lass, and she spoke very kindly to my Sally when in the measles, and she did a deal of good, and folks do say she was parlous learned; and I'd be very sorry, I say again, to believe any ill of her all along of that whey-faced chit they've set up in her place. Heiress forsooth!—they'd do better to keep her in the kitchen to larn manners!"

"Treason and arson," said the soldier angrily. "It's a crime, Tom, any way, that you've done. We've no call to speak agin our commanding officers, and yet you've done it, Tom, and afore a public!"

"Well, well!" said the old man rising; "for my part I don't know much about it. I think Miss Clara was wronged somehow. She was born in the house and brought up in the house, and she oughtn't to have been turned out of the house. If she warn't the heiress she was every bit as good, and a deal better too!"

"So I say," said the man they called Ned—the good-tempered fellow who had opened the conversation. "She was as brave a lass as ever trod shoe-leather, and she made a better mistress than this new thing there. She went about among the poor like, and did what she could, being young, for them. Miss Alice never put her foot inside the door-sill of a cottage since into the Hall she came. Lor-a-mussy! she'd think a poor man's house would swallow her up alive like Dannel and the cave. Miss Clara was a bonny lass too; and I'm like Tom, I don't well believe as how badness and a bonny face go together. She was too good to have turned out so bad as they seem to say."

"Have you seen Hugh lately, Ned?" the old man asked.

"No, I never seen him. That wasn't a nice article—that wasn't," he observed, turning to the ex-soldier. "Do you think Miss Clara would have warned off any old servant as had been so long about the place, and was father too, to her own mother—leastways what she took for her mother so long?"

"Well, I don't like know—it wasn't pretty well I thank you, I admit," returned the soldier. "But Miss Alice is a nice young lady for all that, and she walks so upright! She walks like a drill sergeant. She's no awkward squad—she ain't!"

Before any one could answer, the coach came rushing and bustling through the town. Just as jovial, pompous, gallant, gay, and inconstant as all mail coaches are; appearing to-day and then to-morrow; with the same smile on the faces of guard and coachman—the same saucy compliments to barmaid and landlady—the same insinuation that this spot, this very identical spot, is the centre of the universe to them, and that Eden itself should not tempt them away if government and the post-office in London could do without them—nothing in short, but the leathern bags and the ribbons and the horses; with the same mystery over the interim—the same impenetrable coffin of ignorance for all the melting scenes and stereotyped love-makings at every other place on the road. The same to-day as yesterday—to-morrow as to-day—was the gallant bustling mail coach; always welcome, vile inconstant rover as it was—freighted with tender thoughts and anxious wishes—sped on its way by bright eyes and sunny smiles—the type of careless love to the steady village world of Shorne.

Here came the mail to-day: the south mail from London—with its bags, not very plethoric, of letters, and a few newspapers, varying from one to three weeks' old—with its panting horses and dusty travellers—though these were looked on as base live stock, scarcely to be reckoned after the cattle and the luggage.

The usual bustling reception was given; the usual bustling farewell; when off in a very tempest of horses' hoofs on the frozen ground flew the lumbering machine, rattling over the stones in an ostentatious sort of way that got the girls' hearts fairly out of them. And then, after its departure, the letter-bags were opened at the post office, and their contents thumbed and examined.

Among them was one addressed to—

"Hugh Clayton,

"Shorne,

"———shire."

It bore a London post-mark, and was written in a bold round hand, which a graphiologist—a veluti-in-speculum[79] man—would have pronounced at once to be in the hand-writing of a young but decided person. It might have been from a boy as well as from a girl, except that the "g" and the "y" were too near the verge of elegance—not the clear distinct elegance of the mathematician—but the flowingness of the womanly character: like a robe falling round the words.

The people at Shorne were not graphiologists, and therefore the rough guess that this letter came from Clara, and none other, was more a matter of instinct than of knowledge.

The postmaster laid it in a little pigeon-hole against the wall of his dark room. There were many little pigeon-holes there; a few of them had curious-looking letters in them, and very antiquated newspapers; lying till their owners should come in to town on market-day and fetch them away.

"Where is Hugh now?" asked a gossip to whom had transpired the pregnant fact of a letter for the disgraced old groom.

"No one knows, I fancy," was the answer. "He's been seen about the woods and in the young plantations and such like, but none knows where he bides or what he would be at. It was a hard job, that turning him off. Miss Alice needn't hold her head so high or turn up her nose at decent folk because they be poor; she's known the day when she'd have given much for Hugh's good word!"

"She's a proud huzzy and not worth one's wind!" cried the first. "Why sure!—what's to do now!"

And what was to do?

A crowd of men gathering at the upper end of the street—a crowd of boys and children running as if to a sight—women pressing in among them, some with uplifted hands and some with their aprons to their eyes—and then a parting made in the human atmosphere encircling the cause of this disturbance, and showing an old man with long white beard and silver hair—a broken, tottering, weary man—a helpless monument of weakness and despair—the failing shadow of old Hugh Clayton.

Broken at last! Jaded and foundered—an old horse led to the knacker's[80] yard—was he, this honourable hereditary servant of the great family, brought down now to the village workhouse.

And still he struggled against it; and still he would try to break away from the arms that held him; and still turn his withered face wistfully to the road where the Hall lay beyond, and weep like a child that his home was no longer there. And still and still he strove against the workhouse, as he would have striven against his coffin while in life and strength.

But it was in vain. There was nothing for him but this; and he knew it; and would eventually yield to its necessity; only at the first he could not bring himself to bear the thought of it quietly.

The people pitied him. Though such a rough village set, they felt how great a trial this close of his life must be to him; how painful its rude destruction of all his honourable pride, his hereditary dignity of place. They sympathized with him and cheered him in such homely fashion as they knew; they spoke to him in the same respectful tones that he had commanded when still in place; and this, more than anything else, helped to calm him.

In the midst of all this village democratic demonstration, the carriage from the Hall came dashing down the street; Mrs. Saumarez and her daughter reclining back among the cushions and sumptuous luxuries of its divan-like frame.

It stopped at a small shop for some insignificant article of feminine use—in the very midst of the crowd. Mrs. de Saumarez put up her glass and asked coldly, "What is the matter there? What are they all doing?"

"Oh, mamma, do not ask!" exclaimed Alice. "It is only some tipsy man."

She turned away her eyes haughtily.

At that moment the people gave way; and just in front of the carriage was seen Hugh's aged figure leant against the horse-block by the White Hart Inn, the blood trickling from a small wound—nothing more than a scratch—on his forehead, and mingling with his white hair in a striking and somewhat ghastly fashion.

Mrs. de Saumarez made a movement of disgust—she never could endure the sight of blood! and Alice ordered the coachman to drive on in impatient terms, bidding him harshly to escape out of this "disgusting crowd."

The old man's ear caught the words. As the carriage thundered on, he cursed that pale girl lying there in all her pomp, with words of bitter imprecation. He cursed her now and for ever—withered in her youth—withered in the fruit of her body—withered in her affections, her hopes, her desires—a lasting monument of pride stricken to its base—a living homily on the retribution of a cruel vanity.

But curses carry no stings to the deaf ear: and Alice drove on in her feathers and her pride, and not a shadow fell on her brow—not a cloud gloomed over her heart. Had she even heard them, could the bitter words of a crazed peasant move *her*? The panoply of rank and birth and fortune—triply strong as it was—secured her against all such pigmy onslaughts! The air might be convulsed with the heaviness of such impotent madness as this—it would but prove the might of her strength, and place her all the higher: as a white swan sailing calmly where the grim pool is blackest.

The old man then turned, and voluntarily entered the workhouse.

As his foot crossed the threshold a giddiness seized him; his eyes grew dark, his hearing became a confused rush of many sounds, his limbs failed him, and he sank to the ground struck with paralysis. The excitement and the sorrow were too much for him. He yielded to their pressure as many a stronger man had done before him.

They assisted him to bed, and sent for the parish doctor, who, when he had finished his hand of cribbage with the wine-merchant of Shorne, came and ordered a basin and bandages. The old man was bled very copiously; a dozen leeches were applied to his forehead; and, if he should not be better, a blister and other such pleasantries threatened for the morrow. He was then left to himself, with the belief that he could live strongly impressed on the minds of all those who had seen the energetic treatment of the parish doctor.

"My word, but he did not spare him!" they said.

"Nor himself neither!" was rejoined. "It was hard work to stand over an old body like that, and folk must have a deal of patience who are doctors."

When it is remembered that Hugh had been doing his best to kill himself for some time past—that he had been days without food, at least with so little that it was scarcely worth a name—that he had been weeks and weeks, through all the cold frosty nights of winter, lying out in the plantations and about the home fields of the hall, in a kind of sullen attachment so unreasoning as to become almost a mania—that he had indulged in such wild sorrow as almost broke his heart, and drew consolation from naught—it will seem strange that he survived, if only a few hours, treatment which might have saved a horse, but surely must have killed any man in the world!

However, he was put to bed and told to go to sleep; and the mistress of the workhouse, who was a good, matronly, comfortable body, brought him up a basin of gruel, and tried to make him feel resigned. But he only cried a great deal, and moaned, and said that he was punished for his sins, and that he had not suffered half enough; that wrong never could come right, and that he had done a power of wrong to everybody. All of which the matron took to be a wandering in the head, and so let him talk—which was the best thing she could have done.

It soon became known to all the village that old Hugh's pride had at last been brought down, and that he had been "took really to the workhouse." It created a great deal of gossip; and knots of people got together in shops, and by public-house doors, discussing Hugh's character, and his share in the late transactions at the hall. And though they had all been discussed nearly every day since the occurrence— they came in now as perfectly new; a vigour and piquancy being added by his unhappy state.

Some one with more brains than the rest, hereupon remembered him of a "letter he had heerd tell of, lying at the post-office;" and more than one volunteered to fetch it him. How it ever got safe and whole to Hugh remains a miracle—they were all so curious to have a look at it; and it passed from hand to hand so often, that it must have been of remarkably strong fabric to have withstood all this wear and tear. So many, too, were anxious to be the bearers of this oblong piece of paper, that when they all arrived at the workhouse door, they looked more as if they were going to storm the garrison than cheer a sick man.

The matron relieved them of their weighty charge, and bore the letter to Hugh as he lay in bed, with the leech-bites welling out their little oceans of blood.

"Read it me," he muttered, in the indistinct speech of a paralytic patient.

The matron wiped her spectacles; and having adjusted them, she opened the cover, and read the following letter.

"My dear Grandfather,—You cannot have forgotten me in such a short time as a year after my leaving the Hall, and I do not believe that you will disown me, though you were so angry with my poor mother. I have been unwilling to write to you—nor should I have done it now, had I not been strongly advised by a friend—for I did not know how to address you; nor am I certain of your feelings for me, now that you know I am your daughter's child. While I was Miss Clara I know that you liked me; but now, grandfather, that I have a claim to more than mere *liking*, I trust that you will love me, solitary and almost orphaned as I am, and that I may feel I have one friend in the world, so long as dear old Hugh lives! I hear that very bad reports have been circulated in Shorne about me, and that they have been believed. They are false. You know I never told a falsehood, Hugh, and you may trust me now. If you will come and live with me, you will see that I am speaking the truth; and then your presence will prevent the people saying any more slander of me. As, when I have my dear old grandfather with me, who can say a word against me then? And yet I scarcely like to ask you to come to me. I know how fond you are of the Hall, and how attached to the family, and I fear that I shall have less chance of your affection now that I am your own grandchild, than I had when Miss de Saumarez and the heiress of the estate. But if you think you could make yourself happy here with me, I need hardly say how delighted I shall be to try and make you comfortable, and to prove to you that I am the same Clara you knew at Shorne, with the only change of surname. Will you tell me also where my mother has gone to, and if there is not a chance of my seeing her? I am so entirely alone now, grandfather, so unprotected and so slandered, that I want to be with you and my dear mother—the only people who belong to me or care for me! I hope you will write to me very soon, and tell me if you will come and live with me or not. I have a nice room for you that you can have, and I will try all I can to make you comfortable and happy with me. Where is Fleetfoot now? and who has Juno and Jerry? Tell me all about the old place. Tell me how many dogs and cats and rabbits, &c., there are, and what new pigeons you have got. There is a bird-fancier's near me, but I don't like to see the poor little things in cages. Some of them are so small the bird cannot hop even, not to speak of flying. I do not think this right. Tell me all that has happened since I went away, and remember me to Nancy. Believe me, dear grandfather, your most affectionate and dutiful child,

"CLARA CLAYTON."

"God bless her! God bless her!" murmured the old man, making an effort to rise.

And in spite of his weakness he did rise up in bed, and sit there erect and firm.

The sun came through the narrow casement. It was but a ray—a little broken ray; and yet it was the blessed sun, his old companion and his friend.

"Open the window," he said faintly. "Let me see what is so like her!"

The matron unfastened the casement hasp, and let the small current of fresh air creep in.

"God bless her! she was always good and kind and faithful! She was a princess, though she was but a poor bastard! She was a princess—a real princess! Too late! too late! God bless her!"

He sank down again, murmuring to himself in an inarticulate way; and then he dropped off to sleep, the leech-bites bursting out rather fiercely.

The matron watched him sleeping there so tranquilly for some time. And then a shadow stole into that mean room, and laid a darkening hand on all about. That shadow passed over the sleeping man like a cloud over a still lake; and the woman watching by his side knelt down and prayed—for she knew it was the form of Death.

CHAPTER XIII.

CLARE had an idea. That was very evident. She showed it by her abstraction, by her dreamy eye that did not seem to take in what it saw, by her pale cheek, her compressed lip. She showed it too in smaller things. She put on her garments—several of them—all sorts of ways: some with the wrong side uppermost, some with the back brought round to the front. She walked about her rooms as if not fully awake, and big tears came every now and then into her eyes, as if she was thinking deeply.

And so she was. But it was a strange thought that had come across her, and one in the execution of which she knew not half the dangers.

She would go to Emma Vaughan. She had obtained her address from the slop-worker, and in spite of the locality, and even in spite of what Emma herself had said, she would go down to her lodgings and speak with her. It was her duty. Chance had thrown her into strange connexion with this woman, who had some good in her—much! much!—else she would not have tried to save her. And it was her plain and evident duty to repay the boundless obligation which had been laid on her; and, in turn, to save from a fate so frightful as that into which she had fallen, one who had been her real friend.

And when Clara had such an idea as this—backed by the feeling of duty and self-sacrifice—not all the dangers in the world, nor all the certain misrepresentations of a whole host of detractors, could have turned her from it. What she felt she ought to do in abstract right, that she would do, how far soever it might be conventionally wrong. And certainly she gave good proof of this to-day, in her determination to venture alone through the very vilest parts of Westminster to find out a woman of notorious fame, and to talk with her kindly, gently—ay, affectionately.

"If I'm a Christian at all," said Clara, "I will be one of deed, not only of word. I will act, and not talk. I will, as far as I can, follow the example of Christ—not believe only what one church tells me I ought to believe, and another church tells me I shall be condemned if I do believe. We all have our duties plainly marked out before us, and we cannot be very far wrong if we do them faithfully."

And fortified by what Vaughan used to call her "heated imagination," as to the moral necessity of her action, she set out on her walk she, this innocent girl of seventeen, to find out and to convert yon public woman of hardened years and callous life.

Westminster, though the seat of empire, contains perhaps the worst localities in London. Beneath the shadow of the cathedral—within sight of the stately legislative pile—in the precincts of school and college and courts of law—more rascality, vice, misery, and neglect, are to be found than in any other spot in the metropolis. The streets are scarcely safe for solitary women, certainly many of the by-streets are eminently unsafe; and almost all are of such character as would make it exceedingly undesirable for respectable women to be seen in and amongst them at all, unless for some good or holy purpose. St. Giles's has a pre-eminent name; but Westminster bears off the palm of villany.

Into this tainted quarter—into one of the worst streets even—Clara prepared to go. "They can't hurt me," she said, "if I do them no harm; and I have nothing about me for them to steal. People are not murdered in broad daylight for nothing in the world; and if I don't speak uncivilly to any one, why should I be ill-treated?"

And she found this logic quite sufficient to assure her, even if she had had any hauntings of prudential fear; from which unluckily she was generally perfectly free. She was physically very brave; almost to recklessness; and the last thing in the world which she considered in any of her transactions was the danger that she incurred. If she had been told to go into a den of banditti for the sake of rescuing some wife, or child, or youthful girl, she would not have stayed to calculate the odds, but would have gone without a murmur. In London, she believed herself perfectly safe at all times, and in all places; for there were so many people always about—and then the policemen!—and as she never read the police reports, nor the assize intelligence in newspapers, she was spared a great deal of demoralizing knowledge and terrifying remembrances.

She arrived at Westminster. The grand old cathedral reared its solemn pile, grave and austere, in the clear air. The courts of law looked small and mean beside that splendid House of God; the place of legislature was nothing worth in the shadow of the place of prayer. She stood and gazed with a full heart and reverent; and then she prayed softly for strength to do always that which was pure and holy in the sight of GOD. For she felt in keener force than ever, how different are the ways of man with the words he is so savage to uphold in their intellectual integrity. Those courts of law, with all their foul iniquities—those legislative chambers, with all their criminal delays and guilty opposition to necessary reforms—that splendid cathedral, with its luxurious, pompous, priestly train—all composing these several institutions were men eager for the credo and the ave; but for the spirit of their Master—how slack, how grossly negligent!

And Clare turned her own eyes inward, and asked herself if she too were always willing for her duties when they were painful; and after a few moments she said aloud; " I think I am—I always try to do what I believe to be right."

And she did not boast in this; she spoke the simple truth—as brave to allow herself what she deserved, as she was to condemn, wherein she failed.

People stared at her as she asked her way from street to street, through horrible neighbourhoods of disease and vice. The shopkeepers and policemen spoke to her gently; for she looked so young and innocent, besides possessing the unmistakable bearing of a gentlewoman, that they felt loath to leave her in her intention. One policeman did ask her if she knew where she was going to; and when she answered "Yes, I believe it is a very bad place, but I am going to see a poor woman there," he had nothing more to urge, except a recommendation that she should be careful; which she did not fully understand.

"Careful of what?" she said looking up into his face.

"They are bad people there, Miss," answered the man. "You mayn't know exactly the kind of place you are going to. For, you'll excuse me Miss, but you seem very young to be alone in such a street even as this, not to speak of the other one!"

"But they can't rob me," said Clara with a smile; "for I have nothing with me of any value."

"Yes, Miss, they might. They might strip you of all you had, value or no value. They might take all your clothes from you. Why, where you are going to, none of us dare go down single-handed."

Clara for a moment looked alarmed. But she soon threw off the passing feeling, and thanking the man for his kindness, told him that if she did not come back in an hour's time he must send some one after her body. She gave him the number of the house, and the name of the landlady, and then, with a cheek flushed by the excitement of the very danger against which she had been warned, she took the several turnings indicated, and, gaining the court or alley where Emma lived, walked bravely down.

In a moment the place was alive with human beings. Crowds of faces pressed up against the windows, dirty women and men, dissipated and unwashed, lounged about, talking and laughing with each other in language and on subjects which it was well for Clara she did not understand. The doorways were filled with thick masses of men and girls—the alley swarmed with children—boys chiefly, of the most hardened ugliness of feature, where crime and vice and brutalized formation were stamped as with a brand. They jostled up against her—they begged of her in accents far more menacing than supplicatory—their dirty hands pressed her gown close to her person, to feel where the pocket and the purse might be—and suddenly, without the slightest knowledge of how it came to be so, she was so strangely surrounded that hands and arms and feet were all completely

useless. She never knew how this happened; but for the time it lasted
she was entirely in the power of the men and boys surrounding her.

And yet she did not quail. Her brilliant cheek perhaps gained a
deeper tinge, but her eyes were just as frank and fearless as ever. The
people round her were apt physiognomists. They saw right well that
they had no chicken-hearted fool to deal with; and they whispered and
spoke low, and spoke of her in all sorts of strange slang terms, which
meant their admiration of her steadiness.

"Which is Mary Jenner's house?" she asked, turning to the least
ruffianly of that ruffianly crew.

"Mary Jenner!" screamed the whole mob—a hundred voices all at
once—"the last house on the right-hand side in the corner."

She did not like this very much. The stench of the alley was
intolerable, and so many dirty people clustering round her made her
almost faint. Yet she was thankful that no one had offered any other
annoyance—that no one had insulted or maltreated her. For she saw
now more clearly what her danger might have been, and how utterly
unable she would have been to defend herself.

Still keeping calm through the clamour and the pressure, she at last
gained the door of the house where Emma lived. This too, as all the
rest, was perfectly barricaded by men and women, and the windows
were one mass of elfish locks and bold eyes, and leering smiles of
mockery and menace both.

"I want Emma Vaughan's room," she said, still in the same clear
unshaken voice.

But the crowd in the doorway did not move.

"At the top of the house!" shouted the mob.

"Give way men!" cried one—a young gipsy-looking fellow of about
twenty, who would have been handsome but for his dissipated looks.
"Let the lady go up-stairs," he said aloud; but he whispered something
in slang which Clara did not comprehend, and which made them all
give way at once. I doubt whether even her brave heart would have
carried her up those dark stairs if she had heard what "Flash Jem" said.

Without danger, but still always thus accompanied, Clara at last
arrived at the door which they said belonged to Emma's room. All the
way up the stairs the crowd had been shouting "Emma! Emma! here's
good luck for you to-day!" at the top of their voices; and the uproar
that these noisy tones and noisy feet had made was almost deafening.
But no Emma appeared; and Clara's heart began to die within her as

she thought she might not attain her object after all, and that Emma might be from home to-day. And then what should she do, and how return? However, she opened the door as she was told, and entered.

In the middle of the room—cast down on the floor in a sullen heap, silent and unmoved—sat Emma Vaughan. Her children were playing in the corner with such bits of broken pottery and shreds of linen as they had found; but even the youngest had hushed her childish cries, while the elder one spoke low, as though she had been with death.

The noisy crowd attracted the attention of that wretched woman no more than what an oath betrayed. She raised her hand but not her sullen head; and bade them go from her with bitter curses on their intrusion.

Clara came near to her; she touched her arm with her soft hand, and said in a gentle voice that fell like violets through a hail-storm; "Emma, I have come to see you."

With a cry the woman started to her feet. She put back her hair, she seized the girl's hand in her own feverish hold, she glared at her with eyes that bore too plainly the evidence of insanity by the portal if not within the chamber of her mind, and then she tossed her arms wildly through the air, and crying "'Tis an angel!" burst into tears. The first she had been ever seen to shed—the first sign ever given to that haggard crowd without that one spark of womanly feeling yet remained in her. It electrified them. They stood silent and awed, and spoke in whispers; for it was so unlike what they knew of her that it struck them more with dread than anything else.

But they came. Fast, fast, and burning, still they were tears of good, falling on her heart like water in the desert, and making green and fertile such of the waste whereon they fell.

"Kneel to her!" she cried, holding Clara's hand. "Kneel to this child of purity—this noble maid—this glorious thing of GOD's own making! Kneel to the brave heart that came down through all this curse, that she might bring comfort and relief. Men!—some of ye have heard of a GOD perchance—ye see him now in his angel!"

She flung herself at the girl's feet and kissed the place where she stood. Abandoned, hardened, vile, degraded as was that crowd—men steeped in every crime—women who had lost all sign of womanhood in their sins—though hands were there that had shed human blood, and lips that had sworn away innocence for gold—though every moral sense was deadened, every moral virtue ruined—yet even they were not wholly insensible to the beauty of purity when they saw it; even they could respect the youth and innocence that trusted them. They gave a noisy hurrah, and all crowded on Clara; some shaking hands with her, others blessing her, and others again praising her aloud in quaint but powerful terms. And although afterwards they joked and laughed in ghastly fashion on the want of pluck they had shown in letting the girl escape them so easily, yet for the moment they were subdued, and made to feel an influence of greater softness than they had ever felt before—a something that might have been raised into virtue.

"But what has brought you here?" cried Emma when they were alone, and she had become calm again—preternaturally calm. "My child!—dear lady!—what in GOD's name induced you to come down into such a quarter as this?"

"I wanted to see you," said Clara simply, "and I was not afraid of coming, though I knew the neighbourhood was bad."

"Were you alone?"

"Yes, quite."

"And you came to see me, you say?"

"Yes Emma—for nothing else."

The woman seemed to muse a moment; then drawing a chair forward, she dusted it carefully, and bade her young visitor be seated.

Even in her most reckless moments the voice and accent of this poor creature were pure. She might use coarse language, and she might fall into the ungrammatical fashions of those with whom she associated, but there was always something about her different to her companions; and any one who understood the world, would at once have pronounced her to be what she was—a disgraced gentlewoman. But now, when speaking thus alone with Clara, her manners had an elegance that could not fail to strike the young girl. Her voice was low and softened, better modulated than in general, and perfectly correct in language. She wore an indescribable air of equality, which was not hardened guilt seeking to brazen out its iniquities in the very teeth of virtuous abhorrence, but which was simply the expression of that womanly or maternal feeling which had never left her, through all her most degraded years. As she sat near to Clara, her head leaning on her hand, and her hollow eyes fixed full but with such inexpressible kindness on the youthful face before her, the girl almost forgot the life she had come to change; and her heart, ever ready to acknowledge the dignified affectionateness of a mother, turned towards the woman in simple child-like impulse, and for the time destroyed the tremendous barrier between them.

"And you have come to see me, Miss Clayton—and why?" asked Emma gently.

"Oh! I came to talk with you, Emma, and to see if nothing could be done for you—to see if, by some help, you might not be able to escape from all these wretched companions and wretched surroundings, and gain a peaceful and a happy livelihood. Indeed I feel so much gratitude to you for what you saved me from, that nothing I could do would seem too much for your benefit!"

"You are very good—very very good; you are an angel, if there was ever one on earth. But even angels cannot do impossibilities. How am I to gain a peaceful or a happy livelihood? Who would employ me— with my wretched character—even for the lowest classes of unskilled labour? You know, Miss Clayton, perfectly well what I am—though you may not understand the full degradation of the life. But even you, innocent and inexperienced, must see the impossibility of a woman who has been once lost ever recovering her position again?"

"Oh no! not impossibility, Emma! There are many people who would take you in and help you. In a christian land so few christian hearts? Oh no! you must be mistaken! Difficult though the path of return may be, it is not impossible. With patience and courage you *may* return!"

"So speaks the young and guileless nature. Now turn to facts. Where would you have me go?"

"There are Magdalens."[81]

"Not for such as I am, my child. The very young, the unencumbered, the canting hypocrite, the lucky *protégées* of grand people may find asylums; but for me—independent, proud, a mother—where is mine?"

"Why not because you are a mother?"

"No asylum receives children of any age."

"But the workhouse would, Emma."

A spasm crossed the face looking so straightly into hers.

"Listen," she said quietly. "I have but one affection in life—my children. Clara Clayton, you cannot know the intensity of a One Love. You cannot know the trembling worship of a heart so seared, that it has lost the power of reverence for all save this. You cannot dream of the wholeness of that love, nor how every fibre of goodness is intwined with its existence. And you never will know it; for only those whose souls have sunk as low as mine could fitly understand it. But thus it is with me. My children are my only pleasures—pleasures did I say? Ah! mournful pleasures! reproachful in their innocence—condemning in their very love! Yet such as they are—these nameless children without the pale of the law—they are my very life. I would have died by my own hand years ago, had it not been for them. That eldest one was the first who ever opened the founts of maternal love. She was not my husband's child; she was his—no matter! And for her sake I lived through years of nameless misery, which else would have been speedily ended. Then came that younger thing—born in such a life as you see me in now—and she added another link to the chain which bound me to existence; last was a third, a baby—dead now, and in heaven—happy, poor little one, while its sisters live below! For these I could not enter into any asylum—for these I could not go into a workhouse—for these I have kept out of prison, though sorely tempted at times to deeds which would have sent me there. It is not pride my child, that I would not render myself to the rules of Magdalen or union; it is not even my fierce love of liberty. I can work with my hands like the coarsest charwoman; and I can submit, when I will, like the veriest slave. But do you think that I could leave my children to the cold mercies of a union, to the heartless training of a pauper school? No! no! such as I am now, such I must remain; for causes as strong as fate keep me in my present ways!"

Clara was silent, but tears were in her eyes.

"Why these tears?" said Emma suddenly, and her lip trembled as she spoke.

"I am grieved for you, Emma. I am grieved at my own inability to assist you. I feel that I have come here, with good intentions certainly, but in utter ignorance of what I wished to do. I thought that you had but to be persuaded to renounce your present life, and that all the rest would follow. I did not know that you had children; and indeed if I had known it, I should have thought it an easy matter to have them placed in some asylum or school—where they would have been properly educated and kindly treated. I have been very foolish!—but I came for your good—at least for what I meant to be your good, and I am disappointed that I can do nothing for you."

"Do not say that, my child," she said with real emotion; "your very presence has done me good—your very voice has softened me. To

look into your innocent face there before me—speaking with me as
with an equal—expressing neither pharisaical horror nor sublime pity
for me—this very feeling of sisterhood with one of the pure again, has
been of more real advantage than any simple worldly aid that might
have been bestowed. I am bad now—bad—oh! viler than words can
say!—but I was once as innocent as you, my child; but never never so
true-hearted! In the days of my purity I should have shrunk as from
the plague from anything like communion with one of my present
class. I was taught to name this proper modesty. I have found its true
worth since then!"

"But, Emma," cried Clara, reverting again to the first subject,
"cannot something be done for you? Can you not yourself point out
some means by which you may be able to leave this place, and live in
comfort and respectability? For your children's sake, Emma, can you
not devise something?"

"Nothing," she said gloomily.

"Oh surely yes! in such a large city—with such boundless wealth
and mighty charities."

"Charities!" she cried, starting up with her old fierce glare and
recklessness of manner. "Ay, mighty charities in the name, child!—
mighty generosity in the donors—with their titles and their addresses
printed for all the world to see—but frightfully abortive for general
help! Charities in London? Yes, there are a few that work well; but for
the most part I don't think they are of more use in the removal of vice,
or the assuagement of misery, than a thousand molehills are in the
formation of a mountain! Charities?—no! no! no! they are far more
ostentatious donations than beneficent institutions. Don't mention
them—they are hateful to me, with their cant and their formalism—
their strict investigations and their nullifying rules. If men really wish
to do good, let them do it in a broad, a truly catholic spirit. Don't let
them turn all their waters into such a narrow stream, which, though
it runs farther, does nothing throughout all its course. The broad
mill-dam that turns one single wheel—one single engine of practical
usefulness—is worth half a dozen silver threads through a country,
which simply enliven the landscape and do nothing great or necessary,
though they are so pure!"

"How strange!" said Clara unconsciously.

"What is strange?"

She blushed.

"To hear you speak in this manner—and then to look round and see what a wretched state you live in! Oh! I am so sorry for it all! You are so much too good for this."

"Don't speak like that," said the woman, trembling violently. "I do not wish to be so completely unnerved as you alone have the power to unnerve me. I cannot tell you half I feel for you, nor how your brave, generous, noble action in coming here to me to-day—alone and unprotected—has gone into my very heart of hearts! If my death would benefit you, Clara Clayton, you should be so benefited by it, for this alone could express the deep admiration—ay, and affection— that you have roused up in me! Come, this must end! You must not remain here longer; you have been in this tainted atmosphere quite long enough; and I feel doubly criminal for allowing it. Come! I will take you safely through the court! Come! come!"

Her manner was restless, and the old fever was in her eyes.

"Stay one moment," said Clara earnestly, and she laid her hand on her quivering arm. "Come and live with me until I or Mr. Glynn can get some better place for you. Your children can then be taken care of, and you will have ample leisure, and opportunities too, for finding out some other position which would suit you better."

"What did I hear?" she asked in a hoarse voice. "Are my senses mocking me?"

"No," answered Clara in the same fervent way. "No, indeed, I mean what I say—come and live with me, Emma—in my house, at my charge, and we will then do something really good!"

The woman gave a cry like a wounded bird; she caught the girl by the shoulder and stared wildly into her face.

"You are ridiculing me," she said in a low whisper, like a madman's voice.

"I am not, Emma," Clare said firmly; "I am true and honest."

"Only once! only once!" she cried. "Angel!—goddess!—my child of love and mercy!—God bless thee well!"

She flung her arms round Clare, and kissed her young lips twice and thrice. And then she relaxed her hold, and threw herself on the bed, sobbing in screams rather than in sobs—every fibre of her frame racked with the most painful passion.

Shocked and terrified, Clare knelt by her, while the two children mingled their shrill cries with the mad agony of their mother, creeping into her arms, and kissing off the tears that streamed like thunder rain on her bosom. And long minutes passed thus. She, unable to control herself—her spirit broken before the terrible tempest of memories and remorse which the touch of those pure lips—the accents of those pure words—had wakened up. It was a hideous scene—one that might well blanch Clare's cheek and make her heart beat fast—if not with personal fear, yet with mysterious awe at such dark revelations of feelings that had no name to her, and but a weird existence which terrified by its very power.

At last that wretched woman calmed herself.

She pressed back with a strong hand the remnant of her passion; and after some time longer yet, spent in gaining such mastery as would leave her free, she rose from the bed; and without a word threw on a shawl and bonnet, and prepared to conduct Clare safely through the court.

"And now," she said, turning to her suddenly as she stood by the door, "we have met for the last time. Our paths in life are too diverse ever to lead us in the same track again. You have done your all for me—now leave me to the desolation that even you cannot repair. You have seen how your words have affected me; for pity then—aye for pity, lady—never agonize me so again. My fate is marked out—the die has been thrown—do not force me to look too narrowly at the hideous features which it wears—do not force me to turn back to the peace and beauty that I have lost and cannot regain. GOD bless you, Clara Clayton! and keep your young head unbowed by shame, and your young heart unseared by sorrow! GOD bless you, my child—my beautiful, my noblest one!"

Then taking her hand she led her safely down those dark and reeking stairs—safely through the dense crowd pouring out on them like bees from out a hive. She led her through some streets yet, and then set her face towards her right way, and left her for the last time of her conscious life.

For days and days that woman kept alone in her solitary room. When her children wanted bread she sent out the elder for their food, but she herself would not stir outside the door, nor suffer a human face over its threshold. And then she suddenly came out, and for weeks indulged in one wild career of vice and drunkenness; and at times was utterly mad—a fierce maniac of debauchery and despair, seemingly worse for the very respite she had gained.

CHAPTER XIV.

SOME days in the year are general holidays even to the working world; days when farmers lay aside their spades and fewer hands are in the mills; days when the very theatres are closed and the very Jews taught not to trade; days of idleness to all men saving clergymen and bell-ringers, boyish choristers and deep-voiced clerks, who have then their time of labour and their time of power.

It was on one of these hebdomadal resting-places that Lucretia gave a party, when, as a dominical marvel, there had been no rehearsal at the theatre. For managers do not care much for church bells when they have "novelties" to prepare for the coming week; and Vaughan, being one of those men who delight in shocking religious feelings of all kinds, generally chose a Sunday's rehearsal in preference to a few hours' extra work on Monday. Principally because the better actors objected to such an invariable proceeding on his part; and one of them had once said indignantly, "But, Sir, there is no time left for our religious duties!"

This was Vaughan's standing joke for months after. He thought it such "intolerable affectation that an actor should have religious duties to perform;" he told it at a dinner-table where there happened to be a dean; and then he recovered himself and spoke bitterly of the actor's immorality (which was false), and praised highly "a *real* sense of Christian responsibilities."

However, here was Sunday—one week in the month of March—and here was Lucretia's tea-drinking. An annual affair, to which she was wont to invite some of the lower actors at her theatre—as a kind of patronage. She herself being a theatrical Mahomet's coffin,[82] in equal balance between the stars and the supernumeraries.

Lucretia gave a modest tea enough. She had simply a mountain of muffins and crumpets buttered with salt butter not too fresh, and as much strong coarse tea as would have watered a troop of the line. But her guests knew that something better than this would come; so they saved their appetites, they said; but nevertheless they devoured all her muffins and drank an endless quantity of bohea.[83]

After tea they sat down to cards. One pack was certainly correct, but it was horribly dirty; and the other pack had about equal numbers of three distinct and variously coloured cards, which soon led to a playful advertisement on all sides as to what cards were held—by their backs. There was a whist table, and a loo table, and afterwards *vingt-un*,[84] limited to a dozen halfpenny markers. The whist was very original. Every one had an insane desire for playing out their highest cards at once, no matter whether for or against their adversaries; and no one thought of returning their partners' leads, or of attending to the cards as they fell, still less of letting their partners' best card pass without a trump to back it if their own suit was exhausted. Then they all talked at once; some in the sock and some in the buskin[85] style; and you heard the most extraordinary gallimaufry[86] of several kinds of diction all jumbled up together like property dresses in a carpet-bag.

"Nay, good my lord, but that was e'en my best heart!" said Lucretia's deep tones. For she was a whist-player, and professed to play Major A.;[87] and sometimes endeavoured to stand out for the "rigour of the game."

"Faith! and the jewel has gone and taken my jewel!" roared the wit of the party in an Irish accent, as his partner—Mrs. Jenkins—"a heavy mother"[88]—put her ace on his queen of diamonds while he held the king.

"Good gracious, Mr. Dent, why didn't you trump their spades with all those trumps in your hand?" retorted Mrs. Jenkins, in a shrill voice, when her partner won the three last tricks of the game with the three best honours, after all the other trumps had been made by trumping.

"Lucretia! Lucretia!" said her co., as she called him—a fine-looking man who often played generals and policemen because of his figure— "didn't you see the ace marshalled there? Why did you lead the attack, my good soul, right in the teeth of the enemies' guns?—their greatest gun too!"

"But I led the king, my valiant general," she answered, "and that forced them to expend their great gun; which military tacticians would approve of."

"Yes, and left them with queen and knave! Why, Lucretia, I thought you played better than that."

"Well, you are just as bad," said Lucretia as her co. deliberately trumped her ace of clubs, first time round.

"Ah me! an overwrought brain!" he cried, putting his hand to his forehead, or as he used to call it, "his knowledge-box." But his knowledge-box was something like the treasury of the theatre at times—hopelessly empty. For, like many fine-looking men, he was a most undoubted idiot.

At last, after much laughing, a little undertoned swearing, mutual recrimination and mutual forgiveness—after endless revokes,[89] not one of which were discovered in the inextricable kaleidoscope of "leads" and "suits" all down on the table at once and never responded to—after best cards forgotten and thirteenth cards thrown away—the whist-party broke up and adjourned to inspect *vingt-un*. Mr. Buggins was the hero there, and had the lead at present. He was a desperate fellow this Buggins, and doubled all round, however high the stakes might be; even when he saw two sixpences on the table at once. But he had managed to become the banker too; for he seemed to have a very magnetic power for the "fishes" of his neighbours, to judge by the pile of red and white bone counters—with actually three sixpences shining through the heap—that he had collected before him.

"Make your play, gentlemen and ladies!" he cried in a gaming-house voice. For he was not an infrequent visitor to some of the lower rooms of naughty name.

"Sixpence!" cried one. "Only one," sighed another. "I'm being ruined."

"What shall I go on that, Launce?" asked a little *coryphée*,[90] showing an ace.

"Oh! sixpence, of course!" said Launce; "and I'll go halves," giving her six fish, and a meaning smile.

"Four," said some.

"Two," said others.

"The half of three-quarters," said a wag, putting down a mutilated fish.

"A gentlemanly dozen," said a "heavy father,"[91] counting out his twelve with an air.

"Double!" cried Mr. Buggins; and "Oh dear, what a shame!" cried the whole table.

But the little *coryphée* got a "natural,"[92] and so Mr. Buggins was turned out of the deal, and the table was cleared for supper.

The supper was a grand affair. Lucretia evidently knew the tastes of her company to a hair. There were heaps of shrimps, and dozens of oysters, and no end of porter bottles, and a goodly sprinkling of ginger-beer. There was plenty of bread-and-butter, a round two shillings' worth of radishes and water-cresses—"green meat" as they called it—and lots of brandy and gin, fresh from the gin-shop close at hand. Then there was a large cream cheese in a splendid state of "ripeness;" it was almost "running away," said Mrs. Jenkins; or as Mr. Buggins phrased it, "in a state of lacteal currency." But it was highly approved of; and some of the real gourmands ate all, even to the mouldy outside, with great gusto. And then, after the oysters and the shrimps were gone, in came a huge dish of toasted cheese, that made some of the heavier feeders sigh because it was almost too much after all the good things they had had.

"A gastronomic Pelion upon Ossa!"[93] said Mr. Buggins, who passed for a scholar.

"A gallant rear-guard to the main body," said the military model; and "How nice it smells!" cried the little *coryphée*, handing up her plate, and asking for more porter at the same time.

And when the toasted cheese was discussed they all had some spirits-and-water "to digest it," and sat round the table comfortably, and began to talk.

"I say, Buggins, wasn't I great last night?" asked the military model, slapping his chest.

"With wadding or horse-hair?" cried the wit, Mr. Dent; "or love-locks of the girls—hey, Mat?"

"I've seen Mat's love-locks," said the *coryphée* archly.

"You have?" cried many voices; "and what were they like?" For Mat was held to be a terrible Lothario.

"Oh!" she said, "he gave me a large packet of something that felt like hair, and told me to weigh it, and not to open it on any account."

"Well?"

"Well, I weighed it, and it was just sixteen ounces. That's a pound, ain't it? But I opened it too, and found——"

"What, child?" said Lucretia, in her most tragic voice.

"His poodle's ringlets," she said.

And then there was a roar through the room, as if something very funny and witty had been said.

"Will you take your oath of it some of your own wasn't there, Carry?" cried Mat, chucking her under the chin.

"Well I don't know—I did see some cat's whiskers too."

And then they all laughed again, and called Carry a trump, and voted her another glass of brandy-and-water. And Miss Carry, who was suspected of a weakness for strong liquids, did not even coquet about it, but accepted it with a very good grace, and tasted it like a connoisseur.

"By-the-bye, Lucretia," cried Mr. Buggins suddenly, "when did you see little Clayton last? I mean, to speak to?"

Lucretia looked uneasy. "Not for a long time," she answered. "Why do you ask?"

"Do you know, I think she has got into very bad ways," observed that youth gravely.

"Lord bless the boy, what does he mean! Bad ways—bad ways!—why, what on earth do you mean!" she said in a state of great excitement, and not the least bit affected.

"Why listen here," said that gentleman in an under tone, and drawing close to Lucretia; "I was coming through Westminster the other day, through —— street, don't you know?"

"Know?—of course not! I don't go into any such disreputable places. I know that Westminster is one of the worst places in London, and you had very likely no business to be there yourself. I don't know —— street indeed!"

"Well then—Lord love you! don't look like that! I meant nothing by asking. Well, listen to me now at any rate, and keep your pouting for afterwards. —— street is one of the very worst streets all through Westminster; but who should I see but little Clayton walking first of all by herself, and then with a woman—whew!"—with a whistle—"no mistake about her!"

"Heaven help the girl! What mad trick has she been after now!" cried Lucretia, clasping her hands. "Upon my soul, she's mad! What in the name of ten thousand fiends took her to such a hole, and with such a woman! Are you sure you weren't mistaken, boy? It might not have been Clara after all!"

"Oh no! I couldn't be mistaken you see, because I spoke to her. I looks into her face, and says, 'Good morning my dear Miss Clara—can I do any thing for you or your friend!'"

"Then you were an impudent scoundrel," said Lucretia, savagely. "The girl's got enough troubles—and has fallen low enough too—you needn't help to kick her down! There was a time when you were glad enough to be noticed by her at all—you shouldn't quite forget what the difference was once simply for what it is now—on the wrong side!"

"Well done Lu.! I didn't think you would have stuck up like that for the girl. At any rate she's a plucky little wench for going into such a place at all. I dare say she went after some good or other."

Not that he believed this: he only wanted to soother Lucretia down a bit; as the pseudo Irishman said.

"Come! let us talk of something else!" said Lucretia; "I hate to hear any harm of that girl! When I first saw her she was so grand—the great heiress of the place!—and afterwards she was happy enough, poor child—and now she is just like a swan among ravens, every one picks at her because she isn't as black as themselves. She's a right good heart, and though Vaughan does treat her so brutally, and though she has sunk so low, she shan't be abused before me at any rate. So drink your grog Buggy, and don't talk any more about her!"

And Mr. Buggins did as he was desired, and did not think it necessary to inform Miss Kemble that after he had met Clara, he had gone straightway to Vaughan, and told him what he had seen; and that Vaughan had not been nearly as much obliged to him as he ought to have been. Mr. Buggins was an ingenuous youth, but some things are better kept to oneself too.

So the party went on as gaily and as noisily as such parties generally go on. They all got slightly elevated, and complained of headaches the next morning; and they all talked at once of themselves, and their characters, and what love letters, anonymous and otherwise, they had received, and what handsome men had said, and highborn ladies had looked; and in fact the whole universe laid, according to the superstitions of each, at the feet of each; and he or she had only to stoop to pick up such dirty things as love and honour in as large quantities as could be carried away. All of which being a very comfortable state of feeling, it does not devolve on us to abuse; as happiness is of inestimable price in this world, come by what self-deception it may.

It would have electrified an unprofessional person to have heard the high and noble names which these actors and actresses bandied about. How earls, and countesses, and gentle maids of honour, had given such unmistakable proofs of admiration as even a buzzard could have seen in broad daylight: though when these proofs came down to the touchstone of inquiry, they generally evaporated into hearsay evidence, or looks from private boxes, or mysterious signals in private carriages, which could not be answered because of the intrusive earl or attendant ladies; but which were sure to lead to something more some of these days.

Then, as time wore on, and strong liquids mounted higher in the system, each opened his budget of grievances against the manager, and the "stars." Each showed how much better he could have played that part the other night than the man who did play it. The *coryphée*, Miss Carry, burlesqued Carlotta Grisi, and ridiculed Cerito;[94] and asserted that, had she interest sufficient to be admitted into the *corps de ballet* of the Italian opera, she would soon eclipse them both.

"Unless," she replied, "I was kept back and not allowed to interfere with their success, which"—and she sighed—"would be very likely indeed!"

The Irishman, uttered a cry, "all r's and o's"—flourished a chair over his head like a shillelagh[95]—and then asked whether that wasn't better, gentlemen, than anything we've had on the stage for *this* century?

The wag said, "Oh! John Reeves was very good I dare say—but now, if *I* had played the mummy, I wouldn't have winked my eye so, I would have just done so"—and he put up his hand to his face and touched his nose thoughtfully.

Lucretia's tall figure went through Siddonian attitudes, and her deep voice uttered Siddonian melodrame; and then she declared that not a woman on the stage could take the Siddons air but herself; and being in a very excited state she shed a few tears, and exclaimed; "Oh the tyranny over genius!"

And so things went on; and when they all separated, they called Lucretia a thorough old brick; and some of them tried to kiss her—and Mr. Buggins did accomplish it, though he wiped his lips after the feat. Miss Carry and Mr. Launce, who had been making fierce love all the evening, went away by themselves; and the next week they had quarrelled, and didn't speak even in the green-room. But as they never came on in the same piece—unless by chance—and as they never by any chance at all had to speak to each other on the stage, seeing that Miss Carry was limbs only, and not a voice—they avoided one very fertile occasion of ill-will among theatrical people; which is, to deliver all the stinging speeches in the drama with such point and force, that they become personal and positive insult. Few people have any idea how pleasant this is to the feelings, and how much moral gratification it affords to the speaker.

And when they had all gone, Lucretia went to bed, and slept till past the proper hour of rehearsal in the morning: so that when she got down to the theatre she was sworn at a good deal by the stage-manager, and laughed at by her guests, who gave "very vulgar reasons," she said, for her absence.

END OF VOL. II.

REALITIES

A Tale.

BY E. LYNN,

AUTHOR OF

"AZETH, THE EGYPTIAN," AND "AMYMONE."

"Therefore should I
Be but the essence of deformity,—
A coward,—did my very eyelids wink
At speaking out what I have dared to think."

KEATS.

IN THREE VOLUMES.

VOL. III.

LONDON
SAUNDERS AND OTLEY, CONDUIT STREET.
1851.

REALITIES.

CHAPTER I.

THE disease under which Jane Walcot had long laboured now assumed a confirmed character. The rapid emaciation, frightful cough, hectic flush, and brilliancy of eye, together with other more distressing symptoms, betrayed a positive case of consumption: one of those hopeless cases which must end in death, and against the hideous strength of which specifics and remedies are but as pebbles dropped into the ocean.

Had it not been for Percival's aid—and Clara's too, given in a blundering and unpractical way very often, though so generously—the poor young slop-workers would have been badly off. Jane was unable to do a stitch of work; yet it had been so much more loss than profit with her of late, that it was on the whole a saying that she was thus obliged to be totally idle. Fines for over-time, and work returned because of its incompleteness, had long swallowed up the small earnings that she had gained. And very often more than a week's joint wages of both sisters were swept away in one tremendous penalty. For the sweaters and masters were much like other people. They never believed in physical impossibility, nor reflected on the injustice of fining men for the laws of nature. When a system must be supported, individual sufferings are of no account. It is the same with laws and ethics. Grand principles are laid down—grand resolutions passed—the abstract right is demonstrated—and men are required to believe and perform. Yet all modifications of power—down to patent idiocy—are denied; and the weakling is given the work of the giant, the child is judged side by side with the hero.

However, poor Jane Walcot's trials were nearly over. There she lay—the pale half-starved wench!—in pain and weariness, and apathetic ignorance; groaning through the night—groaning through the day—incapable of amusement—incapable of relief; a mass of grieved sensation without any overruling mind to enlighten or improve.

And yet she possessed the same original conditions of existence as those which formed Aspasia and Corday.[96] She possessed the same material bases for her brute ignorance as those which formed their sublime intelligence. Why then was she so dull, and they so glorious?

Granting all the modifying influences of climate, race, and time—yet had they lived the life of this poor slop-worker—had they been brought up in an atmosphere so foul that it vitiated the very springs of life as they lay in their mothers' arms—had work overtasked, and want left unnourished, their physical powers—had the lack of light, warmth, clothing, wholesome food, and wholesome air checked their growth and stunted their development—had their intellects been unexercised, save in the sharpened savagery of hunger, and their high noble spirits crushed down by the misery of their daily lives—had such as these been the material elements of their nurture—the world would never have worshipped at the shrine of the Athenian wife, nor have bowed before the heroism of the maiden tyrannicide.

We can raise a people into heroes or grind them into brutes as we will. We can elevate them mentally and morally by the laws of material improvement as easily as we have left them to deteriorate by vicious material combinations. There is no natural reason why the lowest of the people should not be educated into an equality with the present moral and intellectual condition of the gentry, as there was no natural reason which prevented the burgher class from rising out of the ranks of the serfdom of the past, or which will prevent them rising still higher in the future. Physical advantages in the daily lives of the poor will work moral advancement, and intellectual development will react on their social condition. In believing this, and in acting on it, we only believe the same truth as that which is demonstrated by an improved class of crops or an improved breed of cattle. The criminal and the pauper are not necessary to humanity. As a race they can be destroyed with the same certainty as a farmer destroys the weeds of his corn-field by better cultivation, or as a grazier annihilates original defects of organization by crossing the breed and improving the food of his sheep and cows. Man lives in nature, subject to every law which controls the other portions of nature. He is neither above nor on one side of the whole; he is simply an excess of the lower types, not a separate creation beyond the range of the chain. And what we want now, is the recognition of grand physical truths, and the allowance of their rights to the poor: those *rights* which are, by the simple fact of humanity, equal and inalienable. And of these are education, the possibility of self-support, the possibility of morality, and a sufficient—if not equal—portion of the goods of life. Yet they are not to be found in the present condition of the labouring classes; the Jane Walcots of society have no share in them.

Sick and weary—the impatient head tossed to and fro on the pillow, and the wasted hands wandering restlessly over the bed-clothes—Jane Walcot awaited her certain doom. Not that she thought she was dying. This was the last thing that she would have allowed, even to herself. If she had but more food, and of a better kind—for she could not eat the stuff they gave her, no not though Percival chose it carefully and managed to have it well cooked—but if she had only something that she could eat, and some fresher air—like what she remembered on Primrose Hill and Hampstead long ago—she would get round fast enough. It was not that she was dying; it was circumstances which any one might help that were keeping her down.

This belief made her peevish and ungrateful; for while she felt so weak how could any effort be making to relieve her? Poor people, like children, exaggerate power to a miraculous extent. They think the very issues of life and death lie in the hands of the rich; and when they suffer—sure it is because no one helps them, not because they have sunk too far for relief!

This was one of Jane's worst days. She was feverish and fretful, and her cough was more distressing than it had ever been before. She was sitting up in the bed; for her breath was so bad now that she could not lie down without the most painful feeling of suffocation, as well as suffering more from her side and shoulders. Besides these miseries, she had become so thin that her limbs were all more or less abraded by the friction of the bed-clothes, and by constant pressure. She was in a bad state—the poor girl!

Sarah sat by the bedside working, very sad and sorrowful, for she knew that her beloved sister must die, and that nothing on earth could save her.

And now she felt in fullest force the depth of tenderness with which she had always regarded her; now she felt how truly apart from any intellectual appreciation is the divine spirit of Love; and how she had cherished her sister all the more carefully because of her very deficiencies.

In that young slop-worker's heart was then a truer instinct than is to be found in all that sickly high-flown sentimentality which disdains to love where it cannot intellectually admire; and which deems the living heart, with all its affections, of less value than a little dry knowledge of facts and scientific causes. It is a false wisdom which holds Love in cheap esteem, which idolizes Intellect alone, and which would make man—that microcosm of hopes and fears and passionate desires—but a mere machine grinding out knowledge only. Knowledge is glorious truly; but oh! how much more ennobling are the affections!—how much more direct from GOD! Knowledge by itself will never make man virtuous; while love, even in the most ignorant, will always sanctify the character and ennoble it. And by love alone had our slop-worker—ignorant, practically criminal by law, degraded as she was—gained a high place among the pure and the holy before heaven; ay, "much was to be forgiven her because she had loved much!"[97]

A stranger's knock was heard at the door. Sarah rose to open it; and a tall, grave, but beautiful young man, dressed as a clergyman, entered. It was Edward Mantell, lately appointed curate of the district, and out on his visiting rounds to-day.

"Your sister is ill, I hear?" were his first words as he entered, spoken in a very sweet but melancholy voice.

"Very ill sir," answered Sarah, the tears in her eyes as she looked up gently into his face.

Her own form and features were delicate and consumptive. A kind of transparent sickliness was about them, that betokened terrible things for the future.

Edward Mantell went to the bed-side. He leant over it, and spoke to the invalid.

She opened her eyes. Bright with fever, but lustreless from lack of intelligence, they were merely the eyes of an animal goaded to irritation by pain; outlets of sensation only, not of thought.

She looked at the stranger for a moment—weariedly and hopelessly; and then she turned her head aside, unroused by his appearance even to curiosity.

"You are very ill, I fear," said the young clergyman, laying his hand on the bed-clothes, and turning them smoothly over with great gentleness.

Clara and Percival came in at the moment. They both remarked, in silence, the extreme delicacy and softness of Edward Mantell's manner. And this was his original nature.

The sick girl gave an impatient moan, and tossed her hands feverishly.

"Do you expect to live, or do you expect to die?" he then asked very gravely, pausing for an answer.

Jane moved restlessly, and Sarah coming to the bed-side, said, with a courtesy; "Maybe sir, you find her dull like, and not very kind; but she's weak, and the doctor says she mayn't be shook much please sir, nor speak to tire herself. So you'll please sir maybe excuse her."

She tore asunder an orange, of which Percival had brought in a supply, and squeezed some of the juice into her sister's mouth.

"I do not mean to keep her long, my good girl," replied Edward, motioning her away, while a peculiar expression of rigid determination came over his face. "But I must do my duty. Tell me," he continued, turning to Jane; "do you ever think of dying?—of what the hereafter will be?—of what you were sent into the world at all for? Do you know that you are to live again?"

"I've heerd tell so," she said.

"And do you not believe it?"

"Maybe no, maybe yes," she answered apathetically. And then a fresh fit of coughing made her moan and cry.

Edward Mantell's face expressed his horror.

"Is it not something more than a 'may be'?" he exclaimed. "If you die in this frightful state of mind, do you not know that you will go to hell?—and do you not know what hell is?—that place of everlasting punishment—of tortures that never cease—of flames and burning, and fiery agony? Do you not know that there is a devil waiting for your soul, who will carry it to this place if you die in such a state of sin as you are in now?"

The girl's attention was arrested.

"What is hell?" she asked; "we had it in a green book of father's once, along with a lot of black monkeys all a-roasting, when we were little uns; but I've not seen it since."

"Tell me first," asked Edward, "have you ever been baptized?"

"I don't know what you mean," said the sick girl surlily.

"No sir," said Sarah, coming to the rescue, "Father never let us be put into the water. He said it only costed money, and did no good.

Father thought nothing of these things. He said they gave carriages to the parsons when the poor wanted bread."

"You are positive that you are both unbaptized?" the clergyman repeated slowly.

"Oh yes, sir, I know we aint! for father said it so often!"

"Have you ever been to church then?" he continued, addressing Jane.

"The big houses?—no, never!"

In spite of her weakness her voice was getting stronger, and her manner more animated. The fever was rising visibly; but the zeal of the young preacher counted this as nothing compared with the chance of saving her soul.

"And why not? why never to church?"

"We'd no clothes—and why should us?" sullenly.

"But you would have heard there precious things; things that would have saved you from hell—that would have taken you to heaven; things that would have made you the child of God, instead of the child of the devil, which you are now unless you believe and repent."

"What's that?" she asked doggedly.

"Being sorry for your sins, Jane;—being sorry for all your past life, with its wickedness and its evil."

"That's it, is it?" she cried, half rising—"and what am I to be sorry for?—for being worked like a brute beast—for being left to the sweaters like a dog in a cart, and no one to look after us?—for keeping sober and honest, when we were hungry and couldn't get nothing to eat by being honest? Am I to be sorry for lying here sick for want and hard work—sixteen hours a day and not sixpence to take!"

A terrible fit of coughing, which seemed as if it would break a bloodvessel, was the consequence of her unusual eloquence.

Clara hurried forward, and took the sick head to her own bosom, while Sarah chafed the burning hands with mingled tears and kisses.

"You had better be silent now," said Clara turning to Edward Mantell, and speaking more sharply than she had ever spoken before. "It is cruel to distress her so much! It cannot do any good!"

"But I will not keep silence," persisted Edward sternly. "Let her die in the hearing, but let her hear the glad tidings before she dies. Better to lose a few hours of breath than to lose her soul for ever!"

"Her soul!—nonsense!" said Clara scornfully. And then she turned crimson for shame.

Edward Mantell took her hand and led her gently away with a magisterial, almost awful, air. She yielded to his touch with drooping head and rose-red cheeks; and Percival received her with an almost imperceptible smile, as she gathered herself close to him like a chastised child; and, holding her hand in his, bade her by a sign be still.

And now, standing by the side of that dying girl—denouncing her sins of ignorance and impiety—Edward Mantell poured forth a flood of Calvinistic sternness, till the very breathing of the invalid came checked and chill, and a cold dark awe crept over the hearts of all.

He spoke not of the sin of those who had left her there uncared for in her long day of toil and ignorance. He spoke not of the rich church with its costly lands and noble names which had counted that young soul as naught, and left that young mind to ruin. He spoke not of the great laws which must be obeyed—else the frightful penalties that come—but which stand forth as avengers only on those who infract them, not as teachers and guardians before such infraction. He spoke not of the mighty legislature which leaves its citizens to pauperism and crime unchecked until it punish. He spoke not of this brute ignorance in a christian nation—of this neglect in a mighty country— this grinding poverty in a wealthy city. All these extenuating causes were unheeded, and only the result, in yon dying thing's infidelity and defiance, was taken by him as matter of condemnation. Physical and moral causes were nothing—if indeed they were not fiendish devices of temptation. He had but one awful truth to teach; the after extenuation of the sinner he left to a higher power than man's. And there flowed on like a river of burning lava, the fiery words of wrath and pain awaiting her in the future. Sick, feeble, dying as she was, she must hear the blessed truth, though that tardy baptism slay her as it falls.

Percival could not oppose him. The appointed minister of the church, Edward Mantell was authorized to utter what hideous doctrines he chose. Yet Percival felt almost a guilty participation in this fanatic cruelty, by standing there silent, and listening to words as false as they were narrow, as unchristian as they were unnatural.

Sobs, bitter and grieving, came from the bed of the poor girl. "She didn't know that she was to be punished for nothing," she said. "She didn't see why she should have been born to hunger and work, and then taken to the fire after. She'd been as good as she could, and she was sure she had done as well as she had been told. If people wanted her to go to church they should have told her—how could she know?" And thus, struggling with her illness and her fears, came up the old spirit of dogged obstinacy and perversity, unconquerable as all brute instincts are.

"At least let me baptize you now!" urged Edward, seizing a small basin of water.

"No, that you shan't," she said, pushing back his hand; "I want nothing with you or your water." And then she added petulantly, among blinding tears and choking breath; "I don't believe in your God or your hell, and you're only making bogies for me."

The zeal of the preacher carried Edward beyond the dignity of the gentleman—the humanity of the man. He took the girl's feeble hand, and wrung it till the bones almost cracked beneath his gripe.

"Do you feel that?" he cried. "Have you senses with the brute, though you have no reason with the woman? If you can feel that—you will know what pain in hell-fire, and with the devils torturing you, will be!"

What ensued was a chaos of excitement. The cries of the terrified girl—the indignant voice of Percival—the shrill sobs of Sarah, and Clare's passionate remonstrances—raised a tumult in the house; which ended by the inmates gathering up into the sick chamber, and with oaths and curses thrusting the young clergyman forth into the street.

What with the irritability of sickness, and her natural peevish temper combined, Jane made more of her hand doubtless than was necessary. She bemoaned herself and wept incessantly; stopping between whiles for her frightful cough, and holding up her hand as if it had been broken at the wrist. In fact, one sinew was displaced, and a small bone was broken.

The room was full of people. Men and women had crowded up in thick numbers at the cry which a girl, passing by the door, had raised, that "some gentlefolks were murdering Jane Walcot." In all probability they would have left two of their own class to murder each other at their leisure; but the antagonism of race drew them to the rescue against a gentleman, as soon as the call had sounded.

"Is this what your parsons do?—is this what your rich men do?" cried one man savagely, striding up to Percival, as he stood with Clara by his side, and shaking his clenched fist in his face. "Do you come into the room of honest folk to murder them? Is this your charity?"

"And maybe you think it like a man to scrouge[98] a poor sick thing like that!" exclaimed a vixenish-looking woman setting her arms a-kimbo. "Maybe you think it grand like to bring trouble to a sick bed, instead of kindness, and call yourself a gentleman all the time. Ugh! Get out with you, you ugly brute you!"

"I was not speaking to her," put in Percival.

"And more shame for you then!" vociferated the man. "More shame, I say! If you'd been a man, and not a dressed-up jackanapes, you'd have kicked the fellow out before he lay a finger on such a poor thing as that!"

"You're no better nor you should be," said a second. "If he were bad you're his cousin—you are."

"I've never seed your face afore, but I know what the gallows'll have!" cried another.

"Your mother was frightened with an ape," said a woman.

"You're a Peeler[99] or a spy," said some.

"An informer," said others.

"And an ugly baste into the bargin," shrieked an Irish woman.

The crowd showed symptoms of proceeding from words to deeds. They pushed up against Percival—hustled Clara from him—insulted them both in coarse language—and threatened them with rough treatment "if they didn't make off with themselves in double-quick time." And one woman clutched at Clare's shawl, and bent her bonnet half over her face.

Clare stood quite composed, but very pale. She simply placed her hand on Percival's arm and trembled a little.

"No, no, you're wrong," cried Sarah, thrusting aside some of her noisy defenders; "these've been the best friends as ever was, and you mustn't hurt no hair of their heads! Hadn't they helped us we must have gone to the house, or broke windows to be took to prison. Th'other gentleman was not them. He was a different sort; but these are the grandest folks that ever crossed a poor body's door."

"To harm this lady or me," then said Percival mildly, "would not punish the gentleman who has just gone. We have done nothing. We did not hurt the poor girl. If you use violence to us you will only harm your friends because you have been wronged by a stranger."

"Friend!" muttered the man, "a pretty kind of friend to see a thief murder a poor creature like that!"

"He had taken her hand before I saw it," said Percival. "I stopped him when I knew that he hurt her."

"And what was the use of that ere?" asked a scowling ragged fellow. "If you'd a stopped him afore he hurted her mayhap you'd a done better!"

At this moment Clare pressed forward. She came quite near the last speakers and cried very fervently—"But we are chartists and socialists, and we love the people, and we'd give our lives for them; we would not hurt them for anything—indeed we would not! I am the daughter of a peasant woman myself!"

Those fierce dark scowling faces crowding in a thick mass of brute hatred softened gradually at this speech. Clare's manner, so heartfelt and earnest—her abandonment to the one overpowering impulse of the moment—the generous warmth of her nature, poured forth so vehemently, so unrestrainedly—all this made that haggard crowd listen with respect; and when she said that she was the daughter of a peasant woman herself, a smile and a low whisper of approbation ran round; and one northern woman said aloud: "The bonnie bairn has a douce voice and a lish[100] figure, whether she be gentle or simple."

"Indeed I am speaking the truth," urged Clara still most earnestly. "We came to-day to see what we could do for these poor girls. And Mr. Glynn has given them a great deal—oh, a very great deal!—and I could give them anything I had, only I am too poor to buy much for them. We would both do all that was in our power to make any of the people happy—for we are your true friends, and would always uphold the people. So you should not hurt us, for we are real chartists!"

"And who hurted yon poor lamb?" asked one of the men, not quite so brutally as before.

"Oh! he was a clergyman," cried Clara, "and he only said what he thought. He did not mean to do any harm—indeed he did not!"

"Mean to do any harm!" returned the man bitterly. "Is scrouging the hand of a dying thing mean to do no harm or not, you dressed-out madam? Was the parson mad or a fool that he dared do such a thing in the house of poor people? Ah! when we have the Charter,[101] won't we see the right side uppermost then!" And he shook his fist full in the beautiful face looking into his.

"All this is folly!" then said Percival suddenly. "I am your friend—and more than one among you know it."

Murmurs of "We do! we do!" interrupted him.

"And being your friend," he continued, "it is scarce likely that I should have encouraged any man—gentleman or not—to behave ill to one of you. I tell you again—that clergyman had hold of Jane's hand before I saw or knew it. That is the simple truth: let it end there. I had no part in it—nor assuredly had this lady, who came here to day simply for the purpose of doing what good she might, and of giving as much aid to these poor girls as she was able. So now my good friends, go back quietly to your rooms. Your anger against me—against us—is useless. We had no part in the matter; and I repeat what the lady said—we are chartists and socialists and your firmest friends. Let the poor girl be in peace now. That is what she wants most. And when you find my hand lifted up against one of the poor, then you may punish me as you like, but not before then. Good morning to you all. Not a few of you have seen me in John Street—not a few have heard what I propose for the people—you know me well—so trust to my word."

The men gave a faint cheer, and the Irishwoman invoked blessings on the head of the "purty lady and lovely gintleman." In a few moments the room was cleared, and Percival and Clara were once more alone with the two sisters.

All this excitement killed poor Jane sooner than need have been. She lay now in a kind of stupor, which, but for that cruel cough and choking breath, might have passed for death.

Sarah knelt by the bed, sobbing loudly.

The dying girl suddenly opened her eyes. She fixed them on Percival and tried to speak. But her lips were too parched, and her tongue rattled between them like dried leather.

They gave her a spoonful of orange juice and water; and then she was able to speak. Percival bent his ear to listen.

"Tell me," she said whispering; "was it all true? Shall I be in pain there, and shall I be in hell when I've done no wrong?"

"No, Jane," answered Percival emphatically: "No; you won't be in pain, and you won't be in hell. You will find a father, Jane, who will receive you—not a devil who will torture. You will find all pain gone—all sorrow—all sickness; you will go to a beautiful place where all that you have suffered here will be remembered, and you will be made happier for it. You will be with GOD, Jane, and not with anything cruel or evil."

A half smile broke over the sharp features.

"Are you sure of it?" she said still in the same sinking voice, but with a strangely beautiful expression breaking through the heavy brutalism of her face.

"Yes, I am sure of it, Jane," he answered. "When you die you will go to heaven, because you have been good as far as you know, and because all your faults have been caused by the evil of others."

The girl sank back. They thought she was dead. But rallying for a fleeting moment she motioned feebly to her sister, and said—but so faint and low that even Love could scarcely hear her—

"Sal, I have oft been unkind to thee, lass, and oft fretted thee more nor I ought. You'll forgive me now Sal, and come—come soon to me there!"

Her head fell back; her lips parted; she looked upward, and a smile of joy lighted up that dying face as in stronger tones she cried; "I see it! I see it!" raising her hand and pointing up.

What she saw, or what comfort and consolation that dying moment gave her, none but her own soul and the Great Father knows. Whether it was the mocking fantasy of fever, or whether it was the true revelation of the opening Life, I cannot say. Her voice then ceased for ever, and her soul went forth into the Dark Beyond that lies on that side death; and all the rest is hidden.

CHAPTER II.

THE usual notice was brought to Edward Mantell of a funeral at four o'clock to-day. It was Jane Walcot's. Here was a difficult question. Did this girl come under the head of Christian—she, who refused baptism—who knew not the very name of Christ—who denied GOD and disbelieved in hell? It was a mockery to give such a one Christian burial! It was an offence against the ordinances of religion—a sin against the sanctity of the church. Sad as it would be to refuse the rite of sacred sepulture, he could not conscientiously bestow it. He must of necessity deny that pallid corpse a ceremony designed only for a professing Christian, and send it out into unblessed ground unsanctified by the holy service which consigns earth to earth and ashes to ashes, "in sure and certain hope of the resurrection to eternal life through our Lord Jesus Christ."

Edward Mantell was a high churchman in all respecting forms, and churchly rites, and churchly discipline; though also holding these mournful doctrines of election, the damnation of the majority, and salvation through faith alone, which are more essentially Calvinistic. Many young clergymen of heated imaginations and ascetic feelings, mingled with some pride of office, combine in this manner the worst parts of two different modes of faith. The narrow formalism of the one, and the narrow spiritualism of the other, appeal to feelings unhappily as dear as they are general; for the self-gratification found in exclusiveness and power is the true reason why Calvinism and Romanism count such ardent followers among their respective priesthoods.

The church was not far from Edward Mantell's lodgings. In a short time he reached the churchyard, where the funeral stood, waiting till he should come down in his priestly robes to receive it within the consecrated ground.

The grave lay near to the gates. It was very shallow; only a few inches below the surface. But this was not the sole corpse in that pit of death. Many and many a coffin lay below in thick ranks of progressive corruption. Between some might be the mockery of a thin layer of earth—merely to hide the mouldering wood. Between others—if they had come near together in point of time—not even this veil of simulated decency hung over the frightful revelations that crowded below. It was the pauper's plot in the yard; and this was the pauper's general grave.

The whole churchyard was crowded with mounds and tombs. There did not seem to be one single available foot of ground left in which to place a suckling's coffin. And yet, had there been a general pestilence—had the firstborn of every family died in an Egyptian night of blood—the clerkly authorities of yon metropolitan burial-ground would have found space for all that came.

No matter that the thousand houses clustered round this tainted spot were struck within and without as by a rod of leprosy. No matter that their inmates sickened at the noxious vapours, which rose so thick from the steaming earth that they were like white-robed ghosts in the air. No matter that all within the range of this churchyard was tainted too—that the waters in the wells ran foul with the corruptions which crept along the earth into their beds—that the air was so laden with the elements of decay as to rot the very meat in the larders—bearing revulsion and disease and death into every chamber round. No matter that fungi grew out on the walls and in the cellars, and that the feet of the walker slipped on floors where the churchyard fulness oozed out in substance and in smell. No matter that every feeling of decency was outraged, every sentiment of respect set at nought. The authorities buried their dead, and laughed at the sentimentality which would rob them of their fees for the sake of a philosophical idea.

Bleached bones were turned up with each stroke of the sexton's spade. Skulls were tossed out of the teeming earth as boys would toss rubble-stones from a field. And once—it was sworn to—a pale corpse was exhumed, on which the spade had struck sharply, and dismembered it in the sight of men. That pale, sad, silent corpse! once loved with all the passionate intensity of the human heart; even now so short time buried—wept for in the silent night—wept for in the busy day—the beloved light of some mournful life whose sun had set when it died out. And there it lay; hacked by that cruel spade; uncovered by the coarse hands of coarse men; seen, witnessed, sworn to, in this refined century; disturbed in its brief rest by the greedy lust of gain that could not let it lie for want of its little space of earth—or rather for want of the pelf which yon little space would bring.

This was the state of that metropolitan churchyard over which Edward Mantell was to read the Christian burial service. This was the enduring mockery of that service—this a plainer evidence of national feeling than can be found in articles or in creeds—this the standing proof that Englishmen—gentlemen—divines—priests, are ready, in rank numbers, to desecrate every holiest feeling and trample on the most sacred instincts of humanity for the cursed love of money only. Ay, blush in the midnight darkness, ye clerkly proprietors of metropolitan churchyards! Blush for your foul desires, ye opponents of the intramural prohibition!

The pauper burial stood waiting for the clergyman. Two women only were mourners. One was Sarah Walcot, carrying thus to the grave the sole tie between her and love; and the other was Emma Vaughan.

What brought this wretched woman there I do not know. But here she stood; and though she shed no tears her face was grave and pale; and something that was not sorrow, and yet was not indifference, lent her features a look that brought back somewhat of their early beauty. Degraded and lost as she was, there was one whole part still left in her; and a skilful physician might have stayed the plague eating through her had he known by what this whole part could be reached.

A few men stood by these two women. Their manner was irreverent and impatient. They handled the coffin roughly, and spoke in no very subdued voices with each other. Why should they show respect? It was but a pauper that they carried! They swore at the parson for being so long a-coming; they jested to each other about Emma, wondering what could have brought "Black Em. to see a burying;" and one of them whistled a loose song, and beat time with his fingers on the coffin.

It was but a pauper—why should they show respect?

It was well for poor Sarah that grief absorbed her too much to allow her to see all this brutality. Her face buried in her hands—sight, sense, hearing, all lost—she knew nothing of what went on about her, and only felt that she leant against some living thing, which every now and then pressed her kindly, but did not speak. It was Emma Vaughan who thus supported her; "for she was kind to my children," she said to herself; "and I never can repay her that!"

At last the clergyman did really come. By this time a few idle boys and lounging men had gathered round the funeral train; that class of people who are always ready at a moment's notice to swell a crowd, or gape at a sight, and who spring out of the earth like human mushrooms, they are so soon brought forth from apparent nothingness.

Edward put a few questions to one of the men with the coffin; and then said aloud, in a slow distinct voice; "I refuse to bury this corpse."

A thrill of startled astonishment went round the group. All pressed nearer to hear what would follow; and a few began to murmur already. Even Sarah checked her tears, and raised her head to look up.

"She was without the pale of the church," continued Edward. "She was virtually excommunicate—unbaptized by her own confession—ignorant of the name of Christ—denying the power of God. She was not a Christian in any sense of the word. She cannot have Christian sepulture."

"But the law will force you, sir," said one of the men fiercely. "We've brought the corpse a precious long way already. D'ye think the parish is a-going to have separate grounds for all your new-fangled notions? We're not a-going to take it back again; so hold your jaw and do your duty—you pale-faced canting cove," he added in an under voice.

"Not bury her?" whispered Sarah in those low tones of terror— "not bury her—and she so poor and good?"

"No, Sal," answered Emma in a loud voice. "The church, as they call it, left her to starve if she liked; it left her to ignorance and want; and now, to punish the very ignorance it made, it will not bury her. This is Christian charity, and he's a Christian priest!" and she laughed bitterly.

Murmurs came from the crowd.

"She wasn't a suicide!" cried one voice, in an educated accent. "You have no right to refuse her burial unless she was publicly excommunicate or a suicide."

A gentleman came forward. He was the speaker; and from his sharp sallow face and shabby black dress-coat, with such wide pockets filled with papers, he looked like a lawyer.

"I have the word of the church on my side," said Edward calmly. "She was unbaptized and an atheist—an avowed atheist—but a short time before she died."

"Hear me, sir; you may get into trouble with this," said the stranger. "Take my advice. Bury the corpse decently and duly; else you will find that the law, as well as popular opinion, will not interpret even the rubric so rigidly as you would have them."

"Popular opinion, under the worst form of indignation, is nothing to me," the young clergyman answered fervently. "While in my duty I can suffer any kind or degree of persecution; counting all gain, so that I keep the testimony and the word undefiled."

"What is that you are saying there?" shouted the man who had spoken before—one of these who had borne the coffin. "Do you think we are to stay here all day that you two men may fight and talk? Here men, lend a hand!—we'll make that puritan bury her fast enough!"

The crowd cheered, and pressed forward. But before they could gain a clear entrance, Edward Mantell swung the church-gates to, and thrust them out with the force of the blow.

"I will not be intimidated against my conscience," he exclaimed. "I have told you quietly and distinctly that this wretched corpse is without the pale of the church, and therefore shall not rest under the blessing of the church Unbaptized, unrepentant, she has no claim to the prayers which the church has framed for its dutiful children, and to offer them up for her would be mockery and blasphemy."

The crowd had now increased to some hundreds. The news went round under different headings—"The parson won't bury the corpse;" while every conceivable reason was assigned; some so gross and cruel that they roused the mob almost to madness.

Curses, yells, and hootings were the first signs of its wrath. Some tried to scale the church walls, but they were high and slippery; others flung their sticks, or picked up anything they could find, to hurl at Edward's head. Horrible oaths, mingled with threats, disturbed the air that should have slept so lightly on that large death-garden. But the cause of all this tumult held his ground as firmly and as manfully as though he stood in the midst of plaudits and of praise.

A few policemen had gathered in among this crowd. Of admirable temper, firmness, and discretion, they tried to pacify the chafed humours of the sovereign people; but every fresh attempt to soothe, only increased, their angry feeling.

A sergeant of police now came up. He called Edward aside, and spoke to him in a low tone.

"No, no!" replied the clergyman. "No! I will not be intimidated! I have the authority of the church and the warranty of Scripture both on my side. The civil laws are less than these—and below them."

"But there will be a skrimmage,"[102] urged the sergeant. "The people are getting impatient, and will insist on it in a rougher way than you'll like. Come!—I advise you to open the gates and put an end to it."

"My own blood shall fill this grave sooner than yon infidel's corpse shall lie in Christian burial," cried Edward. "It is a matter of conscience—of religious duty—of churchly discipline; and I will not yield for any base considerations of selfish safety."

As he stood there—cruel as his action was—he was so firm, so true to his own belief, so resolute even to his own hurt, that he must be respected while condemned, admired while reproved.

The crowd murmured in a kind of low roar during this conference. When it ended, and Edward Mantell withdrew from the wall where he had spoken with the sergeant, the tumult began afresh. He attempted to speak to them, but they would not listen to him. Those who cried—"Hear him! hear him!" were soon overpowered by the torrent of execrations, hisses, groans, and yells, that poured from the increasing multitude.

Making a gesture with his hands, as if signing them away, the clergyman retreated into the vestry, where the summoned church-wardens met him as he entered.

The uproar grew terrific. Screams from frightened women struck by unintentional blows—shouts from men whose blood was up for any deed of violence or outrage—the wild Irish yell—the shrill Scotch shriek—the sobs of children terrified at the rage about them—all formed a hideous requiem for that pale corpse lying within its coffined shroud.

Crying only—"Oh, bury her decent! bury her decent!" the poor sister clung round Emma, stopping in her moans to kneel down by the coffin and to lay her forehead on its hard edge.

Emma Vaughan stood like some dark fiend in the midst of this scene fit only for fiends to enact. Her hatred to the rich, the good, the virtuous, had now full scope and some show of justice. All the personal bitterness which she had cherished so long, came up to swell the passion natural in one destitute of religious feeling, against an action founded solely on religious fanaticism. She raved and swore incessantly. Above all that tumult of maddened men, her voice, hoarse with rage, and uttering oaths far worse than any other there, was heard like a continual scream—a wild fierce cry, more fitted for the maniac's cell than for the quiet of a churchyard. And every now and then she would turn to the grieving sister sobbing in her arms, and endeavour to soothe her kindly; mingling her tenderest words with the foulest language she could frame against Edward Mantell, her husband, the church, society at large, and every institution of the country. Her brain had long been on the very verge of madness: it needed but a slight increase of excitement at any time to destroy the equilibrium for a season.

The church-gates were now forced back. The coffin standing at the entrance was thrown down, the scanty pall trampled and torn, the frail wood broken. No more need be said. The rest was a confused rush, a loud noise, the sudden presence of a large body of police bearing the crowd back, the rescue of the clergyman from hands that clutched him harshly, and the final dispersion of the mob. But in every living heart of that day's crowd was sown a wide harvest of hatred for the church, of hatred for the aristocracy, and of antagonism generally to every species of faith or religion above them.

The next day the whole newspaper press rang with the account.

The conservative journals softened it down, and spoke of the "admirable temper of the clergyman," though they faintly deprecated his "unhappy strictness of view." The liberal press, in proportion with its liberalism, heightened the circumstances into a sad deformity with truth. Some of them said that "the clergyman behaved with unexampled brutality;" others spoke of a "legal tribunal;" and one, more rabid than the rest, regretted that stocks and the pillory were out of fashion, and that the whole clerical body had not a particular mode of punishment of its own, so that all the world might know its particular delinquencies.

But there it was—the eternal fact—and nothing could undo it now. Edward Mantell must make the best of it. At any rate, he was not likely to give way to repentance or concession. He had not acted on impulse merely, nor yet on imperfect knowledge. He had the authority of the rubric on his side, and foregone example in the church; and he was right in following such honoured guides against any lax spirit of the present day. Edward Mantell, like all deeply convinced and resolute men, had not a little of that stuff in him which makes martyrs and steadfast witnesses; men who, when they hold our own doctrines, we canonize and honour, but when they are opposed to us, we name contumacious, heretical, infidel, the servants of Satan, and the disseminators of rebellion and immorality. Yet if the rubric be other than a name—if the ordination vows of the young clergyman be other than formal mockeries—Edward Mantell was right. If the Anglican Church is pure and infallible, her rules ought to be acted up to; and then we should see whether the Anglican people would accept these rules as binding. Consistency in the clergy would at least afford a fair field of trial between the past and present spirit of the nation.

The present uproar was calmed by another curate of the church—more complying than Edward—who read the service over that poor desecrated corpse, and gave it such scant decency of burial as a pauper was entitled to; and thus it did not ensue in any more publicity. The matter was simply talked over by one or two grave divines at a clerical conclave, where some of the more sleepy lamented the "heated brains of the youth of the present day," and others said that "the clergy themselves would pull down the church." But nothing was done. For when the rector thought to chide his young curate, Edward opened on him such a fire of eloquent reasoning and steadfast principle of right, that the old man was fain to be silent, else he would have been completely overborne. He was not one of the voluntary martyrs for church discipline. He was an easy-going old man, fond of quiet; not unfavourable to a genial glass of port; a man who looked to his rectorial rights more than to his cure of souls; essentially one of the sluggish school against which the very church itself has risen up, to cast out such drones from the hive. And thus his very apathy and sloth left Edward free to exercise his fanaticism and cruelty.

While this scene had been performing at the church-gates, a curious world had been passing at the —— theatre.

Just before Clara went down to rehearsal, Percival called on her.

"Am I in time?" he said as he entered.

"In time for what?" she laughed pleasantly, for his coming always cheered her; even more than she confessed to herself.

"To take you to the theatre. You are going, are not you?"

"Yes," she said sighing; "I am going to my prison—to my tread-mill."

"Now don't speak so despondingly! It grieves me beyond measure to hear that tone of voice from you."

"But it is true, Mr. Glynn. I hate my profession now! Oh! my heart is very very heavy!"

"Never to be lighter, Clare?"

His voice had a peculiar accent. It made Clara start and blush and look in his face, as if she had expected him to be transformed in some way. It made her go close to him, and lay her hand on his shoulder, and look strangely like her old baby self when she used to ask Mrs. de Saumarez what she meant by some hard word or other. And then a sudden rush of blood, like the crimson of a carnation, over her cheeks, made her feel as if she had done wrong, and drove her out of the room for her bonnet and shawl a few moments earlier than was necessary.

"I wonder why Percival reminds me so much of Vasty!" she thought, as she tied her bonnet, and could not fail to see her burning cheeks in her small discoloured glass.

She felt uncomfortable as she hurried through the parlour, and told Percival to make haste without looking at him. For she thought he would see "Vasty" in every feature of her face.

As she left her own house, accompanied by Glynn, Vaughan passed with a pretty, blue-eyed, fair-haired girl hanging on his arm; to whom he spoke as gently, bending down and looking into her face as fondly, as ever he had done to Clare in her most favoured days.

Clare was flurried and embarrassed. She had the old brilliant blush and timid glance which Vaughan knew so well, and had revelled in so long—as under an Italian sky with vines and roses trailing over his head. And in spite of the new-born interests and affections that had sprung up, chance-sown, in the barren land of their estrangement—in spite too of the coldness with which he reproached her—of the brutality which she had borne from him—they were not yet so wholly indifferent to each other as to see, what each believed to be visible signs of inconstancy, without a pang in the hearts of both.

Their eyes met. Vaughan's face was earnest, its expression tender; he had evidently been making love; proved also by the coquettish smile and triumphant blush of his little companion. It was long since Clare had seen this gentle expression in his face. It rolled back on her heart a tide of memories, that cast up as stranded gems these hours and moments of thrilling happiness, when first the reality of heaven was evidenced in earthly life. Like withered flowers expanding in the water, forgotten thoughts woke up again to life; feelings that had sunk stone-dead came back to her soul, borne on that rushing tide. Her eyes sank below Vaughan's look. He believed they sank for shame at being seen thus by him, with the crimson cheek of love turned to another.

The girl whose hand he held on his arm looked up, amazed at the sudden start he gave—the sudden impatient stamp with his foot—the quick hand clenched—the muttered oath. She had not seen Clara; and if she had she would have understood nothing beyond what she understood now. As this sudden fit of "muscular contraction" passed away as quickly as it came, it ceased to disturb her; and when Vaughan pressed her hand against his breast, and spoke to her more lovingly than ever, she forgot it altogether.

She was a young "first walking lady"[103] from one of the minor theatres, whose pretty face had caught his eye, and whose superficial cleverness had seemed an advantageous possession. He had engaged her now for his theatre, to take these parts which Miss Gray could not play, and which he would not give to Clare. As for Clara, her theatrical existence had been as brief as it was brilliant. The public had forgotten her. Only one or two inveterate playgoers regretted the glorious girl who came before them so suddenly, all youth and fervour, and who had flashed and faded like a passing meteor. But they supposed it was all right; she appeared every now and then in some minor part; but the Greek Wife was wholly suppressed, and she did her other work but indifferently at the best.

The newspaper critics noticed her absence. Some of them asked why? others said they had always prognosticated her failure, (which they never had done,) and had affirmed from the first that her powers were overrated—for see how ill she played now! Others again hinted darkly at "conspiracy," and "ill-treatment," if the dramatic critic had a weakness for female beauty: and then by degrees this kind of lagging life also burnt itself out, and her name ceased to be spoken or printed at all.

A few minutes after she entered the theatre to-day, Vaughan came in with pretty Mary Smith on his arm. But Mary Smith was too commonplace a name for playbills and theatrical life. It was etherealized into Miss Emmeline de Montfort. A young lawyer's clerk, who fell in love with her at first sight, spent half his fortune and lost his time, and his situation with it, in trying to find out to what particular branch of the great Montfort family the fair Emmeline belonged. He wrote it out in a neat engrossing hand, and sent a large packet of folio to the theatre, containing a genealogical tree, and a full account of the whole Montfort race since the first mention made of them in intelligible history; and asked in return for a lock of her hair: which she sent to him. And thereupon he went into a fit of maudlin sentimentality that lasted, by the help of gin-and-water, many days.

It would be impossible to describe Vaughan's manner to-day: every word was a taunt—every look an insult to Clare, while his attentions to the fair Emmeline were excessive and overpowering. He introduced her to Lucretia, holding her hand in both of his, and saying in a loud voice; "A real treasure this, Miss Kemble!—a true diamond—no false paltry paste," glancing at Clara while he spoke.

And little Miss Emmeline waved her long light ringlets fluttering about her round pink cheeks like locks of spun glass; and laughed and shook her head, and cried, "Oh fie!" and tapped Vaughan playfully with her parasol; moving her small feet as if they were dancing.

Clara, wrapped in a large plaid shawl dimmed by rain and constant wear—her straw bonnet brown and puckered—the ribbon streaked here and there, faded, and very shabby—looked on with a mingled feeling of sorrow and pride. It would be absurd to say that she loved Vaughan still. She did not. And yet she could not see him openly transfer to another the love he had professed for her without feeling some haunting memory of sorrow.

Her beautiful face must be always lovely. But I cannot deny that, at first sight, she looked inferior to the new favourite to-day. She, all flounces and gauze and streaming ribbons and flying hair—a light aërial thing whose atmosphere of vanity did not ill beseem her beauty—moved like a little fairy among the dirty scenes, and through the patched and painted crowd. While Clare, in heavy garments, shabby, dark, and common, sat stiff and motionless, and except for the beautiful face underneath the unfashionable bonnet, might have been a servant to one of the actresses quite as well as an actress herself. She looked neglected—she looked poor. Miss de Montfort was all smiles, and blushes of pride, and gay evidences of wealth, and laughing evidences of happiness. Her light feet clad in silk stockings of the pinkest, and kid shoes of the thinnest, were certainly more attractive than Clare's—albeit these too were small and shapely—in their thick cloth boots, worn at the heel, and splashed. Miss de Montfort's small hands were cased in pale primrose gloves, fresh and delicate, while her arms and wrists were enveloped in a profusion of long hanging lace and muslin, which no one knew where it began, or where it left off, or what purpose it was to answer. And bright trinkets also, that clanked pleasantly and looked aristocratic, depended from these small wrists—pretty fanciful toys that Emmeline loved to exhibit, and was never weary of playing with. Hearts and crosses, red, green, gold, and white—long dangling chains, broad clanking manacles—all the thousand devices for maiden vanity that invention can supply, had she hung on her delicate arms, in lavish profusion of jeweled luxury. Clare had a pair of lavender-coloured cotton gloves much mended, from which the colour had been partly washed; and her sleeves were made tight to the wrist, without bracelets or snowy muslin at all. Miss de Montfort wore a thin light gown all flounces and fringe, over which was thrown a costly mantle of velvet and lace: Clare had a shabby brown merino,[104] dull and faded, scanty and rather short too, for she had been obliged to hem it up round the edge more than once, from being "cut" with walking. Feathers and flowers and a beautiful lace veil all mingled together with those fair flowing ringlets: Clare's heavy hair—not a little disordered by the wind—fell down her cheeks, and not a flower nor a grace was about it. And thus the two stood together.

They were indeed sadly contrasted!—and bitter thoughts might well rise up in that poor child's heart as she remembered how she had once basked in the sunshine of life, and believed in the durability of bliss. And now she was a very bankrupt—a ruined, desolate wreck, stranded on the shore by which she had sailed so short time since, with a bright sun above and a fair wind for her glancing sails—stranded and wrecked, with naught but storm about her!

The love of Vaughan, the chief place in the professional world, the social advantages of wealth, the natural satisfaction found in the esteem of one's fellows, the glittering prospect of success—all the gay hopes that had lured her on far and fatally, were torn from her and hung like gems and gold about the neck of this young stranger.

Clare could not bear it. The contrast was too humiliating; the memory of all she had hoped, and of all she had lost, too painful. Vaughan, passing by, saw tears falling fast on her hands as they lay folded passively in her lap, and gemming the bright brown hair hanging down on her bosom. He saw the full lip tremble; he saw the blue eye droop; he knew all the passion of grief and wounded pride that had called forth those tears. He hated himself. The laughing vanity of Emmeline blasted his sight. He would have given worlds to have gone to Clare, to his best, his only love—ay, in spite of all that had gone before, his only love, his dearest one! He would have annihilated nations if he might but catch her to his breast again, and bid her once more to the sanctuary of his love. But pride restrained him too; and so he passed her with a lingering step, and a tender look, saying involuntarily—"Clara! dear Clara!"

She heard him; and for a moment felt a strange guilty joy. But she had suffered too much to place herself again in danger. She kept her eyes still cast down, as though she had heard nothing. And Vaughan, not knowing that he had spoken, went down into his private room, and sat there long in a death-like reverie.

CHAPTER III.

"CLARA, can you give me half an hour? I have something that I wish to say to you," said Edward Mantell, entering Clare's room early one day.

He was very pale, and his voice was not so strong nor so steady as in general.

"Certainly," she answered with a kind of start; and her voice too trembled.

Edward drew a chair near to her, and sat down. She stood at a little distance from him, looking exceedingly uncomfortable, and rather frightened.

"Come near me," he said, taking her hand gently, and pointing to a chair near his own; "I must have you near me Clara; I wish to look into your face while I speak. Come!"

Clara was accustomed to be treated like a child by most people. It was a peculiarity in her social intercourse—caused by her own manners—which sometimes placed her in unpleasant positions, and often raised false hopes in her male acquaintances. For few men can distinguish between the gentleness of a sensitive temperament and the weakness of a feeble organization; and unless women go about the world in a perpetual state of moral porcupinehood, they are liable at all times to be treated as slaves and regarded as idiots. Because Clara was young and beautiful, she was as yet treated simply as a child; though Vaughan had attempted the slavery too—we have seen with what success.

Clara would have given all her present fortune and future earnings—and that would not have been much—to be a hundred miles at this moment away from Edward Mantell. Yet she did as he told her; mechanically rather than obediently. Quaking and trembling she drew the chair indicated a couple of inches away; and then sat down like a victim, quite upright, and just on the edge—her feet far underneath.

There was an awkward pause. Edward was too much agitated to observe Clara's very evident discomfort, and his heart was beating so tumultuously that it prevented his speaking; he dared not trust his voice—it would have betrayed his weakness too much—and he did not wish to ask fearfully for what he hoped to receive plenteously.

Clara, dreading something unpleasant, and saying to herself, "Oh! is he going to make me an offer?" was glad enough to keep silence as long as she could. She would not therefore break the pause; and so it continued to apparently an indefinite time of uneasiness.

At last Edward spoke.

"You must have seen, Clara, for some time my feelings for you," he began. And then he stopped.

Clara looked down on the ground with persevering industry. Her mouth was unclosed and pouting; and her fingers were twisting in amongst each other, as if they were all at a wrestling match where no one was the winner. This was a favourite habit of hers.

"And I believe—I have had reason to believe from your manners and conduct, Clara—that these feelings are not wholly unreturned."

He paused again. Still Clara was silent—not daring to look up, much less to answer. But she was as much shocked by his assertion as if it had been an accusation. "My manners and conduct!" she thought; "why, does he think that I have done anything wrong?"

"Am I right, Clara?"

"I do not know," she said faintly; "I do not understand you."

"Not understand me!"

"No," she repeated. But she knew that she was telling a falsehood while she spoke.

"Do you not know—have you not seen long months past that I love you?—that you have become my second life?—that I have flung at your feet the whole first love of a heart that loves not coldly nor yet scantily, Clara? Do you not know how I have hung all my hopes of happiness on you—how I have turned to you and the vision of your love as the solace sent me in this weary life of toil and pain? Do you not know all this, Clara, and do you not respond to it?"

He spoke fervently, and took her hands to his bosom; and as he looked into her gentle face, and murmured again and again—"My solace—my delight," he forgot the fierce struggles between conscience and love that he had undergone so long and often—he forgot that she had ever been the Delilah of his soul, binding it to the service of sin.

"No," she said again, much distressed, and attempting to rise.

"Oh Clara! why this averted face?—why this timid voice—this painful hesitation? You love me Clara—you must, you do! A thousand small words—a thousand minute events have betrayed it. You love me Clara as I love you—as you know that I loved you!"

"Indeed, indeed, no!" she exclaimed, "I do not, indeed I do not!"

He released her hands. She rose and turned away towards the window.

"What do I hear?" he said in a deep voice. His face was ghastly pale, and his eyes were sad and anxious. "Have you then trifled with me?—have you meant only my ruin by those caressing ways—those gentle words—those affectionate eyes, which have deluded me so far? Am I to learn today that the very soul of truth and honour is a heartless hypocrite? Is this your morning's revelation, Clara?"

Clara still bent her head from him.

"I am very sorry," she began; and then she burst into tears.

Edward threw his arms round her. How the touch thrilled to his very soul!—how strangely it affected him—this first time when a woman's heart had beat against his own! And that woman one so loved, so worshipped!

"No tears, no tears!" he cried in a peculiar voice; as if he spoke in a reverie, unconscious that he was heard; "No tears, Clara!—they fall on my heart like fire—they are painful—painful;" and he shuddered; then adding, "no tears, bright bird—all must be bright!" he attempted to wipe them from her eyes in a vague dreamy way. But Clara put back his hand gently; then suddenly taking it again between both her own, and looking up into his face, she said ingenuously—through all her grief and sorrow her native kindness more transparent than ever:—

"There has been some mistake, and I have been to blame; I never meant to show you all that you say you have seen in me! Indeed I only meant to show you sisterly affection; nothing more, on my word of honour!"

Edward withdrew his arm. He buried his face in his hands. Not a word was spoken; but once or twice a low muffled groan burst forth as from one in unutterable agony, striving to subdue his pain by pride.

Clara was really alarmed. She sat down by him. She called him by his name. She spoke tenderly—soothingly—and laid her hand on his—on his forehead—on his cheek. She tried to force him to look up; but he resisted her endeavours, and continued his painful position and painful evidences of misery.

"Edward, dear Edward, what can I do for you?" she exclaimed. "Tell me what I can do to make you happy! I do love you——"

"You do love me!" he exclaimed, starting up. "Oh! how can I repay you for the bliss of this one moment of time!—no devotion of a life could fitly express my rapturous gratitude—no holocaust of selfish hopes and selfish desires could be too great sacrifice for such dear words! You love me, Clara—you love me! Life has no other word for me!" Again he strained her to his breast; and then, for the first and last time in life, he kissed her lips.

That touch, that look, recalled Clara to the remembrance of certain laws of formality which she had well-nigh forgotten.

"No! no!" she exclaimed earnestly. "I mean I love you as a sister—as a friend! I cannot love any one again in any other way. Oh! forget this folly, dear Edward, and be my brother—my friend—my dear friend! Forget this! and let our lives go on as they did before such strange thoughts came to you!"

"This is trifling with me!" he cried, pacing the room feverishly. "This is worse than an insult! Sisterly affection!—this to me!—to me, whose whole being is wrapped in one fiery robe of love and suffering! Offer rose-leaves to the starving man—but offer me no such frightful mockery!"

Again that heavy prostration of all energy except such as pain preserved—again that stifled moan—that time of sharpest agony— left Edward Mantell no faculty save that of suffering.

Clare, chilled, and trembling as if with cold, though the summer sun beat down fiercely on the glaring pavement and made the atmosphere dense with heat, sat still on the sofa, keeping her eyes fixed on her companion, but unable to say or do anything which would console him: at least if she kept to truth.

But many times she was tempted to forswear herself, and to soothe this terrible anguish by a false confession of love. Many times the words trembled on her lips; and once she leant over the poor wretch, and calling him by his name said, "I will be—" but she stopped, and then added—"always your friend."

It was too heavy a trial for her. She was unselfish enough in general, but to sacrifice herself—heart and life—to compassion, went far beyond even her notions of duty and sacrificial instincts. Fain would she have ended this painful scene by the only words that could satisfactorily end it; but her repugnance was too strong; she kept silence, and Edward suffered. And there was no help for him in heaven or earth.

"But Clara, you deceived me!" he said after a long pause, looking up with a face so haggard, so grieving, it made her start as if a spectre had arisen.

"No! I did not!" she exclaimed.

"Yes—you cannot tell me you were such a child as not to see that I loved you."

His voice was bitter, yet he seemed to derive some comfort from this accusation, as if he would force her into acceptance from very shame of her inconstancy and deceit.

"Indeed I did not know it!" she cried.

He groaned. "Oh false! false!—what folly!—what falseness!" Still that weary pacing, that weary moan!

"Edward—dear Mr. Mantell—believe me I did not know that you loved me!" she said again.

He came now, and sat down on the sofa by her. He looked inquiringly into her face. Tears which no pride, no manliness could check, rushed down his own cheeks. He did not know they were there, else he might have pressed them back.

"Can you look me honestly in the face and say you did not know this?"

She raised her eyes to his, frankly and steadfastly.

"No, I did not," she said firmly.

"And this is true?—this is true?"

"It is indeed. I did not dream of it, Mr. Mantell!"

"It is well!" he said, and then he started up again, like one who could have walked for ever, but to whom an eternity could not have lightened his sufferings.

Suddenly Clare remembered Percival's warning repeated not so very long ago.

"I did not know till too late," she said in a low voice as he passed her; looking into his face with her own look of ingenuous courage, yet half frightened at her very boldness.

He arrested his steps.

"What mean you, Clara?—what mystery or what deceit is this?" He spoke very harshly.

"Neither, Edward. I mean simply that I never thought of the possibility of your loving me until I was told of it, and warned against to-day."

"Told of it?—warned against me?—and who dared to step in thus between me and my love?—who dared to take on him the control of your heart? But I need not ask! That man—that destroyer of your eternal peace—that underminer of your faith—that frightful slave of sin worse than death—Percival Glynn, has been my secret enemy! He has done this!"

"He has not been your enemy, Mr. Mantell," Clara said, colouring deeply.

"Not my enemy!" he exclaimed. "And what have you been telling me now? Am I a fool?—am I a child?—a deaf dotard, without understanding?—can I not hear what is said? Oh misery! misery!

without this she might have been mine!—mine in the pleasant paths of righteousness—mine in blessed security, in peace, in honour! Saved here—saved hereafter—the saint preparing in the wife—the angel growing in the woman! Misery! misery!—a soul is lost while a heart lies broken!"

"Indeed he never spoke against you," urged Clara earnestly. "He said nothing that you would have disliked to hear. He merely asked me if I——" She hesitated.

"If you loved me, I suppose?" he said with a short laugh.

"Yes," she answered.

"And you denied it—you ridiculed the notion—you helped him in his derision—you laughed at the fond fool who could aspire to such glorious riches—you counted my looks and smiles and words, and told them over for his amusement—you made yourselves merry with this agony—this—" striking his breast, "and planned to-day as you would have planned out a farce? This is what you and your pestilent friend—your pernicious adviser—did, when *he* revealed to you that I loved you!"

"Mr. Mantell—Edward—is this just?" asked Clara in a reproachful tone. "Mr. Glynn has never offended you; he has never spoken ill of you in any way; he has been one of my best friends through all kinds of trouble and distress, and I cannot allow him to be maligned."

"Clara, if you would not see me mad do not, for the sake of every womanly gentleness and virtue, uphold that man in my presence!" he cried passionately. "I do not wish the harm of any one, but if that man had never been born, or had died before he came across your path, I might have been happy to-day; and you—you, Clara, might have been saved!"

"Mr. Mantell, you forget," said Clara somewhat proudly, "there may be other reasons than Mr. Glynn's representations why I should not love you."

"True! true!" he murmured. "She so beautiful—so good—so great in mind though so lost—true, there are other reasons, and I have been blind!"

He turned away, and Clare knew by his action and his attitude what passionate sorrow again possessed him.

"Only one thing," he said, but keeping his face still averted—"only one request—break off all connexion with this man—this socialist—this atheist. Clara, I implore you for your eternal happiness—grant me this request! It is no selfish feeling that prompts it—it is love pure and true for you! Oh hear me, beloved child!—break the snares round you—break from the bands that hold you! Say at least that you will grant me this—this little prayer."

"I cannot," answered Clara. "Mr. Glynn has been far too dear and good a friend to be lightly set aside. I cannot act dishonourably to him, because I do not love you except as a sister!"

Fairly unmanned, Edward Mantell gave way to such a terrible burst of passion, despair, grief, and jealousy combined, as bowed him to the ground, and stamped out all the dignity of the man and the calmness of the Christian. He was as a child in the grasp of a giant; too little accustomed to the presence of passion to be able to control it, as even warmer men might have done who had exercised themselves in mastering, and had not simply evaded, their emotions.

"When will this end!" thought Clara. She was never very patient in misery, being one of those who think that to-day's unhappiness will extend over a whole life, and that the sun can never break through the passing cloud; and this continued wretchedness of Edward's made her nervous beyond words. So hopeless as it was too—so miserable howsoever it should end.

Striving to subdue at least the unmanliness of his grief, but failing in his bitter tears, failing in his choking sobs—now drawing himself up proudly, and keeping his face turned from her essaying to be composed—now leaning against the chimney-piece, and attempting to pray in words that would not come—Edward did his best to overcome his sorrow; but in vain. Ruined hopes, checked passion, wounded love, a life made vain, in the first hours of agony overmastered him, and left him utterly powerless to self-command, powerless even to resignation.

Had he not believed that Clara loved him it would not have been so bad. Had he not set all doubt of this aside when he wrestled with himself, and asked counsel of Heaven for his guidance, he would not have suffered so much. In all his mental struggles, doubt of her acceptance of his hand had never troubled him: he had trembled before his passion as before a crime, but he had never feared for the result, if he should satisfy his conscience that to love yon graceful actress was not a sin against the religion he came to teach. But it was the suddenness of the disappointment—it was the quarter from whence his sorrow came, that unmanned him. In a little time he will be calmer; at present he must bear such tortures as ever companion with a ruined love and hopes razed to the ground.

Clara then rose. She went to him as he stood by the window, looking into the street and appearing to note the passers-by; but seeing only one blurred mass of outer sunshine, in which not a form, not a line, struck intelligibly on his sight.

She laid her hand on his shoulder. He turned round, looking down into her face with an expression of such unutterable grief, such heart-broken misery, that she could not bear up against it.

"Oh do not look like that!" she cried, weeping.

He took her to his bosom and smoothed her hair fondly, but with a kind of unspeakable despair in his action that went to her heart. However, there they stood, before the window, in apparently such lover-like confidence—and Vaughan passing, as he often did, with the feverish restlessness that never left him now, bringing him ever near Clare's door like a haunting spirit of unrest, beheld them standing thus; and he believed that he beheld a happy love.

He paused before the window, his fierce face glaring in like a bird of prey between the sunshine and the dove. He gloated over a sight that brought fire to his heart, like an altar flame lit up to the Furies. He might have passed on quickly, but he did not. He stayed, and lingered, and looked and looked again; and saw still the hand of another smooth down that bright brown hair—saw still that gentle head leant on the bosom of a rival. If Edward Mantell suffered, so did Vasty Vaughan; but anger blood-red made up the pain of the one, a death blackness the despair of the other.

Clare raised her face. She was about to ask some pardon, say some gentle comforting, as far as she might with truth, when the Presence glaring on her made itself felt. She looked toward the street, and saw the face she knew so well, with all its fiend-like rage, its love and passion curdling into hate, as she had seen it once before. She uttered a faint scream and shrank back. Vaughan laughed aloud, and turned rapidly away; rushing frantically to Emmeline, and startling her into fear by the mad passion of his love for her: a love that looked more like the rage of a deserted lion than the soft sweetness of a suitor—the gentle pleading of a wooer; a love that interrupted itself by muttered oaths and convulsive starts—that broke off the kiss with a sudden gnashing of the teeth, and gave back the rosy pressure with a savage gripe of strange excitement—a love that was *not* love, but simply the outlet of intense emotion.

"It was not your fault, Clara," said Edward, when Clara again asked him to forgive her because he loved her, and chose to fancy that she loved him. "It was not your fault, dear child—my misfortune only. GOD has sent me this misery to chasten and correct me. You have been but the instrument."

Yet even from this article of faith he could get no consolation. Ah! the trial he was undergoing was too real for any mere belief to soften.

"No—I have been to blame, Edward," she said. "You would not have made such a mistake with any one else. You are the last man to misunderstand people in general."

"You must not say this, Clara," answered the poor youth. "No blame attaches to you—no sorrow ought to befal you. But Clara, hear me again—answer me—this one question only. Do you love any one? Tell me the truth, even if it should confirm my worst fears!"

"No, I do not love any man in the world now," she said, blushing crimson. "I did once, very deeply and very sadly—but not now."

"Not him?"

She thought he alluded to Vaughan.

"No."

He sighed as if relieved.

"And never loved him?"

"Mr. Vaughan?" she said with some surprise. "Yes, I loved him very much."

"Mr. Vaughan? No! I mean that wretched man—that hideous guide to ruin—Percival Glynn!" His accent, tone, and manner were harsh and bitter. Every feeling of enmity which he could cherish was concentrated on this one head; and Percival stood out to him as the very epitome of evil—a thing to hate which was virtue.

"I love Mr. Glynn very much," answered Clara; but her voice did not change. "He has been, as I said, one of my best—indeed my only friend; and I owe him unspeakable gratitude as well as affection for the kindness he has always shown me."

"Will you promise me never to marry him?" cried Edward, coming nearer to her.

"No," she said coldly and with much displeasure. "The very mention of such a thing is an insult."

He turned away for a moment to hide the spasm that convulsed him. When she looked again his under lip was bleeding fast.

"Oh! Clara, love me! love me!" he then cried, falling on his knees before her, and kissing her hand, abandoning himself hopelessly, without the shadow of restraint left. "Say one little word of hope—promise me at least that you will try to love me—that you will not thrust me from your heart, but will rather nurture and cherish what kindly feelings may be there now into more than kindliness! Promise me this—at least this!"

"Oh! do not stay there, Mr. Mantell! It is unbecoming—it is painful—wrong! Let me beseech you to be calm! If you have any real regard for me you will. All this misery is breaking my heart!"

And indeed she did begin to look pale and worn, with those blue lines around the eye, and those sharp lines about the lip, which mark so plainly the presence of mental suffering.

"One word only—decisive now and for the last! Can you love me? could you ever, under other than the present circumstances, love me? Tell me frankly. The worst pain has passed."

"No," she said, after a long pause and in a low voice; "I could not love you under any circumstances."

He rose instantly. Pale as death, but calm, he bade her farewell.

"God bless you," he said mournfully. "Had it been ordained otherwise I should have made you happy, Clara, and wise, and holy; but you have rejected a love that was true, and oh! How much more pure than the false light of passion which has led you so far from the gates of heaven—the hateful fire which has burnt into your soul! It is a hard trial! but His will be done."

He pressed her hand to his lips, lingered as if irresolute one instant longer, and then with a mighty effort he left her for ever, with a heart so sad, a spirit so broken, he scarce believed it to be life that he felt.

That very night he sent in his resignation of the curacy. It was assumed by the rector and one or two others, that he resigned on account of "that unlucky affair of the pauper burial." For once circumstantial evidence was deceitful. He wished to leave, not because he had done what he believed to be his duty, but because a maid refused her love; he gave up the cure of souls on which he had commenced so zealously, not because he had exceeded his powers, but because he could not marry where he would. But appearances cloaked the truth, and saved him from ridicule and contemptuous pity. And he was glad that they did so.

In a few days he was in Shorne—released from London sooner than he expected by a complaisant brother clergyman: and there he intended to remain, in the atmosphere and among the scenes which had seen *her* young life grow and expand.

CHAPTER IV.

BY the evening post this same day, a legal-looking letter came to Clara. It bore the Shorne postmark, but was not in Hugh's hand-writing; though she had been long anxiously expecting a reply from her old grandfather. She had often wondered why he had not written, and had fretted a little about it, and would have fretted more, had not Percival assured her that she would find some good reason soon, and that then she would be ashamed of her doubts.

She tore open the envelope and read the following:—"Madam, I am directed to inform you that Hugh Clayton, late groom to Bellenden de Saumarez, Esq.—which said Hugh Clayton was I believe your relative, so expressed in a letter from you found on his person after death—expired in the Shorne workhouse on the evening of the — ultimo. His death was occasioned partly by privation and exposure to cold during the late winter, partly by a paralytic stroke—which was the ostensible or proximate cause. He received every attention from the workhouse authorities and died calmly. I have the honour to be, Madam, your obedient servant,—JOHN SMITH, solicitor."

A man who had once said, in his zeal for the great family, that he would rather lose his wife and only child than hear of any harm to Miss Clara, then the De Saumarez heiress. A man who, when Clare had the measles, called regularly three times a day at the Hall, and was actually seen to shed tears when he heard that "they had come out very well;"—and who kept the village in a state of intense excitement, by urging a general vaccination for Miss Clara's sake, because a child had died of small-pox in a farm-house six miles off. And now he writes to her in such studied form of ignorance, and dwells so harshly on the death and state of her old grandfather. Ah well!—she was nothing now—she who had been such an idol for all men to worship! With her name and her future lands had gone every claim to the respect or the affection of others beside this venal steward of the manor. She saw now how little men are loved for themselves—how almost entirely for what they can bestow directly or indirectly. Even amidst her grief the quick proud impulse of disdain had strength to send the blood to her cheek, and to darken her indignant eye.

Hugh's loss was a severe blow to her. It was the first time that death had entered into her own immediate household of friends. She knew of course that people did die. She had heard of many sad bereavements among acquaintances and familiar names, but she had never known before the grief of losing one of her peculiar people—those whose lives made up her own, and without whom her individuality would not be so complete. Coming immediately after her painful scene with Edward Mantell, it more than naturally affected her, for it cut her off now from her mother, whose name and place she had not the smallest means of obtaining, and whom she would probably never see in life again. Yet how she longed to be with her!—how she yearned for her motherly cares, albeit education had so far separated them!—how she dreamed again and again of that tall beautiful fresh figure which she but faintly remembered through the dim vista of childhood; and seemed to feel once more the strong arms that pressed her to the full bosom, and held her there as if enchained. Mother! mother! Oh! thank GOD, all ye who know that blessed name!—thank GOD, all ye who have had through life the holy ark of maternal love, wherein to hide ye from the storm without!—thank GOD, all ye to whom your mother has been spared! Chill and harsh lies the world on thy heart, thou motherless girl. Too often slandered, too often doubted, for need of her care and her guidance—and ever lonely and unfriended in the inner soul—it were as well to lie down and die as to live a youthful maidenhood with no mother's arm around thee. Kneel at her grave, thou desolate, and weep: for death took thy truest friend when he rapt thy mother from thee!

As Clara entered the green-room to-night, the first thing on which her eyes fell were Vasty Vaughan and Miss Emmeline de Montfort standing near each other; he bending over her with all his celebrated grace and pride of manhood, and she talking low and laughing musically, while shaking her long light curls at every pause.

She was beautifully dressed—ready to appear as a fashionable lady in some smart piece that had been written expressly for her by a dramatic admirer. She wore a white silk gown of indescribable lustre, covered by a quantity of lace drapery—like a cloud falling about her—and looped up by white and pink flowers. Her arms and neck were covered with chains and bracelets, and her glossy ringlets mingled themselves amongst light downy feathers, like feathers themselves of more delicate sort. She looked exquisitely beautiful. A small fairy thing who had immunity for every conceivable fault, while her cheek was so fresh and her hair so golden. A gay bird of paradise was she; a useless, lovely creature, which adorned humanity as a flower adorns the earth, but which adds no worth, no dignity, no use, to the sphere in which it lives. And yet that is a harsh word, and a false one; for beauty by itself—ay, mere mindless, lineal, superficial beauty—is a glorious thing—a thing for which we ought to be thankful, and which we ought to cherish well in its degree.

Vaughan had Emmeline's hand in his when Clara entered. He saw her come in by the large cheval glass;[105] and at the very moment he kissed yon little hand, and kissed it again, and spoke tenderly, and seemed absorbed in his pleasant exercise, and very happy in such absorption.

Clare sat down. Vaughan, taking no more notice of her than what a glance of fire betrayed, went on with his love-making, calling on this and on that—on these and on those—to pay homage to his "beautiful little fairy queen." No one was exempt. In his passionate adoration—for so it seemed to those who understood only what they saw, and did not look below the surface—he pressed the whole company into the service of his pretty Emmeline's vanity; and though heroines sneered, and heroes joked aside, he let none escape; he made them all bend before his latest found star.

"Lucretia, come here!" he cried, as the Roman-faced matron entered majestically into the admiring circle. "Come, and tell me if this beautiful little creature is not too good for earth—if she does not look like some rainbow-dyed spirit—some peri[106] of the skies escaped from Paradise, and fallen down among men for her punishment—if she does not look more than human tonight!—Is she not divine?" he added, standing at a little distance from her, and surveying her with excessive admiration.

"Ay! Mr. Vaughan, you say truly, good lord! By my troth, and an angel might that fair young creature be, but for her wings. Where are they, sweetheart?—hast thou burnt them at the torch of love, and given the singed feathers as hostages? Mr. Vaughan, sir, she might act Titania[107] without dressing!"

And Lucretia went off into a rhapsody which soon created her a vacant space, some three or four feet in diameter, and gave her an audience of backs.

The bell rang: the call-boy shouted Miss de Montfort's name; and Vaughan led Emmeline forward to the wings, preparatory to her appearance.

It was her first appearance at this theatre, and was consequently a matter of some little importance to the theatrical *troupe*. Most of them rushed to the side scenes, and Clare found herself alone with Lucretia, and two smoky, dirty men who sat together talking over their wrongs, which consisted in the fact that one was not made chief in the tragic, another in the comic, line at —— theatre; and as they were plain, common-place men without one requisite, physical or mental, for acting at all, their complaints were not to be wondered at, being exactly what might be expected from their condition of intellect.

Lucretia's heart smote her. How well she remembered Clare's *début*! Though but half understood, how she had watched, and watching loved, the very passion of joy which filled that glorious being, and now this painted pretty waxen doll, whose largest sensation was gratified vanity, had usurped the throne whereon she sat crowned, and cast down the star that stood over her for a ballroom bouquet of artificial flowers. Poetry and love had strung Clare's nerves that night; a flippant cleverness which one could scarce understand how it existed at all, was all that Emmeline possessed. Beauty, that was not born only of her fresh youth nor yet of her graceful form and pleasant features, clothed Clare like a garment: a prettiness of mere form—a prettiness grown out of long light hair, and delicate features, and an airy figure, but which had not one single point of connexion with mind or feeling— made Emmeline desirable. Clare was a poetess, Emmeline an actress; Clare felt, Emmeline represented; Clare had loved, Emmeline merely triumphed. Yet the brightest sunshine bathed the home of the one— from roof to basement an unbroken flood of light; while the other lived in darkness which no one sought to cheer, no one sought to dispel.

Lucretia's heart spoke too loudly; it smote her too hard. She came to Clare, and holding out her hand said, but not without embarrassment—"Sweet child! I have seemed estranged from thee—I have seemed perchance to take part with thine enemies, and to league myself with those who desire to do thee hurt. Believe it not! Facts are not always what appearances would make them. Though silent, I am thy friend—though hidden, I am thy defender. In more cases than one I have been the last."

Which in simple truth was merely a poetical figure of speech on the part of Lucretia, seeing that she had never, in any circumstances, defended Clare, present or absent, or indeed spoken of her at all.

"Do not distress yourself, Miss Kemble dear," Clara answered, smiling sorrowfully. "I know that you have a very difficult part to play here, and I would not for the world that you got into trouble about me. I know that Mr. Vaughan would be displeased with you if he knew that you visited me, or continued kindly disposed even in heart; and I am not so selfish as to wish the very least unpleasantness to befal you, for any amount of good to myself."

"Brave good child!" cried Lucretia admiringly; "That speech was like thee! I should have looked for no other from one whom I have been always proud to regard as the most unselfish and the most rational of her sex! Then you believe in my affection, though so silent is it, and so concealed?"

"Yes," answered Clara. "Yes, I believe in you. I lived too long with you, dear Lucretia, not to understand your character. It is a great compliment to me," she added with the same mournful smile, "that you trust to my confidence in you, and do not think it necessary to assure me of your affection twenty times a day before I will rely on it and believe in it."

Lucretia, obtuse as she was, understood this speech. Though no *bonâ fide* tears came to her eyes, there was a certain moistness and redness about them which betrayed her emotion, and answered the purpose quite as well; besides leaving the rouge intact.

"Clara!" she cried, "you are an angel! It's my belief you'll never be happy on earth, for you are too good for ordinary men and women!"

"No, no! Lucretia dear; I am not so bad as Vaughan believes me, but I am a few degrees removed from an angel yet! I know that I do not shine here now; I am so thoroughly disheartened, so thoroughly miserable, that I cannot do anything well. What little power I had, or might have learnt, I have lost entirely—lost too the ability of acquiring it! As for ambition, Lucretia, I have not a spark remaining. It has all gone; and if I were not forced to work for my daily bread, I would give up the stage, and never dream a dream of fame again!"

"Ah!" said Lucretia musingly, "that is sad! And why this dark change from such brilliant light, my child?"

"I do not know," she replied innocently; "unless it be my estrangement with Vaughan. I began my artist life with him; other feelings than mere professional ones mingled themselves so inextricably with my acting, that now since I have lost these I have lost also the impetus, the incitement to succeed. It was a matter of feeling you know, Lucretia dear, much more than of artistic knowledge."

"Yes I know that, my child—I know that. In plain words you mean to say that you lighted the lamp of your intellect by the blazing torch of love, and that now both have gone out because the naughty boy has quenched his!"

Clara laughed a little at this thoroughly Lucretian mode of simplifying an idea. She did not make a more direct answer.

"Then what should you like to do now, my child?" asked the actress kindly, drawing nearer to her in a good-hearted gossiping kind of way, resting her elbows on her knees and thrusting her chin into her hands. "What line would you take now, dear, since you say the professional one has failed to satisfy you?"

"Oh," said Clara warmly, "I should like to read a great deal, and to go among the poor, and know all about their condition, and what could be done to relieve them, and what particular laws press on them the most painfully, and how they might be repealed. I should like to spend my life in this now!"

"Ha! But I advise you my dear to be rather careful in your associates and in your localities. You know, Clara, if you touch gas-tar you will dirty your hands: and it may be that you have gone something deeper into the tar-barrel of improper associates than will do you any good."

"Oh!" cried Clara, "but what does it signify if we are spoken against for doing our duty? I don't care how much I am abused if I know that I am doing right. And it *is* right to help the poor, and try to recover the fallen."

"Hum!" said Lucretia drily. "Pray, my dear, what books have you been reading lately?"

"I don't know—nothing particular I think. But I have heard a great deal about them—the poor I mean—and seen a little of them lately, and that has interested me so much. Though indeed I have always felt very strongly on the subject."

"And who have you been with?—that handsome young man—Mr. What's-his-name—Edward Tippet?—tut! tut!—what is it?"

"Mr. Mantell?" said Clara, turning pale. "No—I have not been with him."

"Then with whom?"

She was silent just a moment—a thought—longer than necessary, and then she said with a sudden blush that crimsoned her face to the very temples, "I have been with Mr. Glynn."

Lucretia stared at her for a long time; then betook herself to a certain attitude of which she was very fond, namely drawing herself up to her fullest height, laying her finger significantly on her nose, and moving her head with the slow solemnity of Friar Bacon's brazen head,[108] saying, "I see! I see! I see!" like an improved version of a Macbeth witch.

"Lucretia," said Clara suddenly: she had not seen this mysterious sibylline attitude, and a long silence had been between them which she was just beginning to feel irksome. "Do you remember the old man—the old servant I mean—who was walking with us the first day I ever saw you?"

She spoke with great hesitation.

"Let me see—do I remember, *imprimis*, an old man—*secundo*, an old servant—in the third place, on that auspicious day when first I met thee? Yes, my fair young querist, I think that I may answer thee with all truth and celerity, yes—I do!"

"He is dead!" said Clare, looking up. But though her face was full of sorrow, there were no tears.

"Indeed!" indifferently; "and you are grieved?"

"Yes, Lucretia, very much." She stopped as if she wished to say more.

"Why, my fair sphinx—why so *very much* grieved at the death of an old servitor? What can interest you so much in this? Methinks your orbit is too far removed now from all that dwells in Shorne—that was the name of the place, wasn't it?—to feel any—I speak advisedly—any interest in the spot or the inhabitants."

"Not in many certainly," she said; "but in dear old Hugh, much; for duty and for inclination."

"Duty!" she interrupted, "you speak in riddles, my fair sphinx."

"Hugh was my grandfather," said Clara quietly, "and he died the other day. I wanted him to come and live with me, but he is gone now;

and I am so alone in the world, Lucretia! I have not a person in the whole world that I belong to, or that has any right to care for me! No one could be more thoroughly solitary than I. Poor old Hugh!"

In general Clare's tears were always ready to flow, the consequence of her youth and temperament. To-night she felt only a strange oppression at her chest, a dull pain about her heart, a giddy fulness in her head; but she could not have wept to save her life.

Lucretia was shocked and sorry. She took her young friend's hand and kissed her face. As she did so the friends and behind-scenes audience of young Emmeline came rushing in; and Vaughan, who led her forward, beheld that action. He saw Clare's face too as he passed; and a glance at that sufficed to tell him that she had been making some revelation which had woke up her griefs. He thought she had been telling Lucretia of her new lover, and that this it was which had so excited her—bringing back all the train of the past, when she loved *him* and was true to *him*.

What devil possessed him to-night no one knew, but he was more fierce, more imperious, tyrannical, rude, passionate, than he had ever been seen before; even than on the memorable day when Clara had refused his love. And he had been unpleasant enough then for the most ardent lover of psychological phenomena.

He called Lucretia to him.

"What have you been talking about to that young hypocrite?" he cried in a loud rude voice.

"Oh! but a little, good my lord, of various subjects—none of any value," she answered with a terrified look.

"Come here, Miss Clayton!" cried Vaughan standing with his face and lips so pale, he looked a breathing statue. But his eyes were bloodshot, and every nerve was strong and quivering, like one in the commencement of a convulsive attack.

Clara rose, and walked proudly towards him.

The people of the theatre gathered round, expecting a scene, from the manager's manner.

"Have you been telling Lucretia of your new lover?" he said in a tone of revolting insolence.

"I do not understand you, Mr. Vaughan," answered Clara coldly.

"By my soul! but this is an excellent actress, anywhere but before the lights," he exclaimed, laughing loudly, and looking round to the group clustered near him. "Not many hours ago—not innumerable minutes even since—I saw her in the window of her house, standing in such lover-like attitude, my ladies, as for sake of her integrity I hope was with a real lover! And now she comes forward to my very face, and minces out her words, and acts the maiden ignorance to the life, and swears 'she does not understand me!' Pray, Miss Clayton," he added still more insolently, "what other historic fact will you deny next?"

"If Mr. Vaughan had asked me frankly the meaning of what he saw to-day I might have given him a truer explanation than the one he has chosen to assume," said Clara haughtily.

"Truer!" he laughed scornfully—"truer?—You will forgive me, I know, but I should take the liberty of doubting any explanation from you that would refine away so indubitable an act! I think I ought to know the probabilities of Miss Clayton's love affairs as well as most men," he said with meaning.

"What do you intend to insinuate by that, sir," exclaimed Clara with indignation, her eyes flashing, and her figure erect.

"Insinuate?—oh, not much! there is not much left for *insinuation* in the affairs of a young lady whose weekly expenses I paid—as Miss Kemble can testify—for months before she appeared on the stage, and whose deficiencies I supplied for weeks afterwards. Is it not true, Miss Kemble?" turning to that lady.

"It is false," exclaimed Clara passionately. "Lucretia!—you never could have done me this wrong!—you never could have placed me in such a cruel, false position—so utterly unknown to me!"

Between two such fires Lucretia thought it wisest to keep silence; spreading out her hands and shrugging her shoulders, endeavouring to make her escape.

"Stay!" cried Clara, grasping her hand with nervous power. "Tell me the truth, Lucretia! Is this so, or is it not? Before all the world exonerate me!"

"I am sorry——" she began.

"The fact!" cried Clara, stamping her feet, and speaking loudly and excitedly.

"Was as Mr. Vaughan represented," answered Miss Kemble. "Never mind, you foolish child!" she continued in a whisper; "no one thinks anything about such things as these. It's only Vaughan's devilish humour that makes him mention it at all!"

Clare released her hold. Everything was very dark and confused before her, and she heard nothing distinctly; but she did not show this in her face or attitude, and it soon passed off.

"I knew nothing of this arrangement in the beginning, and before I thought you loved me," she said in a clear firm voice; "as this scene may have convinced you; but I can only say now, Mr. Vaughan, hold me debtor for all that you expended on me, and you shall not find me dishonourable nor a repudiator of my bond."

"Oh! the money may go!" said Vaughan carelessly. "Men of honour do not take back such gifts as these! I do not care for this, Miss Clayton; nor, had you kept up but the semblance of propriety, should I have considered it in my province to mention any other little lapse into which you might have fallen. I know how unprotected you would be in a really virtuous position, and a man of the world can make allowances for any slight, moderate, respectable departures from strict rule. But your conduct of late has been so shameless— so abandoned—your transfer of affection and person so sudden and disgraceful—your associates are so publicly disreputable—the very lowest women of the streets, my ladies—that for the reputation of my theatre, and for the sake of such as these"—pointing to Emmeline—"I deem it my duty to give you this public warning before your obstinate immorality dismisses you for ever from my company. To others you may, if you can, play the modest maiden. *I* know you—and on me your most practised arts are futile."

He would have turned away; but Clara, whose blood was fairly up, boiling in her veins like fire, and sweeping down prudence and wisdom as straws in an eddying current, made him pause by the tone in which she recalled him.

"Mr. Vaughan!" she said, "this must not end here. I stand in a strange position, and one that I must defend in spite of all disadvantageous appearances, and all my own deficiencies. I know that my character has suffered from many unjust causes: in the beginning from you— and you know how falsely——"

"Do I?" he interrupted her with a low laugh. "Will the world believe that it has suffered thus falsely if I tell them all even of myself—not to speak of others? Will it credit my whining assurances against such startling facts as—visits paid to me unasked—I need not say at what hours of the night; of pleasant excursions out of town—I need not say where, nor for what length of time; of money given for every conceivable requirement—of tender notes in your own hand-writing—of kiss and passionate phrase, till I was fairly weary of their monotonous intensity? Would any one in his senses credit simple words against such truths as these? I may pity you, Miss Clayton, for losing yourself with men who have betrayed you, and leaving one who would have been always careful of you—as a man of honour should be—but I cannot lie to save you even from the consequences of your friendship with me. What you were to me, we both know; and unhappily your own evil ways have rendered it too public to be lied away now. Come, this is folly!" he added roughly, breaking from the crowd. "You have thrown down the gauntlet to me," he said in an under tone as he passed her, "and by heavens you shall suffer for it! You have dared me—defied—rejected—betrayed: and you shall learn when too late how I held you in my hand to crush at my leisure—how I could destroy you with a word—and have so destroyed!"

He left the green-room, and Clare stood there alone in the wreck of her ruined character—in the blight of her maiden modesty. Gone! gone! for ever!

A mass of coarse rude faces—a world of eyes with insolence and familiar wickedness in every lash and glance—a crowd of voices speaking her name, and coupling it with unseemly epithets and unseemly jests, held up Clare's pride, though they made her brain reel with shame. The worst had then really come! No longer a phantom— no longer the mere spectre of imagination—it had come like the inevitable hour of death, and she must learn to bear it as she best might. She must look it in the face steadily, for it was no dream from which she could awake in the morning—no play from which she could escape at her pleasure. It was a reality—a fact that all the years of eternity rolling on could not abolish.

And thus she stood in the midst of that scoffing crowd, with the frightful truth slowly burning itself into her brain; the truth that she was irretrievably lost in the world's esteem—that she had been insulted and could not defend herself—and that her own imprudence, her very innocence, had given such colour to the worst accusations as all the explanations of a thousand volumes could not clear away. Her fair fame lay buried beneath the tomb of slander, and might never rise again. It burnt in deeper and deeper, till at last she heard only those hideous words and saw only the doom of Ruin, standing out like living creatures before her eyes.

She had to appear in the second piece to-night. Mechanically she suffered the dresser to make her ready. Band and gown and ribbon were fastened without her knowledge. She stood before the glass in profound unconsciousness of what was doing to her, and in utter forgetfulness of her existence.

Even the very rouge failed to give brilliancy to her eye or life to her cheek. She moved about like an automaton; her eyes dulled and fixed: and she herself a very mockery of life. The dresser asked her twice "if she was ill?" but Clara did not hear her and did not answer.

No sigh, no tear, no groan; not a movement of grief—scarce the full perception of what she felt.

She was called. More by instinct than knowledge she came to the side-scenes, to wait there until she should be waved on. The actors and actresses playing in the piece with her, whispered to each other as they saw her standing in that death-like stupor. They laughed and jeered, but she heard them not; one or two pitied her, and spoke comfortable words so that they might strike her ear; these too were unheard. She stood in her dumb despair, her stricken solitude; her young heart almost checked beneath the weight that laid there.

So young to be so sorrowed!—so bright as was her entrance into life—and now how gloomy! Poor, poor Clare!—thy fate brings tears to my eyes even now as I remember it, and think on what thou didst hope from life, and how thou once didst dream—and now so rough a waking!

She was waved on to the stage. She went slowly forward, without action or energy. At first the glare of lights confused her. She did not know where she was, or what she had to do there. She tried to clear her eyes—to remember what she had to say—for she knew that she was expected to do something that she had quite forgotten. The actress playing with her gave her the cue, but Clara's senses were not recalled. She looked round her, and into the misty house, and tried to remember what it all meant; but no—she was at frightful fault, and could not be put right.

The audience saw that something was wrong. The actors on the stage looked uneasy, and whispered with each other, still preserving their stage attitudes—as if these private conferences made up part of the written drama. At first she was cheered to reassure her; but that failed too. One actress passed her close and whispered her speech to her, and bade her with an oath repeat it.

She did. As if in a dream she said the words. But she spoke so falteringly—her accent was so strange, so thick and inharmonious—that one voice cried out, "She is tipsy! Shame! shame! Off! off!" And it hissed her.

At first a little sound from the distance—then a louder and a louder noise that took a frightful shape—then groans and cries of "Shame!" and "Off!" came up from the whole house; and loud long hisses that could not be mistaken spoke the disapprobation of the audience.

But she stood, with her eyes fixed on the mist within. She did not stir; she did not speak. Her dull looks only wandered plaintively round, and once she asked softly—"What does all this mean? Percival!—where is Percival?"

At last she was made aware that she must leave the stage. She was taken off, still in the same listless attitude; with the same vacant stare—the same heart-broken apathy. They sat her down, and she remained where and how they placed her. They spoke to her, but she gave no answer; they dashed water over her face and head, but it seemed as if not a hair was wetted, so indifferent was she, so unmoved and unroused. And now they were fairly alarmed—which they had reason to be; and a doctor was sent for, to see what could be done.

He said it was "pressure on the brain," and she was bled. And then she was relieved from the heavy weight of almost idiotism on her: but to a reaction worse than that from which they saved her. She woke from her mental sleep only to the frenzy of madness and despair. Dashing down some that tended her—breaking through those who stood at a little distance wondering—with a terrible cry that went through roof and lane like the cry of death—she rushed from the theatre alone. In her stage dress unfastened and disordered, without shawl or bonnet, she flew through the streets to her desolate home; where at least she was free from those hideous eyes and hideous voices, if she had but solitude to soothe her. And then she sank into insensibility for many hours; and when she woke again the sun was shining on her kindly, as she lay on the parlour floor—her gown wet with blood.

CHAPTER V.

THE next morning, so soon as she could gather strength, Clare hurried off to Percival's house. Not that she knew why she went there. It was not for his assistance in any way; for things had gone too far to admit of amelioration. Neither did she go for his advice—for what could that do for her? No; it was simply instinctive; the unreflecting, unreasoning impulse of a child, seeking to hide itself in its mother's arms when blank faces terrified it.

Percival was not in his sitting-room when she was admitted, and she sat down to wait for him. He presently entered. What a picture of despair met his eye! Cast down on a low stool—her head leaning against the chimney-piece—her checks pale and haggard—her eyes dull and fixed, and all the lines around her mouth drawn sharp and close—she looked the impersonation of deathly dejection; as if sunshine could never brighten over her heart again—as if she might never more know happiness.

She heard his step and started up. As he threw open the door she uttered a cry of pain, and flung herself into his arms—without shame, without reserve, without thought of ill. She could not speak. Large sobs which had no tears, but which seemed as though they would break her heart as they burst forth, were her only greetings. And then with each convulsive shudder she clung closer and closer to him; and would neither loose her hands nor raise her face; she would do naught but press into his bosom as if she would cling there and die.

"Clara! dear, dear Clara! what terrible fate has come upon you! My child! my dear one! Speak to me, Clara!—speak to your friend—your faithful friend! Clara, dear, dearest child! I beseech you to speak to me!"

No, not a word! Nothing but the same long shuddering sigh—the same strong pressure—and once or twice a movement that Percival knew to be her quivering lips kissing his bosom with passionate grief.

He followed her humour. He smoothed her hair, which was rough and disordered; he pressed her to him kindly; he kept silence until she had somewhat wearied herself; and then he led her to the sofa, she holding down her head and covering it with his hand.

And when he had seated her and placed himself beside her, again she threw her arms round him and pressed her face against his bosom, drooping so that he must hold her up, else she would have sunk her head to his knee.

Percival had seen Clare in sorrow—he had seen her in pride, in triumph, in despair, in desolation; but never so broken as she was to-day; never so wholly under the foot of passion. She did not hear him when he spoke to her; she did not answer when he questioned her;

nothing but those heavy sobs and long convulsive quiverings. But oh, what frightful answers were they!

It was a strange feeling which filled Percival's heart now. He grieved truly and unaffectedly at her grief; he sorrowed for it as for a personal misfortune; but yet to hold her thus—to know that she had turned to him the first of all, the only one—to feel her heart beating against his in such innocent abandonment to his love and protection—to feel that he stood in her life as a guardian and a comforter—this was such deep bliss—as made a way of light even through the gloom of her despair.

Many times he besought her to release him for a moment—"she must have some wine." But in utter indifference to his request— almost in ignorance that he spoke—she clung to him with the same tenacity as before, and seemed as if she would have died if he had left her for a moment. At last he forcibly loosened her hold, and poured out a large quantity of opium into a glass of wine-and-water. His hand shook while he dropped the opiate, and more than doubled the dose he intended to give her; which was fortunate; for a common amount would have had no effect whatever on her, excited as her nerves were.

"You must drink this to please me, darling," he said kindly, speaking as to a child, slightly below his breath.

After a little difficulty in understanding what he wanted, Clare took the glass in her trembling hands, and drank it at a draught.

It was strange how soon it calmed her. In a few moments her passionate strain relaxed; she seemed to collect her senses, and to know where she was. She shook back her hair, and made some efforts, though faint, to adjust her much-disordered appearance. But the ribbon hung slack in her nerveless hands, which soon dropped down into her lap like dead things unconnected. Still she never spoke. She might have been struck dumb, for all the power of speech that seemed to be left her.

Percival did not disturb her. He merely sat by her; and when she put her hands in his, which she did without looking at him, he caressed them tenderly, but in silence. And when, after a short time, she laid her head on his shoulder with a deep sigh, he patted the pale face kindly, and smoothed off the hair, and pressed the throbbing head; but let her lie as she would, and did not disturb her by too much attention or interference.

And she remained there—resting against his arm which was round her for support, with her head on his shoulder, and her hands in his; and after a little time of quiet she fell asleep.

She was so much under the influence of the opiate, that when Percival laid her gently down, and covered her with a cloak, she slept too heavily to be roused by the movement. She was like a supple corpse in his arms, resting exactly where and how he placed her. He then rang the bell and bade the servant bring in breakfast; enjoining quiet on her, and telling her in a whisper that "Miss Clayton was very ill."

He busied himself noiselessly about the breakfast, making it comfortable and inviting, lest Clara should awake soon; though there was not much chance of that, for she still slept on in that heavy quiet way which looks so like to death; and there did not seem much probability of its ending for many hours.

Percival as yet was in the dark about the cause of Clara's early visit and frightful distress. She had changed her stage dress before she came, so that he saw no evidence in that of the time and probable manner of her troubles. For when she recovered from her long insensibility this morning, she found her gown wet with blood—the bandages having slipped from her arm which was bent under her in the fall, and the lanced vein thus bursting out again. In the dark dress of her daily life nothing of this was seen. He only judged by her pallor, and the sunken lines and purple veins about her eye, that she had not slept all night, and that therefore something had occurred at the theatre; for if earlier in the day he should have heard of it. But he could not see more than this.

However, there she slept for the present, and his curiosity must remain unsatisfied till she wakes. He could do nothing but watch her, and kneel by her, and bend his face to catch her still breath, and love her, oh how dearly! As she thus flew to him in her distresses, and took refuge in his arms and on his heart against the assaults of fortune!

And how much he did love her! With what deep tenderness, what trembling worship, what gentle cares! All that one hears of fatherly protection, and brotherly pride, and friendly unselfishness, and a lover's warmth, was centred in Percival's love for Clare. He would have given her at the altar to another, without a feature changed—a muscle stirred—and not a soul of all the crowd should have dreamed that he loved her more than a pretty child. He would have rejoiced over her happiness with one worthy of her, as if she had been some favourite sister married to a dearest friend. Her children he would have loved like his own, and would have proved to them in after-life the same devoted friend their mother had known him. As a solitary bachelor, desecrating the glorious image in his heart by no meaner worship, he would have given her all his thoughts as wholly as he did now, and have made her, though the wife of another, as much the object of his cares—as much the duty of his life—and with the same womanlike purity as that which he felt for her now. But if she should ever really bear his name—if he might ever look into her face, and call her his, and know that she loved him and trusted to him alone for happiness—that he was the centre of her existence, the source of all her pleasures, the very sun of her being—oh! then with what anxious care he would guard her from all harm and sorrow!—with what tender idolatry serve her!—with what passionate love adore her! If it could ever be that she would love him and belong to him, and that he might spend his life in confessed affection and untiring energies, what an Eden earth would be to two hearts caught up from the shivering wretchedness of man to the unfading rapture of the angels!

All these thoughts occupied Percival while he watched that sleeping maid, and built up dreams and visions out of the tinted future.

She woke at last; confused and uncertain of her place—of where she was—and what had happened to her—and why that kindly face bent down on her—and why such strange furniture met her eye.

"You have been asleep, dear Clare," said Percival, placing himself by her; for when she awoke she started up from her recumbent position, flinging off the cloak that covered her, and arranging her dress. And now she sat in a bewildered stupor, not knowing what she did.

"Where am I?" she said. "Why am I here?—what has happened?—when did I come?"

"Do not ask now, darling. A good fairy brought you if you like. In a little time it will all come back to you. But don't speak or think just yet."

And true enough it did all come back on her young heart—and that too soon! With a quick harsh hand memory opened the flood-gates of her sorrow, and let despair sweep in like the torrent that swept over the cities of the ancient world.

Burying her face in her hands she burst into a passion of tears, crying; "Oh Percival! Percival! I am ruined—my heart is broken!"

"Come! Come! do not think of it now, darling child! Whatever has befallen you, be sure there is comfort for you somewhere! I must not see you, Clare, the slave of circumstances. I look far higher than this from you. In your time of trial is it that you must prove your strength and show how great and good you are."

But she took no heed of what he said, and continued in her bitter grief, pressing her hands against her side and chest as if to still the thick beatings which went so near to kill her.

"Now calm yourself, my darling child!" he continued, endeavouring to soothe her. "Tell me, Clara, what has vexed you. You must not give way to these frightful paroxysms—for my sake, as well as for your own, you must not! Tell me all, and you will be better then—after you have talked to me about it."

"Oh Percival!—last night!—Vaughan!—the theatre!" sobbed Clara, not knowing where to begin, or what to tell him first.

"This agitation will do you no good, dear child. You *must* calm yourself. Do not attempt to speak until you are more collected. I must not have you so horribly agitated."

"But I want you to know," said Clara innocently. "You are my only friend, Percival, and must hear it all."

And then she put her hands on his arm, and told him of last night—of all that Vaughan had said—and of how she had stood there, stricken into marble among a fierce crowd of insult—each face whereon she looked a portrait of insolence and familiarity—each voice that struck her ear a voice of slander and of wrong. She told him how then a kind of darkness had come on her—a darkness which oppressed her like a heavy veil, and through which she neither heard nor saw, and scarcely breathed; while only indistinct light and confused murmurs broke through its blackness. Yet when it was taken from her chest and eyes, and she remembered what horrible thing had happened— remembered it with tenfold clearness—she told him how that terrible hiss which the stupor of misery had frozen in the air, rushed into sound again as the blood left her surcharged brain; and how she heard, like fiends repeating, the cries of "Shame," and "Off," and knew that the world believed her thus disgraced. She dilated—dwelling with a frightful luxury of self-torture—on how Vaughan had lost her so falsely in the minds of all the theatre, and how he had boldly hinted the terrible lie which had ruined her so irretrievably. Though each word that she said wrung her heartstrings sore, she dwelt on the whole with the same minuteness of dissection, and gave herself up hopelessly to the agony she helped to create. There was something of the recklessness of madness in her manner which alarmed Percival, and made him conceal his own indignation lest it should rouse hers farther; though it was with much effort that he could command himself.

"It will be better, dear child, when your brave old grandfather comes!" he said as calmly as he could. "He will be sure to come!— and then he will guard you from a great deal—certainly from any repetition of such a scene as this."

"Oh Percival! poor old Hugh!" cried Clara.

"Well, darling, what of him? But, Clara, you must positively keep more calm! For my sake, as I urged on you before. You know that I am your friend, and that your sorrows are mine, and all this agony of grief from you fairly breaks my heart!"

"My only friend now, Percival!" she said, in a voice whose very fondness was more mournful than pure sorrow.

"No! no! not your only friend!" he said hastily. "Perhaps as true and sincere as any that you have, but not your only one! Tell me of Hugh—what of him?"

"He is dead!" exclaimed Clara sadly, shaking her head, "And Percival," she added, raising herself from him, and looking in his face; "he died in the workhouse! Oh how dreadful!—My grandfather—my own grandfather—dying in the Shorne workhouse—where I was the great heiress!"

This little bit of pride came in so naturally that Percival greeted it like an old friend. It was a pleasant rampart against the waters of sorrow which had flooded her soul so long; and though at any other time he would have remonstrated with her on it, and have endeavoured to set her right and to give her a higher view, yet now he was so relieved to see any other feeling than the agony she had been suffering, that he could have bidden her be proud for all eternity.

"I am very very sorry, dear Clara," he said gravely, "for I had formed many happy schemes for your grandfather here with us in London. We should have made the poor old man very happy, Clare! He would have loved his life with us."

He looked narrowly at her while he spoke—laying a slight emphasis on the words "we" and "us," and watching what effect they would have. But she did not seem to hear them. Certainly she never heeded their meaning: for not the faintest change of colour spoke an awakened intellect or startled affections. She only said mournfully, "Oh Percival! there will never be any happiness for me again! I was not born to be happy!"

"No, no, Clara! You have not seen your sun set, my child, because a cloud has gone over its meridian—you have not seen your garden laid waste because a rude hand has plucked one of the flowers of its abundance! The cloud will pass away, and leave the golden world of light and life unblemished; and soft sweet winds and kindly skies will bring out innumerable buds yet to beauty and perfection. No, I must not have you despair with all your power and loveliness!"

"Words! words!" she muttered, as if to herself. "They fall on my ear, and have no echo in my heart!"

"Not to-day, perhaps, dear—that is hardly to be expected. But in a short time you will find that I have spoken truths, though now you may think them only follies. You may trust both my sincerity and my knowledge."

"I trust your sincerity," she said.

"But not my wisdom?"

"No! not with me," she answered mournfully. "Just look what my life has been, Percival!—from the very earliest years see how miserable I have been!"

"Not always miserable?"

"Yes," she said. "Now that I look back, I can see the constant presence of sorrow. I loved the fresh air, the sunshine, the flowers, the woods, my dogs and rabbits, and poor old Fleetfoot and Hugh—all these made me happy for the time; but nothing ever took off the heavy weight of loneliness and solitude. I can scarcely explain what I mean! I never heard any one but Hugh say a kind word to me; and all that I said or thought was either ridiculed or thought sinful. My mother did not smile on me for years, and Alice took every pains and care to ruin me; and it was just as if I had been the real daughter, for we all thought I was then!"

"You suffered, darling, as many do—from want of sympathy. Your physical organization, your temperament, and consequently your mental life, were all unsympathetic with those to whom you then belonged. They did not treat you brutally; you were simply alone in your mental life. But this has strengthened you, and made you more independent, and better fitted for real life. Those who are cradled in an atmosphere of love alone, not unfrequently become mentally effeminate, and unable to cope with the trials of life."

"Ah! it may be so—but it has created such a pining want in my life!" said Clara, with tears in her eyes. "And then see how Vaughan has deceived me! How I loved him, and how I trusted to him—and look!—he has ruined me! So kind as he pretended to be to me: and Percival, I was not so old then, and had not too many friends to protect me!—and see how he has taken advantage of my loneliness to destroy all my peace, and my good name too!"

"Do not speak of him!" said Percival hastily. "It is a frightful business, and must be borne with now as well as possible. You have been hardly treated there—I grant this: yet you also owe something to your own want of accordance with the conventionalities of society. And this being so"—and he spoke impressively—"you must exercise strength and grandeur now in the time when the consequences of those acts have come on you. Clara, I should be the last to counsel you to any thing hurtful—I should be the last to tell you to obey your own inclinations and despise the laws of society in matters where no moral principle was involved—though the first to bid you cast down fame and very life itself for the maintenance of the right. But now when the result of your own conduct has really arrived—how dastardly, vile, and mean soever is the source by which it has come—I counsel you to stand up bravely before it—to look it in the face for what it is, believing it no worse—and to live it down, like my noble child whose innate strength no outward adversity can subdue!"

He spoke cheerily—but she shook her head and made no answer.

"This is folly to you?"

"No, not exactly," she said innocently, "but inapplicable. Indeed, indeed, Percival, I have an unhappy fate in me! Look at Edward Mantell! That was my own miserable fault!"

"What of him?" asked Percival, changing colour.

"Oh, yesterday!"

"Well—yesterday?—what then?"

"He proposed to me," said Clara simply; "and because I would not marry him, said we should not be friends any longer; and he said, Percival," she added, looking full into his eyes and speaking very sadly, "that it was my fault—that I had made him believe that I loved him, else he never would have offered to me at all—and that my heartlessness had worked all this misery on him. And I am sure I did not know that I had done so."

"I warned you of this, you know, Clare. Don't you remember?"

"Yes, but I forgot it again," she said. "It was so unlikely! I thought you must be mistaken!"

"And where is he?"

"I do not know. He bade me good-bye for ever—so I lost him as a friend. And I have so few now! And then, after this, poor old Hugh's death came to me; and then that horror—that horror!" She shuddered strongly, and covered her eyes.

"Poor child! It was a hard trial all throughout! I do not wonder at seeing you so broken to-day, Clara. It was indeed a bitter trial, and you have not borne it ill."

"I should bear these things better," she said, "if I had some one to care for me. I mean if I had a father or a sister or a brother. I want some one to love me, and to be always with me; some one that would stand between me and all this misery. Other girls are loved—why am I so desolate?"

Percival was silent. His head swam with a delicious joy that blinded his eyes and thrilled to his heart. He did not dare to trust himself to answer—it seemed like taking advantage of her loneliness—of the impressibility of grief; it seemed dishonourable; and he forbore. For after all she might never love him really; only as a friend; not with every faculty; for he was not handsome—far from it; and he was not rich, nor well placed socially. It might be only from ignorance of her own feelings and views of life, or from self-compassion at her loneliness, if she accepted him as her husband now; and he would not like to owe his wife to that. No; it was better to keep silence to-day. Another time would present itself in the future, when she might have learned to love him for himself, and to be anxious that he should love her. And perhaps he was right.

"You will be happier in the future," he said after a long silence. "You are a person who must, by your own character—and much more so now that you have so anomalous a position—learn a great deal of the realities of life, which few women know. Usually so surrounded by responsible guardians, and hemmed in by the watchfulness of love and the jealous eyes of society, kept in ignorance too by men for various reasons of superiority and sickly sentiment, they know nothing at all of what really exists. They are children all their lives, never using their strength of character or power of intellect; mere dolls dandled in folly and artificiality, most loved when most false to nature. With you it is not so. You have to learn life as it is, and your sufferings will be proportionate. But I can foresee the time when you will get happiness and strength—even from a source undreamt-of now."

"How can I be happy, Percival, with a character gone for ever?" she said with crimson cheeks. "Who will ever respect me again—who will ever care for me? Why, a good woman would not speak to me now—though I have not done anything to really deserve all that I have met with! It might be wrong, running away from home, and yet what else could I have done? I should have gone mad if I had stayed there much longer!"

"Yes, Clare, there *are* women who would love you, though every word now falsely insinuated against you were true. Do not judge the whole sex by the example of a London drawing-room, where prudery is taken as a cloak for irregularity, and where the most faithless wife is loudest in condemnation of infidelity. There are truer and nobler specimens than these, and you will find, as you go on in life, much more freedom of thought among women than the guarded speech imposed on them betrays, and much more of the pure maternal instinct than the strictness of the social laws leaves apparent to the eye."

"No, not to *me!*" she said persistently.

"Yes, to you; why not?"

"Ah! that is what I do not know—what I only feel! I suppose I am worse than people in general, else all the world would not join in using me ill. I do not believe in persecuted innocence," she added with a sickly smile.

"Clara dear, you must no more allow this despondency to gain possession of you than that violence of grief. I tell you—and you must believe me—you have not met with any fate inconsistent with circumstances. You are an impulsive and naturally unconventional person, of warmer blood than English prudery endorses, of profound ignorance of the laws amongst which you live, and breaking twenty times a day the observances which are religious rules to society. In all this there is no mystery why you should suffer from a world whose authority you defy. But then, my child, I must have you remember that there is a holier and a higher life than that which this same society gives; and that though banished from the esteem of men, you can find happiness in the truth of your own heart, and the honesty of your purposes."

Clara listened attentively enough, but was not much benefited. She looked just as miserable as ever, and just as much broken; and Percival felt when she rose to put on her bonnet and shawl that what good soever his arguments might do her in the quiet thoughts of solitude, and when she was physically stronger, they had not made much impression for the present time of depression.

He let her go, as she so earnestly wished it, and he himself took her home, and saw her safely deposited in her own rooms.

Something kept him in the neighbourhood—an undefined feeling of dread, a presentiment of more sorrow. He wandered about always keeping near the street; until late in the evening he saw a female figure leave the house.

It was Clare. She was alone, and walked slowly as if very weak; but yet there was also a feverishness and restlessness in her attitudes that struck him painfully. He followed her; and in due time—though she was a long way off—she got into the New Road, and walked on towards the Regent's Park.

It was a beautiful spring evening—mild and fresh and balmy, with less of the choking dust and soot than general, and more of the freshness of the country in the air. And albeit the New Road, with its swarming population, and gin-shops, and cab-stands, and marble-cutters, and dirt and confusion generally, is not the most inviting of walks, nor the place where one feels most keenly the delights of nature, yet Clare did not mind all these discomforts. She held on her lonely way; and though it was late in the evening, and a great many dubious persons were abroad, no one molested her, and she went forward in peace.

As the flaring open gas-lights from the shops flamed into her face, they showed it pale as marble; with traces of tears still there; and such a look of inexpressible anguish printed, as if in legible type, that more than one woman who saw that face thought kindly of the "poor young thing whose lover had deceived her." For women seldom think their own sex has any source of sorrow but this.

Still she kept on; and now she turned into the gates leading to the Coliseum. The inner park was closed, but she had not remembered that. Keeping close to the side of the road, she walked on as rapidly as her debility allowed; the cool evening air coming fresh on her cheeks, giving her strength, and reviving her with every pleasant breath that came. She turned from the houses, round the circle, still keeping close by the side, while Percival followed her at a little distance. It was now very lonely. They met nothing—not even a policeman or a park-keeper.

Haunted by the smell of running water, and flags and lilies and drooping willows—called to the bosom of nature where she had lain so long as a child drinking in all her greatness and her beauty and her power—she made for what poor translation of nature the art of man can form, as if she hastened to a friend, and rushed to hear loved accents long since silent. At last she gained that beautiful little piece of water scenery in the Regent's Park, where one almost forgives the hand of man for the grace with which he has copied nature—and leaning over the light bridge looked anxiously into the water below.

Her long walk had tired her. She sat down, and bent her face toward the stream. All the stories she had ever read of water-nymphs, and mermaids, and luring spirits of death-giving beauty, came up before her mind with tenfold distinctness of meaning. She remembered the day when first the idea of self-destruction had flashed across her, and then had given way to the desire of a fuller and more active life. She thought of how since then she had gone on and on, still aiming at some bright point that ever vanished as she thought to near it—still endeavouring after a happiness that mocked and eluded her as she thought to grasp it. And now she knew that Death was the true meaning of that long sad desire which had pointed her onwards. She had dreamed of the stage and all its glories of success—this had failed her; she had dreamed of love and all its thousand years of pleasure concentrated into moments—and this had burnt itself to a charred ember of hideous shape; she had thought of the beauties of a foreign land, of the mystic murmurs of the sea, the mysterious voices calling from the distance—the visions of fulfilment in some unknown shape—and now she knew that earth held not that fulfilment—that it was death which all had meant.

She remembered, as she watched the last faint streak of western colour in the water, how she had loved the setting sun; how it had seemed to beckon her on to the land where it then was rising, as if there she could find all that nameless hope for which her soul pined; she remembered how she had yearned for active life—to be in the great centre of the empire—to be one of the thousand veins in the mighty heart of a nation. Her desires had been gratified—but what had she found? Disappointment: for they were but forms of death—forms of the longing for immortality which nothing on earth can quench—forms of the unsatisfying power of the present. She understood now the meaning of the voice in her; and she came here to obey it, and to die—to give back her life to the great elements of nature, and to seek repose where she had so vainly sought for happiness.

Such were Clare's long musings as she sat with her eyes bent downward to the stream, and heard the water ripple by the bridge, and saw the tall reeds move gently in the wavelets. Why should she live? She had lost all that made life desirable; a beggar, an outcast, slandered, reviled—not a path of love or joy lay open to her. She had better die by tortures than live through the friendless loneliness which alone was offered her! How much better then by a way so calm and sweet!

Sickness and sorrow had done their work, and Clare's intellect weakened beneath them.

She felt a gush of divinest pleasure through her heart as she contemplated the peace of death awaiting her; she felt that a home was opening to her, where rest and love stood watching in the portals. The beautiful water!—how calmly it glided on!—how pleasantly it murmured its invitation!

"Yes! yes! I come!" she said in a low voice of exquisite music; and then she lifted her face to the darkening sky, and a light of love and joy lay on it that startled yon watcher with the glory of its beauty.

She made one step forward and would have sprung below, when Percival touched her on her arm, saying calmly—"Clara! here so late?"

CHAPTER VI.

THE spring had really come. Girls cried musk-plants and wall-flowers about the streets, and men shouted "all a-growing all a-blowing," in reference to those cephalic[109] gardens that look so well at a distance, but are of consumptive tendencies under private management. Householders had "done up" their houses; shop-keepers had decorated their shop-fronts, and advertised their last new novelties; dingy windows had become transparent; and the ramoneurs[110] had made their fortunes. Yes, spring was here in all the fresh vigour of her bright maidenhood, and what had man to do, but to stand back and to admire?

A brighter day never dawned over the world than one memorable Thursday when Vasty took Emmeline for a day's pleasure down to Richmond. The sun came out like an unveiled God, and nature was the worshipper lying prostrate before the passage of the divinity. Every tree and herb and grassblade looked a sentient thing in the glorious light. Every pulse which throbbed through the mighty heart of creation seemed instinct with pleasure and confessed emotion. One could not believe in dull dead matter on such a day as this: the Pantheist were the better reasoner than the Geologist under such a sunlight.

Even Emmeline, frivolous as she was, felt more than usual enjoyment in her life when she leaned back in the well-hung cabriolet, and they drove swiftly along through flying showers of garden scents, through broad masses of sunshine and the tremulous shadows of the road-side trees, through the fresh country air that never smells so sweetly as when you have just escaped from London. And though it was but a poor tribute that her happy vanity gave to the grandeur and the beauty of nature, yet it was the best she had to offer up, and must be accepted as it was worth. The chirp of the sparrow is not the song of the divine poet; but yet it has its place in the eternal melodies of earth.

Emmeline's pleasure made her still prettier to-day. Her soft cheeks wore the most beautiful tint of the monthly rose. They were like wax—so smooth and clear. Her blue eyes, though devoid of all intellect and feeling, were full of vivacity; and this lesser quality stands in good stead of all higher expressions with minds of coarse perceptions and low standards. Her pretty little lips laughed always; disclosing a row of small white teeth even and regular. Her light hair, in its profusion of dancing ringlets, glanced in the passing sunbeam like golden threads, and her small hand was every moment raised, under pretence of bringing back some wanderer to its curly brotherhood; which comatose feat never seemed to be accomplished, and was always somehow to be done again. She was beautifully dressed; in the same wonderful profusion of lace, and muslin, and hanging chains, and flowers, and feathers as before. With her *petite* figure all this airy drapery gave her the most gossamer appearance possible. She looked as if a moderately strong puff of wind could blow her away like thistle-down. And when you saw what small feet she had, and how sylph-like they looked in their delicate shoes, and marvellous stockings which showed the pink flesh and blue veins quite clearly, it seemed a miracle how she could withstand the very faintest breath of summer wind that ever blew a rose-leaf from the tree. Altogether she was without doubt a beautiful little creature. And albeit, she had those inane arched eyebrows which give a doll-like expression of surprise to the face, she was much admired by men of all kinds, and had received more than one offer from high station and wealthy rent-rolls.

She created quite a sensation when they drove to the Star-and-Garter, and she stepped out like a walking flower from the handsome cabriolet, looking round with a childish laugh and an exclamation of "Oh how delightful!" Though, as they were standing at that moment in front of the hotel, with only three or four waiters, ostlers, and stable-boys idling about, one cannot see where such immense pleasure could have been found.

Vaughan looked more graceful and manly than ever, as he offered her his arm with an air that said "you may admire, for this is mine," and took her with courtly stateliness to the private room he had ordered for them. It opened on the garden, full on that lovely view which has no parallel; with the river, and the trees, and the scattered houses, and the brave old castle in the distance, and signs of wealth and peace and security everywhere. It is a lovely view! And one does not wish for any greater happiness of the kind than to sit under the trees on a summer's day and gaze for long hours on the scenery of Richmond.

Every attention that a man of gallantry could pay to a pretty woman, did Vasty shower on Emmeline to-day. What he felt few could have told. Perhaps not himself even. He did not love her in any way that could be really called love. Pink cheeks and laughing eyes have little influence in general over a heart inflamed with grief and jealousy and love for another—and if they are taken only to serve the purposes of intoxication, it is but a thin potation a man chooses. However that might be, Vasty did certainly pay Emmeline de Montfort more than even *his* usual attention, and wear more lover-like manners than were absolutely necessary to maintain his acknowledged reputation; hanging on her words, gazing into her face, and seeming as if he tried to shut out all the rest of the world and to look at this portrait alone— as if he had taken up a pair of moral picture-glasses, and could see only the one face whereon he turned them.

Emmeline, reclining in her flounces and her curls, for a short time was happy enough to be so admired. But she soon began to regret that "more men were not there to take some of the trouble off Vaughan's hands;" and then she suppressed a yawn as she wondered if this was to be her day's employment. For after all there is not so much pleasure in flirting alone with one, when no one else is by to envy or admire; and if she had known that she and Vaughan were to sit there talking sentimentalities together and doing nothing jolly, she would have brought down a shepherdess's hat and crook, and not have dressed herself so well. It certainly was getting very stupid, for there was no chance, apparently, of any admiration but this foolish man's; and *she* did not love *him*, though he was so desperately in love with her! If he had not been the manager—and so of some profit and glory in the captivating—she would have seen him at the bottom of the Red Sea before she would have had anything to do with him.

"Shan't we walk?" she exclaimed at last, jumping up in the middle of a speech which Vaughan was making, and which had something about "soul-felt raptures," and "heavenly pleasures," in it. "It's such a pity to lose the whole of this beautiful day in doors! We get enough of that in town."

Vaughan was not disconcerted; and they agreed to go out; at first into the garden, which perhaps was a better arrangement than even the park, Emmeline thought; as the rooms were generally full of gentlemen, and she might see some one she knew. If Vaughan would not be jealous—but he was such a tiger!

Out into the merry sunshine then this gauzy creature fluttered—making the air alive with her shrill laughter; for her spirits suddenly rose so wonderfully as they strolled about the walks, that Vaughan compared her to a butterfly panting on a flower, and to a kid frisking with its shadow, before they had been two minutes on the lawn.

Glancing back at the rooms, Emmeline had cause to rejoice that she had escaped so well from their solitary box where Vaughan seemed to think she could want for nothing so long as he sat by her and talked a quantity of nonsense. The windows were alive with heads, male and female. Large parties come down to dine under the protection of a pair of elderly *chaperons*—with a great many pink bonnets among the ladies, and surprising waistcoats among the gentlemen—were enjoying themselves in one window. Here again was a quiet family, bringing baby and all, for the fresh air; one of those thoroughly

English families that are independent communities in themselves, keeping no society, and devoted to the children and education; and there might be seen a sentimental-looking pair, decidedly in the first weeks of their wedded bliss; and there an unmistakeable affair of love-making, and here an evident case of quarrel. And then Emmeline saw a knot of men lounging together—idlers who had come on chance for any stray amusement they might meet with; and these were the groups that she scanned the most anxiously, always looking out for some mysterious friend who never appeared—like Nadgett's man.[111] Being traditionally rather short-sighted, this fixed idea of hers was still more observable; for she would not remember that other people could see more distinctly than herself. And often, when reminded of this fact by sundry nods and laughs, and pretty speeches, and familiar addresses from strange men—if she wanted to appear very proper to her immediate companions—she would say, "But how could I know that they saw me? I am so short-sighted, and I was only looking to see if there was any one I knew among them!"

Among a knot of male heads of all kinds and descriptions gathered into one of the windows, was one peculiarly striking. Does any English man or woman fail to know the handsome young man of Leech's drawings?[112]—the type of his clever representations of fashionable humanity? The male head I am alluding to now, was just such a one as Leech would have seized on and immortalized. A profusion of curly hair, a profusion of curly whisker, a goodly acreage of spotless shirt with a row of blue studs set in its snowy field—a low collar, and loose dark-blue cravat tied carelessly, and suiting admirably with the chestnut shrubbery above—a fashionable air that cannot be mistaken, and that does look something better than the imitations of the swell mob, (but these are well done too, sometimes)—all fixed Emmeline's attention; and she turned to Vaughan, saying loud enough to be heard—

"Is not that handsome man like Fred Winter?"

But Vaughan thought him exceedingly unlike Fred Winter; and pointed out so many discrepancies, that her short-sightedness must allow itself to be convinced, however unwillingly, and give up the point with a pretty laugh and a shrill cry of "How stupid it is to be so blind!"

The men laughed among themselves, and joked this natural copy of Fred Winter, and praised the pretty little girl; and some spoke of her as if she were a horse, and others as if she were a ballet-dancer; and one man who passed for "a very able man," brought in a few artistic phrases which he did not apply quite correctly. But no one knew any better; and so the inaccuracies passed for "good ideas," which every one appreciated.

By degrees more people came out into the lawn, bringing invisible clouds of patchouli and eau de Cologne and cigars, as they passed in various defile. Vaughan and his fair companion sat down on a garden-seat, watching them; and as Emmeline had a way of sitting gracefully, and looked like a picture in her prettiness and her finery, she was well content to pretend to admire the scenery while gazing from under her parasol at every man who passed. Not that she was worse than vain. But vanity has more than once been the mother of an Eve's serpent.

Among others came out this likeness of Fred Winter. Now Fred Winter was one of Vaughan's "walking gentlemen," and what the papers call "a useful actor;" that is, a man who, being moderately good-natured and not quite qualified for Hanwell[113] by vanity, will play anything the manager gives him, and does not think himself the most ill-used individual on the stage because the whole of the best parts are not laid at his feet. The handsome likeness, "Lord John," would not have been much flattered though, had he known that his lieutenancy in the Guards, his present title and heir-apparency, his beauty and his fashion, only gained him a comparison with a "raffish actor at a second-rate theatre." What a blessing it is that we do not hear half that is said of us both in praise and blame!

Now Lord John, not knowing the dishonourable likeness which that "pretty little girl" found, was amazingly struck with her; and paraded before her with an air of divine nonchalance when Vaughan was looking, though he made up for it, when that gentleman's eyes were turned away, by looks as expressive as they were mesmeric.

The flirtation being thus established, Emmeline became exceedingly happy; delighting Vasty with her childishness and vivacity so much that he resolved on raising her salary next week, and giving her Clara's own Ianthe—which had hitherto been sacred to the memory of his latest love.

And the sun went on, shining down on these happy groups—on the lovers for whom all nature, time, and space seem to have been specially created and designed to form their happiness alone—on the honourable English families who stood in a nook of life, and looked out from their safe place on the passing passions of the world—on the great heart and the vain intellect—on the thoughtful student and the flippant flirt—on the good and the evil—giving out its light equally unto all.

The dinner hour approached, and they now enter the house. With a mutual interchange of ocular electricity the young nobleman and Emmeline parted, though he and his friends still continued to pace through the garden, and to look out for the room where this fair thing had gone. And they were not long in finding her particular locality; for she took care that she should be tolerably conspicuous by some of those thousand arts which women exercise and never betray—if they have the smallest possible amount of tact.

"Champagne, Emmeline?" said Vaughan.

"Yes," she answered laughing, "as much as you like!"

"Oh! you little Bacchante!—what! challenge me in bumpers?"

"To the lip?" she said, with meaning.

And Vaughan took the hint there and then. This was after the dinner had been removed, and while the dessert was on the table—the shining mahogany reflecting pleasantly the plates of fruit and coloured shapes of ice which Vaughan's lavish magnificence had ordered.

And as Vaughan accepted the challenge to the sense, if not to the word, "Lord John," by the merest chance, of course, happened to stroll near that window of Eden.

It chanced also that Emmeline raised her eyes just as Vasty's face bent over her, and that she saw the curly head which had attracted her admiration before, turn round and look in. It made her blush, and laugh, and scold Vaughan for his impertinence, and skip away to the window, and feel a sudden longing for the fresh air which Vasty would not at first indulge. But she begged so hard, and scolded him so gracefully, and kept him at such an awful distance while he was "a horrible ogre," that he thought it perhaps truest economy to lay out so much time on her pleasures now, hoping it would bring him in a valuable percentage after.

The first time they passed by the handsome youth he ostentatiously displayed a piece of paper, so that Emmeline alone should see it; and she, not slow in taking the hint—for it was not the first time she had found such an "adventure," as she used to call it, in her trips of pleasure—let her hand fall by her side when they next met, and received a small note which she hurriedly concealed in her bosom.

Delighted like a child at the success of her deception, Emmeline preserved her good temper even after the disappearance of the curls and the whiskers. And so the time passed pleasantly enough, till all the parties trooped out again when their respective banquets were at an end, and when the sun had set and the fresh air was coming up from the river.

Vaughan left Emmeline, to look after the cab and to prepare for returning to London. He left her very near their own windows; she in a poetic rapture about the rising moon and the summer flowers, and insisting so strenuously on being left out in the fresh air and "not taken back to that dark room," (for Vaughan had a great idea of conventional propriety), that he had humoured her whim, although strongly against his principles. And in that brief interval all the mischief was done; for Miss Emmeline communicated her name, but not her address, to "Lord John," whose name, so far as she knew, was Captain Jones; and a meeting was agreed on for the following day. And thus Vaughan suffered a burglary of the worst description.

Emmeline was now very sleepy and tired; and not all the beauty of the rising moon, not all the balm of the cool fresh air, nor the scent of the flowers though twice as sweet as in the daytime—nothing that had charmed her so much on coming down—had now the slightest influence for her. She yawned in Vasty's face when he spoke to her, and reiterated so often "I am so sleepy," that he began to feel offended. As they drove on in silence, Vaughan asked himself, as he had done thousands of times in his life before, "if it had been worth the trouble?"

Lost in reflections, none of the gayest, Vaughan sat by his fair companion in silence. She was thinking of the chestnut shrubbery and the diamond ring—which had been a conclusive evidence of her unknown admirer's "respectability"—for Emmeline was a judge of diamonds; and he was trying to feel very happy in Clare's disgrace, and to be particularly jocose in his own mind over her discomfiture. But somehow the effort failed, and he could not think of her but with grief, and a certain tenderness for which he hated himself as for an unmanliness. And as he thought and pondered the shadows deepened on his face till not a ray of light was left there. And even Emmeline, opening her fairy eyes, was struck by the somberness of her late so happy host.

And now they reached the thronged streets once more. The calm beauty of nature was exchanged for the flaring gas-light of the gin-palace—the luxury of green fields and wild flowers for the strolling idlers of the evening streets—and in the place of the quiet moon and her gentle beams, the flickering burners of the open shops and the tall lamps about the noisy road shed a yellow light on the air.

The streets were more than usually thronged to-night, or they appeared to be so to Vasty, who had a strange haunting wish for quiet this evening, and for what Emmeline called "stupid sentimentality." Never remarkably fond of the country beyond the day's pleasure out at some metropolitan airing ground, as Richmond or Hampton, he longed to-night to hear nothing but the cry of some solitary night-bird from the distant woods, or the ripple of the water through the sedgy bands that held it. And the hurry and noise and glare of the great city came on him harshly, like an unwelcome face obtruding where you seek a dearer dream.

Through Piccadilly the way was very crowded. Either some large West-end gaiety was going on, or all the world had turned sentimental too; but good driver though he was he had hard work to guide his spirited horse safely through the crush. People crossing and re-crossing made it worse; and frightened women rushing under the horse's very head, and little children starting off where the press was thickest, and seeming as if they tried to get under the wheels and to put themselves in jeopardy, caused Vaughan to swear a great deal, and pull up very often, and to cry "Hie!" as savagely as if he had been the party all but demolished. One particular turn was exceedingly difficult, and Vaughan's horse took to kicking.

A kicking horse in a cabriolet—never a very easy thing to drive—is no trifle on a summer's night in the thickest part of Piccadilly. Several men rushed forward, and a crowd gathered speedily; but Vasty prided himself on his Jehuship,[114] and lashed the hands of those who ran to hold the brute's head, and gave and received no little abuse in the metropolitan vernacular, concerning their interference and his ill-temper.

Emmeline had one good quality. She did not scream when she was frightened. It was strange that she did not; for such a little featherhead as she would naturally have liked the exercise, if more confusion was to be gained by it. But she was wonderfully brave for a pretty woman—whether from lymph or principle I do not attempt to say. She sat back now, very calmly; merely keeping her eyes unclosed, and enjoying the sensation they were creating.

At last Vaughan lashed and strained his horse into obedience, and off it started with a jerk and a dash that nearly broke the reins in his hand. For the first moment it was out of his control. All that he could do was merely to hold the reins tight and straight, so as to prevent if possible any positive mischief. At that moment a woman crossed the street, and immediately behind her ran a child.

There was plenty of room, and they gave the cabriolet a wide berth. The woman took no more care than merely to bid the little one make haste, and to hold out her hand to it. But when nearly over, the child slipped; and the horse making a dash to one side struck it with its fore feet while the wheels of the cab passed directly over it.

Through all the noise of hurrying carriages, and ponderous carts, and omnibuses, and cabs, and clattering hoofs, that child's last scream broke out in frightful clearness. Through the night air rose that little voice to heaven in the unutterable anguish of a frightful death, heralding back from whence it came the prisoned soul of its humanity.

The horse trampled on the tender body and broke the little bones within, and the iron tire ground down the rest and scattered the life in fragments on the wheel; but surely there was something else which these brute forces could not crush, and which was restored by death to the place from whence it had been drawn down to matter!

At that shriek the woman turned; to what a sight! To one that would change the coldest into passionate madness—that would make the most indifferent mother turn back to the instinct of nature, however long forgotten; what then must it have been to a woman whose only affection was in her maternity, and who clung to her children as the last voices of GOD left still audible?

It was the youngest child of his unhappy wife that Vaughan had unwittingly doomed to such a hideous death.

In leaning from the cab, for he dared not leave his place as the horse was still unmanageable, the lamplight fell on his face, and Emma Vaughan beheld her husband as he bent forward to speak with her.

She never knew afterwards why she did not rush on him then, and strangle him in the public streets before a hand could stay her. She never knew what kept back her clutching fingers, nor how he escaped with his life—and the blood of her child wetting his horse's hoofs the while. Whether stricken into stupor by the bigness of her horror—

or whether held back by the influence of that young spirit hovering round her ere it bade farewell to earth for ever—she knew not; but she met those baleful eyes glance for glance, and neither moved nor spoke, neither cursed nor sought to take his life.

Vasty called a policeman. He gave his name and address, and handed him his purse for the use of "the poor woman." And Emmeline addressed some wondering epithets and inane pity; and then they drove off, and the crowd said "the gentleman had done all that became a gentleman and he couldn't do more." While not a few swore at the mother for her stupidity in letting such a young thing cross the street alone.

Without a word, good or bad—of sorrow or of passion—the woman took up the child, and carried it carefully to her own home. She laid it down on the bed and sat by it all the night; but no one could say what terrible thoughts or frightful griefs were in that heavy brow and all those burning sighs—nor how strong the hideous belief which had crept on her that she was doomed to damnation, and that the death of her children one by one was the way in which it was working itself out. For Emma's atheism, like too many of the wretched, consisted but in her denial of the love and mercy of the Great Father, while retaining her belief in all those Judaic attributes of the Avenger which have so long obscured the TRUTH from men. The law of justice was derided and vengeance placed high in its stead; acceptance and forgiveness were blasphemed, but eternal condemnation was held sacred; Heaven alone was blotted out for this wretched woman, while Hell gaped wide, and was her unavoidable doom throughout eternity.

How should it not be so? She had tasted only suffering, and had received no portion of compensation. How then could she acknowledge the love and mercy which she never saw?—how fail to recognise the vengeance that had ever tracked her most secret steps? She had suffered more than she deserved; yes, boldly before heaven would she proclaim that blighting truth! True, she had sinned morally as well as socially; yet did not the first and largest responsibility rest with those who had shared nothing of her punishment? She had been forced into what she was by circumstances. A giant hand of fate had crushed her into the niche of guilt which she had filled so long—she had not gone there all of her own free will—yet she had to bear the fullest penalties alone.

And now this baleful idea took a larger shape, and stretched out its hand beyond the grave, and pointed to eternal damnation there as the completion of her life of forced misdoing. And she forgot partly, while she looked on her dead child, and felt that one other—and the last—round of the ladder of virtue whereon angels clomb between her and heaven, had been broken away, that Vaughan had been the human instrument of its death. She thought only of the visible decree of condemnation which GOD had written in its blood, and bound for ever as a sign between her eyes.

Condemned! condemned! no salvation for her left! Heaven clean gone, and nought but the fiery place of torture left; vengeance for her guilt and no balm of mercy for her weakness; the fact judged of alone, but the temptation and the wrong without set on one side. Aye, that was the religion which men had taught her—that was the last echo which their false words had left.

Oh thou Great Father above mankind, when will thy Second Christ rise to teach wisdom and truth unto suffering humanity!

CHAPTER VII.

"SARAH, take my child," said Emma, suddenly entering the room where the young sempstress sat at her lonely work—in the mournful black got her partly by kindly subscription from those who were as badly off as herself.

"Why, what's come to thee, Emma?" exclaimed the girl, looking in wonder at the pallid face so full of such terrible feelings that they covered it like a veil.

"Nothing, girl!—nothing! I am going away—that's all—and I don't like the child to go to the workhouse. You take care of her, Sally, till I get her back again; and here's the pay!" She threw down a couple of sovereigns on the table, laughing hoarsely as she added—"I'm an honest pay-mistress you see, and don't ask long credit!"

"But Emma, something's happened thee, woman. I'm not to be so easy done. I can see it in thy face and in thy voice. Tell me, woman, what's wrong with thee. Thou'st been good to me and my poor Jane, Emma, and I'll do all I can to serve thee now in turn. But tell me what's happened thee, for I don't like to see thee in such a terrible way."

"What way, fool?" she exclaimed roughly. "What do I look like?— an honest woman trying to be better, or a rogue sinking lower?"

"Neither, Emma," said the young workwoman simply.

"Neither!—and what then?"

"I don't know that neither. Thou seems as if some big sorrow had pulled thee down since I saw thee last. And I don't like it Emma, and maybe if you'll tell me you'll lighten it off a bit."

"It's nothing, girl; nothing," she repeated, but less sullenly than before.

"Yes, there's much," said the child in a whisper. "Fan's dead, and she's crazed," pointing to the mother, as she stood fairly colossal in her misery.

The girl rose, and went to that tall dark scowling woman. Gently she put her wasted arms round the open neck; gently she drew up one of those burning hands with all the veins standing out in feverish prominence, and forced her to look into her inquiring face. Vanquished by her tenderness, by her patience and affection, the rough heart of the poor woman gave way. Oh! how much she would have been saved had tenderness arrested her in time, before it fell only on the sear and the blight.

"Oh, Sally!" she cried, her pride broken like a shattered vase; "my little one's gone!"

"Poor woman!—it's a hard thing to bear, Emma, but what can one do? Death's like nothing else. Rich people may save us from everything else a'most; but death's like an engine wheel, Emma, and nothing can stop it!" said Sarah kindly, her own tears falling fast; for she had earned her right to comfort by sad experience of sorrow.

"Well, sit ye down now and tell me," she continued, "if it'll ease your mind, and don't if it'll make you worse. But sit ye down at any rate, and I'll take care of her," pointing to the child.

"I'll be better soon, Sally," said Emma, struggling to subdue herself. "It was such a hard blow!—so sudden!—so frightful!—before my very eyes too!"

And then she shivered as if she had an ague fit, and pressed her hands on her head, till every vein and muscle worked.

"She was run over," said the child laconically, "and mother was by."

"Yes!" cried Emma; "before my very eyes—run over, Sally, by *him*. Think of that!—*his* horse trod down my child, *his* carriage crushed her to the earth, and *his* mistress looked out and laughed at the anguish of his wife! This is the cup of misery that I have to drink—this the kindness of Heaven to me! And then a canting fool tells me all is good!"

She was silent for a moment, then rising from her seat paced about the room; her chest heaving, her nostril dilating, and all her fiendish passions awake and out on her lip and brow.

"And he'll go to heaven for this!"—she continued. "He's thrust a soul down to farther sin and he will be rewarded, and I punished! He's done a political good, maybe," she laughed, "and rid the country of a pauper or a prisoner; and little any one will think to-morrow of the poor child a rich gentleman's carriage ran over and crushed to death to-night: and much they'd wonder that one heart in all the earth could love a mis-begotten whelp of rags and dirt! But that death shall be revenged! Blood for blood, was the ancient cry, and blood for blood shall be the answer! He that has killed my child, shall perish for his guilt; and the world will lament him and hang me! What justice, Sally, in the great world of man!—the heirs of immortality—the holders of tickets for heaven! Pshaw!—I see no good, and believe in none—here or hereafter—above or below!"

"Hush, Emma dear!—if people heard thee they would maybe take account of thy words and get thee into trouble! The gentleman couldn't have done it on purpose, you know; it was but an accident, woman!"

"Accident, Sally? No! no accident!" she answered, turning round suddenly, and facing the girl. "It was *his* doing, and he is the very impersonation of my misery—the cause of all my wrong-doing and sufferings!"

"But who?" asked the girl wonderingly.

"Who, fool? Why my husband to be sure! that great, proud, rich man, who owns the —— theatre—that mirror to a generation—Vasty Vaughan!"

"Sure! sure!" cried Sally, not understanding any better than before; for she had never been inside the theatres, and only knew of them by tradition—from Emma chiefly—who was passionately fond of them even now. "And he it was that ran over poor little Fan? Ah dear! it was a bad job!"

"Listen girl!" said Emma sternly. "But no—it's no use telling you my history throughout—you would not understand me, nor know why and how such feelings ever came to me. But this at least you can understand. I was born a lady, Sally—a real lady—with horses and carriages, and fine clothes and a fine house: and I married. I married this man, this Vasty Vaughan—and he ill-treated me. I loved him, and he deserted me for such as I am now—and *then* I was what men called beautiful, Sally, and innocent and good; and if he had been kind to me I should have been made far far better. But he nearly broke my heart, and another man took notice of me when he saw my trouble, and got me to love him. And Sally, when I had learnt to love him for gratitude, as well as for hatred against my worthless husband, he deserted me—though I had lost all for him. But he stayed until that girl was born; and then he left me entirely; and was a great lord again in the fashionable drawing-rooms where I was banished; though he had ruined me. Was that justice? Is it fair that these men should have all the honours and glories that they have, and I be looked down on as a monster whose death and damnation no one would care to stop? Is it fair that the man I went off with, after leaving me to the streets, should go back into society, and be loved by the ladies all the more for his gallantries? Is all this fair? Is this a GOD's world, where such things can be—and such injustice given out? No! no! I'm not so idiot blind as to believe that!"

"But, Emma," said Sarah quietly; "why didst thee run away from thy husband at the first? If thou'd a-stayed by him this wouldn't have happened!"

"Stayed by him, fool?—stay by a man whose mistresses ate up his heart like a fire, and whose whole life to me was one of brutal coldness or coarse neglect? Didn't he always teach me that there was no sin in it?—and what's not a sin in a man surely is none in a woman! I can't believe that vice and virtue have a sex in the eyes of GOD! Stay with him?—No! no! not I indeed! And if I had it all to go over again, I would do exactly the same thing; for I say it again and again Sally, I was not so much to blame as the laws of society which drove me to what I am. Don't think because I drink till I forget all that has happened, and seem then the most rollicksome of the set—don't think that I never *reflect*—I do, Sally; and it has driven me almost mad! And sometimes I do believe I am mad! I cannot hear or see when I have been thinking long over it all; and the very life in me seems turned to fire, and the very blood to poison. I must be mad at times!"

"But Emma, listen to me, woman—I'm no scholar, and can't talk with thee—but if people lay the blame when they do wrong on other people and other things, where's the use of right or wrong at all? Isn't it something different to this, Emma?"

"No!" she shouted passionately; "no it isn't—and there is no difference that I can see—in all that the world knows at any rate! Who was that poor woman taken before the magistrate yesterday for pawning her slop shirts? She had committed a theft the gentleman said, and she must go to prison for fourteen days, or pay a fine she couldn't raise. And why?—because she was mad to hear her children cry for bread, after she had worked early and late and got no money to buy it for them. Work as hard as she might, Sal, she couldn't get enough to keep them all. The sweaters and the masters knew this, but still pressed down the wages. Now who is to blame—they who make the poor bad by their laws, and their wages, and their neglect, and all the other wrongdoings of this grand society of ours—or the poor who obey the laws of nature and get food when they can? Remember, it wasn't a question of choice—it wasn't between honest bread and dishonest—it was between starvation and life—a so-called dishonesty to another, and the duty of a mother to feed her young. And so with more things than slop-workers' wages! It isn't always where the punishment falls that it is most needed, as that poor woman and myself both know."

"Oh! that was a hard case, Emma," said Sally mournfully, "and I can feel for the poor mother; I have known what it is to hear a thing you love cry for bread, and you know that all your hard work can't get it. I know that! But Emma, don't the newspapers and the great people say that she was very wicked and ought to be punished? I heard them talking so when I went for work this morning."

"Of course they do, fool! What else could they say when they make the laws and forget what the human nature is they make them for? Of course the magistrates talked a deal about public virtue, and holding out a premium to dishonesty, and kept back the money that was sent her—but, curses on their narrow hearts!—who thought of the temptation?—who measured that by the natural feelings of the mother, and gave a little weight to these against their mouthings of virtue and honesty? It'll have its own way at last!" she added, muttering. "It is too strong to be always in this small coffin of social laws! The first will suffer—I suffer for my share, and the slop-workers suffer for theirs; but when facts accumulate, and men are forced to see that human nature and their rules don't agree, they'll be obliged to square those by that, and to make better laws which don't forget all the necessities and instincts of man!"

Never had the young slop-worker heard Emma speak in this strain before. Usually reserved to a marvel on her former life and present thoughts, this outburst amazed the girl. The language too was so much better than that which Emma generally used, the evidence of her superior birth and education so far more prominent than she had ever before allowed them to be, that she seemed transformed while the girl listened, and grieved in her kindly heart that she should have wasted herself so much!

While she spoke thus, though still fierce and impassioned, Emma's face took a better expression altogether. There was more thought in it, and less of its usual coarseness. She looked great, despite her ragged hair and disordered attire; and something of the grace of her early youth, and its power and its mind, came out as stars seen between the rents of a painted roof: but fleeting—oh how soon!—and leaving her the ruin and the wreck which sin had made her.

"Let that pass!" she said, suddenly resuming the recklessness habitual to her. "You and I are not called to make the laws Sal, we've only got to suffer by them; and obey them though we die, else we'll go to the gallows for our independence. All I want you to do is not to hold me as cheap as most do; for though you are a fool, and know nothing, you've got brains in your heart that are worth half the fine intellects in the world. And when you think of me, Sal, and speak to that child of me, I'd have you remember what I've said to-day, and not call me bad names without adding why they ever came to me. Weeds don't grow without seeds and earth."

"Speak to the child, Emma?" said the girl in amazement. "Why how long art going to leave her me? Where art thou going, Emma: I don't like thy face!—what thoughts have got thee?"

"Least said soonest mended, girl. I'll not tell you where I'm going, or what I'm going about. When that money's spent you'll get some more. This will last you for her keep some good weeks, and you must make her work—slop-working," she added with a bitter emphasis; "and teach her how to keep herself; if the laws of the 'labour-market' will let her," she added scoffingly.

"Why, mother?" asked the child going close to her; "why am I to be sent from you now that baby and Fan are dead? Did you mind only them, and not me?"

"You're getting a big girl now, child, and you must work for your living," answered Emma harshly. "The others were little and had to be taken care of—you can take care of yourself."

"And work?"

"Yes, and work! Are you too proud for that?"

"No," she said with a sigh; "but I should like to play sometimes and have enough to eat always. But I can't yet, and will when I'm older."

"I am going away too, Emma," then said Sarah, in a more cheerful voice; "and maybe I'll run and bolt with the little one too!"

She smiled in a sorry make-believe fashion, looking round as if to her for whom she had always cared to put on her smiles.

"Where to? Where are you going to?" Emma asked in a sullen voice.

"That good gentleman's going to take me to the new lodging-houses. There's one opened now for single women, where the rooms are light and clean, and I shan't pay so much rent for them all as I do for this one alone. And there's plenty of water, and the sewers are all right, and don't smell as they do here—and worse in the court where we lived with you, Emma. And we've a grand kitchen and hall and all that's clean and great—and all for so little rent! And there's a needlewomen's association besides in Red Lion Square; and he's going to put me in the lodging-house, and get me work from the association; and so I'll do better now, and give Mary here a more comfortable home like. And it will be nice for me, Emma, to have her; for since poor Janie went I've been lonely, and it's seemed strange that I've no one to speak to!"

"I'm glad! All this will make you up in the world," said Emma, less sullenly. "Ah! at last they're coming to their senses are they!—and looking after the poor—at least letting them look after themselves—which they won't always do! Well, Sally, good-bye, and bless thee, girl! I'm glad for thy happiness, and I hope to see thee next time we meet prosperous and fat. Take care of her; and Mary, be a good girl, and do as she tells you, and work—work, child, and get your own living honestly. It may be long before I see you again, Sally. I'm going a long journey; Good-bye."

Without a kiss to her child, or a tear, the dark figure of Emma Vaughan went over the threshold and mingled with the crowd below. The little one stood looking from the window to catch the last glimpse of the only friend she knew. And when she disappeared she turned back to the room, and, huddling herself among the clothes, laid there and cried silently, and refused all comfort that Sarah offered.

Emma had now to form her plans. She had set before her the work of Vaughan's destruction with all her energy and concentration of purpose. It was her life's work. Had she to wait years before it could be accomplished she would wait them, and never swerve aside for gain, or pleasure, or even for her re-establishment in the minds of men. All that she had to decide on was the time and manner. When could she gain access to him? But if she did—though she was strong, he was more powerful—and to attempt his open murder by the knife, or even by a pistol, would involve her own certain destruction and perhaps fail in its object. If she followed him secretly at night, and took him unprepared in some dark bye-street—that would be well; and it would be a pleasure to her to see him die, which a little personal risk would cheaply purchase. At any rate she would prepare herself; and accordingly, with some of her ill-gotten gains she bought pistols, powder, and ball, and then set out on her first night of watching.

Little did Vaughan imagine what dark shadow stealthily tracked his path. Little did he see the cloud gathering up in the horizon, which would so soon burst over him—but whether to its own dispersion or his ruin, no man yet could foresee. He went on laughing and drinking, making love and counting hours by timepieces of roses—and he forgot the mother whose brute instinct he had roused—the tigress whose path he had crossed. Else, had he remembered better, he might have found a name for that muffled figure which once had shot before him in the dusky street, with a strange gesture paralysed by some passer-by suddenly appearing. And he would have known whose face, with its dread malignant scowl, always hovered about him. Go where he would, that face was still near; never fully seen, never recognised, but assuming a power and definiteness that gave a shape to his dreams, and woke up an ever-present night-mare round his bed.

More than once the murder had been nearly done. Unweariedly, unsleepingly, Emma watched for that moment. Vaughan never stirred from his own door, night or day, but she followed him. His every movement in the very house itself was watched; and he would have started to have heard the accurate knowledge which that haunting woman possessed of all he did and all he knew. But the hour had never come. She had tracked him through the streets, and more than once she thought her time was at hand; and then some accident, some trifle, had prevented its fulfilment; and so the murderer walked still unmurdered.

But not for long!—and she set her teeth, and sharpened the point of her knife, and planned fresh schemes, which should be more certain than the last.

And then she thought of poison, and of the ready facility which our strange ideas of freedom give for the purchase of arsenic. And she laughed with joy as she hoarsely congratulated herself on the discovery of the true way after all. A worthless witness, a formal caution, a legion of fabulous rats, and you have in your hand the life of such of your fellow-creatures as you may wish under the churchyard sod. And to destroy this facility would be to interfere with the liberty of the subject, in a country that makes the unlicensed death of a hare a misdemeanour against the laws.

"I want two-pennyworth of arsenic," said Emma, boldly entering a chemist's shop in a low neighbourhood. "We're overrun with rats, and we must get rid of them somehow. And this young woman's a witness," she added, turning to a woman she had brought with her by the bribe of a glass of gin.

The man muttered something about "caution," and a "wonderful quantity of rats now-a-days," and wrote "Poison" on the label in a bold legible hand; and being thus out of the clutches of the law, cared little to what purpose this pretended rat-poison was to be appropriated.

With a short growl of triumph Emma caught up the packet, and giving the friendly witness her promised payment, retreated to her lair, to perfect her scheme.

Butter and eggs and spices, flour, sugar, and all that was necessary for confectionary, she bought; and then she got a mould and made a decent-looking cake. In it she kneaded all her two-pennyworth of death; and now she trusted to Vaughan's old predilection for a certain kind of cake to help her out. And if it failed—why she had the steel and the pistol even then! She would try this at first, and then fall back on the others.

She wrapped the cake in a sheet of white paper, strewed some rose-leaves about the inside wrapper, decked it prettily with white ribbon and other feminine fancies, and wrote a small delicate "E. d. M." in the corner. It would do the girl no harm to be suspected on the first blush, if he ate it and died; innocence can always re-establish itself; and it would give her a sobering lesson perhaps, and not be of any real ill to her. So she soon reasoned down her qualms of conscience respecting the poor little butterfly actress Emmeline, and any probable trouble into which this insinuation might get her.

The bait took. This truly womanish present came one day after Vaughan had had a slight quarrel with Emmeline, who, not being quite well, had exhibited more emotion when he left her than he was accustomed to see. She knew his fondness for confectionary, and she had sent this as a consolation of their but half completed reconciliation. He saw it all quite plainly. Dear little Emmeline!—who would have thought the little girl had such a good heart! Vaughan was wonderfully pleased, and looked a long time at the childish prettiness with which her fairy hands had decked this childish gift. And then he cut off a small fragment and ate it.

Passing and re-passing the door was that tall muffled figure. In the deepening dusk—her fittest season—her dark form grew almost giantlike, as she strode again and again past that door, and looked up to the windows anxiously.

And still no hurrying lights, no cries for aid, no shrieks, no groans, no rapid feet hastening for relief. Had he not then fallen into the trap?—was the work incomplete, and to be done over again?—or had he who served her suspected her meaning, and given her some harmless powder for those precious shining grains of death? He ought to have felt its influence by this time! Curse the man!—was he charmed in his life?—could nothing touch him?

Ha! a noise at last! At last the speechless blackness of those vacant windows finds a voice, and lights come out on the gloomy street, and cries break the stillness of the air. She listens with breath suspended, and every faculty tenfold sharpened by desire. Sure she hears him moan and writhe in pain!—sure she hears the feeble voice calling for water to quench the burning fire so suddenly lighted up in his scorching entrails!—sure she knows by sight and sound that his life is ebbing from him, and that his days, his hours, his minutes, are numbered—and her vengeance is complete!

The stifled cry of rapture that burst from yon pallid lips might have startled the archangels in the inner courts of heaven. All passion of revenge attained, of hatred fully sated, of rage and vengeance companioned with a frightful joy, were in that cry. It was the voice of a heart leagued irretrievably to sin laughing at the ruin to which it dragged down others.

And true enough were Emma Vaughan's frenzied fancies. Vaughan *had* eaten of that poisoned food, and *had* discovered, by burning anguish, that it was no food for man.

But this was all. The portion he had taken was so small that no real harm was done, and a very short time sufficed to rescue him from any show of danger. A doctor was sent for, a policeman, and an analytical chemist; and not many hours elapsed before the blood-hounds of the law were on the traces of the criminal, and Vaughan high above the waves of hatred beating at his feet.

Emmeline's terror, surprise, and the utter absence of all criminating proof, together with sufficient proofs on the side of her innocence, soon released her from suspicion; and then Vaughan communicated the name and probable identity of the wretched woman he was forced to call his wife; and a chain of evidence was soon established clear enough for the sharpened faculties of the detective force.

Emma had not wandered about so long unnoticed. More than one guardian of the public peace had watched her as a likely disturber of that peace; and when Vaughan told his suspicions, many of the men on the beat identified his description with the strange woman so often through this street, and so often haunting this very door.

Through the hurrying blindness of her own passions, Emma fell into the snare she had laid for another; and while Vaughan toyed with the "little murderess," and played with her golden hair, that wretched woman was taken by the police, and after a few legal forms convicted and lodged in gaol.

CHAPTER VIII.

IN the silent cell—shut out from all life save what remained of darkest passions in her own breast—Emma Vaughan had time to reflect on the miscarriage of her plans, or to repent her of her intended murder, as she would. Repent? No; this was not one of her characteristics. By conduct and organization alike she was destitute of the instinct; and moreover she had convinced herself so firmly that she had been more sinned against than sinning—that she had done no moral wrong in the beginning, seeing that she had rejected no tenderness of mercy and cast aside no pleading of charity—that she felt nothing of the necessity of repentance. Why should she be sorry for the evil that others had done to her? Rather, she thought, should those others feel remorse for that evil, not she for the natural consequences of it in her own deep degradation.

That she had failed in her designs against Vaughan was a subject of bitterest regret only—not of sorrow. He was so deserving of death! Had he been a deadly reptile crawling through the world of men, she would have had as little compunction in ending his life. He was her evil genius; he was the embodiment of all that was painful and sinful in her life—the concrete crime of her career—and that he should die by her hand was only retributive justice of the most evident kind. He had destroyed her virtue, her social position, her child—and, if her frightful fears were true, her soul—and yet he lived in the sunny places of society, free, loved, and honoured, while she groaned here in the narrow silent cell. Speak of the even-handed balance ye who may—to her the scales had been falsely hung.

And then the dead silence grew alive with horrid shapes and forms; and frightful voices broke out, sounding like a sea of hideous mockeries and scorn; and scenes of her past life started from the sleep of memory, and stood like coloured pictures before her, till her brain reeled with the terrible tumult, and fever leapt up in her veins and licked her blood into its flame.

And oaths that she had heard, and horrible words that she had used, and religious denunciations, and atheistic scoffings, all broke forth into audible sound, which her hands, pressed hard on her ears, could not banish. She shrieked aloud for pain and terror. She flung herself on the pallet, and covered her eyes, and stopped her ears. But the sounds still went on in the same terrible distinctness and volume. Her senses were no inlets to her brain to-day; material organs neither supplied nor restrained this frightful faculty of mental reproduction.

And then she remembered Clare—that blue-eyed modest maid; and pictured her again and again, as she stood in her shabby dress and close-drawn bonnet, looking down on her—unhappy one! as she cowered in such a sullen heap together. And again and again she heard the sweet voice, with its child-like accent, offering her a home—though she herself was so poor and friendless—and though the acceptance of that offer would have been her ruin.

But this moonlight image of gentleness was soon blurred out by others glaring up before her blood-red. Memories of orgies wherein she had led the van in more than devilish debauchery—memories of crimes acted and of crimes desired—memories of moments wherein she had *endeavoured* to debase herself, and had repressed, as if it had been a sin, any haunting impulse unto good—all these broke out like flashes from the furnace-fires of hell; and Clare's gentle eyes faded in their baleful light as the stars fade in the flames of a city's ruin.

This terrible state was broken in upon by the chaplain coming his daily rounds, and halting at her cell for the routine of his office: the dull, unknowing, heartless routine of condemnatory words said parrot-like, without one thought of the causes of crime.

Much as Emma hated the clergy, it was a positive relief to hear the sound of a human voice, and to see a living face break through the spectral ranks of thought that surrounded her. But she was too proud to show any feeling of satisfaction. If she died by her silence she would keep her own heart ever inward—and all that the gaol chaplain saw was a desperate determined face looming darkly from the prison cap, like a fiendish mask to which magic had given life.

He spoke of repentance and of salvation: and she bade him fiercely keep silence; "she understood all about that as well as he could tell her, and perhaps a great deal better."

He took a loftier tone, and dilated on her exceeding sinfulness of life, and on the reparation that she owed to society, not to speak of the repentance that she owed before GOD. And then she turned on him like a wild beast stung to the quick, and cursed him for a pedant, ignorant of the very trade he assumed to have mastered and to teach.

"Do you think," she said savagely, "that it's only those who do wrong by law that are guilty? Are you such a fool as to take legal acts by themselves? I am no teacher—but I know from my own life, and from the lives of my mates, that the real guilt lies often far off the deed, and farther still off the legal criminal."

"I do not come here to argue," answered the clergyman; "I come to instruct. If you think yourself so far advanced as to find it necessary to cavil at all I say, our business with each other is but short."

"Instruct!" she laughed, "you instruct me! Why man I know more of real life, and of human nature as it is, than all your readings and theories could teach you in a thousand years of learning. If you want to know your trade, go about among the people where I have come from, as an equal—but don't expect to convert them, as you call it, when you don't know one requisite of their lives or one peculiarity of their natures."

"You are disrespectful," said the clergyman with displeasure. "If you hold such language to me I must report you for punishment."

"Fool—beast—idiot—out of my sight! Go preach to softer heads than mine—tell things half-witted like yourself, what false lies you want them to believe—but don't attempt to hollow out a rod with clouds and vapours that fear the very name of truth. Out of my sight!—you poison the air even of a prison!"

And ever after this first interview she refused all other intercourse with him, and sat sulking silent when he entered, or cursed him so vehemently that he was obliged to leave—threatening to have his life there and then if he did not let her be in peace. The offence-table of poor Emma Vaughan soon comprised every allowable species of prison punishment for her unmeasured abuse of the prison parson, as she called him. The punishments did her no good—they simply hardened her still more; casting into moulds of deformity which man might never break the rock of marble which might have been so gloriously chiselled. What was wanting to her now, was a teacher to show her the TRUTH, and to bind her to repentance by love. Dogmatism had failed; strict morality with all its virtuous abhorrence had failed; punishments in the present failed, denunciations of punishments to come also failed—indeed these last had roused her courage rather than her fears; hardening, not breaking her strong nature; making her feel proud of her steadfastness, not penitent for her sins. A resolute sinner she had lived and would die—what cared she for a world which had discarded her, or for a heaven that already had prejudged?

And hours passed on in this narrow silent cell, with but one long train of horrors for its wretched inhabitant of vice and misery. Work she had none, and only the light of the passing day. Though this was not so bad as it would have been in the winter, when prison populations spend two thirds of their time in idleness and darkness—for what purposes of reform or wisdom none can tell but the upholders of the model theory.

She had a few books in her cell. The Bible, and one or two religious tracts published by the Christian Knowledge Society, of inflammatory character and unstable theories, comprised the whole library allowed her. She read the tracts, then tore them up as drivelling lies, and flung the fragments in the face of the matron when she was reproved. And she hurled the Bible through her opened door on the first opportunity. She preferred the fang of memory, she said, to any falsehoods that could blunt it. At any rate she would keep to truth. But she had a long term of punishment for her violence. She was put down into the "strong cell," or black-hole, as it is sometimes called, and fed on bread and water. And when she was brought up again, they thought she might be tamed; but her insubordination was more fierce, and her whole conduct more violent than ever; and the governor's harshest threats only made her flout his authority to his face.

"She is a perfect savage," he said when he left her.

"An irreclaimable demon," added the clergyman.

The deputy-governor—a sharp military man—advised various kinds of punishment unsuited to a gaol; and the matron declared solemnly that she was afraid for her life. Only the doctor kept silent, and when appealed to recommended strict medical attendance mixed with great kindness. But doctors who know their profession, and act up to it, are ridiculed as pedants or shunned as atheists. Medicine and physiological treatment for moral crimes!—who but a Materialist would dare to recommend them? And the gaol doctor was reprimanded by the gaol chaplain, and spoken to severely by an evangelical visiting justice. He held his peace, for he was not a self-martyrizing man; but he kept to his opinion for all that; and told his wife in a whisper, that calomel would do her more good than cant, and that antiphlogistics might reform her sooner than church services.[115]

Emma fell sick after some time; but she concealed it from the matron, though the doctor discovered it. Yet when he questioned her, she swore savagely that she was well and didn't want his help; and she broke his bottles before his eyes, and trampled on his powders as soon as they were brought, and would not accept anything that would make her happier or healthier. She wished to die; and though the way of her death was by torture worse than an hour's term of sharpest agony, she would die game to the last—she would never yield! Too mad now to care for relief, she managed to evade the infirmary; and then her hideous solitude was peopled thicker and thicker with visions that eat like a canker into her brain. An old she-wolf was she— dying in her lair unpitied, unvisited, yet steadfast to the end—seeking neither sympathy nor aid from earth or heaven.

She asked for no work—she sought no communion. When they came she was utterly dumb, though so crazed with the silence and the loneliness that the chirp of a hedge-sparrow had been as the voice of a god. Yet she defied them all—punishments, terrors, texts, exhortations—she would have none of them. Had her breast been of granite and her temples of cast iron, she could not have been more resolute than she was now, as a lonely, diseased, mad, dying woman, defying dissolution itself to weaken her mighty will.

At last the silence grew so oppressive she scarcely dared to listen to her own breathing. This loneliness was so terrible, she was afraid to think of herself as of a human being. She dared not look round; often in the twilight she dared not raise her eyes, but pressed them down with her iron hands, and yet could not shut out the consciousness that something not palpable but still living was standing by her. And if an accidental voice was heard, this strong fierce woman started, and shrieked like a helpless child.

Faces pressed up against her; leering and mocking eyes stared into hers, till the glaring balls touched her very lashes. Skinny fingers clutched her throat, and tore down her streaming hair, and played round her heart like death-worms writhing there. Ha! no longer alone!—no longer silent!—no longer the solitary prisoner was she! Thronging thick as summer bees, rushed out that long train of phantom faces—sounding loud as a cataract falling, broke out those hoarse voices. She was no longer alone in very truth—for her company was the demon train of madness.

Shriek upon shriek burst forth. Cries and oaths, and sometimes tender wailings for the dead, startled the warders of the gallery. And when they entered, they found her with her head covered up in her coarse prison dress; a hopeless maniac, whose last likeness with humanity was ground out of her soul, that a theory might be upheld.

The solitary system had made another victim to the perfection of its forms: and this unhappy creature, who might have been brought out into such a divine power of womanhood had her early education led her upward and not thrust her down—whose first beginnings of vice might afterwards have been arrested had any cared to so arrest them—and who now might have been reclaimed, perhaps, had prison discipline been reformatory and not simply punitive—practical and not theoretical—now lay for ever unredeemed in her hardness and iniquities—a mere meeting-point of brute forces without any hope of after spiritualization. And her soul, sadly stained as it was, had a larger claim on mercy than on vengeance, from the lethargy of a morality which might have reclaimed her but forbore, and from the injustice of a system of punishment which had not one rational element throughout its whole character.

"One man of the present day might have saved her," said Percival after Clara had been to see the poor maniac in her cell; with a hope, though but a faint one, that her presence and her voice might enkindle some spark of memory, and lighten up the brute mass which, alas! was all that she was left now.

"Who is that?" asked Clare, "yourself?"

"No, my child, not myself. A man whom I met with some years ago, and whom I have known intimately since—a man who to me has not his equal living—the best and truest specimen of Christianity that I have ever seen—that great and good reformer, Captain Maconochie."[116]

"I have heard you speak of him before," she said. "And would he have saved Emma from madness, do you think?"

"Yes; I do think so."

"How?"

"By his manly nobleness—his temperate severity—his Christian kindness—his knowledge of the human heart—and his adoption of means that must, by fixed laws, affect the individual. Were prisons to be managed on his system we should have fewer commitments and more reformations than our model theories or old abuses have given us under the most favourable conditions of trial."

"And what is his system?"

"The substitution of labour for time."

"How? I do not understand you. But I am so stupid!"

"He would make criminals perform a certain amount of labour, instead of remaining in prison a certain length of time: giving thus to each man the power of shortening or of lengthening his term of imprisonment by the exercise of industry and self-denial. I cannot go into the whole of his system with you now; but its distinctive feature and main element is simply a labour instead of a time sentence, as affording opportunities for improvement and self-culture, which present systems do not give now."

"And is it not adopted, Percival?"

"No, dear; nowhere."

"Why not?"

He shrugged his shoulders.

"Who can tell?" he answered. "Party prejudice— misrepresentations—unfriendly tongues busy at slander—all these are good and cogent reasons why great reforms are not tried during the lifetime of the reformer. A man must die before he is canonized—in social politics as well as in religion."

"Poor Emma!" ejaculated Clara.

"Ah, Clara! we have a great work before us!" cried Percival. "We have but one thing to look to now—and that is justice."

She looked up into his face, and came nearer to him—as was her way when much interested.

"The poor and the criminal, Clara, claim their rights now as the burgher class in the days of noble tyranny claimed and won theirs, and as the maniac class in our own days have gained theirs. The proud noble scorned the working citizen. His blood ran in another stream— his life was hewn from another block. The pure marble of aristocracy disdained all brotherhood with the coarse granite that shaped out the plebeian type. Yet by moral strength the burghers won their place, and by moral strength they have surpassed their ancient masters. The middle class of England is now her true aristocracy, and in turn the tyrants of the third estate."[117]

"But with the charter, Percival?"

"The people will gain such a footing as will enable them in their turn to compete with the wealth and influence that crushes them to the ground now. Once fitly represented—once heard in the legislature by right, and not by pity—once forming part of the legislative economy—and the third estate may doff its cap to none; it will then have a fair field before it, wherein it may win all that it deserves."

"And will this ever be, Percival?"

"I believe so. A spirit has gone abroad among the people which it will not be very easy to suppress. A feeling of wrong and of oppression has been excited, which will take more wit than any living statesman possesses to sneer down into nullity. The people know that they are not represented—they know that, though they are the back-bone of the empire—its sinews and its very life—they are held of no value in its councils, excepting in the minds of some half dozen philanthropists whose organs of benevolence are somewhat elevated."

"It seems all very dreadful!" cried Clara.

"So it is, my child! The poor and the criminal, I say again, are struggling for their rights—and will have them. As for the criminal— the morally diseased—the maniac to virtue—we shall find after a time that brutal punishment is not the means of moral reformation, and that changes as large and as wise as those which have been made in our lunatic asylums must now be wrought in our prisons, if we would do any real good among the guilty."

"Oh, Percival! I wish that all men thought as you do!" exclaimed

Clara with fervour. "How different you are to other people! Why do not others think with you?"

He smiled—a very sweet and pleasant smile—and then he answered gently: "I believe that the real reason lies in the bigotries and prejudices of mankind. People have thrust their minds into a mould, or mask; and therefore their ideas cannot expand. We all believe, of course, that our own peculiar way is the best, so I am not singular in believing that if all men would be free they would be also as I am in matters of opinion. I cannot get at any other results than those I have already arrived at, by an independent process of reasoning. By one based on foregone conclusions of course I could—but with perfect liberty of thought I see no other end."

She rose to go: for she had been at his house all this time. She had gone to him immediately after she had seen Emma; her pretty eyes still wet with the tears of mingled terror and pity which the dark fierce madwoman had made her shed. Yet more of pity; for she had had a strange influence in that padded cell, where even the keepers durst not venture without precautions. The wild scream had been hushed, the wild laugh had died away, the blasphemous oath had checked itself on the lip, and the glaring eye had become dulled and subdued. Mad as yon woman was, one little portion was untouched; and Clara, like some sweet fairy in the desert, took off the curse while she rested there in that waste of ruined intellect.

Percival was now Clare's life. He was what a father would have been—what a brother or a mother. He was the centre of her existence—the prop and stay of her faltering steps. How she loved him! Not specially, not consciously—but deep in her young heart fervently—a pure, inexhaustible, life-fulfilling love, that was as unlike the feverish passion given to Vaughan as the star of the morning is unlike the noonday lightning.

"May I go to see her again?" she asked as she took her leave; speaking with a child-like accent of trust.

"*May* you, Clare?—may you not do what you like with me, and for me?"

"Not always," she laughed.

"No?—and when are you checked?"

She blushed and looked down; then raised her eyes again; and then laughed in a constrained fashion enough.

"Oh!" she said, "when I wish to do wrong you will not allow me. That is all."

"Well—wait until you do wish to do wrong before you doubt my ready acquiescence in all your desires."

And Clare remembered the time when Vaughan had said those very same words to her. As she walked home she thought of the strange difference there was between Percival and Vasty, and wondered wherein that difference consisted, and why she felt so safe with Percival—why she had always felt so timid with Vaughan.

And then she began to reflect on all that Percival had said to her to-day on the condition of the people, and on the rights of the criminal. And she reasoned and reasoned—in a circle truly—till she reasoned herself into the positive conviction that Percival Glynn, and no other, was the coming man of present superstition.[118] Oh how great he was!—how good!—how true!

"How I wish he had been my brother!" she thought, when she sat down in her shabby parlour and wrote out the heads of her late conversation—embodying them in an essay, of which form of composition she was very fond.

Percival once found this essay. It bore a rough but capital likeness of himself, traced right in among the lines—and on one side a piece of poetry—of no small merit—addressed "To my own Friend" and containing lines which set forth that she, the writer, did not "love" the said friend, but that she "thought of him day and night," and believed him to be the most "perfect type of noble manhood," save some sundry antediluvian heroes of historic fame. How they both laughed the day on which this memorable essay was found!—and how Glynn made her repeat it to him till she was tired of her own voice, and he was tired of thanking her in his own peculiar fashion!

Ah! when that piece of paper was found they were both very happy—very, very happy—rather different to the anxious man who watched her now so carefully, and to the pale wasted girl whose whole face was one of suffering and sickness. And they deserved their happiness; for it was based on virtue and experience—on self-control and on clear insight—on true love, as love ought to be rendered unto men.

CHAPTER IX.

EDWARD MANTELL was received at the hall, when he returned to Shorne, with a cordiality really wonderful from people so undemonstrative as the De Saumarez family. Even Mr. de Saumarez left his important treatise on the laws of moral sympathy—which he was rewriting for the last time—having been obliged to remodel it *ab initio*[119] in consequence of some new discoveries in electro-biology, and a new mesmeric theory. And it was a proof of no common interest when he could lay aside those small scratched scraps, whereon was traced what he fondly believed would upset every foregone belief the world had ever held; more especially when it was to welcome a young clergyman who was, *ex-officio*, a natural enemy—a man he was to demolish as speedily as possible.

"You have been long a stranger to our quiet country place," said Mrs. de Saumarez with a courtly smile: for Edward's fortune, birth, and "correct views," had long gained him a most favourable verdict from that lady's judgment. "Have you found London so very fascinating? I am afraid we shall appear but small in our humble village after your great doings there; unenlightened and lagging."

"It was not the fascination of London that kept me," answered Edward; "but my duty. I had the temporary charge of one of the most populous and ill-conducted districts in the metropolis, where I laboured with more love than hope."

"Beyond your strength, I fear? You are pale and thin, and look wearied in mind."

"It was a trying cure," he said, evasively. "I had a population composed of the worst characters in London; and it was no easy matter to make an impression on minds so brutalized by vice as theirs."

"I pity you! I, in my small way, know the mental condition of the poor; and I sympathize with any one who has to work among them for their good. So ignorant and unimpressionable—so ungrateful too as they are! The best of our voluntary gifts they accept as their right, and neglect the most precious opportunities of improvement offered to them."

Mrs. de Saumarez spoke almost warmly, for she had been made rather sore of late on the subject of gifts and privileges. The case was this. On the estate was a large plot of waste land which grew only bulrushes and king-cups,[120] and was of no use to the tenants, and of no profit to the landholder. This piece of ground Mrs. de Saumarez had persuaded her husband to let out in garden allotments, at so much per acre. The tenants were to drain and prepare the land, without any help beyond permission to build a brick-kiln for making draining tiles; and the rent was to be at the rate of four pounds an acre.

"For," reasoned Mrs. de Saumarez, "if it is let to them at a high rate, they will be obliged to farm well; and so, industry and foresight and prudence will be forced on them, if they wish to make a profit of their land."

I dare say this was a wise theory; but the cotters unfortunately did not see its beauty; and only a very few of the allotments were taken—and these mainly by rich farmers who wished to please the landlord, and could afford to lose the rent. This was one instance of the ingratitude of the poor.

The other was the Mechanics' Institute.

Shorne was a quiet, secluded, behind-the-day kind of place. It stood back from any great road, in a corner by itself like Golden Square.[121] It led nowhere, and meant nothing; and might have been wiped out of the map and no one in the great thoroughfares of England would have missed it. There would have been a branch mail coach the less; and that would have been all. And being this primitive place it is easy to imagine what the people were like. A rough, uncultivated, honest, ignorant set, in whom time made the only distinction of birth and death. They were in a manner mentally stereotyped after the fashion of the Tony Lumpkins and Hodges of our rustic superstitions;[122] and nothing changed them. A few of the tallest youths might go off as 'listers in the army; but for the most part the sons followed in the steps of their fathers; and constant imitation had made such deep ruts in their clodded minds that Mrs. de Saumarez' æsthetic ploughs and harrows were useless. She formed schools, and the little urchins stole away birds'-nesting and fox-following. She opened a Mechanics' Institute, and her lecturers spoke to empty benches; for the whole village was inside the travelling caravan, or on the green with the itinerant juggler. She bought an orrery,[123] and the men, after a few minutes' gaping, lounged off to the cricket-ground. She offered prizes for literary composition and mechanical inventions, but a fair was held a few miles off on the day of the award, and half her tenants were losing their money on the race-course, or trying their luck at the thimble-rig[124] table. She could do nothing with them. The Mechanics' Institute gradually got the look of a premature ruin, and the books and the maps mildewed on the walls. The Shorneites were not up to concert pitch yet, and their intellectual patroness complained bitterly of the want of co-operation.

It was from these two failures, therefore, that Mrs. de Saumarez spoke so warmly of the poor and their stupidity; and it really was very provoking to an æsthetic lady to be thus thwarted by the coarse propensities of willful human nature. But so it was, and so it ever will be while people attempt to sow rare seeds in undressed grounds, and expect a flourishing crop of exotics before they have taken the trouble to break one clod or remove one stone.

"And did you go into those dreadful places?" asked Alice with evident interest.

"Yes," he said kindly; "I passed through some awful scenes! Ill as I believed of humanity left to itself without the incessant culture of spiritual religion, I own I was not prepared for the revelations of the London bye-streets, and their doomed population."

"It will have a serious end!" Mr. de Saumarez said. "If strong measures are not soon taken, these dangerous classes will break out against all established authority, and we shall have an English Jacquerie[125] of a worse description."

Mr. de Saumarez, it must be remarked, was theoretically a strong Tory—a divine-right-of-kings man, and a believer in the virtue of coercion above all other modes of government. "He, for his part," he would say, "would rather bring back the pillory and the stocks, and leave all these new-fangled ideas to such scoundrels as the French or the republican Italians. A little wholesome severity was the best way of managing the poor! What else could they understand? Depend upon it," he would add, "England was never so happy as when her labouring classes were kept in their proper places, and before such pestilent notions as equality and education got abroad."

Which theories, doubtless perfect though they were, nevertheless were not destined to be acted on; for Mrs. de Saumarez had the moral management of the estate, and her husband's energy expended itself in fragmentary diatribes when occasion offered, and in the scientific pursuits of his laboratory. He was far too learned to be practical.

"I am opposed to the March of Intellect as it is called," said Edward; "but the force of the age is too strong for us. This is the spirit which demagogues and factious politicians have evoked, and now we must do our best to guide it. The time of laying it has passed."

"I am afraid Mr. Mantell will not approve of all my plans for the improvement of our people," Mrs. de Saumarez observed with a gash-like smile, turning to her daughter.

"I do not know, mamma," that young lady replied; "you have mingled religion with them all."

"If so, dear Madam, they must be good," said Edward fervently. "All that is wanting to the whole human race is the knowledge of the truths of the Christian Religion: the only book—indeed the complete library of every peasant—is the Bible. Teach the poor to read this—teach them to study it night and day, to understand its divine precepts, to draw consolation from its wonderful promises—and you have given them the marrow of learning. All else is dry bone. As I said before, the march of intellect has begun, and we cannot stop it; we can only point out the way, and lend our strength in directing it through the portals of the Bible—leaving the issue in the hands of Him whose Church must prevail!"

Edward's fervour—shown in his very stillness of attitude, his very pallor, and his concentration of warmth to the heart inward—charmed Mrs. de Saumarez and subdued Alice. Until now the lady had connected enthusiasm with boisterous warmth—like Clara's early outbursts; she had not been accustomed to this gentle manner of intense conviction, which shocked no sense and took captive every feeling. It broke over her like a spell to which she *must* yield an assent.

"I shall be pleased," she said, "if what I have done meets with your approval. I have had many arguments with Mr. Tiffin, our vicar, but he is so old and so little enlightened—so wedded to the undesirable systems of the past—that I pay his opinion less respect than perhaps his office demands."

"The Church has a sacred office," said Edward drily.

"But its members unequal gifts, my dear Sir," she answered.

"That may be; yet to the most sparingly gifted in worldly or intellectual goods belongs the robe of sanctity, from the first hour of his ordination; a robe that, if it falls not to his feet, yet covers up his head. And to that must all pay respect who stand without the altar-rail."

"And you allow nothing to individual judgment?—nothing to the conscious superiority of mind?"

"Against the decree of constituted authorities? No! The Church alone has power of rule in the land—the Church alone holds the keys of heaven, and binds laws on men's consciences. If you once permit private interpretation, where do you stop?—at unitarianism and dissent!"

"But is not this the High Church doctrine, Mr. Mantell—and are not you what is called Low Church?"

"I am neither, dear Madam. I am simply a Christian clergyman, obeying as far as I may the laws of the religion I serve, and carrying out the institutions of my church. But I hold no divine grace in the forms of the Puseyite,[126] and I do not despise the power of authority with the Low-churchman. To me Religion means the possession of the Spirit—the walking with GOD in faith and prayer—the regeneration of the soul in the baptism of repentance—the strict separation of the saints and the castaways. If you can find any other code than this in the gospels and the epistles (which last contain our more immediate directions—the first rather by implication and an exemplar to which we cannot attain), I will cordially follow you. But to keep this religion pure and dogmatically correct, we must have a visible authority—a visible source of rule; and that we find in the Church and its appointed ministers."

"I am not quite of your opinion," answered Mrs. de Saumarez, in her cold determined manner, but very ladylike withal. "The human mind has its own power of authority—I mean of course such minds as have educated themselves, and fathomed, by their own reflections, the tremendous depths of truth."

"So think the Socinians,"[127] said Edward quietly.

"But they are painfully mistaken!—they have no authority in the Bible. Nothing can be more imperfect than Socinianism carried to its farthest development."

Edward looked relieved, and Alice puzzled. For in truth most of Mrs. de Saumarez' opinions started from the same basis with Socinianism and all other forms of dissent—namely, her cherished faith in the individual authority of the mind, provided it were well educated and "correct;" provided, in short, it went as far as she did, and no farther, and sympathized alike in her disagreements with the Church and in her disapprobation of dissenters. Mrs. de Saumarez wished to be what so many of the more intellectual classes attempt—a lamp not only to her own feet but to the human race generally. She was not content to hold her own ideas of truth, but every one else must hold the same; and all who passed her were "undesirable and untrue," and all who lagged behind her were "imperfect." Never was there a more complete example of the tyranny of independent judgment than she displayed in her censures and her lauds. And this it was which gave her so much the air of inconsistency in a long continuance of argument; for it was difficult to discover when she really approved, or why she sometimes dissented. Once hold the key—once understand that she was not only her own guide but assumed to be also the model of all mankind—and then her heart was an opened book, and you might turn the pages at pleasure.

Edward Mantell saw this, and decided on her conversion to the humility suited to a daughter of the Church. By degrees he acquired so much influence over her as to make her patient and attentive; and then he said that the divine influence was manifesting itself in her. But a shrewd observer would perhaps, had he been profanely inclined, have defined it as the struggle for supremacy between two minds equally fond of control, and the final submission of the weaker to the mysterious power of manhood.

Alice used to be present at these conferences; and they made a deep impression on her. Hitherto she had lived in an atmosphere of mental calmness, so undisturbed by passion or unartistic emotion that she believed all must be right within. The chief lesson that Mrs. de Saumarez taught her, repeated under various forms and on every occasion, was the virtue of serenity. In this consisted her summary of all the virtues—the apex of the pyramid. No matter that it was the result of physical organization, no matter that it was the product of haughtiness and self-conceit—Mrs. de Saumarez, metaphysical as she was, did not stop to inquire the remote cause; the present effect was all she asked for. By the blessing of a temperament three parts lymphatic, this serenity of manner and of thought was the natural characteristic of Alice, as it had been of the mother; and to this, education could only add a few dogmas and a few lady-like pursuits which the uninitiated find tame and dry, but which the hierophants of this school of calmness feed on as divine food.

All was changed now. Alice learnt, under Edward Mantell's teaching, to look on this state of mind as one eminently sinful and hazardous. She had not received the true awakening spirit; he assured her of this, and she believed him. Her religion, he told her, had been cold and lifeless. She needed more strength of faith, more fervour of prayer, more consciousness of sin. And as he enlarged on this, insisting with the fervour of an apostle on the innate depravity of the human heart, and the doomed condition of a soul unawakened to a knowledge of this depravity, the young girl trembled at the frightful abyss suddenly opened before her.

And by prayers and frequent studyings of the Bible and its orthodox commentators—by intellectual inflammation generally—Alice believed she was obtaining admission into the band of the elect, and making her future salvation sure. But no warmth of love, no pity, no forgiveness, no wider word of charity, no casting down of pride, no imitation of the example of Christ, was the result of her increase of religious fervour. A little spiritualism, a few intellectual assents, a round of disagreeable actions—and that was all. The seal of grace was given, and her soul was now destined to the company of the elect.

And this is the sum and substance of a religion which lays such stress on these mere intellectual assents as to deny all power of good without their influence—making a life of active virtues of no account if not coupled with a belief which the mind by its very constitution may reject.

On Edward also, this calm still life wherein the awakening of those two slumbering souls was his only work, had no little influence. When he contrasted the docility of this gentle girl with the unmanageable independence of Clare—when he marked how this young mind bent itself under his hand, and took what shape he gave, and then remembered the wayward will which *appeared* only to yield and soon sprang back still stronger than before from the very seeming of subjection—he felt that wheresoever the palm of loveliness and the meed of love might be bestowed, in Alice was the richest casket of feminine virtues, the strongest hold of submission and obedience.

And oh, ye independent women, remember how many Edward Mantells there are in the world! Remember that the majority of men make submission and virtue their feminine synonymes, and endorse that woman alone as loveable who takes such hue as they bestow, and speaks such words as they indite. Nay; an independent life they may forgive; some may be even found to admire the strength and energy which help her through so bravely; but an independent thought unsexes her; and love shuddering weeps, and spreads his wings, if opinions be retained, intellectual admiration continued, an author read, or faith upheld, contrary to masculine authority. And this notwithstanding her most passionate love which, though it lead her to the docility of love in act, yet cannot constrain her intellect any more than whips and chains. Simply because the reason is beyond the power of the will, and large brains are not wholly the slaves of passion. Yet for all this love—for all this great heart and greater mind—she must be rejected, reviled, undone, because she cannot intellectually obey.

From this superstition Edward Mantell was by no means free. He had not kept pace with the age in the higher appreciation slowly granted to women, any more than in the necessity of a liberal scale of education to the poor. To him the *tacens et placens uxor*[128] was his matrimonial ideal; the independent thinker his dreaded bane. And nothing but Clare's marvellous beauty, and the mesmeric influence of her affectionate nature, could have ever made him love an individual of the hostile ranks. But sometimes he asked himself now, "If it had not all been for the best? and if it was not a wise ordination, evident in its wisdom?" And he always answered "Yes," if he had been much with Alice de Saumarez. It seemed impossible that Clare and Alice should live in the same heart. Even to the peasants, no one person liked them both; and the very dogs which had loved Clare snapped and snarled if the new heiress came within the length of their chain. They were so wholly antagonistic—there was so wide a gulf between them—that no one love could overshadow them—no one heart was large enough to contain both.

It was fine weather; and the lives of Mrs. and Miss de Saumarez were regular; and Alice was young; but for some unknown cause she lost her colour: not so much the rosy cheek of robust health, for that she never possessed, but the clear complexion which is quite as indicative of health in a weaker frame. Her eyes had a deep purple line round them; the orbit was more or less discoloured; she grew thin, and failed in appetite; and altogether showed evident signs of loss of health.

Mrs. de Saumarez anticipated consumption; but Alice rejected the idea, and tried to make light of her appearance. "She felt nothing," she said.

Edward Mantell noticed it too, and spoke of it one day.

"Are you ill, Miss de Saumarez?" he said gently. "You have grown pale and languid lately. What is the reason of it? Do you read too much at night?"

"No," answered Alice, with a slight smile. "I am not ill, and I do not read much at night."

"*Much?* It is a bad habit to cherish in ever so mitigated a form. You ought to give it up."

"I do not think it hurts me," said Alice rather coldly.

"But you are not well—your countenance bespeaks your delicacy. Do you require change of air and scene, think you? the sea breezes, or a milder climate—which?"

"Neither," she answered laconically.

"You will think me impertinent if I press the subject further," returned Edward; "but you must allow me to say how grieved I am at your altered looks, and how much I wish you would try change of air."

"Thank you for your interest in me"—and Alice smiled a strange smile, not all of pleasure nor all of satire, yet both were there—"but do you wish me to leave Shorne so very much?" and again she smiled.

"Wish you to leave? Dear Miss de Saumarez, how can you ask me such a question! Why should I wish you and your mamma to leave? Would it not derange all my plans, and undo a great portion of the work begun? If you left, who would manage the school, or take your districts?"

Alice, whose face had betrayed some simplicity of pleasure at the commencement of this speech, looked blank and hurt. Though very religious, she had not quite attained to this point of self-abnegation. She would rather that Edward had spoken of his own loss—not of hindrance to the works they had undertaken together.

"The school and district could be managed by some one perhaps more competent than myself," she answered, with a scarcely perceptible shade of petulance in her voice; "and then," she added, turning a sickly smile on him, "then you would have gained by the exchange."

Not exactly understanding what, Edward Mantell knew quite well that something was wrong with his young friend. Her colour had mounted to a small but definite spot of red on each cheek, and her eyes were darker than usual—the pupil dilating, though not much.

"I should gain by your recovered health," he said very kindly; "in no other way."

"Well, let it pass," answered Alice rising, for she had been sitting near the open window while they spoke. "I believe there is no present intention of our leaving Shorne, nor do I wish it in the least degree. I am quite content to remain at home, and even to suffer, if it be the will of GOD to send me suffering."

Edward's answer was checked by the entrance of Mrs. de Saumarez, who had been engaged in her own room, drawing out what she was pleased to call her "winter syllabus"—otherwise, the heads of sundry lectures to be given in the Mechanics' Institute.

"Have they your approval, Mr. Mantell?" was her first question, handing him the paper.

"'Popular geology,'" said Edward, reading. "Yes—if made an exposition of the truth of the Mosaic account. This can do no harm; but on the contrary, if strictly dependent on and illustrative of that sublime account, may lead to higher things. 'The History of Music.' Pardon me, my dear Madam, if I object to this—decidedly object. Music, as a science and an amusement is unfit for the poor. It is an idle taste, which leads to worse than idleness in its practice, and totally beyond their range in its theory or history. If you like to substitute a description of the sacred instruments of the Jews, it will not be so pernicious—though even then I cannot see much moral good in it. What the poor want most, is enlivened faith, not social acquirements or scientific knowledge. However, give them the history of the Temple of Jerusalem, and an account of the sacred musical instruments, if you choose; and if coupled with a few forcible remarks on the poverty of our churches, and the coldness of our love to GOD compared with the fervour of the Israelites, some Christian doctrines might be educed, and some practical good attained."

"I see yours is an eminently practical mind," said Mrs. de Saumarez, submitting with wonderful outward patience to these emendations of her young friend.

"Practical to that one end, my dear Madam, for which I believe we were designed, and which alone constitutes the glory of humanity. Else, I am by nature inclined to metaphysical subtleties and philosophical abstraction. But faith has made me practical."

"Will you read the remainder of the lectures?"

"'Great reformers.' Good—for of course you mean great *Protestant* reformers. 'Scientific inventors'"—he paused. "Dangerous ground, Mrs. de Saumarez!"

"Dangerous ground?—no! In what way? Are not the inventions of the present day its characteristic?—are they not the true revolutionizers of the time? They are facts which have worked social miracles—they are facts which have given our age a name distinct from all preceding ages. I think you must leave me the lives and inventions of scientific discoverers."

"No, I cannot—they are too generally infidel or unorthodox. Did they work for the furtherance of the truth?—did they give the glory of their discoveries to GOD?—did they acknowledge His inspiration in their minds leading them to such results?—No, none of these things! They blasphemed the power by which they wrought, in ascribing it to the natural progress of the mind, and they worked for men—and for the worldly advantage of a corrupt generation—and not for the furtherance of religious truth. No: the 'lives of scientific inventors' savours too much of that idolatry of intellect which is the ruin and the shame of the present day. That must not be upheld in the lecture-room of a Christian woman! We must erase this, if you please."

And Mrs. de Saumarez was obliged to see her intellectual syllabus thus torn piecemeal to fragments, and reduced to simple sermons.

With everything it was the same. Not an event, not a word, would Edward Mantell have allowed—could he have arranged all as he would—that had not a direct reference to religion. Mrs. de Saumarez thought to make the people intellectual: Edward cared only to make them pious. Mrs. de Saumarez, leaving out the earliest and humblest steps, did begin half-way in the building: Edward boldly raised his stones in the air, and thought to fashion a temple from the roof downwards. And neither of them succeeded, because both ignored the laws of human nature, and both formed their schemes of improvement from theories extraneous to the minds they sought to teach, and not by the natural order of progress.

When he handed back the paper, marked in pencil with his erasures and substitutions, it was headed—"A course of Christian Lectures, to be delivered in the Shorne Mechanics' Institute, from the first of November to the first of June inclusive, comprising the following subjects:—The Truth of the Geology of the Bible exemplified by modern discoveries. The History of Jewish Sacred Music, with a description of the Temple at Jerusalem. Great Reformers of the Church. The Translators of the Bible. The Compilers of the Prayer-book. The Life of a Missionary (Henry Martyn), &c. &c."

"I think you will find this more appropriate than your own," he said quietly, making no apology for his corrections.

"Thank you," answered Mrs. de Saumarez. "I will re-consider the subject."

"I hope not to the restoration of any of the lectures I have effaced," persisted Edward, in his calm determined way.

Mrs. de Saumarez, not too well pleased—for he had trenched on her most favourite province—was yet obliged to acknowledge his earnestness of purpose, and unable to repulse his encroachments while his manner was so gentle. She tried to smile, but the effort died on her lip; and when she would have answered haughtily, the clear eyes, with their hidden sorrow and their fervent zeal, their faith and their truth, destroyed that too; and she was fain to make what composition with her pride she might, and to accept his determination for her own.

This was only one of innumerable instances wherein Edward Mantell proved to himself, as well as to them, that he had acquired an undoubted and well-nigh unlimited influence over the minds of both mother and daughter. Well for them was it that he was so honest and practically so good, else they might have suffered from his power. As it was they suffered, in no mean manner, from the narrowness of his views and the sternness of his principles. What they both needed of mental reformation was the inculcation of more tenderness— more love and universal charity—not a still further drying up of the shrunken fount of their sympathies.

The paleness and meagerness of Alice continued, and at last the mother became seriously alarmed. She spoke first to her husband, who immediately proposed to administer his own medicines on the spot; but this she firmly refused, and a doctor was finally summoned. Not the Shorne doctor, but a learned man who lived a long way off, and charged by the mile.

"Any cough, young lady?"

"No."

"Pain in the chest—so?" and he pressed her chest just below the collar bones.

"No."

"Nor now?" and he laid two fingers on the same place and tapped them pretty hard.

"A little"—which was very natural.

"Difficulty of breathing?"

"Sometimes."

"When?"

Alice hesitated. She seemed to reflect, and then she blushed slightly, as she answered, in a cold voice; "When I have walked or run very quickly."

The doctor smiled.

"Appetite good?"

"Not very."

"Sleep well at night?"

"No."

"Nervous?"

"Yes."

"Hysterical?"

"Sometimes."

"Allow me to feel your pulse."

She gave him her long white hand, and he held the slender wrist.

"One—two—three—ten—twenty—Ah, I see! a weak pulse—jerky—tremulous. Allow me again, Madam."

And he repeated the process once more. A male figure passed the window—(they were in the breakfast parlour which looked on the terrace of approach)—and suddenly Alice's wrist burst into a torrent of pulsations, which made the doctor start and count his decimals at a rapid rate.

"Very nervous!—very nervous! Must have soothing medicine. Pray who was that visitor?"

"I saw no one," answered Mrs. de Saumarez. "Who was it, my dear?" to her daughter.

Alice raised a pair of cold blue eyes, and said, without a muscle changing; "It was Mr. Mantell, mamma."

When the doctor tried her wrist again after a short time it was as quiet as before, and even less tremulous and less "jerky;" as if a weight had been laid on her heart.

"Bless me, you are very nervous!" he repeated again; "very uncertain."

"But I have some self-command," said Alice quietly.

And she had. She could by a strong effort of will, still even the beating of her heart. I have known more people with that power.

The learned man then took his leave; and in due time his

prescription arrived, consolidated into a "bottle" which tasted of almonds and opium.

But though Alice swallowed this bottle, and another and another, very diligently—"a sixth part three times a day"—they had not the least effect on her. She wasted rather more perceptibly than before; and her eyes were bluer and larger, and the purple lines about them more distinct.

Mrs. de Saumarez was much distressed; for the only thing she really loved in the world was her daughter; and if she had lost her, I doubt if all her æsthetics, or her spiritual religion, or her boasted self-control, would have reconciled her to the loss, or have ever healed the wound.

It was decided they should go to London. In vain Alice pleaded rather warmly to be allowed to remain in peace at home; in vain she urged that she was getting much—very much better. The lady had spoken and it must be done. And to London they drove; posting all the way like real gentlefolk.

During the journey, Mrs. de Saumarez more than once fancied that she detected tears in her daughter's eyes. But if she did, they were so evanescent—so soon gone—that she never rightly knew if her suspicions were correct or no. Afterwards she used to think they were, and feel something annoyed that her child should have shown such weakness, and manifested so much approach to passion.

Poor Mrs. de Saumarez!—what a pity it is that facts will upset thy theories so rudely—and that even lymphatic human nature will assert a strength superior to thy notions of propriety.

CHAPTER X.

"MR. MANTELL!" cried Mrs. de Saumarez in some surprise, as that gentleman was ushered into their rooms at the private hotel where she and her daughter had put up.

Alice, who was lying on the sofa, reading through a pile of halfpenny tracts, looked up for the first instant in evident emotion. She cast down her eyes immediately however, and continued her reading; and no one knew that she had been disturbed from her intellectual and improving employment.

"Oh! Mr. Mantell," she said, in the tone of a person just aroused to the knowledge of a fact—when her mother called her attention to his presence. "How do you do? quite well?" and she rose from her reclining position with a studied elegance that struck Edward as exceedingly graceful.

Her face was paler than when he saw her last, and her form slighter; but though evidently suffering, she had lost nothing of the cold composure and serene self-control which she inherited. She was indeed an evidence of the power of the will, and the influence of mind over matter, at eighteen!

"What brought you from Shorne?" asked Mrs. de Saumarez. "I hope that nothing unpleasant has occurred in our absence? The school is flourishing, and the people orderly?—Mr. de Saumarez is well?"

This was all said interrogatively.

"There has been nothing unpleasant," replied Edward; "but I was called to London on sudden family business. And I was not sorry that it happened now; for I was lonely when you left," he added ingenuously.

At that moment Alice stooped.

"What is it Miss de Saumarez?" he asked. "Allow me to assist you!"

"Thank you, it is in my hand," she said, indicating her handkerchief; "I thought it had fallen."

"I fear you are very weak," said Edward gently, looking at her with much interest; "your face changes its colour so suddenly! Even with that slight exertion it was crimsoned, and now it is pale as death!"

"I am better," she answered quietly; but she cast down her eyes and looked somewhat embarrassed.

"I need scarcely ask if you have been very gay," the young clergyman then said, addressing Mrs. de Saumarez; "Miss de Saumarez does not look equal to much exertion."

"We have been to two sacred concerts—but to no other public place," she replied. "My daughter expressed so much fatigue, that I resolved on keeping quiet for the remainder of our stay."

"Will that be long?"

"No—not more than a fortnight longer—to give the physician sufficient time to study her case carefully. We shall then return with a more scientific regimen than we could obtain from a country physician. Already I think I see a perceptible advance."

"Thank heaven!" said Edward. "It has grieved me much to see Miss de Saumarez fade so like a flower! We must not suffer you to become a confirmed invalid," he added, speaking to Alice in his gentlest voice, for her delicacy interested him much, and her increasing weakness seemed to give him a sort of official right to that interest.

Mrs. de Saumarez opened her hard blue eyes rather wide at this speech. But Edward's manner was so entirely respectful, while in fact familiar, that she could not take offence. He was too right-minded and too well-bred to advance a step beyond the line, and she felt she might safely allow him to be interested in that important item of humanity—the heiress of the great De Saumarez family. He would never presume.

It was but natural, now that he had come to London, that Edward Mantell should often find his way to their rooms. The De Saumarez were solitary enough; and it was his duty to cheer them, as far as he could, with religious books and religious disquisitions. And of course he was always ready to do his duty—more especially when it came in such gentle shape as this. Once established as visiting chaplain not many hours in the day passed unaccompanied by Edward and his kindly attentions to the young invalid.

In all this there was no hypocrisy. Alice de Saumarez was evidently enough, to most eyes, in love with Edward Mantell, and his manners and words were calculated in their extreme kindliness to strengthen the feeling. But he was blameless—even if he never intended to marry her; for in honest sincerity he did not perceive her attachment, nor did it ever cross his mind as probable. She was interesting to him because of the spiritual good he was labouring to effect. She was young, and beautiful for her style of beauty; and this must have also had a strong though unacknowledged influence over him. But still he did not know of her love for him; and continued day after day in her society, lavishing on her every care consistent with his reserved character, without dreaming that he was heightening the disease he deplored, and adding to the debility he lamented.

Mrs. de Saumarez, long strangely blind, was now beginning to be aware of the state of her daughter's feelings. It did not escape her, that in Edward Mantell's presence, the painful weakness which had increased so much since their arrival in London, was changed for a freshness and vivacity that left her trebly prostrate when he was gone. She saw how she read his books and adopted his opinions; she saw how carefully she preserved the flowers he brought her, and would not have them removed—though once when she, Mrs. de Saumarez, asked coldly, "why they should not be destroyed?" Alice had flung them away without a murmur. She saw it all plainly now; the struggle of pride with love—the conflict of temperament with instinct; and she felt as if a heavy misfortune had befallen her, and one which she had unwittingly helped to create.

Yet, why should it be a misfortune? Edward was young, rich, and well-born, and of such right-thinking and desirable opinions! There was nothing so unequal in the union! Besides—are not all men equal, and is not the gift of mind, and the possession of correct views, a better dowry than title? Birth was much; even if unaccompanied by any distinctive name of honour it was a grand thing; and Edward Mantell had good blood in his veins; he had nice hands too, and clean-cut nostrils; and he was not a person to be ashamed of in any way, even without the recommendation of his very perfect views.

Mrs. de Saumarez reasoned thus till she consoled herself for this prefatial[129] failure of her hope, that Alice would marry into the aristocracy. And as the equality of such a nature as hers means exactly what it says—emphatically equality, neither condescension nor progress—she was not so far wrong in her recognition of her daughter's inclinations. Never imagining it possible that Edward could not be so deeply in love as her child.

But Edward made no sign. She treated him with maternal tenderness; she flattered his love of control by the most impressive submission to his opinion; she made him feel that he was all-important to her now, and that he stood in the dearest place that could be accorded to a friend; but it all fell like dew on the barren sand, and showed no evidence of germination.

She thought it was humility—but he spoke one day of a friend of his, in much the same social position with himself, who had married into one of our noblest families, as having made an "inauspicious union." And when Mrs. de Saumarez asked him "why?" with much and evident astonishment, he answered quietly; "She was not suited to him in mind, and he might have well looked for one of higher development."

Then if it was not humility, what could it be? It was not in the range of Mrs. de Saumarez's probabilities to dream that it was the want of love. I believe it would have almost annihilated her if she had thought that her child could by any probability have loved without return. Yet it puzzled even her clear vision, and she could not understand the aspect of affairs at all.

Mrs. de Saumarez patronised paintings more as an admirer than a connoisseur. Alice liked them too, but tepidly. Indeed of late it had been a mental question with her, whether representation was not something savouring of idolatry, and whether the Mahometans, frightfully in sin though they were, had not a better creed on such matters than ourselves. Perhaps the real reason of her coldness for art was her want of early education. She had not that warmth of temperament which makes it an instinct—as it was with the Greeks and Italians, and with a few individuals in colder climes, whose blood runs something clearer than the rest: and since her conversion to such stern simplicity of faith—such spiritualism of idea—as she now held, it was almost a virtue not to be able to appreciate the divinity of creative art. For did it not savour of the pomps and vanities which she had sworn to renounce?

Edward admired her for her simple judgment; and when he heard her reasonings, though they were crude and one-sided, he was too much gratified by the progress in the way of truth which they evidenced to be moved by their imperfectness.

To-day, however, they were to visit an exhibition of paintings, and Alice expressed an amazing degree of pleasure at the prospect. Edward Mantell was to accompany them.

They drove to the place, and entered. The room was not over crowded. There were just enough people in it to give it the air of a frequented exhibition, but not so many as to block up the best pieces, and offer you the choice between backs of individuals or glazed faces of pictures hung full in the glare of light, and undiscoverable as to their meaning by mortal eye.

Edward was a good judge of landscapes. Statuary and figure pieces he did not understand, and did not much value. And Mrs. de Saumarez agreed with him in this division of taste; looking narrowly after the heathenish pictures of Etty's school[130], as things to be specially avoided and indeed unacknowledged altogether, though so very explicit in their intentions. The only recognition that she gave the finest studies from nature was one of unmitigated disgust. And though she was too modest to mention them even with reprehension, yet she betrayed her notice of them by her studied silence quite as much as the loudest censure could have done. How keenly she looked after those tabooed nymphs!—and how bitterly she deprecated their admission at all, when she spoke on the subject with her husband!

As they stood in raptures before a landscape which was made up of a rock, a sea beach, a fisherman's hut, and a very white gull—and spoke eloquently of the "nice feeling in the composition," two well-known voices struck Edward Mantell's ear. Not daring to turn and meet such eyes as he knew shone in their dangerous brilliancy behind him, he was obliged to stand there, listening to Clare's fervid expressions of admiration at some female studies, while Alice and her mother spoke to him on their side of this exquisite unpeopled rock.

"But don't you see, dear Clara, that the shoulders are too narrow?" said Percival, pointing to one of the figures—some nymphs bathing—at which they were looking.

"That may be—but the whole attitude is graceful," said the voice whose least accents thrilled to Edward's heart. "I like the picture altogether—it is so very natural—so unartificial; and there is such a warmth of atmosphere about it."

"What do you think of this?" said Percival, pointing to a figure of piety—a very long female draped in dingy red, and standing out against a violently blue sky. She was a fashionable beauty; treated in the pre-Raphael style.

"That is a lovely thing, Mr. Mantell!" said Mrs. de Saumarez, pointing to the same picture. "What stillness and repose in the figure—what artistic management of the drapery—and what grace in the whole attitude, though so dignified!"

"Oh shocking!" cried Clare; "it is like a wooden doll! It is too long, too stiff and cold! Such a picture as that would make me ill! No; I like my beautiful nymphs better than anything else I have seen yet."

"Lost! lost!" murmured Edward to himself. "In everything it is the same!—from the largest to the smallest, the most important to the most insignificant—the one certain evidence of depraved associates and depraved tastes! Lost for ever—though so glorious in her fall!"

"Percival!" cried Clare in a low voice of terror, clinging close to him, and laying her disengaged hand on his arm. "Percival, look there!"

"Where, dear? What is the matter with you?" And he looked kindly into her blanched face.

She pointed towards Edward Mantell and the De Saumarez.

"Oh, I see!" he said quietly, following the direction of her hand. "Mr. Mantell! Never mind, dear child. We will go into the other rooms. He has not seen you; and if he has—what does that signify!

You are not alone, and he shall not annoy you while I am here. Cannot I protect you, Clara?" His voice was like music, it was so full of love.

"But, Percival—no—more," she said, gasping. "Not him—those!"

"Who? I do not understand you! Don't look so terrified, my child!—you cannot be annoyed while you are with me."

"It is mamma—Mrs. de Saumarez and Alice," she said at last, clinging still closer to him. They turned, and Percival saw their faces clearly; and they saw Clara.

Overcome by all the memories of home and the dear pleasures past of youth—believing that all the world must feel as keenly and must have the same amount of affection as she herself—trusting in her conscious innocence too much to remember all that had been spoken to her disadvantage—at least for the first moments—she forgot that she might well receive a repulse; and leaving Percival's arm, she rushed forward to the party, holding out both her hands, and crying; "Dear, dear Mamma!" Nay, she even touched the lady's arm, and that in no cold manner.

Mrs. de Saumarez turned frightfully pale. What terror or revived disgust came up I do not know; but as if involuntarily she caught her daughter's hand in hers, while she shook off Clare's grasp with a shuddering vehemence.

"I do not know you," she said hastily. "We are strangers, and must ever remain such."

"Oh! speak one word to me kindly," pleaded Clara. "I know I was tiresome and undutiful, and that I did a great deal I ought not to have done—but if I failed I have been punished for it; for indeed, dear mamma, I have suffered very much!"

"Must I repeat that I do not know you?" said Mrs. de Saumarez very sternly. "Must I tell you again, more plainly, that I do not wish to hold the slightest intercourse with you, and that I think your very presence dishonouring to my child? I blush for you!—so young to be so destitute of shame—lost as you are in the esteem of all good people! I desire you will pass on; I do not know you."

"No, I will not pity you," said Percival, taking her hand in his, and looking into her eyes as they raised themselves to him, with an expression of wondering sorrow in them. "You must learn more discrimination, and know better to whom you can be natural and to whom you must be reserved. To be impulsive to such natures as Mrs. de Saumarez' and her daughter's is to fling a bar of heated iron into water—you will only cool the metal and scald your own skin. You have committed the mistake once, and it must be future experience to you. Another time you will know better. Don't be so foolish again, and forget it now."

But poor Clara could not forget it, and was very unhappy and very humiliated all the day after.

The De Saumarez too were disturbed; and Edward Mantell's emotion did not escape either Alice or her mother. The more so because he made such evident efforts to conceal it, that he betrayed its depth by those very means.

"You know that person—or at least knew of her—I believe?" the lady said after a short silence.

"Slightly," he answered.

"Indeed!—did you know her personally?" asked Alice with her peculiar smile.

He did not answer at first, and then said hurriedly; "What a charming Stanfield![131] Mrs. de Saumarez, this will delight you! Did you speak?"—to Alice—"I beg your pardon. Yes, I did know her personally—by mere chance. Pray examine this Stanfield—it is exquisite."

"She is a most undesirable acquaintance for you, Mr. Mantell," said Mrs. de Saumarez coldly. "I hope you have no further intercourse with her?"

"No—not any," he said, still in the same hurried and careless manner, pretending to be absorbed in the catalogue. "Not any, I assure you."

"How did you know her, Mr. Mantell?" persisted Alice. "Is she then admitted into good society? I thought you said she was discarded by every one."

Edward felt he must make a stand somewhere. "I knew her chiefly in my district," he said, prevaricating like many other good people who would tremble to tell a direct falsehood. "She used to visit among the poor."

"Oh! she was always fond of vulgar people," said Mrs. de Saumarez; and then the conversation, turning on rather a delicate subject as connected with Clare and Alice, dropped stone-dead; and they looked at the rest of the pictures in a gloomy unsatisfactory way.

To Edward the shock of meeting Clare again was very great. It takes a long time to break the spell of the voice. Even the face loses its power before the voice. Once love, and years of separation and of coldness will not suffice to weaken the magic of one word in the old familiar accents; even while you may be able to look on the form and into the very eye without emotion. And Edward, who had often brought before his memory with tolerable calmness the expression and features of Clara Clayton, was thrown down again to his former weakness by the few words—the few sounds—of the beloved voice.

Distressed and terrified he strove to crush out the feelings which this unexpected meeting had revived. He contemplated Alice, and thought of her gentleness and orthodox piety, and tried to exaggerate Clare's minutest defects into mortal sins. He pictured the impatience with which she had often received his admonitions, and the obstinacy with which she had clung to this wretched man, this Glynn, against all his entreaties and forewarnings; and then he saw Alice, meek and womanly, accepting what he bestowed and believing what he taught without opposition or argument. What! shall he be such a slave of passion as to love that thing which he cannot esteem?—shall he peril his soul for the sake of brighter eyes and fairer lips? Far be the thought!—far the temptation! He will rise superior to it and stamp it out, or die.

And he raised his eyes, which had been cast down in reflection so earnest it was almost prayer; to meet the blue orbs of Alice fixed steadily on him.

That look went to his heart. Despite his want of vanity, despite his chastened blood—and notwithstanding her coldness of temperament—Edward Mantell understood its love. And then the veil dropped off from the mystery of the past, and he read for the first time clearly the meaning of the riddle that had puzzled him so long.

Alice saw him start, and change colour. She knew that he turned his eyes on her again; if not with any intensity of love, at least with earnestness and mildness; and something seemed to have sprung up between them, as if they had spoken when no one else was by, or as if they knew a secret which no one else possessed.

When they arrived at the hotel, Edward asked Mrs. de Saumarez to give him a few minutes' interview—a request granted without difficulty—and then and there, with one burning pulse of ardent love for Clara rushing headlong through his being, he demanded her permission to regard Alice as his future wife; to which Mrs. de Saumarez gave a cold assent, though the tears were in her eyes at the moment. But long habit had tutored her so effectually that it was no effort now to appear calm under any circumstances. It would have been a greater trial to have been demonstrative, or, as she used to call Clare, "expansive" in her manners.

When Mrs. de Saumarez left her room to inform her daughter of what had happened, Edward flung himself on his knees, praying for power to withstand all future trials, and to hold fast by the salvation offered to him. And in this temper he married; sincerely believing that Alice was his visible release from sin—the consecrated power, sent spiritually to deliver him from Egyptian bondage, as typified in Clare.

Alice believed the same thing for her own share; and though their marriage was never a very volcanic affair, not much surpassing in demonstrativeness or warmth the philosophical loves of the elders, it was at least calm and mentally sympathetic; and for that reason it may be called a happy marriage. And since Alice could not, constitutionally, know any violent passion, and Edward Mantell held its indulgence sinful, they were admirably suited in their temperaments, and believed each other almost perfect because they were cold in their manners and measured in their feelings.

The villagers of Shorne went on in their old way; and Mrs. de Saumarez died in the belief that Mechanics' Institutes, schools, and lectures were infallible, and that it was the fault of the people that they had not become popular on her estate. It could not be for any want of practical wisdom or common sense in herself.

CHAPTER XI.

AND now the dark shadow which had so long lain over Vasty's fairest prospects was removed, and the sunshine might pour down unchecked and undiverted. It is true he had not allowed himself to be much concerned at any time about the fate of his wife. He did not love her, and so cared nothing for her miseries. He did not wish to marry again—at least he had not until lately—since he knew Clara—and so felt nothing of the tie which bound him to a nominal union; and he was too proud, as well as too pleasure-loving, to take to himself any reflected disgrace from her career, which after all was known to very few, and never thought of now by any. Under these conditions therefore, he had lived more happily and less disturbed than any other would have done; but yet, when he heard of Emma's death, a sensation of joy and freedom, such as he had not experienced for a long time, told him that he had felt the burden heavier than he had acknowledged; else he would not have rejoiced so much when it was taken off.

"And are you really truly free?" cried Emmeline, bending her blue eyes pleasantly on him; "and can you marry again? They have been telling me about it at the theatre. How well you kept your secret! Poor Vasty! And so you can marry now?"

"Yes, my little beauty. I can make you my wife to-morrow, if I choose."

"Me?" she laughed shrilly; "if *you* choose. And is there no other consent to be asked but yours, you vain man? Suppose I didn't choose, if I were asked. Hey, what then?" and she made a saucy movement such as a pretty scold indulges in on the stage.

"But then you wouldn't refuse," returned Vasty in a careless debonair kind of way; "you would be only too glad to have some one whose name you could pawn, and on whose substance and station you could draw your bills of pleasure. I know the sex well enough by this time. I ought, for I have had a few years close experience."

"But you don't know me Vaughan, and so I tell you; and child as you think me—"

"You are deeper than I suspect? Is that it, my pretty one? No, you are not, Emmeline! I know you a vast deal better than you think I do, and I see further too, and clearer than I care to say."

"That he doesn't," thought Emmeline with a heightened colour; "else he would not be sitting here now!"

Perhaps he would though. He was not very strict in some cases, and Emmeline was one; and very likely, after the first burst of constitutional jealousy, he would have overlooked her infidelity and allowed it. Provided always he was supreme in position and power, and that she did not desert him, nor rob him of his usual hours, for the sake of another; then he would have been furious and probably would have left her altogether; but if he might have had the lion's share he would have given the refuse to the fox.

"Oh! but you would not marry me at all events?" she cried after a short silence, arching her eyebrows and pouting her lips; "even if I would marry you, you would not!"

"And why not, fairy?"

"There's that other girl—that good, amiable, dear Miss Clayton," she said maliciously; "the one who used to come to the theatre in one eternal straw bonnet and woollen shawl. Don't you know who I mean?"

"Yes," answered Vaughan, making a strong effort to conceal anything like emotion. "Yes, I know who you mean, what of her?"

"Why, don't you like her better than any one else in the world? At least you did. All the theatre was talking of it before I came."

"And who told you this gossip? What impertinent chatterbox presumed to meddle in my affairs?"

"Now don't be cross; Lucretia told me."

"Hem! and what else did she say? I know that it would be impossible for a woman to make only one confidence at a sitting. The flood-gates of Lucretia's eloquence once opened, truth and reason would not long find a dry footing. Give me some more of her revelations, pretty one."

"No, I shan't! She told me nothing more—positively. She only said that you nearly broke Miss Clayton's heart. Vaughan, why hasn't she been to the theatre lately? I am sure there is some reason for it. Now tell me—why hasn't she?" speaking gravely.

"Who do you mean, child? Lucretia?"

"Lucretia? No! How stupid! You know I mean Miss Clayton. She has never been once since that night when she was hissed; that night when you spoke so sharply to her in the green-room. And yet Lucretia says she is not dismissed."

"The devil take Lucretia and all her pratings!" cried Vaughan angrily. "What! may I not have the power of giving any of my people leave of absence if I like, but it must be canvassed, and talked over, and made into a mighty state secret! You will make me seriously angry, Emmeline, if ever you mention the subject again! Miss Clayton goes away when she is allowed, and that is my business; not yours or Lucretia's. Suppose I let her go into the provinces for a run—what is that to any one else?"

"But you haven't let her go into the provinces," persisted the little damsel.

"And how do you know that?"

"Because I met her yesterday—with some one," she answered, with meaning.

"And where pray?—and with whom?" asked Vaughan trying to

look undisturbed, playing with the little hand that lay on his, and recovering his equanimity with marvellous celerity.

"In the Strand—with a gentleman."

"Oho! a gentleman? indeed!" he said, still playing with the rosy fingers; "and what was he like? What an exquisite little hand! it is like a white satin cushion lined with pink, as I once heard a school-girl say! And what was this man like, fairy queen?"

"Is it a pretty hand?" she cried, holding it up in admiration. "Well, upon my word it is! I never knew that before, Vaughan!" and she laughed with a childish delight at her wit, which at any other time would have quite enchanted the manager, but which now tortured him to death.

"Yes! a beautiful hand! and don't tell stories: it isn't a good habit to get into. I have often told you how lovely it is, and you knew it long before. Who was with Miss Clayton?"

"Goodness! how should I know? I didn't know the man! Some vulgarian or other that I could not be expected to know!" tossing her head.

"But what was he like?" urged Vaughan, his face on fire, and his lips quivering.

"Good gracious, Vasty! one would think you were in love with the girl! I really cannot tell you what he was like. I did not know him, and I never saw him before, and I should not know him now if I were to see him again. Now, are you satisfied?"

But Vasty was not satisfied at all; only he was obliged to pretend that he was in the seventh heaven of contentment, else his capricious little maiden would have made his visit very unpleasant. And as he had nothing to do to-day he had come intending to remain a long time with her, which would have made a fit of ill-humour very embarrassing.

Now, so quick as Vaughan was, he soon perceived a great change creep over Emmeline. For the first half-hour she was charming; vivacious, graceful, prettily pert, and delightfully saucy; just what pleases a *blasé* man in a frivolous beauty. As he leaned back in the easy-chair which was his appropriated place, he had something of the feelings of a grand Turk watching a dancing girl, or a newly bought slave, or any other hired thing of amusement. He felt that all this grace and beauty was displayed for his pleasure; that his sovereignty was undoubted, and his lordship confessed. Half shutting his eyes he gave himself up to the most delightful feelings of superiority—even more definite than those which men usually cherish; and for the first half-hour everything went smooth. But the half-hour had passed now.

Then Emmeline began to grow rather fidgetty. Her cheeks flushed, and her eyes were restless. Her manners, though more determinedly gay, were constrained and evidently forced. Something was manifestly wrong.

"I thought you were going to be very busy to-day, Vaughan!" at last said Emmeline with an air of vexation she could not conceal. "You told me so yesterday, and that you would not come here at all!"

"So I thought, fairy; but I managed better than I hoped, and got released. Are you not glad?"

"Oh, of course—but—"

"If of course, why a but?" he interrupted.

"Nothing," she said, turning away with a look of indubitable annoyance.

"Come, Emmeline, what is it? I see something is going wrong with you; tell me what it is! Am I in your way? are you expecting another lover?" and Vasty's jealousy, never thoroughly in a state of coma, woke up in a blaze in his eye.

"Nonsense!" cried Emmeline. "I—I—" she hesitated and glanced at her watch.

"You what, Emmeline?" very sternly.

"I have made an appointment," she exclaimed with a sudden burst of confidence, turning on him the most guileless face imaginable.

"With whom? if I may ask."

"Lucretia," she said making a bold dash.

"Lucretia! that is strange, too!" Vaughan exclaimed in a musing tone. "I saw her this morning, and she said she was a prisoner, studying her new part—at least restudying an old one. Why did she tell me such a falsehood?" he added inquiringly.

"I don't know I'm sure," said Emmeline; who, now that she had fairly embarked in the concern, was resolved to venture her whole capital of brains, and not shrink from a scientific defence of the first falsehood. "Perhaps she was afraid."

"Afraid?—afraid of what?"

"Oh I don't know! Don't look so dreadfully cross! *I* am not Lucretia—*I* did not tell you a story."

"You are not a Lucretia certainly," returned Vasty; "but the rest of the sentence I won't endorse," he added a little below his breath. "And when is your appointment, and where?" he asked addressing the little girl, who sat half-frightened, and wondering if she had done wisely or not in endeavouring to cheat him.

"At half-past two," she said; "and it is two now."

"And where, I asked before?"

"Oh"—she hesitated now very much—"here."

"Lucretia is to come here? Is that it?"

"Goodness, Vaughan! one would think you did not believe a word I said! You cross-question me like a counsel. I never saw any thing like it!"

"Don't pout, Emmeline. If you do, I shall be disagreeable to you for the next half-hour."

The terrified look the little actress threw!

"Oh Vaughan!" she cried in desperation. "I wish you would go!"

"Go Emmeline! Why should I go?" he answered with the utmost coolness. "I should like to see Lucretia here this morning, very much. I want to speak to her about that hideous headdress she will persist in wearing as Constance, and I forgot it at the theatre. Don't look so terrified, child. I will not follow you, nor find out your business. As soon as I have seen her I shall leave."

Emmeline's temper and terror were beyond her control. Almost crying from vexation, yet frightened too—for Vaughan held her in great physical awe of him; he was so tall and strong, and she felt such a mite in his grasp—she did not know how to get rid of him; for as may have been guessed, it was no Lucretia she had appointed to meet, but her new lover, Lord John, who was coming at half-past two. And then they were going to all sorts of sights and places of amusement, and she had been in the very gayest spirits about it for the last three days; for a new admirer was to Emmeline as enchanting as a new gown— she loved it so much till wearied of it.

There Vaughan sat like a handsome Quilp, or the occupant of Glengulphus's[132] chair. He had a savage pleasure in fretting this little girl. He could not feel his power so sure in any other way. She was too slight and small to treat roughly, personally. One grasp rather harder than usual would have broken her to pieces like a barley-sugar doll. On her affections he never dreamt of any hold. One cannot control what does not exist; and of all synonymes with nonentity, Emmeline's affection was the most complete. On her vanity and her love of pleasure, therefore, he had his only leverage; and it gave him a fierce delight to make her feel his power, and bend under it, and acknowledge it.

"But Vaughan," she said at last, "I want to talk to Lucretia—I don't want you here at all."

"I don't doubt that, my dear; but I shall not hear a word you say. I am going as soon as she comes. Don't be alarmed—I shall not interrupt your private conference by my senseless shadow even! Come, 'Smile again my bonny lassie;' this sudden gravity—and what a vulgar person would call fidgettiness—make you lose half your beauty! There's your guitar. Go and sing to me; it is long since I have heard you sing. I want that little French thing, 'Voulez-vous à voir.' Do you remember it?"

"No," said Emmeline, pouting.

"No? then something else; some English ballad, if you like that better; a 'Moorish' melody or a 'nigger song' even, if you can't soar higher."

"I can't sing at all." And then she said, piteously and almost crying, "I want you to go, Vaughan—I don't want you any longer!"

"When Lucretia comes," Vasty answered calmly. "I'll go then, and not before; so don't ask me. It is very odd!" he added, turning on her a look as dark as night, "that you should wish me to leave you so very earnestly! I cannot understand it at all! Have I offended you? or are you wearied with me? or why should you desire me so passionately to leave you?"

Before Emmeline could or would answer, a loud knock came to the door, and a private cab dashed up to the kerb. She flew to the window.

"There's Lucretia," said the impenetrable Vasty. "What a fashionable knock the old lady gives!"

Emmeline was rushing from the room, to tell the servant to say, "Not at home," trusting that she would be able to diplomatize matters afterwards, but Vaughan held her by main force, and the servant ushered in "Captain Jones."

"Oh! I see!" said Vaughan drily, taking up his hat. "This was your Lucretia, then? I understand!"

"Am I intruding?" said the stranger, with a freezing bow to pretty, guilty, fibbing, little Emmeline. "Shall I call again, Miss de Montfort?"

"By no means on my account," said Vaughan, quietly. "I am going now; my business is at an end."

And the cruel slanderer of Clare—the unmoved witness of his

wife's ruin—did one of those generous things which the worst men sometimes do, and helped to conceal Emmeline's delinquency, that she might not lose the lover for whom she had deserted him. But his pride was severely wounded, though he affected not to heed it; and he did deserve some praise for self-control when he walked away so calm in manner, while he was so little calm in feeling.

And Emmeline told Captain Jones how Mr. Vaughan had been on business, and was scarcely known to her—not at all beyond their professional connexion; and when the handsome guardsman expressed his wonder at that—for "had he not seen him at Richmond with her?"—Emmeline uttered such an audacious falsehood, that she there and then won the youth's heart for ever, "for her plucky way of getting out of a scrape."

Vaughan walked home in no enviable mood. A gay man does not like to feel himself gradually becoming *passé*; tripped up by the hurrying youngsters of the coming generation. Conceited as he might be—and he wanted for no form of pride, ranging from the most artistic haughtiness to the smallest personal vanity—Vasty was obliged to allow that he was not only growing older with all the world, but growing visibly older past one-half the world. This Captain Jones, now—he certainly was some years younger than himself (he was about five-and-twenty,) and that gave him an advantage; though he, Vaughan, was infinitely his superior in looks and manners, and acquirements generally. And what that little fool could see in this beardless boy—though he *was* a little younger—superior to his own merits, he was at a loss to understand! But these women—heaven keep them!—they never know what is really good in a man! A nursery hero would please them better than anything else; one of the rising generation that ought to be birched and sent to bed, would carry off half-a-dozen hearts from a manly well-grown fellow like himself!

But all this was hollow reasoning. Vaughan felt the ground slipping from under his feet; his day was nearly at a close; the sun almost setting; and oh! that he had cherished better that last sweet flower which opened to his rays!—oh! that he had repaid that fervent love with greater truth, with greater gentleness, and safe protection! *She* would not have jilted him like this vain thing of folly; *she* would have stood by him in all and every trial: in sickness, poverty, disgrace, age— though every gem were plucked from out his coronet of manhood— she would have loved him still! No flippant foppery would have turned

her steadfast eyes aside; no brilliant fortune would have lured her from
her simple troth—firm as the ivy round the oak, true as the needle to
the pole—his last and best love would have been! Yet he had sacrificed
her to his cruelty, his pride, his jealousy; when he could control a just
and natural indignation to shield yon heartless thing from censure.
The human heart is a strange study; and not every one can unravel the
motives of his own actions.

Vaughan was destined to humiliation to-day. Humiliation too in
his most sensitive part. Passing through the park, he saw two figures
before him walking slowly, arm in arm. Surely he knew them! Surely
he had seen that girl's light step before, and knew the free movement
of her limbs, and the graceful poise of her body! Surely he recognised
the actions he had so often watched with admiration, as so far superior
in their unfettered ease to the taught grace of the schools!

He was right. It was Clara Clayton that he saw before him. Quite
different to the slow swan-like movements learnt in a school, and from
posture-mistresses and drill-sergeants and dancing-masters, the natural
grace of an untaught woman is also infinitely superior. The drawing-
room belle may dance with precision, and walk with stateliness, and
make all her movements expressive with their studied elegance; but
the free firm step and unconscious actions, beautiful because the frame
is perfect and the limbs symmetrical by exercise, are worth all the
artificial graces of the most graceful drawing-room in the world.

It was like an old remembered picture to see this well-known
figure moving there before him. He could almost hear her voice now;
and indeed if the air blew a moment fresher, he did catch those low
sweet accents—so much more mournful than they used to be—but
with even more trembling music in them, more fervour and more
love. And now, by walking on the grass to deaden the sound of his
footsteps, he could approach them nearer, and catch once more the
rich drops into his cup, and brood over them as the enchantress over
her flowers—taking in very life with each breath of her presence.

No, pride was nothing; jealousy was nothing; his savage cruelty
was nothing; his determined hatred was nothing. They were all mere
straws in the path of the flame, and for every one he threw down the
fire rose all the stronger. And though his jealous heart quailed and
quivered to see this man—this hated Glynn—standing there by her
side, and receiving the whole weight and care of her life—yet that too
must pass and fade, and leave only passionate love alive within him.

He stole softly behind them. He heard her speak to him gently—kindly—and sometimes almost fondly. He saw him turn his eyes on her with a meaning in their looks that could not be misunderstood. He saw the gentle all-absorbing love that stole like moonbeams over his face, and stood like a sainted glory round them both; he saw, and felt, and knew—knew deep to his writhing soul—that they loved each other; that whether the word had passed their lips or not—whether they had confessed it to themselves or not—they loved. Plainly, unmistakeably, with him; with her a sweet affection which, though she might not understand to the utmost now, would sooner or later make itself heard, and own the shape it wore. He saw her look up into Percival's face as he had seen her look into his, with eyes in which affection played like the summer's mist over the earth, making tender and divinely beautiful all on which it rested. He saw her cheek flush beneath his gaze, and flush again still deeper at the gentle pressure of his hand. He saw the parted lip and downcast eye of emotion modest to itself, and he cursed himself bitterly! bitterly! when he thought that all this was once his own, and he had suffered it to fade away; nay, he had repulsed it roughly, and strangled the guide which Heaven had sent to lead him to peace.

He rushed homeward, stricken but not conquered, wounded but not subdued. Still rose up his old indomitable pride; still rose up his fiery passions and immortal love; and then, twin-born came hope and flattered him: but underneath the mask it was a painted skeleton—a hideous phantasm which mocked him while it appeared to offer comfort.

Hope? No, no! He had better lay aside that fancy. There was no hope now of Clara's love!

And Vasty might have been pitied by the coldest as he cowered beneath his anguish, and endeavoured still, and still again, to battle with himself, and to rise superior to his weakness. And in the face of the world, with spectators and an audience, he could easily have risen so superior; but alone, with only truth for his companion, it was of no avail to dress her in false garments; through every garb she would have thrust out her face and scoffed him for his endeavour.

And Vasty sat there, and suffered such tortures as men of passion and of pride must suffer when their hopes are overthrown, and they themselves have helped to dig down the foundations. Then suddenly starting up, he flung himself from the house, and in a shorter time than he believed it possible to have traversed the distance, he found himself half mad at Clara's door.

CHAPTER XII

ONCE more standing alone in her presence—once more by the gates of Paradise unrepulsed—Vaughan forgot the gnawing misery he had suffered so long and tried to conceal even from himself. Clara's breathless astonishment when she saw him enter, seemed to him, blinded by passion as he was, the excitement of rapturous pleasure; her agitated voice when she uttered his name, and starting from her seat stood half turned away in terror, seemed shy emotion. It could not, should not be; she did not love Percival—that frigid pedant, that unlovely prater;—she could not love that while he was by!

"Clara," said the deep voice, shaken and low, "have you so forgotten me as to offer me not one word of welcome?"

He advanced towards her, holding out his hand. She trembled, but placed her hand within his, though coldly. Still not speaking.

"Not a word from you to your first friend, Clara?" he asked again, grasping her hand nervously.

"It is so long since Mr. Vaughan was my friend, that I have almost forgotten him as such," she said, her voice trembling very much, and her lips quivering.

"Never!—never! I have never been anything but your friend—your lover!" he cried passionately.

"Have you?" she said, and her accent was mournful and her eyes sad; "when you disgraced me before the world, when you degraded me in my profession, when you sought for long months past to ruin me in the esteem of all men—were you my friend and lover then, Vaughan?"

"I was!" he cried fiercely, "I was, Clara!—I loved you then as truly as I did the first day my lips ever breathed the word—the first day;" and his voice sank to a whisper, "that my lip took back that word from yours!"

Clara blushed painfully.

"Ah, then," she said, "I believed you to my sorrow!"

"No, no, not to your sorrow!" he cried vehemently. "To your eternal happiness, to your joy, to your salvation! Clara, there has been a dark cloud between us—a dark time of deathly misery! It must pass, and pass for ever! Henceforth we must be all in all to each other—we must heal up the wounds that an unhappy fate has graven on our souls—we must rush back to the only fountains where we can gain health and peace—we must love each other as we did, and die in that love—die in each other's arms!"

He would have taken her to his breast, but she drew herself away.

"No, Vaughan—that can never be again. The past is emphatically the past. There has been too much misery ever to bind it with the future!"

"Clara! Clara! this is folly! I love you—deeply—fervently—with a fire that preys on my very heart, and that will destroy me if it is not quenched. And you love me too!—you cannot have changed to such chill distrust of me!"

"And can you ask me to love you again, Vaughan—can you expect it—after all that you have done? Do you not believe that in the tenderest moment the words, the actions, which have sunk me to such a low place of degradation as I stand in now, will come back chilling and dark? Do you not believe that I shall hear again the hiss which completed that night's frightful range of misery?—that I shall see again the insolence of men, lost to all knowledge of good, whom you let slip against me to hunt me down?—do you not believe in this? You surely cannot think the human mind is so plastic as to forget all that has gone before, for any little pleasure of the present! Love?—No! you have destroyed that power yourself." And she turned away with a mixture of scorn and sorrow that struck Vaughan like a heavy blow.

"But I was mad then!—it was from jealousy of you, Clara—it was the insanity, the fierce madness, that your coldness woke up in me, coupled as that coldness was with such intense affection for others! It was not Vaughan—not your lover Vasty, that spoke then—it was a maniac, the key of whose reason you held and had ruthlessly thrown away."

"And what warranty, Vaughan, could I have that you would not be the same again? No! no! you have cast me off in no gentle fashion, because I would not continue in a state I believed sinful, and you cannot take me up again at your pleasure."

"I did not cast you off, Clara! I swear I did not! Was it not yourself who repudiated me? It was not I who rejected you."

"And when did I repudiate you, Vaughan? When I found that for long months you had deceived me, and practised a fearful falsehood which made me sin unknowingly; then it was that I rejected you, and then only! Had I ever disobeyed you before? Had I ever deceived you? Had I not given up every thought and wish to you, and was it anything but the commonest virtue and delicacy that made me leave you? You cannot accuse me of coldness, whatever else I may have done wrong. Few women ever loved more truly than I loved you—nor shall I ever love another with anything of the same fervour that I felt for you!"

"This is all of the past," repeated Vaughan tremulously. "It is of the present—the moment—that I want you to speak! It is of your love for me now, Clara, that I wish to hear, and your promise to become my wife that I thirst to receive! I am free, Clara—my hand, my heart, my faith, love, protection, care, all I offer to thee, my fondest hope; all I consecrate to thee, now and for ever—darling, darling, Clare!"

"You have destroyed my power to marry you, Vasty," she said, not so coldly now as sorrowfully; for his manner was tender and impassioned as it used to be; and women never wholly forget.

"No! no! no! mere folly! How have I destroyed it? I, who would give lives to secure it!"

"My character has been blighted through you, Vaughan——"

"Through me to be re-established tenfold stronger!" he cried, interrupting her hastily.

"No!—I will not have it said that I owe my husband to compassion—to honourable restitution," she exclaimed proudly. "What I have lost I cannot take back by your sacrifice!"

"Clara, this is fencing with the question! It is not a sacrifice on my part—oh! you know how far wide of the truth that word is! You know how all that earth has of divinest bliss lies in the small space of your heart! Crowns and empires, Clare, would I shatter to dust for one such word as used to bless me—for one such kiss as used to greet me! Clara, dear, dear Clara, love me as you did, and you fill my veins with the blood of a God!"

"I cannot, Vaughan."

"Yes! I must not hear that word!" he cried, speaking very rapidly. "I cannot hear it! We will go to some place where our names were never heard—where the young earth will pour out its blessings in like profusion with our loves. We will leave England, Clare, and escape from all the viperous tongues that have blasted our peace—from all the cold laws that would have frowned on our happiness! We will go to some dear spot where we may be blessed without reserve—bound by every tie of God and man. Clara! it is not to poverty or to disgrace that I would wed you—but to pleasures of the purest, the most exalted kind; to love that shall never fail you, darling, while the heart on which you rest beats in a human breast! Come, come with me, Clare! I am weary of waiting!"

She shrank farther from him. His voice and air terrified her.

"No," she said again; "let us rather part for ever. Give me back my bond, and release me from your control. We could not be happy now, Vaughan, and my theatrical connexion with you is a mockery on both sides. Give that to me, and let us part friends."

"I cannot understand you!" cried Vaughan with a howl of despair. "The words fall on my ear, but I cannot understand them!"

"And yet they are my final answer," said Clara in a low voice.

He drew back, stiffened and dumb.

"What did I hear?" he said very slowly. His blood-shot eyes glared like burning flames on her—his lips were open, feverish and blackened—his hands were clenched till the nails dug into the palm—and his chest heaved with thick breathings that seemed to burst forth like the gusts of a rising tempest. It was so hard for him to quit his hope! He clung to it, and fought against increasing conviction like a giant against death. He struggled to escape it, as it clutched him in its cold marble hand and froze the blood within his heart. He would not yield to it—he would not sink. Clara should love him though she died—he would not release her yet!

"This is too painful for us both," said Clara moving towards the door. "Vaughan, we must part! I cannot marry you; I do not love you now; and I would rather work at the humblest trade than be forced into any contact with you. And yet I do not feel unkindly to you, Vaughan. Though I see in you my whole misery, I do not feel one shade of anger or revenge. Let us part now for ever."

She was going, but he caught her back, and held her with one arm as in a vice.

"Shall I kill her now?" he hissed, through his closed teeth.

She did not scream, nor cry, nor faint. She simply put back his hand, and looked calmly into his eyes.

It sobered him, and he let her go; and then he cursed her with such frightful oaths mingled with such passionate love as made her blood curdle with horror and with shame together.

"This must end, Vaughan," she said sternly, "I cannot submit to this conduct! You have no right to treat me thus! Our connexion is at an end—our love—our very friendship—if these are to be the conditions of its existence! Be calm—be rational—be at least *manly* to a woman you can insult and torture and destroy as you please! At any rate, let this scene end now—I cannot submit to it longer!"

Taking back, as a strong man plucking at his chains, his power of self-control, in a moment Vaughan was outwardly the calm, the suave gentleman of the drawing-rooms, which was his public character. No one who had seen him in his late transports could have believed that his face could have thrown off so suddenly all traces of his furious passion. Only in his flashing eye and the nervous quiver of the muscles round his lip, could be read the evidences of his excited feelings. But on all that he *could* control he had thrown an impenetrable coat of mail of serenity.

"Your request shall not be granted, Miss Clayton," he said with a satirical smile. "On the contrary, you must consider your leave of absence in which I have weekly indulged you of late at an end. You will present yourself at the theatre, if you please, at the regular hours; and I must have you play with more precision and correctness, else I shall be obliged to degrade you still lower in the ranks. It was a courageous thing to ask for!" he added with a short savage laugh. "You reject a man who offers you all that love, protection, and wealth can give, and quietly add to your refusal a request that he will do you a favour at his own expense! You have improved in moral courage since I had the honour of knowing you, Miss Clayton!"

"Must I then appear at the theatre to-morrow?" she asked coldly, restrained by shame from appearing weak or frightened. "In the morning?"

"If you please; you will find work for you then, doubtless. In fact I will give orders about it."

How strange his calm voice sounded!—how unnatural his still attitude and manners, after the ferocious energy which he had so lately displayed!

"I will obey you," she said quietly.

"And I leave you now?"

"If you please; I am engaged."

He started and quivered, and seemed about to speak, but he

checked himself; while Clara stood waiting for the leave-taking, cold
and proud and pale.

"And your decision is really taken, Miss Clayton? You prefer the
miseries of a low, a very low walk in the theatrical profession, with
all the disagreeables incident on your unprotected position and your
imprudent conduct, to the safety and honour of my wife? Am I to
understand this?"

"You are," she said firmly. "I will suffer anything—the worst that
can befal me—rather than accept the alternative."

"When you *do* suffer, remember that it was by your own free
choice!" he cried fiercely.

And then he turned to go, but still lingered.

She looked away, and kept silence. There was no help for it;—the
time had really come.

And then and thus parted the two hearts which had once loved
each other so fervently; thus Clara separated from her first, her
dearest lover, and saw the doors close for ever on the earliest temple
which she had raised in her youthful heart.

The cloud came down—the deep purple pall fell over the altar's
glories, and hid it from the sight for ever: and whether those glories
had been false or true—whether they had been tinsel and paint lighted
up by gaslight, and dazzling by their very falseness—or whether they
had been true gems in the sunshine of heaven—she might not now
determine. Perhaps in the future, when she understands the Reality of
Feeling, and fathoms the source from which it springs, she will know
if that passionate love was of the sanctity it appeared, or if it did not
rather owe its beauty to the blindness and the poetry of youth.

"Percival," said Clara, a few hours after this interview, when Glynn
came on some trifling errand—but such as he usually found important
enough to take him constantly to her lodgings. "Vaughan has been
here."

Percival at this moment was standing near the fire-place—one foot
on the fender, and his head leant on his hand, while his elbow rested
on the low chimney-piece. The other hand was on his hip.

When she spoke, Clara walked softly towards him, and went close
to him, playing with the lapel of his coat, and bending it back among
the buttons.

He looked down on her with that sweet gentleness which made his generally plain features so beautiful, and said softly; "Well, and what then?"

Still busied with the coat and the buttons, she answered—she herself speaking below her breath, and a strange oppression, not disagreeable, at her chest—

"He wanted me to love him again."

"And what did you say?"

"I could not."

"And why could you not, Clara?" bending his face till he almost touched her hair.

Clara's heart beat very fast. A gentle pleasure thrilled through her whole being. She felt strange and agitated, but very happy, as if some pleasant tale was telling.

"I do not know," she said, creeping nearer to him.

"No?"

He placed his arm round her waist. She yielded to the pressure, and leant against his bosom, his face bending lower and lower, but not touching hers.

She looked up, and their eyes met. Without a thought or doubt she put her arms round his neck and—unasked, unsolicited—her lips were on his.

"Beloved! beloved!" he whispered, straining her to him. "Was that the reason why you could not love him again?"

She did not answer, excepting what answer could be found in a child-like abandonment that made her clasp her hands tighter round his neck and bend her face close into his bosom.

Oh! how happy they both were! Let us stand aside for a moment, and view them in the blessed fulness of joy—and reverence the sacred silence that befits it.

At last Clara raised her eyes.

"But, Percival—the world thinks so badly of me?"

"Then they cannot speak evil of you now, darling. As my wife, who can assail you?"

"But you?"

"But I could not but be proud of my Clare, let the world say what it would! What character soever she held, she would never be aught to me but the dearest and the noblest thing on earth! Clare, so far from feeling the shadow of disturbance from the false reports abroad concerning you, I care as little for them as for the raindrops on the grass blade! Do not be shocked, darling, but while you were so good, so honest, so loving, as you are now, I would hold you to my heart, were you even worse than what some believe you to be. Is not this the way in which you deserve to be loved?—or would you rather the cold pedantry which wants only a reflection of its own virtues in the thing loved? Which shall it be, my angel?"

"Percival! dearest Percival!—oh! I do love you!" she cried, looking up to him with an expression of intense devotion, like a prayer to a superior being. And Percival's lip had in its kiss both less and more than a lover's passion as it thanked her for her words.

"But, Percival," she said after a long pause, "why did you not love me before?"

"Before I saw you, darling?—for I have loved you ever since I first knew you."

"No!—I did not see it!"

"I know you did not. I hid it from you."

"Why?"

"First come and sit here by me, and let me feel my hand in yours, and your soft warm hair on my face. There, now—question me; I will answer. What will you know?"

"Why you did not let me see that you loved me?" she said playing with his hand, and sometimes kissing it fondly.

"Because you loved Vaughan from the first, and I knew that you could not be turned to me then. I knew also, Clare, that your fancy for him could not last long—that you would grow out of it as out of any other phase of mental immaturity. If you could be preserved in the mean time, and influenced gently—not too evidently—if your mind could be led up and educated higher and higher, I felt confident of the result. And I hoped ever, Clare—though not strongly—that in time I should hold you as now, and feel that your heart had recognised its true home, and joined its best friend."

"But, Percival," she said, raising herself from his arm and looking into his face; "I do not love you as I did Vaughan. Why is that?"

"Because you are older, darling, than you were, and because you love me differently. I did not covet the love, beautiful as it was, which you gave to Vaughan; for I knew how ignorant you were of the real nature of your own feelings, and of the character of the man you had chosen. And I would rather that you loved me consciously—I mean understanding me thoroughly, and feeling a mental sympathy as well as a personal liking—than have possessed all the poetry and fancy of your early blindness. I have lost nothing, darling, I have rather gained by waiting."

And he kissed her tenderly.

Again another interval of silence—of most exquisite delight— brought down heaven to earth, and filled that small poor room with an atmosphere that angels might have lived in.

This was broken in due time by Clara. She had been thinking very deeply whenever she could rouse herself from the delicious dream in which she lay. And now she stole her soft small hands round his neck once more, and said, in a sweet caressing way, beginning as usual—

"But, Percival—my position at the theatre, and my poverty, and Vaughan's certain displeasure and tyranny. And then I am bound to him, and cannot get away; but must suffer everything he chooses. How will you like that?"

"Listen, beloved, to me, and accept as true every word I say. We are both poor; we must live in mean lodgings, in a mean street, and fare meanly. We have both to work, and we shall know little relaxation and little pleasure. I do not regret it, even for you. For myself, work is as necessary as air or food. But even for you—soft, childish, sensitive, as you are, pleasure-loving and fond of luxury and art—even for you, my child, I do not regret the necessity of work, nor do I fear the influence of poverty. I know you, my darling; and I know that you will come out of such trials as these, doubly strong. And for your painful position at the theatre, Clare, with me by your side you will find its ghastliness decrease more than you believe now; and, as my wife, helping me in my work, you will see among the really poor and wretched such scenes of misery which you have relieved, perhaps, as will make you blush for any weak repining at your own comparatively slight misfortunes. Remember too that all your sorrows will be conventional: you will not be hungry, but your fare will be plain; you will not be an outcast, but the rich and the great will ignore your existence; you will not be in pain, but the ignorant and the prejudiced will despise you. In all this, what truth is there? None! On the contrary, it is a phantom-world which you must confront and subdue. No, Clare, you will rise higher and higher the greater such pressure as this is laid on you! It will be a disagreeable school, but a salutary one; and now that your affections will not be wounded, I cannot pity you for its rough teaching! Come, kiss me, darling, and fear nothing! You have to learn the realities of life yet—that is all. You have to make poverty your bosom friend, side by side with love; you have to learn patience from suffering, and strength from oppression; you have to rise superior to those who would crush you, and to find charity for all who sin, and for all who fall; you have to perfect your moral character at the expense of your personal ease; but I will be with you, darling, and will help you forward as I best can. And together I believe that we shall arrive at the Peace which is beyond circumstances, and at the strength which is got from Truth. No fear, no doubt, beloved! Life has a grand lesson for us both—one far greater than that to be gained from the sybaritism of social well-being. And in action, charity, reliance on the comprehensiveness of the faith that we hold, and in moral courage superior to every extraneous power, that lesson is alone to be learnt, and in these must my wife be taught!"

And Clara found that Percival spoke the truth.

When I saw her last she had developed into such a woman as I would to Heaven we had thick among us! With an intellect guided by her glorious heart, giving practicality to the charity which covered even the very lowest in its angelic robe of womanly tenderness—with love unfailing, shedding a light as from heaven over all with whom she was connected—with a grandeur of recognition that took its limit only from the visible laws of GOD in nature, and meted out its judgments by another measure than man's narrow prejudices—with a firmness of faith that heeded not the denunciations of a sectional faith, but believed in GOD alone, and gave nothing of His work to the devil—did Clara grow up to the light and the truth; an evidence of what humanity may become if it will but take counsel of its own heart, and believe in the instincts of nature rather than in the false theories of an artificial society, and fashion its religion from the laws of toleration and of love rather than from the deadening prejudices of a condemnatory creed.

THE END.

NOTES

1   The goblin page of Lord Cranstoun in Sir Walter Scott's poem "The Lay of the Last Minstrel" (1805).

2   Seems to refer to Zoël, alias Zebel, seventeenth-century astrologer and metaphysician, author of *Liber Imaginum*.

3   A particular way of speaking characteristic of a group of people (see Judges 12).

4   Harry Hieover (1796-1859), author of numerous books about management of the stable.

5   Strong female character in Sir Walter Scott's novel *Rob Roy* (1817), known especially for her propensity to sport, particularly riding and fox-hunting.

6   The art of shoeing horses.

7   Sarah Stickney Ellis (1799-1872), British author known especially for conduct books, the most famous of which is probably *The Women of England, Their Social Duties and Domestic Habits* (1839).

8   Referring to *Des Compensations dans les Destinées Humaines* (1810) by Pierre Hyacinthe Azaïs (1766-1845).

9   Paving.

10 Raphael Sanzio (1483-1520), Italian Renaissance painter. Antonio Canova (1757-1822), Italian sculptor.

11 Publisher of the most famous genealogical guide to the British aristocracy.

12 An innermost room or shrine.

13 The Siamese were thought to be serene and civil as compared, for instance, to rough and brutal Europeans, or loud and hardworking Chinese.

14 *Vestiges of the Natural History of Creation* (1844) by Robert Chambers (1802-1871) was an important pre-Darwinian exploration of the idea of evolution.

15 Adam Sedgwick (1785-1873), British geologist. Michael Faraday (1791-1867), British chemist and physicist known for his work in the fields of electromagnetism and electrochemistry.

16 In his fondness for facts, Mr. de Saumarez is a striking utilitarian contemporary of Thomas Gradgrind, Sr. in Charles Dickens's novel *Hard Times* (1854).

17 Robert Pollok (1799-1827), Scottish poet best known for "The Course of Time." William Cowper (1731-1800), British poet. Henry Cary (1772-1844), Gibraltarian author, whose translation of Dante's *Divina Commedia* appeared in 1814. Oliver Goldsmith (c.1730-1774), Anglo-Irish

author, best known for his novel *The Vicar of Wakefield* (1766). Honoré Gabriel Riqueti, Comte de Mirabeau (1749-1791), writer and statesman, undertook secret negotiations between the French monarchy and the Revolution. Georges Danton (1759-1794), major figure in French Revolution. Maximilien Robespierre (1758-1794), associated with the Terror of 1793-94. Georges Couthon (1755-1794), associate of Robespierre. Gilbert du Motier, Marquis de Lafayette (1757-1834), French royalist. Pierre Terrail, Chevalier de Bayard (1476-1524), considered the ideal knight, the "chevalier sans peur et sans reproche" (knight without fear and without reproach). Jean Sylvain Bailly (1736-1793), mayor of Paris during French Revolution. Marie-Jeanne Roland de la Platière "Madame Roland" (1754-93), Girondist during French Revolution. Charlotte Corday (1768-1793), assassin of the Jacobin Jean-Paul Marat. Joan of Arc (1412-1431), youthful French leader, burned at the stake for heresy and later beatified. Augustina Zaragoza "the Maid of Saragossa" (1786-1857), hero of the Siege of Saragossa in 1808. Camille Desmoulins (1760-1794), author of *La France Libre* (1789) calling for a republic. Sir Thomas Moore (1779-1852), author of *Lalla Rookh, An Oriental Romance* (1817). Hafed: Persian who falls in love with Hinda in *Lalla Rookh*. François Mignet (1796-1884), French historian, best known for *Histoire de la révolution française* (1824).

18   Silvio Pellico (1789-1854), Italian poet imprisoned by Austria on account of his sympathy for the Carbonari, a nationalist group associated with the Italian Risorgimento.

19   Daniel O'Connell (1775-1847), Irish political leader and champion of Catholic Emancipation.

20   John Mitchel (1815-1875), Irish nationalist.

21   Lord Edward FitzGerald (1763-1798), Irish aristocrat, revolutionary, and conspirator.

22   Immanuel Kant (1724-1804) and Johann Gottlieb Fichte (1762-1814), German philosophers.

23   Euclid (fl. 300 BCE), known as the "Father of Geometry."

24   Astley's Amphitheatre, a circus founded by Philip Astley in London in 1770; the Surrey, a circus founded by Charles Dibdin (who also coined the word "circus") in London in 1782.

25   The Kembles were a family of English actors, two of the most famous being Sarah Kemble Siddons (1755-1831) and John Philip Kemble (1757-1823).

26   Lucretia was a Roman matron who committed suicide after being raped by a member of the ruling Tarquin family of Rome. The outcry after her death led to the expulsion of the Tarquins from Rome.

27   Eliza O'Neill (1791-1872), Irish actress.

28   Micher, a sneak.

29   (Lat.) All other things being equal.

30   (Fr.) Good fortunes.

31   A rushlight is a tallow candle with a rush (grassy marsh plant) used as the wick.

32   The Gorham case and the so-called Papal Aggression were two religious controversies that had roiled England in the years immediately preceding the writing of *Realities*. In the former, evangelical clergyman George Cornelius Gorham (1787-1857) was challenged in 1847 by Bishop Phillpotts over Gorham's belief in baptismal regeneration. The term "Papal Aggression" was used by "no-popery" Englishmen to describe Pope Pius IX's reclassification of Catholic organization in England from a mission-style to a bishop-led diocesan arrangement.

33   "Hark, hark! the lark at heaven's gate sings" from Shakespeare's *Cymbeline* II:ii.

34   Two rooms on the second floor facing the front of the building.

35   A theatrical production repeated regularly.

36   (Fr.) snub nose.

37   Haidee is one of the hero's discarded lovers in Lord Byron's (1788-1824) *Don Juan* (1819-24).

38   Civil and ecclesiastical court located in London, ruling on cases of "blasphemy, apostasy from Christianity, heresy, ordinations, institutions to benefices, celebration of divine service, matrimony, divorces, bastardy, tithes, oblations, obventions, mortuaries, dilapidations, reparations of churches, probates of wills, administrations, simony, incest, fornication, adultery, pensions, procurations, commutation of penance, right of pews, and others of the same kind" (http://www.londonancestor.com/leighs/crt-docoms.htm).

39   Makers of cheap garments, paid by the piece.

40   Pottery style originating in Holland, usually characterized by a white glaze and a blue overglaze design.

41   A wealthy part of London.

42   A home for reformed prostitutes.

43   The workhouse.

44   Home of the Labour Association.

45   John Hampden (c. 1595-1643) Puritan landowner who opposed taxation without representation and died fighting Prince Rupert's royalists during the First English Civil War. William Tell, semi-legendary Swiss hero known for shooting an apple off his son's head with a crossbow; his defiance of Habsburg rule helped lead to the founding of the Swiss Confederation.

46   Tadeusz Kościuszko (1746-1817) led what came to be known as the "Kościuszko Uprising" by Poles against imperial Russian rule. Lajos Kossuth (1802-94) demanded Hungary's independence from Austria in 1848; Kossuth's government collapsed after Russia joined the war, and

he fled to Turkey, where he was imprisoned until 1851, when he moved to the United States.

47 The metallic embellishments of cabinet work.

48 Tonans (Lat.), thundering; an epithet for Jupiter.

49 Jean Antoine Watteau (1684-1721), French rococo painter; Sir Peter Lely (1618-1680), Dutch/English portrait painter; Sir Thomas Lawrence (1769-1830), British portrait painter.

50 (Fr.), well-placed.

51 Calcium fluoride, a mineral of many colors, the principal source of fluorine.

52 An alloy of copper and zinc used for ornamental gilding.

53 A kind of velvet.

54 Division of the family shield into quarters, with the various sections denoting marriage alliances.

55 A Greek goddess, the embodiment of ruin, folly, and delusion.

56 From "The Sensitive Plant" (1820) by Percy Bysshe Shelley.

57 Severe stabbing pain in the side of the face caused by irritation or compression of the trigeminal nerve.

58 The division of the High Court of Justice responsible for civil cases, including actions for the recovery of property or debt.

59 "A bruised reed shall he not break, and smoking flax shall he not quench, until he sends forth judgment unto victory." (Matthew 12:20)

60 Having to do with dress.

61 A shrub of the honeysuckle family, with white or pink flowers.

62 Gentlemen in the audience who were allowed entry backstage.

63 A sick-nurse in the novel *Martin Chuzzlewit* (serialized 1843-44) by Charles Dickens (1812-1870).

64 Miss Kemble mistakes her reference. Jesus refers to the disciples as the "salt of the earth" (Matt. 5:13).

65 Literary expression for a "wood-pigeon or ring-dove" (*OED*).

66 (Fr.) We shall see.

67 "A water-works official entrusted with the turning on of the water from the mains to supply-pipes" (*OED*).

68 (Fr.) Literally, warmed-over; figuratively, hand-me-down.

69 (Span.) Literally, rotten pot; figuratively, a mish-mash or stew.

70 (Lat./Gr. and Aramaic) Cursed, excommunicated.

71 In ancient Greece, a large public sacrifice.

72 A ladies' man.

73 The "new" poor law was the 1834 Poor Law Amendment Act, which assigned parishes to a union, in order to spread out the cost of maintaining workhouses for the poor.

74 Cold feet.

75 An early muzzle-loading gun, ancestor of the musket.

76 Leashed.

77 Hanged.

78 Arthur Wellesley, 1st Duke of Wellington (1769-1852).

79 (Lat.), as in a mirror.

80 A person who slaughters old, worn-out livestock in order to sell the hide or the meat.

81 Asylums for the reformation of prostitutes.

82 That is, according to legend, suspended in the air between heaven and earth.

83 A kind of black Chinese tea.

84 (Fr.), twenty-one.

85 A thin sock was worn by ancient Greek comedic actors; a buskin, or elevated boot, was worn by tragedians to elevate them above other players on the stage.

86 Hodgepodge.

87 "Major A—" was the anonymous author of the popular 1835 book *Short Whist: its Rise, Progress, and Laws*, which promised "to make anyone a whist player."

88 In theatrical slang, a stern bossy mother.

89 A whist player revokes by failing to follow suit on a play. Other whist references here include the bad play of leading the king to be taken by the opponents' ace, thus "establishing" the queen and jack (knave) as top cards in that suit. Another cardinal sin is to play a trump card on one's partner's winning ace, thus taking the trick twice and wasting a good card.

90 (Fr.), a ballet dancer who functions as a minor soloist, just above the *corps de ballet*.

91 In theatrical slang, a ponderous unbending man, especially one who wishes to control his offspring's choice of spouse.

92 Scoring 21 with only two cards, *i.e.* an ace and a ten or face card.

93 Heaping Pelion upon Ossa, that is, one mountain upon another, refers to the unsuccessful efforts of giants attempting to storm Mt. Olympus in Greek legend. Figuratively, it denotes any huge but fruitless attempt.

94 Carlotta Grisi (1819-1899) and Fanny Cerito (1817-1909), Italian ballerinas.

95 An Irish club or cudgel with a strap.

96 Aspasia (c.470 BCE-c.400 BCE), consort of Pericles, was considered to be the wisest woman in Athens. Charlotte Corday (1768-1793) assassinated the antimonarchist Jean-Paul Marat, and was herself executed.

97 "Wherefore I say unto thee, Her sins, which are many, are forgiven; for she loved much" (Luke 7:47).

98 Squeeze.

99 (Br. colloquialism), a policeman.

100 (Scot. dialect) douce: gentle, modest; lish: active, nimble.

101 The People's Charter of 1838 demanded "universal suffrage, vote by ballot, annual parliaments, the division of the country into equal electoral districts, the abolition of property qualification in members, and paying them for their services" (*OED*).

102 A rough or disorderly struggle.

103 The actress who plays minor female parts after the leading lady, and after the second lady.

104 A wool cloak.

105 A tall dressing mirror.

106 In Persian legend, peris were descendants of fallen angels; the term is used to refer to women.

107 Queen of the fairies in Shakespeare's comedy *A Midsummer Night's Dream.*

108 In Robert Greene's 1594 play *Friar Bacon and Friar Bungay*, Friar Roger Bacon made a head of brass, which was supposed to become an oracle. After saying "Time is," "Time was," and "Time's past," the head broke and never spoke again. Roger Bacon (c. 1214-1294) was a Franciscan friar and philosopher, sometimes credited with originating the modern scientific method.

109 In other words, imaginary or ideal gardens "of the mind."

110 (Fr.) Chimney-sweeps.

111 In Charles Dickens's novel *Martin Chuzzlewit* (1843-44), Mr. Nadgett, "man of mystery to the Anglo-Bengalee Disinterested Loan and Life Assurance Company," seemed always to be waiting for a "man who never came."

112 John Leech (1817-1864), artist credited by some with the popularity of *Punch* humor magazine.

113 Hanwell Asylum in west London opened in 1831 and was the "pauper lunatic asylum" for the county of Middlesex.

114 Jehu was a general, later a king of Israel, known for aggressive chariot-driving (see 2 Kings 9:16-27).

115 Calomel: mercury chloride, a strong laxative often given to patients in the nineteenth century to purge their bodies of illness. Cant: obscure language deliberately used to conceal meaning. Antiphlogistics: anti-inflammatory drugs, or fever reducers.

116 Alexander Maconochie (1787-1860), Scottish penal reformer.

117 The three "estates" were traditionally identified as the clergy, the nobility, and the common people.

118 The Rev. James E. Smith's book *The Coming Man* (1848) described this eponymous individual as a "great personage who was to come in amongst the chaos of society like a sunbeam through the clouds of heaven and shed light upon the world. No nation can be great which does not labour to produce such a man, but the greatest nation is not

content with a merely national man, for that is a small, a limited idea. It conceives the idea of a conquering man who will unite all nations under his law" (*The Coming Man* Vol. I [London: Strahan, 1873 ed.], 256).

119 (Lat.), from the beginning.

120 Flowers which grow in swampy areas, also known as marsh marigolds.

121 Golden Square, in the Soho district of London, was described by Charles Dickens as "not exactly in anybody's way to or from anywhere" (*The Life and Adventures of Nicholas Nickleby*).

122 Tony Lumpkin is an oafish comic character in Oliver Goldsmith's play *She Stoops to Conquer* (1773). Hodge is the stereotypical rustic bumpkin in Thomas Arne's opera *Love in a Village* (1762).

123 "A mechanical model, usually clockwork, devised to represent the motions of the earth and moon (and sometimes also the planets) around the sun" (*OED*).

124 A game played with three thimbles and a pea.

125 A peasant revolt in France in 1358, during the Hundred Years War.

126 A follower of the doctrines of Edward Pusey (1800-1882), founder of the Oxford Movement, which sought to move the Church of England in the direction of Roman Catholicism.

127 Any of a number of Antitrinitarian sects, including, for instance, Unitarians.

128 (Lat.), quiet and pleasing wife.

129 "Of, relating to, or of the nature of a preface; prefatory" (*OED*).

130 Referring to William Etty (1787-1849), an English artist known for his paintings of nudes.

131 Clarkson Frederick Stanfield (1793-1867), English marine painter.

132 Daniel Quilp is the deformed lecher who pursues Little Nell in Charles Dickens's *The Old Curiosity Shop* (1841). The murder of St. Gengulphus is revealed when his chair fastens itself to his two-timing wife, who is sitting upon it, by pieces of his beard hidden in its cushion.

Appendix: Contemporary Reviews of *Realities*

Rev. of *Realities*. *The Spectator* (May 24, 1851), 499.

The author of this work, when she tried her hand at a remote place and a distant period, did not exhibit that imagination which is necessary to embody the spirit of the past, or that aptitude for a perception of the events of life which is necessary to form a story. The advantage of being contemporary with the state of society chosen as the subject of *Realities* does not change the nature of her qualifications. It seems from the preface, that the writer's friends advised her not to publish this tale; and request of friends may generally be safely complied with in *this* direction.

Rev. of *Realities*. *The Leader* (May 31, 1851), 517-518.

Having gained a name by her treatment of those difficult subjects—Egyptian and Grecian life—Miss Lynn now attempts the still more difficult subject—Realities! To the uninitiated it seems so easy to be natural, and to describe realities! Yet so difficult is it that not one in a thousand can write as he *thinks*, but each writes more or less according to a pattern; that is to say, *not* as he thinks, but as he thinks he *ought* to write! If this be true of the mere diction, it is glaringly so of the modes of representation. Difficult as it is to write the phrases you think, it is still more difficult to describe truly what you see, or to represent what you imagine. In fact the difficulty is only to be overcome by Genius. As authors in general do not write according to the idiom of their own minds, but according to the idiom of the literature of the day, gathering together all the current phrases, worn images, and familiar turns which belong to no one writer but have become common property—as they aim at a conventional smoothness and harmonious adjustment of sentences, rather than at vivifying their style with the infusion of their own personality—so likewise in describing or in representing they follow conventions, and sacrifice individual truth to the so-called poetical effect. The first test we should apply to a young writer, in a consultation as to whether he had genuine artistic power, would not be whether his style were harmonious, his images captivating, or his command of language remarkable; we should set him to describe the brick wall opposite! Ten to one he would fail miserably. Twenty to one he would exaggerate!

The attempt to describe the realities of Life is singularly ambitious, because the difficulties of Art become intensified the nearer its subject and form approach to the Actual, while retaining the purposes of the Ideal. A tragedy in prose, taken from modern life, is ten times as difficult as a tragedy in verse moving amidst the ill-understood fashions of the past. Hence the modern novel, unless mainly satirical, is scarcely ever a faithful representation of society; its characters, its action, its scenery, are all—except in rare instances—so unlike the actual truth, that in proportion to the seriousness of its aim becomes the greatness of its failure. Miss Austen stands alone in her incomparable pictures of life; and the subtlety and genius, restricted though the scope of that genius may be, which created *Emma*, *Pride and Prejudice*, and *Mansfield Park*, have found no rivals. In a higher sphere, and representing life under more impassioned phases, George Sand may be cited as a master of the art, though she often sins against the truth of reality.

Such being our view of the difficulty there is in giving an adequate representation of that complex drama moving before our eyes, it will not surprise Miss Lynn, for whose eloquence and general power we have the highest respect, if we pronounce her picture of social life to be one which falls short of its aim. Whatever may be thought of the interest of the story, the passion and eloquence thrown into it, or of the antagonism against conventions which rises up in every chapter, there will be no one, we believe, to accept this work as giving shape and substance to the Realities of our life. We do not say that Reality has not formed the groundwork, we say it is not in the work. The brick wall may exist from which the copy is made, but the copy is untrue. It is not the fact we doubt; it is the Art. Singularly unfortunate we must call the choice of her subject, which, lying of necessity beyond the sphere of her own actual experience, frustrates all her efforts. How is it possible for her to know theatrical life with anything like the accuracy needed for artistic reproduction? How can a woman know enough of the slopworker's modes of existence, to give anything but a partial representation of them? Yet we are in this work mainly thrown behind the scenes of a theatre, and into the dread alleys where slopworking rises hideous amidst so many horrors.

Her aim has been a philosophic aim. She has undertaken to portray the trials and perils which a free, impulsive, truthful nature must necessarily encounter in a world of convention, compromise, and repression. Clara de Saumarez, the heroine, is charmingly introduced to us as a madcap, impulsive child, who "shocks" her mother, and makes life a burden to all the "proprieties." Her mother is happily touched in this passage:

"Moreover, Mrs. de Saumarez was a woman [. . .] mutual dissent between mother and child."

And throughout the character is sustained. Clara does not seem like her child. In course of time it turns out that she is *not*. Put out to nurse, the nurse thought to benefit her offspring by a substitution:

"At the proper time Clara was returned home [. . .] all the rest of the household combined."

The want of sympathy between the "proper" mother and the impulsive child strikes the keynote. The same antagonism Clara finds when she comes forth into the world; if her father and mother misjudge her, how can strangers appreciate the purity of her motives? She is driven from home, and in London a new experience begins: there she knows love and triumph, and sorrow, and humiliation; there she is imprudent and misjudged; loses her character from carelessness of "what will the world say"; and there she is made acquainted with some of the social diseases of our time. The intention is, as we said, philosophic; but we cannot applaud the choice of machinery. Of all places, perhaps the theatre was the worst for such a drama. It admits of considerable independence in the actors, and irregularity in their modes of life; but it is itself a half-real, half-fictitious existence.

Clara, however, chooses the stage as a profession and falls in love with her manager, Vasty Vaughan, seeing him only through the inexperienced eyes of girlhood. We will extract a bit from the account of her début:

"The morning never passed her rosy fingers [. . .] diligence with which he paced those creaking boards."

Her success is immense—the sort of success artists win in novels. But the failure in her affections soon robs her triumph of its charm. She learns the true character of the man she loves, she suffers the consequences of her imprudence, she learns in her misery the misery of others, and, after many trials and much experience, finds refuge and a home in the constant, honest love of Percival Glynn. But all that you must read in the volumes for yourself.

Rev. of *Realities. The Athenæum* (June 14, 1851), 626-627.

Miss Lynn's dedicatory preface, addressed to Mr. Landor, will acquaint the public that her novel has been published in spite of the almost unanimous alarm and disapproval of her friends and counselors. She announces this fact, it may be presumed, with the view of bespeaking the credit due to one who acts courageously for conscience sake. About this valour a word in season seems required. There is such a thing as plain-speaking presumption disguised under the garb of honest and pains-taking sincerity. In Miss Lynn's eagerness to preach, it is possible that she may have contented herself with a most imperfect ordination. In place of enlarging the world's store of wisdom, she has added another to the proofs that daring and infallibility do not always imply self-knowledge or due preparation. The topics of her novel—female reputation—the constraint of the marriage tie—the plea of poverty against wicked wealth—the right divine of private judgment to overrule the ordinances of Pharisaical respectability, though among the most confessedly difficult objects of philanthropical and philosophical inquiry, she handles with great flippancy, great inconsistency, and a conspicuous ignorance of her premises and of the facts by which they are illustrated. This proclivity belongs to the times we are living in,—which are times of energy, progress and transition;—but that *My Lady Gathercole*, when she hears of the Crystal Palace, should prattle about *Belshazzar*—and that *Rosa Matilda* should rate Kings and Ministers, Church and Law, as so many living lies because the sight of beggary afflicts her—are "utterances," not so much illustrating the enlightenment of the several ladies, as their being touched by the morbid influence of disease. We admit Miss Lynn's courage;—we recognize now, as heretofore, her literary power to be considerable; but in this tale she ranks herself with the *Mause Headriggs*, who have fancied that fiery zeal would atone for prejudice and ignorance. The world which she here displays is a world of people extravagantly vicious and extravagantly innocent and extravagantly cold-blooded,—a world existing in the chambers of her own imagination, and not in any highways or by-ways of London, or any other city with which we are conversant.

Her heroine, Clare, to give but one instance, is the reputed daughter of one of those persons in whom commonplace respectability and narrow benevolence are made to look almost diabolical by the caricaturing ingenuity of their antagonists. While she is yet a girl, Clare becomes an enthusiastic contemner of authority and of class-distinctions—not reasonably but passionately so. She insists on the cold-hearted Mrs. De Saumarez adopting a beggar child,—and is supplanted by the new comer. This "strange turn" is explained by the Minerva Press device of proving Alice to be the real heiress, and Clare to be a changeling,—

A base-born child of passion and of shame.

—Again, in the days of Clare's prosperity, she patronizes a draggle-tailed, fustian-spouting actress, who calls herself Miss Kemble. When she becomes unhappy, Clare rushes up to London in search of this second-hand Siddons, and insists on going on to the stage. Mrs. De Saumarez, at this period of the history, still believing Clare to be her daughter, makes no effort to reclaim her nor to provide her with money—but at once coolly cuts Clare off from her love as one abandoned, and a Pariah. Still stranger vicissitudes await our heroine. The manager who undertakes to bring her out is a manager of the *Lothario* genus. Though he is many years older than herself, and a scheming voluptuary, she is made to fall in love with this being; in reality innocent, she lends herself to a manner of living with him by which her character is irretrievably damaged. While, however, Clare is so blindly child-like, it was necessary to Miss Lynn's story that her heroine should not yield to circumstances. Although, therefore, she loves this man dearly, she extricates herself from what the world calls shame,—and henceforward becomes the victim of his vengeance. The scene in which Vaughan openly denounces the guiltless girl as having been his mistress, in the green-room, before his whole *corps* of "heavy fathers" and low comedians, men, women, and children—though necessary to show how sublime Clare could remain under an Ossa of ignominy—is one of the most outrageous exaggerations ever produced. We will not here inquire whether women are or are not well occupied in undraping the profligacy and corruption which exist for the public good,—but we must repeat that Miss Lynn's Quixotic enterprise has led her to deal with imaginary monsters, and not human beings,—has made such a woman as never existed, and placed beside her such a fiend as would not have imposed on her purity for half-an-hour. None of the conventionalisms against which she raves like a Pythoness are half so artificial—do a violence to nature half so extreme—as the respective stratagems and forbearances of her hero and heroine. Let it be added, that this strange drama is written in scenes where there is no innuendo for plain speaking, but "a spade" is called a spade. Miss Lynn's lovers have not learned, like the actors and actresses in the Trianon theatre, *"faire jabot,"* by way of evading lip-familiarities. She has no reserve either in dialogue or in colour. Fearless our young authoress is ambitious of being thought, and fearless she is to a point of temerity almost unparagoned:—whether felicitous, is another question.

There is not a word of the above character that could not be illustrated by a host of passages;—but enough has been done in recording our opinion as an act of severe friendliness due to one whose early efforts in Art inspired no common hopes. We are not sanguine, however, as to any present return to truth and soberness on her part. There is a positive untruth to the very principles which she thinks she is here maintaining which convinces us that she wants either earnestness or thought. Good and evil are alike attacked by her simply because either is established. The former becomes the latter the moment it has authority on its side. We own to the fullest the weight and the sorrow of the social enormities and inequalities which Miss Lynn's book denounces; but we cannot see her in the pulpit without declaring that as a preacher she is naught,—and reminding her of the *animus* of Dr. Johnson's celebrated rebuke of Hannah More, when that Lady had administered more flattery than it suited the author of 'Irene' just then to swallow:—"My good Miss Hannah," said the sage, "before you are so lavish of your praise, consider its value!" "Be not too bold!" was the last motto on the door which thrice encouraged the Pilgrim Knight "to be bold."

"The Novels of the Day." *New Monthly Magazine* (June 1851), 231-235.

The three volumes of "Realities," which we now take up, have their purpose also; and if we are to accept the author's definition of her object, that purpose is as comprehensive as, if successful, it would be beneficent. Miss Lynn declares herself the advocate of "The Social doctrines taught by Christ;" and to this advocacy and the enunciation of opinions whereby she interprets those doctrines, she ascribes an amount of private reprehension such as never before, perhaps, attended the baptism of an unpublished work. There must have been some singular misgivings as to the effect which these "Realities" were likely to cause, to have induced the author so widely to circulate her manuscript before it was presented to the public, for she tells us that "for three months" her book was "a species of literary Caliban" to her friends, "a monstrous thing of wickedness and deformity, advocating all that was abhorrent to reason and good morals." Nevertheless, undeterred by the "hard names which flew like hailstones around her," Miss Lynn withstood the "battery of condemnation" with which she was assailed, and persevered in her determination to give the world the benefit of her labours [. . .]

It was to say the least of it, a bold venture; but, having read Miss Lynn's book, we are not surprised that she should have made it, for moral courage is certainly not amongst the attributes that are wanting to her literary character.

We now pass from the dedication, in which the untoward circumstances above adverted to are set forth, to the body of the work, which we shall allow to speak for itself as often as we can, convinced that we should otherwise fail in doing justice to these remarkable volumes.

Miss Lynn's heroine, Clara, is the reputed daughter of Mr. and Mrs. de Saumarez, the antiquity of whose family ascends to the Conquest; but there is so little art in the construction of the story, or, rather, Miss Lynn has cared so little for her plot, that we see at once that Clara is a changeling, the real heiress being a girl of her own age, named Alice, the alleged illegitimate offspring of Martha Clayton, the daughter of an old groom in the De Saumarez family. Mr. de Saumarez is a cold, pedantic, scientific ass, considerably under the domination of his equally cold but really clever wife, who has established a reputation for granting the degree of "respectability."

Clara is described as a creature full of impulse and imagination, and the opposite in every respect not only to her supposed mother, but to the *protégée* Alice, who, having been ridden over by Clara when each was thirteen years old, has been taken into the house of Mrs. de Saumarez, and brought up as the companion of the young heiress. Though cold to all the world beside, maternal nature warms towards the *protégée*, and Alice occupies that place in the affections of Mrs. de Saumarez which Clara imagines is hers by right. Hence, and from the antagonism of their characters, arise situations which embitter the girlhood of Clara until the age of sixteen. At this period she accidentally encounters a strolling actress, who calls herself an offshoot of the Kemble family, and the presumed scion of the noble house of De Saumarez breaks through the restrictions of "the Hall," keeps the servants up till past twelve at night, and, on her return from Miss Kemble's dramatic readings in the village, is confronted by her father, who lays on her with a dog-whip "across her neck and shoulders," and orders her into the solitary confinement of her chamber. Clara had previously made an attempt to run away, and now carries her intention into effect. She joins Miss Kemble on her way to the railroad by which the latter returns to London, places herself under the actress's protection, is not pursued by her family, and, experiencing no further let or hindrance, resolves at once to realise the dearest aspiration of her soul by becoming a regular candidate for dramatic fame. She is introduced to the manager, with whom, *par parenthèse*, she very soon falls violently in love, in spite of his incipient bald head and the forty years which had passed over it.

This personage, whose name is Vasty Vaughan, is further described as "agreeable, gentlemanlike, a systematic *roué*, and a thorough-going atheist, skeptical of all virtue and all goodness;" and, besides being handsome, "one of those manly, frank, benevolent, and pleasure-loving people who win women sooner than any other class of men." Miss Lynn might very well add that "he was a dangerous person to become the arbiter of a young girl's fate." Such, however, is the case, and the consequence of being exposed to so much fascination is speedily developed. This "manly, frank, benevolent" manager, in the course of a dozen pages from this description, has "his arm round Clare's waist while her hands are clasped in his;" and before the chapter closes Mr. Vasty Vaughan asks her for a kiss! This favour Clara does not instantly grant, but the manager has not long to wait; he gives her a dinner at Windsor, and the kiss comes off—and something more. We extract the scene to show Miss Lynn's power in this particular line:

"What made you blush so much Clara [. . .] this present hour of bliss."

Was the above amongst the passages "abhorrent to good morals" to which Miss Lynn's friends objected before she decided on publishing?

It seldom happens that the heroine in a novel has only one lover. The second string to Clara's bow is Percival Glynn, the master of elocution, who is to prepare her for the stage. On his character Miss Lynn has bestowed much earnest writing, with the view, no doubt, of asserting those opinions which it was the aim of her work to uphold. Her views are not ours with regard to the Magdalen-worship, in which it would seem her idea of the charity of Love consists; we refrain, therefore, from quoting more of her description of this man's creed than she has herself summed up in the following sentences:

"He was politically a socialist, religiously a non-sectarian—a freethinker in the positive sense of the term—and practically the unshrinking protector of such poor sinners as a moral society has discarded and a Christian people anathematized."

This gentleman, who seems a little too good for mankind as we find it just now, is exposed to the suspicions of Vasty Vaughan, and the scene that takes place between the rivals at a more advanced period of the story, is described by Miss Lynn in language rather more forcible than agreeable, as follows:

"Vaughan laughed loudly [. . .] frightful oaths."

We pause here to ask a question. Are scenes like this and the preceding one calculated to add to the dignity or advance the objects of literature, and is it by the advocacy of a work which abounds in similar passages that "the social doctrines taught by Christ" are to be inculcated?

It may be said that in these extracts there is no exposition of doctrine, and that to cite them only is to leave the author's opinions unrepresented; but, to say the truth, our impression, in going through these volumes, is that the whole work is one tissue of the same exaggeration, violence, and too often prominent writing, and that we do her most service when we say the least. Miss Lynn is a determined social reformer, and that our social system requires reform on many of the points which she attacks, there can be no doubt; but we shall be very much mistaken if the defective condition of our laws, and the ugly vices which she dissects with such an eager hand, are cured or mended by her novel. Amongst the many repulsive portraits which we meet with in it, Emma, the abandoned wife of Vaughan, is the most hideous. From the moment of her first entrance, "a woman, bold, ragged, and untidy," sitting in "a dirty room overlooking the fetid river," to that of her last appearance, "an old she-wolf," "an irreclaimable demon," a convicted felon only saved from the scaffold by madness, she shocks and disgusts us more, perhaps, than we have ever before been shocked and disgusted by any fictitious creation.

Here is a taste of her quality: "She felt that she would like to see blood [. . .] in his heart's drops." The clergyman in prison attempts to instruct and soften her; she makes answer as follows: "Fool—beast—idiot—out of my sight! Go preach to softer heads than mine—tell things half-witted like yourself, what false lies you want them to believe; but don't attempt to hollow out a rock with clouds and vapours that fear the very name of truth. Out of my sight! you poison the air even of a prison." The prison-governor might well call her "a perfect savage." But why make such a character? For the purpose of showing such a condition of mind to be the inevitable result of the law of divorce as it now stands; and this is the argument which Miss Lynn employs to justify her view of the case:

"Our age is too spiritual to contemplate [. . .] the very fact that society condemns." [. . .]

We are sorry to have been compelled to comment with severity on the work of a writer of so much undoubted talent as Miss Lynn, but the very fact that she writes with vigour and ability is a reason the more for not refraining from silence. We fear, however, from the example afforded us in the rejection of that friendly counsel which advised the suppression of her book, that any advise of ours as to her future literary career would be useless.

Rev. of *Realities. Bentley's Miscellany* 29 (1851), 669-670.

Talent every one will readily accede to Miss Lynn, and her courage is as great as her talent. Here we have before us a young lady, a sort of English George Sand, preaching Socialism and Chartism, in a novel which sometimes startles by its power, and then revolts by its sentiments. The heroine, a very handsome girl, impulsive and generous, is a socialist, as Miss Lynn would have socialists be, and her life is spent in a constant warfare with the received opinions of the world. She looks upon kings as the curse of nations, has a secret approbation for Danton and Mirabeau, thinks "Madame Roland the grandest woman (except Charlotte Corday, Joan of Arc, and the Maid of Saragossa) that the world ever saw." She is the reputed daughter and heiress of wealthy and aristocratic parents, but in reality a changeling. Froward,—a girl who will have her own head, she does what she likes, is at length disgusted with home, and comes to London to be an actress. And here commences the interest of the story, which in spite of some improbabilities, is considerable. She falls in love with Vasty Vaughan, the manager of the theatre, a libertine and a married man (but of this last circumstance she is ignorant), makes a triumphant *début*, lives in the same house as the manager, spends a day at Richmond with him, finds out by means of his wife, who is a street-walker, that Vaughan is married, leaves him, falls in love with and marries Percival Glynn, an elocutionist and a chartist. A young clergyman of the Calvinistic order is introduced who is made to pour out "fiery words of wrath and pain," and Edward Mantell is offered by Miss Lynn as a type of what is now called the Low Church. His character is well-drawn, his enthusiasm, earnestness, and courage, redeem him from the dislike usually invited by a bigot. But he is not a type of the Low Church, which ranks amongst its members many of the really working clergy, men who have as much charity as those who have more form.

As a foil to Clara, the heroine, Emmeline de Montfort is brought on the stage, becomes the new love of Vaughan, and herself loves a noble lord. She is a well-depicted character-less character, with long light ringlets, blue eyes, small hands and feet, and a host of dangling chains, charms, bracelets, &c. There are some minor characters introduced, more or less well sustained, Old Hugh perhaps being the best of these.

We are afraid that Miss Lynn will find that the publication of this work will draw upon her the censure of those who are not altogether the "slaves of convention," "Christian ladies and gentlemen," and so forth. The work has no doubt been suggested by the letters which have appeared from time to time in the Morning Chronicle, and which have aroused the public mind, which will not rest satisfied until the social condition of the lower classes is considerably ameliorated. The author has seen these letters through a magnifying glass; her strong imagination has cast a dark colouring over what was before sufficiently hideous. She has given us no Rembrandt picture, such as would really represent life; no gleam of light relieves the revolting misery and crime which she exhibits. Rich men do not step in to aid the struggle of poverty; poor people are driven by a necessity to commit sin in order to live. Fatalism, materialism, Chartism, and socialism are the doctrines inculcated in "Realities." When we add that the Divine Author of Christianity is here styled the first socialist, we have said enough to disgust most people.

The perusal of the work leaves a very painful impression, and not all its eloquence can compensate for its unhealthy tone. It is a protest against the laws which bind society; a vehicle for the publication of all the immoral doctrines, the propagation of which has caused such misery in France; and a sad stain on the literary reputation of one of the most gifted authors of the day.

George Henry Lewes, "The Lady Novelists." *Westminster Review* 58 (July 1852), 70-77. Present selection from Elaine Showalter (ed.), *Women's Liberation and Literature*. New York: Harcourt Brace Jovanovich, 1971, 171-183.

Miss Lynn occupies a strange and defiant position. In her first work, "Azeth," she astonished by the recondite reading exhibited in her Egyptian colouring, and by the daring voluptuousness of her eloquence. In her second romance, "Amymone," she quitted Egypt for Greece, showed an equal amount of laborious study and of exuberant rhetoric, but assumed a still more hostile position against received notions by a paradoxical defence of Aspasia. In "Realities," a novel of our day, the antagonism was avowed, incessant, impetuous; it was a passionate and exaggerated protest against conventions, which failed of its intended effect because it was too exaggerated, too manifestly unjust. Splendour of diction, and a sort of rhythmic passion, rising oftentimes into accents of startling power, have never been denied her; but one abiding defect of her novels we must allude to, and that is, the want of that Observation which we have insisted on as a requisite in fiction. In "Realities," this want was singularly apparent, and gave it the air of unreality so detrimental to such a work. The realm of imagination is better suited to her powers than that of fact; she feels deeply, paints vividly what she feels, but she sees dimly. (182)

9781934555736